ASCEND
Numen Chronicles

T. Csernis & Julia Bland

ASCENDANT
NUMEN CHRONICLES VOLUME FIVE

NO ACCENT EDITION

ASCENDANT
Numen Chronicles | Volume Five

Copyright © 2025 by Tate Csernis (T. Csernis).

All rights reserved. No part of this book may be used or reproduced in any form whatsoever without written permission except in the case of brief quotations in critical articles or reviews.

Without limiting the author's exclusive rights, any unauthorised use of this publication to train generative artificial intelligence (AI) technologies is expressly prohibited.

This book is a work of fiction. Names, characters, businesses, organizations, places, events, and incidents either are the product of the author's imagination or are used fictitiously. Any resemblance to actual persons, living or dead, events, or locales is entirely coincidental.

For more information on the world, this series, other books, or to contact the author, head to: https://www.numenverse.com/

Cover designed by Tate Csernis
Cover drawn by Simon Zhong
Cover edited by Julia Bland

ISBN – Paperback: 978-1-917270-16-8
ISBN – Hardcover: 978-1-917270-17-5
ISBN – E-Book: 978-1-917270-18-2

THE NUMEN CHRONICLES™ is a collaborative work written by

Tate Csernis (T. Csernis) and Julia Bland (Julia B.)

Each Party retains ownership over their respected Intellectual Property created outside of this collaboration, including but not limited to names, characters, stories, etc. All Collaborative Intellectual Property shall be jointly owned by the Parties, and each Party shall have the right freely to use all Collaborative Intellectual Property for all purposes and uses.

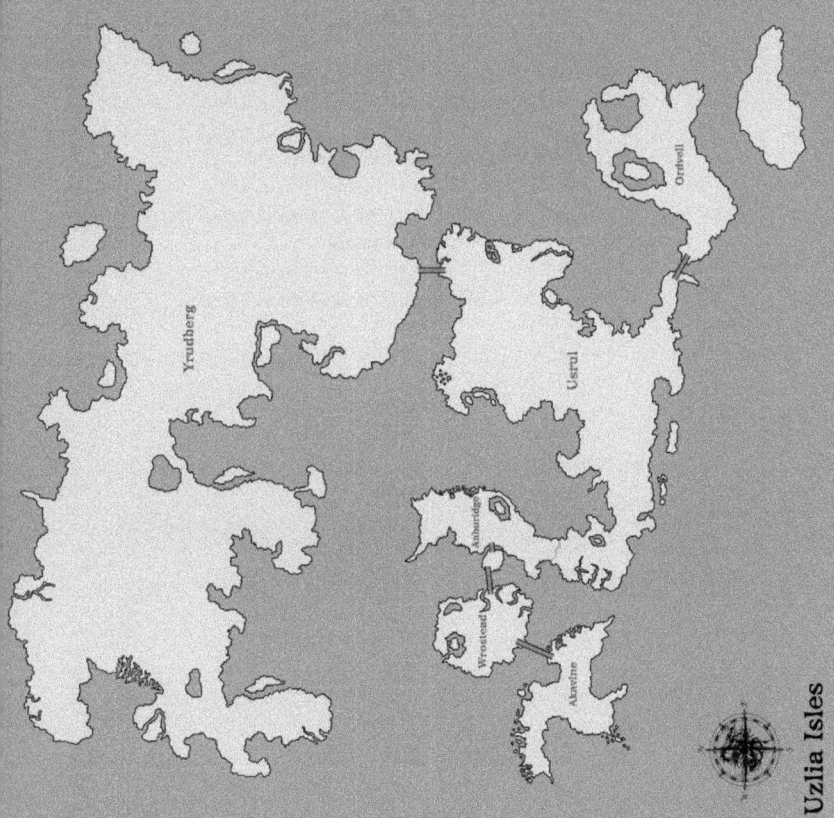

ASCENDANT
Numen Chronicles | Volume Five

GLOSSARY

Ethos [ee-thos] - The energy within someone that can be used to create or manipulate other energies

✝

Dor-Sanguis [door-san-goo-wis] - Translates roughly to Pain *[Portuguese]* and blood *[Latin]*
(aka, Romania)

✝

Nefastus [neh-fas-tus] – Translates to Unlawful *[Latin]*
(aka, the Americas)

✝

Eltaria [el-tar-ia] – Zalith's homeworld

✝

Numen [noo-men] - God-like beings that chose to show themselves to the world rather than remain anonymous

✝

Aegis [ee-gis] - The Dragon Gods, children of Letholdus

✝

DeiganLupus [day-gan-loo-pus] - Translates roughly to 'refused to turn to the wolf' *[Icelantic, Latin]*
(aka, UK)

✝

Lumendatt [loo-men-dat] – Numen crystals containing the power to create life

✝

Obcasus [ob-cass-us] – Knives capable of putting Numen in a frozen statis

✝

Proselytus [pros-elly-tus] – A heart-like organ which creates ethos inside a body

✝

Scion [skee-on] – ethos-crafted children of the Numen

✝

Înfățișare [in-fuh-tsee-SHAH-reh] – vampires able to shift into animal forms

✝

The Seven Realms:

Aegisguard [ee-gis-guard] - The world
(aka, Earth)
Mareaeternum [Mar-ay-ter-num] Translates to eternal tide *[Latin]*
Glaciaqua [Glass-ee-aqua]
Letholdus [Lee-fold-us]
Tengetso [Ten-get-so]
Celitrianas [Sel-it-ree-a-nas]
Yilmana [Yeel-mana]

ASCENDANT
Numen Chronicles | Volume Five

The Months and Currency

Months

January – Primis
February – Cordus
March – Tertium
April – Aprilis
May – Quintus
June – Iunius
July – Quintilis
August – Tria
September – Novem
October – Decem
November – Undecim
December – Clausula

Currency

Copper – Equivalent of $0.01
Bronze – Equivalent of $0.20
Silver – Equivalent of $2
Gold – Equivalent of $10
Coronam – Equivalent of $100
Cidaris – Equivalent of $1 million

ASCENDANT
Numen Chronicles | Volume Five

CONTENTS

ARC ONE || CROFORD AND FORKAND

1	Challenger	Pg11
2	A Slowly Healing Wound	Pg18
3	The Month That Had Passed, The Dismay…	Pg28
4	My Love	Pg34
5	Of Life's Torments, and its Pleasures	Pg42
6	A Letter By Owl	Pg59
7	Soren, and the Eimwood Collusion	Pg68
8	Ordvell	Pg77
9	Talk Over Bourbon	Pg88
10	Glimpse	Pg94
11	Forkand	Pg103
12	Over Two Hundred	Pg111
13	Cleaning Wounds	Pg121

ARC TWO || THE INSECTUMOID CONUNDRUM

14	A Blade and a Box	Pg129
15	A Lamentable Morning	Pg136
16	Sleep	Pg146
17	Notes	Pg154
18	An Impromptu Lesson	Pg161
19	Shell	Pg168
20	Careful Mistake	Pg172
21	Apologies and Forgiveness	Pg177
22	Insectumoid	Pg183
23	A Morning of Pleasures	Pg189
24	News from Rasmus	Pg196
25	A Discussion of Updates	Pg204
26	The Cave	Pg209
27	The Strawberry Saloon and Restaurant	Pg218
28	Dream-Eaters and Favours	Pg223
29	The Prelude to Cecil's Downfall	Pg232

30	The Townhouse Meeting	Pg239
31	Talk of the Town	Pg246
32	Plans for the Inevitable Future of Eimwood	Pg253
33	Wedding Planner	Pg263
34	Sleeves	Pg266

ARC THREE || TIME AWAY

35	A Short, Tropical Escape	Pg275
36	Pina Coladas and Pasta	Pg283
37	Tolerable	Pg294
38	Portrait	Pg301
39	The Tortoise	Pg308
40	Dining Under the Setting Sun	Pg316
41	Their Last Night Away	Pg322
42	Four Hundred and Twenty-Three Years Ago	Pg333
43	Souvenirs	Pg342
44	Until Late Afternoon	Pg353
45	One Final Day in the Sun	Pg358
46	Play Fighting	Pg366

ARC FOUR || EXTERMINATION

47	Aniani Tortoise	Pg379
48	Back to Work	Pg384
49	Temptations	Pg395
50	Intoxicating, Devouring	Pg405
51	Utterly Entranced	Pg410
52	The Final Predicament	Pg420
53	Queen Syllia Caivarus of Yrudberg	Pg428
54	The Protestors	Pg438
55	Silas and Ezra Wright, Lords of Eimwood	Pg443
56	Burns	Pg452
57	To Fort Rudă de Sânge	Pg460
58	The Vampire Conundrum	Pg467
59	Behind the Heart	Pg473

ASCENDANT
Numen Chronicles | Volume Five

This book contains explicit sexual content, dark fantasy themes, and mature subject matter. Reader discretion is advised.

Arc One
✝
Croford and Forkand

ASCENDANT
Numen Chronicles | Volume Five

Chapter One

— ⊰ † ⊱ —

Challenger

| **Zalith**, *Friday, Tertium 10th, 960(TG)—Avalmoor, Croford Island* |

From the shadows of the murky tree line, Zalith crouched in silence, his gaze fixed determinedly on the meadow at the bottom of the hill. Beside him, Alucard and their fighters held their positions, breaths quiet and steady, their anticipation thick as the night air. The glade stretched out before them like a grim tableau, illuminated by the kaleidoscopic light of the six full moons and the flickering orange glow of a solitary campfire; its flames danced and cracked, casting eerie, shifting shadows over the carnage that lay scattered across the open field.

A lone, crimson-eyed man hurried towards the fire, his movements jerky and frantic, like a rat darting through a predator's territory. Fallen trees littered the field, their gnarled branches clawing at the air, and beneath them lay lifeless bodies, half-hidden in the gloom. It was hard to discern whether they were human, humanoid, or beast; death had rendered them shapeless, their forms contorted in unnatural stillness. The stench of decay hung heavy in the air, mingling with the acrid tang of burning wood and the faint metallic scent of blood that the breeze carried.

Zalith's muscles coiled with restrained tension, his claws lightly scraping the bark of the tree beside him. The faint rustle of the forest canopy above and the distant chirp of crickets were the only sounds that punctuated the ominous quiet. Even the man below didn't glance at the corpses, his crimson gaze fixed solely on the campfire, as if its warmth might shield him from whatever darkness haunted the edges of his vision.

Exactly fifty-seven pairs of crimson eyes ignited in the darkness across the glade, their eerie glow flickering like embers in the dense gloom. The air shifted as every demon lurking within the meadow stiffened, their attention snapping to the lone man making his way forward.

Zalith watched closely, tracing the man's hurried path towards the demons' Alpha— a broad, dark-skinned figure perched casually on a throne of ashen wood. The Alpha sat as though the glade were his kingdom, his broad form exuding an air of dominance that dared anyone to challenge it. His grin, sharp and wolfish, split across his dirtied face with the confidence of a predator who believed himself untouchable.

A flicker of amusement broke through Zalith's otherwise calm demeanour. This Alpha clearly thought that he was special—dangerous, even. Zalith couldn't deny the theatrics were well-rehearsed: the torn, battle-worn attire designed to convey both savagery and control, the lean of his body into the throne as if he were the very embodiment of untamed power. It was all so contrived, so predictable. Zalith had seen this performance before, and it always ended the same way—with a man like this proven far less extraordinary than he believed.

In the Alpha's right hand, a golden chalice gleamed, catching the campfire's light. Within the cup, crimson liquid swirled lazily, thick and dark, as though imbued with some ominous power. Zalith's eyes flicked to it briefly before returning to the Alpha; it was all just another layer of the show, a shiny prop to reinforce the illusion of invincibility. But Zalith wasn't here to be impressed or cowed. He was here to take everything this self-important Alpha thought was his. The amusement lingered, quietly sharpening his focus as he prepared to dismantle the illusion piece by piece.

The man who'd hurried towards the Alpha stopped before him, his deference clear in every nervous shift of his body. At the Alpha's feet, two women knelt, their fingers clutching desperately at the edges of his throne, their soft pleas falling unheard; with a dismissive wave of his hand, the Alpha sent them away without even a flicker of acknowledgement, his fathomless black eyes fixed instead on the man in front of him.

"What?" the Alpha uttered, setting his eyes on him.

"The perimeter's clear, Sirrus," the crimson-eyed man answered cautiously.

Sirrus' wolfish grin returned as he lightly waved his hand in dismissal. "Good," he mumbled, and as the crimson-eyed man wandered off to join the group of spectating demons, Sirrus returned to admiring the moons above.

As the night deepened, the air grew bitter, carrying with it a baleful fog that crept across the glade. The hum of the surrounding wildlife faded to a deathly silence; even the faintest breeze had stilled, leaving the meadow unnaturally quiet. Zalith's sharp eyes flicked towards the wide-open tent across the camp, filled with treasures that glinted faintly in the dying firelight. He noted how the Alpha's gaze kept darting back to that tent. It wasn't hard to piece together: the gold and trinkets mattered more to Sirrus than the lives of his pack.

Zalith's lips curled in quiet disdain. Typical. The man thought himself a king, but his priorities showed his weakness.

Sirrus suddenly shot to his feet, baring his claws and grinding his teeth as he glared into the blackness beyond the fog; he'd clearly sensed that *something* was wrong, but the confusion in his eyes was growing—he had no idea what lurked on the borders of his territory, did he?

Zalith held his position, silent and still, his amusement flickering again as he watched the Alpha's posturing. The dull grey fog that had begun to snake through the camp now darkened, staining black and pulsing with faint flickers of crimson light as Alucard's power took hold of it. It slithered between the trees, coiling like a serpent and climbing as high as the canopy, suffocating the campfire's light.

Sirrus' Betas moved instinctively, darting towards the treasure-filled tent. Wings flared, horns gleaming faintly in the distorted light, they positioned themselves protectively, their stances tense and aggressive. The rest of the pack stood frozen, their gazes flicking between Sirrus and the encroaching darkness, waiting for orders that never came.

Zalith glanced at Alucard, admiring the focused stare on the vampire's face as he weaved his ethos, crafting the fog using the blood that oozed from his cut wrists, ensnaring Sirrus' camp in an ocean of power that he nor his pack would be able to escape. And then he shifted his focus back to Sirrus, whose composure was already unravelling. The Alpha's hesitation spoke volumes, and Zalith's dark eyes glinted with predatory intent. Sirrus might not have realized it yet, but his time at the top was rapidly running out. All Zalith needed to do was wait for the perfect moment to strike.

And that moment came when Alucard unclasped his fist, infecting the glade in a deafening explosion of dark and red. As the serpentine power ensnared every demon before they could even try to attack or flee, Sirrus panicked. He clearly had no idea what to do—he looked left, he looked right—he stared in utter disbelief as Alucard's fog gripped and pulled his men into the darkness, and as the Betas guarding his treasures were torn away into the dark, he rushed over to defend it himself.

It was time to move. Zalith led his own demons down the hill, disappearing into Alucard's fog, where he could see perfectly in every direction. As Tyrus led the fighters across the glade to deal with Sirrus' pack, Zalith fixed his scowl on the Alpha. The panicking leader skidded to a halt in front of his treasure, and as Alucard began clearing the fog, the Alpha's eyes darted around frantically; his men were revealed, each and every one of them struggling in the grip of Zalith's demons, and once Zalith and Alucard stopped twenty feet away from the man, the vampire commanded the remainder of his fog to return to him.

As they revealed themselves, Zalith stood protectively in front of Alucard, urging him behind him; he didn't want Sirrus to attack his fiancé thinking that he was the man there to challenge him.

With a furious snarl, Sirrus' anxious eyes shifted between Alucard and Zalith. "Who the fuck are *you*?" he growled.

"A challenger," Zalith announced tonelessly. He wanted this to be over quickly; Sirrus wasn't the first Alpha he'd challenged since escaping Nefastus, and he certainly wouldn't be the last. Zalith would beat him, and Sirrus' pack would join his and Alucard's growing army.

Sirrus scoffed, snarled, and stretched out his dragonish wings as his oryx-like horns gleamed in the moonlight. He grinned, waiting, evidently proud of his display.

Zalith responded, moving forward and adorning his own dragon-like wings and his tall, dark horns. And as he stretched his wings outwards, he prepared to engage in battle. He didn't want to leave Alucard's side, but the challenge was between him and Sirrus, so he reluctantly prowled towards the man, and in the corner of his eye, he saw his vampire back off and join Tyrus and their fighters, who held Sirrus' people firmly.

This wasn't like the first challenge, though; he knew what he was doing, and he knew that his demons would rush to protect Alucard if they had to. Sirrus was only the third in a long line of Lilidian demon Alphas whose packs Zalith planned to take, the third challenge since he escaped Nefastus. There were many more he planned to deal with before the month was over, and he wasn't going to waste a second longer.

Zalith began circling, as did Sirrus, their scowls locked. He'd wait for him to attack first—that way, he'd be able to work out what kind of man this was. A single move or two would tell him whether Sirrus was actually trained in combat, or if he was just an irrelevant idiot who knew no more than to flail his claws around when battle came his way. Zalith was already sure that he wasn't as much of a threat as he might make himself out to be—after all, he seemed far more interested in protecting his treasures than his pack, and his pack might even be relieved to be free of this man's rule.

Sirrus laughed, grinning as they kept circling one another. "What are you waiting for? Coward!" he snarled, scowling.

Zalith rolled his eyes. He had nothing to say to him.

Scoffing, Sirrus came to an abrupt halt, his crimson eyes narrowing in frustration. Zalith mirrored the motion, standing still and unyielding, his expression calm but calculating. With one final snarl, Sirrus lunged forward, claws bared and teeth flashing. Zalith didn't flinch; he waited, timing his move perfectly. As Sirrus closed the distance, Zalith shifted smoothly to the side, catching the man's arm mid-strike. With effortless precision, he twisted and flung Sirrus face-first into the nearest tree.

The impact reverberated through the glade, the sound of wood cracking and Sirrus' grunt of pain cutting through the still air. Zalith stood motionless, watching as Sirrus struggled to his feet, using the tree for support. The Alpha swung around with an aggravated huff, his gaze locking onto Zalith. The look in Sirrus' eyes betrayed his growing frustration—and perhaps a glimmer of fear. Zalith scowled back, his stance steady, every muscle poised for the next move.

It was clear to Zalith now: Sirrus wasn't used to a real fight. His bravado was crumbling, and it was painfully obvious that he relied more on intimidation than skill. This would be over much sooner than Zalith thought.

Sirrus lunged again, this time throwing wild punches. Zalith blocked the first with his forearm, the force rippling through his muscles but not breaking his stance. The second punch he dodged effortlessly, tilting his head aside with a grace that only fuelled Sirrus' growing rage; the Alpha snarled, stumbling slightly as Zalith shoved him back. Normally, Zalith might have enjoyed dragging this out, toying with the overconfident fool. But not tonight. He wanted this done quickly.

He could end Sirrus with a single move, with one lethal touch—but there was no need. Zalith preferred to show a shred of mercy. After all, someone would need to lead this pack once it belonged to him, and he didn't want Sirrus' demons thinking that *his* rule would be just as cruel as that of their current master.

But Sirrus wasn't finished yet. With a feral roar, he surged forward, his wings flaring wide as he used them to propel himself at Zalith with surprising speed. Zalith braced himself, catching Sirrus by the wrists as the man collided with him. Their strength locked for a moment, but before Zalith could counter, Sirrus twisted sharply, his right wing snapping around and slamming into Zalith's side with brutal force.

The blow sent Zalith off his feet, his body hitting the ground with a thud. But his recovery was instantaneous—before Sirrus could press his advantage, Zalith surged upward, closing the distance between them in a single motion. Sirrus barely had time to react before Zalith's hand clamped around his throat.

With a growl, Zalith slammed him into the ground, pinning him beneath his weight. His blood-red eyes burned with cold fury as he leaned in, his grip firm but controlled. Sirrus' crimson gaze widened in shock, his earlier confidence all but shattered. Zalith stared down at him, unmoved by the pitiful defiance that lingered there.

This fight was already over. Sirrus just didn't know it yet.

Sirrus choked and struggled, trying to pull Zalith's grasp from his throat with the only free hand he had, his other pinned above his head. He tried to move his wings, but Zalith pinned those down, impaling the man's carpals with the talons on his own wings.

"You can either work under me…or die," Zalith offered as Sirrus grunted angrily. "Either way, your pack is mine."

With yet another snarl, Sirrus still tried to break free, but Zalith tightened his grip, depriving him of air. He glared down into the man's eyes, waiting for him to answer. If he had to kill this man, then he would. He didn't *need* him.

Sirrus kept struggling, trying to pull free—he wasn't going anywhere.

At least that was what Zalith thought.

Before he could comprehend it, Sirrus spat venom into his face—Zalith's eyesight immediately blurred as he gritted his teeth and snarled in revolt; pain surged through his head as the venom burned into his skin, and Sirrus managed to pull his left wing free and smashed it into Zalith's side, sending him tumbling along the ground until he hit what felt like a tree.

Zalith got up, dragging his hands over his face in an attempt to wipe the venom off; however, his eyesight cleared just enough only for him to see Sirrus grab him by his throat. He gripped Sirrus' arm, but the man yelled furiously and threw him back into the centre of the glade. Zalith wouldn't let him throw him off like that again; he recovered as quickly as he could, climbing to his feet—Sirrus reached him and went to grab him again, but Zalith dodged, and Sirrus stumbled past him. The Alpha swung around quickly, slashing his claws forward; his talons cut Zalith's chest, but he didn't care—Zalith snarled and grabbed the back of the man's head; he forced him forward, smashing his face into the closest tree with an aggravated huff, and as Sirrus' face broke, the man grunted painfully and dropped to the ground, where he lay in silence.

It was over.

As he then let his horns and wings crumble away, Zalith lifted his hand to wipe the venom from his face again—

Alucard snatched his wrist and stopped him. "Don't wipe it," he said with a concerned frown. "It'll only burn more," he mumbled. He used his coat sleeve to gently dab away the venom from Zalith's face as he stared at him, waiting. Once Zalith's face was clean, Alucard's eyes then wandered down to the three slashes on his chest—

"I'm okay," the demon said, placing his hand on the side of Alucard's face.

The vampire's frown thickened as his gaze shifted from the bloodied wounds visible through the torn fabric of Zalith's shirt and blazer to the demon's face. His eyes lingered there, searching, before darting back to the injuries. "You don't look okay," he said quietly, the concern etched across his face unmistakable.

Zalith smirked a little, his focus shifting from his victory to his desire to assure his fiancé that he was just fine. "What *do* I look like?"

Alucard pouted, running his fingers through Zalith's hair and tucking the loose strands of his fringe back over the top of his head. "You look hurt," he said.

"I'll heal—I'll be okay, I promise," he said with a smile, moving his hand to Alucard's right bicep and squeezing it.

He nodded in response, but he looked hesitant—he clearly didn't want to make a scene in front of Zalith's people. "Okay," he replied, taking hold of Zalith's hand.

"Are *you* okay?" the demon then asked, dragging his hands down Alucard's arms and turning his wrists, revealing the healing wounds.

"I'm fine," he said.

Zalith watched the cuts heal, and once they closed, he took his eyes off Alucard and watched as the pack of demons he'd just won from Sirrus were cautiously released, and then they made their way towards him, each and every one of them lowering their heads in submission, keeping their eyes off him to let him know that none would question his authority. Zalith's own people moved closer, too, standing behind the crowd of new demons in case anything might happen—not that it would, though; these demons now belonged to him, and they would follow his orders without hesitation.

"Which of you is the highest ranked behind him?" Zalith asked, glancing over at Sirrus' lifeless body.

A dark-haired, crimson-eyed man stepped out of the crowd, keeping his eyes on the ground. "I am, sir. Julius Lafayette at your service."

"This is Idina," Zalith said, holding his arm out towards her as she made her way through the crowd and stood beside Tyrus. "You and everyone else will listen to her and do whatever it is she tells you, or there will be problems," he ordered.

Julius nodded.

"Once you've logged them, find them a suitable Alpha or assign them to existing packs that would benefit from them," Zalith told Idina.

"Of course," she said with a nod.

"The rest of you, go with her," he instructed the new demons.

As Idina then made her way over to Julius, the new demons followed.

"Let's move out," Zalith called and started leading the way out of the trees. The battle was over, and now it was time to head back to the ship. There were many more fights ahead of him, and he needed to take whatever chances he got to rest and recover. But he knew that he wouldn't find respite; his thoughts wouldn't stop racing, eager to plot for the next challenge. All he could do was take a break... and breathe. And maybe he could enjoy a moment or two with the man he loved.

Chapter Two

— ⟨ ✝ ⟩ —

A Slowly Healing Wound

| **Alucard,** *Saturday, Tertium 11th, 960(TG)—Avalmoor, Croford Island* |

Once they emerged from the forest, the dense canopy gave way to open skies, and Alucard glanced back at the shadowy expanse behind them. The trees stood tall and ominous, their twisted branches clawing at the twilight, while the air still carried a faint, earthy scent of damp moss, decaying leaves, and rotten bodies. In contrast, the hill ahead was alive with motion, the grass bending and rippling under the push of the wind. Alucard and Zalith climbed steadily, their boots leaving faint prints in the soil, and at the crest of the hill, the dirt road stretched out like a promise of respite. Half a mile further along, their waiting carriage sat framed by the fading glow of the horizon.

Alucard kept hold of Zalith's hand as they made their way along the road, his grip firm but tender. He stole a glance at his mate, a small smile lingering on his lips. A content, victorious feeling swelled inside him. Another pack had been claimed, and their army was slowly growing—a slow but steady march towards their shared goal. But more than that, Alucard relished the memory of Zalith in battle. He loved watching the demon fight, he loved the way his aggression burned with precision, and he loved the way he delivered lessons that were well deserved.

But then his gaze flickered to Zalith's face, catching the faint wince that marred the demon's otherwise confident expression. Alucard's eyes dropped to his chest, seeing the deep wounds that were still bleeding through the torn fabric of his shirt; concern twisted in his stomach, though he said nothing just yet.

"Well, that's one more down," Zalith said as they continued walking, his voice calm but laced with exhaustion. "Next, we'll face one of Lilith's bigger congregations," he muttered, his words edged with both determination and weariness.

That was the plan. Since leaving Nefastus, Alucard and Zalith had been working tirelessly to grow their numbers, preparing for the inevitable confrontation with Lilith,

Damien, and anyone else who stood in their way. Zalith's people had tracked Lilith's followers, targeting smaller, scattered demon packs first. Each time, Zalith would challenge the Alpha, defeat them, and absorb their demons into his and Alucard's growing army. The attacks served a dual purpose—not just to bolster their ranks but also to provoke Lilith into revealing herself.

Her whereabouts remained frustratingly elusive. Orin was scouring the lands in search of her, but so far, he'd uncovered nothing of value. Without knowing where she was or the size of the force she had at her disposal, Alucard and Zalith couldn't yet make their move. But they were certain of one thing: Lilith was hiding because she was afraid. She knew Alucard had her Obcasus, one of two things needed to render her comatose permanently. He had the strength, the skill, and the resolve to use it; all they needed was a Pandorican to trap her inside—and Crowell was still hunting for the one that had last been in Ysmay's possession. Until then, they would keep advancing, dismantling her forces piece by piece, waiting for her to show herself.

Snapping out of his thoughts, Alucard worriedly asked Zalith, "Will you be okay?"

"Of course I will," he said with an assuring smile, glancing at him as they approached their carriage.

"The Alpha of the next pack might not be as stupid as that guy back there," Alucard mumbled. "He's most likely one of Lilith's scions."

"Well, he's going to feel very stupid when he loses," the demon said as they stopped beside their carriage.

Alucard pulled the door open, inviting Zalith to climb in first. "Do we have a name yet?"

Zalith climbed in. "Thank you," he said, and as he sat down, he sighed deeply. "Erasmus, I believe."

The vampire groaned, sitting beside him. "Well, I stand...*sit* corrected," he said amusedly. "I know of Erasmus. He's not very intelligent, but he *is* really strong and dangerous," he warned him, pulling the carriage door shut.

"Then I'll outsmart him," Zalith said confidently, smiling at Alucard.

Alucard smiled shyly in response, making himself comfortable as the carriage started moving. "Do we know exactly how many demons are in Erasmus' pack?"

"One-hundred-and-thirty-four," Zalith answered.

"That will give us...what? Over three hundred demons?"

"It will," his mate said with a nod. "Three hundred and twenty-two to be exact. Three hundred and seventy-four including those I just won, and including Tyrus and Orin's people, we'll have five hundred and thirty-five."

"Five hundred and sixty if we include the demons I took from Ysmay."

Zalith nodded again, a quiet sigh upon his breath as he glanced out the window.

"What's wrong?" Alucard asked.

"Nothing's wrong," he said, looking at him, "I'm just not content with the numbers yet."

"We'll get more," Alucard said with certainty. "And...there are always Ysmay's other packs, too," he said—but he knew that Zalith wanted to keep as far away from the Diabolus and Lucifer as possible.

"Soon enough," the demon said.

Alucard sighed and sat up straighter as the carriage rattled along the uneven road, the quiet clatter of wheels and the rhythmic creak of wood filling the air. His gaze drifted to Zalith, his hand instinctively moving to rest on the demon's shoulder. When Zalith turned to him, offering a faint smile, Alucard's chest tightened, and his own lips pressed into a frown. His eyes were drawn again to the tears in Zalith's blazer and shirt, the jagged slashes exposing raw, angry wounds across his chest. The bleeding had stopped, but the gashes were still open, the edges dark and inflamed. Zalith sat there as though nothing were wrong, his casual demeanour doing little to convince Alucard. He knew his mate too well; the pain was there, hidden behind that smile, and it was likely far worse than Zalith let on.

"Will you let me help you?" the vampire asked quietly, his anxious gaze lifting to meet Zalith's eyes.

"Maybe," the demon replied, his smile growing. "That depends on how."

Alucard's eyes wandered down again; first, he wanted to see how severe the cuts on Zalith's chest were. So, he unbuttoned the demon's blazer.

"Oh," his mate said in what might be realization as he smirked suggestively. "I get it now."

Alucard kept the faint pout on his face as he slid Zalith's blazer off, his fingers lingering longer than necessary against the fabric and the warm skin beneath. Was it awful of him to be thinking about something far more intimate right now? Probably. Zalith was injured, and his priority should be helping him...but a part of him—the part that had been simmering ever since he watched Zalith dominate yet another fight—couldn't ignore the desire curling low inside him. The sight of Zalith's strength and aggression had always done something to him, and now, sitting here in the dim confines of the carriage, that feeling was only growing stronger.

Still, he justified to himself; this wasn't just selfish. If Zalith gave in, it might even help him heal faster. Demons thrived on intimacy and connection, didn't they? Especially an incubus. That thought—half rationalization, half raw truth—was enough to keep Alucard's hands steady as he tossed Zalith's blazer onto the seat across from them and moved to the torn, bloodied shirt beneath.

He began to unbutton it, his movements slow, his gaze flicking up to meet Zalith's. The demon didn't say a word, his dark eyes fixed on Alucard with a quiet intensity that only made the vampire's pulse quicken. When the last button was undone, he pulled the shirt away, tossing it aside to join the blazer, leaving Zalith's chest bare.

Alucard's eyes settled on the three deep slashes marring his mate's chest. They looked about an inch deep, the raw edges still inflamed; the wounds weren't bleeding anymore, but they hadn't started healing either, their stillness a reminder of Zalith's unnatural restraint. Alucard reached out hesitantly, his fingers brushing just shy of the injured skin, his desire momentarily tempered by a surge of concern. Whatever else he wanted, he needed Zalith to be okay. And maybe, just maybe, he could make that happen—for both of them.

"Does it not hurt?" Alucard asked, his voice soft but heavy with concern as his gaze flicked from Zalith's wounds to meet his dark eyes.

"I've had worse," the demon replied with a casual shrug, his tone steady, almost amused. "Someone cut my entire hand off once," he said, smirking as he lifted his left hand. "It was in…nine hundred fifty-two in Aegisguard years. Some asshole called Bateman."

Alucard frowned sadly. "That's not funny."

"I know," he chuckled. "I really am okay, though."

The vampire's eyes dropped back to the deep slashes across Zalith's chest. He hesitated for only a moment before moving his hand to the demon's right pec. His fingers brushed against the torn skin, and then, with a shyness that melted under the weight of his desire, he leaned closer. Without a second thought, he dragged his tongue slowly and lightly over the bloody wound.

A quiet, contented sigh slipped from Zalith's lips. He leaned his head back, his posture relaxed and inviting as his hand found its way to Alucard's head. His fingers slid into Alucard's hair, caressing it with a gentle yet possessive touch, his dark eyes half-lidded as he clearly revelled in the sensation.

The moment Zalith's blood touched his lips, Alucard felt the familiar euphoria flood through him, its pull as irresistible as ever. His eyes fluttered closed as he savoured the taste, his restraint hanging by a thread. The metallic sweetness carried a rush of heat, a spark that ignited every nerve in his body. He shifted instinctively, nuzzling against the demon's neck, breathing in his scent, the combination of blood and strength intoxicating.

His fingers moved of their own accord, trailing lightly down Zalith's chest, over his firm abdomen, and lower still. He wanted more—he *ached* for more. The urge to sink his fangs into Zalith's neck surged within him, a hunger so raw that it was almost painful. But he held back. Zalith needed to heal, and Alucard refused to let his own desires overshadow that.

Instead, he pressed his lips to the demon's neck, the kiss lingering, warm and reverent. His hand slid back up, tracing the contours of Zalith's body before coming to rest against the side of his face. Alucard lifted his head, his fiery eyes meeting Zalith's, his touch gentle but possessive. He leaned in, his lips brushing just shy of the demon's as he whispered, "Let me take care of you."

Smiling, Zalith threaded his fingers through Alucard's hair, his dark eyes smouldering as they met Alucard's. "I love when you take care of me," he murmured, his voice low and rich, carrying a warmth that sent a shiver through Alucard. There was no smirk this time, only a soft, genuine smile that left Alucard's heart pounding harder in his chest.

Alucard returned the smile, his resolve melting as he leaned closer, capturing Zalith's lips in a tender yet hungry kiss. Their mouths moved together, the soft press of lips quickly growing deeper, more insistent. Zalith's hand tightened in Alucard's hair, and Alucard felt his breath hitch, his pulse quickening as heat surged through him.

The need for Zalith's touch had grown into an almost desperate ache, but Alucard held himself back, channelling that need into something more purposeful. Right now, it wasn't just about sating his own desire—it was about Zalith, about making him feel good, cared for, and whole. As they kissed, Alucard let his hand slowly trail down the demon's chest, his fingers brushing over every curve of muscle, lingering just enough to feel Zalith shudder beneath his touch.

When his hand reached Zalith's waist, Alucard gripped the demon's belt, his kisses unbroken as he began to unbuckle it. His mate responded with a low, satisfied hum, his hand sliding up Alucard's back before tightening in his hair. That possessive grip sent a thrill coursing through him, spurring him on as he tugged the belt free and discarded it.

Alucard didn't hesitate, unbuttoning the demon's trousers with steady hands before reaching inside to grasp his arousal. Zalith let out a quiet, breathy sigh, leaning his head back as Alucard's lips moved from his mouth to his jaw, then down the side of his neck. Each kiss was slow and reverent, as though Alucard was savouring every inch of him—*he was.*

Zalith's quiet sounds of enjoyment filled the carriage, sending Alucard's desire into a burning crescendo. He kissed lower, his lips brushing over the demon's collarbone and chest, trailing a path down his body with the same care he'd reserve for something sacred. Every touch, every kiss carried an unspoken promise: Zalith wouldn't have to wait for anything—Alucard was there to take care of him completely.

The taste of Zalith's blood still clung faintly to the vampire's lips, adding a heady edge to his growing hunger. When he reached Zalith's waist, he didn't hold back, his tongue tracing a slow path along the length of the demon's hardening shaft.

A soft, pleased sigh escaped Zalith as his fingers slid through Alucard's crimson hair once more. Alucard closed his eyes, letting the heat of the moment consume him as he worked his mouth over the tip, teasingly gradual, revelling in every reaction that trembled through Zalith's powerful frame. The demon's quiet moan sent a thrill coursing through

Alucard, and he felt his own arousal burn brighter, fed by the satisfaction of seeing his mate begin to relax under his care.

Zalith's hand tightened in Alucard's hair, the grip firm yet laced with a tenderness that sent a jolt of pleasure through the vampire. It only urged him further, his tongue swirling in slow circles around the demon's wet tip; the taste of his pre-cum mingled with the lingering notes of his blood, creating a flavour so rich, so intoxicating that it overwhelmed Alucard's senses.

It was more than just the taste of blood, more than the metallic tang that usually drove him into a frenzy—it was deeper, sweeter, carrying a warmth that seemed to seep into his very core. The pre-cum added a complexity, a subtle saltiness that was unexpectedly pleasing, heightening the euphoria already coursing through him. It was unlike anything he'd ever tasted, headier than any wine, and more potent than any blood alone could ever be.

Alucard closed his eyes, savouring the way it coated his tongue, the way it seemed to spark an insatiable hunger in him, a hunger that wasn't just about feeding—it was about Zalith, about the connection between them, raw and unfiltered. He tightened his grip on Zalith's hips, steadying him as he took more, his tongue tracing a languid path down his length before dragging back up, teasingly slow.

The sound of Zalith's soft groans, deep and reverberating, filled the carriage, and Alucard grew more content with each passing moment knowing that every flick of his tongue, every movement of his lips was driving the demon to the edge. The warmth of Zalith's arousal mixed with his intoxicating scent, wrapping around Alucard like an intoxicating haze.

He couldn't get enough. Every taste seemed to pull him deeper, stoking the fire inside him as he moved a little faster, his fangs brushing lightly against Zalith's sensitive skin, a silent promise of just how far he was willing to go to please him.

The soft, breathy moans spilling from Zalith's lips were like fuel, igniting a deeper need to please him, to make him forget everything else; the faint flicker of pain still visible in the demon's expression began to fade, replaced by pleasure that softened the tension in his jaw and the line of his shoulders. Alucard pressed his hands against Zalith's hips, holding him firmer as he quickened his pace, dragging his mouth along his inches. The demon's quiet groan in response sent a wave of satisfaction through him, and he relished the thought that he alone could make Zalith feel this way.

This wasn't just about healing Zalith, though; it was about showing his mate just how deeply he cared in a way words never could. Alucard poured every ounce of his devotion into every touch, every motion as if this was the only way he knew how to express what he felt. And as Zalith settled with a contented moan, his hand still gripping Alucard's hair, the vampire couldn't help but feel victorious. This moment belonged to them, and nothing else mattered.

Alucard felt a rush of satisfaction, not just in knowing that he was helping Zalith heal faster but in the undeniable pleasure he was drawing from his mate. The way Zalith's body tensed beneath him, the quiet growls deep in his throat, and the way his hands gripped Alucard's hair sent a thrill of pride through him. He loved this—he loved how he could unravel Zalith, reduce him to nothing but raw, primal pleasure, and Alucard exulted in the control and intimacy of it all.

When Zalith finally climaxed, a deep, delighted moan escaped his lips, filling the small carriage like a rumble of thunder; his fingers moved through Alucard's crimson hair, stroking gently before sliding down to the side of his face. His touch was warm and reverent, the pad of his thumb brushing over Alucard's cheek as if to wordlessly express everything he felt.

Alucard felt the hot rush of release against his tongue, the warmth strikingly intense, almost searing in its sensation, but he loved it. The taste was richer, darker, and far more intoxicating, carrying a hint of the same essence that made Zalith's blood so enthralling but with a deeper, more primal edge. It filled his mouth, coating his tongue in a way that felt utterly decadent, and Alucard couldn't help the soft, satisfied hum that escaped his throat. The sheer heat of it sent a shiver down his spine, igniting a deeper sense of connection to his mate, and he swallowed it eagerly, savouring every moment of the intimate exchange.

Zalith then lightly gripped Alucard's chin and tilted his face upward, pulling him into a heated, lingering kiss. It was slow and deep, carrying an unmistakable note of gratitude and affection. Alucard felt Zalith's hand move to the back of his head, holding him close as their lips melded together, the demon's body still shivering faintly from the aftermath of his climax.

"Perfect," Zalith murmured against his lips, his tone low and saturated with satisfaction. He pulled back just slightly, tucking a stray strand of Alucard's hair behind his ear as his dark eyes locked onto the vampire's face. A playful smirk curved his lips, though his gaze held a comforting softness. "You always know how to take care of me, baby."

Alucard's chest swelled with pride, his own smile curving his lips as he glanced down, his hands moving deftly to button Zalith's trousers and re-buckle his belt. "You're welcome," he said quietly and rested his forehead against Zalith's. For a moment, he lingered there, enjoying the closeness and the warmth of Zalith's breath against his skin. Then he leaned back, settling comfortably beside Zalith, who rested the side of his head on Alucard's as the vampire's hand brushed lightly against the demon's thigh, a small, pleased smile remaining on his lips. He felt complete in that moment, knowing he'd given Zalith what he needed—not just healing, but the pleasure and care that came with it.

For a short while, they sat in comfortable silence as the carriage bumped and swayed along the dirt road. The muffled creak of the wheels and the soft clopping of the horse's hooves filled the air, accompanied by the occasional rustle of wind brushing through the nearby trees. But as the landscape began to open up, the distant screech of seagulls broke the quiet, sharp and piercing against the softer sounds of the journey. The salty tang of the ocean reached Alucard's nose, carried on the breeze that drifted in through the small front window of the carriage, mingling with the faint scent of damp earth and the musk of the horse.

Through the window, Alucard caught a glimpse of the coastline ahead—the grey-blue expanse of water stretching endlessly towards the horizon, its surface glittering like stained-glass in the colourful moonlight. The masts of distant ships swayed gently in the port, their sails furled tightly. Beside him, Zalith leaned closer, pressing a kiss to the top of his head before slipping his hand into his with a reassuring squeeze.

Alucard let his gaze linger on the approaching shore but found his thoughts straying elsewhere. He was looking forward to boarding the ship and beginning the long journey home. It would take at least ten hours, and he and Zalith would be sleeping aboard. Yet, as much as he yearned for rest, he couldn't shake the question gnawing at the back of his mind. Would Zalith plan to head straight to their next target as soon as they returned tomorrow, or would they finally take some time to recover?

Lately, Zalith had been relentless in his work—dedicated to a fault. Alucard had noticed the way his mate threw himself into every task, every fight, rarely sparing a moment to pause. If he wasn't out challenging Alphas and claiming their packs, he was locked in his office, buried in plans and preparations.

Alucard frowned slightly, his fingers tightening around Zalith's as he glanced at him, wondering if now might be the time to convince him to rest. "Will we be leaving for Drydenheim the moment we get home tomorrow?"

Zalith nodded. "I had Edwin put our things for the trip near the door; I also had him pack your white shirt." He paused and smirked at him. "I hope that's okay—I like you in white."

Alucard pouted, trying to hide his fluster. "I thought I wasn't allowed to wear white anymore," he joked.

The demon laughed softly, trailing his fingers up beneath Alucard's shirt, grazing his skin with a teasing touch. He pressed a kiss to the side of the vampire's face, his lips lingering for a moment before moving down to nuzzle against his neck. As he did, his other hand found its way to Alucard's top button, fiddling with it absentmindedly. "Are you going straight to bed when we get to the ship?" he asked, his voice smooth and quiet, tinged with playful curiosity.

It was late. Alucard's thoughts drifted back to when they disembarked the ship earlier, just as the clock had edged close to ten. Now, hours later, he was sure it had to be well past midnight. "Probably," he murmured, his eyes already heavy with fatigue. The weight of the long day pressed against him, and he leaned slightly into Zalith's touch. "You should too—you need to rest," he added, his tone soft but firm, laced with concern as his gaze flicked towards his mate, noting the faint tension in his expression despite the warmth of the moment.

The demon nodded in response. "Okay. I'll try."

Eventually, they arrived at the empty docks, where their steamship awaited them. The vessel was a curious blend of function and sophistication—its polished brass fixtures and intricate piping glinted in the moonlight, while the dark wooden panels of its hull bore the weathered charm of a well-used craft. The smokestack loomed above, hinting at the power beneath its elegant facade.

As the carriage rolled to a halt, Alucard pushed the door open and stepped out, offering a steadying hand to Zalith. His concern for the demon's injury lingered, though it was healing rapidly now, much to his relief.

Keeping hold of Zalith's hand, Alucard led the way along the creaking docks, the faint scent of salt and tar mingling in the crisp night air. They ascended the ramp onto the ship, greeted by the crew who immediately began preparing for departure. The hum of machinery and the rhythmic clatter of boots against the deck added to the ship's lively atmosphere as Alucard and Zalith retreated into the cabin.

The cabin was simple and efficient, reflecting the ship's practical purpose. A sturdy table occupied the centre of the room, while a double bed stood at its far end beneath a large, circular window that framed the dark, rippling waters outside. To the left of the bed sat a plain dresser, and to the right, a modest cupboard. A black, patchy rug covered the floor, its edges curling slightly from wear. If this ship were anything more than a temporary means of travel, Alucard would have taken the time to make it more inviting—more like a home. But this vessel served its purpose well: inconspicuous and unremarkable, exactly what he and Zalith needed right now.

He led Zalith to the bed, his hands careful and attentive as he helped him out of his trousers. Alucard gradually undressed the demon and guided him into bed before climbing in beside him. Fatigue pressed heavily on him, and he could see the same weariness in Zalith's eyes. As he lay down, the vampire shuffled closer, his body drawn instinctively to his mate. He wanted to rest his head against Zalith's chest, to listen to the steady rhythm of his heart, but he hesitated—he didn't want to risk causing him pain. Instead, he settled as close as he could, draping an arm gently across Zalith's stomach, holding him in a way that still brought comfort and closeness without pressing too hard. The warmth of the demon's body beneath his hand was grounding and soothing, and Alucard felt himself begin to drift, secure in the knowledge that they were together.

As much as he wanted to lay there and talk, though, he knew that they both needed as much rest as they could get. He exhaled deeply, closing his eyes. "I love you," he murmured.

"I love you, too," Zalith said contently, moving his arm around Alucard and hugging him tightly as he turned his head to kiss the vampire's forehead. "Goodnight," he added.

"Goodnight," Alucard replied sleepily. And to the sound of the waves and the warmth of his mate's embrace, he let himself slowly fall asleep.

Chapter Three

— ⊰ ✝ ⊱ —

The Month That Had Passed, The Dismay That Still Remained

| **Zalith**—*The Ocëanthar Ocean, The Steamship* |

Zalith lay beside Alucard, his dark eyes fixed on the ceiling, a deep frown carving lines into his face. No matter how he shifted—turning onto his side, adjusting his position, tucking an arm beneath his head—comfort eluded him. His mind refused to quiet, spinning endlessly with thoughts he couldn't suppress. The steady sound of the waves crashing against the ship and the rhythmic creaks of its wooden frame did little to soothe him. Even the gentle rise and fall of Alucard's breathing beside him, so peaceful and steady, failed to bring him the calm he desperately sought.

He moved closer, resting his head lightly on Alucard's chest, listening to the slow, reassuring beat of his heart. It helped, just as it always did, but it wasn't enough. Beneath the comfort was a gnawing unease, a war waging in his mind that he couldn't win. His thoughts whispered cruel truths, telling him he wasn't doing enough, that he didn't deserve to rest while there was still so much to be done. His chest tightened as he let out a quiet sigh; it had only been a month since they'd fled Nefastus, and though he'd worked tirelessly—gathering hundreds of demons, expanding his influence in the city near their castle, and forging alliances—it all felt inadequate.

What right did he have to rest when so much still hung in the balance? His paranoia fuelled his restlessness. He couldn't stop imagining the worst—what if something happened to Alucard while he slept? The thought was enough to make his hold on his vampire tighten, his arms wrapping securely around him as though that alone could ward off any threat. But even that small comfort wasn't enough to keep the tension from knotting his shoulders and clawing at his mind.

He opened his eyes and stared into the dim cabin, the faint flicker of moonlight spilling through the round window offering little to focus on. Alucard stirred beside him, rolling over to tug the blanket back around himself, and Zalith froze for a moment, watching his vampire settle again. A pang of guilt stabbed through him; he didn't want to disturb Alucard's rest—at least one of them deserved peace tonight.

With a quiet sigh, Zalith sat up slowly to avoid waking Alucard. The dull, lifeless room stretched out before him: the plain table, the worn rug, the darkened fireplace. His eyes lingered on the cold hearth, and a thought struck him; if he wasn't going to stay in bed to keep Alucard warm, he could at least make sure the room was comfortable. Raising a hand, he lazily waved it towards the fireplace, and with a soft crackle, it roared to life, the white flames shimmering in the dimness and casting a gentle glow across the room.

Zalith stared into the flickering light, his mind still buzzing, even as he tried to convince himself to rest. He closed his eyes for a brief moment, knowing it would be another long night—just as every night had been since they fled their old home. The dread that clung to him had yet to fade, and no amount of firelight or reassuring heartbeats seemed capable of chasing it away.

Thinking about losing his home stirred a painful memory, one Zalith tried to avoid but could never truly escape. Nefastus wasn't the only home he'd lost, but it cut far deeper than the others. It wasn't just a place—it was a reflection of something sacred. He had built it to mirror the house he'd grown up in with his family back in Eltaria, every detail carefully chosen to preserve the warmth and comfort he'd once known. Losing Nefastus felt like losing his family all over again, a cruel reminder of how much had been taken from him.

He cursed himself for dredging it up, but he couldn't stop the thoughts from unravelling. Talking about losing his hand had been enough to open the floodgates, forcing him to confront the other horrors of that battlefield. That night had cost him far more than a hand—it had taken his mother. Her bloodied, terror-stricken face surged to the forefront of his mind, so vivid that it felt like a fresh wound. He clenched his jaw, trying to push the image away, but it refused to fade. No matter how much he wanted to fight it, he didn't have the strength. He was too tired—too drained to fight another war with his own mind. All he could do was sit in the oppressive silence of the memory, its weight pressing heavily against him.

But sleep would bring no respite. He'd either dream awful, terrible things, or he'd wake up twenty minutes later under a thick avalanche of guilt. Or both. It was often both.

With a quiet sigh, he pulled himself out of bed, made sure the blankets were firmly over Alucard, and then made his way over to the nearby desk as he pulled his trousers back on. A lingering soreness clung onto his chest—his wounds were almost healed, but they still ached. He didn't care. There were things he had to do that were far more important than his discomfort…and his need to rest.

He quietly pulled out the desk's chair and slumped down into it. Tucked between the desk and the dresser beside it was his leather briefcase; he'd been quite sure that this would happen, that he wouldn't be able to sleep, so he'd brought his work with him. He placed it onto the desk, unclipped it, and pulled out the papers from within.

Eimwood—the city an island over from his and Alucard's castle. It had been a cesspool of poverty and struggle before he had decided to do something about it. After all, he'd need more than just an army of demons for what he had planned. The more people he and Alucard had trusting in their cause, the better, whether they be demons, humans, elves—the latter were a species that had caused Eimwood's fall.

The elves of Yrudberg Island had exploited Eimwood for decades, their grip tightening year after year. They had cut off vital supply lines, forcing the city into a constant state of scarcity. Food, water, medicine—everything a city needed to thrive was rationed to the barest minimum. The people were left to scrape by, their spirits eroded by hardship. Then, the pandemic struck. Despite his and Alucard's tireless efforts to contain it, the same virus that had once infected Zalith escaped Nefastus, spreading like wildfire through parts of Aegisguard. But, curiously, it didn't reach Eimwood. Zalith had acted swiftly, determined to protect the city and reshape its future.

He and Alucard had been more than generous in their efforts. They had funded the construction of high, fortified walls to keep the infected—and other dangers—out. The streets, once overrun with rat infestations and stray monsters that prowled after dark were now patrolled and secure. Zalith had forged new relationships with supply lines, ensuring the city received the provisions it desperately needed—food, clean water, medicine, and the materials to rebuild homes that had been falling apart for years. Families who had once huddled together in damp, crumbling buildings now had roofs that didn't leak, walls that kept out the cold, and floors that didn't rot beneath their feet.

The children of Eimwood, who had once wandered the streets barefoot and threadbare, now had clothes on their backs and warm beds to sleep in. The marketplace, which had once been eerily silent, was alive again with the sounds of trade and laughter, the stalls stocked with goods that hadn't been seen in years. All of this was because of him and Alucard. Their names—well, alias'—were spoken with reverence throughout Eimwood—and even across Yrudberg—as the ones who had brought the city back from the brink.

Of course, the elves weren't pleased. They had profited from Eimwood's suffering, and now their influence was slipping through their fingers. Their discontent hung like a storm cloud on the horizon, but Zalith was ready. Eimwood was his city now, and he would do whatever was necessary to protect it—and the people who called it home.

But he wasn't where he wanted to be—not yet. Eimwood still had a Lord, and it wasn't him, nor was it Alucard. Lord Cecil, an arrogant and self-serving man, had done nothing for the city he was meant to govern. Instead, he skulked about, content to scrape by on whatever meagre scraps the elves deigned to offer him and his people, showing no backbone, no leadership, and certainly no care for the city's future. A faint sneer crossed Zalith's face at the thought of him. That man had no business sitting on a throne.

Zalith's plans to pry Cecil from his seat of power were already in motion, though he was in no rush. All in good time. When the moment came, he would claim the throne not for himself alone, but for Alucard as well. Together, they would rule—not with the cowardice and complacency of Lord Cecil, but with strength and purpose. Eimwood deserved better, and Zalith intended to give it just that.

For now, there were other matters to focus on.

Croford. That was the place they had just left. He dragged the tip of his pen through the name; he had just killed the Alpha of the pack that resided there, and next— *tomorrow*—they would head to Adenaville, a city on Lerkand Island, which was just off the coast of Drydenheim. One of Lilith's larger cults was currently residing in a small town not far outside the city, a pack of over a hundred demons. He had the numbers to subdue them and challenge their Alpha; he was sure this attack might draw Lilith out. Orin was searching for her, but she hadn't shown herself despite their recent attacks on her people. She was losing followers, yet it didn't seem to matter. Why didn't it matter?

Zalith pulled a world map from the stack of papers in front of him, his dark eyes narrowing as he spread it across the table. His gaze moved over the marked locations, each one representing a report from his scouts—places identified as homes to packs of Lilidian demons. He studied them intently, his expression sharp with focus, as though willing the map to give him more answers than it held.

Tonight marked the third pack he'd taken from her, and yet...there had been no retaliation. Why? Zalith's jaw tightened as he considered the possibilities. He had no idea where Lilith was hiding, and he wouldn't know unless she chose to reveal herself. For now, his strategy remained the same: force her hand by continuing to dismantle her power base. The more packs he stole from her, the fewer demons she'd have under her sway; with each loss, her influence would dwindle, her grip on her followers weakening. Surely, she couldn't ignore this forever. Sooner or later, she'd have to react—and when she did, he would be ready.

The demon clenched his jaw as his thoughts turned to Lilith. He knew why she was hiding—it was because Alucard had her Obcasus, the very weapon that could destroy her just as it had when they'd escaped her wretched temple. Her fear was keeping her in the shadows, and he could use that. Tomorrow's plan to take the larger pack from her was designed to provoke her, to force her to react. If she showed herself, they'd finally have a lead on her whereabouts, and they could move forward with the next phase of their plan.

But Zalith wasn't ready to face her just yet. He needed more people, more power before that moment arrived. Alucard had suggested branching out, targeting other groups like Damien's followers or even Lucifer's cults, but Zalith wasn't convinced. Such moves could draw the attention of the other Numen, and that was a risk he wasn't willing to take—not yet. Lilith was isolated for now, and no one was coming to the aid of her packs. He intended to keep it that way.

The idea of expanding their targets could be explored later, but for now, his focus remained solely on Lilith. Until tomorrow, when the next strike would bring them one step closer, there was little else he could do but wait—and he despised the waiting.

He pushed the map aside and pulled a small book from the briefcase. There wasn't much more he could do about Lilith for now, but Eimwood demanded his attention. The city was thriving under the changes he and Alucard had brought—its people already held them in high regard for their contributions. The next step was clear: he needed to remove Lord Cecil from power. Zalith smirked faintly at the thought. Taking the throne wouldn't be difficult; the people wouldn't mourn Cecil's absence. But how to deal with him without drawing suspicion or unwanted attention? He'd figure it out soon enough. All he needed was to get the man alone.

The elves were another matter. Alucard's vampires were guarding Eimwood's borders, keeping an eye out for any elf that dared try to come near. Zalith had banished them from the city so they could no longer do harm, but obviously, they weren't at all happy to lose it. He was sure they were planning something, and he had a few of Greymore's men investigating a nearby town the elves enjoyed drinking in—he had to wait for answers. But if the elves were planning an attack on the city, he was ready—*they* were ready. Where his demons were out all over the world, Alucard's demons were in the city ready for anything. Eimwood was his city now, and he'd make sure it stayed that way. All he had to do was get rid of Cecil…something would turn up, he was sure.

The elves were another problem entirely. Alucard's vampires guarded Eimwood's borders, ever watchful for any elf bold enough to attempt an approach. Zalith had banished them from the city, cutting off their ability to manipulate and harm its people, and their fury over losing control was palpable. He had no doubt that they were scheming. To that end, he'd sent a few of Greymore's men to investigate a nearby town where the elves were known to gather and drink. All he could currently do was wait for answers. If the elves were plotting an attack on Eimwood, Zalith was prepared—*they* were prepared. While his own demons worked across the world, Alucard's demons remained stationed in the city, ready to act at a moment's notice.

He closed the book, tired of poring over his calculations. The money he'd poured into Eimwood wasn't concerning in the slightest—it was nothing more than a drop in the ocean compared to what he was willing to spend. Leaning back in his seat, he let out a quiet sigh, tapping his fingers rhythmically against the papers spread across the desk. As much as he itched to dive headlong into his plans, he knew better than to rush. Tomorrow, when they returned home, he'd let Alucard rest while he turned his attention back to Eimwood.

The city council was surely wondering where he was by now, and his presence there was overdue. Beyond that, his investigation into Cecil needed to move forward. Perhaps speaking directly with the citizens could reveal information he hadn't yet uncovered. Zalith also understood the power of visibility—showing his face would strengthen his reputation as someone actively working for Eimwood's future. He intended to personally delve into Cecil's involvement in the city's decline, ensuring that the people saw him taking action firsthand.

Of course, more eyes searching for answers meant better results. Danford was already looking into anything that could help remove Cecil from power. Discretion was essential, and Danford excelled at it, especially with his new vampire skills. Zalith trusted him to uncover what others might miss, and he knew that, with time, the pieces would fall into place. Cecil wouldn't remain a problem for long.

Zalith pulled out his pocket watch, the gold casing catching the flickering light of the white flames. Nearly 4 a.m. It was late—or early, depending on perspective—but the weight of exhaustion hadn't yet pushed him to surrender. He was tired, yes, but not enough to force his restless mind into sleep. Not with so much work still demanding his attention.

With a quiet sigh, he reached for his briefcase, pulling out a fresh stack of paperwork. The rustle of the pages filled the otherwise silent cabin as he spread them across the desk, his eyes scanning the lines of text and figures. This would keep him occupied, a distraction to anchor him against the storm of thoughts swirling in his head. It wasn't a cure, but it was something—something to stop him from sinking too deeply into the darkness of his own despair.

And so, as the ship rocked gently against the waves, Zalith settled into his work, his focus sharp and unwavering. The light of the fire cast long, shifting shadows across the walls, and somewhere behind him, Alucard slept soundly. Whatever battles awaited them tomorrow, Zalith would be ready—he had no intention of losing. Never again.

Chapter Four

— ⊰ ✝ ⊱ —

My Love

| **Alucard**—*The Ocëanthar Ocean, The Steamship* |

The soft creak of wood stirred Alucard from his slumber, though his eyes remained closed at first. For a fleeting moment, he thought it might be the ship groaning against the waves or the faint hum of the wind brushing past the cabin. But something about the sound—or perhaps the feeling that accompanied it—unsettled him. Slowly, he blinked his eyes open, the dim glow of the white fire casting flickering shadows across the room.

Sitting up, Alucard instinctively reached out to the space beside him where Zalith had been. The sheets were cool to the touch, the absence of his mate's warmth sending an odd pang through his chest. His gaze moved towards the desk across the room, where Zalith sat hunched over, papers strewn before him and the gold of his pocket watch catching the light. Even from a distance, Alucard could sense the weight pressing down on him—the kind of despair that clung like a shadow, silent but oppressive.

For a moment, Alucard simply watched, his fiery eyes tracing the tense set of Zalith's shoulders, the way his hand paused just slightly before picking up the pen again, as though the act of writing required more effort than it should. He could almost feel it radiating from the demon, that gnawing frustration, the restlessness that kept him awake when he should be resting.

Alucard sighed softly, his voice barely a whisper against the crackling fire, "Zalith?" The sound of it wasn't enough to draw Zalith's attention, and the vampire's frown deepened. He swung his legs over the side of the bed, the cool floor biting against his bare feet as he rose; he wrapped the fur throw around himself to keep the cold from gnawing at him and took a slow step towards the demon. "Zalith," he said quietly, his voice steady but laced with concern. "Is late. You need to be vesting."

His words hung in the air between them, soft yet insistent, as he waited for Zalith to look up.

When the demon finally turned his head to look across the room at him, a flicker of guilt slithered across this tired face. "Oh...I'm sorry. Did I wake you up?"

Alucard's frown became despondent. "Why aren't you in bed?"

"I couldn't sleep," he answered sadly.

"What's wrong?"

Zalith shrugged. "Nothing...I just can't sleep."

A deep ache settled in Alucard's chest as he lowered himself onto the edge of the bed, his fingers curling against the rumpled sheets. This wasn't the first time he'd found Zalith working when he should be resting, and each time it happened, his worry grew heavier. He could see it in the tension across Zalith's shoulders, feel it in the air—the struggle, the quiet suffering that his mate refused to voice. All Alucard wanted was to ease that burden, to help him find peace. But no matter how much he wanted to fix it, he knew he couldn't. All he could do was try.

"Come back over here," he murmured, his voice low and gentle as he patted the empty space beside him. With a soft pull, he tugged the covers aside, inviting Zalith back into the warmth of their bed.

The demon nodded, a sullen stare on his face. "Okay," he mumbled. He cleaned up his work, stacked his papers back into his briefcase, stored it under the desk, and then made his way back over to the bed. He pulled off his trousers and climbed in, shuffling closer to Alucard as he moved the blankets over him, and the vampire pulled the fur throw back over the covers.

Once Zalith was comfortable, lying on his side to face Alucard, the vampire rested his forehead against Zalith's and asked, "Why can't you sleep?"

Zalith shrugged. "I just...can't," he said softly. "When I'm laying here, I think about all the things I have to do, and...I figure it's better to do something than just lay here and do nothing—especially when I have so much to do."

Alucard frowned, guiding his hand up Zalith's arm and to the side of his face. "You need to rest," he said, something he found himself saying so very often lately. "You *deserve* to rest. You've done so much already, Zalith—but you don't have to do this all by yourself, and you don't have to keep overworking yourself. You do more than enough, and you *are* enough. Let yourself take a break," he pleaded quietly, caressing the side of Zalith's face.

"I've been trying," Zalith sighed sullenly.

The vampire's frown thickened with sorrow; he closed his eyes, stroking his hand down to Zalith's neck. "I love you," he hummed, moving his face as close to Zalith's as he could. "I see how hard you work—everyone sees how hard you work. We *all* love you, and we all appreciate what you do for us, Zalith. But you don't have to work yourself to death to make up for what happened in Nefastus—none of that was your fault. And you got everyone out of there alive. Stop blaming yourself," he begged, opening his eyes to stare into Zalith's. "Let yourself see that all of this—everything you've done since we got to the castle—…is all *more* than enough."

"I just don't want to be unprepared for any more surprises," the demon said despondently.

Alucard shook his head. "We won't be. No one knows where we are; we have people all over the world keeping an eye on our enemies, and Lilith is still hiding. Damien is nowhere to be seen, either—we are safe, Zalith, and we are safer every day because of you."

His mate looked hesitant, conflicted. "I don't want to do us and everyone else the disservice of getting comfortable again and creating opportunities wherein our enemies strike again—"

"I know," Alucard interjected, moving his hand to the side of Zalith's face again. "I know that you're worried they might find us again, and I know that you just want to protect everybody. And I don't blame you for being so worried—I'm worried too…but more about you and what this is doing to you. There's only so much you can do, and…there really isn't much more *to* do. Our castle is the safest place in all the seven realms," he said with a quiet laugh. "We made sure of that, and we make sure every single day that no one will know where we or your people are. We have hundreds of guards and people out there searching for even the slightest little hint that our location has been exposed—and it hasn't. We are safer here than we ever were in Nefastus."

Zalith nodded, closing his eyes. "Yeah," he murmured sadly.

Alucard didn't know what else to say. He knew that what he was saying wasn't helping, and it hurt him to know that he couldn't help Zalith out of this dismay he had sunk so deeply into. But that didn't dishearten him—he'd keep trying. He'd keep making sure that Zalith knew he loved him, and that everything he was doing and had done was more than enough—because it *was*.

He frowned again, guiding his fingers through Zalith's tousled hair. If he couldn't help him feel better, then maybe he could help him take his mind off it for a while. "I love you," he said again, and then he kissed Zalith's lips.

"I love you too," the demon said, trailing his hand up the blanket and to the side of Alucard's face. "Thank you…for trying to help me. I'm sorry if I'm frustrating to deal with sometimes."

Alucard shook his head, staring into Zalith's eyes. "You don't have to be sorry— and you're not frustrating to deal with. I just want to do whatever I can for you—there's nothing I won't do," he said with a smile, stroking his cheek.

Dismay flickered across Zalith's face for a fleeting moment, but he closed his eyes and exhaled softly. "Thank you," he said.

Alucard smiled again and kissed his lips once more. "I'll lay here with you until you fall asleep. And if you can't fall asleep, then we can lay here and talk about anything," he said quietly.

"No, it's okay," the demon said, shaking his head. "You need to get some sleep too."

"I'm okay," Alucard assured him. "I just want to lay here with you."

"Okay," he said sadly, caressing the vampire's hair.

Alucard moved his hand down from Zalith's neck, dragging it over his arm. He thought about the fact that he always felt safe in Zalith's arms, so maybe Zalith would feel a little more relaxed in his. He shuffled closer to him. "Turn around," he said.

Zalith smirked slightly. "Why?"

"Because I want to hold you," he said, pouting. "But I don't want to hurt you," he said, glancing down at what he could see of Zalith's chest. His wounds had healed a lot since earlier, but the scars still looked sore and were probably sensitive. He didn't want to cause Zalith any discomfort.

"Oh, okay," Zalith said with a smile, and then he rolled over onto his right side.

Alucard turned onto his right side and moved his arm around Zalith, hugging him tightly as he rested the side of his head on the side of Zalith's. "Do you want me to tell you a story?" he offered.

"Sure," the demon said curiously.

The vampire thought to himself for a few moments. He hoped it might help Zalith fall asleep, and if not... then he'd still lay here with him. "I had a horse... a hundred or so years ago—her name was Rocinante."

"Rocinante?" Zalith replied. "That's a cute name. What does it mean?"

"It's Aguilian; it means formerly a workhorse."

"I like it," the demon said.

Alucard smiled and continued, "We were walking along a cobblestone path on our way to a nearby town, and it was quite windy that day. A leaf blew across the trail, and Rocinante was terrified—she bucked me off and ran. I broke my arm in the fall," he laughed quietly. "It took me about twenty minutes to find her, and when I did, I slipped in this huge puddle of mud, and *that* scared her too, so she ran again. She was in the town when I found her... and I had to walk in there covered in mud—it was one of the most embarrassing things to ever happen."

Zalith chuckled amusedly. "Aw," he said sadly. "I've heard mud can be good for your skin, though."

The vampire shrugged. "You would never catch me willingly putting mud on my body."

"What if it's at a spa?"

"No," he said, pouting. "It just... feels wrong."

"It can make your skin very soft," he said with an assuring tone.

He pouted again. "Is my skin not soft?" he mumbled.

"It's soft," his mate assured him, stroking the arm Alucard had around him. "But imagine it after a mud bath...like satin," he mumbled, pulling Alucard's hand closer to his face so that he could kiss it.

Alucard smiled as the demon then held onto his hand and hugged his arm. "I'll try it if you do."

"I'd try it," he said with a shrug. "But only somewhere clean."

"Maybe that's something we can do together when we get back from Adenaville," he suggested.

"I don't think there's anywhere near the castle that does it, but we can ask around."

"Okay," Alucard said, closing his eyes.

Fatigue tugged heavily at Alucard, his body yearning for rest, but he resisted, unwilling to let sleep claim him while Zalith remained so visibly burdened. He wanted to stay awake, to be there for him—to make him feel even a fraction better in whatever time he had before his own exhaustion inevitably won. The vampire's arms tightened instinctively around his mate, his frown deepening as his thoughts churned. Maybe he could say it again—those words Zalith always seemed to need, even when he didn't ask for them. But even as the thought crossed his mind, he hesitated. It felt like telling him he loved him wasn't enough, not tonight.

A new idea surfaced, and he smiled faintly. Zalith always had a way of making him feel adored with the names he used: *baby, darling*—words that felt so natural and tender when Zalith said them. Alucard wanted to offer him the same, something that would let Zalith know how deeply he cared, how much he was cherished. But what could he call him? His frown returned as he considered it, the question circling in his tired mind. It needed to be something special, something that felt as intimate and unique as Zalith himself.

Alucard exhaled quietly, his exhaustion settling over him like a heavy blanket. Despite the fatigue, a faint nervous flutter stirred in his stomach as he thought about calling Zalith something new—something just for him. He didn't know why it made him so anxious; it was such a simple thing, yet the idea left him feeling shy and unsure, and that only frustrated him. Zalith deserved more than hesitation, more than the words that always felt too few.

But as he looked at Zalith, the answer felt clearer. There was no one else, no other thing in the world that meant as much to him as this demon who held his heart so completely. Zalith was *his love*—the words were so simple, but they carried everything he felt, everything he couldn't always say.

He smiled softly to himself, brushing aside the lingering nerves. "Goodnight, my love," he murmured sleepily, his voice low and warm as he hugged Zalith close. He nuzzled into the curve of his neck, feeling the quiet comfort of his presence, and let the fatigue finally take hold.

"Goodnight, baby," Zalith replied, his voice carrying a warmth that hadn't been there in a long time. There was a brief pause, just enough for Alucard to notice the subtle shift in his tone—surprise, softened quickly by something deeper, something almost reverent. The contentedness in Zalith's voice was unmistakable, like a quiet, unspoken happiness that lingered in the space between them. The demon squeezed his hand, and Alucard felt him finally relax.

With a soft, contented smile, Alucard let sleep claim him once more. As the warmth of exhaustion pulled him under, one thought lingered: he hoped that when he woke again, Zalith would still be beside him—and that, somehow, he'd managed to find even a little rest.

| **Zalith**—*The Ocëanthar Ocean, The Steamship* |

Zalith wasn't sure how long he'd been laying there since Alucard fell asleep. He frowned in dismay as his thoughts slowly consumed him; he didn't want to make Alucard sad or worried—he could see it in the way his fiancé had looked at him, in the softness of his words. That familiar pang of guilt settled in his chest, heavy and suffocating. He just wanted things to go back to how they used to be, when everything was fine, when no one had to worry, when he wasn't such a problem. He was tired of being the source of Alucard's concern.

Still, he had tried to smile earlier, forcing a fragile facade so Alucard wouldn't be any more troubled than he already was. That kindness, the way Alucard had spoken to him tonight—the tenderness of *my love*—had warmed something deep within him, even if he felt unworthy of it. Alucard's willingness to love him so wholly, to always try to help was something Zalith felt he didn't deserve. He didn't deserve someone like Alucard, someone who would do anything for him.

Closing his eyes for a brief moment, he tried to bury the despair threatening to rise. "Thank you," he said softly, the words feeling both necessary and inadequate, even if Alucard didn't hear them.

Now, with Alucard's arms wrapped around him and the sound of his slow, steady breathing filling the quiet room, Zalith felt himself relax ever so slightly. He smiled faintly as Alucard's earlier words echoed in his mind. *My love*. He had never heard Alucard call him something so endearing before, and it brought an unexpected ease to his heart. He loved Alucard so much, more than he could express, and moments like this reminded him just how deeply they were connected.

But even as Alucard slept, Zalith knew that sleep wouldn't come for *him*. He lay still, careful not to disturb his vampire, and frowned as his eyes wandered the dimly lit room. His gaze eventually fell on the desk across from them, and an idea struck him. He couldn't work—that might wake Alucard—but he could *read*.

Holding out his hand, he used his ethos to pull a book from the desk. It floated silently through the air before settling into his grasp. *A History of Yrudberg and Its Sister Islands*. Zalith had been gathering as much information as possible about the places he and Alucard were working to restore. Currently, his focus was on the elves of Yrudberg and the reasons Eimwood held such importance to them. As he opened the book, he let the familiar act of reading anchor him, hoping it might keep his restless mind at bay, even for a little while.

With a quiet sigh, he flipped through the page he was last on, and he read, taking in as much information as he could. Yrudberg was once a sacred place to the Yrudyen Elves; they worshipped the God Khila, an angelic being believed to grant them immortality through tribute and unconditional devotion. It sounded like a cult to Zalith, and he wouldn't be surprised if it were. The Numen and their cults... this Khila was most likely one of the known Numen using a different name, or perhaps one of their children. But Khila was said to have died saving their people from Aresphis, a colossal serpent that arose from the ocean and plagued Yrudberg and its sister islands with war, death, and famine.

He flipped to the next page. Since Khila's death, the Yrudyen Elves had followed one single queen. Like all elves, the Yrudyen cherished the natural world, the 'natural order', and despised those who wished to alter the world that the gods had already made perfect. And *that* was why elves loathed humans and their cities.

Zalith frowned. If they hated humans and their cities so much, why had the Yrudyen been using Eimwood before he had arrived and sent them running? Why not just tear it down as their beliefs would urge them? Perhaps these elves had been led astray. He wouldn't find the answer in this book—it was over fifty years old, and the Yrudyen Elves appeared in Eimwood roughly twenty years ago, according to the people Zalith had spoken to.

With another quiet sigh, he returned to the book's contents and searched the page for a chapter that might tell him more about Khila and Aresphis. And to his relief, his eyes hovered over: *page 347—Khila and Aresphis*. He flipped to the correct page and delved into the information laid out before him.

From what was written, Zalith was able to assume that Khila seemed to possess the likeness of an elf but might not actually be one. He was described as a god, after all, and unless he was a false god, he could only be a Numen or a Numen's child... perhaps like

Alucard? Or similar to the Aegis, Letholdus' children. Whichever it was, it didn't seem like it would matter, for Khila was dead, and so was Aresphis. Whoever they were, they didn't seem to grab the attention of the Numen—there was no mention of them here.

Aresphis, on the other hand…a giant serpent? The information didn't lead Zalith to believe that he was a Numen, a scion, a Numen's child, or an Aegis. Perhaps he was just some old, powerful creature that had chosen the wrong island to take a vacation on.

Zalith sighed, reading through the pages…but as he turned each one, the more his fatigue began to get to him. His eyes were getting heavy, and his mind wasn't absorbing as much information as it normally would. He flipped through the pages…however the book became looser in his weakening hands…and soon enough, the book dropped to the floor, and Zalith gave in, allowing himself to slowly sink into his exhaustion. It had been a long night…and he had to rest.

He *hoped* that he'd rest.

Chapter Five

— ⊰ ✝ ⊱ —

Of Life's Torments, and its Pleasures

| Zalith, *Quintilis, 344(TG)—Eltaria, Chronia, Andora* |

Zalith found himself running towards the redwood forest that stretched wide and imposing behind his childhood home. The towering trees rose like sentinels against the clear blue sky, their reddish-brown trunks glowing softly in the sunlight. Around him, familiar faces raced alongside, their laughter and hurried footsteps blending into the distant rustle of leaves. On his left were his two cousins, their playful jabs pushing each other to run faster. On his right, Xurian, his older brother, darted forward with his usual confidence, and next to him—Alucard.

The demon's heart twisted. The memory was achingly familiar, one he had relived so many times in quiet reflection. He knew this day well: he had been just eleven, Xurian thirteen, and his cousins fourteen. But Alucard—Alucard had not been there. As much as it felt natural, as if his mate belonged in this memory, Zalith knew better. Alucard wasn't a part of this moment in the past. This wasn't real. It had to be a dream.

Yet the thought didn't bother him. He didn't want to wake up. This dream, however altered, wrapped around him like a comforting cloak, and he let himself revel in it. He could smell the faint sweetness of pastries baking in the kitchen, carried on a gentle breeze that mingled with the earthy aroma of pine and moss. The warmth of the sun on his skin, the freedom of his youthful stride—it was all so vivid, so alive.

"Don't you dare come back filthy!" his mother's sharp voice cut through the air, breaking the harmony of the moment. From the balcony of their home, she leaned forward, her arms crossed, her expression hard and commanding. "And if you ruin your clothes, it'll be the end of you!"

They all shouted back half-hearted acknowledgements, their voices a chaotic jumble of irritation and defiance. Zalith felt the echo of his childhood rebellion, the fleeting freedom of racing towards the forest, away from her critical gaze. His cousins laughed, pushing ahead, and Xurian glanced back, grinning with a playful challenge.

Alucard ran beside him as if he had always been there, his presence a seamless part of the memory. Zalith couldn't bring himself to question it further. It felt right, even if it wasn't. And as the shadow of the redwoods fell over them, Zalith let himself sink deeper into the dream, unwilling to let it go.

"You're it!" one of his cousins shouted, slapping Zalith's arm before taking off with a burst of laughter.

The others scattered like leaves caught in the wind, their voices echoing through the trees as they raced ahead. Of course, Zalith was it—he was always it. They were all so much faster than him, but that didn't matter. He didn't want to be left behind. Determined, he launched into a sprint, his feet pounding against the soft forest floor as he chased after them.

As the group split in different directions, his gaze locked on Alucard. He set his sights on him, his legs burning with the effort to keep up. Alucard was just a little faster, just a little more agile—he always had been. But Zalith didn't care. He chased him anyway, weaving through the towering redwoods, dodging low-hanging branches and the occasional patch of undergrowth. The laughter of the others rang in the distance as they eventually regrouped, all heading towards a familiar opening deep within the woods—the place they always gathered, their little sanctuary.

When they reached the clearing, Xurian and their cousins immediately resumed their chaotic antics, snatching up sticks and whacking each other with wild abandon. Their laughter filled the air, carefree and unrestrained, while Zalith and Alucard wandered to the edge of the clearing. They sat on an old, weathered log, its surface rough beneath their hands.

Zalith fidgeted, his fingers brushing against the bark as he stared down at the ground. He had always been shy as a child, and now, sitting so close to Alucard, that shyness tightened in his chest. His hand rested on the log, close but not quite touching Alucard's. He glanced sideways, trying to muster the courage to move just a little closer.

When he dared to look up, he caught Alucard doing the same—sneaking a glance at him. A flutter of nervous excitement twisted through Zalith's heart, making him hesitate. His gaze darted towards Xurian, who was now whacking one of their cousins over the head with a stick, drawing a loud yelp and more laughter. The distraction gave him the smallest burst of courage, and slowly, cautiously, Zalith began to edge his hand closer to Alucard's.

When their fingers finally brushed, he froze, his breath hitching as a nervous frown tugged at his lips. He turned his head, meeting Alucard's eyes, his heart pounding in his chest as he searched for a reaction—something to tell him what this moment meant.

"Hey!" Xurian then yelled, startling them both.

Zalith took his eyes off Alucard, pulling his hand away as he looked at his brother.

Xurian, who was standing a few feet away from their cousins as they whacked one another, stared at Zalith and Alucard. "Get over here and play—come on!" he yelled.

He didn't want to play 'whack each other with sticks'. "No," he said, a sullen pout on his face. "I don't wanna get hurt."

"You'll be fine! You always complain that we don't involve you enough—let's go!" his brother insisted.

Zalith sighed and gave in; he actually didn't want to be left out, and if he played, he could protect Alucard—maybe that would make him like him back. He sighed and stood up but looked back at Alucard as he stood up, too. "You don't have to play if you don't want to, but I'll protect you so you don't get hurt," he said with a shy smile.

Alucard smiled, looking down at the ground to hide his face. "Okay," he said quietly.

Smiling nervously, Zalith reached out and shyly took hold of Alucard's hand, the warmth of the gesture grounding him for just a moment. Then, with a flutter of newfound boldness, he turned and hurried towards Xurian and his cousins, ready to join in their games.

But his steps faltered as a sharp, unnatural shift rippled through the world around him. The air turned cold and heavy, a suffocating emptiness settling over the clearing; the carefree laughter and rustling leaves gave way to an eerie silence, broken only by the sudden, slicing whistle of an arrow cutting through the air.

Before Zalith could process the sound, Alucard's hand jerked, pulling him back. His brother and cousins stood frozen, their faces pale and drained of joy, their wide eyes fixed on something behind him. Zalith stopped, dread curling in his chest like icy fingers. Slowly, he turned, his movements stiff and hesitant, but as he looked back, Alucard's hand slipped from his grasp.

A muffled thud struck the ground, sharp and final. Zalith's breath caught in his throat, his body seizing with an overwhelming wave of dread. His gaze dropped, and what he saw made his stomach twist violently. Alucard lay crumpled on the ground, his neck skewered by an arrow that protruded from both sides. Blood spilt from the wound in sluggish rivers, trickling down his pale skin and pooling beneath him. The air, now thick with the metallic tang of blood, felt too still, too wrong.

Zalith's knees buckled, and he collapsed beside Alucard, his legs numb and useless beneath him. His chest heaved with laboured breaths as horror and confusion crashed over him in a relentless tide. He couldn't move, couldn't think, couldn't process what just happened. His cousins darted past him, their movements frantic as they raced towards the trees where the arrow had come from, but their panicked shouts barely registered.

"Get up! Get up!" Xurian's voice cut through the haze, raw and desperate, but it sounded distant, as though coming from underwater. The words faded into an eerie void as Zalith's trembling hands hovered over Alucard's neck, helpless and unsure of what to

do. Tears blurred his vision, spilling over his cheeks as he stared down at Alucard's face. The vampire's lips were slick with blood, his breaths shallow and wet, each one a desperate struggle. Blood seeped from the corner of his mouth and down the curve of his jaw, staining the dirt beneath him.

Zalith's heart twisted with an unbearable weight, his mind screaming for this to be a nightmare, something he could wake from. But as he reached out, his trembling hands aching to stop the blood, to do anything, the cold, unforgiving truth settled over him. This was no dream—it was a nightmare he could not escape.

"We need to take it out!" Xurian's panicked voice rang out, sharp and desperate.

Zalith tore his eyes away from Alucard, his heart hammering as he saw Xurian kneeling across from him, his trembling hands hovering near the arrow embedded in Alucard's neck. The sight jolted Zalith out of his frozen silence, his entire body trembling as fear and urgency collided within him. "T-take it out!" he stammered, his voice breaking as he turned his gaze back to Alucard and clutched his hand tightly.

Xurian's hands edged closer to the arrow, his fingers twitching as if drawn by an invisible force. But just as he was about to grab it, he recoiled, shaking his head violently. "I-I can't—I can't do it! You do it!" he cried, his voice cracking as tears welled in his eyes.

Zalith's breathing quickened, his panic mounting as he looked back at Alucard. He knew Xurian wasn't going to do it. Alucard couldn't. That left only him. His hands shivered uncontrollably as he reached out towards the arrow, his mind screaming against the weight of what he had to do. "W-we have to—we ... I ...." Words failed him, choked by the lump in his throat, but he forced himself to act. He couldn't let Alucard suffer for another moment.

Muttering frantic apologies under his breath, Zalith gripped the arrow's shaft. His fingers wrapped around it, the sensation sickeningly real as he snapped the tail end off. Alucard let out a sharp, agonized gasp, blood bubbling at the edges of his lips as he struggled to breathe. Zalith's heart shattered at the sound, but he knew he had to keep going. He tightened his grip around the arrowhead, his hands slick with blood, and in one swift but careful motion, he pulled it free.

But the relief he'd hoped for didn't come. Instead, it unleashed something far worse. Blood poured from Alucard's neck, a relentless, horrifying torrent that Zalith couldn't stop. His hands flew to the wound, pressing down desperately, trying to stem the flow, but it was useless. The warm, viscous sensation of blood seeped through his fingers, unstoppable, unyielding.

Tears streamed down his face as he watched the life leave Alucard's eyes, the light fading into a cold stillness. His body trembled as he clutched Alucard, his voice breaking into anguished sobs. The world blurred around him, collapsing into a void of despair as he realized that he was losing the one he loved all over again. The dream unravelled into *darkness, swallowing him whole, leaving him with nothing but the ache of his heart and the echo of his failure.*

| **Alucard,** *Saturday, Tertium 11th, 960(TG)—Aegisguard, Uzlia Isles* |

When Alucard stepped back into the cabin, the muted sounds of the ship and the sea greeted him. The rhythmic hum of the steam engine thrummed softly beneath the floorboards, blending with the distant cries of seagulls outside and the gentle lapping of waves against the hull. Yet, his attention was immediately drawn to Zalith, who lay beneath the blankets, his body tense and flinching as though caught in a battle only he could see.

Alucard's heart ached at the sight. He knew all too well what his mate was enduring. Nightmares were cruel and merciless, inflicting confusion, pain, and despair that lingered long after waking. He would never wish such torment on anyone, least of all the man he loved.

Without hesitation, he crossed the room, setting the plate of eggs, bacon, and toast on the table as he passed; the faint clink of the dish against the wood was almost lost beneath the cabin's quiet symphony of sound. Reaching the bed, he lowered himself to the edge and gently shook Zalith's arm, his voice soft and steady. "Zalith?" he murmured, careful not to startle him.

Zalith jolted awake almost instantly, his body flinching as he turned his head, his gaze locking onto Alucard. Confusion clouded his dark eyes, his expression thick with dread and disorientation. But as he stared at the vampire, the tension on his face began to ease, the shadow of his nightmare fading with each passing second. Slowly, his pupils dilated, just as they always did when their eyes met.

"Are you okay?" Alucard asked worriedly, rubbing Zalith's arm.

With a deep, relieved exhale, Zalith nodded and smiled a little. "Yeah. Just a bad dream."

Alucard resisted the urge to ask what he'd dreamt; he wasn't going to make Zalith relive it. So he glanced over his shoulder at the table. "I got you some breakfast," he said before setting his eyes back on him.

Zalith smiled again. "Thank you. It's very sweet of you."

The vampire got up and fetched the plate. He sat back down and handed it to Zalith. "Did you sleep okay?" he then asked.

Zalith shrugged, looking down at his food. "I've slept better. How about you? Did you sleep okay?"

Alucard nodded, but as Zalith lifted his head to look at him, the vampire frowned worriedly. "Are you really okay?"

He nodded and smiled *again*. "I'm okay," he assured him. "Are *you*?"

"I'm okay too," he said, smiling back at him. "We're about twenty minutes away from home."

Zalith sighed quietly. "Okay," he murmured.

"What's wrong?"

He shrugged and said, "I just… don't really want to go to Adenaville the moment we get home, but… we can't waste time. I want to get it out of the way."

Alucard frowned in concern. "We don't have to go right away; we can rest for a day or two. The pack in Adenaville won't be going anywhere; they've taken over the city, so… they'll be staying there a while."

Zalith shook his head. "I just want to get it over with."

"Are you sure?" Alucard asked sadly.

The demon shrugged again.

Alucard's concerned frown thickened with worry. He could see the sadness in Zalith's eyes, the confliction on his face. He clearly wanted to rest—of course he did. He must be exhausted; he was working so hard, getting so much done. He needed a break, and Alucard needed to find a way to convince him that it was okay to rest.

He took Zalith's plate and placed it on the bed behind them. Then, he moved his hands onto Zalith's shoulders and stared into his sullen eyes. "You've been working so hard lately. Take a day to rest… please?" he pleaded.

"I just… don't think I'll be able to," Zalith mumbled.

Staring at him, Alucard did his best to keep himself from trying endlessly to get Zalith to agree. As much as he wanted his mate to rest, he knew that he couldn't force him—and he wouldn't. He didn't want to upset him, anger him, or make him feel any worse than he already did. The best he could do right now was be there for him. So, he nodded. "Okay," he agreed. "But after tonight, we're staying home for at least a day," he said sternly.

"Maybe," the demon said. "We'll see how things go."

"Okay," Alucard said. Then, he handed Zalith his plate back and kissed his lips—he wasn't sure what more he could do.

Zalith started eating, but after a few moments, he took his eyes off his food and looked at Alucard. "Have you eaten?"

"No… but I'm not really hungry."

"Do you want blood?"

Yes...he did. An irritating hunger was simmering within him, and it had been since the moment he'd woken up this morning. But he could wait. He didn't want to be latching onto Zalith's neck like an irritating tick the moment he woke up, especially while Zalith was feeling so downhearted. He felt awful for needing so much from Zalith...and all he wanted to do was try and give just as much back. The least he could do was spare him the annoyance of a bite on his neck.

He shook his head and smiled. "I'm okay. Thank you."

"Are you sure?" he asked. "I don't mind."

Alucard looked down at his lap. He didn't want Zalith to think he didn't want *him* because he *did*...so much, so often—*right now*. "When you're done eating," he said, lifting his head to look at him. "Eat first."

"Okay," Zalith said, and then he resumed eating.

While they sat there together, Alucard shuffled around, making himself more comfortable as his mind worked to find something—*anything*—that might help Zalith feel better. His thoughts drifted to their engagement, to the promise of their upcoming wedding; the mere thought of it brought a warmth to his chest, a happiness so profound that it had chased away the shadows of his own sorrows. For once, the future seemed brighter, filled with hope instead of loss, and it was all because of Zalith.

But Alucard couldn't ignore how much they'd lost—how hard Zalith had taken it, and how merciless he was being on himself. Maybe if he spoke about their wedding, about the life that they were building together, it might ease some of that weight. Their future was something worth holding onto, something good, and if anything could lighten the burden in Zalith's heart, perhaps it was that.

"So...I was thinking," he started, smiling at the demon. "About our wedding."

Zalith smirked softly. "What were you thinking?"

A surge of excitement flooded through him, lighting up every corner of his heart. The thought of marrying Zalith, of sharing a life together filled him with an overwhelming sense of joy and eagerness. There was nothing he wanted more—it was the kind of happiness that made everything else seem distant and unimportant. Unable to contain the warmth building inside him, Alucard moved closer, his hand reaching out to rest gently on Zalith's leg, still draped under the blanket. The simple touch grounded him, a quiet expression of the love that overflowed within him. "Well...I was thinking about places where it could be—we still didn't get to go to Samjang, so...maybe we could have the wedding there? Or...if you don't want to go far, we could always have it at the castle," he suggested, glancing down at his lap as his nervousness started to return.

"I think we're better off visiting first to see if we like it there," he said, finishing his toast. "I don't know how I feel about the castle. We're rich," he said, his smirk growing, "and people usually have a backyard wedding when they don't have a lot of money."

Alucard nodded, looking down at his lap again.

"But it *is* a castle, and it would be nice to put it to use."

The vampire shrugged. "We can think more about it; there are a lot of places to choose from."

"I'd like to have it somewhere with mountains," he said, pondering. "In the background, maybe. Or something nice with water."

Alucard smiled, picturing a beautiful valley.

"But we have to ask ourselves who we're inviting. It would be rude to have it too far away from our guests."

"That's true," the vampire agreed, looking down at his lap as he fiddled with his engagement ring. "Well…I don't have any family…I don't really have any friends—maybe Thomas and Soren," he said with a shrug.

"Who?" Zalith asked.

Alucard pouted. "Greymore and Becker," he mumbled.

"Oh, I remember now," he said with a quiet, teasing laugh. But then he sighed, placing his empty plate on the bedside table. "I don't have any family or friends either…but Orin, Tyrus, and Idina should be there. I'd say perhaps *Thomas* too, but he's your guest," he said, smiling at him. However, a saddened frown then appeared on his face as he looked down at his lap. "I'd like Varana to be there, but…."

Guilt gripped Alucard tightly. He knew that Zalith was devastated by how things had turned out…how Varana had chosen Ysmay and Lucifer over him. He didn't know what to say, but he didn't want to leave Zalith to sink into his sadness. "Have you…heard from her?" he asked.

"No, but I'm almost thankful that I haven't."

Alucard nodded. He was certain that Zalith didn't want to talk about her, and neither did he. So, he placed his hands on Zalith's shoulders, pushed him down onto his back, and straddled his lap, smiling down at him. "So," he said, making himself comfortable. "Are there any foods you know you want at our wedding?"

Zalith smirked again, gently gripping Alucard's waist with both his hands. "Something lavish," he said. "Only the most expensive cuts of meat, and fruits and vegetables imported from somewhere fancy," he laughed. "And we can have a blood fondue fountain just for you, vampire," he teased. "No double dipping."

With an amused smile, Alucard laughed with him. "That sounds like a plan, but you know I prefer to drink straight from the source, no?" he flirted, lightly dragging his fingertips from behind Zalith's ear, down his neck, and to his shoulder.

The demon kept his smirk. "We can put a tube in my neck and you can suck on it all night like a straw," he joked.

Alucard pouted. "We won't be doing that."

"Suit yourself," Zalith said with a shrug.

Still pouting, Alucard moved his hand to Zalith's chest, resting it there. "I prefer to be able to bite you," he said quietly.

Zalith softly rubbed Alucard's hips with his thumbs. "Hmm...well, you better get your bites in while you can because I don't think we should do that in front of guests."

"What if I drag you away into a dark, empty room where no one will find us?" he asked, leaning a little closer to Zalith's face.

The demon laughed quietly. "Tell me more."

A flicker of nervousness began to creep in, but Alucard pushed it aside with quiet determination. He was tired of letting his shyness hold him back, tired of hesitating when he already knew exactly what he wanted. This time, he wouldn't let his nerves win. He slid his hand upward, his fingers brushing along Zalith's neck. His touch lingered, gentle yet purposeful, as he focused on the warmth of Zalith's skin beneath his fingertips, doing his best to exude confidence instead of uncertainty. "We could slip away from the party...I could bite you—maybe more than once," he said, taking his eyes off Zalith's face to gaze at the demon's neck. "I get a little carried away sometimes...because you taste really good," he murmured, dragging his fingers down from the side of Zalith's neck and around to the front of it. "Maybe you will then decide that you want to fuck me—maybe more than once."

Zalith laughed quietly as he guided his hands up Alucard's body and pulled him closer so that their faces were but inches apart. "We should get some practice in in the meantime, so we really nail it on the night of," he said, moving his fingers through Alucard's hair.

"Maybe we should," Alucard agreed as his hand moved to gently grip Zalith's throat. His fingers rested there, firm yet tender, while his gaze drifted from Zalith's eyes to his lips. Without hesitation, he leaned in and pressed a soft kiss against them, savouring the fleeting moment before his hand shifted to guide Zalith's head. Tilting it slightly, he exposed the right side of the demon's neck, the faint warmth of his breath brushing against his mate's skin as he prepared to claim the moment fully.

Zalith exhaled softly, a sound laced with anticipation as Alucard leaned in closer to his neck. The vampire's lips hovered just above his skin, and Alucard could feel the faint, intoxicating pulse of blood beneath it, each beat calling to him like a siren's song. He was starving for it—the taste, the warmth, the way Zalith's pleased sigh would always follow the first pierce of his fangs. But he didn't want to rush. He wanted Zalith to feel the weight of his need, the tension building with every passing moment.

Widening his jaw, he pressed his fangs lightly against Zalith's neck, teasingly close to biting. But instead of sinking them in, he paused, letting his breath ghost over the demon's skin. After a moment, he pulled back and dragged his tongue slowly, deliberately, along the spot he'd chosen to bite, relishing the way Zalith's body tensed beneath his touch.

A quiet laugh came from Zalith, low and enticing. He pushed Alucard's head closer, his hand firm but coaxing. "Do it," he murmured, his voice rich with anticipation.

Alucard smirked, letting his lips trail along Zalith's neck as he nuzzled against it, his voice a low tease. "Make me," he mumbled.

Another quiet laugh escaped Zalith, but this time it came with a touch of challenge. His hand tightened, pulling Alucard even closer, holding him in place. He didn't need to say another word; his patience was enough of a command.

And Alucard couldn't resist any longer. The scent of Zalith's skin, the sound of his blood coursing just beneath the surface—it was too much. With a quiet growl, he widened his jaw again and pressed his fangs firmly against Zalith's neck before biting down. The warm rush of blood filled his mouth instantly, sweet and intoxicating, sending a wave of euphoria crashing over him. Zalith sighed deeply, content and relaxed, while Alucard let out a muffled sound of delight, the taste of the demon's blood consuming his every thought. For a moment, the world around them vanished, leaving only pleasure and relief.

"Bite harder," Zalith urged, pulling him nearer.

The vampire complied, his fangs sinking deeper into Zalith's neck as he bit down harder, earning a low, pleasured moan from the demon. Alucard moved instinctively, pinning Zalith's free hand above his head, holding him firmly in place. His mate's moan deepened, his fingers tightening in Alucard's hair, pulling at it with a mix of need and encouragement.

Alucard swallowed the gush of blood, warm and thick as it coated his tongue and slid down his throat. The taste was indescribable—rich, dark, and uniquely Zalith, with an underlying sweetness that ignited something primal within him. Each gulp sent a rush of euphoria through his veins, a warmth that spread like wildfire, flooding his senses and making his whole body hum with pleasure.

The feel of Zalith's pulse against his lips, the way his blood flowed so willingly, so perfectly, was intoxicating. It grounded him and yet made him feel untethered, as though nothing else in the world mattered but this connection. He gulped again, his grip on Zalith's wrist tightening slightly as a low, satisfied sound escaped his throat. Each drop seemed to fuel him, heightening his awareness of every movement, every sigh that passed Zalith's lips, until Alucard felt drunk on the sheer intimacy of it.

Not too long later, Alucard forced himself to let go, though it took all his willpower to do so. He pulled his fangs from Zalith's neck, and the demon's blood still lingered on his tongue, burdening him with an overbearing delight that clouded his thoughts and made his body tremble with satisfaction. But he knew he had to stop. As much as he craved more, as much as the rush of Zalith's blood threatened to overwhelm him, he couldn't take too much—not now.

Zalith hadn't been resting enough, and with the battles they would soon face, Alucard needed him strong, not weakened by his own indulgence. Worse, he could feel himself slipping, losing control in the flood of pleasure that came with every drop. If he didn't stop now, he wasn't sure he'd be able to.

He loosened his grip on Zalith's wrist, letting his hand fall away as he rested his head on the demon's shoulder. His body softened, relaxing against Zalith's, the steady warmth of his mate grounding him as he fought to regain control of himself. For a moment, he simply breathed, letting the intoxicating haze begin to subside, though the connection between them lingered, as tangible as the heat of their embrace.

The demon started gently rubbing Alucard's back, guiding his other hand down until he reached and squeezed the vampire's ass.

Alucard smiled faintly, his voice thick and languid as he murmured, "Thank you...my love." The words slipped from his lips slowly, as though he were savouring every sound. His hand trailed upward, brushing over Zalith's chest, his touch light and unhurried. The blood-high coursing through him was intoxicating, wrapping around his senses like a warm, glowing haze.

His mind felt unmoored, floating just out of reach of coherent thought, leaving only the vivid sensations of the moment. Every touch, every beat of Zalith's heart beneath his palm seemed sharper, more vibrant, as if the world had narrowed to just the two of them. The euphoria swelled within him, pulling him deeper into its grasp, making time feel stretched and slow. Alucard's entire body hummed with warmth, the remnants of Zalith's blood thrumming in his veins, filling him with a bliss so overwhelming that he didn't want it to end.

"Any time, baby," came the demon's content reply.

Alucard relaxed completely, the lingering euphoria of the blood-high pulling him deeper and deeper into a blissful haze. His body felt weightless, warm, and pliant, but the moment didn't end there—Zalith clearly had other plans.

Zalith carefully rolled the vampire onto his back, the motion smooth and unhurried. He straddled Alucard's lap, his dark eyes glinting with a playful intensity as he smiled down at him. The warmth of his body pressed against Alucard's was grounding and electric all at once, pulling him further into the moment. The demon leaned closer, capturing Alucard's lips in a kiss that was both tender and commanding, sending a fresh wave of heat coursing through him.

Alucard's hands moved instinctively, sliding up Zalith's body, savouring the firm, defined muscles beneath his fingertips. Every touch felt heightened, as though he could feel the strength and heat radiating from Zalith with every caress. When his hand reached his mate's left arm, he paused to grasp the demon's bicep, marvelling briefly at the power there, before his other hand slid up to tangle in Zalith's tousled hair. His fingers curled into the silken strands, pulling him nearer as their kiss deepened, leaving Alucard breathless and utterly captivated.

As their lips parted, Zalith's hand slipped under the blanket draped around his waist, moving with precision and intent. Alucard barely registered the quiet clink of his belt being unbuckled before Zalith's hand slipped into his trousers, wrapping around his arousal with a firm, teasing grip. A sharp breath escaped Alucard, his body shuddering as pleasure surged through him like lightning.

Zalith smirked, his expression dripping with confidence and mischief as he stopped kissing Alucard to stare into his glazed, half-lidded eyes. "How does my chest look?" he asked, his voice low and teasing, the words laced with a mix of amusement and seduction.

Alucard blinked, struggling to focus as Zalith's hand moved over him, coaxing his body to respond in ways that made coherent thought almost impossible. He reached up, his trembling hand brushing over Zalith's chest, feeling the smooth, unbroken skin beneath his palm. "It's all...healed," he murmured, his voice uneven as another wave of pleasure shivered through him, leaving him gasping softly. His gaze locked onto Zalith's, a mix of awe and desire flickering in his eyes as he clung to the overwhelming intimacy of the moment.

Zalith smirked, still caressing the vampire's hardening shaft. "So, I'm still hot?"

The vampire nodded and groaned quietly, struggling to hide the sheer delight that coursed through him. "You are...the hottest thing I've ever seen."

"Thank you," Zalith said with a light grin. "So are you."

Alucard smiled widely as he turned his head to the side, a quiet, breathy moan slipping past his lips as Zalith's hand continued to stroke his dick. The warmth of the demon's touch sent shivers rippling through him, his heightened senses amplifying every sensation. Zalith chuckled softly, the sound low and teasing, before leaning in to kiss Alucard's neck. The vampire exhaled a contented sigh, his lips parting as his body melted further into the moment.

He was certain that he knew where this was heading, and the thought alone made him pulse with anticipation. A flicker of eagerness surged through him, and he began unbuttoning his own shirt with slightly trembling hands. But before he could finish, Zalith's hand replaced his, gently batting Alucard's hands aside to take over. Alucard groaned softly, sliding his hand to the back of Zalith's head and pulling him closer, guiding the demon's lips firmly to his neck. His eyes fluttered shut as Zalith's kisses turned slow, each one igniting a fresh wave of heat that coursed through his veins.

Unable to resist, Alucard let his free hand trail down Zalith's chest; he stroked the firm planes of muscle beneath his fingertips before slipping under the blanket. His hand found Zalith's arousal, and he wrapped his fingers around his thick dick, stroking him in a way that earned a quiet, pleased growl from the demon. Zalith's kisses became aggressive, eager, his lips grazing Alucard's throat before he pulled the vampire's shirt open and slid it off, exposing his skin to the cool air.

Zalith exhaled a soft sigh, the sound vibrating against Alucard's ear as he removed the vampire's belt. Alucard's own breathing hitched as he felt Zalith's warm breath so close, every sensation amplifying his need.

Impatience flared suddenly within Alucard, the remnants of his blood-high making his desire all-consuming. He couldn't deny how badly he wanted Zalith, his whole body aching with longing. Hoping the demon would understand the urgency of his need, he hooked his left leg over Zalith's back, pulling him closer until their bodies were flush. His hand slid back into Zalith's hair, gripping it tightly as he tilted his head further, offering his neck while his body trembled with desperation. Every part of him seemed to hum with desire, silently pleading for Zalith to match his fervour.

Zalith seemed to understand perfectly. He chuckled softly, his lips brushing up Alucard's neck, then across his jawline, before capturing his lips in a heated kiss. Meanwhile, his hand worked gently, massaging cold, slick lube into Alucard's ass, the sensation drawing a quiet, shivering moan from the vampire. Alucard tilted his head to the side, his chest rising and falling as he took a moment to catch his breath, only for Zalith's kisses to trail back down to his neck, igniting another wave of pleasure that coursed through him.

When Zalith began easing his dick into Alucard's body, the vampire let out a low, breathy sigh, the sensation both intense and deeply satisfying. His fingers slid down from Zalith's head to his back, where his claws dug in lightly, his grip firm enough to express his pleasure but careful not to hurt. The sharp edge of desire unfurled within him as a delighted, unrestricted moan escaped his lips, his body arching slightly beneath the demon's as a spiralling warmth spread through him, growing more intense with every hard, thick inch pushed into his ass.

Alucard turned his head, his blue eyes locking onto Zalith's dark, smouldering gaze; the sunlight didn't sear his sights this time—either that or he was too enthralled to care. A faint smirk curved the demon's lips, and Alucard couldn't resist reaching up to cradle Zalith's face, pulling him down into another kiss. The connection was fierce and unyielding, a dance of passion that left Alucard struggling to focus. As Zalith pushed deeper, a small frown of strain tugged at Alucard's brow, his body caught between the intensity of the moment and the growing ache of overwhelming pleasure. His fingers slid back to tangle in Zalith's hair, gripping tightly as he turned his head to exhale deeply, his heart pounding harder as Zalith's rhythm began to quicken.

Leaning closer, Zalith let out a low, pleasured moan, his warm breath brushing against Alucard's ear. He playfully nipped at the lobe before kissing his way down the vampire's neck, lingering for just a moment before slowly sinking his fangs into his skin. Alucard flinched at the initial sting, but the sensation quickly melted into a deep, consuming contentment as the demon's venom spread through him, heightening every nerve and amplifying the intensity of his desires—so much that he felt himself edging nearer to his limit.

Alucard breathed deeply, his entire body trembling as he surrendered to Zalith. His mate always knew how to unravel him, to give him exactly what he needed while taking just enough to drive him wild. The feel of the demon's body pressed against his own, the intoxicating rush of his bite, and the knowledge that Zalith was enjoying him just as much—it was everything he craved.

A soft, broken moan escaped him as he turned his head again, pulling Zalith's face back to his so he could claim his lips once more. The kiss was deep, desperate, a collision of need and love that left Alucard gasping into Zalith's mouth. As an overwhelming surge of sensation shot through his body, he moaned again, his voice muffled against Zalith's lips. He grimaced slightly, struggling to contain the torrent of exhilaration coursing through him, but his trembling body betrayed him, shifting restlessly beneath the demon.

Zalith's smirk returned, full of knowing confidence as he pressed a kiss to the side of Alucard's face. Slowly, his lips trailed back to the vampire's neck, his movements unhurried but intentional. His pace quickened, each thrust drawing another gasp or moan from Alucard as their bodies moved in perfect rhythm, the intensity between them building with every moment.

Alucard was seconds from his peak, his body trembling beneath Zalith's with the relentless, electrifying pleasure that the demon gave him. Every movement sent an intense surge of sensation through him, his skin burning and his heart pounding as he gasped for air. Zalith's hands gripped his wrists, pinning them firmly above his head. The shift in control sent a shiver down Alucard's spine, and he let out a soft whine, frowning as he struggled against the restraint. His breath hitched when his eyes fluttered open to meet Zalith's burning gaze, the demon's seductive smirk pulling him deeper into the moment.

A flicker of nervousness gripped Alucard, but it was quickly drowned out by the overwhelming pleasure coursing through him. Zalith leaned down, his lips capturing Alucard's in a deep, demanding kiss. Alucard moaned into it, his chest rising and falling as he struggled to breathe through the intensity. His body trembled beneath Zalith's, anticipation coiling tighter and tighter and tighter until it finally broke. He moaned loudly, his fists clenching tightly as he climaxed, his body arching against the demon's, his shaft throbbing between their touching bodies. Zalith's grip on his wrists held firm, grounding him as waves of pleasure rolled through his trembling form, making him wince, moan, and cry out as the overwhelming release devoured him.

Zalith didn't relent, his lips trailing down to Alucard's neck as he thrusted faster, harder, his rhythm unyielding. The vampire's breath came in shallow gasps, his head tipping back as he moaned and whined and grimaced, utterly inundated by the sheer intensity; his heart raced wildly, each beat echoing in his ears as Zalith leaned closer, his breath hot against his skin.

Alucard's vision blurred, the world around him dissolving into a haze of heat and sensation. The consuming flood of pleasure pulled him in so entirely that it felt as though the bed beneath him had fallen away. His grip on reality teetered dangerously, his mind spinning as his body trembled under Zalith's relentless pace. Every thrust, every brush of the demon's lips against his neck, sent him spiralling further into the abyss of sensation, his breath hitching erratically as he fought to hold on.

His muscles tensed, his body caught in a shuddering rhythm of its own as he felt himself slipping closer to the edge—of what, he couldn't be sure. The intensity drowned out everything else, leaving him lightheaded, dizzy, and so utterly overpowered that for a fleeting moment, he thought he might pass out. But just as his grip on consciousness faltered, Zalith nipped at his neck, the sharpness grounding him enough to cling to the fraying threads of awareness. Reality blurred at the edges, but all that mattered was Zalith, the heat of him, the strength, the connection that tethered him to this moment.

And then the demon let out a deep, resonant moan thick with pleasure and satisfaction. It sent one last shudder through the vampire, leaving him entirely spent, completely devoured, and at the utter mercy of Zalith's power, of his desires and his hunger. The demon's dick, buried deep inside Alucard's shivering body, throbbed thickly, and as the heat of his cum oozed into him, the vampire barely managed a pleased but exhausted moan.

Zalith finally stilled, his weight settling against Alucard's body as he slowed his breathing, his chest rising and falling unsteadily, his face nuzzled into the curve of Alucard's neck, and his warmth and closeness soothing the aftershocks that still rippled through the vampire, who, with a deep, shaky exhale, let himself relax beneath the demon, his body sinking into the mattress as the tension drained away.

"Fuck," the demon breathed, his voice carrying the weight of a burden finally lifted. But beneath the relief, there was a faint note of something else—concern? The sound barely registered in Alucard's mind, hazy and distant through the lingering high that still clouded his senses.

Alucard's body felt heavy, his limbs tingling as though they weren't entirely his own. The intensity of everything—the blood, the heat, the unrelenting pleasure—had left him teetering on the edge of consciousness. The world around him seemed both hyper-vivid and strangely blurred, each sensation amplified yet dreamlike. Dizzy and slightly disoriented, he managed a soft, contented smile and let out a deep sigh, his breath shuddering as he tried to steady himself.

He moved to pull his wrist free, intending to rest his hand on Zalith's head, seeking the comfort of touch to ground himself. But the demon's grip didn't loosen. Confusion flickered through the haze, and Alucard frowned slightly, tilting his head to glance at Zalith. His thoughts felt sluggish, swimming through the remnants of his high, making it difficult to focus.

Before he could speak, Zalith nuzzled closer, the warmth of his breath brushing against Alucard's neck. The demon pressed himself tighter, his presence grounding but firm, the grip on Alucard's wrists tightening—not painfully, but with an unmistakable possessiveness. It was a silent gesture, a reminder of the connection they had just shared, of everything that lingered unspoken between them.

The tension in Alucard's body eased, his frown softening as he closed his eyes again. The dizziness still swirled at the edges of his mind, but he let himself sink into the quiet intimacy of the moment, his breath slowing as the haze began to settle. The sound of Zalith's unsteady breathing and the weight of his body against him felt like an anchor, pulling him back from the edges of his spinning thoughts and into a place where only the two of them existed.

"Alucard?" came Zalith's voice, clearer this time.

He slowly opened his eyes to stare up at the demon.

"Are you okay?" he asked worriedly. "I'm sorry. I got carried away. I—"

Alucard shook his head as he said, "No…it's okay." He breathed deeply, slowly relaxing a little more. "It felt…*really* amazing." He was now certain that he'd just experienced a mere glimpse of what Zalith—possibly the only incubus in existence—was fully capable of.

"Are you sure? I'm just…tired—*very* tired, I guess. I never lose control like that."

He shook his head again. "It's okay, Zalith. I feel really good."

Zalith smiled and exhaled deeply. "I love you so much," he said and kissed Alucard's neck.

The vampire smiled, too. "I love you too—more than anything."

As Zalith's soft smile grew, he released his grip on Alucard's wrists, the possessive hold giving way to a more tender touch. Zalith's hands slid down the vampire's body slowly, deliberately, his fingers tracing the ridges of Alucard's abs with an almost reverent ease. A deep sigh escaped the demon as he reached for the blanket, pulling it over them both before shifting to lay beside Alucard. His head came to rest on Alucard's shoulder, his breath warm and steady against the vampire's skin.

Alucard moved an arm around Zalith, holding him close as he stared up at the ceiling. His breathing, still uneven from before, gradually steadied as the haze of his blood-high began to ebb away. The lingering warmth and dizziness faded with it, leaving behind a subtle ache in his body and a quiet sense of grounding. He could hear the distant cawing of crows—the ones he kept circling above the tallest tower of their castle. The sound felt both familiar and soothing, a gentle reminder that they were only minutes from home. Five minutes, he guessed—five minutes away from another day of responsibilities.

As much as Alucard wanted to stay like this, wrapped in the warmth of Zalith's body, he knew better. The demon would want to get straight to work the moment they arrived home, throwing himself back into his relentless routine. Alucard frowned faintly at the thought but sighed, already resigned to the futility of arguing. He knew Zalith too well; trying to talk him into resting would only lead to frustration on both sides.

Still, he'd decided that once their business in Adenaville was done tonight, he would make sure Zalith took a proper day to rest. No excuses, no distractions—just time for the two of them. Until then, though, he would follow at Zalith's side, wherever the day might take them.

Pressing a gentle kiss to Zalith's head, Alucard held him tighter, letting out a content exhale. If they only had five more minutes to lay there, then he would savour every second of it, imprinting the closeness of this moment into his mind. Whatever awaited them beyond this fleeting peace could wait just a little longer.

Chapter Six

— ≺ ✝ ≻ —

A Letter By Owl

| **Alucard**—*Uzlia Isles, Usrul, Castle Reiner* |

Alucard and Zalith rode side by side, their horses' hooves kicking up soft clouds of golden dust as they followed the winding path towards their castle. This side of the island had always been Alucard's favourite, and every time he travelled this way, he found himself admiring its beauty anew. Vast meadows of soft, blue-green grass stretched out on either side of the path, dotted with jewel-toned flowers that swayed gently in the breeze like scattered gems against a vibrant canvas. It was a sight that always erased the lingering distaste that came with seeing the dark, miserable territories claimed by Lilidian demons.

Here and there, apple trees stood tall, and despite the winter, their gnarled branches were heavy with ripe fruit that glimmered in the morning sunlight. The air carried the sweet, crisp scent of the apples, mingling with the faint saltiness of the sea breeze. To the right, the black-sanded beach shimmered faintly, the dark grains glittering like obsidian. Two towering willow trees stood sentinel at the water's edge, their sweeping branches dipping low, as if bowing towards the gentle waves lapping the shore.

Between the docks and the castle lay roughly a mile of meadow, with the final stretch giving way to a wide, rocky path that ascended the hillside in gradual curves. The castle itself loomed in the distance, its stone towers and battlements rising above the landscape like a silent guardian.

As they neared the base of the incline, where the meadow met the start of the hill trail, Alucard turned his gaze towards Zalith. The sunlight caught in the demon's dark hair, adding a faint warmth to his striking features. Alucard smiled softly, his heart lifting at the sight of his mate. Amid the serenity of the island, the peaceful rhythm of the horses, and the breathtaking scenery, it was Zalith's presence that truly made this place feel like home.

"It's really beautiful here," Zalith said, looking at him. "I'm still so happy that you gave all of this to me."

"I'm glad you love it," Alucard said as he took the lead, guiding his horse up the hill trail. "I took a very long time to make sure everything was perfect."

"It *is* perfect," Zalith assured him.

Still smiling, Alucard turned his head to set his eyes on a herd of wild horses, watching as they grazed on a plateau, chewing the grass. Then, he looked back over his shoulder at Zalith. "What do you have planned for today?" he asked.

"Catch up with my correspondence for the most part," he said.

Alucard nodded, and as the path became wide enough for them to walk side by side, he slowed his horse a little so that he could walk beside Zalith. "I think that I might go fishing with Thomas—that's if there isn't any work waiting for me when we get home."

"Where?" Zalith asked, sounding a little worried.

"He said something about a good spot on Ordvell—the small island north-east of the village," he said.

Zalith glanced at him as they continued up the hill. "Do you mind if I come?" he asked. "I'll probably read the whole time, and I can stand off to the side or stay on shore if you want some time alone with your friend."

Alucard frowned faintly as he glanced at Zalith. He knew that his mate wasn't particularly interested in fishing, hunting, or any of the other activities he often did with Greymore. And this wasn't the first time the demon had accompanied him, either. In fact, Zalith had been at his side nearly every minute of every day, and Alucard knew why: he was still paranoid, still carrying the weight of everything that happened to them in Nefastus; it lingered in his every move, an unspoken fear that something terrible might happen again. And he knew that Zalith wasn't willing to take that risk; he needed to be there, close enough to act if anything went wrong.

He understood, and he didn't resent it. If their situations were reversed, if Zalith had been the one to endure what he had, then he wouldn't let the demon out of his sight, either. The thought alone was enough to tighten something in his chest, a protective instinct that mirrored Zalith's own. So he didn't question him. He didn't try to talk him into staying behind or taking time for himself. He wouldn't do that to Zalith, not when he understood him so completely. Besides, Alucard loved having him with him. He loved his company—he always had. There was a quiet comfort in Zalith's presence, a reassurance that balanced out the chaos of his thoughts. Truthfully, Alucard was relieved to have this time with him, even if the reasons for it were shadowed by their shared past.

"You can come," the vampire replied. "But… why don't you join us?"

"No, it's okay," Zalith said, smiling at him. "I have a lot of work to do."

Alucard patted his horse's neck, murmuring softly as it whinnied in response to a flock of birds taking off ahead of them. His frown deepened, a flicker of confliction tugging at his thoughts. He knew Zalith would stay at his side no matter where he went—there was no doubt about that. But he also knew that his mate had work to do, responsibilities that demanded his attention. If Alucard decided to go out with Greymore, Zalith would follow, sacrificing his time and focus to remain by his side. The thought left a pang of guilt in Alucard's chest. Zalith would never complain, never hesitate, but Alucard couldn't ignore the strain it might put on him.

And yet, staying at home didn't feel right, either. Alucard didn't want to work—he wanted to do something, *anything* that would pull him away from the monotonous grind of daily responsibilities. But the simple truth was that whatever he chose to do would inevitably hinder Zalith, tying him to Alucard's side instead of allowing him the space to handle his own tasks. The realization left Alucard feeling restless and uncertain, caught between his own desires and the knowledge of how they might affect the man he loved.

He sighed quietly, sitting up straight. "Okay," he said. "Well…I don't know if I'll go yet. If I have things to do that have been waiting for me, then…I will probably just work until it's time to leave tonight."

"It's okay—you can go. I want you to have fun with your friend and enjoy yourself," Zalith said quietly.

Alucard shrugged. "Thomas can wait," he muttered. "If I have work to do, then I have work to do."

Zalith laughed quietly, smiling at him. "You're always telling me to have fun—you should have fun too, you know."

He sighed deeply, glancing at him. "I know…I just…I like to get things done when they come up rather than leave them until later. But if I don't have anything waiting for me, then I'll go with Thomas."

"Okay, well let me know," the demon said.

Nodding, Alucard then stared ahead, continuing towards the castle.

Once they reached the castle courtyard, Zalith and Alucard dismounted their horses, handing the reins to the two waiting groundskeepers. Alucard's fingers lingered on the leather briefly before he turned, his hand slipping easily into Zalith's. At the touch, Zalith smiled at him, and Alucard felt a flicker of warmth that chased away the remnants of his earlier restlessness.

They began walking to the front doors, Alucard keeping his gaze on Zalith as they moved. But when he noticed the demon's eyes drifting towards the castle, his expression soft with quiet admiration, Alucard couldn't help but follow his gaze. He lifted his head and let his eyes take in their home—a sight he often overlooked in the routines of daily life. The black-brick castle loomed above them, its immense towers reaching into the sky, a commanding presence against the backdrop of the island's vibrant landscape. The red-oak drawbridge they'd crossed moments ago spanned the shimmering moat, its waters teeming with fish and fed by the hill streams that flowed down to form a river across their domain. The stained-glass windows, radiant even under the muted light, caught Alucard's attention, their vibrant colours demanding to be admired.

He let his gaze drift lower to the white cobblestones beneath their feet, which gleamed faintly in the sunlight, the stones forming the courtyard where they now stood. It was beautiful—every inch of it—and the thought filled him with a sense of pride. This wasn't just a castle—it was *theirs, a* place they had claimed together, a home that represented everything they had endured and built. For a moment, Alucard allowed himself to linger in the feeling, grateful for the sight and for the man at his side.

The vampire followed at Zalith's side until they reached the tall, redwood front doors to which only he, Zalith, and their butler possessed the ability to open. Alucard reached forward, twisting the doorknob, and as he pushed the door open, he invited Zalith to enter first.

His mate smiled and walked in, saying, "Thank you," as Alucard closed the door behind them. He then let go of the vampire's hand and helped him take his redingote off.

Alucard gave the demon an appreciative smile, but once Zalith took his own coat off, Alucard saw his eyes shift to the archway that led deeper into the castle—to his office. Although the vampire knew that Zalith wanted to get to work, seeing him so eager to get to it admittedly made him a little sad. He was working *far* too much lately.

Before Zalith took a single step, though, and before Alucard could try thinking of a way to convince him to rest, hurried footsteps echoed towards them. Moments later, Edwin walked quickly through the archway and to Zalith and Alucard. In his hand was a sealed white envelope in his right hand... and when Alucard glanced at Zalith, he saw the aggravation on his face—he was thinking the same thing as him, wasn't he? What could it possibly be now—more problems, a death, a threat? Evidently something that either one of them needed to see to.

"A message came for you by owl, sir," the butler said to Alucard, holding the envelope out to him.

Alucard took it from him and sighed. "Thank you," he said, sure that whatever was written inside wasn't something he wanted to read. But he wasn't going to procrastinate. As Edwin wandered off, the vampire headed through the left archway into the waiting room, where he lazily slumped down on the white couch beside the window.

As Zalith sat down next to him, he looked down at the envelope, making himself comfortable. "Who do you think it's from?" he asked.

Reaching over to the small table beside the couch, Alucard pulled open the drawer and took a letter opener. Then, he started opening the envelope. "I hope it isn't something that's going to take up my day," he muttered. "It's probably from Soren or Attila, and I don't want to have to deal with either of them right now—it might even be from Crowell, and I don't want to talk to him," he mumbled, pulling the folded paper from within the envelope. He unfolded it, placed the envelope and letter opener down, and then stared at the Dor-Sanguian writing.

A,

I've received your latest batch of demons. I'm working on giving them all something to mask their auras, and they'll soon be ready for you to come and do whatever it is you do—send them on their way, put them to work. Business as usual.

In other matters, Crowell's reported back to me. He has information regarding the items you have been looking for. At your earliest convenience, come and collect this information. But it is dire—Crowell insists the information he has for you will only help you for so long.

G. Eb

"G. Eb?" Zalith questioned.

"Gabriel Erichblood," Alucard grumbled with a sigh, slouching back in his seat. "He says he has news from Crowell—and apparently, it's dire. I'll probably have to go and see him before I meet Thomas."

Zalith nodded. "Okay. I'll come with you."

"Maybe he's located the Pandorican," the vampire suggested, *hoping* that he was right. "Or more of Ysmay's people…maybe even Ysmay herself. I guess we'll find out," he said, placing the letter on the table beside him.

"I suppose we will," Zalith agreed.

He didn't see any point in waiting—the sooner he got this out of the way, the sooner he could get on with his day. "We may as well go now," he said, standing up. "Maybe you can personally assign jobs to some of the new demons while we're there," he suggested. "Boost morale or whatever they say."

"Maybe," Zalith said, also standing up.

Alucard led the way back through the hall, took his redingote from the coat rack, and pulled it on as Zalith pushed the door open and stepped outside. They walked through the courtyard and to the stables, which sat to the right of the drawbridge. "We can just take our horses—I can't be bothered to wait for them to set up the carriage," the vampire muttered, nodding over at the two groundskeepers, who were sweeping up straw outside one of the horse paddocks.

"Okay," Zalith said with a smile, following him to where their horses were hitched.

"Maybe we can get coffee or something while we're in the city, hmm?" he suggested, glancing at Zalith as they both grabbed the reins of their horses and led them out into the courtyard.

Zalith stopped to mount his horse and said, "That could be nice."

With a content smile, Alucard mounted his horse and then tapped its side with his boot, making it trot forward as Zalith's horse followed. "And maybe some cake, too," he added.

The demon laughed quietly as they made their way over the drawbridge. "What kind of cake?"

Shrugging, Alucard stared ahead, setting his eyes on the two small islands a few miles over the ocean. "Maybe… chocolate. Will you have anything?"

"I think I'm okay with just coffee," the demon replied, walking alongside Alucard as they turned right onto the wide, rocky path that traced the edge of the river moat rather than descending towards the docks. "But you can have whatever you like," he added with a soft smile, his tone warm and teasing.

Alucard returned the smile, though his gaze soon drifted to the path ahead. The gentle murmur of flowing water accompanied the clipping of their horses' hooves as they followed the river's course; the moat glistened in the sunlight, its surface rippling faintly as it moved towards its destination. The path eventually led them to the cliff's edge, where the water spilled over, cascading in a smooth sheet into the lagoon far below. The distant sound of the waterfall blended with the hum of the island, a quiet harmony of nature and motion.

From the lagoon, the water broke into two vast rivers. One stretched straight ahead, carving a path towards the small village nestled further inland, its rooftops just visible through the trees. The other curled around the base of the hill, winding its way like a silver ribbon towards the black-sand beach that lay behind the castle. Alucard took it all in—the rivers, the lagoon, the way the island's beauty was shaped so perfectly by its waters—as they continued along the path, the air cooler here, tinged with the faint mist rising from the waterfall.

It was peaceful, and for a moment, Alucard allowed himself to appreciate the journey, his eyes flicking briefly to Zalith beside him. Even amid all their responsibilities, moments like this—a simple walk with the man he loved, surrounded by the beauty of their home—felt like a rare, grounding gift.

Alucard's gaze drifted ahead, taking in the vast, sweeping view that stretched before him. From this vantage point, the castle truly dominated the landscape, offering a perfect overlook of both land and sea. The Uzlia Isles unfolded like a map beneath him, each island distinct in its place. Grandest of all was Yrudberg, connected to their island by a vast white stone bridge that arched elegantly across the ocean. Even from here, Alucard could make out the silhouette of Eimwood City sitting close to Yrudberg's shore—a city whose soft glow could be seen from their castle towers on clear nights.

Beyond Yrudberg, Ordvell sprawled to the southeast, a slightly larger island covered in dense forests and pockets of swampland—a haven for hunters and fishermen. To the west, Anburidge, Wrostead, and Akavine sat in quiet isolation, their wooded expanses barely touched and brimming with secrets that Alucard still intended to explore. Perhaps someday, when the weight of responsibilities wasn't pressing so heavily on his shoulders, he'd allow himself the indulgence of wandering those forests and villages that lay within, the perfect quiet and secluded sanctuaries for those of Zalith's people who didn't want to live in the bustling city.

As he and Zalith began their descent down a winding path towards the meadow below, Alucard's eyes settled on the bridge to Yrudberg. The sight brought thoughts of Eimwood, the city he had grown to admire. Its elven architecture had always been beautiful, even if its origins were tainted by the occupation that had plagued it. He and Zalith had changed that—driven out the invaders, reclaimed the city, and turned it into something worth calling their own.

Of course, the matter of the Yrudyen Elves still lingered at the edges of his mind, uninvited and persistent, but Alucard pushed it away. This wasn't the time to think about them. His focus remained on the present: the path before them, the man at his side, and the day that lay ahead.

He did, however, let himself think about the city that he and Zalith had transformed in such a short amount of time. What they'd accomplished there was undeniable; the city had been on the brink of collapse, but now it thrived. They had given its people everything they needed—supplies, safety, and hope. And in return, the people looked at them as though they were kings.

It was no secret that Zalith intended to become something close to that, to claim a rightful position of power over Eimwood. Their current leader, Lord Cecil, was an incompetent fool, unfit to lead, and both Alucard and Zalith knew it. The man had not only allowed the city to fall into ruin but had actively contributed to its suffering, indulging in corrupt dealings that had once thrown Eimwood into debt, famine, and filth. Many of the city's people wanted him gone—desperately so—and Zalith was already working on a way to remove him.

Unlike Alucard, who might have taken a more *direct* approach, Zalith was determined to handle it without bloodshed, to ensure Cecil's removal was swift, decisive, and above all, untraceable. Alucard wasn't sure yet how his mate planned to accomplish it, but the quiet confidence Zalith carried suggested that he had something in mind. Alucard found himself curious—he knew Zalith well enough to trust him, but part of him still wondered what shape that plan would eventually take.

He turned his head, gazing at Zalith as they continued down the hill. "Do you know what you plan to do with Cecil yet?"

The demon shrugged. "I could blackmail him...or find out what secrets he's hiding."

"You're so sure he's hiding something, no?" he teased, smirking.

Zalith nodded, returning a smirk and a glance. "I've had Danford snooping around—little Lord Cecil leaves his home every night at eight and doesn't return until the very early hours of the morning. His wife seems oblivious, as do his children, but the groundskeepers who take care of his estate haven't failed to notice his strange habits. He returns covered in sludge, as Danford has described it, and he believes it to be the same kind of sludge that might be dirtying the city's main source of water, thus causing this 'common' sickness that the people of Eimwood are dealing with," he explained, grimacing a little.

The water. Alucard frowned, his thoughts darkening as he considered one of the city's most pressing issues. Both he and Zalith were certain that Eimwood's primary water source had been compromised. The signs were everywhere. The city's people were perpetually sick, plagued by relentless fevers, bouts of vomiting, and weakness that kept entire families bedridden. Children suffered the worst, their small bodies unable to fight off the illness brought by whatever poison lingered in the water.

And the damage wasn't limited to the people. Along the Eimwood River, the flora had withered into brittle husks, and any greenery within the city itself was either dead or struggling to survive, leaves curling brown at their edges, the grass turned brittle and flaky. A once-vibrant city now carried the quiet weight of decay.

For now, Zalith had taken charge, paying workers to haul clean water from a nearby reservoir, an effort that kept the city functioning, but it wasn't a sustainable solution. They couldn't rely on temporary measures forever. Until they uncovered what—or who—was poisoning Eimwood's supply, the city remained vulnerable, and Alucard knew that Zalith wouldn't stop until he rooted out the cause.

"So, you think this is connected—that Cecil knows what's poisoning the water there?" the vampire asked.

"I do," Zalith confirmed. "I'm going to send someone to see if what's been seen on Cecil's boots matches the mud upstream—then we'll know for sure that he's involved. Perhaps...once we return from Adenaville, I'll wrap up this investigation and have Cecil kicked out of our new city home," he said, smirking again.

Alucard laughed quietly—he *loved* when Zalith plotted, when he smirked and scoffed and looked so devious and conniving. "I don't know..." he replied slowly. "I've come to like that little townhouse the people think we live in—it's...quaint. And I hear the staff we have in there really like the place, too."

Zalith shrugged, smiling at him. "I'm sure you'll like the Lord's Manor once we've had Cecil's stench removed from it."

Staring ahead as they gradually reached the bottom of the hill, Alucard smiled. "What will we use this manor for?"

"We should probably pretend we live there, too, so no one wonders where we are," he said. "I was actually thinking of giving it to Idina or Greymore."

Alucard shrugged as they followed the golden dirt path towards the white stone bridge gate. "I'm sure a manor like that would be too fancy for Thomas—he'd probably make use of about…two of the forty rooms that place has," he said amusedly.

Zalith nodded. "You're right. But he's been working with me for so long; I feel like he deserves an upgrade."

"That's true," Alucard said with a light shrug. "Well, maybe a change of scenery will be good for him."

The demon smiled and nodded, his expression calm but unreadable, and together, they made their way towards the bridge in comfortable silence. The rhythmic clopping of their horses' hooves echoed against the dirt path, mingling with the distant rush of the rivers.

Alucard kept his gaze forward, though his thoughts began to wander. Once they reached the city, there would be no shortage of work waiting for them—there never was. But what lingered at the edges of his mind was the thought of Soren and whatever he had to tell him. He cast a glance at Zalith—who rode beside him, stoic and focused—as the bridge loomed closer ahead, its white stones gleaming under the morning sun. Had Crowell found a Pandorican? Or had he failed to make it through *another* mission? If it were the latter…then Alucard felt it was time to demote him. But he'd not know until they got to where Soren was waiting.

Chapter Seven

— ᛉ ✝ ᛋ —

Soren, and the Eimwood Collusion

| **Alucard**—*Uzlia Isles, Yrudberg, Eimwood City* |

As they rode across the meadow and onto the white stone bridge, the gates creaked open ahead, granting them passage. The bridge itself was a marvel, stretching half a mile over the calm, glistening sea below. Alucard glanced at the smooth, pale stones beneath his horse's hooves, certain that the bridge had been built around the same time as their castle, using the same white stone that made up the courtyard's ground. Elven architecture was nothing short of extraordinary—imbued with ethos, it allowed structures to rise impossibly high, span vast distances, and endure for centuries without faltering.

But the bridge wasn't the only evidence of elven craftsmanship. As they reached the far end, the path curved towards the gates of Eimwood, where an immense wall of white brick loomed in the distance. The wall, still under construction, stretched proudly around the city's perimeter—a defence that Alucard and Zalith had committed themselves to funding and overseeing.

The world beyond had become a dangerous place. Ever since Lilith's infection had broken free from Nefastus and spread across distant lands, chaos followed in its wake. Cities fell. Nations crumbled. And though Eimwood had remained untouched thus far, both Alucard and Zalith were determined to keep it that way. They had vowed to protect this city and its people, to ensure its walls could withstand anything—be it plague, invaders, or monsters.

In return, Eimwood had embraced them. Alucard could see it in the way the guards nodded respectfully as they passed through the gates and onto the bustling cobblestone streets. The people of the city held them in high regard, their contributions to Eimwood's survival impossible to ignore. For now, at least, this place was safe—and it was theirs to defend.

As they emerged into the bustling city square, the red brick pavement beneath them seemed to glow warmly in the sunlight, its rich tones a stark contrast to the pale stone of the surrounding buildings. The square hummed with life—market stalls lined the edges, their colourful awnings fluttering in the breeze as merchants called out their wares, limited as they were, and the scent of fresh bread and herbs mingled with the faint tang of salt carried inland from the sea.

The moment Alucard and Zalith came into view, the lively murmur of the crowd shifted. Many of the townsfolk turned towards them, faces lighting up with recognition. Smiles spread quickly as people stepped away from their stalls or hurried across the square to greet them. There was warmth in their words, in the way they called out their hellos, and Alucard and Zalith nodded graciously in return, faint smiles tugging at the corners of their lips as they continued on.

They made their way past the stables, where the rich scent of hay and horses lingered in the air. Like many of Eimwood's buildings, the stables were constructed with a blend of sturdy wood and pristine white stone, giving it a refined yet rustic charm. The craftsmanship was undeniable, each arch and beam a testament to the city's elven architectural roots.

Behind the stables, rising into the sky like a watchful sentinel, stood the white-marble tower Alucard knew well. Its smooth surface gleamed under the sun, an unmistakable landmark in the heart of the city. Within its walls resided the Eimwood Guard, the city's law enforcement—a force tasked with maintaining order and ensuring the people's safety. Though Alucard's gaze lingered on the tower only briefly, its presence was a quiet reassurance, a symbol of the peace that he and Zalith had worked so hard to preserve.

They rode deeper into the city, Alucard's sharp gaze sweeping over the elven architecture that surrounded them. The marble pillars stood tall and immaculate, their intricate carvings whispering of a time long past. To his right, the colosseum loomed at the end of the road, its grandeur repurposed into a temporary camp for those still waiting to be housed. It was a sobering sight, but Alucard took comfort in knowing that it was only temporary. The sound of hammers and saws filled the air as construction continued in earnest—up ahead, several homes were already taking shape along the road, while more were being built a few streets over.

Much of the unused space near the market had been reclaimed, repurposed with care and efficiency by Zalith's contractors. Rows of cleanly laid foundations and framework promised a brighter future for Eimwood's residents, and Alucard couldn't help but feel a flicker of pride at what they were building together.

The path they followed, however, led somewhere far more serene. After several minutes, the redbrick road beneath them gave way to smooth white marble, gleaming faintly in the soft light. Emerging into a wide, open garden square, Alucard slowed his horse to a stop, his gaze taking in the quiet beauty of the space. The square's edges were bordered by elegant marble pillars, each one supporting triangular arches that framed the scene like a work of art. Between each pillar stood carefully sculpted bushes in whimsical shapes—some trimmed to resemble horses mid-gallop, others carved into fierce lions and majestic bears. These animals had once been symbols of worship here, relics of a time before the elves had left the city.

At the centre of the square rose a tall white fountain, its carved tiers cascading with clear water that sparkled in the sunlight. The path leading to it circled gracefully around the fountain before branching out in three directions—one to the left, one to the right, and the final path stretching straight ahead towards the grand structure that dominated the square's far end. Cecil's palace stood there, an immense cathedral-like building that exuded an air of forced majesty. Unlike the rest of the city, its front-facing wall featured more glass than brick, the tall windows reflecting fractured light that scattered across the square like shards of colour. It was an impressive display, but to Alucard, it reeked of arrogance—something befitting the man who lived there.

To the right of the square, another path led towards the finer district of the city, where wealth and influence clung to every stone. Alucard gave the palace one last glance before he and Zalith nudged their horses forward, turning right as they reached the fountain. The rhythmic clip of hooves echoed softly off the marble, the tranquil atmosphere at odds with the quiet anticipation building in Alucard's chest as the same question circled inside his head: if Crowell *had* found a Pandorican, how soon would he and Zalith face Lilith?

They followed the white marble road, the steady rhythm of their horses' hooves echoing softly between the rows of tall, elegant townhouses that lined the street. Each building stood as a testament to the city's refined beauty—constructed from pristine white brick with polished black panelling that gleamed under the afternoon light. The subtle, intricate details carved into the facades spoke of wealth and sophistication, their grandeur a stark contrast to the city's working districts.

As they passed, the socialites of Eimwood made their presence known, their fine attire and composed expressions accompanied by warm smiles and polite waves. Alucard and Zalith nodded back in return, the exchanges brief but respectful. These people held the pair in high regard, their admiration evident even in these fleeting interactions.

It wasn't until they reached the townhouse at the very end of the street that they slowed to a stop. This house, while no less grand, held a quiet distinction, its position apart from the others lending it an air of exclusivity. Dismounting their horses, they hitched the reins to a nearby post, the faint jingle of leather and metal breaking the otherwise still air.

Alucard led the way up the wide marble steps, the smooth surface cool beneath his gloved hand as it brushed the railing. Reaching the polished black-wood door, he knocked firmly, the sound resonating through the quiet street. As they waited, Alucard's gaze lingered on the intricate iron knocker, shaped like an ivy-wreathed serpent, its craftsmanship no doubt a nod to the city's elven roots. His sharp ears caught the faint creak of footsteps within, and he straightened, ready for whatever news awaited them on the other side of the door.

"We can get coffee on the way home if you like," he said, smiling at Zalith.

"Okay," the demon replied, returning a smile.

The door unlocked with a faint click before swinging open, revealing the man on the other side. He was one of Alucard's vampires; the moment his crimson eyes landed on Alucard and Zalith, they widened with unmistakable recognition.

Alucard and Zalith both frowned expectantly, their expressions calm but commanding.

The butler, clearly intimidated despite his well-practised demeanour, quickly stepped aside and extended his arm in a formal gesture, inviting them in. "Welcome, My Lord, and welcome, Sir Zalith," he said humbly, his voice tinged with reverence. He knew exactly who they were—*what* they were—and what they had done to earn such fear and respect.

Alucard led the way into the house, their footsteps echoing faintly through the narrow entry hallway before they emerged into a large, dimly lit lounge. The room, though clearly intended to be refined, bore the unmistakable signs of a man consumed by his work. A heavy mahogany desk dominated the far corner, papers and ledgers scattered across its surface in a chaotic sprawl. A few empty coffee mugs sat haphazardly among the mess, their rims stained and forgotten, while a half-empty bottle of bourbon rested dangerously close to Soren's outstretched hand.

Soren lifted his head at their approach, his silvery eyes narrowing with that perpetual look of irritation so often plastered across his pale, tired face. A strand of his ear-length black hair had fallen loose, partially obscuring his left eye as he leaned back in his creaking leather chair and exhaled a deep, heavy sigh. His unkempt stubble and the deep shadows under his eyes betrayed his lack of sleep, as though he hadn't so much as glanced at a bed in days.

Nearby, the trash bin overflowed with discarded papers, crumpled notes, and empty liquor bottles, their labels peeling and glass smudged with fingerprints. Flies circled lazily over a plate perched on the edge of the desk, where a sandwich—undoubtedly days old—lay forgotten, its bread hardened and its filling all but abandoned.

The air smelled faintly of stale coffee, old bourbon, and the subtle mustiness of a room that had seen little fresh air. It wasn't filthy—Soren wasn't *disrespectful* to his space—but the sheer volume of clutter, both physical and emotional, spoke to the weight of his responsibilities.

As Alucard's sharp gaze settled on him, Soren tilted his head back slightly, his shoulders sagging with an exasperated weariness that bordered on theatrical. "Well," he drawled, his voice hoarse from disuse, "look who the wind dragged in." He held out his arms in mock grandeur, his tone dripping with sarcasm. "Well, if it isn't Lord *fucking* Alucard—or is it Aleksei, Ezra, Nosferatu? Hard to keep up."

Alucard scowled at him. He hadn't changed at all.

Soren's silvery eyes narrowed as he crossed his arms, the irritation deepening the lines on his face. "I wasn't expecting to see you so soon—you usually avoid this place when it's crawling with the people you lumbered on me," he grumbled pointedly, his gaze flicking towards the demons lingering in the room. At the sound of his voice, they scattered quickly, their hurried exit leaving behind a faint, uneasy silence that hung in the air.

With a scoff, Alucard stood in front of the window and glared at Soren. "I have been busy," he said with just as much aggravation in his voice as he could see on Soren's face.

Soren stood up, throwing down his pen as his eyes shifted from Alucard to Zalith. "And of course, we never see one of you without the other," he said with a smirk, making his way over to them. "What's it like living up there in that castle while the rest of us wallow down here with poison water, huh?"

"I'm sure not nearly as entertaining," Zalith said tonelessly.

Soren snorted half-amusedly and stopped in front of them both. "Quite," he said. "I assume you're here for the information I mentioned and not here to tell me how much you love and appreciate all the things I do for you," he said with a smile, setting his eyes back on Alucard.

Zalith rolled his eyes.

"You had something important to tell me," Alucard muttered.

Soren lost his smile and sighed. "Crowell came by. He had a lot to say and eagerly awaits your response," he said as if citing from a book. "He's located Ysmay and her Diabolus goons—they're holed up in some abandoned farm. Ysmay has apparently been trying to contact Lucifer with little success. Crowell is quite sure that she's in possession of one of the six Numen Pandoricans—if you want it, now would be the perfect time to attack. He estimates there are roughly fifty to sixty Diabolus with her, as well as her sister. She moves every two days, and this information was delivered this morning. Crowell would like to know what you want him to do."

Alucard glanced at Zalith, who looked to be pondering. They weren't focusing on Ysmay right now, and Alucard knew that Zalith wanted to keep away from her and Lucifer as much as possible. The current plan was to simply keep an eye on her. "Tell him to keep watching and following her—we're not ready to attack yet," he said, glancing at Zalith to ensure that he didn't disagree. He paused, waiting, but once he was sure that the demon agreed, he asked Soren, "What about Attila? Has he been following your leads?"

"He has," Soren said with a nod. "And he hasn't found much information on the location of any of the other Pandoricans. If you want my opinion, going after Ysmay is the best option if you want to obtain a Pandorican—"

"I didn't ask for your opinion," Alucard snarled.

Soren frowned, but he didn't argue. "Right…" he mumbled. "Nothing from your vampires—no elf sightings, no unusual activity across Yrudberg. You're looking into the water, right?"

"We are."

"Need me to do anything?"

"No," Alucard denied. "Keep doing what you're doing—there will be more demons on their way to you tomorrow."

With a quiet sigh, Soren dragged his fingers through his hair. "All right. But look…I've been thinking; you've got people out there looking for Lilith's cults all over the world. Orin is looking for Lilith, Crowell is watching Ysmay and searching for signs of the Pandorican she has, and Attila's out there searching for the Pandoricans, following the leads *I* give him. Your vampires are guarding the city, more of them are out there trying to kill off this plague, and I'm just…sitting here behind some desk. Come on, Alucard—you know I'm more useful than that. Let me do something. You and…Zalith…you're too busy working on these Lilith cults. *I* could lead an attack on Ysmay and the Diabolus; I could get that Pandorican for you," he offered, almost insisting. "Let somebody else do the desk work—like Idina, for example," he said, glancing into the room behind him, where Idina was talking to a few of the demons Zalith had won last night.

"If she could do it, we wouldn't be asking you to," Zalith said.

He sighed again. "But I have a point, right? Why not go for Ysmay now?"

"We need to think about it," Zalith said before Alucard could answer. "But we'll get back to you."

Soren sighed again. "Right, yeah, sure," he uttered.

"I like you here," Alucard said. "You're a very skilled craftsman, Soren," he smirked. "No one can make jewellery quite like you."

He scoffed. "*Anyone* can make jewellery, Alucard. The only thing I'm actually doing here is enchanting it—hiding your little demon friends back there so none of the Numen know you're building an army…empire, whatever it is. Am I really going to go down in the history books as the guy who sat in some grubby little house making rings and necklaces for your soldiers?"

"Is that so bad?" Alucard laughed. "You'll become a widely known craftsman—people will come from all over to buy your wares, no?"

Soren shook his head, a slight smile on his face. "I don't want to be a famous jeweller, Alucard. I want to fight. Why can't you—"

"Your time will come," Alucard assured him. "But for now, this is what I need you to do. Make sure Crowell gets my message."

"All right," he said with a deep exhale and went back to his desk.

Alucard turned to Zalith. "Do you want to go and get coffee now?"

"Yeah, let's go," he said with a smile. "But let's make sure we get it from somewhere using the clean water," he added, taking Alucard's arm as he started leading the way towards the door.

"Alucard," Soren called.

They stopped so the vampire could look back at him.

"If little Danford needs help with spying on Cecil, let me know—I'm dying to get out of this house," he muttered, returning to drawing whatever he had been before he and Zalith arrived.

Shaking his head, Alucard followed Zalith towards the front door, stepping back out into the quiet, empty street. The stillness was almost soothing as they made their way to their horses, but it didn't last. A faint scuffling broke the silence—footsteps fumbling hurriedly across the redbrick ground.

Both Alucard and Zalith halted beside their horses, their movements instinctively synchronized. Turning slightly, they glanced back over their shoulders, sharp eyes narrowing as they searched for the source of the sound. A small woman raced towards them, huffing and puffing.

"U-uh…S-Silas, Ezra," she said, gripping tightly onto the torn scarf around her neck as she stopped in front of them.

Silas and Ezra Wright—that was who Zalith and Alucard were here. Of course, they kept their real names hidden, for they didn't want to expose their location. Here, to the people of Eimwood, they were Mr and Mr Wright, the wealthy husbands who had come to this city to escape the spreading virus and were helping the city in any way they could.

"I-I'm sorry to bother you—I know you must both be *very* busy," she said, creeping closer. "But I've just come from the camp, and…some of us were just wondering when the new houses might be ready. Th-they look amazing already…and pretty cosy," she said with a nervous laugh. "We really appreciate everything you're doing here for us…it's just…it's so cold, and it's only getting colder."

Zalith smiled at her. "They're going to be done by the end of this month," he said, when in actuality, they were going to be ready in less than a week, and Alucard was sure that he was planning on surprising the people waiting for their new homes.

"O-oh, really?" the woman asked, clearly relieved. "That's wonderful news—th-thank you so much—both of you. I-if there's any way we can repay you, I—"

"Don't worry about that," Zalith assured her. "Everyone just being happy and healthy with a roof over their heads is enough for me."

Alucard frowned, his eyes slowly wandering down to the ground. Was it…wrong that Zalith's kindness to others seemed to…arouse him, for the lack of a better explanation? Sure, he loved to see Zalith yell and fight and snarl and growl, but…seeing him act so caring and selfless—Alucard loved that, too, and it made him want to hold him, kiss him, and just be close to him. But there was a time and place.

"We'll let you know as soon as they are ready," the vampire said, setting his eyes on the woman.

"Okay. Thank you again," she said, and then she turned around and wandered off back down the street.

"Do you like to surprise people?" Alucard asked with a smile as he and Zalith mounted their horses after pulling their reins from the post.

"Mostly only when it's going to make people like me more," the demon laughed.

"I see," he said amusedly, leading the way back towards the garden square.

"The more these people like me, the better," Zalith said, following at his side.

"Oh, I am sure they all love you already, Silas Wright," he teased, smirking.

Zalith laughed quietly. "They better."

Shaking his head, Alucard stared ahead. "Let's go and get our coffee."

But Zalith then frowned. "Wait, you have something on your face—come here," he said, moving his horse as close as he could get it to Alucard's.

"What's on my face?" he asked, dragging his hand over his face, afraid that it might be a spider or something worse.

"No, you missed it—let me get it," he offered, holding out his hand.

Without hesitation, Alucard leaned closer, and Zalith then swiftly kissed his lips, startling him. As the demon laughed in response to his reaction, Alucard made his horse stop and pouted.

Zalith stopped his horse, made it turn around, and halted beside Alucard. "What's wrong?" he laughed.

"There's something on *your* face now," he muttered.

"Oh, really?" he asked, grinning slightly.

"Yes," Alucard grumbled, moving his hand to the back of Zalith's head. He stared at his mate for a moment, slowly pulling his face closer to his own…and then, as he slanted his head to the side, he closed his eyes and pressed his lips against Zalith's.

The demon held onto the kiss for a moment. "Copycat," he then teased, his face mere inches from Alucard's.

"Whatever," Alucard replied, smirking a little. He kissed him again…and again until they were making out in the middle of the street—and Alucard didn't care. He just wanted to kiss Zalith. And he did. They kept kissing…a short moment became a long moment, and Alucard enjoyed every second of it. But he knew that they couldn't sit there like this forever. They had places to be, things to do… so after one more kiss—no… *two* more—he sighed and moved his face from Zalith's. "Let's go and get our coffee now."

"Okay," the demon said, smiling at him.

And then, as Zalith turned his horse around, they began making their way back up the street, heading towards the city's centre.

Alucard lingered in his thoughts as they rode, the rhythmic clip of hooves filling the quiet between them. He felt a flicker of relief knowing that Crowell was successfully tracking Ysmay. It was a small comfort in the midst of everything—they *would* face her eventually, and the Pandorican they needed to finish off Lilith would soon be within their grasp. But even so, he couldn't help but wonder when they would finally shift their focus to going after her.

He didn't dwell on the thought for long, though. Now wasn't the time to ask or to pressure Zalith. He knew where Zalith's attention was: strengthening their army, securing Eimwood, and ensuring that the city was on its way to thriving once again. Zalith had to rise to power here, and Alucard understood why that mattered so much to him.

So, Alucard said nothing, instead allowing himself to sink into the calm of the moment. They rode side by side through the quiet streets, the path ahead leading them back into the heart of the city and towards whatever awaited them next.

Chapter Eight

— ⊰ ✝ ⊱ —

Ordvell

| **Zalith**—*Uzlia Isles, Usrul* |

As they crossed the white stone bridge back to Usrul, Zalith took his eyes off their castle in the distance and looked at Alucard. Despite the fact that he would be going with his fiancé, he couldn't fight the growing worry and guilt inside him—and what made it worse was that he *knew* it wasn't normal for him to feel so clingy and needy and anxious. Before what happened in Nefastus, he would have been fine with Alucard going off to do his own thing, but right now...he didn't want to be away from him for even a second.

He tried to push the worry aside, though, and asked, "What are you and Greymore planning on doing today?"

Alucard shrugged, sighing quietly. "Well, we *were* meant to go fishing, but I don't feel like it. I want to do something that requires a little more effort, so...I think I'm going to ask if he'd like to go hunting instead."

"What are you going to hunt?"

"There are usually deer over there—Arieto sometimes, too," he said and glanced at Zalith. With a smirk, he asked, "Are you going to join in?"

"Maybe," the demon said, smiling at him.

"Okay. Well, I need to get my rifle from the castle, and then we'll go to the Anburidge village and meet Thomas. *Then*, we'll head to Ordvell."

"Sounds good," Zalith replied, but as he set his sights back on the castle, his heart started beating a little faster. His anxiety was starting to conquer him, urging him that even their fortified, rune and ward-protected home might not be safe. What if someone or something had gotten in while they were out? He scowled for a moment but shoved the paranoia away. Yet...it still lingered in the back of his mind, and he knew that it would eventually devour him.

They continued through the meadows and up the hill, and once they reached their castle, they left their horses in the courtyard and went inside for what should only be a few minutes. Zalith knew that Alucard kept his rifle in the same room where he kept his other weapons and inventions, so while his vampire went to fetch it, he'd do his best to calm his nerves.

"I have to get something too," the demon said as he followed him into the entry hall.

Alucard nodded. "Okay. I'll meet you back here in a few minutes?"

"Yeah," Zalith said and kissed his lips. He then watched Alucard turn around and head through the lounge before disappearing deeper into the castle. Seeing him leave worsened the growing sadness within, but he did his best to ignore it and got to work. He only had a few minutes.

He hastily made his way through each room, making sure that there was nothing to be panicking about. But even when he was sure that the castle was empty, he checked as many windows and doors that were accessible from outside as he could for signs of tampering. He didn't like this—he didn't like that he felt so paranoid all the time, but he knew that his mind wouldn't silence if he didn't check. But when he heard Alucard return to the entrance hall, he snatched a book off the shelf beside him and hurried back to the entrance hall.

"Did you get what you needed?" Alucard asked as Peaches nuzzled his blazer, resting on his left arm.

"Yeah," he said with a smile, making his way over to him. "Did you?" he asked, but the rifle in Alucard's right hand made it pretty obvious that he had.

Alucard nodded, placing Peaches down on the floor. As she hurried off into the lounge, the vampire led the way to the front door.

Zalith followed at his side and made sure that the front door was securely locked, and then he trailed behind Alucard as they headed to their horses. Once they climbed atop their steeds again, they left the courtyard and started their journey down the hill.

And Zalith did his best to keep his paranoid thoughts at bay.

| **Alucard—*Uzlia Isles, Usrul*** |

The path to Anburidge stretched to the left of the hill, the narrow dirt road cutting through the gentle slopes of blue-green meadows. Alucard let his gaze drift sideways to Zalith, his worry gnawing at him like a dull ache that refused to fade. He was always worried about him—he had been since they left Nefastus. Zalith never let him go anywhere alone anymore, and this outing with Greymore was no exception. The paranoia still gripped his mate, a shadow that clung to every step, every glance over his shoulder. Alucard wanted nothing more than to help him through it, but a question lingered in his mind, heavy and uncomfortable. Was this constant closeness helping Zalith…or hurting him? Would spending a little time apart ease Zalith's burdens, even a little? Or would it only deepen his anxieties? Alucard didn't know, and that uncertainty stung. He couldn't stand the thought of Zalith sitting alone, stewing in his fears, but he also couldn't shake the feeling that maybe—just maybe—being with him every minute of every day wasn't the answer.

His eyes flicked down to the rifle stowed on his horse's saddle. Despite the steady rhythm of the ride and the serene beauty of the island, guilt pooled in his chest. It sat there like a stone, cold and immovable. Zalith did so much for everyone, *always*—and yet *he* was the one left to wrestle with paranoia and dread. He didn't deserve this constant unease. Alucard wished that he could do more for him, but what? Telling Zalith time and time again that he'd done enough and that they were safe didn't seem to help. Words couldn't erase what Zalith had been through; they couldn't chase away the ghosts haunting him. Zalith needed to *see* it—*feel* it—to believe it for himself. Alucard knew that far too well.

But how could he make that happen?

The truth was, he didn't know. Maybe there wasn't anything he could do except be there, unwavering and constant. And that left him feeling utterly helpless. A pang of disheartened frustration flared within him as his thoughts churned; there he was—safe, sound, and trying to live his life, spending time with a new friend—and there was Zalith, trailing after him, clinging to him out of an all-encompassing fear that something might happen. The imbalance gnawed at Alucard; he hated seeing his mate like this, and though his instincts urged him to keep asking if there was something—*anything*—he could do to help, he held his tongue. He already knew what the answer would be. It would either be the same gentle reassurance that he always got or something else, something guarded and simmering that might lead to anger or upset. And Alucard couldn't bear to make Zalith feel worse than he already did.

With a quiet sigh, he looked at Zalith. "Zalith," he said quietly.

"Yes?" the demon asked, smiling at him.

Alucard hesitated. He'd just told himself that he wasn't going to talk about it. He had to just bury his overbearing concern and hope that time really would help Zalith. So, he shrugged and stared ahead. "When should we talk about the Ysmay situation?"

Zalith exhaled deeply. "I supposed we should soon, shouldn't we?"

"We don't have time now. Maybe tonight…on our way to Adenaville?"

"Okay, that sounds good," the demon agreed.

And then they continued towards Anburidge village in silence. It was probably best to give Zalith a little time to think, so Alucard focused on their journey.

| Zalith—*Uzlia Isles, Usrul, Anburidge Village* |

Zalith's thoughts didn't give him a moment of peace.

Not through the *entire* journey.

He didn't want to deal with the Ysmay problem yet. Right now, he knew that she was doing her best to stay out of their way—but she possessed not only an Obcasus but a Pandorican, too, something they sorely needed. However, if they went after Ysmay, he'd have to face Varana, and he wasn't ready for that. A suffocating sadness still ensnared his heart when he thought about her betrayal, and he couldn't stand to see her face again so soon. Not just that, but he didn't want to get involved in anything Lucifer-related. *He* was who had nearly taken Alucard from him, and he knew how dangerous he was—he didn't want to risk Alucard. He knew that they'd have to deal with him eventually, but not now. He needed to be stronger first. So he'd continue focusing on the Lilith problem: take her followers, wither her influence, drain her source of power, and kill her—or lock her away, at least. *That* was all he wanted to think about.

When they reached the entrance to Anburidge village, where all of Zalith's people lived, he tried to relax a little. He glanced at Alucard, and as they came close to Greymore's home, they slowed down and dismounted their horses.

Greymore—who was sitting on a bench on his porch with half a beer in his hand, laughed as he held out his arms. "Well, well, well, I was wondering when you'd get here," he called, standing up.

Hitching his horse beside Zalith's, Alucard shrugged. "We got caught up in the city."

"That's fine. The fish aren't going anywhere."

"About that," Alucard said, walking over to him. "I don't feel like sitting around on a boat today—I thought we could go hunting instead," he said, tapping his rifle, which was still stowed on his horse's saddle.

"Oh, that makes sense. I was wondering why you had that," Greymore chuckled. "I thought you were gonna shoot the fish."

Alucard rolled his eyes as he grabbed his rifle. "That would be quite a skill."

Greymore laughed and said, "Let me just go grab my stuff." He downed the rest of his beer and disappeared into his house.

"Are you sure you want to come?" Alucard then asked Zalith.

"Yeah," he immediately answered. "I'll probably just stay out of the way and read my book." So long as Alucard was within his line of sight—or at the very least within earshot—then he *should* be able to remain calm enough to let his vampire enjoy some time alone with his friend.

"Okay," the vampire replied, smiling at him.

Zalith smiled, too, hoping that his paranoia wasn't visible on his face.

Then, Greymore burst out of his front door and hurried down his porch. "All right, let's get the hell out of here," he said, throwing his bow over his shoulder, gripping tightly onto a few arrows in his other hand. He made his way over to a nearby brindle stallion, stowed his bow and arrows on its saddle, and then climbed atop it.

Zalith mounted his horse, as did Alucard, and then the three of them made their way towards the village's exit.

"So, how've you two been?" Greymore asked, looking at them both.

"Good," Alucard answered. "I trust that everything is fine with your new home? The city is still having trouble with their water."

"Yep," Greymore replied. "Everything's fine—everything's good, good, good," he said, but then he sighed very heavily. "Everything's peachy keen—great, even."

Zalith rolled his eyes. Something was evidently wrong.

"You don't sound very sure about that," Alucard said with a frown. "What's happened?"

"Oh, nothing's happened," he assured him. "Don't worry. I'm just used to having everybody around all at once, you know? Back in the day, I might have shared the place with Danny or someone, but he's off living with my wife," he said with an amused chortle.

"I'm sorry that it didn't work out," Alucard muttered.

"Eh, don't worry," Greymore said with a shrug as they left the village and started following the path down towards the bridge that led over to Ordvell Island. "It wouldn't have been a love connection anyways—she's not my type."

"What *is* your type?" the vampire asked curiously.

"Oh, I don't know…nice…doesn't have much of an attitude—some attitude's fine, though. Likes the outdoors…preferably a werewolf, but what can you do?" he laughed.

"A lot, actually," Alucard said with an amused smirk. "I know more than just Freja. My people deal with werewolves every day; there are many other packs out there that would love to join this little inner circle we have going on."

"Aw, you're gonna help me find a wife?" Greymore laughed.

The vampire shrugged. "It's the least I can do—I know a lot of people."

Greymore chuckled and shook his head. "Thank you. If I knew how to bake, I'd bake you a big ole cake shaped like your head and fill it with blood or something."

Alucard grimaced. "Eh, cake and blood—they don't go well together; a cake, though, I would like that."

"Good, 'cause I don't feel like killing anybody," he replied.

"Well," Alucard said with a sigh, "if you really do want me to reach out to some of the werewolves I know, I will. You could all…meet up and do whatever you do. Maybe having more werewolves among our numbers would be good, no?" he asked, looking over at Zalith.

"Couldn't hurt," the demon said.

"We got space," Greymore agreed.

"Then it's settled—I'll reach out to my werewolf contacts sometime this week."

"You're the best," he said.

Greymore then started singing some godforsaken song that Zalith wished he didn't have to listen to. But there was no escaping it.

The short trek to Ordvell took a little over ten minutes. They eventually reached the crooked, narrow bridge that would take them over to the island, and on the other side, the construction workers that Zalith had hired were working on extending the village.

As they walked over the bridge in a single-file line, Greymore looked back over his shoulder at Alucard and Zalith. "Ya'll better get to fixing this bridge before someone breaks their neck," he laughed as his horse snorted in distress, the wooden bridge beneath him creaking loudly.

Zalith rolled his eyes again.

"I'll get someone to look at it," Alucard replied.

Once they reached the end of the bridge, they trotted through the village and construction sites to get to another narrow bridge; this one led through the marshland, and on the other side sat a thick forest. They all slowly crossed and then dismounted their horses at the tree line, and after Alucard took his rifle from his horse and Greymore grabbed his bow and arrows, Zalith followed them into the woods.

The three of them moved in silence, making their way deeper and deeper into the forest without uttering a word until they stopped in a copse clearing.

"This is a good spot to start," Alucard said, pointing to what looked like tracks in the mud up ahead. "It's close."

"All right," Greymore said with a grin.

Zalith was sure that it was best he didn't follow them while they tracked whatever they were tracking, so he placed his hand on Alucard's shoulder, and as the vampire looked back at him, he kissed his lips and frowned worriedly. "Be careful," he pleaded.

"I will," Alucard said with an assuring smile.

"Okay," Zalith said. He trusted him, but the worry would still linger.

The demon reluctantly let go of Alucard's shoulder and made his way over to a tree stump. He sat down, pulling out his book; he felt more and more paranoid as Alucard started moving into the forest and away from him, but he had to try and wait where he was. He didn't want to ruin their hunt, and he didn't want to be too overbearing. So, he opened his book and stared at the pages, but he kept *all* of his senses focused on the world around him. If anything happened, he was ready to run to and defend the man he loved.

| Alucard—*Uzlia Isles, Ordvell, Ordvell Woods* |

"So, how are things going with the old ball and chain?" Greymore asked quietly as he followed at Alucard's side.

Tracking what he believed to be a deer, Alucard frowned. "What?" he asked, unsure of what he meant by that.

Greymore laughed quietly as they continued following the deer's tracks. "How are things with you and Zalith?"

Alucard glanced at him. "You've asked me that twice now—we're fine. He's just…taking a little longer to adjust to being here than me."

"I'm mostly just wondering about him…; he seems a little more clingy than usual these days—which is fine if you don't mind it of course, but I've never really seen him like this before."

With a conflicted frown, Alucard kept following the trail. If it were anyone else asking, he'd tell them to stop—but Greymore was his friend, someone he trusted, and he was so worried about Zalith; maybe talking about it would help. "I don't know," he mumbled and sighed deeply. "I died, we both lost a lot—he took that really hard, and…he's constantly worried about losing me again. And I get that—he always wants to be with me in case anything unexpected happens again. I feel so guilty and useless, to be honest. I wish I could do more to help him feel okay," he admitted.

Greymore shrugged. "Maybe he's getting a little better one piece at a time—he's all the way back there instead of here with you right now," he said. "Progress, baby," he added with a wink.

Alucard shook his head. "I guess so."

With a quiet sigh, Greymore placed his hand on Alucard's shoulder. "He'll be okay, I'm sure. He probably just needs some more time. Not having Varana around is probably kicking his ass, too—I've never seen them apart like this ever."

"She betrayed him," Alucard grumbled. "He trusted her completely, and she chose Ysmay over him. Zalith deserves better," he said, letting his anger and hatred of Varana surface. But then he exhaled deeply, crouching to examine the deer tracks. "I try to be there for him; I worry about him all the time. He probably feels like he deserves to lose her—he blames himself for everything," he mumbled sadly.

"He shouldn't, especially when it comes to her," Greymore mumbled. "That whole situation with the family versus you and Zalith was precarious to begin with—I'm actually surprised things haven't gone worse than they have. And I don't know Ysmay, but I know Varana, and she's as vindictive as they get, and I'm sure her sister's no better."

Alucard nodded, taking his rifle from over his shoulder. "It's close," he muttered, starting to lead the way again. "But..." he paused and sighed, "do you think..." he hesitated, but the thought had crossed his mind, and he felt like asking Zalith wasn't the best thing to do right now. "Do you think...Zalith might...to an extent, regret that I came into his life?" he murmured, trying to hide the sudden, growing dismay. "I mean...if it wasn't for me, Varana would still be with him, and none of this would be happening. I kind of...feel like all of this is my fault—because this *is* all my fault, really."

"Buddy, if he regretted it, one: he would definitely not have proposed to you, and two: he'd be scrambling to undo everything."

The vampire nodded, trying to take in his words. "I know, I just...I know he's so sad, and...I don't know what to do for him."

"Maybe you two need to get away from work for a day or two," Greymore suggested.

That sounded like a good idea; maybe a weekend away somewhere quiet and peaceful. He and Zalith had talked about taking a vacation some time ago. Maybe now was the time to talk about it again. "Maybe," he agreed.

Alucard froze behind the cover of a dense bush, his sharp gaze locking onto their target. The deer stood no more than twenty feet ahead, its slender frame still and unaware, the delicate rise and fall of its shoulders betraying the calm rhythm of its breath. The vampire lifted a hand and nodded in its direction, catching Greymore's attention. Without a word, Greymore slipped behind the trunk of a nearby tree, leaving Alucard to take the lead.

Raising his rifle, Alucard steadied his aim, the polished barrel glinting faintly through the shadows of the forest. The deer grazed idly, its head dipping towards the lush grass at its feet, completely oblivious to the danger lingering so close by. For a moment, Alucard hesitated. A flicker of guilt crept up his spine, curling its way into his chest. The creature was defenceless, blissfully ignorant of the fate closing in on it, and there was something almost...unfair about that.

But that was the way of things. Life was harsh and indifferent, and survival often came at the expense of another. This deer would feed Greymore's pack for a few days, and he'd not take that away from them because he felt guilty.

Alucard exhaled slowly, dismissing the thought and narrowing his focus. His grip on the rifle firmed as he pressed the stock against his shoulder. The world fell into stillness—his heart, the breeze, even the distant rustling of the trees seemed to pause.

The deer lifted its head, its large, dark eyes scanning the clearing for unseen dangers.

Alucard didn't give it the chance to sense him. He pulled the trigger. The shot cracked through the forest like a whip, the rifle's recoil kicking back into his shoulder as the sound echoed into the distance.

| **Zalith**—*Uzlia Isles, Ordvell, Ordvell Woods* |

Zalith waited, the minutes stretching endlessly. *Ten...fifteen...thirty*? He couldn't be sure anymore. Each second without Alucard gnawed at him, the quiet surrounding him only amplifying his unease. His fingers tightened subtly around the edges of his book, though the words on the page blurred into meaningless shapes beneath his distracted gaze.

He glanced up again, his eyes drifting to the tree line where Alucard and Greymore had disappeared. The forest stood still and indifferent, the branches swaying lazily as if mocking his mounting anxiety. Zalith's jaw tightened. He told himself that he was fine for the *hundredth* time. Of course he was fine.

And yet, the longer he waited, the harder it was to hold back the storm of unease clawing its way up his chest. His mind whispered dark possibilities, every rustle of leaves or distant call of a bird making his pulse quicken. He *wanted* to act, to move, to run into the woods after his fiancé—but he couldn't let himself give in to that fear. Alucard would come back. He *would*.

Zalith forced his gaze back to his book, his eyes skating over the lines, though he didn't take in a single word. How long had it been now? How long was he going to be?

The sudden gunshot shattered the silence like glass.

Zalith flinched violently, the book slipping from his hands as his heart pounded against his ribs, wild and erratic. The noise echoed in his ears, sharp and startling, and his mind splintered with panicked *what-ifs* before he could rein them in.

But he stopped himself—just barely. *Alucard*. It *had* to be Alucard. He had the rifle. It was Alucard who fired the shot. That was the rational thought, the truth, but calming down wasn't so easy.

Zalith clenched his fists, his breathing shallow as he stared into the shadowed trees ahead of him, willing himself to stay where he was. But the book lay forgotten at his feet, and any attempt to appear at ease had vanished entirely. Now, all he could do was sit there, his sharp gaze locked on the tree line, waiting—*hoping*—for Alucard to come back to him.

And the very moment he saw Alucard emerge from the trees, the demon shot up, hurried over to him, and gripped his free hand. He wanted to hug him, but he didn't want to do it in front of Greymore. "Hey," he said with a smile. "Did it go okay?"

Alucard nodded. "It went fine—we found it a lot faster than I thought—"

"Our quickest kill yet," Greymore smirked, standing with the deer over his shoulders. "I'm gonna go put this somewhere safe—see ya'll in a sec," he said, strutting off into the woods in the direction they had left their horses.

Once he was gone, Alucard put his rifle over his shoulder and placed his hand on the side of Zalith's neck. "Are you okay?" he asked quietly.

"I'm okay. Did you have fun?"

Alucard nodded. "Thomas wanted to look for more, but I didn't want to leave you by yourself for too long."

"Oh...you could have—I'm fine," he said, guilt starting to grip his once anxious heart. "You can call him back if you want."

"It's okay. It looks like it's going to rain," he said, looking up at the grey sky. "We can go back—maybe he can come up to the castle for a bit before we have to leave?" he suggested.

"That sounds good. We can probably have the kitchen do something with that deer for him to take down to the village."

"We should probably see if he even wants to come up to the castle first," Alucard laughed, starting to lead the way back through the forest.

"I'm sure he does; he loves to spend time with you."

The vampire smiled a little. "I actually like to spend time with him too—he is...a good friend."

Zalith nodded as they came out of the forest. "He is," he agreed, and then he looked at Greymore, who was finishing stowing the deer on his horse, singing once again.

Alucard let go of Zalith's hand as they reached their horses. "We're going to head back now," he said to Greymore.

"Head back where? Home?" Greymore asked with a disappointed look on his face.

"Yes," Alucard replied. "It's going to rain. But I'd like you to come back with us—to the castle. We can...drink...or something—Zalith says the kitchen can do something with that deer for you to take back to the village."

"Drinks in the castle with the future Lords of Eimwood and possibly all of Yrudberg?" he asked in a snooty voice. "I simply couldn't say no."

"All right," Alucard said, mounting his horse, clearly trying to hide his amusement. "I hope our fancy, rich-people alcohol won't be too much for you to bear," he added with a smirk.

Zalith smiled discreetly as he got up on his horse; he enjoyed seeing his vampire having fun.

Greymore laughed as he mounted his horse. "You should be hoping for the opposite actually because I might drink you out of house and home, and then it'll be *my* castle."

Laughing, Alucard shook his head. "Let's go before it starts raining," he said, glancing at Zalith.

The demon smiled at him, and when Alucard smiled back, something shifted within Zalith—subtle but significant. The burden of his worry and sorrow lightened; Alucard's presence alone was enough to dissolve the dark fog clinging to his heart. He breathed in deeply, steadying himself, the tightness in his chest loosening just enough to let him feel grounded again. Alucard was here. He was safe.

But as they headed for the crooked bridge, Zalith's gaze flicked up to the sky. The clouds above had grown heavy, a deep charcoal grey swallowing the last of the light, and he caught the shimmers of skyfish. A faint patter broke the quiet as the first droplets of rain began to fall, cold and thin against the ground, and the breeze picked up, carrying the scent of damp soil and wet leaves.

Zalith exhaled softly, pressing his lips into a faint line. "Let's get back," he muttered, glancing at Alucard. "Before it rains harder."

They quickened their pace, the sound of hooves mingling with the soft rhythm of the rain on the forest canopy. The crooked bridge loomed ahead, its wood slickening under the growing drizzle. Zalith cast one last glance over his shoulder at the tree line, now shrouded in deepening shadow, before turning forward again. And as the rain fell harder, tapping against his shoulders and soaking through the fabric of his blazer, Zalith felt an odd sense of urgency...but also relief. He was heading home with Alucard safe at his side, and that was enough to bury the paranoia.

For now, at least.

Chapter Nine

― ⊰ ✝ ⊱ ―

Talk Over Bourbon

| **Alucard**—*Uzlia Isles, Usrul, Castle Reiner* |

When they got back to the castle, Zalith headed up to his office, and Alucard took Greymore to one of the bar lounges. The room was an elegant retreat— a space of polished mahogany and gleaming brass fixtures; a grand mirror adorned the wall behind the bar, its gilded frame reflecting the dim glow of crystal chandeliers overhead. Plush velvet armchairs and tufted sofas in deep burgundy hues were arranged in inviting clusters around small marble-topped tables, and the air carried a faint mix of aged leather and the bourbon that they were drinking.

Alucard refilled their glasses, the amber liquid catching the flicker of gaslight.

Greymore shook his head with a low chuckle, his easy grin lit by the warm glow of the bar lamps. "So, I'm laying in bed like this—like this, right," he said, resting his right arm on the bar and stretching his left out as he tried to move his legs to show Alucard that he had been lying on his side, leaning on his arm. "Anyway…I was just waiting for her, you know, and she comes in the room and she looks absolutely disgusted," he said, taking his now full glass as Alucard placed the bottle back down. "And I'm like—oh shit, like did I do something wrong? Are we moving too fast? What's going on? So I say what? And she looks at me and she says 'I didn't know you were a werewolf'. And I said what? Because how do you *not* know, right?"

The vampire nodded with an amused smile on his face.

"And she says, 'I didn't know.' And I said babe, I was talking about pack stuff for an hour earlier, what do you mean you didn't know? And she's like 'well I can't be with a werewolf I'm sorry', and she turns to leave—and I'm scrambling right I'm running after her calling her name and stuff, and eventually I ask her what she's so afraid of, and she says 'well I don't want you to bite me or hurt me or anything', and I say—no offence Alucard—but I say, I'm not a vampire, I'm not just going to bite you. And then she goes into this whole monologue about monsters and what's right and what's wrong and anyways, long story short, that's why I don't date humans anymore," he said and took a sip of his drink. "They're all either skittish, fragile, or religious—and *do not* get me started on those crazy Lethy cultists."

Alucard frowned and asked, "What made her realize that you were a werewolf if not the conversation you had earlier?"

"Oh, I have a pack tattoo right here," he said, patting his right pec.

The vampire nodded, sipping from his drink.

"It's some ridiculous old-world bloodline cult thing that my family was tied up in for generations. I got it when I was twelve or thirteen," he said with a roll of his eyes.

Also rolling his eyes, Alucard sighed and glanced down at his glass. "I hear that word at least five times a day. There's a cult in every direction you look here," he mumbled. But then he set his eyes back on Greymore. "So, you are…what? An Alpha, or…I don't know if there's a word for an Alpha of Alphas, but Zalith never really told me your role in his work."

Greymore placed his glass down and exhaled deeply. "Back home, we were called Primes; I was one and so was Addison," he said with a disgruntled look on his face. "We basically had the whole country's werewolf population split in half between us. To be honest, I think one day we would have probably duked it out for control of the whole thing, but Varana and her council made rules that we all had to listen to, so Addison and I didn't end up doing it. I would have won for sure, though," he said confidently, finishing his drink.

Alucard frowned irritably; just the thought of Addison reminded him of the anger he'd felt when he found out that Addison was the reason Adellum knew where Zalith was…and Zalith very nearly died because of it. "I wish I made him suffer more for betraying Zalith," he grumbled, but he didn't want to sit there and dwell on that moment. He took the almost empty bottle of bourbon and refilled his and Greymore's glasses. "Maybe now that we're building our numbers, you'll get your old job back. I don't know how Zalith feels about the idea of going out there and having you battle werewolf packs, but I think it would be wise—especially since some subspecies of demons here are highly susceptible to werewolf venom."

"I don't know—does the job come with a castle?"

The vampire laughed quietly. "It might if you really want one—or perhaps an estate would suffice?"

Greymore also laughed. "That would be nice, but it would probably be a bit of a waste because I'd only ever use like…two rooms."

"That's exactly what I said to Zalith when we talked about who we'll let live in Cecil's estate," he laughed.

Still laughing, Greymore shook his head. "I mean, I'll take it if you're offering, but if you want it to get some good use out of it, I might not be your guy."

"We'll see what happens once we've removed Cecil."

"No rush, brother," Greymore said with a smile, leaning his arm on the bar as he picked up his glass. "We got all the time in the world," he said, and then he sipped from his drink.

"Well, if you really do want to meet some of the werewolves I know, I can get Soren to arrange a meeting."

"Do I have to fight them?" he asked, staring at Alucard.

Alucard laughed once more and shook his head. "No. I said I would help you find a wife, so I'll introduce you to the werewolves I know—no one has to fight anyone, unless you fall in love with someone else's wife and decide you want to steal her away," he said, rolling his eyes. "Werewolves."

"Wouldn't that be something?" Greymore laughed. "Me taking a page out of Danny's book."

The vampire took a sip of his drink and frowned as he placed his glass back down. "I never really got why both demons and werewolves have these rules—I understand the challenging Alphas for one another's reign or pack, but taking somebody's wife or husband or whatever... what if they don't want to go with the other guy if he wins?" he questioned, looking down at his drink. "I guess... we're no better than humans when it comes to our women, no?"

Greymore nodded. "Yeah. In all honesty, I agree; I wouldn't be able to actually steal away someone's wife unless she wanted to be stolen. It just wouldn't feel right."

Alucard sighed deeply. "Maybe when you and Zalith are kings of your species, you can bend some of the rules."

He laughed and shook his head. "I don't think I could ever bend rules quite like Zalith does, but I'll certainly try. I'm not as charming as he is."

"I hope you're not falling in love with my fiancé, Thomas."

Greymore laughed loudly. "Oh, please. Even if I was, he wouldn't give me the time of day anyway," he exclaimed amusedly. "What I mean is, I don't have the money or that little smile—how does it do that? Like this?" he asked, trying to smile like Zalith did.

"Not bad," Alucard said. "Two out of ten. You need to add a little bit of 'I'll kill you if you say no', and probably some 'I'm going to kill you one day anyway'. That might do the trick. And maybe some fangs, too."

"Two out of ten is not bad to you?" Greymore questioned, humoured. "That's two away from being the worst!"

Alucard shrugged. "Or eight away from being utterly perfect."

Greymore chortled. "That's a lot of numbers."

The vampire laughed with him but shook his head and glanced down at his drink. "You don't need a smile to twist people around your fingers. You just need influence, really. A reputation. Fear is a very powerful tool, and it's probably stronger than hope. Somebody I hate told me that, and I used his advice for a long time," he muttered, and it left a bad taste in his mouth. He didn't like to think about Damien, but he couldn't deny that he'd learnt a lot of useful things from being around him so often.

"Was it Zalith after not letting you eat ice cream past ten at night?"

Alucard deadpanned. "No, but I would have preferred that," he grumbled. With a heavy sigh, he lifted his glass and finished his drink. "Zalith and I have to get ready to head out soon, so we're going to have to end this right here."

"Oh, yeah, okay. I'll get out of your hair then" Greymore said and downed what was left of his drink. He then stood up, stretching as he groaned loudly—they'd been sitting there for quite some time, after all.

"Someone will bring the deer down to the village when it's ready," Alucard said as he also stood up, straightening his shirt as he did. "It's been nice to have you here—I had a good time," he said with a smile. "Maybe…we can do this again some time," he suggested as he led the way out of the bar and into the entrance hall.

"Yeah, we should. Next time, drinks will be on me, though," Greymore said with a smirk. "Maybe we can take the boat somewhere."

When they reached the entry hall, Alucard opened the front door and turned to face Greymore. "Boat?"

"You'll see," he said with a wink, stepping out into the courtyard.

Intrigued, Alucard frowned and asked, "What is this boat called?"

"Nothing exciting that you'll recognize," he said, walking backwards. He then raised his hand and waved. "Byeeee," he called, turning around, "love you."

Watching him leave, Alucard laughed quietly. He really had enjoyed his time with Greymore, but soon, he and Zalith would have to leave for Adenaville…and Zalith had been in his office this entire time. He was sure that his mate hadn't yet eaten, so as he closed the door, he thought he'd head to the kitchen and see if dinner was ready.

| **Zalith**—*Uzlia Isles, Usrul, Castle Reiner* |

In his office, Zalith sat behind his mahogany desk, where he'd remained since he and Alucard had returned home. The room was quiet, save for the faint crackle of the fireplace casting flickering shadows across the walls lined with leather-bound books. He wasn't entirely sure how much time had passed—it felt like hours—but it had been long enough for him to finish responding to all the letters piled on his desk. Things appeared to be running smoothly; everyone was doing their jobs, and nothing troubling had occurred yet—not even the smallest inconvenience. For now, at least, everything seemed under control, and Zalith hoped it would stay that way.

Leaning back in his chair, he picked up a sheet of paper, scanning the details about Adenaville and the pack he'd be facing tonight. His dark eyes traced the words, though his mind briefly wandered. He paused, thinking about how he felt right now. He supposed he was fine—steady, as always—but it wasn't the same as feeling *good*. He remembered what it was like to feel truly at ease, to be so far ahead of everything that he didn't have to lift a finger for days, sometimes weeks. He missed that effortless sense of control, the freedom to breathe without the constant weight of responsibility pressing down on him.

These days, he felt…strained, stretched thin by the sheer volume of work required to rebuild what he'd lost. He was determined to climb back to that place of comfort and confidence, but the road there felt endless. His chest tightened with the thought, but he quickly pushed it aside, unwilling to let himself linger on anything that might slow him down.

He sat for a moment longer, staring at the flickering flames. He didn't resent being in charge—he liked working; it was what he'd done his entire life. But…just for a moment, a break would be nice. Even ten minutes to let go of everything. He wanted to feel what it was like to not be the one carrying it all, to let go of control, if only briefly. And as his lips curved into a faint, almost wistful smile, an idea came to him—one that made him feel just a little lighter. He knew exactly how he'd like to spend those ten minutes.

Just then, his office door opened, and Alucard walked in with a plate in his right hand and a smile on his face. "Hey," the vampire said. "Dinner was ready, and I know you're working, so…I brought it up here for you," he explained, closing the door behind him before making his way over to Zalith's desk.

"Oh, thank you," the demon said with a smile, watching him walk over. "I didn't even realize the time," he said, tidying his desk as much as he could, moving the papers aside and stacking them atop each other as he made room for his plate. Alucard then handed it to him, and as he placed it on his desk, he gazed up at Alucard. "Have a seat," he offered, nodding at the seat across from where he was sitting.

Alucard sat down and leaned his arms onto the desk. "What were you working on?" he asked curiously.

"Just refamiliarizing myself with the plan for tonight," he said and started eating the venison steak sitting on his plate next to a bed of vegetables. "Did you have a nice time with Greymore?"

"Yes," he replied, looking content. "We just had drinks and talked a lot—well…he talked more than I did, but that's just Thomas for you. I like to talk to him."

Zalith laughed quietly. "Once you get him going, he really doesn't stop, does he? I swear I heard him laugh a few times from all the way up here."

The vampire laughed, too. "We were talking about his past…seventeen girlfriends."

"That must have been a very interesting conversation."

Alucard shrugged. "It was interesting to learn what a Prime is, and we discussed the possibility of him becoming one again. It could help us to have more werewolves."

"It would," he agreed. But then his attention averted to the usual concern he felt for his fiancé. "Have you eaten anything?"

He shook his head. "No…I'm not really hungry."

Zalith smiled, but he felt conflicted. He wanted to feed Alucard, but last time, the vampire had become upset when he'd tried giving him food even after he'd said no. So, he refrained from attempting to do so. "Are you sure?" he asked. "I can share."

Alucard smiled, shaking his head. "I'm okay—thank you. Maybe I'll be hungry later tonight."

"Suit yourself," Zalith said with a shrug, enjoying his dinner.

"Do you want me to get you something to drink?" he offered.

"That would be very nice, thank you."

"What do you want?"

"I was going to say maybe some wine for the two of us, but I'm sure Greymore made certain that you drank with him already."

Alucard shook his head. "Wine sounds good—I'll go and get some."

"Okay," Zalith said softly, his voice carrying a note of appreciation.

As Alucard stood and left the room, the demon's gaze followed him, lingering on every graceful step. He couldn't help but admire the fluidity in the way his vampire moved, the quiet confidence that seemed to radiate from him without effort. And, of course, he didn't miss the opportunity to appreciate the view from behind, a faint smirk tugging at his lips.

For a moment, the weight on his shoulders felt a little lighter. With Alucard by his side, even the most daunting of tasks seemed manageable. The thought made him feel just a little steadier, a little more sure of the path ahead. He leaned back in his chair, exhaling a quiet sigh as his eyes drifted towards the flickering fire. Yes, there was still much to do, but for now, he could let himself feel…better.

Chapter Ten

— ⋞ ✝ ⋟ —

Glimpse

| **Alucard**—*Uzlia Isles, Usrul, Castle Reiner* |

Alucard descended the winding staircase leading from Zalith's office, his footsteps echoing softly against the polished stone walls. The castle was quiet, a stillness settling over the halls that made every sound seem amplified. Passing through the grand entrance hall, he walked down a dimly lit corridor, the familiar path guiding him to the wine cellar's heavy oak door.

Once inside, the cool air and earthy scent of aged wood and wine greeted him. He knew exactly what he wanted. At the far end of the cellar, nestled in the largest wine rack, was a bottle of red Barolo—a vintage he favoured and one he'd been meaning for Zalith to try. The room felt cavernous, its shadows stretching long under the dim lights as Alucard made his way to the back.

He opened the glass cabinet door and scanned the bottles, his fingers trailing along the engraved labels until they found the one that he sought. With a soft hum of satisfaction, he plucked the bottle from the rack and closed the glass door—

Alucard froze, and his breath hitched sharply in his throat.

There…in the glass's reflection, crimson eyes stared back at him, cold and unblinking, framed by hair the same blood red as his own. His heart clenched violently, terror coursing through him like ice as he recognized the face that he thought he'd never see again.

His father.

The bottle slipped from his grasp before he even registered his trembling fingers, shattering on the marble floor in a burst of sound and spreading dark red wine like blood across the pale stone. He spun around, the fear choking him as he braced for what he'd see—but there was nothing.

No one was there. The room was empty.

The shadows loomed quietly, undisturbed, their edges soft in the dim light. His rapid breathing echoed faintly off the cellar walls as he clutched the edge of the wine rack for balance. Slowly, the grip of terror began to ease, though his heart still hammered in his chest. He stared down at the mess of glass and wine, the crimson pool stark against the pristine floor, and swallowed hard. His father was not here. He was alone. And yet, the chill lingering in the air suggested otherwise.

Alucard stood frozen for a moment longer, his mind racing as he tried to make sense of what he'd just seen. The image of those crimson eyes bore into his thoughts, unshakable and vivid. Had it been real? Or was his exhaustion playing cruel tricks on him? He frowned deeply, his gaze dropping to the spilt wine. He let out a shaky breath, trying to convince himself that he was just tired, but the unease in his chest refused to subside. His scowl deepened as he reached for a towel hanging from a nearby rack and threw it over the puddle of wine; the cloth quickly soaked through, the dark stain blooming like ink on parchment.

Wiping his shoes on the edge of the towel to ensure no trace of the spill followed him, he avoided glancing at the glass cabinet again. His hands moved on instinct, reaching into the cabinet for another bottle, though he didn't bother to read the label this time. He grabbed it quickly, along with two glasses, eager to leave the cellar and the unnerving sense of being watched.

The clink of glass in his hands echoed faintly as he ascended the stairs, his thoughts still tangled in the haunting image of his father's eyes. Even as he stepped back into the corridor's warmer light, the chill from the cellar seemed to cling to him, refusing to let go.

"Edwin," he called, spotting the butler heading into one of the lounges as he emerged into the entrance hall. "I spilt something in the wine cellar—get somebody to clean it up, please," he instructed.

"Of course, sir," the butler replied.

Alucard then continued through the castle and back up the winding staircase to Zalith's office. When he reached the door, he pushed it open, stepped inside, and closed it behind him before making his way over to Zalith's desk. "I hope...Merlot is okay," he said, looking down at the bottle he'd hastily taken from the cellar.

"Thank you," Zalith said with a smile, and once Alucard reached the desk, the demon stood up, leaned over it, and kissed his lips.

The vampire sat down, and as he poured them both a glass, he did his best to smile, trying to put out of his mind what he'd seen just now. "Are you ready for tonight?" he asked.

"More or less," Zalith replied, taking his glass as Alucard handed it to him. "I'd like to brush over everything another time or two before we get there, though."

Sitting down, Alucard nodded. "Okay. We can probably go over it on the ship."

Zalith nodded in response.

Alucard then leaned back in his seat, staring into his glass as Zalith ate his food. His thoughts spiraled, tangling around the dread that had settled deep in his chest. Or was it fear? He wasn't sure. Whatever it was, he hated it. It gnawed at him, sharp and relentless, leaving him feeling unsettled and strangely vulnerable. Why had he seen Lucifer's face? Why had the crimson-eyed figure loomed behind him in the glass reflection like some lingering spectre of the past?

He frowned, trying desperately to rationalize it. Perhaps he really was just tired, his mind playing cruel tricks on him in his exhaustion. Or maybe…maybe the scars left by his time in Lucifer's prison-place still lingered, buried deep beneath his conscious thoughts. That made sense, didn't it? But if that were true, surely his dreams would betray his fears. And yet, they didn't.

His dreams of late had been peaceful, even pleasant. He dreamed of the future he wanted to share with Zalith, of their wedding and the life they were building together. Occasionally, a memory of his time with Damien might surface, but it never lingered long or disturbed his rest—not anymore. Maybe that was thanks to his new dream-eater. Whatever the reason, his nights were calm, untouched by the terror that haunted his waking thoughts.

Sighing, he raised his glass to his lips and took a slow sip of wine, the rich, velvety warmth doing little to soothe him. His gaze shifted to Zalith, who was focused on his own thoughts, and hesitated. Should he tell his mate? This wasn't the first time he'd seen Lucifer since escaping his prison. He'd seen him before, standing in the forest when he first regained his human likeness. The memory was as vivid as ever—the confusion, the terror—it was the same as what he'd felt ten minutes ago.

But Zalith already carried so much. The demon was stressed, overworked, and juggling more than any one person should. Alucard didn't want to burden him with something that might turn out to be nothing. It could just be fatigue…a fleeting trick of the mind. He would wait. If it got worse, if it started to happen again, then he would tell Zalith. But for now, he'd keep it to himself, clinging to the hope that it wouldn't happen again.

He exhaled slowly, his fingers tightening slightly around the stem of his glass. He had to believe he was just tired. He had to. Anything else was a possibility that he wasn't ready to face.

"What's your schedule looking like for the rest of the day?" Zalith suddenly asked, pushing away his empty plate.

Alucard frowned confusedly. Had he really been thinking so long that Zalith had managed to finish his dinner? He shrugged and replied, "We have…thirty minutes or so before we have to head down to the ship…but other than that, nothing."

"Oh good," Zalith said with a smirk, leaning back in his chair. "Because I want you to fuck me."

Alucard froze mid-sip, his eyes flicking over to Zalith. The familiar flutter of nervousness stirred in his chest, but he wasn't about to let it take over. Instead, he set his glass down with a faint clink and smiled curiously. "Is that so?" he asked.

"It is," Zalith replied smoothly, his smirk deepening. "Unless, of course, you're too busy."

Alucard's smile widened, a flicker of heat igniting behind his icy gaze. Zalith's request wasn't just tempting; it was irresistible. Not only would it sate the constant desire that Alucard harboured for his mate's attention, but it would also help him drown the lingering unease still clinging to his thoughts. There was no better distraction than Zalith—no better way to ground himself than being so close to him, touching him, feeling him, and pleasing him.

Without hesitation, Alucard stood up and made his way around the desk. Zalith watched him with a steady, amused gaze, but before the demon could voice whatever smug remark was brewing behind that smirk, Alucard gripped the front of his shirt and yanked him to his feet. Zalith barely had time to react before his back met the wall, not with a jarring thud but a firm press—the vampire was mindful not to hurt him.

"Careful you don't break my castle," Zalith quipped, his smirk unshaken, though his dark eyes betrayed the spark of excitement he clearly tried to mask.

Alucard pouted faintly in response, his lips curving into a mock expression of reproach before he leaned in and claimed Zalith's mouth in a kiss. The demon responded immediately, meeting him with equal fervour, his hands sliding up Alucard's back. The kiss was slow at first, but it quickly grew heated. Alucard pressed closer, pinning Zalith firmly against the wall, their mouths moving together with a frantic urgency.

His free hand trailed down Zalith's body, and when he gripped the demon's arousal through his trousers, his mate groaned softly into their kiss, the sound reverberating between them as Alucard tightened his hold slightly. Whatever nervousness lingered in his mind was long forgotten, replaced by the singular, overwhelming focus of giving Zalith exactly what he wanted—and taking the same in return.

"Alucard," Zalith then breathed, sighing pleasurably as he pulled his face from Alucard's.

"What?" he questioned with a frown, desperate and quickly growing frustrated as the seconds stretched between them.

The demon smiled at him and asked, "Can you do me a favour?"

"Okay," he replied, waiting.

"I want you to fuck me like you hate me—like it's all I'm good for," Zalith murmured, his voice low, rough, and dripping with need.

Alucard's eyes darkened, his frown lingering as he stared into his mate's pleading gaze. A question hovered at the edge of his mind—*why?*—but he didn't ask. He didn't want to break the moment or risk pulling Zalith from the raw vulnerability in his plea. If this was what Zalith wanted, what he needed, then Alucard would give it to him. Aggression wasn't foreign to him, but being the one to wield it with Zalith was rare—and exhilarating.

Without a word, Alucard leaned in, capturing Zalith's lips in a fierce, unyielding kiss. There was no hesitation, no gentleness—only heat and intent. As their mouths moved together, Alucard's hands dropped to Zalith's belt, the buckle clinking softly as he unfastened it with quick, deft fingers. He tore it from Zalith's waist, the leather hissing through the loops before landing with a thud on the desk.

Alucard's hands were back on him in an instant, unbuttoning Zalith's shirt impatiently. The demon responded in kind, his hand sliding down to grip Alucard's arousal through his trousers. The touch sent a sharp jolt of pleasure through him, and he groaned softly against Zalith's lips, his restraint slipping further away with each passing second.

Desire coiled tighter in Alucard's chest, feeding his eagerness to take control. He wasn't the timid man he once was, and now, with Zalith's words echoing in his ears, he felt bolder than ever. He wanted to give Zalith exactly what he'd asked for, to unravel him completely. With a growl of determination, he deepened the kiss, his hands sliding beneath Zalith's shirt to press against the heat of his bare skin.

Alucard pulled back just enough to stare into Zalith's eyes, his own icy gaze smouldering with intensity. His voice was a low, velvety murmur, vibrating against Zalith's lips as he asked, "Is that what you want, my love? For me to ruin you?"

Zalith's smirk faltered, replaced by something raw and desperate. "Yes," he breathed, his grip tightening as Alucard's fingers curled possessively against his chest.

"Then I'll make sure you won't forget this," Alucard promised, his tone dripping with dark, seductive promise as he captured Zalith's lips again, growing hungrier, more unrestrained.

Once Zalith's shirt hit the floor, Alucard turned him around, guiding him to bend over the desk. The demon smirked, his hand moving to the desk's right drawer. As the drawer slid open, Alucard's sharp gaze followed, catching sight of a small bottle of lube nestled beside neatly arranged papers. Without hesitation, he reached for it, setting it aside briefly as he pulled Zalith's trousers down, exposing him fully. Alucard then looped an arm around Zalith's chest and gripped his throat, pulling him upright so his back pressed firmly against his chest. The vampire's touch was firm and commanding, his other hand working the lube between his fingers before he began massaging it into Zalith's ass.

Without warning, Alucard then tilted Zalith's head to the side and sunk his fangs deeply into the side of his neck, eliciting a low, shuddering moan from the demon. Zalith's hand flew to the back of Alucard's head, fingers curling into his hair, but Alucard wasn't about to relinquish control. He snatched Zalith's wrist mid-motion and pinned it to the desk with enough force to make his dominance clear.

He slowly pulled his fangs from Zalith's neck, the heat of the bite replaced by a cool rush of air as he trailed his lips down the demon's spine. Alucard's grip shifted, his hand pressing firmly against Zalith's back, guiding him to lean forward once more until his forearms rested on the desk's polished surface. The sound of Zalith's quiet sigh of anticipation filled the air as Alucard stood behind him, his icy gaze burning with focus and hunger.

Alucard's hands moved with precision—one sliding down Zalith's back, the other gripping his own shaft. He pressed the tip of his arousal against the demon's ass, his breath hitching as he slowly eased into Zalith's body. Every inch was an exquisite sensation, drawing a satisfied sigh from both of them as Alucard sank as deeply as he could. His grip on Zalith's shoulder tightened, claws pressing against his skin as pleasure rippled through his body.

But this wasn't about tenderness. Zalith's words echoed in Alucard's mind, driving him to meet his mate's request; he abruptly pulled back and thrusted forward again, his movements unrelenting as he began to build a rhythm. His grip on Zalith's shoulder dug deeper, his claws leaving faint marks as he increased his pace, thrusting harder, faster.

The sound of Zalith's moans spurred him on, each one a melody of delight that only fuelled Alucard's need to please him. The heat of Zalith's body and the friction between them sent spirals of pleasure coursing through him, and Alucard leaned closer, his breath ghosting over Zalith's ear. With every thrust, his determination to meet the demon's desires intensified, his movements a mix of control and feral passion that left no room for hesitation.

Alucard's claws pressed deeper into Zalith's shoulder, piercing the skin as blood welled and seeped against his fingertips. The coppery scent mingled with the heat of their movements, intoxicating him further. Leaning forward, he braced his right arm on the desk beside Zalith's, his breath ragged and uneven. His left hand slid down Zalith's body, trailing over the taut muscles of his back before gripping his thigh firmly. He sunk his fangs into Zalith's neck once more, a feral growl escaping him as he thrust harder, his rhythm relentless.

Overwhelmed by the sensations, Alucard's claws unconsciously dug into Zalith's thigh, leaving faint streaks of crimson in their wake. The demon's low, contented moans reassured him, the sound vibrating through the air like a song meant only for his ears. Zalith's hand moved to cover Alucard's, fingers lacing together in a moment of grounding intimacy amidst the chaos. The vampire kept moving, his focus wholly consumed by the heat of Zalith's body and the euphoric pull of his blood.

Alucard felt his peak approaching, the mounting pleasure spiralling uncontrollably through him. He moaned against Zalith's ear, his voice breathy and laden with satisfaction as he pulled his fangs free. The taste of Zalith's blood lingered on his tongue, an indulgence so potent that it threatened to unravel him completely. His hands shifted to Zalith's waist, gripping tightly as he moved faster, harder, every thrust a desperate effort to prolong the bliss.

Zalith's pleasured groans filled the room, mingling with Alucard's own strained sounds as he fought to hold on just a little longer. His body trembled, his grip tightening before finally loosening as his climax overtook him. The wave of pleasure surged through him, leaving him breathless and shaking as he rested against Zalith's back, his chest heaving.

Alucard exhaled deeply, his forehead brushing against Zalith's shoulder as he closed his eyes. The warmth of the demon's body beneath him grounded him, pulling him slowly back from the edge of euphoria. He let his hands trail lightly over Zalith's sides, a silent expression of affection as he worked to calm his racing heart, savouring the quiet intimacy of the moment.

"You did a really good job," Zalith breathed. "If I didn't like you so much, I'd recommend you to all my friends," he laughed.

Alucard laughed a little, too, stroking his hand down Zalith's side. "I'm all yours, Zalith, and you are mine," he hummed possessively.

"Which suits me just fine because I don't like sharing very much."

"Neither do I," Alucard concurred. "I love you," he then said with a pleased smile and kissed Zalith's shoulder.

"I love you too, baby," his mate said contently.

But it wasn't over yet. Zalith hadn't climaxed, and Alucard wanted to ensure that he did. "Do you want me to suck your dick?" he asked quietly.

"Yes, please," the demon breathed.

Alucard slowly pulled his dick from Zalith's body; he tucked himself back into his trousers and adjusted them. Then, turning his attention back to Zalith, he gently guided the demon to sit down in his chair, his gaze lingering on the flush of satisfaction still painted across Zalith's features. Alucard knelt before him, his hands sliding up the demon's thighs with a touch both possessive and tender.

Zalith's hand moved to the back of Alucard's head as the vampire leaned forward, his mouth brushing against the hard length of Zalith's shaft. Alucard's lips parted, his tongue trailing a slow, teasing path along the demon's dick, savouring the way the demon's body responded beneath his touch. He took him into his mouth fully, each pass of his tongue thorough, as though he wanted to memorize every inch of him.

His mate hummed contentedly, his fingers curling into Alucard's hair, gripping it just enough to urge him forward. Taking the hint, Alucard began to suck faster, his mouth sliding over Zalith's inches with a growing rhythm. His hands tightened on Zalith's thighs, his thumbs pressing into the tense muscles as he steadied himself. The quiet, pleased sounds Zalith made were intoxicating, each sigh and groan spurring Alucard on with a mix of satisfaction and pride.

Alucard worked him with increasing fervour, his focus unwavering as Zalith's grip on his hair tightened. He could feel the tension building in Zalith's body—the subtle shudders, the way his thighs flexed beneath his hands, the sharp hitch in his breath. Then it came, sudden and overwhelming, as Zalith moaned low and deep, his climax surging through him.

The vampire felt the warm release hit his tongue, the taste uniquely Zalith's—intoxicating, potent, and laced with the faintest hint of something otherworldly that made his head spin in the best way. He swallowed instinctively, savouring the moment, his movements slowing as he eased Zalith through the peak of his pleasure. The demon's fingers tangled tightly in his hair, his breaths coming in shallow gasps as the last waves of his release washed over him.

Alucard didn't pull away immediately. Instead, he let his lips linger, brushing softly against Zalith's sensitive skin, his hands sliding gently up the demon's thighs in a grounding, affectionate touch. Finally, he leaned back, gazing up at Zalith with a faint, satisfied smile that carried both pride and affection. His hands remained resting lightly on Zalith's thighs, anchoring them in the quiet intimacy of the moment. For Alucard, the taste, the closeness, and the sheer rawness of the moment was fulfilling in a way that nothing else could be—a reminder of how deeply they belonged to one another.

"Thank you," the demon said with a long, relieved sigh, caressing Alucard's hair as he looked up at him. Then, he moved his hand to grip the vampire's chin and pulled him closer. Alucard leaned forward, resting his hands on the chair on either side of Zalith's legs, and with a smile on his face, the demon urged him nearer and kissed his lips.

Alucard smirked and said, "You're welcome."

Zalith leaned in, capturing Alucard's lips in a kiss that was both gentle and lingering. Alucard tilted his head slightly, deepening the connection as he shifted forward, straddling Zalith's lap to close the distance between them completely. Their movements were unhurried, savouring the quiet intimacy as their hands wandered in gentle, familiar touches. For a while, there was nothing but the warmth of their shared space, the soft sound of their breaths mingling in the stillness of the room.

Alucard relished every second, his fingers threading lightly through Zalith's hair as their lips met again and again, each kiss more tender than the last. But as much as he wanted to stay in this moment, reality tugged at the edges of his thoughts—a reminder that they would soon need to leave for the docks. He lingered for a few more minutes, stealing every last second he could, before finally breaking the kiss with a quiet, reluctant sigh.

Resting his forehead against Zalith's, Alucard closed his eyes for a brief moment, letting their closeness soothe him.

"We should get ready," Zalith said before Alucard could.

The vampire nodded. "We should," he agreed, fiddling with Zalith's tousled fringe. "Maybe…tonight we can do something?" he suggested. "Go for a walk…sit around, listen to music and eat something really expensive—or…cuddle for a really long time," he mused with a smile, moving his hand to the side of Zalith's face.

Zalith nodded and said, "That sounds wonderful."

"Okay," Alucard replied. Then, he stood up and handed Zalith his clothes back—but as Zalith went to take them, he pulled them away and smirked. "I like to see you like this," he said, looking him up and down.

Zalith rested his elbows on the arms of his chair. "Well, if we had longer, I might just sit here and let you admire me."

Alucard smiled, handing Zalith his clothes. "Maybe you can do that for me later, no?" he asked, leaning in to kiss him.

The demon gently snatched his jaw in his hand and stared into his eyes. "Maybe I will," he said quietly, and then he kissed Alucard's lips.

After letting their kiss drag on for a few moments, Alucard stood up and sighed deeply, picking up his glass and downing the rest of his wine as Zalith swiftly got himself dressed. Once Zalith was ready, the vampire turned to face him and asked, "Are you ready?"

"I'd like to take a quick shower first," the demon replied.

With a nod, Alucard said, "Okay."

Zalith then took the vampire's hand and started leading the way over to the door.

Alucard let a small, determined smile curl at the corners of his lips. Tonight would go well—he was sure of it. Zalith hadn't lost a single one of these challenges, and Alucard held an unshakable confidence that he never would. Zalith's strength, his resolve, and his unmatched skill made him unstoppable.

But more than tonight's victory, Alucard's thoughts were on what came after. He was determined to see that Zalith got the rest he so desperately deserved. After tonight, there would be no excuses, no work pressing enough to pull Zalith away from the break he needed. Alucard would ensure it.

With that thought anchoring him, he exhaled deeply, tightening his grip on Zalith's hand as if grounding himself in the here and now. Whatever challenges awaited them, they would face them together—stronger, unyielding, and ready for whatever came next.

Chapter Eleven

— ⟨ † ⟩ —

Forkand

| **Zalith**, *Sunday, Tertium 12th, 960(TG)—Drydenheim, Lerkand Island, Forkand* |

Zalith sat quietly in the ship's cabin, sprawled out on the plush couch in front of the softly crackling fireplace. The early morning hour—around 3 a.m., by his estimation—hung heavily in the room, the kind of stillness that only came when the world was caught between night and dawn. During the journey, he'd watched the sky shift outside the narrow windows. What had started as the deep, star-dappled hues of late night had gradually lightened into the faint, murky grey of early morning as they crossed into Adenaville's time. The changing light was a reminder of how far they'd travelled, both in distance and intent.

The white flames he'd conjured cast the room in an ethereal glow, their ashen light dancing across the polished wood walls and floor. The faint smell of salt from the sea mingled with the smokiness of the fire, creating a comforting yet sobering atmosphere. The ship creaked faintly with the rhythm of the waves, the soft sounds underscoring the quiet weight of the moment.

Alucard lay against him, his head resting on Zalith's chest, his soft breaths steady and calm despite the tension that hung in the air. Zalith shifted slightly, his dark eyes catching the subtle shimmer of red as the firelight reflected in them. He knew they were about fifteen minutes from Adenaville's shores, but their ship would dock further down the coastline—an extra precaution to ensure their enemies wouldn't be tipped off to their arrival.

He ran through the plan in his head again, meticulously reviewing each step. Before their departure, he had briefed everyone on the attack strategy, ensuring there were no gaps, no uncertainties. Still, despite the apparent strength of their plan, Zalith felt the familiar weight of unease creeping in. He didn't doubt Alucard or their fighters—he doubted the unknowns, the variables that he couldn't yet account for.

The sound of the waves outside was steady, a calming rhythm against the hull of the ship. Alucard's warm presence against him was a welcome solace, but even as Zalith ran his fingers absently through the vampire's crimson hair, he could feel the tension lingering in him. He glanced down as Alucard buried his face in his shirt, a small frown marring his fiancé's otherwise serene expression. Zalith's gaze softened; he could sense the storm in Alucard's mind even without him saying a word, the way his body shifted ever so slightly in a telltale unease.

Zalith hugged Alucard tightly. He was tired—not just physically, but in a way that went deeper, settling into his very bones. All he wanted was to reach Adenaville, win this fight, and go home. For a fleeting moment, his thoughts wandered to Tyrus, his best fighter. He wished Tyrus was here instead of out there somewhere, always on the move to distract Lilith and the demons tracking him. Tyrus's presence, along with the small army of skilled demons who followed him, would have made these fights so much easier. But Tyrus had his assignment, and it wasn't here. The fighters Zalith had with him were enough—he knew that. Still, he couldn't shake the gnawing feeling of wanting everything to be more than enough.

The demon tightened his arm around his vampire, his other hand trailing soothing circles across Alucard's back. He couldn't know what was weighing so heavily on Alucard right now, but whatever it was, he'd support him as much as he could. There was little time before they'd have to step into the chaos waiting for them on shore, but for now, they had this. And Zalith was determined to make it enough.

The fire crackled softly, its warmth a stark contrast to the icy dread that lurked beneath Zalith's calm exterior. But even as his own worries whispered at the edges of his mind, he let himself focus on the vampire in his arms, grounding himself in the connection they shared. If nothing else, Alucard's presence was his anchor, and in moments like this, it was all he needed to keep moving forward.

"Zalith," Alucard then said. "Do we...both have to have a best man for the wedding?" he asked, glancing up at him.

He smiled down at his vampire. "We don't *have* to, but that's usually how these things go. Do you want one?"

Alucard shrugged. "I was...thinking of asking Thomas."

"I'm sure he'd love to do that for you," Zalith agreed.

"Do *you* have anyone in mind? Or...do you not want one?"

Zalith sighed quietly, sadness starting to build up within him. "Under normal circumstances, I'd probably ask Varana, but..." he paused and shrugged, staring into the fire. "Other than her, I'm not too sure. I'm not close with anyone else besides you."

"What about...Orin or Idina?"

"Sometimes, I'm not sure if they're my friends or just employees I've taken a shine to," he admitted. "In an ideal world, I'd want it to be my brother...maybe even my father," he mumbled, trying not to let himself become too upset.

Alucard then sat up, moving his hand to the side of Zalith's neck as he stared into his eyes. "We don't have to have a best man—we can just invite everyone we want there and have a good time," he said with a warm smile.

Although he appreciated Alucard's attempt to lighten his mood, he felt guilty. "I don't want to rob you of the experience of having one just because I don't have any friends...especially since it's going to be your first and only wedding," he said, smirking a little. "Right?"

The vampire smiled amusedly. "I'll think about the best man thing," he said, moving his hand down from Zalith's neck and over his chest. "I want to have some sort of chocolate there, though—maybe cake."

"The wedding cake can be chocolate if you want—I don't mind."

"Okay," Alucard said contently. "Maybe...we can have one of those chocolate fountain things, too," he suggested.

"Absolutely we can."

"And some of those éclair things you got for Yule."

Zalith laughed, remembering the joke he'd made with an éclair, but he knew that if he brought it up, he'd want to have sex again, and there wasn't time for that. "Okay," he agreed, fiddling with Alucard's hair.

"Is there anything you know that you want to be there?"

"Admittedly, no...but I can imagine it all in my head, and it's beautiful," he said, smiling as he thought about it.

"Well, I'm really excited."

"I'm excited too," he said, moving his hand to the back of Alucard's head; he pulled him closer and kissed his lips a few times before sighing and gazing into his hell-fiery eyes. "We should probably get ourselves a wedding planner so that we can balance planning with our work a little easier," he suggested.

"That's a good idea," the vampire agreed. "Maybe we can look for someone over the weekend?"

"Sounds good," Zalith said with a smile on his face.

The demon noticed the subtle shift in the ship's rhythm, the steady hum of its steam engine easing into a softer cadence. His gaze shifted to the window on his left, where the curve of a sandy beach came into view, its pale expanse glinting faintly under the dim early morning light. They were nearing Adenaville. As instructed, the captain was steering towards a secluded stretch of the coastline, well away from prying eyes or any potential lookouts. From there, they'd proceed on foot to the town not far from the city, where Zalith would face the pack's Alpha in yet another battle for dominance.

Onboard were two hundred and thirty demons, handpicked from his growing army. The number was deliberately chosen to exceed the count of the local pack, which his informant had recently reported as being one hundred and thirty-four strong. Zalith wasn't taking any chances—he wanted their strength to be undeniable, their arrival unassailable. The element of surprise was theirs, and the enemy was blissfully unaware of the storm about to descend upon them.

He exhaled softly, the weight of the moment pressing against him as he turned his attention back to Alucard. Leaning in, he kissed his vampire one more time, savouring the fleeting calm they shared before the chaos to come. "It looks like we're here," he murmured, his voice steady but carrying the faintest undercurrent of tension. He moved his hand to the side of Alucard's face, his touch lingering there for a moment. "We'd better get ready and get this over with."

Alucard nodded and stood up. As he made his way over to the table where he'd left his coat, Zalith watched him with a smile on his face. But he couldn't escape the fatigue. He just wanted this to be over with and hoped it wouldn't take up too much of his night.

"Will you kill this guy, too?" Alucard asked with a smirk, pulling on his redingote.

Zalith hadn't actually decided yet whether he was going to kill this Alpha. "If he spits on me," he said, pulling on his blazer as he stood up, "yes."

Making his way over to the door with Zalith, Alucard shrugged and said, "Maybe he will accept defeat—we have more numbers than he does, so…he doesn't really stand a chance."

"If he doesn't, I'll just kill him—he's not that important," he said, pulling the cabin's door open.

Zalith stepped out onto the deck with Alucard at his side, the crisp sea breeze brushing against his face. His gaze immediately locked onto the shoreline ahead—a crescent of pale sand framed by jagged rocks and the dense shadow of the surrounding forest. The ship slowed further, its engine humming softly beneath their feet as it drifted closer, though the lack of a proper dock made their approach less than ideal.

He tightened his jaw, already anticipating what would come next. The ship couldn't pull in, and they'd have to fly the rest of the way. Zalith wasn't particularly fond of shifting into his demon form unless it was absolutely necessary, but practicality would win out here. His wings would carry him and Alucard to the beach swiftly and safely, but the thought still brought a flicker of irritation. Shifting wasn't about discomfort—it was about control, and he preferred to use that part of himself sparingly, deliberately.

As he surveyed the shoreline, his dark eyes glinted faintly red in the dim firelight from the ship's lanterns. The beach looked deserted, as it should. They'd chosen this spot specifically for its isolation; the distant roar of waves crashing against the rocks underscored the stillness of the moment, but Zalith knew that silence was fleeting. Soon, they'd reach the town where the Alpha and his pack waited, and the real work would begin.

He glanced at Alucard, who was staring out at the horizon with a calm yet focused expression. With a quiet sigh, Zalith shifted his gaze back to the beach, steeling himself for what came next.

"Would you like me to fly you over to that beach with me?" Alucard suddenly offered. "Or do you want to fly yourself?"

"I would like you to take me," he said with a relieved sigh, moving his hand to the side of Alucard's neck.

"Okay. As soon as the boat stops, I'll take us over there," he said, and as Zalith's demons started emerging from below the deck, following behind Idina, Alucard glanced back at them and frowned. "It's a good thing this is a big ship," he said, turning his head back to face Zalith. "Or some of the new demons might have to fly to Uzlia."

"I'm sure they'd love that," Zalith said sarcastically. "We're turning their lives upside down already; killing their Alpha, and then we're going to make them fly all the way to Uzlia—a two-day flight," he laughed.

Alucard laughed and stared out at the beach as the ship came to a halt. "They will have no choice but to do whatever you say. If they have to fly, they will fly." He paused and looked at the demon. "Are you ready?"

"I'm ready," he said with a nod.

Alucard wrapped his arms around Zalith, his touch firm but fleeting as their forms dissolved into a swirling cloud of vermillion smoke. The transformation was seamless, the crimson haze drifting effortlessly towards the white-sand beach below. Above, Zalith's demons unfurled their dark wings, the leathery sound faint but unmistakable as they took flight and followed.

The beach glowed faintly under the early morning light, the pale sand shimmering like powdered pearls. When Alucard landed, the vermillion smoke coalesced, and he and Zalith rematerialized. Turning back, Zalith watched as his demons descended, their wings folding sharply as they touched down, forming into a tight, disciplined group before him. The quiet was heavy, broken only by the distant crash of waves and the faint rustle of wings settling.

Zalith scanned the assembled faces, his sharp gaze ensuring that no one was missing. Satisfied, he exhaled quietly, his breath visible in the cool air. "You all know where you're meant to be and what you're doing—head to your positions and await my signal," he called.

Everyone dispersed, seamlessly blending into the shadows with the innate stealth that came naturally to demons, their movements silent and invisible to the untrained eye.

Zalith felt Alucard's arms encircle him once more before their forms dissolved into the familiar, swirling vermillion smoke. Together, they glided soundlessly across the ground, weaving through a forest of pale birch trees, their silvery bark gleaming faintly in the muted light. The forest gave way to a steep, grassy incline, which they ascended effortlessly, the smoke slipping over the terrain like an ethereal mist.

They halted at the edge of a cliff, the wind tugging gently at the grass beneath them. Zalith rematerialized alongside Alucard, crouching low as his sharp eyes swept over the view below. The small town, Forkand, stretched out beneath them—a cluster of dark rooftops, dimly glowing streetlamps, and winding streets that seemed unnervingly quiet. In the distance, just visible on the horizon, lay Adenaville. The city's sprawling expanse was marked by its towering chimneys and scattered lights, their faint glow a stark contrast to the dark countryside surrounding it. Every detail of the town closer to them was clear, the deceptive stillness masking the confrontation that was waiting to unfold. Zalith took in the scene with calm precision, his mind already calculating their next move.

At first glance, everything appeared just as his spy had described it—quiet, still, and seemingly abandoned by all but the demons who were said to control the place. But it didn't take long for Zalith's gaze to pick out details that didn't sit right. The mud-lined streets bore the unmistakable imprint of heavy traffic—deep grooves from carriage wheels and countless hoof prints. Someone—or many someones—had been coming and going from this town frequently and recently. Yet, as Zalith scanned the scene below, there were no horses, no carriages, nothing to explain the activity.

His jaw tightened. Had his spy been incompetent enough to overlook something so obvious? Or worse, had they been compromised? Unease prickled at the edges of his thoughts, but he forced himself to remain focused.

And then there were the fire pits. They sat conspicuously in the town's open spaces, their charred remains flanked by neatly arranged tents that hadn't been there in his spy's earlier reports. It was all too orderly. And the silence…the streets were unnervingly empty, yet every building glowed brightly with the flicker of candlelight or lamps within. Zalith stretched his senses, searching for the telltale signs of demonic auras or scents, but there was nothing. Not a trace. It was as if the town itself was an illusion—a hollow shell masking something far more insidious.

His grip on the cliff's edge tightened, his crimson-tinted eyes narrowing as he began to piece together the unsettling scene. Whatever this was, it was far from the simple ambush he had planned for. Something was wrong, and Zalith knew better than to let his guard down.

"Something's wrong," he uttered.

"Agreed," Alucard concurred. "It looks like no one is here…or there could be more people hiding here than we know. I can scout the area—in one of my animal forms," he said, looking over at Zalith.

"No," he denied—he didn't want to risk Alucard in any way whatsoever.

But Alucard frowned. "Zalith, we don't know what might be waiting for us. And I'm as inconspicuous as anything," he insisted. "We need to know what we're dealing with."

"I know," he said, his eyes rapidly searching the place below for answers, his mind racing, working to find a solution that didn't involve Alucard... but there really wasn't anything else he could see or do. Maybe he could send someone else to investigate... but he didn't want to send anyone into what could be a trap. He didn't know what to do.

"The owl I turn into is as common as the trees around here—if there are people there, they won't spare a second glance my way. Or a fox—they love empty streets. There's no way for anyone to know who and what I really am, and if anything happens, I can fly out of there; after all, there's barely anything that can stop my mist form," he said, trying to convince him.

Zalith didn't know what to say. Under normal circumstances, he'd be fine with letting Alucard scout the place, and he knew that; though he'd become overly paranoid recently, and he wanted to go back to the way he used to be... but he was scared for Alucard's life. "I'll just go," he said.

Alucard snatched his arm before he could move. "No," he denied. "It won't be as easy for you to get away if something happens."

"But I don't want you to get hurt," he said sullenly.

"I won't. I'm just looking around—I'll be out of there the moment anything happens; you know I will."

"I know," he said quietly, and surely with a worried look on his face.

"I'll be okay," Alucard assured him. "This isn't the first time I've done something like this—this is basically what I spent my life doing while I worked for Damien, and I came out fine every time. I know what I'm doing—I know how to stay hidden, and I know how to get out of somewhere if I need to," he said, looking down at the town again. "These are just demons. I used to do this with scions and Aegis'—it will be simple," he said with a smirk.

Zalith sighed heavily. Alucard was right. He wasn't a child, and he knew that he wasn't going to get better at letting go of his paranoid thoughts if he didn't at least try. So he frowned in confliction and nodded. "Fine," he said.

"I'll be okay," the vampire told him again, moving his hand to the side of Zalith's neck.

The demon nodded but then wrapped his arms around his vampire. "Be careful," he pleaded quietly.

"I will, my love," he mumbled.

As Zalith released him, Alucard's form dissolved into a swirling plume of vermillion smoke before reshaping itself into the sleek figure of a great-horned owl. The rich brown of his feathers gleamed faintly in the dim light, and his hell-fiery eyes glowed with an intensity that sent a subtle shiver through the air. With a single powerful beat of his wings, the owl took flight, gliding silently towards the town below.

Zalith's gaze remained fixed on Alucard, unwavering as a familiar pang of worry clenched at his chest. Every instinct in him screamed to stay alert, to prepare for anything. If Alucard encountered trouble—if he even so much as faltered—Zalith was ready. He didn't care about the mission, about the town, or the pack he'd come to conquer. None of it mattered compared to Alucard's safety. If it came down to it, he'd abandon everything without a second thought just to ensure Alucard was unharmed.

His fingers flexed against the ground as he crouched there, tension coiling through his body like a tightly wound spring. Every beat of Alucard's wings, every second that passed sharpened his focus. For now, he could only watch and wait, his readiness to act overshadowed by his unwavering determination to protect what mattered most.

Chapter Twelve

— ⟨ † ⟩ —

Over Two Hundred

| **Alucard**—*Drydenheim, Lerkand Island, Forkand* |

As Alucard glided silently down towards the town, his sharp eyes scanned the streets below. Spotting a lamppost near the centre of the square, he adjusted his wings and landed gracefully atop it, his talons gripping the cold metal. For now, he didn't immediately begin searching; instead, he paused, ruffling his feathers and running his beak through them in a convincing imitation of a bird preening. Subtlety was paramount—he wanted to appear as inconspicuous as possible, avoiding any suspicion while he assessed the situation.

After a few moments, Alucard tilted his head, his fiery eyes catching the faint glow of a window in the tavern to his right. Turning his attention towards it, he peered inside. As expected, the tavern was packed—every table was occupied, and clusters of people stood in every available corner, their faces shadowed by the dim lantern light. At first glance, the room appeared eerily quiet, but the longer he watched, the more he noticed the subtle movement of their lips. They were speaking, but no sound reached his ears.

His gaze narrowed as he shifted his focus to the building across the street. The same unsettling scene unfolded there: every space was crowded, their mouths moving in silence. The sheer number of them was unnerving, but what disturbed him more was the absence of any detectable presence. He couldn't sense their auras, smell their blood, or even feel the faint hum of life that he would usually pick up on. It was as though they didn't exist—not in the way living beings should.

Alucard's feathers bristled slightly. If he didn't know better, he'd assume that these demons had gone to extraordinary lengths to mask their presence. An effort to obscure themselves—one that hinted at a deeper strategy. They knew someone was coming for them. But how? Had they been warned? Or was this some trap laid for him and Zalith?

The weight of uncertainty pressed against him, and for a fleeting moment, Alucard considered returning to Zalith with what he'd seen. But no—he needed more information. So he waited, his sharp gaze fixed on the unnatural stillness of the buildings, the eerie quiet of the town sending a chill through him that even his infernal blood couldn't dispel.

He spread his wings and glided silently to a bench further down the street, perching atop it as his eyes swept over the buildings. The eerie pattern repeated itself—behind him and across the street, more buildings packed to the brim with unmoving, silent figures. Alucard couldn't detect even a flicker of their life force, couldn't feel the familiar pulse of blood or the distinct aura of demons. And yet, there they were, unmistakable. He counted at least a hundred so far, their presence visible only to his eyes but cloaked in every other sense.

The vampire flew further up the street, landing this time on a weathered wooden crate beneath a cracked window. Peering inside, his suspicions deepened. These weren't ordinary demons lying low; they wore their true forms openly—wings, horns, and crimson eyes all on display. The sight unsettled him. Demons who wanted to remain hidden wouldn't flaunt their forms like this. It was a statement—or a distraction.

His unease sharpened as he reached the sheriff's office. Through the barred window, his eyes locked on a battered and bruised figure slumped in the corner of a cell. Zalith's spy. The man was barely recognizable, his face swollen and bloody, his movements sluggish as he shifted weakly against the wall. A bitter knot formed in Alucard's chest. This wasn't a coincidence—it was confirmation. These demons had known someone was coming.

Zalith's spy had sent a report just after they'd left the castle for Adenaville. The timeline didn't add up; his capture must have happened recently. Had the demons dragged the information from him? And if so, what else had he told them?

Alucard's thoughts raced. This wasn't a defensive strategy born of fear; it was calculated. They were drawing Zalith and their forces here, likely to eliminate them in one fell swoop. But clearly, they didn't know who they were dealing with. If they'd realized it was Zalith leading the attack, they would have done more than just increase their numbers and hide their presence—they would have informed Lilith herself. And if Lilith knew that Zalith was here, this town would look very different. Reinforcements would already be crawling over the area—scions, monstrous constructs bred for battle, the kinds of forces Lilith had unleashed centuries ago during her war with Damien. But there was none of that, at least not yet. That small mercy gave Alucard hope, but it didn't erase the sharp edge of caution digging into his mind.

This wasn't going to be as simple as they'd hoped. Alucard perched silently, his fiery eyes narrowing as he prepared to return to Zalith with what he'd uncovered. They needed to be ready for the unexpected—and for the possibility that this was far from the worst of what awaited them here.

Alucard spread his wings and launched into the air, determination fuelling his every movement. He needed to assess the full scope of the threat, to get an accurate count of how many demons were actually here. His and Zalith's forces totalled two hundred and thirty—a formidable number, but if the enemy's numbers exceeded that, retreat might become an unfortunate necessity.

He swept over the town, gliding silently from building to building, peering into windows with a keen, predatory focus. Room after room was packed with demons, their auras carefully masked, their forms unmistakable. Alucard's unease deepened with every tally. This wasn't a mere outpost or a lightly guarded pack—this was a trap, one that was meant to overwhelm them.

By the time he reached the farthest edge of the town, he'd counted well over two hundred demons, at least seventy more than Zalith's spy had reported. A grim scowl settled on Alucard's face as he hovered near the final building, casting one last sharp glance into its window. Every muscle in his body was tense, his mind racing with calculations. This wasn't going to be as straightforward as they'd hoped, but at least Zalith had made the decision to bring over two hundred of their own fighters.

With a final sweep of the area, Alucard pushed off into the air, the wind carrying him swiftly back towards the cliff where Zalith was waiting. The town faded into the shadows behind him, but the weight of what he'd seen stayed with him, pressing down on him like an iron shroud. There was no time to waste; Zalith needed to know everything.

When he reached his mate, Alucard dematerialized into vermillion smoke and shifted back to his normal self, crouching beside Zalith.

"Are you okay?" the demon immediately asked.

"I'm fine," he said with a nod.

Zalith reached out, using his thumb to wipe off a spec of ash from Alucard's right cheek.

"There are over two hundred demons here," Alucard told him cautiously. "Your spy has been compromised—I saw him locked up down there, so they must know that *someone* is coming for them. If they knew it was you, they would have contacted Lilith, and she would have sent more than a few extra people. The Alpha is also in that tavern there," he said, pointing down at the first tavern he'd investigated. "There are about thirty people in each of the larger buildings and ten to fifteen in the rest. They're all masking their presence, so there could be more where I couldn't see, but it looked like they were all hanging out in the same rooms, ready for the attack they know is coming."

Zalith sighed, looking down at the town. "I guess it's a good thing we brought extra people."

"Are we still going ahead with this?"

"Yeah. Let's get it over with."

"Okay," Alucard said with a single nod. "Everyone is waiting on your signal."

The demon sighed again. "All right. Let's go."

They moved without hesitation. Just as with every other attack, Zalith and Alucard coordinated seamlessly, their timing a deadly testament to their partnership. On Zalith's signal—a telepathic command issued to every demon under his command—their soldiers sprang into action. Alucard wrapped an arm around Zalith, and in an instant, they dematerialized into swirling vermillion smoke, descending swiftly to the ground.

Once they rematerialized, Alucard stretched out his arms and used his claws to cut his wrists upwards; as the blood oozed from his wounds, he imbued his ethos into it, transforming it into a dense, otherworldly fog that poured through the town. It writhed and pulsed, its black depths laced with shimmers of crimson and silver, a haunting, living thing that cloaked everything in its reach.

The fog was more than a cover—it was an extension of Alucard himself. Through it, he could sense everything: the pulse of movement, the vibrations of footsteps, the presence of every being caught within its grasp. He stood still, his glowing eyes scanning the shifting shadows, every detail laid bare to him within the mist's eerie embrace.

Zalith remained at his side, his imposing figure a steadying presence amidst the chaos. As the fog swallowed the town, it began—hostile demons spilled out of the buildings, their masked auras no longer able to hide them. At the same time, Zalith's soldiers surged forward, colliding with the enemy in a cacophony of roars and the tearing of flesh. Chaos erupted, the sounds of battle rising into the night.

The air crackled with tension as Zalith flexed his claws; his wings unfurled, their dark span framed by his sharpened horns, and he met Alucard's gaze briefly. No words were needed; his determination was clear. Then, with a powerful leap, Zalith vanished into the swirling fog, his form disappearing into the melee as he hunted for the Alpha.

Alucard stayed rooted, allowing Zalith and their fighters to see everything within the murk while their enemies were blinded—no movement escaped his awareness. The screams, the clash of claws, and the guttural cries of combatants filled the air, a symphony of chaos that would only end when Zalith stood victorious.

But once all of Zalith's people were within the town, Alucard noticed that hostiles were still pouring out of the buildings. There were more enemies than there were Zalith's soldiers, and Alucard could do a lot more than stand there. He knew that his part in Zalith's plan was to only submerge the battleground in fog and then back off, but... there were a lot more people than they had first anticipated, and he didn't want Zalith to lose any of his soldiers—not now. So once his fog was imbued with enough ethos to stand on its own for a few minutes, he joined the battle.

Alucard moved swiftly, a lethal shadow within the fog. His first target was a skirmish where three enemy demons were pressing two of Zalith's soldiers. He struck with precision, pulling one of the enemies into the dense fog and snapping his neck with a single, brutal motion. A pang of regret flickered through him—every life taken meant one less to bolster Zalith's ranks later—but survival was more important, and he wouldn't allow Zalith's soldiers to fall.

Dispatching the second enemy with similar efficiency, Alucard turned his attention back to the two allies, leaving them to subdue the final hostile. His steps were soundless, his movements fluid as he sought his next target.

Not far ahead, he spotted another group: five enemies overpowering two of Zalith's demons. Without hesitation, Alucard lunged forward, grabbing one of the hostiles by the arm and hurling him with such force that he crashed into the side of a nearby building; the man crumpled to the ground, motionless. The remaining three adversaries spun around in shock, their focus abruptly shifting from Zalith's soldiers to the sudden, unseen attacker. Alucard's intervention provided the opportunity Zalith's men needed. With swift coordination, they seized two of the hostiles, leaving the third to Alucard. He wasted no time, gripping the demon by the shoulder and throwing him back towards his unconscious ally in the mud.

The skirmish was over in moments. Alucard's sharp eyes scanned the scene briefly, ensuring his allies were unharmed before disappearing once more into the fog. There were still too many hostiles, and his work was far from done.

Alucard took a moment to assess the battlefield, his sharp eyes cutting through the swirling fog. Zalith was closing in on the Alpha, dispatching enemies with ruthless efficiency, and his soldiers were holding their ground, subduing hostiles wherever possible. Yet, as the fog began to thin, the advantage it offered started to wane. The enemy, still outnumbering Zalith's forces, was gaining clarity, and Alucard couldn't afford to let them turn the tide.

Determined, he surged forward through the dissipating fog, his focus zeroing in on a chaotic skirmish ahead. A cluster of hostiles clashed with Zalith's demons, the fight a blur of snarls, claws, and desperate blows. Without hesitation, Alucard darted into the fray. Grabbing one of the enemy demons by the arm, he flung him backwards with such force that the man crashed into a wooden crate, splinters scattering as he crumpled to the ground. Before another hostile could strike one of Zalith's men, Alucard intercepted, pulling him away just as his claws hovered near his ally's throat.

The demon in his grip growled, struggling against him, but Alucard held firm. However, the man's furious yell rang out above the din—a call to arms. Whether he was a Beta or held some other rank, Alucard couldn't be certain, but the effect of his command was immediate. Hostiles from all directions abandoned their fights and charged towards them.

Four demons converged on him at once, their eyes blazing with violent intent. Alucard didn't flinch. He hurled the demon in his grasp into the mud, straightened, and turned to face the approaching attackers. His fiery eyes gleamed with predatory focus as he braced himself, ready to meet their challenge head-on.

Alucard fought alongside Zalith's soldiers with fierce determination, their coordinated efforts holding back the advancing hostiles. One of Zalith's demons grabbed an enemy by the arm, subduing him with raw force, while another tackled another foe to the ground. Alucard, moving swiftly, caught the throat of a third demon, his grip unyielding. But before he could act further, a sharp, searing pain tore across his back, radiating through his entire body like wildfire.

The agony was immediate and all-consuming, but worse than the physical pain was the memory that it awakened—a visceral flash of torment from his past. The force of it shattered his focus, and his grip on the demon before him faltered. In that vulnerable moment, a hand grabbed him roughly from behind, yanking him off balance, while the man he had just been holding slammed a fist into his face. The impact sent him sprawling to the ground, his cheek pressed against the damp grass. The world around him blurred, the cacophony of battle muffled by the high-pitched ringing in his ears.

For a heartbeat, Alucard lay still, overwhelmed by the familiar dread that the pain had stirred within him. It wasn't just pain; it was a cruel echo of something far worse—something he had fought so hard to bury. His body trembled under the weight of it, a deep-rooted instinct screaming at him to submit, to stop struggling, to let go. He clenched his teeth against it, but despair coiled tightly around his heart.

He forced himself to move, rolling onto his back just as another demon lunged at him, claws poised to strike. Alucard caught his attacker's wrist mid-swing, his arms trembling under the strain. The demon's crimson eyes burned with feral intent, his weight pressing closer as Alucard struggled to hold him back. His strength was fading—the pain tearing through his back was unrelenting, each pulse eroding his resolve.

His mind screamed for him to let go, an insidious whisper of defeat rooted in old trauma, but Alucard fought against it. His grimace deepened, his jaw tightening as he pushed back against the tide of despair. He couldn't give in—not here, not now. He managed to shove the man away, giving himself time to get up, but the moment he was on his feet, his foe grabbed him, grinning maniacally.

Alucard wasn't alone, though. A blur of motion broke through his disorientation, and before he could fully register what was happening, the demon bearing down on him was yanked backwards. Alucard's wide eyes tracked the scene as Zalith, his wings flared in a menacing display, tore the man's head from his shoulders. Blood splattered across the fog-drenched ground, the crimson stark against the pale mist. Before the other attacker could react, Zalith swung around, his claws slicing through the air; he drove his fist into the second man's face, the impact shattering bone with a sickening crunch, before ruthlessly tearing his throat out.

The vampire stumbled back, his shoulder brushing against a nearby wall. He pressed his back against the cold, unyielding stone, using it as a crutch to steady himself. His chest heaved, his breaths shallow and erratic as he watched Zalith mercilessly dispatch their enemies. But even as the immediate danger passed, Alucard couldn't shake the tremor in his hands—or the way his body seemed to tremble uncontrollably. The searing pain across his back remained a relentless reminder, but it wasn't the physical agony that had him frozen.

Memories came unbidden, sharp and cruel. The last time he had felt such pain, it had been inflicted by Damien; the flashes of that moment assaulted him—Damien's face, the twisted smirk, the echo of his sadistic laughter. It all collided with the present, leaving Alucard feeling small, exposed, and utterly vulnerable. His carefully constructed defences, the strength he had fought so hard to build in defiance of Damien's torment... it felt like they were crumbling under the weight of the memory.

He clenched his fists against the tremors, his claws digging into his palms as he struggled to ground himself. But no matter how hard he tried, the fear seeped into every corner of his mind. He felt as though he was trapped in that moment all over again, and the walls of his resolve were threatening to collapse entirely.

"Alucard?" came Zalith's voice. "Are you okay?" he asked, frantically looking him over.

Alucard stared at him—*was* he okay? He couldn't find his voice, nor could he get over the startle... the recollection.

Zalith placed his hand on the side of Alucard's face. "Alucard?"

He snapped out of it. The pain was still throbbing in his back, but the harrowing memories that had come with it started to wither. "I'm okay," he said, digging his claws into the wall behind him. Then, he took his eyes off Zalith and stared into the crowd of struggling demons. "Go," he insisted. "You have to fight him," he said, setting his eyes on the Alpha of the hostile pack.

"Are you sure?" he questioned worriedly. "I'm not leaving you if you're not okay."

He nodded. "I'm fine," he assured him as best he could, staring into Zalith's eyes. "Go."

The demon stared at him for a moment, his stern, concerned frown fading into something despondent. But he didn't argue—he clearly knew that Alucard was right and accepted it. "Okay, but just... can you take cover in one of these buildings, please?" he pleaded. "I can't fight if I don't know that you're safe."

A part of Alucard wanted to protest and keep helping Zalith's fighters, but he knew that he'd only be a burden at this point—to his mate and their people. So he nodded and murmured, "Okay." He let Zalith usher him into the nearest door, and after the demon hastily kissed him, he watched his mate hurry off into the fog, leaving him alone in the doorway of an empty, foggy tavern. But he wouldn't let his trauma devour him entirely.

Through the fog, he watched the battle, and if Zalith needed him at any moment, he'd not hesitate to run to his aid.

| **Zalith**—*Drydenheim, Lerkand Island, Forkand* |

Zalith clenched his jaw as he moved swiftly through the thinning fog, the weight of his decision heavy on his shoulders. Leaving Alucard alone, especially after what had just happened, gnawed at him. But he had no choice—if he didn't deal with the hostile Alpha now, more of his people could end up hurt, or worse. He would finish this quickly and return to Alucard's side. He needed to ensure that his vampire was truly okay, both physically and emotionally.

The dissipating fog revealed more of the battlefield as Zalith telepathically instructed three of his soldiers to watch over Alucard. He trusted them to do their duty, but the ache of leaving Alucard lingered. His thoughts churned, replaying the moment he had seen his fiancé hurt, the moment he'd seen the fear and shock etched into his vampire's face. It wasn't just the wound—it was the way Alucard had frozen, the haunted look in his eyes. Zalith knew it wasn't just physical pain that Alucard was struggling with; something deeper had been triggered, and the thought that he might have been the cause made his chest tighten with guilt. He had brought Alucard here, and now his vampire was suffering for it.

Pushing his emotions down, Zalith focused on the task ahead. His sharp gaze locked onto the Alpha standing in a small clearing. The man was tall and broad, his pale skin contrasting starkly with his crimson eyes that gleamed with malice. Zalith approached silently, his wings spreading wide, a menacing display that made his shadow stretch long across the muddy ground. The Alpha's attention shifted from the skirmishing demons nearby to Zalith, his expression hardening as he recognized the challenge in Zalith's stance.

Zalith stopped, his scowl deepening. He didn't want to exchange words, he didn't want to waste a single breath on this man. The emotions he'd suppressed threatened to resurface—disappointment, frustration, and an overwhelming sense of blame. Whatever Alucard had endured, whatever horrors he had been reminded of, it all felt like Zalith's fault. And now, all Zalith wanted was to finish this fight swiftly so he could return to the one who mattered most. He flexed his claws, his sharp gaze unwavering as he stared down the man who dared to stand in his way.

The man grinned but scoffed as he straightened his jacket and spread out his bat-like wings. "I see you're the reason for this shit," he called, aggravated. "Here to…what? Steal my land? My money?"

"Your people," Zalith answered. He'd already decided that he was going to kill this guy. He wasn't in a very good mood at all, and his anger was only increasing—he needed to let it out.

"My people?" he scoffed, dismissing the two demons at his side.

"I hope they have better comprehension skills than you do," Zalith replied.

The man scowled and gritted his teeth. "You're going to regret coming here, you ignorant fuck."

Zalith smiled slightly. He was about to make him understand that that wasn't going to be the case.

Without further hindrance, the Alpha propelled himself forward using his wings. Zalith charged forward, too, and the moment they collided, *everyone* stopped struggling and fighting to observe their fight.

Zalith wanted this over quickly, and he already knew how he was going to kill this man. He threw the man back, and as he stumbled, Zalith crashed his fist into his chest. The Alpha flew back, but he recovered quickly and ran at Zalith—he threw his fist forward, but Zalith dodged and smashed his wing into the man's side, sending him tumbling across the ground. And then he hurried over to him to finish him off, but as he was climbing to his feet, the man swiftly swung around and crashed his wing into Zalith's chest, sending *him* flying back.

As Zalith hit the ground, the Alpha propelled himself up into the air and dived down towards him—Zalith rolled out of the way and hurried to his feet as the Alpha landed, crashing his fists into the ground, which cracked and split beneath him. This man was obviously a lot stronger than the Alpha Zalith had faced yesterday, but he wasn't unnerved. He backed off, standing his ground as the Alpha ran at him again. He needed to grab him, and he kept trying to do so as the man threw one, two, three punches at him; he dodged every one, but the Alpha also dodged his claws—he obviously knew that Zalith was trying to grab him, and he was trying his best not to let it happen.

But Zalith was determined—he needed this to end so he could get back to Alucard. As the Alpha missed another punch and stumbled past him, Zalith took a moment to glance over at Alucard—he was still standing in the tavern doorway…watching, but with a disoriented look on his face. Something was definitely wrong, and Zalith wasn't going to leave him to suffer alone a moment longer.

He swung around and gripped the Alpha's wing—he flung him forward, and as the man rolled along the ground, Zalith charged at him, ready to grab him—but the Alpha recovered much faster than before and slammed his fist into Zalith's face. He didn't care. It didn't startle him. He returned a punch to the Alpha's chest—the man stumbled back and threw his fist forward, but Zalith dodged and took his chance to grab hold of the man's neck.

It was over.

Zalith chose to use an incubus ability that he didn't often utilize; it required skin-to-skin contact, and once he had achieved it, all he had to do was drain every ounce of his victim's life force...and that was exactly what he did. Gold, fiery vein-like marks appeared at his fingertips, spreading up his fingers, over his hand, and up his arm beneath his sleeve as he started to drain the man's energy along with every piece of useful information within his mind. The man choked, he struggled, and he tried to fight, but Zalith concentrated harder, stealing his life force and his ethos faster—he wanted it finished, he wanted to go home—he wanted to get to Alucard. And after just a few more moments, the life started to fade from the Alpha's crimson eyes; his pale skin shrivelled, and his ragged breaths silenced.

With a revolted snarl, Zalith threw the man's husk of a body into the mud, and as he turned around, all the dead Alpha's demons dropped to their knees or bowed their heads in submission. They were his now, and the battle was over. But he had so much additional ethos that he didn't need—he could feel it swelling and raging inside him—and he didn't want to find out what would happen if he held onto it. He had to expel it. So he held out his arms and spread white flames across the ground, but he made sure that his fire didn't burn, thus using up more of the new ethos he'd taken from the Alpha. And he kept the fire lit for a few moments until he had burned away the new power.

He then set his eyes on the once hostile demons. He wasn't going to waste any more time. "Which of you is next in command?" he called.

A woman stepped out of the crowd, and at the same time, Idina joined them.

"This is Idina," Zalith said, nodding over at her. "Do what she says." Then, he made his way through the gathering of demons and returned to Alucard. He placed his hand on the side of his vampire's face, but he wasn't going to see to him here. Instead, he scooped Alucard up in his arms and immediately took off, disappearing into the night sky. Another fight was over and won, and now it was time to get as far away from Adenaville as possible.

Chapter Thirteen

— ⸰ ✝ ⸰ —

Cleaning Wounds

| **Zalith**—*Drydenheim, Lerkand Island* |

Zalith carried Alucard into the ship's cabin, and when he reached the bed, he carefully laid the vampire down, mindful of his every movement. He placed two cushions beneath Alucard's head, gently adjusting them until his fiancé looked as comfortable as possible. Yet, the discomfort etched into Alucard's face didn't fade, and Zalith's worry only deepened.

Sitting on the edge of the bed, he stared down at Alucard, his dark eyes scanning his pale, weary expression. Guilt clawed at him. What had happened to make Alucard freeze like that? And why hadn't he been there when he needed him most? They wouldn't have been in that town or faced those dangers if it weren't for Zalith's mission. The weight of his choices pressed heavily on his chest.

He reached out, his fingers brushing through Alucard's crimson hair in a soothing gesture, but his movements faltered when he noticed the blood staining his own sleeve. His heart thudded painfully as his gaze followed the smear up his arm and towards his chest. Was it his blood? He hadn't felt any pain…. Panic flared as he shifted his focus to Alucard, frantically scanning for a wound.

That's when he saw it—the tears in the back of Alucard's blazer. Leaning over him, Zalith's breath hitched as he set his eyes on the three bloody slashes across Alucard's back, the dark fabric torn to reveal the angry, ragged wounds beneath. The look of horror on Zalith's face deepened as his mind raced, piecing together what had happened.

It was his fault. Every cut, every drop of blood—this never would have happened if he hadn't brought Alucard to Adenaville. Guilt twisted his heart as he imagined the pain that Alucard must have felt, the memories that the injury had undoubtedly dragged to the surface. He knew what Damien had done to Alucard, the scars that lingered not just on his body but in his mind. This must have reopened them all.

But Zalith wouldn't let Alucard suffer alone. He wasn't going to sit there and do nothing. He gently moved his hand over Alucard's, his voice quiet but firm, laced with a tenderness meant to ease the vampire's pain. "Is it okay if I clean your wounds?" he asked softly, his thumb brushing lightly against Alucard's hand in reassurance. He'd do whatever it took to help Alucard, to make him feel safe and loved, no matter the guilt that weighed on his soul.

Alucard closed his eyes, nodding faintly, though a distressed frown slowly carved itself into his face. The sight only tightened the knot of guilt in Zalith's chest.

Zalith brushed his fingers through Alucard's hair, the tender motion a silent promise to take care of him. "It'll be all right," he murmured, his voice soft but resolute.

Rising from the bed, the demon moved to the small bathroom to the right of the cabin's door. Inside, he grabbed a cloth from beside the sink and rummaged through the small medical box beneath it, retrieving bandages and gauze. On his way back, he paused by the side cabinet, picking up a bottle of vodka. Placing the supplies on the nightstand near Alucard, he turned back to the bathroom, spotting the fruit bowl on the counter. He emptied its contents, washed it thoroughly in the sink, and filled it with warm water before returning to the bedside.

Zalith set the bowl beside the other items and sat beside Alucard once more, his hand resting gently on his fiancé's arm. "Do you think I should disinfect it?" he asked, his tone low and cautious. Demon physiology didn't require it—wounds couldn't get infected—but it might help the healing process, and above all, he wanted Alucard to feel better.

Alucard opened his eyes, gazing up at Zalith with a faint flicker of trust, though his voice remained quiet and strained as he replied, "Okay."

Zalith nodded, the weight of Alucard's quiet agreement pressing heavily on his chest. He uncapped the vodka, pouring a small amount into the bowl of warm water before dipping the cloth into the mixture. Gently, he helped his vampire sit up, his guilt twisting tighter as Alucard winced and uttered a faint sound of pain. He carefully eased the blazer off Alucard's shoulders, then removed his shirt, his hands steady despite the turmoil inside him. Once Alucard was bare to the waist, Zalith helped him shift onto his front, ensuring that he was as comfortable as possible before tending to the three slashes on his back.

As Zalith picked up the vodka again, he hesitated. The idea of causing Alucard more pain tore at him. Pouring the alcohol directly on the wounds would undoubtedly sting, but the thought of leaving them untreated—of risking infection, however slim the chance—was unacceptable. He sighed, his resolve hardening, but before he began, he decided to use what tools he had to ease Alucard's discomfort.

Placing a warm hand on Alucard's back near his waist, Zalith focused his energy. As an incubus, he had the ability to influence sensations, and he channelled that now, willing Alucard's pain to subside. The tension in the vampire's body slowly eased, a subtle but reassuring change that steadied Zalith's own resolve. Only then did he begin cleaning the wounds, starting by carefully disinfecting them with the vodka.

Alucard grimaced and winced quietly under his touch, and Zalith's heart ached.

"I'm sorry," the demon murmured, his voice heavy with regret as he worked with the utmost care to avoid causing more pain.

Zalith carefully cleaned the three gashes across Alucard's back, his touch gentle as he wiped away the blood with the warm, damp cloth. The water in the bowl quickly turned crimson, but as the blood was washed away, Alucard's tense grimace began to fade. Gradually, his body relaxed under Zalith's care, the vampire's breathing becoming steadier.

Once the wounds were clean, Zalith helped Alucard sit up again, mindful of his movements to avoid causing further discomfort. He placed gauze over the injuries, the sterile fabric soft against the vampire's back, and began wrapping bandages around his torso to hold it securely in place. His hands worked with meticulous care, ensuring the bandages were snug without being restrictive. When he finished tying them off, he gently guided Alucard to lay back down on his front, smoothing his hand over the vampire's shoulder in a silent gesture of reassurance.

For a while, he sat there and softly massaged Alucard's shoulders, his arms, his neck—he wanted him to feel comfortable and relaxed, and he wanted to help him in whatever way he could. "How are you feeling?" he asked quietly.

"Tired," he mumbled sleepily, his voice slightly muffled, half his face buried in the cushions.

"I'm sorry," Zalith said shamefully.

"Why are you sorry? It wasn't your fault."

"I should have been paying closer attention."

Alucard opened his eyes and looked up at him from the corner of his eye. "It was *my* fault," he said. "I knew what I was supposed to do—I should have just backed off once I was done with my part, but *I* decided to ignore the plan and go in there and fight," he murmured, closing his eyes again as he sighed deeply, moving his arms under the cushions a little more so that he could prop his head up.

Zalith didn't know what to say—he didn't want to start an argument with him...he just wanted Alucard to feel better. So he kept massaging his arms and shoulders with a sullen look frown. Nothing was going to convince him that this wasn't his fault.

The vampire then rolled onto his side, looking up at him. "Will you lay with me?" he asked.

Nodding, Zalith turned around and laid on his back. As Alucard moved closer and rested his head on his chest, the demon carefully moved his arm around him and held him firmly.

Not long later, the ship started moving, and Zalith held his fiancé a little tighter. With a quiet sigh, he said, "We're never leaving home ever again."

"Well, at least not for the next week or so," Alucard agreed. "We both need to rest."

"Or maybe the next six years," Zalith mumbled.

"Maybe," the vampire said sleepily.

"Or we could stay there for our entire lifetime and die there."

Alucard frowned, opening his eyes to look up at him. "Well...we are immortal, so we would be living there until the end of time...if that ever comes."

"So be it," Zalith said. "As long as we're safe."

The vampire sighed and moved his hand down over Zalith's chest. "We have work to do...we can't stay at home forever."

Zalith exhaled deeply, staring up at the ceiling. "I know," he mumbled sadly.

Alucard then moved closer and nuzzled the demon's neck. "Did you get anything useful out of that Alpha?"

Holding him, Zalith thought to himself for a few moments. He'd made sure to extract everything that Alpha knew, and he'd stored it within his mind for later...but he hadn't actually looked at what he'd found. So he did it now, searching through his own mind for the information he'd taken from that Alpha—Alegan, his name had been...and it turned out that he actually knew where one of Lilith's scions was.

Vila. She was one of the first scions Lilith had made after Zalith wiped them all out to ensure that Damien wouldn't kill him years ago. Just like the rest of Lilith's scions, Vila had been aged at an incredible rate and was already an adult, but she was only a few years old, which meant she wouldn't have the strength or experience that someone much older would. She was currently living on a small island just off of Sinéad with a group of succubi and other Lilidian demons. Finally, some good information...and Zalith didn't yet know what he wanted to do with it, but he'd think about it.

"He knew where one of Lilith's scions is," he said, almost forgetting that Alucard had asked, and *that* was why he had looked at what he'd found in the first place. "An island just off Sinéad; her name is Vila, and she's with a small group of succubi and other Lilidian demons."

Alucard frowned. "Are we going after her?"

"I don't know," he answered because he *didn't* know. He didn't want Alucard to get hurt again, and he didn't yet feel ready to do something that might encourage Lilith to come after them. He needed more numbers first.

The vampire nodded, resting his head on Zalith's chest again. "We should probably increase our numbers some more before we go after scions."

Zalith nodded, too, staring up at the ceiling. "It would be for the best. I'm not ready to deal with Lilith right now."

"Then...what's next?" Alucard asked. "Are we waiting for your people to locate more Lilidian packs?"

"Yeah. Hopefully, they'll get back to me soon."

Alucard nodded, nuzzling Zalith's neck again.

Zalith knew that his vampire was tired, and he wanted him to get some rest. So, he fell silent, moving his hand to Alucard's head; he started caressing his hair, and as Alucard moved his hand over the demon's chest and to his shoulder, Zalith frowned. "You should get some sleep," he said quietly.

"So should you," Alucard mumbled.

"You more," Zalith argued.

"*You* are the one who had to fight that guy, not me. And then you carried me all the way back here. You need to get some rest, too."

"I don't think I can sleep right now, baby, but I'll be okay," he insisted, kissing Alucard's forehead.

"Okay," the vampire murmured tiredly.

As Alucard drifted off to sleep, his breathing soft and steady, Zalith remained awake, his gaze fixed on nothing in particular. The faint rhythm of the ship's movement over the waves filled the cabin, but it did little to quiet his restless thoughts. Sleep was a luxury he couldn't afford—not now, not when so much still needed to be done.

His mind churned with plans and possibilities, each thought weaving into the next as he stared into the dim glow of the cabin. The ship was bound for the Uzlia Isles, carrying them steadily towards their island, Usrul. Once there, Zalith resolved to stay for a while, at least long enough to consolidate their growing power. His immediate focus would be Eimwood—removing Lord Cecil from his position and addressing the inevitable conflict with the Yrudyen Elves, who would undoubtedly resist his takeover.

He exhaled quietly, determination settling heavily in his chest. Whatever challenges lay ahead, he would face them. He had no intention of delaying what needed to be done. It was time to act, to secure what he and Alucard had worked so hard to build. As the waves carried them closer to home, Zalith steeled himself for the battles yet to come, his resolve unwavering as the chapter of tonight gave way to the dawn of what awaited next.

ASCENDANT
Numen Chronicles | Volume Five

ARC TWO
✝
THE INSECTUMOID CONUNDRUM

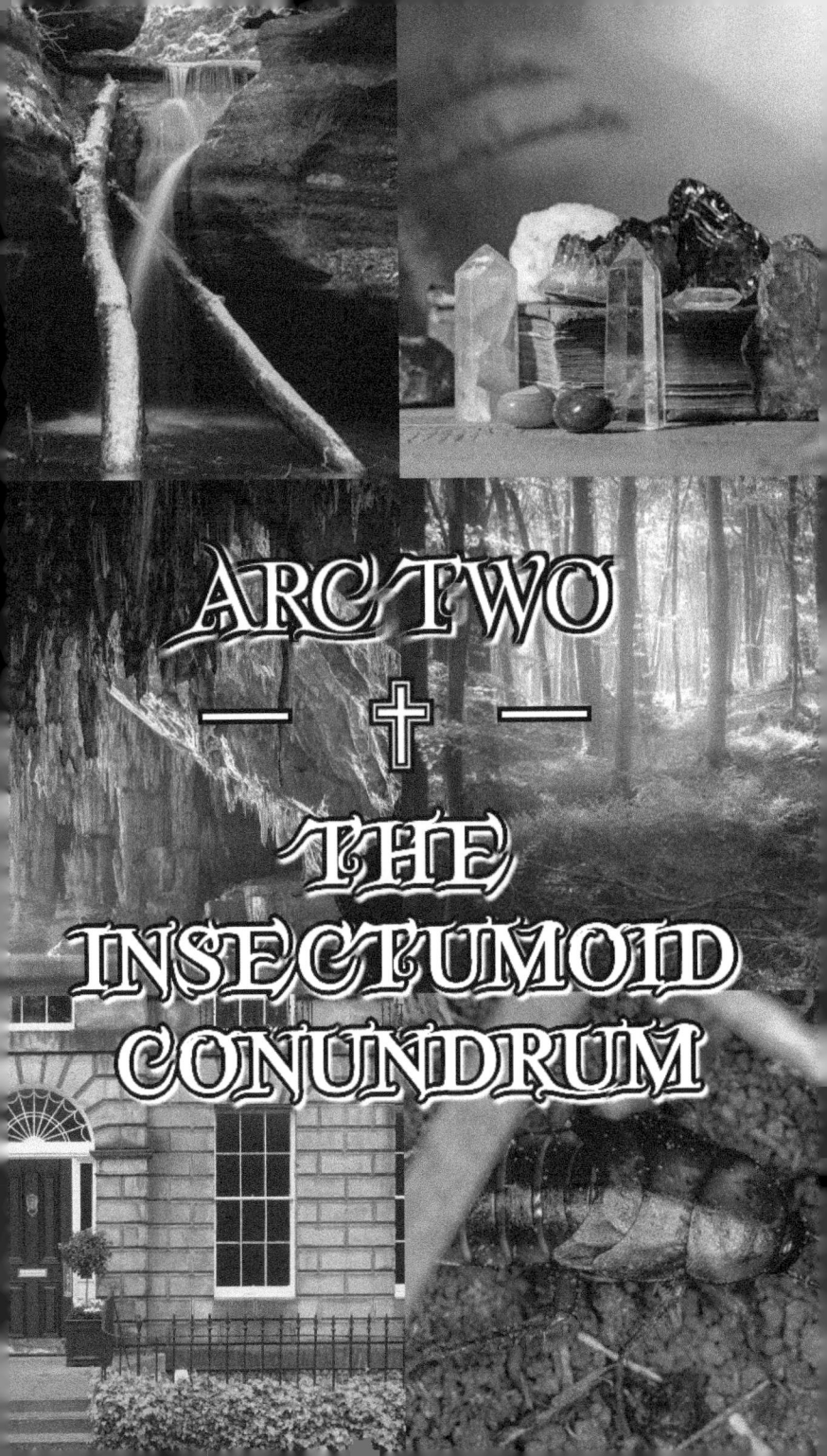

ASCENDANT
Numen Chronicles | Volume Five

Chapter Fourteen

— ⟨ ✝ ⟩ —

A Blade and a Box

| Alucard, *Aprilis 4th, 833(TG)—The Underworld, Damien's Castle* |

*A*lucard knelt on his hands and knees, trembling as his gaze remained fixed on the blood-slicked floor beneath him. The metallic tang of it filled the air, deep and suffocating, and he fought the rising bile in his throat. He wasn't in the room he shared with Zalith anymore. The familiar comfort of their space had been replaced by something far darker—a place that could only be a nightmare... or worse, a memory. His breath struggled as the whip cracked behind him, its merciless edge slicing into his back once again. The sharp, fiery pain stole the air from his lungs, each strike worse than the last, and his body shuddered under the weight of it.

His teeth clenched so hard that it felt as if they might crack, his fists curling against the slick floor as the punishment continued. But even through the unbearable agony, he couldn't bring himself to cry out, to plead for it to stop. He deserved this—he told himself that over and over again, forcing the thought to anchor him against the overwhelming torment. He knew why he was here, back in this cursed room.

This was where Damien had dragged him nearly every day, a chamber of anguish that had become his waking nightmare. Just over an hour ago—was it an hour? Time felt meaningless—he'd returned to Damien's castle with Lucifer's Pandorican. But he'd failed to retrieve Lucifer's Obcasus. Damien hadn't explicitly ordered him to bring it, but Alucard should have known. He should have anticipated Damien's desires. And now, he was paying for his failure.

Another searing crack of the whip ripped through his back, drawing a hiss of pain from between his clenched teeth. His blood painted the floor beneath him, and the weight of his torment threatened to crush him entirely. Yet he dared not utter a single word in defiance. To do so would only make it worse, and Damien's shadow loomed too large, too oppressive for him to bear anything more.

Later, Alucard found himself lying on the cold, unyielding floor of his room—the room in Damien's castle, the room where he had spent centuries of his existence. Everything about the place was suffocatingly familiar. The red, cracked brick walls loomed around him, seeming to pulse in the dim, hellish light; the air was thick and humid, clinging to his skin, and it reeked of ash and blood—a stench that seemed embedded into the very stones.

His breath hitched, uneven and shallow as his chest heaved with lingering pain. The ghostly echoes of the whip's lash still burned across his back, and he felt the phantom weight of Damien's shadow pressing down on him, unrelenting. Was this real? A memory dragged back to life by his broken mind? Or some twisted nightmare conjured by the depths of his subconscious? He didn't know, and the uncertainty clawed at him, driving him closer to panic.

Alucard turned his head slightly, his gaze catching on the jagged cracks running through the bricks of the far wall. He wanted to wake up—to escape this suffocating room, this cursed castle. But no matter how much he tried to will himself away, he remained trapped, pinned in place by the oppressive weight of his surroundings.

Alucard pushed himself upright, his body trembling under the strain. The searing pain radiating from the wounds on his back made it nearly impossible to find any semblance of comfort. His breath struggled as he shifted, trying to ease the sting, but the ache only served as a cruel reminder of his failure. He'd hoped—foolishly, perhaps—that this time, he might finally earn a word of approval from Damien. But like every time before, his efforts had been met with agony, not gratitude. Damien's standards were impossible, his punishments unyielding; one tiny misstep was all it ever took, and Alucard always seemed to falter... at least, according to Damien.

He moved his gaze to the corner, where his blood-soaked, tattered shirt lay in a heap. The sight of it made his chest tighten with shame. Why was it never enough? Why could he never do anything right? His fingers curled into fists, claws digging into his palms as he wrestled with the despair creeping in. Would he ever truly please his overseer? He doubted it, but he knew he couldn't stop trying. He had to keep going—this was his life, wasn't it? Serving Damien, striving endlessly for approval that never came.

Self-pity had no place here, he reminded himself bitterly. Feeling sorry for himself wouldn't change anything. He deserved the pain that burned through his body, didn't he? He told himself he did. And he wouldn't rest—not until Damien looked him in the eye and told him, just once, that he had done well.

The vampire stepped out of his room, his footsteps light as he navigated the familiar corridors. Each step sent a faint pulse of pain through his back, but he ignored it. He needed to find Damien, to ask what he could do to make amends, to find a way to prove himself again. His every thought was a tangled web of desperation and determination, *but as he descended the staircase, a familiar sound froze him in place—the echo of Damien's voice reverberating faintly from the far end of the corridor.*

Alucard's heart quickened. The tone of Damien's voice was sharp yet subdued, a telltale sign of whom he was speaking to. That man. The one who always spoke to the Daegelus as if he had the upper hand, as if Damien—the fearsome overseer Alucard served without question—was somehow beneath him. Alucard had never understood it, but it unnerved him deeply. There was something about that man that even Damien, with all his power and cruelty, seemed almost cautious of.

The vampire hesitated, but curiosity gripped him tighter than fear. Every time he overheard one of their conversations, he learned something—something important, something Damien would never willingly tell him. He crept closer, his movements silent, his presence cloaked in the shadows of the dim corridor. As he neared the source of the voices, he paused just outside the door, his head tilted slightly. He strained to listen, his breath shallow as he tried to make sense of the muffled words spilling into the quiet hallway.

"I told you," Damien uttered angrily. *"I have it."*

"You were supposed to get them," the voice snarled. *"I asked for both."*

Damien scoffed. *"My insolent errand boy forgot—"*

"Don't lie to me," the voice growled. *"I know when you're lying, and I know when you're planning something. I want that Obcasus, Damien."*

"And you'll get it," he insisted. *"I just need more time."*

"You've had years! You could be doing this shit yourself, yet you sit around and send Lucifer's spawn to do it instead?! Why?"

The Daegelus scoffed again. *"I don't have time to be running around—"*

"But that's your job," the voice growled. *"I tell you to go somewhere… get something, and you do it. Or have you grown tired of our cause in your old age?"*

"No," Damien snarled. *"I have not."*

"Then get off your fucking ass and get what I asked for."

"Fine," Damien hissed.

Just then, a crash shattered the tense quiet—Damien's chair slammed into the wall with a resounding smash that reverberated through the corridor. Alucard froze, his breath catching in his throat, before disappearing into a swirl of vermillion smoke. Within an instant, he reappeared in his room, his heart pounding in his chest. He sat on the edge of his bed, gripping the torn, bloodied covers tightly, his mind racing.

He strained to listen, hoping that Damien would open a rift and leave, vanishing into one of his countless unknown errands. But no such sound came. Instead, he heard the echo of footsteps, each one growing louder and more menacing as they ascended the stairs. They were coming closer. His dread only deepened with every heavy thud of Damien's boots against the cracked stone floors, and his mind spiralled into panic.

Had Damien heard him? Was he coming to punish him?

Alucard's heart raced, its erratic beat thundering in his ears as the steps drew nearer. He gripped the fabric beneath him tighter, his knuckles whitening. He tried to steady his breathing, but the suffocating weight of dread settled over him like a shroud. The sound of Damien's final step outside his door made him flinch, his stomach twisting into a painful knot. Waiting felt unbearable, each second stretching into an eternity.

The door swung open with a sharp crack, and Damien stormed in, his presence filling the room like a devouring storm. "Get up," *he snarled, his voice low but brimming with impatience.*

Alucard immediately rose to his feet, his body tense, his mind spiralling.

"Put a shirt on. There's more shit for you to do," *Damien barked, leaning against the doorway with a scowl etched deep into his face. The faint stench of ash and smoke clung to him, mingling with the humid air of the castle.*

Alucard quickly obeyed, grabbing a clean shirt from the haphazard pile of clothes beside his bed. He slipped it on, careful not to wince as the fabric brushed against his still-throbbing wounds. Once dressed, he stood there, silent and waiting, his eyes lowered to avoid meeting Damien's.

He felt the weight of Damien's unrelenting gaze on him, and his mind reeled with possibilities. Surely, he was about to be sent to search for Lucifer's Obcasus—just as the voice had been instructing Damien earlier. His chest tightened at the thought. It didn't matter how impossible the task felt or how much pain he was already in; if Damien told him to go, he would have no choice but to comply. It had always been that way.

"I need you to go and find your father's Obcasus," *he snarled.* "Letholdus probably has it—he had all the Pandoricans, all the Obcasus'... even yours," *he sneered cruelly.* "Go and get as many as you can... and if you return with less than half, I'll do worse than tear your skin from your body," *he hissed, pointing at him.*

Alucard lowered his head, staring down at the ground. "Yes," *he answered obediently.*

"Move!" *Damien yelled.*

Without question, Alucard hurried out of his room, preparing to head for Avalmoor—

⟵❖⟶

| Alucard, *Sunday, Tertium 12th, 960(TG)—Aegisguard, Uzlia Isles* |

The oppressive darkness of his dream dissipated, and Alucard blinked into the warm glow of the cabin. It wasn't Avalmoor that greeted him now; it was the ceiling of the room he had fallen asleep in. The gentle creak of the ship's hull grounded him, yet the ache in his back snapped him fully into the present. A sharp inhale escaped him as he grimaced and carefully rolled onto his left side, the pain flaring with the movement.

Across the room, Zalith sat on the couch, papers scattered across his lap and the small table in front of him. The demon's dark eyes glanced over his shoulder, softening with concern at the sound of Alucard's discomfort. "Are you okay?" he asked, his voice low but weighted with care.

Alucard managed a nod, though the tension in his body didn't ease. "What are you doing over there?" he asked, his tone quieter than usual, still touched by the remnants of his dream.

"I couldn't sleep," Zalith admitted, placing the papers down. "I didn't want to wake you with my tossing and turning."

Alucard frowned slightly, shifting his arm under the pillows as he exhaled deeply. The dream lingered at the edges of his mind, its visceral weight pulling him down. He remembered every detail—the harrowing truth of his past that had resurfaced so vividly, and the raw discomfort that it brought with it. The pain in his back was more than physical; it was a reminder, a scar of memories that he would rather leave buried. But he couldn't ignore it. As much as he wanted to push the shame and self-consciousness aside, there was something in that dream—a detail that had stirred in him, something important he had learned centuries ago. And perhaps it was something Zalith needed to know.

He hesitated, his fingers lightly curling into the edge of the blanket as he stared at Zalith's back. "Zalith," he started softly. "I...remembered something."

"What did you remember?" the demon asked.

"I think I know where we might be able to get a Pandorican instead of waiting on Attila and Crowell to find them."

Zalith made his way over and sat on the edge of the bed. "Where?"

Alucard sighed and looked up at him. "Well...a long time ago, Damien had me looking for the Pandoricans. I didn't know I had one made for me until Damien said so. I also learnt that...if an Obcasus is used on another Numen rather than the one whose name is on the knife, that sends them into a temporary coma of sorts. If they're stabbed by the one that has their name on, they're made comatose unless the knife is removed by someone with the stabbed Numen's blood. But the most important thing I learned is that any Numen can be locked away in any Pandorican, so...we don't need Lilith's Pandorican specifically to lock her away forever. We could...use mine," he explained, recalling more of the buried memory as he spoke.

The demon frowned as a *very* concerned look appeared on his face. "Why...is there one for you?"

"I don't know where they came from, but Damien said both items just...appear when a Numen is born—or the blood offspring of one. Scions don't have them, but...I do."

"I don't like that," Zalith said worriedly, looking a little nauseous.

"Well, I'm sure you won't like what I have to say next—Detlaff probably has my Pandorican," he said, watching as Zalith's look of worry became something horrified. "Damien had no idea where my Obcasus was, and neither did I. We found out a few months ago that Detlaff had that, so I suspect he has my Pandorican, too."

"I don't like that even more," the demon exclaimed.

Alucard sat up. "We have Detlaff locked up, so...we could probably find out from him where the Pandorican is, and then we could use that against Lilith."

"If he's even alive down there," his mate muttered.

The vampire frowned. "You get updates from the people checking on him every day, no? He's still sitting down there crying," he said, a small, amused smirk breaking through the lingering dismay.

"I'm speaking it into our reality," Zalith said, smiling at him.

Alucard shrugged and said, "Well, it was just an idea. I can keep Attila looking for the other ones."

Zalith nodded.

"How far away are we from home?" he then asked.

"About thirty minutes," the demon answered. "You should get some more rest," he said, fiddling with Alucard's hair.

Alucard frowned in confliction. "Are you going to keep working?"

"Probably...at least until we get home."

Nodding, Alucard laid back down and sighed deeply, relaxing. "Zalith..." he said, unable to shake the discomfort that his recollection of the past had forced onto him.

"Yes, baby?"

He didn't really know what he wanted to say, all he knew was that he wanted to see Damien die...and suffer. "I just...I don't know," he said with a sigh.

"You don't know about what?" Zalith asked with what almost sounded like angst in his voice.

Alucard looked up at him. "I was just...thinking about Damien—I want to kill him already, but... there's so much we have to do before we would even be able to hurt him," he muttered.

"I know," he said sullenly. "I want him dead, too."

"We will get there eventually," Alucard said, trying to assure not only Zalith but himself, too. "Lilith first, though."

"Lilith first," the demon agreed.

Alucard made himself as comfortable as he could with the healing wounds on his back. "Don't overwork yourself," he said, turning onto his left side. "And when we get home, it's bedtime," he said sternly.

"Maybe for a few hours," he said. "I don't want to waste the day away."

Alucard glanced up at him. He wanted to tell him that he needed to get more than just a few hours of sleep, but he didn't want it to turn into an argument. If Zalith wanted to work, then…he'd let him work. He'd just keep trying to get him to rest more. "Okay," he said quietly.

Zalith kissed the vampire's forehead, pulled the blanket over him, and made sure that he was comfortable.

As the demon then made his way back over to the couch, Alucard sighed quietly and closed his eyes. He just hoped that Zalith would eventually get some sleep, too.

Chapter Fifteen

— ⟨ ✝ ⟩ —

A Lamentable Morning

| **Zalith**—*Uzlia Isles, Usrul, Castle Reiner* |

Waking from a dream he had no desire to recall, Zalith opened his eyes to the familiar contours of his and Alucard's bedroom ceiling. A flicker of irritation gripped him almost immediately, a bitterness that came with the recurring nightmares; he was tired of seeing horrifying visions of the people he loved—the helplessness, the pain. It made him wish he could keep himself awake indefinitely, even though he knew it wasn't a solution.

Turning his head, he caught sight of the clock. Almost 6 a.m. They'd only returned to the castle a few hours ago, yet it felt like an eternity had passed. Exhaustion weighed on him, but sleep wouldn't come even if he wanted it to—not after those dreams.

He sighed quietly, dragging a hand over his face. And that was when he heard soft purring.

His eyes shifted to the left, landing on Peaches, who was curled up contently on Alucard's back. The vampire was still fast asleep, his face peaceful in repose as he lay on his front, arms tucked beneath the pillows. Peaches blinked lazily at Zalith, her blue eyes half-lidded with a feline smugness that made his brow twitch.

Zalith stared back at her, frowning. He didn't particularly like her being in the room, least of all on their bed. But he didn't dare try to remove her—not with her claws so close to Alucard's already sore and bandaged back. The thought of those tiny daggers piercing his vampire's injured skin was enough to quell any desire to shoo her away.

Instead, he leaned back with a resigned sigh, his dark eyes drifting to Alucard. There was something grounding about seeing him so at peace, even if the quiet couldn't drown out the lingering unease from his dream. For now, he decided that he'd leave them both be—the vampire and his stubborn little guardian.

Zalith knew there was no point in trying to fall back asleep. The restless weight of his thoughts wouldn't allow it, and he didn't want to risk another nightmare. Instead, he decided that a shower might help clear his mind while letting Alucard rest a little longer.

Careful not to disturb him, Zalith slowly and gently shifted out of bed. Peaches watched him with disinterest before settling her head back down, her purring undisturbed. Zalith's gaze lingered on Alucard's face for a moment, his concern momentarily quelled by the sight of his fiancé's serenity.

He headed across the room towards the bathroom, leaving the door ajar; a habit intensified by his growing paranoia—he wanted to be within earshot in case Alucard woke up or if he needed to step out quickly.

The demon stepped into the shower, the cool tile underfoot a brief contrast to the warmth he intended to envelop himself in. Sliding the glass door shut, he turned the knob, and warm water cascaded down over his body, steam quickly rising to shroud the small space. He exhaled deeply, closing his eyes as the steady stream worked to ease the tension in his muscles. For a moment, at least, he allowed himself to be distracted by the soothing rhythm of the water.

As the water poured over his face, Zalith exhaled heavily. He tried to anchor his restless mind, to sift through the noise and focus on what needed his attention. Today, his focus would shift to Eimwood and the final steps of its inevitable takeover. The thought stirred his irritation, though, as it always did when his mind lingered on Lord Cecil.

Cecil's incompetence wasn't just a thorn in his side—it was a problem that had long hindered Eimwood's stability. Zalith had no doubt that Cecil's dealings played a significant role in how the Yrudyen Elves had managed to exploit the city so effectively. Worse still, he was almost certain that Cecil was involved in the tainted water supply that had left the city's people weak and sickly. Danford's reports only strengthened his suspicions: sightings of Cecil sneaking back to his home in the pre-dawn hours, his boots coated in the same mud found along the polluted stretch of river that fed the city's main water source.

Zalith sighed, pressing his left forearm against the sleek black tiles of the shower wall, the steam curling around him like an oppressive fog. He would find out exactly what Cecil was up to, root out whatever schemes the man was hiding, and remove him from power once and for all. His path forward was clear—Eimwood would be his, and the Yrudyen Elves would follow. Whether they were persuaded to work for him or were dealt with permanently, Zalith didn't much care. They had made themselves an obstacle, and obstacles had no place in his vision for Uzlia.

Once Eimwood was under his control, the final piece of his plan would fall into place. Every island in Uzlia Isles would be his, and he would transform them into a network of safety and strength—an unshakable foundation for his people and Alucard. But first, he had to deal with Cecil. And he didn't intend to fail.

| **Alucard**—*Uzlia Isles, Usrul, Castle Reiner* |

Alucard woke to the soft sound of pouring water, his consciousness stirring slowly to meet the dim stillness of the room. To his relief, he wasn't greeted by the searing headache that he'd half-expected. The heavy black curtains remained sealed shut, keeping the bright morning sunlight from invading; a thin line of light stretched across the floor beneath the drapes, its faint glow the only sign of the world beyond.

The lingering ache in his back reminded him that he wasn't fully recovered, though. He became aware of a small weight atop him, one he immediately recognized. Of course, it was Peaches. He'd let her in last night when he'd gotten up to use the bathroom, her familiar presence offering a quiet comfort that he didn't want to deny himself. He knew Zalith wouldn't approve, but he couldn't bring himself to care—not yet. Sleeping without her felt strange now, and he wasn't quite ready to break the habit.

He sighed softly, resisting the urge to roll onto his back, knowing that the movement would only aggravate the wounds. As if sensing his discomfort, Peaches leapt gracefully from his back to sit beside him on the bed. Her striking blue eyes blinked up at him, a look of feline indifference masking what Alucard liked to think was concern.

Carefully, he shifted his pillows and leaned them against the headboard before easing himself into a sitting position; his movements were slow and struggled, the pull of his healing back keeping him cautious. Once he was comfortable, he patted his lap in invitation, and Peaches didn't hesitate to oblige, curling up in her usual spot. Her warm, soft weight was grounding, and Alucard gently ran his fingers over her pink skin, tracing the dark splotches he had grown to adore.

His gaze drifted towards the wide-open bathroom door. The steady sound of water continued, and though he couldn't see Zalith, he knew that his mate was just out of view, showering to the left of the doorway. The thought of joining him crossed Alucard's mind, but he quickly dismissed it. The water would sting his back, and he wasn't keen on inviting more discomfort. So instead, he stayed where he was, absently stroking Peaches as he waited for Zalith to return to him.

Eventually, the water stopped, the gentle cascade replaced by silence. Moments later, Zalith stepped out of the bathroom, steam curling faintly behind him. Alucard's gaze flicked towards the doorway, where Zalith appeared utterly unbothered by his nudity, a towel draped over his shoulders as he used it to dry his damp hair.

Alucard frowned, realizing that Zalith wouldn't be pleased to find Peaches lounging in their bed. He carefully lifted her from his lap, intending to place her on the floor, but the feline had other ideas. She squirmed and mewled in protest, her small claws catching at his shirt as she struggled against his grasp.

"Alucard," Zalith said, his tone mildly disapproving as his dark eyes narrowed. "You know I don't want the cat on the bed."

The vampire's gaze darted towards Zalith, and despite his guilt, he found himself momentarily distracted by the sight of his naked mate. Zalith's damp skin shimmered faintly in the dim light, the carved lines of his musculature captivating. Alucard's pout deepened as he reluctantly tore his eyes away, looking back at the stubborn kitten in his hands. "I know," he muttered, his tone tinged with defeat.

Peaches continued to resist, her small but insistent strength making the task harder than it needed to be. A sharp sting shot through his back as he struggled with her, the movement pulling at the edges of his healing wounds. He grimaced but pressed on, carefully prying her away from his chest and setting her down on the floor.

"I'm sorry," the vampire added softly as Peaches let out a final huff of displeasure before scurrying away to hide beneath the curtains nearest the door. Alucard leaned back against the headboard with a quiet sigh, his expression one of both pain and resignation as he avoided Zalith's gaze.

"It's okay," Zalith said, making his way over to him. "I forgive you. The sheets are due to be washed today anyway."

Alucard shrugged. "She was just here when I woke up...and I wanted to say hi to her."

Zalith sat down beside him. "How did you sleep?"

Looking down at his lap, Alucard exhaled deeply and shrugged. "I kept waking up," he mumbled. "I couldn't get comfortable. And then my back started hurting again, so I was debating whether or not I wanted to try and go back to sleep. But then I guess I fell asleep while lying there thinking about it," he said, glancing at Zalith. "Then I woke up just now when I heard the water running. I would have joined you, but I don't think I've healed yet, and I didn't want to deal with that discomfort."

The demon guided his hand up Alucard's arm and to the side of his face. He started fiddling with his hair as he worriedly asked, "Is there anything I can do for you?"

Alucard shrugged again. He wanted *and* needed blood; not only would it help him to heal faster, but it might also help him fight against the exhaustion gradually devouring him.

"Do you want blood?" Zalith asked just moments later, as if he knew exactly what Alucard was thinking—he *always* had a way of knowing.

He wasn't going to say no. The vampire nodded and said, "Yes, please."

Zalith's hand gently cupped the back of Alucard's head, his fingers threading through the vampire's hair as he guided him closer. Alucard moved willingly, nuzzling the demon's neck; his hand traced a slow path up Zalith's chest, over his shoulder, and then lightly gripped it as he steadied himself. The ache in his back throbbed faintly, but he ignored it, focusing instead on the closeness between them.

He hesitated for a moment, resisting the urge to bite immediately. He didn't want to seem desperate, and he didn't want to risk hurting Zalith more than necessary. Instead, he trailed soft kisses along the curve of Zalith's neck, deciding where to sink his fangs. And when he finally bit down, his fangs piercing the demon's skin with careful precision, Zalith sighed quietly in contentment. The sound alone was enough to ease some of Alucard's lingering tension, but it was nothing compared to the rush of Zalith's blood filling his mouth. Alucard's eyes fluttered shut as the pain in his back began to fade, replaced by a calm, soothing euphoria that coursed through him like a gentle tide.

The vampire sighed softly, his grip on Zalith shifting. His hand wandered from the back of Zalith's head to his thigh, his fingers lightly pressing into the muscle as he hummed in satisfaction. The sweet, warm taste of Zalith's blood was everything he needed—a reprieve from both physical pain and the emotional weight he carried. With each sip, he felt more at ease, more relaxed…until all that remained was the quiet intimacy of the moment they shared.

"Thank you," Alucard hummed as he pulled his fangs from Zalith's neck and rested his head on the demon's shoulder.

"You're welcome," Zalith replied and kissed Alucard's forehead.

For a short while, they stayed wrapped in silence, Alucard sinking into the comforting haze of his euphoria. The tension in his body had ebbed, leaving only a lingering fatigue. He still felt tired—his eyelids were heavy with the weight of interrupted rest—and part of him longed to curl back into the sheets and let sleep reclaim him. But another part, the determined part, refused to let him give in. He wanted to go with Zalith to Eimwood, to stand beside him and help see the takeover through.

"We should probably change your dressing," Zalith murmured, his voice heavy with concern.

Alucard hesitated, his thoughts knotting with conflict. He knew Zalith was right—his bandages needed changing—but the memory of yesterday's pain and the dark thoughts that it had dragged up loomed in his mind. Still, he knew the alternative: leaving the wounds untreated might slow his healing, and he didn't want that either.

Pushing his apprehension aside, the vampire gave a small nod, sitting up straighter despite the ache it caused. "Okay," he replied softly, his voice quiet but resolute.

"Wait here," Zalith said as he stood up and wrapped the towel that he'd been drying his hair with around his waist. "I'll go and get Edwin to find some medical supplies."

Alucard nodded and watched Zalith leave their bedroom—but as the demon opened the door, he was greeted by Sabazios, who pounced to his feet, wagging his tail.

"Stay off the bed," Zalith uttered, letting the dog into the room, and then he closed the door and made his way downstairs.

Alucard smiled at his hellhound as he made his way over and sat in front of him, resting his head on his lap. "What have you been up to this morning, hmm?" he asked, patting Sabazios' head.

Sabazios growled quietly, flicking his ears as he lifted his head and tilted it.

"I'm okay," Alucard assured softly, his fingers gently scratching behind the hound's ears.

Sabazios tilted his head, his concerned crimson eyes fixed on the vampire, and let out a quiet whine, his tail swishing faintly against the floor.

"I promise," Alucard added, rubbing the dog's head.

But the hound remained unconvinced, his gaze flicking briefly to Alucard's back before a sound at the door caught his attention.

The bedroom door creaked open, and Zalith stepped inside, his tall frame illuminated briefly by the light spilling in from the hallway. Sabazios let out a soft huff and trotted out of the room, casting one last glance at Alucard before disappearing into the corridor.

Zalith closed the door behind him and approached the bed. In his right hand was a small white box, one of the castle's medical kits kept well-stocked by their staff. He set it down gently on the bed and sat beside Alucard; he placed a warm hand on the side of the vampire's arm, giving it a reassuring squeeze as he asked, "Are you ready?"

Alucard hesitated briefly but nodded, his resolve outweighing his lingering apprehension. He turned carefully, positioning himself so that his back faced Zalith, and braced himself for the pain that he knew was coming.

"I can make sure you don't feel any pain," Zalith murmured, sliding his hand down Alucard's arm, his touch lingering before settling at his waist.

Alucard nodded, welcoming any relief that the demon could offer. He closed his eyes as a wave of Zalith's power began to flow through him, warm and soothing, like a balm against the ache in his body. The sharp sting of pain faded quickly, replaced by a soft, all-encompassing comfort that seemed to spread through every fibre of his being. A quiet, contented sigh left his lips as the tension in his muscles eased; he let himself relax fully, the lingering traces of discomfort dissolving under Zalith's care, leaving him at peace for the first time since waking.

Zalith began untying the bandages wrapped around Alucard's torso. Alucard could feel the subtle tugging as the fabric shifted against his skin, the tension easing with each loop that was unwound. Despite the soothing veil of Zalith's power, there was still a faint, residual ache—a dull throb beneath the surface that flared slightly as the bandages were peeled away.

When Zalith gently lifted the gauze from the three long, jagged gashes across Alucard's back, the vampire tensed briefly, a ghost of the earlier pain sparking through his nerves. The cool air against his exposed skin made the area feel oddly raw, a reminder of how deep the wounds had been. But the relief of not feeling any fresh tearing or sharp agony allowed him to exhale quietly, settling into the moment.

As Zalith worked, Alucard couldn't help but think about how much worse it could have been. He was healing—albeit slower than he would have liked—but there was a strange sense of gratitude in having Zalith there, ensuring the process wasn't as agonizing as it might have been.

"How do they look?" the vampire mumbled, fighting the ache.

"A little better," Zalith assured him. "But it still needs time."

A grimace crossed Alucard's face, though it wasn't just the faint remnants of pain that gripped him. Despite the comfort and trust he shared with Zalith, an unwelcome wave of embarrassment swirled within him, tied to the scars marring his back. No matter how much he told himself that Zalith wouldn't care—that the demon would never judge him—he couldn't fully shake the anxiety that came with being so exposed. His thoughts intruded, whispering doubts that he wished he could silence, but the soothing warmth of Zalith's presence worked to unravel his tension, helping him to let go just enough to sit still.

Alucard's gaze drifted, focusing on the small crystal sculpture perched on his nightstand. Its soft shimmer served as a quiet reassurance, a charm he'd crafted to shield himself from his most harrowing dreams. The idea formed swiftly in his mind—Zalith. He thought of how much his mate had been struggling with his own nightmares, and how powerless he often felt to ease the burden of the demon's trauma. But this... this he could do. If he couldn't take away the pain itself, he could at least offer Zalith some respite in his sleep.

A quiet determination settled over Alucard as he resolved to create a dream-eater for Zalith—a delicate token imbued with the same care and ethos that he'd poured into his own. It wasn't a solution, but it was something, and in that moment, it felt like enough of a start.

But it wasn't enough to distract him from the pain of his sore, healing wounds. "What's today's plan?" he asked almost desperately as Zalith started wrapping new bandages around him.

"We're going to head to Eimwood," the demon said quietly, carefully working. "I'm going to find out what Cecil is hiding, and then we'll remove him. It might not be today, but I hope we'll be the new Lords of Eimwood by tomorrow—maybe the day after depending on how the people of the city take it."

"Well, I don't see that being a problem. The people love you already, Silas Wright," he said with a smirk.

Zalith laughed quietly, starting to tie the bandages firmly in place. "They better after all the money I've put into their city. But I suppose I am pretty loveable," he said amusedly.

The vampire smiled. "That you are," he agreed. "Are we going to investigate the river ourselves?" he then asked, remembering that Zalith had said he suspected Cecil knew why the city's main water source was tainted.

"Might as well," the demon said, finishing with Alucard's bandages. "We should meet Danford first, though, and see if he has any updates."

"Okay."

Zalith made sure that Alucard's bandages were secure, and then he packed away the medical supplies.

"Thank you," Alucard said, looking back over his shoulder at him.

"You're welcome, baby," Zalith said with a smile, moving the medical box to the edge of the bed.

"When are we leaving?" the vampire then asked, turning around to face him.

"After breakfast, maybe. Do you need time to write?"

Alucard shook his head. "I can do that when we get back." With all his altered, hidden memories slowly returning to him after Zalith removed the block, he'd decided to write everything down to help him process it all, but no harm would come from waiting a few more hours to write down what he'd remembered earlier. "I guess… we should get dressed, then," he muttered.

The demon sighed. "I guess we should."

But Alucard didn't move. He stayed where he was, reluctant to move; he didn't want to get up just yet. Instead, he reached out, placing a hand on Zalith's shoulder, and gently pulled the demon down with him as he shifted onto his side. Zalith leaned on his left arm, his dark eyes softening as he smiled down at Alucard.

For a moment, they stayed like that, a quiet intimacy filling the space between them. Alucard felt the pull of sleep still lingering, a tempting weight urging him to close his eyes for another hour or two. But a flicker of guilt kept him awake—he didn't want to waste time that Zalith could be using to further his plans in the city. Still, he let himself savour the moment, basking in the warmth of Zalith's presence, knowing how fleeting such peaceful mornings could be.

And just as he felt himself sinking into the fatigue, he sighed deeply and looked up at Zalith. "Okay," he said stubbornly. "Let's get ready."

As he got up, however, Zalith didn't move and stayed where he was, staring up at Alucard with a smirk on his face.

After shuffling to the end of the bed, Alucard frowned and looked back over his shoulder at him. "Are you coming?" he asked.

"Yeah," he said, smirking. "I just wanted to take some time to admire you first."

With a curious smile, Alucard laid back down beside him. "I can stay here a little longer if you like."

"I'd like that," the demon said, moving closer to him.

Alucard smiled softly, leaning forward to rest his forehead against Zalith's. His hand slid up to cradle the side of the demon's face, his thumb brushing gently against his cheek. Zalith tilted his head, closing the space between them as he began to kiss him, his lips warm and inviting. His hands moved down Alucard's body, settling at his waist with a firm but tender grip.

The vampire kissed him back, the growing heat between them sparking a familiar desire. It didn't take long for the stirring of arousal to rise within him, and while he enjoyed the way Zalith's touch made him feel, a flicker of reluctance crept in. His body was still healing, and as much as he wanted to indulge in the moment, he knew that pushing himself too far might not be the wisest choice.

After a few lingering kisses, he sighed quietly and let his head fall back against the pillow. His gaze softened as he looked up at Zalith, a faint smile playing on his lips. "What's for breakfast?" he asked.

"I'm not sure," Zalith replied, looking like he was pondering. "We'll have to go and find out."

"All right," Alucard said, but he still didn't feel like getting up.

Zalith started kissing him again, pulling him closer. "I'd rather have you, though," he flirted, staring hungrily at him before kissing him again.

Alucard smiled through their kisses, and when he took a moment to breathe, he gazed into Zalith's eyes. "Well...I'm right here," he said, trying to entice him, ignoring his concern; the desire always won.

Zalith kissed him a few more times before sighing softly and moving his hand to the side of Alucard's face. "But...I don't want to hurt your back any more than it already is."

Alucard exhaled quietly, nodding. "You're right. It'll probably take a day or two to heal completely," he muttered.

The demon smirked, a teasing glint in his eyes. "Okay, well...I'll have you *then*—later."

Alucard smiled, doing his best to suppress the lingering arousal that stirred at Zalith's words. He sighed deeply and sat up, steadying himself against the ache in his back. "Let's go and see what's for breakfast," he said as he swung his legs over the side of the bed.

Zalith nodded, standing and following him to the wardrobe.

Pain or not, there was work to be done, and no wound was going to stop Alucard; he'd been through much worse, and he wouldn't let the agony devour him now.

Chapter Sixteen

— ⚔ ✝ ⚔ —

Sleep

| **Alucard**—*Uzlia Isles, Usrul, Castle Reiner* |

Out on the terrace, Edwin and two kitchen staff members were busy arranging the breakfast table. A large crystal bowl of vibrant fruit salad took centre stage, surrounded by a neatly stacked tower of golden pancakes and an array of beverages—both steaming and chilled—waiting to be enjoyed. Once everything was in its rightful place, they bowed respectfully as they passed Zalith and Alucard before quietly retreating into the castle.

Alucard and Zalith sat down, and as they started eating, Alucard began thinking about what crossed his mind the other night. He still felt that Zalith needed a break, and a vacation might be the best way to go about it. So he asked Zalith, "How would you feel about maybe going on a little vacation or something?"

Zalith sipped from his coffee. "When?"

The vampire shrugged. "Maybe…this coming weekend—after we're finished in Eimwood."

Rather than the curiosity or contemplation that Alucard had expected, Zalith's expression was shadowed with worry. A pang of uncertainty tugged at Alucard's chest—perhaps this hadn't been the right time to ask. He knew how much Zalith relied on his work, how it served as both a distraction and a means to regain control over the chaos of his past. Was it selfish of him to keep trying to pull his mate away from it? Alucard's gaze lingered on the demon, torn between his desire to see Zalith rest and the understanding that, for him, work was a kind of solace.

He looked down at his plate, staring at his half-eaten pancake. "We don't have to go," he said. "It was just an idea."

"No, I want to," Zalith said. "I'm just worried."

"I know," he said, pushing the blueberries around his plate with his fork. "Now probably isn't the best time anyway. We have a lot to do before we should even start thinking about taking some time away."

Zalith nodded. "Hopefully we can make time for something soon."

Alucard didn't want to think about that stupid idea anymore. He knew they wouldn't have time for something like that for a while—maybe ever. Zalith had things he wanted to do, and Alucard shouldn't be trying to hinder him. "I need to get a few things when we're in the city," he mumbled. "I can go and get them while you see Danford and meet you after," he said, now focusing on his idea to make Zalith a dream-eater.

"I'd rather just go with you if that's okay," the demon said.

Zalith's response left Alucard feeling conflicted. He had wanted to surprise his mate, to do something thoughtful without ruining the moment by involving him in the process. But now, uncertainty gnawed at him. Would Zalith even want something to help with his nightmares? The demon never asked for help, despite knowing Alucard had the means to ease his troubled sleep. Instead, he simply chose to sleep less, pushing through the exhaustion as if it were just another burden to bear.

Alucard often found himself caught in this same cycle—torn between his desire to help and the fear that he was overstepping, imposing when Zalith might not want him to. He didn't want to force his support on him, but doing nothing felt just as wrong. Maybe he should just let it go...but the thought of Zalith struggling alone night after night bothered him. No—he wanted to do this, even if Zalith didn't think he needed it.

He stared down at his plate and nodded. "Okay," he said—if he stayed silent too long, Zalith might ask why.

"What are you getting?"

Alucard shrugged. "I need a new crystal for my dream-eater. One of them is cracked."

"How did it crack?"

"Sometimes they just get overwhelmed. I forgot to empty them," he mumbled, and then he pushed his plate away. He wasn't hungry anymore.

Zalith nodded. "Do you think they'll have what you need in the city?"

"Maybe. If not, I can just get someone to go and get it from somewhere else," he said, resting his arms on the table. "Where are we meeting Danford?" he asked, changing the subject again.

"We'll meet him at his home in Eimwood," Zalith said, sipping from his coffee.

"Okay, well...I'm ready to go whenever you are."

"I'll just finish my breakfast."

The vampire rested his arms on the table, staring down at them as a heavy sigh escaped him. He couldn't quite pinpoint why he felt so despondent—nothing was particularly wrong, yet unease settled within him. His gaze flicked towards Zalith, watching as the demon slowly worked through his meal. The exhaustion on his mate's face was impossible to ignore, the shadows beneath his dark eyes deeper than usual. Alucard was certain that he hadn't had a proper night's sleep in...how long now? Too long. Zalith just kept working, pushing himself past reason, past exhaustion until his body had no choice but to catch up.

Alucard wanted to make him stop—force him to rest—but he knew better. Zalith wouldn't take it well. And deep down, it felt selfish to even try. Maybe this relentless drive was the demon's way of coping, his way of keeping the ghosts of his past at bay. Alucard knew what it was like to have nothing but work to cling to, and the bitter truth was, he couldn't take that from Zalith—not when he had nothing else to offer in return.

His eyes drifted to his half-eaten pancake, his appetite long forgotten. Another glance at his mate, and the thought struck him again: if Zalith weren't a demon, he might have worked himself to death by now. But his nature allowed him to push further, to endure longer, especially with Alucard's help. That fact twisted something in him. He didn't want Zalith to keep going like this, he didn't want to be complicit in it.

He wanted Zalith to rest...even for just a few hours.

But asking would get him nowhere—Zalith would brush it off with that stubborn insistence that he was fine. The only way to make it happen would be...to trick him into it. The thought made Alucard's stomach turn with guilt, and he could already picture the demon's fury when he woke. But if it meant Zalith getting the rest he so desperately needed, Alucard would take the scolding. He'd sit there and let Zalith fume because at least *then* he'd know that his mate had finally—if only briefly—let himself breathe.

"Are you okay?" Zalith then asked.

Alucard lifted his head to look at him; he wasn't going to tell him that he was worried—that would only make Zalith become guarded. "I don't know," he mumbled.

"Is it your back?" he questioned, pushing his empty plate away.

The vampire shrugged. "No—it's fine."

Zalith adorned a concerned frown. "Then what is it? Do you feel sick?"

"No," he said, shaking his head. "I just...feel tired. I didn't sleep much last night."

Zalith frowned sympathetically. "Do you need to lay down? We can head to Eimwood later if you like."

Alucard nodded.

"Do you want me to come with you?"

He nodded again. "If you don't mind."

The demon stood up. "I don't mind. Let's go."

Alucard got up, his fingers curling around Zalith's hand, and without a word, he led his mate inside the castle, their footsteps echoing against the polished marble floor. The towering archways loomed above them, their intricate carvings casting light, elongated shadows beneath the dim flicker of chandeliers suspended from the vaulted ceiling.

They passed the sweeping staircase that ascended into the upper levels, its mahogany banister gleaming under the muted glow of wall-mounted candelabras. The air carried the familiar blend of old parchment, faint incense, and the ever-present chill of the castle's ancient stones; beneath it all, their own scents wove through the atmosphere—subtle yet undeniable. It was an instinctual claim, an unspoken declaration of territory that all demons left upon the spaces they inhabited, a quiet but primal assertion that this place belonged to them, their presence etched into every darkened corner and velvet-draped alcove. And every time Alucard was reminded of it, the safer he felt within the castle walls.

Reaching the living space, Alucard slid open the doors, the hinges releasing a hushed creak that seemed almost reluctant to disturb the stillness. Within, an air of understated opulence awaited—elegant white couches arranged with careful symmetry around a dark, intricately carved table. Heavy, brocade drapes framed the towering window that overlooked the shadowed courtyard beyond, their fabric pooling onto the floor like forgotten whispers. Beneath the window, a daybed rested in quiet invitation, its velvet cushions offering a place of solace beneath the sun's distant glow filtering through the leaded glass panes.

Still holding Zalith's hand, Alucard led him to the daybed and all but collapsed onto his right side, exhaling a long, weary breath of relief. The familiar plushness welcomed him, and he cast a sidelong glance at Zalith, expecting—*hoping*—he'd follow suit. Instead, Zalith merely sat beside him, easing back until he seemed settled in his own way.

Alucard frowned, shifting restlessly against the cushions, a quiet pout tugging at his lips. He fidgeted, adjusting his position with exaggerated subtlety, hoping that Zalith might take the hint. But the demon's gaze remained fixed on some distant point, unfocused and aimless, his expression carved from exhaustion.

The vampire sighed softly, watching him for a moment longer. He could see it—how fatigue clung to him like a weight he refused to acknowledge. And yet, Zalith didn't yield, his posture rigid even in rest.

But Zalith soon noticed Alucard's fidgeting and laid down on his side, facing the vampire.

Alucard smiled contently, shuffling closer to Zalith so that he could rest his forehead against his. "Thank you," he said, moving his arm around him.

"You're welcome baby," Zalith mumbled, moving his hand to the side of Alucard's face.

Alucard then sighed quietly, closing his eyes. He knew Zalith wouldn't fall asleep himself, and he didn't want to immediately try to put him to sleep because the demon might suspect that was his plan—it wouldn't be the first time he'd done it, after all.

Instead, he tried to think of something they could talk about. "If you could...pick anywhere to go for a few days, where would it be?" he asked.

Zalith thought to himself for a few moments. "Somewhere warm. And on the ocean, maybe."

"Sinéad has some really nice beaches."

The demon nodded. "Or maybe one of those little houses that sit right above the water."

"Zhat could be fun," he agreed, and then he frowned curiously. "Did Eltaria have any nice beaches?"

"It did," Zalith said with a small nod. "My favourite was a pink sand beach that my mother and father used to take us to when we were growing up. There were little hermit crabs everywhere."

"Maybe...we can go there someday?" Alucard suggested.

"Maybe," Zalith said with a smile, but the pain that flickered across his face was as clear as day.

Alucard closed his eyes, his fingers trailing to the side of Zalith's face with a touch both tender and possessive. He knew—*he'd always known*—how much Zalith longed for Eltaria, the distant homeland that called to him in quiet moments like this. And Alucard missed their home in Nefastus just as fiercely. The ache of it clawed at him, a silent yearning buried beneath duty and survival.

He would do anything for Zalith. Anything.

As he lay there, the thought surfaced like a dark whisper in his mind—Eltaria, drenched in blood, its streets cleansed of Zalith's enemies by his own hand. He could go there. He could hunt Adellum down—if the bastard was even still alive—and rid the world of him once and for all. He could lay waste to every human foolish enough to have stood against Zalith, reducing them to nothing but ash and memory. And then, once the world had healed from the carnage, Zalith could return, unchallenged, to the home he deserved.

But it wasn't possible. Not yet.

The resources it would take to crush Adellum and his followers were needed here, on this battlefield, in this war. Every ounce of strength, every plan, every calculated move was required to bring down Lilith, Damien, and whatever other Numen dared stand in their way. He couldn't afford to be reckless, not with Zalith's mission hanging in the balance.

If he had the means—if he had the time—he would do it without hesitation. But for now, their war was here. And Zalith's vengeance, like so many other things, would have to wait.

He should try to change the subject a little; he didn't want to cause Zalith further despair. So he opened his eyes and stared into Zalith's. "Do you like beaches?"

"I do," the demon said, smiling. "Do you?"

The vampire shrugged. "Well...I do and I don't. I don't like finding sand in my shoes...and my feet...and places that I have no idea how it got there. But other than that, I like to be by the water."

Zalith laughed quietly, fiddling with Alucard's hair. "Well, you should be more careful with the sand then, vampire," he said, smirking.

Alucard pouted. "I *am* careful. I don't even know how it ends up where it does—all I did was stand by the water."

"Are you sure you were just standing?"

"Yes," he mumbled, still pouting.

"You weren't rolling around like a dog?"

"No," he grumbled. "Why would I do that?"

"Because the beach is so fun," he teased, squishing Alucard's cheeks together with his hand. "And you love it so much."

The vampire rolled his eyes. "Whatever," he muttered. "Anyway...I was going to say that maybe we can go to the beach together sometime."

Zalith laughed again. "We can do that."

"Okay," Alucard said, closing his eyes again as he sighed quietly, moving his hand up from the side of Zalith's face and to his head, where he started fiddling with his fringe. "Do you still have nightmares?"

"Yeah," the demon murmured sullenly. "All the time."

"I could...try to help with that," he said—he didn't want to give away what he was planning, but he *did* want to know if Zalith would even want his help.

"How?" he asked.

Alucard shrugged a little. "Well...I could..." he paused and sighed; he couldn't think of anything else to say. "I could make you one of the dream-eaters...or something."

"That would be very nice—thank you," the demon said and kissed the vampire's lips.

Alucard then smiled contently. "Okay. I'll work on it this week."

Zalith smiled in response.

With a quiet sigh, Alucard pressed closer to Zalith, his eyes slipping shut as he tried to relax. But his mind refused to settle. He needed to figure out how to get Zalith to sleep—truly sleep. He already knew what it would take; he would have to do it himself. The thought sat heavy in his chest. Zalith couldn't know what he was planning, and Alucard despised the deception. His hand was already resting against the demon's head...all it would take was the precise placement of his fingers.

But he felt so guilty that it was making him nauseous.

He didn't want to force Zalith into anything, least of all something so intimate, but there was no other way. Zalith would never give in willingly; he would keep pushing himself beyond reason, beyond exhaustion until his body failed him. And Alucard couldn't—he *wouldn't* let it come to that.

He would put him to sleep... and more than that, he would use his ethos to ensure Zalith's rest was truly peaceful. The spell would drain him—it always did, especially without crystals to imbue—but he didn't care. Zalith mattered more. He always had.

Fiddling gently with his mate's hair, the vampire let the moment stretch between them, waiting for the right time. Slowly, carefully, he shifted his fingers into place, pressing them against Zalith's left temple and the curve of his face. He focused, channelling his power, coaxing Zalith towards sleep inch by inch.

Zalith stirred, his body tensing slightly as his eyelids grew heavier, fighting against the pull even as exhaustion weighed him down. He struggled to stay awake, his instincts resisting the inevitable, and the sight of it made Alucard's heart ache. Watching Zalith try to fight off the rest that he so desperately needed almost made Alucard falter, his fingers twitching with hesitation.

But he steeled himself.

Zalith wasn't going to sleep any other way, and Alucard refused to stand by and watch him collapse from sheer exhaustion. This was necessary, even if Zalith wouldn't see it that way.

"Sleep," Alucard murmured. He watched as Zalith's eyes almost instantly closed, and his tense body started to relax against the vampire's. But he wasn't done yet. "*Somnus pacificae*," he mumbled, and the frown on Zalith's face then withered into something peaceful. Hopefully, he'd stay asleep for at least four or five hours—longer, even. Alucard still felt so very awful about it, but... there really was no other way to get Zalith to rest properly, was there?

Alucard sighed, his gaze lingering on Zalith's sleeping form for a long moment. He knew without a doubt that Zalith would be angry when he woke. He'd figure out what happened soon enough, and Alucard could already feel the weight of that inevitable confrontation pressing down on him. The very thought of Zalith's frustrated voice cutting through the air sent a ripple of unease through him. And worse still, he dreaded the look that would follow—the quiet betrayal, the disappointment etched into those dark eyes.

But he would endure it.

He would sit there and take every word, every glare, every accusation Zalith threw his way, because in the end, it would be worth it. If it meant Zalith had finally gotten some real rest, Alucard could bear the weight of his anger.

But now... what to do while Zalith rested? Alucard exhaled softly, his mind already drifting to Eimwood. He'd handle their business there himself—what he and Zalith had planned to do together today, he would see through alone. Or, perhaps, not entirely alone. If he brought someone with him, Zalith might be a little less furious when he woke. After all, if something *did* happen, having backup would be a reasonable precaution.

Greymore. The name surfaced almost instantly. He was the only one Alucard could tolerate for more than ten minutes without wanting to strangle, and more importantly, he was one of Zalith's best—if not *the* best—fighter in his service. If anyone could keep things from spiralling into disaster, it was him.

Alucard sighed again, his fingers lingering in Zalith's hair, twirling the dark strands absently as a small ache settled in his chest. Then, with quiet resolve, he shifted closer, pressing a lingering kiss to Zalith's lips, then his forehead. A silent promise. He eased himself off the daybed, careful not to disturb the demon's hard-won rest.

Crossing the dimly lit room, he retrieved a thick fur blanket from the nearby wardrobe, draping it gently over Zalith and smoothing it down with a tenderness that belied the sharp thoughts racing through his mind. He took one last look at him—at the way exhaustion had finally softened his usually tense features—before turning away.

Without another word, Alucard slipped out of the room, sliding the doors shut behind him with a quiet click, leaving Zalith to his well-deserved sleep.

Chapter Seventeen

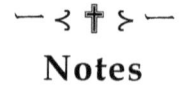

— ⟨ ✝ ⟩ —

Notes

| **Alucard**—*Uzlia Isles, Usrul, Anburidge Village* |

Alucard pulled his fur-collared cape around his shoulders as he stepped out into the courtyard, the crisp morning air biting against his skin. His gaze flickered briefly towards the stables, considering the thought of taking his horse—but time was not on his side. He needed to get to the city and see things done without delay. With a sigh, he dismissed the notion and instead reached for his cane, gripping it firmly as he tapped it lightly against the stone underfoot.

It wasn't just any cane, of course. Hidden within was a slender, lethal silver blade— far more practical than openly carrying a sword through the city streets. He'd left his old rapier behind in Nefastus, abandoned in the frantic rush of his escape. There had been no time to retrieve it, no time to look back. And while he missed the familiar weight of his trusted weapon, the cane-sword offered a discreet advantage. In a city where flashing silver would only stir fear and suspicion, the cane presented an illusion of refinement, an innocuous accessory to those unaware of its true purpose.

Satisfied, he adjusted the dragon-shaped grip, letting the cool metal rest comfortably against his palm. Then, without another moment's hesitation, he dematerialized into vermillion smoke, rising swiftly into the sky. The castle shrank beneath him, and once he reached the right height, he fixed his eyes on Anburidge Village and raced towards it, the wind tearing through the misty morning air.

He landed with a soft thud, his form solidifying at the village entrance in a swirl of dissipating vermillion smoke. As he strode along the well-trodden dirt path, he returned each murmured greeting and polite *good morning* with a nod, his mind already set on his task. The village stirred with the usual early bustle—merchants setting up their stalls, the scent of baking bread curling through the air—but Alucard paid little attention, his focus fixed ahead as he approached Greymore's house.

Stepping onto the creaking wooden porch, he rapped his knuckles against the door, the sound sharp in the quiet morning air. He waited, but before long, a familiar, thunderous snoring rumbled from the open window above. Alucard stilled, exhaling through his nose. Greymore—clearly still entangled in the throes of yesterday's indulgence—was in no state to be of use.

Typical Greymore. Amusing but *frustrating* Greymore.

Alucard considered waking him, a flicker of irritation stirring, but it passed just as quickly. It wasn't worth the effort. Greymore could sleep off his hangover undisturbed. He'd find someone else.

With a quiet sigh, he turned away, stepping off the porch and dissolving into a swirl of vermillion smoke. The village blurred around him as he drifted towards Eimwood, the morning sun doing little to chase away the lingering chill in his chest.

As Alucard drifted over the water that stretched between Usrul and Yrudberg, his thoughts, as always, circled back to Zalith. Worry gnawed at him; guilt, regret, and a familiar thread of sorrow coiled within him, whispering doubts that he couldn't quite silence. Maybe he shouldn't have forced Zalith into sleep like that. Maybe he shouldn't be out here doing this alone—*their* task, meant to be handled *together*.

But he just wanted to make things easier for his mate. Zalith worked himself to the bone, never stopping, never yielding. And Alucard—more than anything—just wanted him to rest, to ease the weight that Zalith refused to acknowledge.

A sharp gust of wind stirred the mist over the water, and Alucard forced himself to push the thoughts aside. If he dwelled on them too long, he knew he'd cave—turn back, return to the castle, and spend the rest of the day at Zalith's side, watching over him like a fool.

Eimwood loomed on the horizon, and Alucard latched onto the task ahead. Once he arrived, he'd head straight to Danford's house and retrieve whatever information he had managed to dig up on Cecil. That, at least, was something he *could* control.

With a tired exhale, Alucard touched down at Eimwood's docks, the scent of brine and damp wood curling around him as he adjusted his coat and set off towards the main street. The town bustled with morning activity—merchants arranging their wares, the distant clang of a blacksmith's hammer ringing through the crisp air. His path led him towards the Bauwell Residential District, nestled higher up the steep, paved hill where the wealthier residents resided. Danford's home wasn't far from the townhouse that he and Zalith had claimed as their own, and the route was all too familiar.

As he walked, Alucard offered small smiles and polite nods to those who waved or called out his name. Their gratitude came easily, sincere in their praise for all he and Zalith had done for Eimwood and its people. He responded in kind, though his mind was already preoccupied with what lay ahead.

When he finally set eyes on Danford's townhouse, he sighed, bracing himself. The stately redbrick home stood tall and dignified amidst its neighbours, a reflection of the district's quiet affluence. Intricate wrought-iron railings framed the porch, curling in elegant, elven-inspired patterns. The tall, narrow windows gleamed in the morning light, their delicate lace curtains drawn just enough to grant privacy without denying the outside world.

Alucard climbed the porch steps, the wood creaking softly beneath his boots. He paused before the navy-blue door, its brass knocker shaped like a curling vine. He knocked, the sound echoing in the stillness…and then he waited, already dreading the inevitable conversation to come. Danford was, without question, one of the last people he wanted to deal with right now. But he was the one watching Cecil, so like it or not, he had no choice but to face him.

In the silence, however, he couldn't shake the nagging guilt that crept in whenever he thought about how he truly felt about Danford. Sure, there'd always be a lingering dislike of him because he was someone who Zalith had slept with a few times, but he'd made Danford a hybrid, and all he'd done was teach him how to survive; he hadn't taken an interest in teaching Danford to master his abilities himself—if he had any, that was; he'd just handed him over to Păzitoarea. Danford hadn't complained, though, so she must be teaching him well enough.

The door then unlocked from the inside; the maid answered, smiling up at Alucard. "Oh, good morning." She bowed humbly.

"Get Danford," Alucard grumbled.

"Sure," she said with a nod. "Please wait here." She then wandered off into the house.

Alucard let out a deep exhale, leaning against the wrought-iron porch railing as he waited. The quiet morning air pressed around him, broken only by the distant hum of the city beyond. He stared out into the street, absently tracing patterns on the metal with his fingertips, his mind restless despite the stillness.

After a few moments, the faint creak of footsteps echoed from within the house, moving steadily across the wooden floorboards. Straightening, Alucard pushed off the railing and turned back to the door.

Danford pulled it open, and as he set his eyes on Alucard, he frowned anxiously. "O-oh, hey," he said nervously. "M-My L—"

"You don't have to call me that."

He nodded stiffly, his anxious expression growing. "Uh…what's up?"

"I'm here for the updates on Cecil," he muttered.

"Oh, o-okay…sure," he said, pushing the door open as wide as it would go. "Do you wanna come in?"

Alucard nodded and stepped inside, immediately greeted by the unmistakable scent of wet dog that clung to the air like an unwelcome guest. He resisted the urge to wrinkle his nose, reminding himself that it was to be expected—werewolves lived here, after all. The house itself, despite standing in the upper-class Bauwell district, bore a ruggedness that spoke of occupants more accustomed to the wilderness than fine city living. The polished wooden floors were scuffed in places, and the walls, though adorned with tasteful paintings and decorative sconces, lacked the pristine upkeep one would expect of a home in such an affluent neighbourhood.

Danford led him through the dimly lit hall, where the faint aroma of pine and damp earth mingled with the lingering musk of wolf fur. Alucard's keen eyes took in the worn furniture, the heavy coats hanging haphazardly by the door, and the faint scratches marring the baseboards—likely from claws that hadn't been fully retracted in time. It wasn't filthy, just… lived-in, in a way that spoke to a life of practicality over appearance. He could understand it, even if it wasn't quite to his tastes.

Once they reached the lounge, Alucard paused near the fireplace, letting the warmth seep through his clothes while his sharp gaze settled on Danford. He expected him to get straight to the point, but instead, the werewolf stood there, an awkward frown pulling at his face. After a few moments of tense silence, he cleared his throat and smoothed down his shirt, a telltale sign that he was hesitating.

Alucard frowned, waiting patiently—but not too patiently—for him to speak.

"Uh… do you… want anything?" he asked. "We have some… uh… water… beer… we have wine, too."

"No, thank you."

"We have um… cheese… if you'd like some cheese," he offered.

The vampire sighed a little, trying his best not to snap. "I'm not hungry, but thank you." He crossed his arms and leaned his shoulder on the wall; for some reason, fatigue was creeping up on him, like he hadn't slept in days—well… he hadn't slept as much as he would have liked, but surely, he'd slept enough to avoid feeling so exhausted. He brushed it off, though. "I came here for the information Zalith and I have you gathering."

"S-sorry," he said, patting his trouser pockets. "Um… let me just grab my notebook." He scurried out of the room.

Alucard sighed again and decided to sit in the armchair not too far from where he was standing, hoping that it would help relieve some of his fatigue.

"Sorry," Danford then said, hurrying back into the room. "I wasn't expecting you."

The vampire looked up at him, waiting as Danford flipped through his notebook in search of the right page. With his impatience already growing, Alucard snatched the book from him and rolled his eyes. "Give it to me," he snarled.

"Y-yeah, sure—s-sorry," he stammered, stepping back. "There's a bunch of stuff in there from other jobs—sorry."

Alucard flipped through Danford's notebook, his sharp eyes skimming over page after page of cramped, meticulous handwriting. The werewolf's notes were sprawled in tiny, almost obsessive script, interspersed with small doodles and sketches—some of which, to Alucard's reluctant acknowledgement, were surprisingly well-done. Not that he'd ever say as much. Offering Danford a compliment would feel too much like encouragement, and Alucard wasn't in the business of stroking egos, least of all his.

He continued flipping through the pages until he found what he was looking for—Cecil's whereabouts. His gaze sharpened as he read, confirming what Zalith had already mentioned yesterday. Danford had been keeping a close watch on Cecil and had uncovered an unsettling pattern. Cecil had been slipping away from his home under the cover of darkness, only to return in the early hours of the morning. The same mud always coated his boots—the distinct, dark silt found along the riverbank that snaked through Eimwood, weaving beneath the city walls and stretching into the dense forest beyond.

Alucard's lips pressed into a thin line. The water was poisoned, tainted by some unknown force, and Zalith suspected Cecil either had a hand in it or at the very least knew why it was happening. Yet Danford's notes revealed another troubling detail—he had been unable to follow Cecil beyond the midpoint of the forest. There, the trail simply...vanished. No scent. No tracks. No heartbeat or lingering aura. Cecil disappeared as though swallowed whole by the shadows themselves.

Interesting.

Alucard tapped a finger against the edge of the notebook, thoughtful but wary. Whatever Cecil was up to, it wasn't something as simple as clandestine meetings or petty treachery. Something was covering his tracks—something unnatural.

Sighing, he looked at Danford. "Is there anything else that you haven't written down yet?"

"N-no, I write everything down."

And he certainly did. The notebook was crammed with meticulous details—right down to the exact clothing that Cecil had worn each day, noted with almost obsessive precision. Danford had even recorded the man's scent, which, more often than not, consisted of damp earth, sage, and lavender. Alucard scanned the descriptions with a mixture of intrigue and mild exasperation. Was it Cecil's chosen perfume? His wife's? Or perhaps he frequented a local herb shop—lavender was a common enough ingredient, after all.

But what would someone like Cecil want from a herbalist? Alucard tapped a finger against the edge of the page, brow furrowing. Sage and lavender weren't just for pleasant scents; they had their uses—medicinal, ritualistic. Protective. It could mean nothing...or it could mean far more than he'd already assumed. And with Cecil's evasive behaviour, he couldn't afford to dismiss any possibility just yet.

He sighed again, closing Danford's notebook. He had to investigate, and he'd decided that he wasn't going to go alone, so…he might as well ask Danford to go with him. He was better than nobody. "Thank you," he said, handing the notebook back to Danford.

"No worries," he said, stuffing it into his pocket. "Should I go back out there and watch him again? Zalith didn't tell me to today, so…I wasn't sure when I got up this morning."

"No," the vampire replied. "Zalith and I are going to bring this to an end today."

Danford nodded. "Uh…where is Zalith?" he then asked, looking around the room.

"He's busy. So, *you* are going to come with me in case I need anything."

His eyes widened in startle. "O-oh. Sure—uh…right now?"

"Yes…unless you have something better to do," Alucard grumbled.

"Uh…n-no, not really," he said, shaking his head. "I just need to get changed."

"Then go. I'll wait here."

Nodding, Danford went to scurry out of the room, but just as he was about to leave, Freja stopped in the doorway, and both of them gasped in shock.

"S-sorry," Danford said with a smile.

As Freja muttered something that Alucard didn't care to listen to, the Boszorkián bulldog at her feet waddled into the room and hurried over to where the vampire was sitting.

Alucard smiled, letting the dog pounce up into his lap as Freja and Danford spoke to one another. The dog panted happily as he scratched its ears, smiling down at it while it wagged its tail excitedly.

"Oh, sorry about him," Freja then called as she made her way over once Danford had left the room. "He gets overexcited whenever someone new comes in."

The vampire glanced up at her as she sat down in the armchair across the room from him. "I don't mind," he said, patting the dog's head.

Freja smiled, making herself comfortable. "How are you and Zalith?"

"Fine," he mumbled—he didn't like talking about his personal life with the people who worked for him. "I hope you and Danford are comfortable here."

She nodded. "It's certainly better than a tent," she laughed. "Danny tells me you're taking him along with you—do you need my help, too?" she offered.

"No," he denied. "You shouldn't really be doing anything but sitting around—I hope Danford hasn't been making you do too much," he said, admittedly concerned.

Freja shook her head, absently pressing a hand to her belly as if feeling for the quiet flutter within. "He insists that I either stay in bed all day or sit in some chair and do nothing—it gets boring after a while. I've read more books than I can count this past month."

Alucard laughed quietly. "Maybe you should try something else—you could write," he suggested.

"I honestly don't have the patience," she admitted with a sigh.

The bulldog leapt off Alucard's lap as Danford strode back into the room, now clad in fresh, dark attire. His coat was buttoned up neatly, the fabric sturdy yet unassuming, designed for both warmth and discretion. The muted tones of his vest and trousers blended effortlessly into the dim surroundings—practical choices for someone accustomed to moving unseen. Clearly, he was prepared to sneak around and knew exactly what he was doing.

Alucard felt a flicker of relief; at least he wouldn't have to waste time explaining the basics to him. He stood up and straightened his cape. "Let's go."

Danford nodded. "Okay," he said. Then, he made his way over to Freja. "I'll be back later," he said quietly before kissing her a few times. "Stay off your feet."

"Be careful," Freja insisted.

"I will," Danford said with a nod.

"I'll make sure he gets back here in one piece," Alucard said, glancing at Freja.

Freja nodded as Danford made his way over to Alucard. "Don't stay out too late—it looks like it's going to rain later," she said.

With one last nod, Danford left the room, following behind Alucard.

The vampire stared ahead, his thoughts already racing as the maid pulled open the front door. Stepping onto the street alongside Danford, he inhaled the crisp air, letting it settle him. First, Cecil's estate—he'd go there and see if the man was still lurking about. If he was, Alucard would wait, shadow him when he left, and follow him deeper into the unknown—further than Danford had managed.

Whatever Cecil was up to, Alucard was determined to uncover it. And whatever it was…he only hoped that he could get as much done as possible before it was time to return home and wake Zalith. His jaw tightened at the thought. If Zalith woke up on his own and discovered that he was gone—wandering the city, prying into this mess without him…the demon's anger was not something he particularly wanted to face, especially not when he was already nursing his own guilt.

Alucard exhaled slowly, pushing aside the nagging anxiety curling in his chest. He would do what he could while daylight remained, gather whatever pieces of the puzzle he could find. And when the sun dipped below the horizon, he'd return home—he'd face Zalith's aggravated, upset response if he must—and tell him everything that he had uncovered.

For now, all he could do was focus.

Chapter Eighteen

— ⋜ ✟ ⋟ —

An Impromptu Lesson

| **Alucard**—*Uzlia Isles, Yrudberg, Eimwood City* |

Alucard led the way down the street in silence, and Danford followed slightly behind. He had no desire to speak to the man, nor any inclination to start a conversation. He wasn't here for small talk—he was here to get a job done, and he intended to do it quickly and efficiently. The sooner he finished, the sooner he could return home. The thought of Zalith alone in the castle gnawed at him, a faint sadness creeping in with every step that carried him further away.

His icy gaze remained fixed ahead, though he couldn't help but notice Danford's fidgeting in the corner of his eye. The werewolf kept glancing at him, awkwardly twiddling his fingers, and Alucard had counted at least four times now where Danford had opened his mouth to speak, only to think better of it and fall quiet. Alucard almost smirked. He was sure that Danford was intimidated by him—and rightly so.

He felt no guilt about it either. It wasn't that he despised the man; there was no deep-seated hatred simmering beneath the surface. He simply didn't *like* him. Danford was tolerable, at best, but their personalities were oil and water. To put it plainly, they were never going to be friends, and Alucard was perfectly fine with that.

The vampire continued up the street towards Cecil's estate, his expression warm and inviting as the people of the city smiled and waved at him. He returned their greetings, a polite smile here, a nod there, carefully maintaining the cheerful, approachable demeanour of Ezra Wright. He and Zalith portrayed their human personas flawlessly—the benevolent guardians of Eimwood, always kind, always enthusiastic, with the people's best interests at heart. The city adored them, and Alucard was determined to ensure it stayed that way, just as much for Zalith's sake as for his own.

As they turned onto a quieter street, leaving behind the bustling main road, Alucard caught Danford glancing at him again, his fingers fidgeting nervously.

The werewolf hesitated before finally speaking, his voice unsteady as he asked, "S-so...how...are you?" The words tumbled out awkwardly. But before Alucard could respond, Danford shook his head, a flush of embarrassment crossing his face. He looked down, frowning as though regretting the question entirely.

"I'm fine," Alucard grumbled, slipping his hands into his trouser pockets as a bitter breeze raced through the alley beside them.

Nodding, Danford hurried to catch up with him and walk at his side. "Uh...how...how have you been settling into your castle?"

Alucard glanced at him. Surely Danford knew that he didn't like him, yet...the guy was still trying to make conversation anyway. "It's been fine," he uttered, staring ahead as they left the narrow street and emerged onto another wide, busy sidewalk. The white brick road led straight up to Cecil's estate, and Alucard could see a horse-drawn carriage waiting outside, so he thought it was best that he wasn't seen, just in case Cecil was in the carriage or would soon be getting into it. He led the way across the road and into another narrow alley, following it around the back of several houses as Danford followed.

"What do you even do with all those rooms?" the werewolf asked.

"Most of them are lounges," he mumbled, stopping behind a confectionary store.

Danford laughed slightly. "What do you do with all those lounges?"

"We lounge around in them," the vampire muttered under his breath, taking a key from his pocket and sliding it into the lock. Once the door clicked open, he tucked the key back into his pocket and pushed the door wide. It creaked softly, revealing a narrow staircase that wound upward to the room perched above the confectionery shop. The faint, lingering scent of sugar and vanilla drifted up from below, a subtle reminder of the bustling business beneath their feet.

"I'd turn one of them into an art room," Danford said, closing the door behind him as he followed Alucard up the stairs. "I'd have canvases and shit everywhere and just paint all day."

"Don't you have room for something like that in your new house?" he asked, stepping into the room at the top of the stairs. The space was utterly bare, save for a single table and chair positioned near one of the three windows. Of the trio, only that window had its white curtain drawn, its pale fabric filtering the faint light that seeped into the otherwise stark and lifeless room.

Danford shrugged, following Alucard over to the window. "Nah," he said. "I've been kinda reluctant to get set up because we're always having to pack up and leave and have been doing so for years now. A part of me can't really accept that this is real, I guess. I almost didn't even want to get the dog, but Freja wanted him, so I didn't wanna say no," he said, sitting down.

Alucard leaned his back against the wall beside the window, setting his eyes on Cecil's estate not too far across the street.

Danford continued, "And besides, we'll need somewhere for the kids to sleep, too. We might have to get a bigger house, actually... depending on how many kids we have."

Alucard kept his eyes fixed on the estate, watching as the butler, who had rushed out to greet the carriage driver, scurried back towards the house. The man was red-faced and breathless, beads of sweat glistening on his brow as he huffed and puffed his way across the manicured lawn with all the grace of someone clearly unused to such exertion. "You can always have your current home extended," he mumbled—he knew werewolves always had at least two children at a time, and Danford and Freja's home consisted of only three bedrooms. "All it really takes is a little construction—maybe someone can knock out the wall to the house next to yours, and then you will have both houses."

Nodding, Danford leaned back in his seat. "That's true," he said with a shrug. "We'll see what happens later on, I guess. I'd hate to go through the trouble and get excited just to have it all ripped away again."

The vampire sighed as an almost irritated frown started to appear on his face. "It's not going to get ripped away," he said firmly. "Zalith and I have done everything possible and are still doing everything possible to make sure this is the safest place in Aegisguard. No one will find us here, and no one will be chasing us away," he muttered.

With a wide-eyed look of startle, Danford glanced around nervously. "I know... and I don't doubt either of you, but there's just... always that tiny little bit of lingering fear, you know? I just... can't help it."

"I guess everyone feels that way," Alucard said, waiting for Cecil to make an appearance.

"We'll just all have to try and get used to a new normal," Danford said, shrugging as he looked at Alucard again.

Alucard exhaled deeply, trying to make himself comfortable. Leaning back against the wall was beginning to irritate the wounds on his back, and as he scowled and rested his arm and shoulder on the wall instead, he grunted restlessly.

"Are... you okay?" Danford asked.

"What time does Cecil usually leave?" the vampire questioned, ignoring him.

"Uh... he usually leaves at one every afternoon and doesn't come back until between two and four in the morning."

Nodding, Alucard kept his eyes on Cecil's estate.

Danford kept talking. "So, uh... do you know when you and Zalith are having your wedding?"

The question weighed heavily on Alucard, deepening the sadness already tugging at him. It had only been a month, yet he and Zalith hadn't made much progress with the planning. Zalith had suggested hiring a wedding planner, and Alucard had wanted to look into it, but a troubling thought crept into his mind—would Zalith want to postpone the wedding until he felt their work was complete? No...surely not. Zalith was just as excited as he was about it...wasn't he?

Alucard sighed softly, his gaze remaining fixed on Cecil's estate, though his thoughts were far away, tangled in doubts and questions he couldn't quite silence. "Not yet," he replied. "Probably sometime next year—maybe later."

Danford nodded. "Nice—so you'll have a lot of time to plan." He paused for a moment. "I was kinda thinking that...maybe I wanna propose to Freja soon—since she's pregnant...and it's the right thing to do. But we haven't been together for very long, so I always wonder if it's better to wait. But I *do* love her a lot; I don't want to do it because I feel like I have to."

Alucard frowned at him. "You already sealed your bond, no? Marriage would cause discord among the packs."

"I know, I just...I feel so right about her. I've always had to work so hard to make sure that everyone I've been with was happy in our relationship, but everything's so effortless with her...and I'm getting old," he laughed.

The vampire turned his head and glared out at Cecil's estate again. "You would have to talk to Thomas about that; I don't want to get involved in those kinds of werewolf politics."

"Yeah," Danford agreed quietly.

Alucard shifted his focus back to Cecil's estate, though Zalith lingered stubbornly in his thoughts. Zalith was always on his mind, whether he was near or far. His fingers toyed absently with the rings on his left hand as he frowned, trying—*failing*—to concentrate solely on his mission. But the worry never quieted, an unrelenting hum beneath every thought. Worry for Zalith's well-being, his exhaustion. Worry for his reaction when he woke and found Alucard gone. And beneath the worry, an ache—a deep, insistent yearning.

Even now, while standing there trying to work, all he wanted was to be with Zalith. To lay with him, to hold him, to feel the comfort of being held in return. Every inch of his being longed to return to the demon he loved, and this wasn't the first time he'd caught himself debating whether he should go back—not just out of concern for Zalith's anger, but because he simply *missed* him. The distance was unbearable.

Alucard exhaled a long, measured sigh, forcing himself to focus on the task at hand. Cecil would leave his home every afternoon at one and not return until the early hours of the morning. What could he possibly be doing outside the city for such a long stretch of time? Whatever it was, Alucard was determined to find out.

"It looks like he's getting ready to leave," the vampire mumbled, remembering that Danford was with him. He stared out the window, his gaze fixed on Cecil as the man exited his home and made his way towards the waiting horse-drawn carriage. Dressed in a sharply tailored grey suit, Cecil carried himself with a self-assured strut, his greying hair slicked back neatly over his head, and a pair of rounded glasses perched on his nose, drawing attention to the rather prominent wart that sat at its tip. The man's appearance was as meticulous as it was peculiar, a reflection of someone clearly accustomed to presenting a polished façade.

"He usually takes the carriage about ten-fifteen minutes or so up the road as a fake out in case anybody's watching," Danford said, standing up. "He then gets out and heads further into the forest—he changes out of his suits, too," he explained.

"Okay," Alucard muttered, watching as the carriage started heading towards Eimwood's exit once Cecil was inside. "We'll wait a few minutes, and then we will follow."

Danford nodded and stood in silence, waiting for Alucard.

For the next few minutes, Alucard stood by the window, leaning his arm against the wall; he kept his eyes on the carriage as it was pulled through the Bauwell Residential District, and once it disappeared behind the tall houses of Oklens Market, Alucard decide it was time to go.

"Let's go," he said, leading the way down the stairs as Danford followed. As they left the building, and once Alucard had locked the door, he frowned and set his eyes on Danford. "Has Păzitoarea taught you to shroud yourself yet?"

"No..." Danford said with a nervous frown. "What's that?"

"Vampires can hide themselves from pretty much every type of detection and sensory ethos—it's called shrouding and is similar to how demons can disappear."

"Oh," he said, a wide-eyed stare on his face. "How do I do that?"

"Did she teach you what blood magic is?"

He frowned. "I know what it is, but...I've never done anything remotely close to that before."

Alucard led the way through the Bauwell Residential District; he and Danford didn't need to hide themselves just yet, so he'd have time to tell him what he needed to know before they had to shroud themselves from detection. "Vampires are...well...blood magic," he started, leading the way out onto the main street, following the revolting smell of damp soil and what he could only describe as rotting fish, a scent that belonged to Cecil. "You are made from my blood, and everything you do and have comes from my blood within you. To use any of the abilities you have as a vampire, you have to focus on the vampire blood within your body. It's similar to drawing ethos from a rune or a vessel. You find it, you focus on it, and then you tell it what you want it to do. In this case, you want to hide yourself from any and all detection—you want to hide your scent, your aura, and any sound that you and your body make. And then you hide the fact that you are a visible creature," he explained, hoping that Danford understood so that he didn't have to explain it twice. "It's simple," he added, approaching the wooden bridge that stretched over the river that separated Bauwell from Oklens.

Danford's eyes widened in what looked like shock and confusion. "Uh...how...how do I tell it what to do?"

"You just think," Alucard grumbled. "In your head—think...think about yourself completely immune to location and detection ethos—tell yourself you are undetectable, and it will happen. Always keep your ethos in check, though. You only have so much, and once it's gone, it will take time to come back. Blood helps your ethos to regenerate faster, but if you use too much without a break, your vampire blood will take hold and you won't really be able to stop yourself from killing everything and everyone in your way."

"How do I know when it's gone?" he asked, bewildered.

Alucard sighed quietly, trying not to lose his patience. Why would Danford know anything about ethos? He had been a werewolf all his life, and werewolves had only basic ethos, the kind that made shifting possible. He glanced at Danford and said, "Ethos...feels like...hmm...it's hard to really compare what it feels like, but when it starts to decline—when you really should start thinking about stopping is when you start to feel tired—fatigued. Your body will start to feel heavy, your legs will get weak, and it will be hard for you to fight the worsening dizziness," he explained slowly. "And if you keep going, even after that, you will eventually pass out and won't wake up until your body has recovered enough of the ethos you lost—which takes a very long time to regenerate, just like all blood magic-sourced ethos."

Danford nodded, following Alucard over the bridge. "Okay...sorry, I've never done anything like this before—I didn't even know I could. Păzitoarea *has* been trying to get me up to speed, but it's all just...well, a lot."

"All of this would be so much easier for everyone if there was a brood nurse around, but I haven't had the time to look for one," he muttered. "They could teach you everything you need to know much more efficiently."

"Are they hard to find?" Danford asked as they made their way over to the bridge and into Oklens Market.

"Not hard to find, more so...hard to create. Only experienced vampires can really take on the role of a brood nurse—one with at least two or three hundred years behind them. They also need to be particularly patient and skilled with teaching—the only person I have who is old enough is Attila, but he is not patient, and I value him in the field too much. All of my older vampires are out there working, and I need them out there, so there's no one left other than Păzitoarea for me to get to look after you and any other Fledglings that might so happen to be created," he mumbled, but there wouldn't be any more Fledglings besides Danford because he had ordered his vampires not to turn anyone right now; any vampire who was old enough to become a brood nurse was out there with Crowell looking for and following Ysmay and the Diabolus.

"Oh," Danford said, still walking at Alucard's side as they made their way through Oklens and headed for the city exit.

Alucard was certain that the conversation had reached its end. Without a word, he turned and silently led the way through the city gates. Ahead, Cecil's carriage disappeared into the shadowed tree line, its wheels creaking softly along the north path. The vampire followed, his gaze narrowing as the forest loomed in the distance. Whatever Cecil was up to, the answers that Alucard sought lay somewhere ahead—hidden among the trees and shadows, waiting to be found.

Chapter Nineteen

— ⟨ ✝ ⟩ —

Shell

| **Alucard**—*Uzlia Isles, Yrudberg, Yrudberg Woods* |

As Alucard and Danford approached the tree line, the vampire adorned a cautious stare. "Once we hit the tree line, we will shroud ourselves," he mumbled.

Danford nodded. "O-okay," he said nervously, following behind him. "Hopefully I can figure it out."

Alucard rolled his eyes. "If you can't, then you can just wait outside the forest," he grumbled. "I don't have time to wait around."

"I'll try my best," the werewolf insisted.

Alucard sighed quietly, following the dirt road towards the forest. Danford had said that Cecil took his carriage ten or fifteen minutes along the road and then got out, and Alucard was sure that he was close to hitting that mark. It was time to disappear.

"We are going to disappear here," he said, but he didn't wait for Danford to figure it out. The vampire shrouded himself, disappearing into the space between the real world and the astral plane. He left Danford—who stood there trying to work it out—and hurried into the forest, following the trail of Cecil's carriage. He kept himself utterly hidden, and when the carriage came into view, he stopped moving and watched as the door opened.

Cecil stepped out, no longer wearing the grey suit that he'd left the city in; instead, he wore an olive-green hooded cloak. As he stepped out of the carriage, he looked around cautiously and then scurried into the trees.

"I-I'm here," came Danford's voice—he appeared at Alucard's side.

Alucard glanced at him, seeing that he'd worked out how to shroud himself. "Good," he said. "Let's go."

Silent and unseen, Alucard travelled through the forest, setting his sights on Cecil, who was moving rather quickly—as if he was in a rush. But Alucard kept up with him, determined to find out where he went every night.

However, when Cecil turned behind a tall, wide willow tree…he *disappeared*.

Alucard halted when he reached the tree, searching for any sign of the man or his tracks, but there was nothing. He frowned, looking around, up, down, left, right—there was no scent, no aura, no sound...it was as if Cecil had just...vanished—like he hadn't even been there at all.

"I don't know where he went—or...where he goes," Danford said, stopping beside Alucard. "Unless...he can fly," he said with a shrug.

"Humans can't fly," Alucard muttered. "Unless he's *not* human and you failed to notice," he muttered irritably.

"He *looks* human...and smells human. But...so do we, I guess."

Danford wasn't wrong. Cecil's aura was that of a human, as was the scent of his blood, and the rhythm of his beating heart. Cecil *was* human...so where could he have gone? A portal? A rift? Was there something Alucard couldn't see? No...if there was any kind of ethos present, he'd be able to detect it. So where had Cecil gone?

Alucard sighed, glancing at Danford. "So, you have no idea what he might be if not human?"

He shook his head. "I couldn't detect anything other than human."

The vampire huffed, searching the ground with his eyes for any hint as to where Cecil might have gone. "Maybe he's an elf...or a seer—he could be a mage; they are very good at hiding that they have ethos."

Danford looked around for tracks, too. "That's true. I should have thought of that."

"He probably hid well. How *could* you have known?"

Shrugging, Danford looked down at his boots.

"Help me look," he ordered, continuing forward a little, searching for even the smallest trace.

Nodding, Danford resumed scouring the ground.

Alucard sighed, keeping his eyes on the flat dirt below. As he searched, he tried to wrap his head around it—how did a human just disappear? Cecil couldn't be human, surely.... Maybe he *was* something that could hide the fact that it wasn't human, just like demons could.

He shook his head, his sharp eyes scanning the ground beneath him for anything unusual. As the clouds above shifted, allowing sunlight to filter down through the canopy of trees, something in the corner of his vision caught his attention—a flash of green that shimmered faintly in the dappled light. His head snapped in that direction, every instinct on high alert.

There, at the base of a tree, sat something peculiar, glinting brightly as if demanding his notice. Frowning, Alucard moved closer; he crouched down, narrowing his eyes at what, at first glance, looked like a shard of glass. But as he picked it up, his fingers brushing over its smooth, cool surface, he realized that it was something else entirely.

It was a carapace—or so it seemed. An emerald green shell with an iridescent purple sheen that shifted subtly as he turned it in his hand. But what truly unsettled him was the faint ethos-imbued aura clinging to it, a pulsing energy that he could feel humming against his skin. The vampire's frown deepened. To his knowledge, no insect—not even in the unnatural corners of the world—possessed ethos.

And yet...there it was.

"Did you find something?" Danford asked, appearing at his side.

"It's a shell," he said, holding it up so Danford could see. "Maybe a beetle or something...but beetles don't have ethos, and this shell *does*."

"Oh," the werewolf said with a curious frown.

Alucard then noticed a few fallen leaves where he found the shell—so he looked up, and directly above him was a rather large break in the treetops. "Something really big took off here—far too big to be an insect, though," he said, standing up, still holding the shell.

Wide-eyed, Danford gulped a little. "Uh...an insect-person?" he suggested, but when Alucard looked at him, he frowned in embarrassment and shook his head as if he was telling himself that he shouldn't have suggested that.

"It's possible," the vampire said, looking up at the gap in the trees again.

"W-wait...so...Lord Cecil is a giant roach?"

Alucard laughed quietly in amusement. "He sure does look like one, so I wouldn't be surprised," he said. "I can follow this shell's aura—maybe it'll lead us to Cecil. If he *is* a giant roach, then...we will probably need a lot of insect repellent," he muttered, looking around, searching for a trail using the shell in his hand.

"U-uh...oh god...okay," Danford said in what sounded like confliction.

Alucard didn't care to ask him why he sounded hesitant, though. Once he caught the aura's trail, he immediately headed deeper into the forest.

For a while, Alucard followed the trail. He walked through the birch forest until he stepped out of the tree line and onto the riverbank. *Of course* they'd end up near the river; Danford had reported that he'd seen Cecil returning home with the same mud on his boots that could be found by the riverbed, so Alucard was certain that they had to be close now.

He followed the river, and eventually, they came close to the northern waterfall. Alucard stopped walking, setting his eyes on a large cave entrance just visible behind the falling water, but he hesitated. Usually, he'd just enter the cave and continue following the trail, but...as he focused on the cave ahead, the aura seemed to vanish, and as hard as he concentrated, his sensory ethos couldn't see past the water. *That* had to be where Cecil was; it made sense that the place he kept visiting would be enchanted.

"Are...we going in there?" Danford asked, stopping beside him.

Alucard didn't plan to go any further. As much as he wanted to solve this problem to save Zalith the work, he didn't want to do something as reckless as walk into what might be a trap. He was sure there was something inside, and whatever it was, it had to be pretty powerful to be able to block *his* sensory ethos. So, he'd not risk hurting himself. He'd leave with what he had and return home to Zalith. At least he now had an idea of what Cecil might actually be, if not human. A creature with a beetle-like shell? He'd not heard of such a thing, but he'd look into it once he got home.

He looked at Danford. "No," he replied. "It's time to go."

"Oh…okay…really?"

"Yes," he grumbled, turning around and starting to lead the way back towards Eimwood.

"Okay," the werewolf said unsurely, following him. "Sorry." Then, without another word, he followed Alucard in silence.

As he made his way back towards Eimwood, Alucard's thoughts returned to Zalith. He still dreaded the imminent scolding that he was going to get—he knew Zalith would be angry with him for not only putting him to sleep but for heading out on his own. But Alucard had stayed out of danger; he'd not gone alone, and he had chosen *not* to continue into that cave without his mate. He hoped that the precautions he'd taken would make Zalith a little less mad.

He frowned, slipping his hands into his pockets. Maybe if he got Zalith something nice, *that* might also make the demon a little less angry. He recalled that the room where Danford would watch Cecil's estate was atop a rather cosy-looking confectionary store—maybe he could visit before he went home.

Once they reached Eimwood's entrance, Alucard sighed and stopped walking. "Go home," he said to Danford. "Thank you for coming with me."

"Oh, okay…if you need anything, let me know," the werewolf said.

Alucard nodded, and then Danford walked off, heading home.

The vampire continued up the street, heading for the confectionary store. He already knew what he was going to get for Zalith, and once he had it, he'd head home and search one of the castle's libraries for a book that might tell him about 'insect people', as Danford had called them. It was entirely possible that Cecil was such a creature, and Alucard wanted to find out as much as he could so that later, when he and Zalith went to that cave, they'd know what they were up against.

Chapter Twenty

Careful Mistake

| **Alucard**—*Uzlia Isles, Usrul, Castle Reiner* |

Orange light filtered in through the half-drawn curtains, signalling the approaching end of the afternoon. The hours passed by fast while Alucard sat cross-legged on the end of the daybed, silently watching over Zalith, who slept peacefully. He'd gotten about halfway through a book about insectoids, but he hadn't found anything that matched the description of the shell he'd found out in the woods.

When he flipped over to the next page, he felt Zalith stir. He looked down at the demon, watching as a confused frown struck his face—Zalith panicked as he woke, but when his eyes locked onto Alucard, he calmed a little. The vampire smiled at him, putting down the book.

"What time is it?" Zalith asked, sitting up.

"It's about... six-thirty," he said, placing the book on the cabinet beside the bed.

"What?" the demon questioned, an almost mortified look on his face. "Why didn't you wake me up?"

"You needed the rest," he insisted, resting his arms in his lap as he watched Zalith tidy his clothes as if he were preparing to head out. "You haven't been sleeping well lately, and... I want you to get all the rest you can."

Zalith frowned. "But it's *six-thirty*." His eyes then shifted to Alucard's hair, and his frown thickened. "Were you in the woods?" he questioned, an argumentative tone in his voice.

Alucard hesitated for a moment. He knew that the demon would know, and he wasn't sure how, but... *he knew*, and he wasn't going to lie to him. He looked down at his lap, angst swelling inside him; he *hated* when Zalith was angry with him, he hated hearing the demon's aggravated voice directed at him, to see that irritated look on his face as he glared at him. It all made him feel so anxious—so... panicked, even. But he quietly answered, "Yes."

The demon leaned forward and reached out his arm—

Alucard almost flinched as Zalith moved his hand closer to his face—he didn't mean to, his body just reacted on its own. But he didn't push Zalith away. He let his mate fiddle with his hair for a moment. When Zalith moved his hand away, though, he held a small yellow leaf in between his fingers, and Alucard understood how the demon knew he'd gone outside.

"Which woods?" Zalith asked sternly.

"Yrudberg," he mumbled sadly.

Aggravation smothered Zalith's face, along with a confused stare. "What?" he asked, almost astounded. "Why?"

"I wanted to let you rest," he insisted, glancing at him—but he couldn't stare at his face for longer than a few seconds. Zalith's angered expression hurt his heart. "I know you wanted to get this Cecil thing out of the way today, so…I thought I would go and find out what I could while you slept. I took Danford with me, and we found out where he's been going—and I also discovered that he might not even be human," he explained. Then, he reached behind him and grabbed the wrapped-up piece of coffee cake he'd got from the confectionary store for Zalith. "And I got this for you, too," he said quietly, holding it out towards him.

Taking it, Zalith glanced down at the wrapped-up cake and then looked back at Alucard. The irritated look on his face hadn't faded at all. "What if something happened to you while I was all the way over here asleep on the couch in the middle of the day?" he questioned.

The vampire shrugged, looking down at his lap again. "Nothing bad happened to me. I was careful—I'm always careful. I know I shouldn't have left, but I just wanted to make today easier for you," he said despondently.

"I thought you were tired."

"I was. And I still am, but you're more important to me than my own need to rest."

"And *you* are more important to me than *my* need rest, which is why I'm up all the time worrying about you because I'm scared you're going to do something like this or be separated from me when I'm not prepared and something horrible is going to happen," he said, raising his voice a little. "You could have at least said something."

Alucard hung his head in shame, and he didn't know what to say. He could sit there and try to argue with him about the fact that Uzlia was the safest place in Aegisguard; he could sit there and insist that he would be fine and that nothing would happen, but he knew how Zalith felt, and it wouldn't make any difference. "I didn't want to wake you up," he said meekly. "I wanted to do something to help you so that you'd get to have a few hours to relax…because you don't stop," he said, lifting his head to look at him. "You're going to work yourself to death, and all I want to do is stop that from happening."

"Just please at least let me know that you're leaving next time," Zalith said, still angry.

Alucard nodded stiffly. He wasn't going to do anything like this ever again. It had only upset Zalith and hadn't made him feel any sort of relief, clearly. But Alucard wouldn't sit there and sulk and feel sorry for himself. He knew what he'd done, and he wasn't going to try and wiggle his way out of the scolding. "I'm not going to do it again," he said quietly, staring down at his lap.

The demon still had a vexed look on his face. "Thank you. I don't like being like this, Alucard; I want you to be able to go wherever you want and do what you want to do, but I'm just not capable of that right now—I'm sorry."

"I know," he mumbled. "I understand."

Zalith then held out his arms. "Come here," he said, inviting Alucard into a hug.

The vampire didn't look at him—he didn't want to see the aggravated expression that he knew was still on Zalith's face. The irritated tone in the demon's voice made him hesitate, but he didn't want to upset or annoy him any more than he already had. So he moved closer; he shuffled over to him and leaned into him, resting his head on Zalith's shoulder as the demon wrapped his arms around him.

"I'm glad you're okay," Zalith said—but still, that aggravated tone remained in his voice.

Alucard moved his arms around him. He felt like an idiot right now. He'd gone out there on his own against Zalith's wishes—he knew Zalith was paranoid, and the last thing he would want is for Alucard to go off and do something on his own in case he got hurt... or worse. But Alucard had decided to ignore that, and even though he hadn't been hurt, that didn't outweigh the fact that he'd done something so reckless and ignorant.

He scowled at himself. Why did he keep doing this? Why did he keep ignoring the people who just wanted to keep him safe? Maybe Damien had been right. Maybe he really was incapable; maybe he really shouldn't keep continuously trying to prove that he could do more. All it ever did was cause either himself or someone else unnecessary pain.

"Thank you for thinking of me, though," the demon then said, holding him tightly.

"It's all I ever do," he mumbled despondently.

The demon sighed sadly, resting the side of his face against Alucard's. "I love you."

With a sullen sigh, Alucard lowered his head and nuzzled Zalith's neck. "I love you, too," he said. And then he just sat there, sinking deeper in the disappointment he felt in himself. He shouldn't have been so stupid. He knew Zalith would be upset with him, yet he'd still gone and done it anyway. He was tired of upsetting Zalith—he was tired of angering him with his stupid little decisions, and he felt as if he didn't deserve Zalith's affection right now. As much as he wanted to kiss him, as much as he wanted to let himself sink into the comfort of Zalith's embrace, he didn't deserve it, so he ignored what he needed, staring sullenly at the wall behind where Zalith was sitting.

"Do you want some cake?" the demon soon asked—and despite the small silence that had just fallen between them, the demon still sounded aggravated.

"No," Alucard murmured. "I'm not really hungry."

"Me neither," Zalith said, placing the wrapped-up cake he'd been holding this whole time on the table next to the daybed.

Alucard shrugged, still staring aimlessly. "You don't have to eat it," he said, thinking about how stupid it was of him to think that giving Zalith something would help him feel better about what he'd done. "I got it from the store near Cecil's place, so it's probably not even that good."

The demon laughed a little. "I'll try some later."

Nodding, Alucard closed his eyes, his sadness slowly twisting into fatigue.

"I should get to work," Zalith said quietly, still sounding upset. "I'll be in my office."

Zalith was still mad at him; Alucard was certain that he would be for the rest of the night, and maybe even tomorrow, too. He wasn't going to argue with him, nor was he going to ask him to stay. He didn't deserve anything from Zalith right now other than his anger. So he leaned back out of their hug and stared sullenly down at his lap. He wanted to ask the demon not to leave—he wanted to tell him that he didn't need to keep working constantly, but... he'd already upset his mate enough, and he was beginning to understand that there wasn't anything he could do to help Zalith but stay at his side and be there for him.

The demon got up and left the room without saying another word.

Hearing Zalith's footsteps echo through the castle, Alucard sank back onto the bed, his gaze fixed sullenly on the door. A smouldering ache constricted his chest, frustration and guilt twisting together into something heavy and inescapable. He'd done it again—tried to do more than he should, more than Zalith had asked of him. It was a pattern that had haunted him since childhood, this constant need to prove himself, to help in ways that often ended in failure or pain for someone else. Why couldn't he just stop? Why couldn't he listen when Zalith told him there was nothing more he needed to do?

With a low grunt of discomfort, he rolled onto his back, his healing wounds protesting the movement. A sharp pang of anger flickered through him, and he turned onto his side instead, burying his scowl into the pillow. His heart burned with a mix of disappointment and quiet despair, a weight so potent that it stung his eyes. He didn't want to keep fighting against what Zalith needed—not when it only seemed to frustrate the demon further. Zalith had chosen to cope with his grief through relentless work, and if Alucard couldn't help ease that burden, the least he could do was stop making it worse.

He closed his eyes, exhaling deeply. The idea of a vacation, of getting Zalith to rest was pointless. He knew that now. Even the thought of tricking Zalith into taking a break only filled him with guilt; it would only anger him further. No, he'd stick to Zalith's plans, offer his support where it was wanted, and leave the rest alone. At the very least, he could be there to help replenish Zalith's energy when he needed it—though even that had its limits. Alucard's own energy and stamina weren't endless, and the knowledge of how finite his help could be left a bitter taste in his mouth.

The vampire opened his eyes, staring at the cushion in front of him with a glare that held more at himself than anyone else. Zalith would likely be furious for the rest of the night, and Alucard knew better than to chase after forgiveness. He wouldn't try to comfort himself or plead his case—it wouldn't fix anything. Instead, he'd wait. He'd wait for Zalith to be ready to talk, and when that moment came, he'd own his mistakes. It was all he could do now.

Chapter Twenty-One

— ⸰ ✝ ⸰ —

Apologies and Forgiveness

| **Zalith**—*Uzlia Isles, Usrul, Castle Reiner* |

Zalith spent the next few hours sorting through his letters. He answered those that he had to, looked over the plans he'd made regarding demon packs and his gradually increasing army, and did everything he could to try and take his mind off what happened earlier with Alucard. He didn't want to think about their conversation—he wanted to work. He'd missed out on so much time today that he had to get as much work done as quickly and efficiently as he could to make up for it.

But Alucard remained on his mind. He felt frustrated—this was stupid. He didn't want to be mad because Alucard was only trying to be helpful, but...he *was* mad. *Anything* could have happened, and he knew that Alucard was confident that they were safe here, but they had only been here a month, and Zalith wasn't yet ready to let himself believe that was true. He'd love to believe it, but every time he let himself relax and believe that he and the people he loved were safe, some of them were killed.

He sighed, resting his arms on his desk as he dragged his hand over his face. He wished Alucard wasn't as upset as he knew he was, but his fiancé was the one who caused the problem in the first place, so...if he *was* upset about it, then that was his problem. Zalith wasn't going to baby him. Alucard knew how he felt about all of this—he knew how terribly he worried for the vampire's safety, and yet he'd still gone and left the castle while he was sleeping.

With another sigh, Zalith sent off his final message and pushed away his finished paperwork. He leaned back in his seat, exhaling deeply; he was done with everything he had to do today, and he couldn't get Alucard off his mind, so he was going to go and check on him. He was sure that his fiancé was beating himself up about it, and although it was his fault, Zalith still didn't like knowing that he was upset.

He got up out of his seat and left his office; he made his way down the stairs, through the castle halls and eventually into the lounge where he'd left Alucard. The vampire was asleep on the daybed with his back to Zalith, and Peaches must have come in the open window because she was curled up at Alucard's feet. The book that Alucard had been reading earlier had also fallen to the floor—it looked like Alucard might have fallen asleep while reading it.

Zalith walked over to the bed and sat beside Alucard. He placed his hand on the sleeping vampire's arm and leaned back so that he could see his face. "Alucard?" he asked quietly.

His fiancé didn't reply, though.

With a quiet sigh, Zalith caressed Alucard's hair and let him sleep a little longer. He knew that his vampire sorely needed the rest.

| **Alucard**—*Uzlia Isles, Usrul, Castle Reiner* |

Alucard felt something warm beside him, and something soft caressed his hair. He frowned as he stirred, waking from his sleep, and when he opened his eyes and turned his head ever so slightly, he saw Zalith sitting beside him. He wasn't sure what he felt—dread? Shame? He was worried that his mate was back to yell at him, or maybe he was there to tell him how disappointed he was in him. His heart ached, and his frown grew thicker with angst.

"How are you feeling?" Zalith asked—he didn't sound mad, and his touch rested against Alucard with quiet attentiveness. "Is your back any better?"

He sat up and shrugged. "A little," he answered. "Did you get your work done?"

Zalith nodded.

The vampire moved closer, and Zalith shifted instinctively, allowing him to nestle even nearer. Alucard rested his head against Zalith's chest, his right arm draping over the demon's shoulder in a slow, tentative embrace. Without hesitation, Zalith's arms wrapped around him, holding him tightly, grounding him. Alucard wanted to speak—he wanted to find the right words—but the need faded almost as soon as it surfaced. He didn't want to talk. He just wanted this. To be here, held by Zalith, the lingering tension between them melting away in the warmth of his presence.

He lifted his head, his gaze searching Zalith's face for any trace of lingering anger. But there was none. No frustration, no sharpness—only exhaustion, and perhaps a quiet sadness that twisted something deep in Alucard's chest. He didn't want Zalith to be sad.

And he certainly didn't want to say something that might push him further into it. So instead, he leaned in, closing his eyes as he ignored the surge of quiet anxiety tightening in his ribs. He pressed his lips to Zalith's, a silent plea wrapped in the softness of the kiss.

When he pulled back, he studied Zalith's expression, gauging his reaction. There was no irritation, no cold withdrawal—only a faint, almost sullen frown. Zalith's hand moved to the side of Alucard's face, his dark eyes searching his own, and Alucard took it as an invitation. He leaned in again, closing the space between them, kissing him once more. His mate kissed back, though his usual fervour was absent. It didn't make Alucard hesitate, though, nor did it make him stop. He understood—Zalith was tired, drained, maybe even hurting in ways that he hadn't admitted, and Alucard wanted to ease that, even just a little. This was what *he* needed, and maybe…maybe it was what Zalith needed, too.

His hand drifted from Zalith's shoulder, down over his chest, trailing lower towards his waist—until Zalith suddenly stilled. He broke the kiss with a quiet sigh, his frown deepening into something more despondent.

"Alucard, I don't want to do this while we're upset with each other," the demon said.

Embarrassment then enthralled Alucard. He turned his head, looking away to try and hide his face, and then he shuffled away from Zalith, convinced that he probably shouldn't get too close for comfort. Zalith was still mad at him, clearly, and he didn't want to add to his irritation.

"I'm sorry," his mate said.

Alucard frowned in dismay. He'd just made yet another stupid decision. He really did suck at reading Zalith's face, didn't he? "Why?" he asked sullenly, staring down at his lap as he sat cross-legged—it was the only position he could sit in that didn't hurt the healing wounds stretching down his back. "I'm the one making all the stupid decisions."

"Because I don't want you to be upset," Zalith answered.

The vampire shrugged. "It's not your fault. It's my own."

"Can you look at me, please?" Zalith then asked calmly.

Alucard felt his angst increase, but he wasn't going to ignore Zalith. That might only make it worse. So, he turned his head to look at him, trying to keep his eyes focused on some region of Zalith's face.

"Yeah, I'm a little angry with you," his mate continued. "But I don't think any less of you as a person."

He shrugged again. "I should have known not to go; I know how worried you are," he admitted, his eyes shifting from Zalith's cheek to his eyes and back to his cheek. He felt so ashamed of himself, and seeing the disappointment on Zalith's face only made him feel worse.

"I agree," Zalith said. "But I'm ready to start moving past it, and I don't think you should be sitting around beating yourself up over it."

Nodding, Alucard took his eyes off Zalith's face and looked down at his lap—but he quickly looked back at him, trying his best to keep his eyes on him. "I'm sorry for leaving earlier," he said, looking down at his lap again.

"It's okay. I understand why you did it. I'm sorry that I've been having issues lately."

Alucard shrugged. "You don't need to be sorry for that. You're going through something, and instead of helping you with that the way you asked me to, I keep trying to do more, and…I don't know why," he confessed sullenly, still staring down at his lap. "Well…" he mumbled and sighed. "All I want to do is help, but I only ever end up getting hurt or hurting someone else. I think…maybe I'm still trying to prove that I can do more—maybe I just wish I could do more to help you feel better. And I *know* I can't, but I just…can't seem to understand and accept that no matter how many times you tell me, no matter how many times I tell myself. It's like some sort of instinct—*that* feels like the best way to explain it. I *need* to try and do more, and I know I can't—it's just…some vicious cycle. And I don't know what to do about it," he said shamefully, glancing at Zalith and then back down at his lap.

Zalith frowned slightly. "It hasn't happened *every* time. There have been times you've done things for me and you made me really happy. In fact, it *rarely* happens."

Still staring at his lap, Alucard shrugged. He didn't know what else to say. He wasn't going to be able to do anything to surprise Zalith as he had before because if he left the castle alone, it upset his mate—and he understood why; Zalith was terrified that something might happen to him. He couldn't go to the city to buy or do anything to surprise the demon, and although he could get someone else to go and get what he needed, it didn't feel as exciting or as special as it would if he were to do it himself. And admittedly, it frustrated him. He wanted to do things for Zalith, and for himself, but he was restricted to how much he could do without worrying his mate.

He sighed, trying to banish his frustration. "I won't leave by myself again," he said—he knew that was what Zalith wanted, and all he wanted to do was make him happy.

Zalith frowned and shook his head, but he didn't say anything.

And silence fell between them.

Alucard glanced at the demon, and the moment he noticed Zalith's look of disappointment, he frowned sullenly and stared down at his lap again. "Do you want me to go?" he asked, unsure whether Zalith wanted more time to be mad alone.

"No—why would I want you to go?"

He exhaled quietly and sadly. "You're still mad at me, and I don't want to make it worse by trying to explain why I did what I did."

"I'm more mad at myself right now, to be honest."

Alucard's frown became a confused one. "Why?"

"Because my problems are the root of this issue."

"But it's not your fault," he said, turning to face him. Shifting one leg over the side of the bed, he let his foot touch the floor, uncrossing his legs so that he could move closer to Zalith. "You just...want to make sure I'm safe, and you need longer to see that this place is safe for us—I get that. You went through a lot—you had to deal with so much, and I don't blame you for feeling like this. I just wish I could help."

Zalith frowned despondently, moving his hand to the side of Alucard's face. "You *do* help," he said, fiddling with the vampire's hair.

Alucard stared at his mate's sorrow-smothered face and slowly moved his hand over the demon's shoulder. "Just tell me if you ever need me to do more," he pleaded. "I only want to make you happy."

"I know," the demon said quietly. He then moved closer and rested his forehead against Alucard's. "I love you," he mumbled, closing his eyes.

Closing his eyes too, Alucard exhaled quietly. "I love you, too," he said, guiding his hand to the side of Zalith's neck. "And I'm sorry I upset you."

"I forgive you," Zalith said before kissing him. He then hugged him tightly.

Alucard felt as if it might be time to try and change the subject; Zalith wasn't feeling great, and *he* wasn't feeling great, either. He rested his forehead against the demon's again and stared into his eyes. "What do you want to do now?" he asked. It was only eight-thirty—a little too early to be thinking about heading to bed...well, for Zalith, anyway.

"I'll do whatever you want to do," the demon said.

He thought to himself for a few moments. Maybe leaving the castle for a little might help them both feel better. "We could...go and walk Sabazios," he suggested.

"Okay," Zalith agreed.

Alucard smiled. "Let's go and get ready," he said, slipping his hand into Zalith's as he stood up.

The demon got up and followed Alucard as he led the way out of the lounge and through the hall.

Alucard went into the cloakroom, grabbed one of Zalith's black redingotes, and handed it to him.

"Thank you," the demon said as he took it and pulled it on.

The vampire then went to grab one of his own coats, but he didn't feel like having to struggle to put it on with his healing wounds. Instead, he grabbed his fur-collared cape and pulled it on over his shoulders.

They both slipped their shoes on, and once they were ready, Alucard took hold of Zalith's hand again and led the way out of the cloakroom.

"Sabazios," the vampire called, waiting with Zalith by the front door.

Moments later, the four-foot-tall Hellhound came running. The thumping sound of his giant paws hitting the marble floors echoed through the castle, and once he reached the entrance hall, he slowed down and trotted over, his claws clicking on the floor beneath his feet as he panted happily.

Alucard smiled and kneeled as Sabazios hurried over to him. "What have you been doing?" he asked with a babyish tone. "Did you scare Peaches earlier?" he asked sternly.

The dog adorned an innocent stare and whined quietly.

"Mm-hmm," the vampire hummed doubtfully. "That's not what she tells me."

Sabazios wagged his tail and crouched down, panting excitedly.

"Okay," Alucard sighed, patting his head and scratching his ears. "Let's go." And then he led the way outside, hoping that they could escape from all of the despair and frustration for a while.

Chapter Twenty-Two

Insectumoid

| **Alucard**—*Uzlia Isles, Usrul* |

Sabazios raced around the fountain, his white fur a ghostly blur against the moonlit courtyard. Every few bounds, he skidded to a stop, glancing back with bright, eager eyes, waiting for Zalith and Alucard to catch up before darting ahead once more. When they finally got down to the meadow, the hellhound fell into step beside them, his tail flicking excitedly as they moved through the open expanse.

The soft, blue-green grass stretched out before them, rippling like silk beneath the cool night breeze. Vibrant, jewel-toned flowers dotted the landscape, their delicate petals shifting under the faint glow of the moons. To Alucard's left, a stone pathway wound through the meadow, flanked by a handful of apple trees, their branches heavy with ripe fruit. The scent of them—sweet and slightly crisp—drifted through the air, mingling with the freshness of the open field.

"What did you learn about Cecil today?" Zalith asked, glancing at him.

Watching Sabazios as he chased a pheasant, Alucard frowned, recalling what he learned from the insectoid book before falling asleep. "A lot—well…maybe. I found where he's been going—some cave in the Yrudberg woods. I couldn't see in there, though—there was some sort of barrier blocking my ethos. I found a shell near the place where Cecil would always disappear when Danford followed him, and the thing had ethos in it, so…I followed the aura to that cave. I suspect that Cecil might be an Insectumoid—it's a sort of…bug…person," he said, not really sure how else to explain it. "They disguise themselves as humans and usually sit around living off unsuspecting ones."

Zalith frowned, intrigued. "Oh?"

Setting his eyes on the willow tree not too far from where they were, Alucard continued, "They are…shapeshifters; some of them are actually humanoid-looking, but they often have wings and shells—exoskeletons. They evolved to hide their true selves so that they could live among humans and live off them. There is a possibility that his wife and children don't actually know what he is—well...the children might. Male Insectumoids usually choose to seduce and reproduce with humans—the book I read didn't exactly say why, but...I assume it's because they live best when they live among humans, and having a normal family is good cover." He sat under the willow tree, and Zalith sat beside him. "I don't know *which* Insectumoid he is, though. The shell looked like that of a millikar, rochkin, or irwinth."

"I have no idea what those are," Zalith said with a small laugh.

"Well, millikar are millipede-looking humanoids, rochkin are essentially giant cockroaches, and irwinth are these earwig-looking people."

"Well, I wonder how the city will react to that."

"Are we going to expose him?" the vampire asked, taking his eyes off Sabazios, who was running around in the distance.

"It depends on whether or not we think the people are going to react poorly. Although...I *do* feel bad; it's not his fault he's a bug."

With a conflicted frown, Alucard looked out at Sabazios again. "Well, bugs aside, do you still think he has something to do with the water? The river runs through the cave he's been going into—we should find out what he's doing in there before we think about exposing him."

The demon nodded and laughed a little. "Maybe he's laying eggs in there."

"Maybe," Alucard said unsurely. "The only way we'll find out is by going in there. Maybe he has a whole family of bug people in there that haven't got themselves human bodies yet—they...take people and crawl up into their bodies, eat them from the inside, and then walk around in their skin," he said with an amused smirk on his face as he ran his fingers up Zalith's body, over his chest, and then prodded his neck. "Maybe he's planning to use this whole city for that."

Zalith leaned back away from his hand and chuckled. "Ew."

Alucard shuffled closer; he climbed onto Zalith and straddled his lap, sighing quietly as he relaxed and guided his hand to the side of the demon's face. All he wanted right now was to be with Zalith—to be as close to him as he could get. He was convinced now that his mate wasn't as angry with him as he had been earlier, but...he didn't want to assume and start seeking affection that Zalith didn't want to give him again.

"Are you still mad at me?" he asked quietly.

The demon moved his hand to the side of Alucard's face and frowned despondently. "No."

With a quiet, relieved exhale, Alucard leaned forward and rested his forehead against Zalith's. "Are you okay?"

"I'm okay," he said with a small smile.

Alucard studied him for a moment, his gaze lingering. Despite the dismay that had weighed on him earlier, his need for Zalith only seemed to grow—an ache that always burned hotter after an argument, as if conflict only deepened the pull between them. Slowly, he leaned in, closing his eyes as he pressed his lips softly against Zalith's. Uncertainty flickered in the back of his mind—he wasn't sure if Zalith wanted him, not right now. But the demon kissed him back, and something in Alucard eased. Maybe Zalith *did* want this too.

Their movements deepened, unhurried yet consuming as Alucard slid his arms around Zalith's shoulders. He settled into his lap, fitting against him and letting himself sink into the warmth and solidity of him. For now, there were no words—only this, only *them*.

After a few more kisses, he stopped to stare at and admire the demon's face. "Did you eat yet?" he asked.

"Edwin brought something up to my office, but I didn't want it—I'll be okay, though," his mate said, tucking a loose strand of Alucard's hair behind his ear.

Alucard frowned in concern, starting to fiddle with Zalith's loose fringe. "You need to eat something, though."

"I'll be fine. I'll have something when we get home."

Nodding, Alucard looked down at his lap for moment but then looked back at Zalith's face. "We don't have to go yet."

Zalith's fingers trailed back to the side of Alucard's face, his touch warm, his smile slow and knowing. "We can stay as long as you want."

Alucard's own smile mirrored his, though there was something deeper beneath it—something smouldering. He leaned in, capturing Zalith's lips again, the kiss unhurried yet charged with a growing intensity. They lingered like that for a while, lips meeting and parting, breaths mingling, each kiss stoking the fire building between them.

His body hummed with need, the ache curling low and insistent. Tilting his head aside, he silently invited Zalith closer, offering his throat. He barely had a moment to anticipate the heat of Zalith's lips before they brushed against his skin, and a quiet, shuddering breath left him. The sensation sent a thrill down his spine, making his fingers tighten against Zalith's shoulders.

He swallowed, his pulse quickening as he leaned into the demon's ear, his voice barely more than a whisper, edged with want and nervous anticipation as he said, "I want *you*."

Zalith dragged his hands down Alucard's body to grip his waist as he kissed his neck one final time. "I want you, too," he murmured. "But what about your back?" he asked, their gazes meeting.

The vampire shrugged as a conflicted look made its way onto his face. His wounds hadn't yet healed, and he struggled to sit or lay in most positions without them hurting.

But his need for Zalith outweighed the concern for his wounds. "I'll be fine," he assured him.

"You don't look very confident," Zalith said with a quiet laugh.

He sighed and moved his hand over the demon's shoulder, letting his other fall into his lap. He didn't really know what to say. "I guess I'm not," he mumbled. "It's taking a lot longer than I thought for them to heal."

Zalith frowned sympathetically and placed his hand on Alucard's cheek. He then dragged it down the vampire's body and gripped his waist. "Here," he said and turned them around, making Alucard sit with his back against the tree.

Alucard's frown lingered for only a moment before Zalith leaned in, capturing his lips in a kiss that left little room for doubt. As the demon's fingers unbuckled his belt, understanding dawned, quickly followed by anticipation. A slow smile curved Alucard's lips, his excitement igniting as Zalith's hand slipped beneath the fabric of his trousers, wrapping firmly around his growing arousal.

The rough bark of the tree pressed against his back, an irritation he barely acknowledged, his focus wholly consumed by Zalith—by the heat of his touch, the way his mouth moved against his own. And then, as the demon began trailing downward, Alucard exhaled a soft, contented sigh, tilting his head back against the tree.

The first brush of Zalith's lips against his shaft sent a shiver down his spine, and when his mouth closed around him, Alucard's fingers instinctively tangled in his mate's dark hair, gripping tightly. Pleasure pulsed through him, intoxicating and consuming, making it impossible to think of anything else. A quiet moan slipped free of his breath, but as he tried to relax, the ache in his back became harder to ignore. The roughness of the tree dug deeper into his skin, making him shift uncomfortably. He grimaced, his body caught between discomfort and ecstasy, his pulse quickening as desire overtook him.

Zalith paused, looking up at him with quiet concern. "Are you okay?" he asked.

Alucard nodded, exhaling steadily as he shifted his weight. He pressed his right hand into the grass behind him, leaning onto his arm to keep his back from pressing against the rough bark. The adjustment was a relief, easing the dull ache enough for him to focus on what really mattered. His left hand remained tangled in Zalith's hair, guiding him back down with gentle insistence.

Zalith obliged without hesitation, his tongue dragging teasingly over Alucard's shaft before resuming his slow, intoxicating rhythm. Finally able to relax a little more, Alucard melted into the sensation, his body responding eagerly. A quiet moan escaped him as he let his head tip back, eyes fluttering shut, surrendering to the pleasure unravelling within him.

The demon hummed in quiet satisfaction, his pace quickening, the warmth of his mouth drawing Alucard ever closer to the edge. Fingers tightening in the demon's hair, Alucard let out another soft moan, his breath hitching as tension coiled in his core.

Normally, he might try to hold out longer, prolonging the moment, indulging in Zalith's attention for just a little more time—but the strain on his arm, coupled with the lingering discomfort in his back, made it impossible to resist for long.

His teeth clenched as his pleasure peaked, a final moan slipping free as he climaxed, his body trembling beneath the force of release. His right hand slipped across the grass, his elbow giving out until it hit the ground. He almost let himself collapse entirely, but he fought against it—giving in fully would only invite a fresh wave of pain that he wasn't willing to deal with.

Breathing heavily, he sighed, his heartbeat still racing as he tried to ease himself into something resembling comfort. It wasn't easy, not with the awkward way he was laying, but he did his best to steady himself.

Zalith hummed in delight as he buttoned Alucard's trousers back up, re-buckling his belt before crawling over him, his dark eyes searching his face. "Are you okay?" he asked, his voice low and edged with concern. "How's your back?"

Staring at him, Alucard huffed uncomfortably. He didn't want to lay there like that anymore. So, he sat up and gently pushed Zalith back against the tree so that he could straddle the demon's lap once more. Then, he rested his head on his mate's shoulder and sighed a deep, relieved sigh. "It's okay," he answered quietly, relaxing. "Thank you."

The demon slowly dragged his hands up Alucard's arms, over his shoulders, and then moved his right hand to the back of his head. "You're welcome," he said, starting to caress his hair.

Alucard exhaled deeply, steadying himself as the lingering tension drained from his body. A sense of relief washed over him, as though a weight had finally lifted from his shoulders. He craved Zalith's affection so fiercely that when denied, the frustration and longing would gnaw at him, turning into something almost unbearable. At times, he felt selfish for it—he knew there would be moments when Zalith simply didn't want to give him his attention…like earlier. But that was behind them now. They'd moved past it, and with the last remnants of his frustration fading, only one thought remained: sinking into bed, wrapped in Zalith's arms, where everything felt right again.

And it seemed he might get his wish sooner than expected.

A deep crash of thunder rolled through the nearly blackened sky, the distant rumble vibrating through the air. Alucard felt Zalith shift, lifting his head to glance upward, his sharp eyes catching the flicker of approaching storm clouds.

"We should head back," the demon murmured as the sound of Sabazios' paws tore across the field. "It's going to rain."

Alucard frowned, reluctant to move. He didn't want to get caught in the rain any more than Zalith did, but the thought of trudging all the way back felt tedious, *exhausting*, when all he wanted was to stay right where he was. Maybe…Zalith would carry him? The idea curled temptingly in his mind, and before he could stop himself, he was already trying to figure out how to convince him. But as the thought lingered, guilt followed close behind. He felt selfish for even considering it—worse still for actually plotting how to make it happen.

With a quiet sigh, he sat up, his gaze settling on Zalith's face. It wasn't just the walk back that made him hesitate; he wasn't quite ready to pull away from Zalith's embrace. He *wanted* to stay—wanted to keep holding him, to keep being held, to sink deeper into that comfort just a little longer. He knew he could relax with him once they were home, but the simple thought of moving made exhaustion weigh heavier on him.

His lips pressed into a pout as he dropped his gaze to his lap. He wasn't going to act *that* childish. Zalith had said he wasn't angry anymore, but Alucard wasn't entirely convinced, and he wasn't about to push his luck. The last thing he wanted was to *actually* irritate him.

Nodding, Alucard took hold of Zalith's hand and stood up, pulling the demon up with him. "Okay," he said as Sabazios joined them, holding a large stick in his mouth.

The vampire smiled down at his dog as he sat down and barked, dropping the stick at Zalith's feet. The demon picked it up and threw it, and as Sabazios sprinted off to fetch it, Alucard started leading the way back towards the castle—and he hoped that they'd get back before the rain started falling.

Chapter Twenty-Three

— ⊰ ✝ ⊱ —

A Morning of Pleasures

| **Zalith**, *Monday, Tertium 13th, 960(TG)—Uzlia Isles, Usrul, Castle Reiner* |

Zalith jolted awake, his body tensing instinctively as the remnants of yet another nightmare clung to him like a suffocating shroud. He didn't want to remember it—he didn't *need* to. They came every night now, without fail, lurking in the edges of his mind, waiting for the moment he dared to close his eyes.

There was no escaping them. Not really.

The only way to avoid them was to stay awake, to keep himself from slipping into the vulnerable embrace of sleep. But even he couldn't do that forever. Eventually, exhaustion always won.

Beside him, Alucard stirred, his head rising slightly from Zalith's chest. His hellish eyes, still heavy with sleep, blinked up at him in the dim light. "Are you okay?" he mumbled.

"I'm okay," he assured him. "I just had another bad dream."

"What happened?" the vampire asked as he leaned over him, his touch gentle as he rested a hand against the side of Zalith's face, his thumb grazing lightly over his skin.

"The same thing as always," he said, staring into Alucard's eyes. "You die, my family die, and there's nothing I can do about it," he said sullenly, *tiredly*. He was so tired of these dreams and so tired of the way they made him feel.

Alucard frowned sadly, softly caressing the side of the demon's stubbly face with his fingers. "It was just a dream," he said quietly. "I'm not going anywhere."

"I know," he said, guiding his hand to the side of Alucard's face. He knew that they were just dreams, but he appreciated that Alucard was trying to comfort him.

The vampire exhaled sadly, stroking his hand up Zalith's face to start fiddling with his fringe. "Do you want to get up?"

"Yeah. I have to catch up on yesterday's stuff."

"What time are we leaving to go and find Cecil?"

"He usually leaves his place at one every afternoon, right?" he asked, sitting up. "We'll leave at twelve and watch him for a little before he leaves."

Alucard nodded, also sitting up. "Okay, well… I'm going to work on things too, then. I'll come and see you when I'm done?"

"Okay," Zalith said, smiling at him. "Do you want breakfast first?"

His fiancé smiled, too. "Are you having breakfast with me?"

"Of course," he said with a nod. "How's your back?" he then asked, fiddling with Alucard's tousled hair.

He shrugged. "It feels better."

"Good. Can I have a look at it?"

Alucard nodded before shifting off him, moving to sit at the edge of the bed. He began unwrapping the bandages from his body, and Zalith followed, settling behind him to help. He moved carefully—he didn't want to cause Alucard any pain; it took a few moments, but once the last strip of cloth was removed, the demon's gaze fell to what remained of the once-deep wounds on Alucard's back. The gashes had faded, now nothing more than raised scars, their edges smooth and nearly invisible against his pale skin. Another day, maybe less, and they'd be gone entirely.

"They're looking a lot better now. You probably don't need these anymore," he said, dropping the bandages to the floor. He then moved closer, gently massaging Alucard's back around the healing scars; he leaned forward and kissed his back a few times before resting his head on Alucard's shoulder, hugging him tightly.

Moving his hand to the top of Zalith's head, Alucard sighed deeply and gripped Zalith's left wrist with his other hand. "Thank you," he said quietly. "For taking care of me."

"You're welcome, baby," Zalith said and kissed his cheek. "I'm glad you're okay."

Alucard smiled, fiddling with Zalith's hair for a few moments before turning around and gently pushing Zalith down onto his back. He crawled over him, resting his chest against his, and then he sighed, placing his hands on either side of Zalith's face. "I'm always okay," he said, staring into his eyes. "Because of *you*, my love." He stroked the right side of Zalith's face.

Zalith let out a quiet chuckle as he guided his hand to the back of Alucard's head. With an easy pull, he drew him closer, capturing his lips in a slow, indulgent kiss. Alucard responded eagerly, returning each kiss with growing intensity, his touch trailing lower along Zalith's bare skin. Zalith felt the shift in him—the hesitation that always lingered beneath his desire, the quiet war between nervousness and longing. But this time, the vampire didn't pull away.

Instead, his fiancé lingered for a few moments, pressing another kiss, then another, before his lips wandered downward, over Zalith's jaw, then his neck, and finally paused near his ear. Zalith could hear the faint hitch in his breath, he could sense the way he fought against his nerves, pushing past them in favour of something deeper.

"Can I fuck you?" the vampire mumbled, still stroking his fingers down over Zalith's body until he reached the demon's crotch.

Zalith smiled delightedly, equal parts surprise and excitement flickering through him. It wasn't often that Alucard took the lead like this, and though Zalith relished being in control, there was something undeniably intoxicating about those rare moments when the vampire seized it for himself.

With his hand still tangled in Alucard's hair, Zalith tightened his grip just enough to make the vampire shiver, tilting his head to the side as Alucard nuzzled into his neck. "Okay," he murmured, his voice edged with anticipation. He felt Alucard smile against his skin, a brief moment of warmth before the vampire's fingers wrapped firmly around his growing arousal.

A deep, contented moan escaped Zalith's breath, tapering into a low, pleased hum as Alucard playfully caught his earlobe between his teeth, sending a sharp thrill through him. The vampire's mouth trailed lower, pressing heated kisses along his throat, his touch both teasing and intent.

Zalith let his own hand drift downwards, fingers curling around Alucard's shaft in response. He caught the vampire's chin with his other hand, guiding his face back towards him before capturing his lips in a kiss that deepened almost instantly. Their breaths turned uneven, swallowed between each slow, hungry movement. As Zalith began stroking him, Alucard moaned into his mouth, his body pressing closer, his need evident in the way he moved—desperate, eager, and completely *his*.

The demon smirked as Alucard pulled back, his breath coming in quiet, uneven gasps. He felt the vampire nuzzle into his neck, his heart pounding against him, excitement thrumming in every touch. Zalith let out a slow, pleased exhale as Alucard's hand dragged up his body, his fingers warm against his skin. The moment Alucard leaned over him, reaching for the nightstand, Zalith took the opportunity to tease him. As soon as the vampire's fingers curled around the first tincture bottle of lube he could find, Zalith dipped his head and bit down on his nipple—playful, just enough to make him flinch.

Alucard tensed, a sharp little pout crossing his lips as he turned back towards him with a glare that only made Zalith chuckle. With a quiet laugh, he reached up, pulling Alucard's face back down to his own, kissing him again before the vampire could voice his protest. Alucard kissed him back, his touch eager, unsteady with anticipation. Zalith felt him move, his fingers slicking with the tincture before pressing between his thighs, working the lube into his ass with slow, teasing strokes. A quiet hum of delight escaped Zalith, his grip shifting from the back of Alucard's head, trailing down the curve of his spine before gliding over his shoulder. His fingers found the vampire's throat, wrapping lightly around it, feeling the way Alucard swallowed, how his breath quickened at the contact.

The vampire broke the kiss, exhaling deeply, his lips brushing against Zalith's skin as he buried his face into his neck once more. His movements turned hurried, his need bleeding into every touch. With a shaky breath, he quickly coated his dick with lube before finally pressing forward, slowly easing inside. Zalith inhaled sharply, his fingers tightening against Alucard's neck as the vampire breathed heavily against his skin, his body trembling with restraint; he felt every inch slip inside him, each more satisfying than the last, and Alucard's delighted hum only satisfied him further.

Zalith smirked to himself, tilting his head back against the pillow. He could *feel* how badly Alucard wanted him, and that more than anything sent heat curling through him. He let out a deep, pleasured moan, his fingers tangling once more in Alucard's hair. He tried to pull him back down, craving another kiss, but Alucard had other plans. Before he could move, the vampire seized his wrists, pinning them firmly above his head. Excitement thrummed through the demon as his fiancé pressed closer, still nuzzling into his neck. Then, with a slow thrust, Alucard buried his hard, pleasing dick as deep as he could go, exhaling a shuddering breath before resting his head against Zalith's shoulder. The demon exhaled just as deeply, the weight and heat of him sending sparks of euphoria rolling through his body.

A moment later, Alucard shifted, hooking Zalith's right leg over his back, securing it in place with a firm grip. His other hand still held Zalith's wrists above his head, keeping him pinned as he finally started to move. Each slow, measured thrust sent jolts of pleasure spiralling through Zalith, making him moan softly beneath the vampire.

Alucard nuzzled against his throat, his breath hot against his skin. Zalith could *feel* the restraint in him, the quiet tremor in his body as he fought the primal urge to sink his fangs into him. His grip tightened around Zalith's wrists, his free hand gliding up his body before tangling roughly in his hair. Then, with a sharper exhale, the vampire picked up his pace, his body moving faster, more desperate now.

Zalith smirked against the delight curling through him. He could feel just how much Alucard *needed* him—and that was the most intoxicating part of all.

He revelled in the pleasure unravelling between them, his moans slipping freely as Alucard thrusted with increasing urgency. Every roll of the vampire's hips sent another wave of pleasure surging through him, tightening the coil of heat low in his stomach. He could hear it—*feel* it—in Alucard too, the way his breath hitched, the quiet, desperate tremble in his movements as he struggled to hold himself together.

But then, control slipped.

With a strained, shuddering breath, Alucard sank his fangs into Zalith's neck. A sharp gasp left Zalith's lips, his back arching at the sensation. The bite was brief, but the rush of warmth—his own blood spilling into Alucard's mouth—sent a heady shiver down his spine. The vampire exhaled against his skin, a quiet, satisfied sound as he drank. Zalith could feel the tension easing from him, the way he melted into it, lost in the intoxicating taste.

And then, just as quickly, Alucard pulled away. His tongue swept over the fresh wounds, warm and slow, licking away the evidence of his hunger. Another sigh left him, this one softer—content, *sated.*

Zalith barely had a moment to breathe before he freed one of his hands, threading his fingers into Alucard's hair. With a firm tug, he guided his face back down and kissed him, swallowing the last of his pleasured sighs.

Their mouths moved feverishly against one another, lips parting only to gasp for breath as Alucard kept moving, his pace quickening. Zalith's grip tightened—on his hair, on his waist, anything to ground himself against the rising pleasure that threatened to pull him under.

He knew Alucard was close, his body tense with need, barely restrained. Sheer delight surged through him, his body arching beneath Alucard as the vampire thrust harder, faster. A deep, satisfied moan slipped from his lips as the vampire pulled back, breathless, before diving in again, capturing his lips in another desperate kiss. Zalith's body tensed, a shiver of raw pleasure rolling through him as Alucard pushed deeper. The demon let his hand curl around Alucard's jaw, gazing up at him, watching his expression twist in aching struggle. He could *feel* the vampire's need, the way he fought to hold back, but control slipped fast. Alucard moaned loudly, his grip tightening on Zalith's wrist before fisting into the sheets. With a final, shuddering gasp, the vampire succumbed, his body trembling as he whined euphorically, his forehead dropping against Zalith's as his dick throbbed inside him.

The satisfaction of each pulse devoured Zalith, enthralling him tighter and tighter as he savoured the feeling of Alucard's cum oozing into his body. He exhaled slowly, his fingers idly playing with the vampire's hair as he felt him relax against him. After a moment, Alucard shifted, pulling away before resting his head on Zalith's shoulder, his touch lingering as he stroked Zalith's cheek.

"I love you so much," the vampire murmured.

Zalith smiled as he turned his head and pressed a kiss to Alucard's temple, his grip tightening around him. "I love you too, baby," he said quietly. But despite the delight of Alucard's climax, he wasn't ready to calm down. He rested the side of his head on Alucard's and ran his fingers down his back. "Can I fuck *you*?" he asked.

The question made Alucard tense, and as he caressed Zalith's stubbly face, he said, "You can."

Zalith didn't wait; he had his answer. As anticipation flooded through him, he got up, gently gripped Alucard's waist, and made him lean on his hands and knees. He carefully massaged lube into the vampire's ass, but before he could slide his dick inside him, his fiancé hesitated.

"Can I lay down?" Alucard asked quietly, glancing back at him.

"Of course," he said with a smile.

Alucard laid on his front, moving his arms under his pillow, where he rested his chin.

"Are you comfy?" Zalith asked.

Nodding, Alucard relaxed. "Yes. Thank you."

Zalith then pressed his left hand into the blanket beside Alucard's head as he leaned forward, slowly easing his dick into him. A deep sigh left his lips, pleasure unfurling through him as the warmth of Alucard's body enveloped him. Beneath him, the vampire moaned quietly, his fingers twisting into the sheets, his body responding so perfectly that it only made Zalith want him more.

Leaning closer, Zalith rested his face against the side of Alucard's. He started to move, each slow thrust deepening his pleasure. He could feel Alucard tremble beneath him, he could hear the way his breath shook, and how his moans grew needier. The demon smirked, nuzzling into his neck before dragging his lips over his skin, biting down just hard enough to make Alucard whine. The sound only spurred him on, making his movements quicker, rougher, his body tightening as the pleasure built impossibly fast.

And it didn't take very long for him to reach his peak.

With a deep groan, he buried his throbbing dick fully, his release ripping through him in waves of bliss as Alucard cried out contently. Zalith moaned into Alucard's ear, his fingers gripping the sheets as he pressed his body against the vampire's back, riding out every last pulse of pleasure. For a few moments, neither of them moved, their breaths mingling, their bodies still locked together. And then, as the last tremors faded, Zalith exhaled slowly, relaxing against him, feeling the steady thrum of Alucard's heartbeat beneath him as they both came down from the high.

Zalith rolled onto his side, pulling Alucard against him, their bodies still warm from the lingering heat of pleasure. The vampire settled easily against his chest, exhaling a quiet, contented sigh as he wrapped an arm around him. Zalith could feel the way Alucard clung to him, how he nestled in closer, his breath soft against his skin. He hummed in amusement as the vampire nuzzled into his neck again, the familiar, affectionate gesture bringing a rare sense of ease. Zalith knew him well enough to sense when he wanted to say something—*three particular words,* no doubt—but his fiancé hesitated. Instead, he sighed, dragging his fingers lazily up the demon's torso, tracing the contours of his skin before coming to rest at the side of his neck. Zalith smirked in response, tilting his head slightly into the touch, letting him linger. He didn't need to hear the words to understand. He already knew.

"How much work do you have to do today?" Alucard asked quietly.

"A fair bit," he answered. "I answered all my messages yesterday, but I have to catch up on some Cecil shit."

Nodding, Alucard rested his head on Zalith's shoulder again. "I'll probably finish my things before you, so...I'll come and see you when I'm done, and then we can leave to go and watch Cecil when you're ready," he said. Then, he moved his hand to the side of Zalith's neck and frowned despondently. "I'm sorry again...for yesterday," he said quietly.

Zalith turned his head. "It's okay baby; don't worry about it," he said and kissed his forehead.

Alucard closed his eyes, hugging him tightly. "Do you need to go right now?"

"No," Zalith said. "But I'd like to have a shower."

"Okay," Alucard said with a small smile. "Can I join you?"

"Absolutely," Zalith said, a satisfied smirk tugging at his lips as he leaned down, capturing Alucard's mouth in a slow kiss. Then, without another word, he slipped out of bed, stretching briefly before leading Alucard to the shower.

He definitely felt better than he had when he woke up—*much* better. The weight of exhaustion still lingered at the edges of his mind, but it was dull now, pushed aside by the satisfaction thrumming through his body. And while the thought of heading to Yrudberg later to uncover exactly what Cecil was up to sparked a certain anticipation, for now, there were other matters to handle.

There was still work to be done.

Chapter Twenty-Four

News from Rasmus

| **Alucard**—*Uzlia Isles, Usrul, Castle Reiner* |

Once Alucard finished writing down the memory that he recalled this morning, he set his pen aside and leaned back in his chair, exhaling as he let his gaze drift to the ceiling. For a few quiet moments, he simply sat there, allowing himself to relax before shifting his focus back to his work. He was going to begin making Zalith's dream-eater; the preparations had already been set in motion—yesterday, he placed an order at a crystal store in town, and the owner had assured him that the materials would be ready by this morning. Rather than retrieving them himself, Alucard sent Edwin to collect them, and the butler should be returning soon.

With little else to occupy him, Alucard idly flipped through the small pile of letters on his desk, skimming over each one as he waited. The first was from Attila—he was the only one who wrote to him in Dor-Sanguian; the familiar script barely held his attention before he set it aside, moving on to the next.

The handwriting on the second letter belonged to Crowell, and the sight of it stirred a flicker of urgency within him. Crowell had been tracking Ysmay and the Diabolus, and any update on their movements was worth his immediate attention. Breaking the seal, he scanned the message quickly. It wasn't much—just confirmation that Crowell was now following Ysmay to what could be yet another hideout. Meanwhile, a few of his men had been assigned to tail two separate groups of Diabolus that Ysmay and Varana had sent off to unknown locations. Once their destinations were clear, Crowell would send word again.

Alucard sighed, setting the letter down. It wasn't the breakthrough he wanted, but at least progress was being made. It made him wonder, though…*when* were they going to do something about Ysmay and the Diabolus? He knew that Zalith was consumed by the fight against Lilith and her people, but Alucard couldn't keep ignoring the fact that the Diabolus had played a direct role in the destruction of his home—his entire country.

They had spent months slaughtering his people in an attempt to draw him out of Nefastus, but he'd refused to retaliate, unwilling to risk exposing himself or his mate. And then, when patience wasn't enough for them, they had reduced his castle to rubble, wiping out most of his council.

Of course, there had been evidence that Lilith's hand had guided that attack. She was the only one who knew about Zalith's weakness to rhodium, and that cursed metal had been laced into the poison cloud that swallowed Dor-Sanguis.

Alucard sighed, leaning his arms onto his desk. They *knew* where Ysmay was. They *knew* she had a Pandorican—and even an Obcasus—two things they desperately needed. Yet Zalith was focused on finding one of the other lost Pandoricans instead. It was the safer choice, but Ysmay was vulnerable with fewer Diabolus under her command than Alucard had initially feared. He and—well, *Zalith*—had over three hundred demons in his army now. It would be enough to overwhelm her, and in the process, Alucard could kill her, take her demons, and add them to his own pack, strengthening Zalith's numbers in the process.

But Zalith wanted to avoid Ysmay entirely—*anyone* tied to Lucifer. Alucard understood why. He *did*. But that didn't dull the hunger burning inside him. He *wanted* revenge. He *deserved* it.

The thought had crossed Alucard's mind more times than he cared to admit—growing his following, increasing his influence, transforming himself into a fully-fledged Numen so they could *end* Lucifer—so they could *end* them *all*. He and Zalith both knew the only way to eradicate the Numen was to create one of their own, and Zalith—no matter how many demons he commanded—could never become one. It had to be Alucard. Only *he* could wield pure Numen ethos.

But did he *want* that? Did he truly want to become one of *them*?

He still wasn't sure. However, if it meant protecting Zalith, if it meant securing a future where they could live freely, safely—then *yes*. He would do it. He would *become* it.

Though not yet. Not now.

Zalith didn't want to think about Lucifer or the Diabolus, and Alucard couldn't be naïve. So he'd wait.

With another sigh, he ignored the third letter sitting on his desk—he knew that it was from Soren, and he didn't want to read his complaints.

A quiet knock then came at his door.

"What?" he called irritably.

The door opened, and Edwin stepped in with a small black cardboard box in his hands. "Your order from the emporium, sir. I collected it as soon as it was ready."

"Thank you," he said, tapping his desk. "Put it here."

Nodding, the butler made his way over and placed the box on his desk. "Is there anything else I can get for you, sir?"

Alucard shook his head. "No. Did you feed Sabazios and Peaches?"

"Yes, sir. The chickens have also been fed; it looks like it's going to be a cold day today, so we put them in the shed."

"Thank you," he said, leaning back in his seat. "Can you take some coffee to Zalith—if he hasn't already asked, please."

Edwin bowed humbly. "Of course, sir." Then, the butler turned around and left, closing the door behind him—and Peaches slinked inside just in time.

Alucard's gaze softened as his hairless cat scurried over to him, her small paws pattering against the floor. He smiled, tapping his lap in invitation, and without hesitation, she leapt up, settling comfortably against him. She meowed, staring up at him with wide, expectant eyes, and his brow furrowed slightly in concern.

"What's wrong?" he asked as she lifted a paw and patted his chest. Gently, he took hold of it, inspecting her tiny claws, where dirt had started to gather between them again. *Of course.* Hairless cats didn't have fur to help keep their paws clean, and without regular care, grime built up easily. He could have Edwin or one of the staff take care of it, but he'd much rather do it himself. "I have to make something for Zalith first, then I'll do them, okay?" he murmured with a small smile, giving her paw a light squeeze before releasing it.

Peaches meowed and pounced onto his desk; she strolled over to the cardboard box and sat beside it.

"It's a dream-eater," he said, pulling the box closer to himself as he took the lid off. "It'll stop Zalith from having bad dreams. These are the things I need to make it."

Peaches mewed softly before curling up in his lap again, her large eyes fixed curiously on his hands as he began unpacking the crystals and small rods of metal from the box.

Making the dream-eater would take time—careful work, precision—but Alucard knew exactly what he was doing. And more than that, he *knew* this would help Zalith. That alone steeled his resolve, sharpening his focus.

So with a determined expression, he focused and got to work.

⸻ ❖ ⸻

Two hours passed in quiet focus. Alucard worked meticulously, shaping the rose-gold metal rods into an intricate, tree-like structure. Each branch and twig was carefully bent, extending from the sturdy base—a large obsidian crystal that anchored the piece upright. He hadn't put nearly this much effort into his own dream-eater; his was a simple design, resembling the curve of a dragon's wing. But for Zalith, he had allowed himself a touch of creativity. He wanted it to be more than functional—he wanted it to be *beautiful*, something that would blend seamlessly into their bedroom without drawing too much attention.

With careful precision, he bent the last piece of metal into place, forming the tree's final branch. Once satisfied, he leaned back in his chair with a quiet sigh, stretching his fingers after hours of delicate work.

Peaches stirred, getting up from where she'd moved earlier and making her way towards him, her tiny paws stepping carefully around the scattered crystals and metal fragments on the desk. She meowed softly before leaping into his lap, curling up and purring as she kneaded at his leg with her front paws. Alucard huffed a quiet chuckle, knowing exactly what she wanted—he *had* promised to clean her paws once he was finished. But this was taking longer than expected.

"Okay," he said, scratching Peaches' ears. "I'll do them now."

Peaches let out a happy meow, shifting onto her back with a lazy stretch, exposing her tiny paws. Amused, Alucard reached into one of his desk drawers, pulling out a small pair of tweezers. He then carefully took hold of her front left paw, his fingers gentle as he began cleaning the dirt from between her claws and toes.

She purred contentedly, her tail flicking in satisfaction, and Alucard couldn't help but smile. There was something oddly soothing about the task, the simple act of tending to her bringing a quiet sense of fulfilment. Knowing that Peaches was grateful in her own small way only made it better. As he worked, he flicked the bits of dirt into the small trash bin beside his desk—the same one already filled with discarded labels and paper wrappings from the crystals he'd been working with earlier.

"Does that feel better?" he asked as he finished her last paw, tapping her nose with his own, and as she meowed happily, he kissed her head. "Good. You can sit here while I work if you want to," he then said, patting her head as he put the tweezers away.

Peaches curled up in his lap and purred quietly as Alucard prepared to get back to work.

Next, it was time to attach the crystals to the tree's branches. Like his own dream-eater, he'd gathered pieces of shungite, black onyx, fire agate, and smaller shards of obsidian. He took the thinner metal rods and began carefully wrapping the crystals into delicate wire cages, securing them without restricting their natural shapes. One by one, he hung them from the branches, ensuring balance in both form and function. The design was intricate, almost elegant, but more importantly, it would *work*.

As he worked, Alucard's thoughts drifted once more to the things he had done and the things he *wanted* to do for his and Zalith's cause. He supposed he could call it that. Zalith was building an empire, expanding his army with the sole purpose of destroying Lilith, Damien, and any Numen who dared to stand in their way. Alucard was certain that soon, demons and mortals alike would begin hearing whispers of Zalith's growing power, and some might even *choose* to join them. But they weren't there yet. Not quite. They needed something *big*, something that would send ripples across Aegisguard, and Alucard suspected that moment would come with Lilith's defeat. Not her *death*—not yet. The plan wasn't to kill her outright but to stage her downfall. A shapeshifter, disguised as Lilith, would fall before Zalith in a grand display, a spectacle meant to break her followers' loyalty and turn them to his side. Meanwhile, the *real* Lilith—wherever she was—would be left weakened, her power dwindling to nothing. And when the time was right, *then* they would strike, sealing her away forever in a Pandorican.

If they could get their hands on one.

But what could *he* do? Yes, he fought in battles—disorienting enemies, aiding their allies—but it wasn't enough. He *knew* that he could do more. The thought of expanding his own pack surfaced again, but that, too, had to wait. He had connections, influence, vampires scattered across the world, and his hand in countless businesses and organizations. *Surely* some of the people he knew could be of use.

Sighing, he fixed another caged crystal to the tree's branches, his mind still turning. He already had his best people working across Aegisguard. Crowell was tracking Ysmay and the Diabolus, Attila was searching for Pandoricans, and Soren was here, managing the demons that Zalith brought back from his fights. Luther… as much as Alucard didn't want to think about him, he'd been one of his best when it came to finding things. Maybe they'd have secured a Pandorican by now if Luther hadn't turned out to be who he was… *what* he was. And Felix… a well-trained brood nurse—he was dead, too. If he wasn't, Alucard could have been expanding his vampire numbers, strengthening their forces in ways only his kind could.

Maybe that was something to focus on: finding a new brood nurse. But that, too, would need Zalith's approval. Would he even *want* vampires in his army? They weren't true demons, just… *an echo* of one—a subspecies most demons saw as abominations. That was another conversation he'd have to have. Eventually.

Alucard sighed, fastening another piece of fire agate to the tree before glancing down at Peaches. She purred softly as he patted her head, the small comfort doing little to distract him from the quiet ache settling in his chest. It had been some time since he and Zalith parted to focus on their work, and already, he found himself missing him.

Back in their old home in Nefastus, their offices had been side by side. Even when buried in his own work, Alucard could hear Zalith's voice drifting through the walls, catching snippets of conversation whenever the demon spoke to someone. But here, their offices were in entirely different towers—too far apart for such familiarity. He loved this place, but there were things about it that he *didn't* like. The layout, for one. There hadn't been two rooms large enough to place their offices side by side, and those that *were* suitable either lacked en-suites or had configurations that didn't suit either of them. It was a small thing, but today, it weighed on him more than usual.

After fastening two more pieces of shungite to the tree, Alucard decided that it was time for a break. More importantly, it was time to see Zalith. He picked up Peaches and set her down in his chair before standing and heading for the door. But just as he went to leave, a barn owl swooped in through the open window, cutting through the air before landing on the nearby perch. Alucard frowned, turning towards it just as he noticed the brown envelope clutched in its beak.

With a quiet sigh, he made his way over. The owl tilted its head before extending the letter towards him, and the moment he took it, the bird flapped from its perch, settling instead on the window ledge. Alucard's frown deepened; if it was expecting a reply, then whatever was inside had to be important. Without hesitation, he slid a claw under the seal, tearing it open and pulling out the parchment within. His gaze flicked over the script—and immediately, he recognized the bold strokes of Dor-Sanguian.

It was from Rasmus, the only council member aside from Crowell who had survived the Diabolus' attack on his castle last Yule. Since then, Crowell had rebuilt the council, but it was *Rasmus* who led them now.

Alucard's grip tightened slightly around the letter. What could he possibly want?

My Lord,

I understand that now is a rather busy, strenuous time for you, so I held out writing this for as long as I could. But no longer can I manage this matter alone.

As per your order, the Coven Masters have been meeting every two weeks to share information and updates regarding the vampires under their care. The covens of Drydenheim, Boszorkány, DeiganLupus, Eleymond, Aresham, Olnstead, Antamont, and Noridge are all settling well with their new members, and the people of said places aren't causing any problems the Coven Masters can't handle. The same, however, can't be said for Atheson. Eyra, the Coven Master, has been taking part in some questionable activities, and the people of the city her coven lives close to have started searches and protests. Three vampires have been killed already, and Eyra has suggested she go to war with these people. I felt it necessary to inform you of her actions.

It may not be my place, but I also feel urged to mention our decline in numbers. Our people have suffered many losses and continue to suffer every other day because of issues such as that in Atheson. It has admittedly been hard scaring the humans into submission since the Lilidian cults and Diabolus have been sweeping the world without halt. Just as the Coven Masters start to make progress, these demons raid and pillage, and the humans are much more afraid of them than they are of the vampires. Please advise.

Rasmus. K.

Alucard exhaled a heavy sigh, sinking onto the couch near his office door. There was always *something*...something that refused to go right. Adjusting had been difficult for the Dor-Sanguian vampires; many had struggled to settle into the widespread covens scattered across Aegisguard, preferring the security of his presence. Now, they had to find new homes in unfamiliar places without him there to shield them. It gnawed at him; he *needed* to do something. They had to know that they were safe. They had to *feel* safe. But beyond that, he had to ensure that they could *stay* in their new homes without fear, without being cast out. And yet, in the places where they now lived, the people were too afraid—too consumed by their terror of the Lilidian cults and the Diabolus to even acknowledge the covens. That, too, was something he had to fix.

The vampire let out another sigh, dragging a hand over his face before dropping the letter onto the seat beside him. His first priority had to be Eyra, the leader of the Atheson coven. He couldn't allow her to start a war with the humans there—not now. That was the last thing he needed. He couldn't even make up for the losses that they'd *already* suffered, let alone the destruction that would follow if tensions escalated into open conflict. And then there was the matter of their dwindling numbers. He *needed* to find another brood nurse—*more than one*, if possible. Only then could he begin to rebuild, to replenish his people and strengthen the covens once more.

Exhaling, he pushed himself up from the couch and strode back to his desk. Lifting Peaches from his chair, he settled her in his lap before pulling out a fresh sheet of parchment and an envelope from a drawer. He nudged Zalith's nearly finished dream-eater aside, along with the crystals still waiting to be attached, clearing space before him. Then, he reached for his quill, uncorked a bottle of ink, and dipped the tip inside.

Alucard began writing. He instructed Rasmus to gather all Coven Masters and their eldest members at Fort Rudă de Sânge—the council's meeting ground, a place Alucard only visited when necessary. In two weeks, he would meet with them all. Not only would he address the tensions in Atheson, but he would also begin seeking candidates to become brood nurses, a necessary step towards rebuilding their dwindling numbers.

Beyond that, he suspected that he might need to personally visit the covens to ensure they had the strength to stand against the Lilidian cults and the Diabolus. But with greater numbers, that task would become far more manageable. If the covens could grow, if they could expand their reach, they could keep the Diabolus and the cultists from tightening their grip on the regions where they lived.

Sealing the letter with wax, he gestured to the owl, holding the envelope out. The bird took it without hesitation and then launched itself into the air, vanishing through the open window, heading back to Rasmus.

Now all that was left was to speak with Zalith.

Alucard wasn't about to waste more time lingering in his office—he'd already decided that he was going to see him.

He stood up, lifted Peaches, and set her down in his chair before turning towards the door. And without another thought, he left.

Chapter Twenty-Five

― ᐸ † ᐳ ―

A Discussion of Updates

| **Alucard**—*Uzlia Isles, Usrul, Castle Reiner* |

Alucard made his way through the dimly lit corridors. He followed the familiar path—through the hallway, down a quiet passage, and finally to the spiralling staircase that led up to the tower where Zalith's office sat. As he ascended, the sound of the demon's voice echoed from above, low and steady. Who was he speaking to? His curiosity grew as he reached the top of the stairs and stepped towards the office door, and without hesitation, he pushed it open.

Zalith sat behind his desk, his expression unreadable as he extended a shimmering gold coin to a small izuret. The delicate, winged demon chirped in gratitude, clutching the coin tightly before gliding effortlessly towards the open window. With a final flutter, it disappeared.

"Hey," Zalith said with a smile, looking across the room at Alucard, resting his arms on his desk.

Closing the door being him, Alucard smiled and said, "Hi. What did the izuret want?" He walked over to Zalith's desk and sat in one of the leather armchairs.

"He was just bringing updates from Orin."

"Has he found anything yet?"

"He's still working on it," he said with a sigh. "But he believes he has a lead—one of his men heard from some of her cultists that Lilith may be attending a gathering for some sort of ritual at some point. He doesn't have too many details. I also had him send one of his men to watch Vila—the scion we learned of from Alegan."

Alegan, the Alpha Zalith killed the night before last. "The Numen sometimes gather their followers—or as many of them as they can—and they do things for them...grant their wishes or whatever. That increases their belief and loyalty. Lilith hasn't done anything for anyone in a long time—maybe never. She's never really had to do anything for her followers because no one ever stopped believing in her. Her scions would enforce her will, so a lot of people followed her out of fear. It's also very easy to be a Lilith cultist—you don't have to do so much to praise her and worship her," he muttered. "But now that she's losing followers, maybe she's decided to start doing things for those who remain to keep them from leaving," he suggested.

"Well, she certainly ignored my parents all the time, and they were obsessed with her. I can't see why, though."

Alucard shrugged. "A lot of people spend their lives believing that they just have to keep praying and offering, and one day, the gods will answer. It's strange that she didn't answer your parents—they were scions, no?"

Zalith nodded. "If my memory serves, I think she said something about being mad at them for leaving Aegisguard."

"Why *did* they leave Aegisguard?" the vampire asked. He didn't actually know why Zalith's parents had chosen to leave this realm and head into a smaller pocket world with no Numen presence other than Erich, who never showed his face there anyway.

The demon shrugged. "To start anew in unclaimed territory. I never really asked. But I do know that a lot of Lilith's scions moved over to Eltaria, and that's where my parents met—they weren't together when they and the other scions left Aegisguard."

Alucard nodded, leaning back in his seat. "And then *you* decided to move back over here," he said, smiling. "Do you think…we would have still met if you didn't live in Eltaria?"

Zalith thought to himself for a few moments but smiled at him. "I still would have found you," he said confidently.

With a flustered smile, Alucard looked down at his lap. He laughed slightly, glancing at him again. "What would you have done if I wasn't interested? I could have been straight, you know," he teased, smirking.

Leaning his face on his hand, Zalith hummed, "I'd love you from afar. I might have turned into an Elvin and always been at your side."

Amused, Alucard laughed and looked down at his lap again. "I never really knew what I wanted back then—I wasn't exactly looking. But then you came along, and I realized that I'd been waiting for you for a very long time without even knowing."

"I realized the same thing about myself, too," Zalith said quietly.

"And now we're engaged," Alucard said contently.

Zalith smirked seductively. "And have sex all the time."

Alucard pouted, certain that embarrassment now smothered his face. "What would you have thought if I was one of those weird Letholdus believers that think premarital sex is a sin? Three years without it?" he teased him.

The demon laughed. "Well, we would have been married by now, that's for sure. But I think I might have been able to convince you to go against your beliefs."

Alucard shrugged. "I don't doubt that."

Zalith rested his arms on his desk again. "Speaking of getting married, we should talk about our wedding plans soon."

Immediately, excitement enthralled Alucard. "Do we need to look for a planner to hire?"

"I think that's probably the smart thing to do."

"When should we look? Maybe…tonight…after we're done with Cecil? Or tomorrow, maybe?" he asked, a little eager.

"I don't even know where to look in a place like this," his mate said. "We'll probably have to bring someone in from overseas."

"I can get Soren to find someone," Alucard suggested. "If you want."

The demon nodded. "Good. That might shut him up for a while."

Alucard laughed quietly. "I'll send him a letter before we leave today."

"Okay," Zalith said, smiling again. "Thank you."

"Did you get all of your work done?" Alucard then asked.

"Never," the demon replied with a sigh.

He nodded slowly. "Well…there's something I need to talk to you about."

"What?" Zalith asked, a little hesitation in his voice.

"It's nothing bad," Alucard assured him. "Well…nothing that will hinder this mission."

"What is it?" the demon questioned.

"I need to go to Fort Rudă de Sânge to meet with the Coven Masters. Things in the world of vampires have been…tough lately. Rasmus has done a remarkable job of keeping everything and everyone in check, but he has brought to my attention that there are some things he cannot manage."

"What can he not manage?" Zalith asked, looking concerned.

"A lot of the vampires I saved from Dor-Sanguis are struggling to settle into their new homes. They're used to having me around; my presence makes them feel safer. I have to go to them and make them see that everything will be okay. One of my Coven Masters, Eyra, is causing problems. The people of the city close to where the coven lives have killed a few vampires, and Eyra is threatening to start a war—I don't need that right now. I have to help them scare the humans into submission, but the humans are too busy being scared of the Diabolus and Lilidian cults that make their way through that place every week. I need to find another brood nurse so that I can increase the numbers in these covens, and then they can fight off the cults and make sure these cities belong to the vampires," he explained. "It's been a struggle for everyone since the Numen started looking for us, and it's only getting worse. I have to do something."

Zalith nodded. "Okay. How long do you think it'll take?"

"I told Rasmus to have everyone convene in two weeks. I don't know how long it'll take, but the meeting should only take an hour or two—maybe more if they all have things for me to do," he mumbled.

"Do you want me to go with you?"

Alucard nodded. He didn't want to go anywhere without Zalith again—he knew how he felt, and he just wanted him to be happy. And...he didn't exactly want to go alone anyway. It was often stressful and annoying talking business with so many of his subordinates, and he knew that all he would want after was Zalith and his embrace. "I do," he replied. "As long as you're not going to touch my leg under the table again and make me yell at you," he said with a pout.

Zalith laughed quietly. "What if I touch it a little? But platonically—like a friend?"

The vampire pouted again. "Friends don't touch each other's legs like that, Zalith. And I don't want you to act like my friend; just don't touch my legs," he said as sternly as he could through his pout.

"What about your butt?" Zalith asked with a smirk.

Alucard grew more flustered by the second as he scowled and looked away from him. "Only when we're not in the meeting."

"What if my hand is on the chair that you're sitting on by accident and you don't notice and sit down?" he asked, still smirking.

"Then I guess it's an accident," he said with a shrug.

"Okay, good, because I'd probably just leave my hand there so you don't get embarrassed in front of your vampires."

The vampire sighed and smiled. "Do you want to touch my butt, Zalith?" he asked, sure that that was what his mate wanted—*he* admittedly wanted it too.

"Always," the demon said.

Alucard got up and made his way around to Zalith's side of the desk. As the demon swivelled in his seat to face him, Alucard climbed on the demon and straddled his lap, moving his arms around his shoulders. "You can touch it," he said, resting his forehead against Zalith's.

The demon laughed again. "Oh, thank you," he said, and then he moved his hands down Alucard's body and gripped his ass.

With a deep exhale, Alucard rested his head on Zalith's shoulder, wrapping his arms around him. He wanted to enjoy his attention for a little while, but they both had work to do, and today, they couldn't really afford to hang about.

He nuzzled the demon's neck. "When do you want to start getting ready to leave?"

"We might as well right now," he said.

The vampire nodded. "Okay, well, I'm going to go and write that letter for Soren, and then I'll be ready. Meet me in the hall in...fifteen minutes?"

"Okay," Zalith said, tucking a loose strand of Alucard's hair behind his ear. "I'll see you then," he said and kissed his lips.

With a content smile, Alucard slipped from Zalith's lap and left his office, his steps light as he made his way downstairs, through the hall, and back to his own office. The moment he pushed the door open, Peaches greeted him from atop his desk, sitting beside the nearly finished dream-eater he'd been crafting. He'd hoped to complete it before tonight, and he still intended to—he'd work on it more once they returned from Eimwood.

Settling into his chair, he pulled out a piece of parchment and dipped his quill into ink, quickly drafting a letter to Soren with a simple request: find a wedding planner. When he finished, he summoned an owl, handing off the letter before watching it vanish through the open window.

Without wasting another moment, he scooped Peaches into his arms and left, descending the stairs once more.

As he stepped into the main hall, his gaze immediately found Zalith, who was already waiting for him, his redingote draped over his shoulders. Over one arm, the demon carried Alucard's cape, and as soon as he noticed him approaching, he turned fully, his lips curling into a knowing smile.

"Thank you," Alucard said, taking his cape from him. "Do you want me to fly us over to the city?" he asked, putting Peaches down as he pulled his cape on.

The demon smiled again as Alucard took hold of his hand. "Sure," he said, walking at Alucard's side as the vampire led the way over to the door.

"We can head straight for the watchpoint near Cecil's estate, and then we can wait until he leaves and follow him," the vampire said as they stepped out into the courtyard.

Zalith nodded. "Sounds good."

Alucard then wrapped his arms around the demon and dematerialized them both into vermillion smoke. Without any falter, he took off, heading towards Eimwood.

Chapter Twenty-Six

The Cave

| **Alucard**—*Uzlia Isles, Yrudberg, Eimwood City* |

Once they landed in the alley behind the confectionery store, Alucard unlocked the door to the room upstairs. He led the way with Zalith following behind him, and as they ascended, he looked back over his shoulder at the demon. "Did your parents ever work for or with Lilith?" he asked, still curious about Zalith's family.

"They did," his mate confirmed.

"Did they still work for her when they had you? Well…they moved to Eltaria, no? So…I would guess not."

Zalith nodded as they reached the top of the stairs. "Yeah, they pretty much stopped working for her when they moved to Eltaria," he confirmed.

"Did *you* ever work for her?" Alucard asked, making his way over to the only uncovered window.

"No," the demon said, standing on the opposite side of the window.

"I don't know why anyone would *willingly* want to work for any Numen."

Zalith nodded in agreement. "So far, the ones I've met have been extremely unlikable."

"I guess a lot of people are either afraid or crave recognition," Alucard said with a shrug.

The demon shrugged too.

Alucard then scowled, setting his eyes on Cecil, who was waddling through his grounds, waving around a dishcloth as his wife, Mirabella, yelled at him from the porch. "He usually leaves around now," he said to Zalith.

"What are they arguing about?" his mate asked as Cecil and his wife yelled at one another.

Focusing, Alucard listened in on their argument. "She's…tired of him disappearing for half of every day and night, and he's tired of her and her boring taste in tablecloths," he said, watching as Cecil threw the dishcloth at his wife. "He also hates the material their dishcloths are made out of...and she's tired of telling him that dishcloths aren't meant to be used...in the bathroom," he continued—he cared not to repeat Mirabella's vulgar words.

"He sounds like quite the catch," Zalith said with a quiet laugh.

Alucard shook his head. "We might be doing that woman a favour by getting rid of him," he mumbled.

Zalith nodded again.

"Do you think his wife knows what he's doing in that cave?" the vampire asked, glancing at Zalith.

"I'm not sure. Did Danford say anything about his family?"

Alucard shook his head. "No."

"Oh well," Zalith said with a sigh.

Cecil walked back out of his home, now wearing a coat. Alucard watched as he strutted down to his carriage, and as he always did, he climbed inside and had it head for the city's exit.

"He's leaving," the vampire said. "Let's go."

"Okay," Zalith said, following as he walked towards the stairs.

Alucard had no intention of wasting time. The sooner they uncovered whatever Cecil was doing in that cave, the sooner they could drive him out of the city—and when that happened, both he and Zalith would claim their rightful place as its new Lords. But if Cecil truly *was* an Insectumoid, things could become complicated. A *giant beetle* would be far more troublesome to deal with than a mere man if they were caught. Still, neither of them intended to let that happen. They knew what they were doing, and they had no plans to reveal themselves.

Without a word, they slipped out of the building, heading towards the main road as they began trailing Cecil.

Alucard led them down a narrow street, keeping a firm grip on Zalith's hand as they turned into a shadowed alleyway. Silently, they cloaked themselves with their demon ethos, masking their presence as Cecil's carriage rumbled along the stone roads ahead. They followed it as it crossed the bridge from the Bauwell Residential District into Oklens, but rather than taking the same path, the vampire veered towards a more discreet route.

At the edge of the city, nestled near the river's end, stood a crooked bridge—a weathered, decaying structure that few dared to use. It had long since fallen out of favour with the locals, its unstable appearance making it unappealing to most. But for Alucard and Zalith, it was perfect. With no prying eyes to worry about, they crossed swiftly, slipping unseen into Oklens as they continued their pursuit.

Once they reached Oklens, they navigated the winding alleys of the docks, keeping as close to the main road as possible without exposing themselves. Moving unseen through the narrow passages, they shadowed Cecil's carriage as it rolled through Oklens Market, through the district, and finally out of the city's main gate.

From there, they used the cover of the trees, ensuring that they remained neither seen nor heard. As expected, Cecil's carriage came to a halt about ten minutes into the forest; the door opened, and Cecil stepped out.

Alucard knew what would happen next—Cecil would disappear, just like before. But it didn't matter. The vampire had already committed the route to memory; he knew the way to the cave that Cecil had been visiting.

Still concealed by their ethos, Alucard tightened his grip on Zalith's hand and silently took the lead, guiding them deeper into the forest, towards the cave at the river's end.

"Did you survey the area?" Zalith asked quietly as they neared the river, his voice barely audible over the increasing roar of the waterfall cascading over the cave's entrance.

"No," Alucard answered. "I couldn't see past the entrance, so I didn't want to look around in case there was anything dangerous. It was probably stupid of me not to, though," he added with a shrug.

The demon shook his head as they approached the tree line. "No, it wasn't. I'd rather have you safe than out there alone with only Danford as backup."

"Is he any good in combat?" Alucard asked. "I've never seen him fight."

The demon nodded as they stopped at the edge of the tree line. "He was a lone wolf for about nine years before he joined Greymore's pack, and all the while, I had him working on money dealings on his own with questionable people. Those things tend to go south on occasion," he said with a quiet laugh. "He can handle himself, but if you two were to come across something that could hurt *you*, then Danford would be no match, I'm sure," he explained.

Alucard glared ahead at the cave. He wasn't even sure why he'd asked; he didn't like Danford, nor did he care to learn anything about him. But…he did find himself often wondering if the werewolf had once had feelings for Zalith—or he still did. "At least he isn't obsessed with you," he mumbled.

Zalith laughed again, glancing at him. "Why would he be obsessed with me?"

Shrugging, Alucard kept his eyes on the cave. "I don't know. If you and I had a thing for a while, I wouldn't be able to get over it, and I'd probably scramble around trying to get you to notice me again," he said with a pout. "Danford seems like the type to scramble around in search of your attention."

With an endearing smile, Zalith placed his hand on Alucard's shoulder. "He *does* seem like the type, but he and I never had an emotional connection—especially not one like we have."

The vampire smiled a little and then looked back out at the cave's entrance. "Okay," he said. "I just...don't like him much," he admitted. "And when I try to at least tolerate him, he just...annoys me."

Zalith laughed quietly. "I was surprised to hear that you took him instead of Greymore."

"Thomas was sleeping in—he snores louder than a thunderstorm," he said with a roll of his eyes. "Either he couldn't handle the hangover from what we drank the day before, or he had more to drink when he got home. The latter seems more like him."

He laughed again. "His snoring is a small part of why Varana stopped staying with them in Eltaria during the war."

Alucard smirked amusedly. "I'm surprised we didn't hear it from the castle," he said, glancing at him. "Anyway, are you ready to go?" he asked, nodding at the cave.

"I'm ready," Zalith confirmed.

As they emerged from the tree line, Zalith extended an arm, a silent signal that he would go in first. Alucard slowed his pace, falling in behind him as they approached the waterfall, its crashing roar masking their movements. Beyond the curtain of water lay the cave entrance, dark and yawning, its depths still a mystery.

Alucard wasn't sure what they would find inside. He *suspected* that Cecil was an Insectumoid—but there was still a chance he was wrong. The shell he'd found yesterday *could* have been unrelated, just some other Insectumoid wandering these woods. But something told him that wasn't the case.

No—his instincts screamed that this was *Cecil*.

And he was certain that very soon, they'd find out.

| **Zalith**—*Uzlia Isles, Yrudberg, Yrudberg Woods* |

Zalith stepped into the cave, leading the way into a wide cavern that stretched deeper into the darkness. The air was thick with damp and stagnant rot, the walls slick with moisture, but beneath it all was another scent—one he couldn't quite place. It was repulsive, cloying, like something long dead had been left to decay. He scowled in disgust but ignored it, glancing back just once to make sure that Alucard was close. His vampire moved beside him, silent and steady, prompting Zalith to turn his attention forward once more.

A frown tugged at the demon's brow. He could no longer sense the world outside. The ethos-blocking barrier that concealed the cave worked both ways—those outside couldn't see in, and those inside were just as blind to what lay beyond. It left an unsettling weight in his chest, but he pushed it aside. Whatever was ahead, he would handle it. More importantly, he wouldn't let anything happen to Alucard. No matter what.

Moving carefully, Zalith advanced through the cavern, his focus divided between his fiancé at his side and whatever lay in wait. He reached out with his sensory ethos, scanning the area ahead. At first, he picked up nothing unusual—bats, rats, the small insects one would expect in a place like this. But as he pushed his reach further, something shifted.

A mass of energy. Twisted. *Distorted.*

He looked at Alucard. "Did it mention anywhere in your book about Insectumoids being able to distort sensory ethos?" he questioned quietly.

"No. But there wasn't a lot in there—whoever wrote the book clearly hadn't researched them much."

Zalith sighed. "I hope there aren't any more surprises."

"I'm sorry," Alucard said despondently. "I should have done more research."

"It's okay," he assured him, keeping his voice hushed. "I'm sure we'll be fine."

As the vampire nodded, they both glared ahead, continuing deeper into the cave.

The cavern began to slope upward, leading them higher into the depths of the cave. Before long, they reached the edge of a jagged cliff, the ground dropping off sharply below. From here, the distorted energy pulsed stronger than ever, thick and unnatural, pressing against Zalith's senses. Whatever was hiding here, it was down there.

Moving silently, he crouched low and crept towards the ledge, motioning for Alucard to stay close. As he leaned forward, peering over the edge to see what lay beneath, a wave of putrid air hit him—rancid, festering, *wrong*. The stench was so overpowering that his stomach twisted, but it was what he *saw* that made him fight the urge to gag.

Sitting in the lagoon that connected to the stream feeding the waterfall outside was a grotesque, muddy-green-skinned creature unlike anything Zalith had ever seen. Well…*not quite*. He knew that it was a troll—he'd encountered plenty before—but none quite like *this*. Draped over its massive frame was a patchwork gown, crudely stitched together from at least fifteen different expensive dresses—undoubtedly stolen from Cecil's human wife. Atop its misshapen head, four short, stumpy brown horns jutted out, while its left ear—elf-like in shape—was ragged and half-torn away. Two disturbingly human teeth protruded past its upper lip, lips that were smeared in garish red lipstick, and its long, rotting fingernails were painted the same shade—*badly,* Zalith noted—as were the nails on its thick, calloused feet.

But what *truly* turned his stomach was what sat at the troll's feet.

One of its bloated legs rested outside the water, stretched out in eerie relaxation, as something large nuzzled against it. A *human-sized cockroach* clung to the crusted, filth-covered skin, its mandibles working away at the grime in slow bites.

Zalith's entire body recoiled. A sharp wave of nausea curled through him as he brought a hand to his face, covering his nose and mouth. The stench was near unbearable—thick, rancid, potent enough to make his head spin. The last thing he wanted was to inhale the same foul air as *that* creature and *that*…thing.

But the *thing*—he focused, pushing past his revulsion, sharpening his senses. And there it was. The unmistakable signature of *Cecil's* aura.

Cecil. The Insectumoid. The man who played Lord of this city was nothing more than a giant, man-sized cockroach, making a meal out of a troll's festering foot.

And that troll? *That* explained the distortion in his sensory ethos. Zalith had encountered trolls before, and all of them had the same unnatural resistance to ethos—it made them difficult to track and even harder to fight.

But the troll was not the problem here.

The *real* problem sat at its feet. And now, Zalith knew exactly what they were dealing with.

However, the sickening sight *did* bring a smile to the demon's face. This was everything he needed to have Cecil removed from Eimwood.

He glanced at Alucard, seeing the nauseous look on his face—not only did he look like he was going to throw up, but he seemed almost afraid.

"Are you scared?" the demon whispered.

Sharply turning his head, Alucard glared at him.

Before the vampire could speak, the sudden splash of water below yanked their attention back to the troll—and to *Cecil.*

Zalith's stomach twisted in revulsion as they watched the troll lazily pull her leg back into the lagoon, sending ripples across the murky surface. As she shifted, the giant cockroach scuttled over her other leg, then up her bloated torso. And in that moment, it became *painfully* clear that the troll was female—blindingly obvious as she moved her arm, revealing far more of herself than Zalith ever wanted to see. *Three* almost rectangular breasts, all coated with grime.

But what made his skin *crawl* was what happened next.

Cecil reached her face, his mandibles twitching, and instead of stopping, he leaned in, his mouth—*his disgusting, insect mouth*—nibbling at her lipstick-smeared lips.

Alucard retched quietly, turning his head away as the troll opened its mouth, letting the giant cockroach clean her teeth.

The demon laughed quietly, glancing at his fiancé. "Do you need to leave?"

Shaking his head, the vampire kept his eyes off the creatures below.

Zalith refocused. Every fibre of his being recoiled in disgust, but this was *good* for business. If the people of Eimwood saw *this,* Cecil would be ousted without Zalith or Alucard having to lift a finger. He could spread the word—subtly, carefully—without positioning himself as an antagonist, and once the rumours took hold, the people would come looking. Just as he and Alucard had, they would find the *truth* lurking in this cave.

And that truth would destroy Cecil.

But before Zalith could dwell on the idea further, his attention snapped back to the horror unfolding below.

Cecil, having apparently finished cleaning the inside of the troll's mouth, began making his way down her body. His spindly legs twitched as he reached for the tangled straps of her patchwork gown, and then he started to unfasten it.

Alucard shook his head. "Okay, we're leaving—"

"Wait," Zalith said, gently snatching his arm. He wanted to make sure that the relationship Cecil had with this troll was sexual. After all, maybe he was just helping this troll, but if he could confirm their relationship, it would only strengthen his case when it came to revealing everything to the people of the city.

So he watched as the giant cockroach pulled off the troll's dress and started chewing the warts off her body. But once Cecil started crawling down past the troll's waist, Zalith was certain that he'd seen enough. It was time to leave. He scowled in revolt and turned around—he didn't need to see anything more. All he needed to do now was work out how he was going to go about revealing this to the city.

The demon took hold of Alucard's hand and silently led the way out of the cave. Relief struck him once he stood in fresh air and sunlight, and he felt Alucard relax a little, too.

His fiancé took out his sunglasses, putting them on as Zalith led the way to the forest. "So...you have a plan?" he asked.

"I do," Zalith confirmed. "I'm going to send Danford and Greymore to two separate taverns in the Bauwell District to spread word of Cecil and this cave. I'll get them to talk to some well-known gossipers so stories will spread fast. They'll talk about how they've both been suspicious of Cecil for a while now—that they followed him together to that cave and perhaps they might even mention that they saw him turn into an insect," he started.

Alucard nodded, staring at him as they walked through the forest.

"I have a meeting with the council tomorrow to talk about handing out medicines and supplies. They're bound to ask me about the water situation—they always do—so I'll tell them that I've had some people doing tests on the water and that whatever's going on with it could be dangerous, so I want them to finish the tests before anyone goes investigating anything. That will give the gossip more time to spread. Then, I'll tell them that if the tests come back inconclusive—which they will—I'll send some of my people to investigate the cave. When the time comes, I'll say I don't have enough people to spare, and some of the city people will volunteer, I'm sure. They'll head to the cave at the right time to see Cecil and the troll together to confirm the rumour that I had Danford and Greymore start."

"It's a really good plan. You really are so smart," Alucard said with a smirk. "You come up with plans so fast—I love that about you."

Zalith smiled at him. "Thank you. We might have to make a few changes along the way, but I'm glad you like it."

Alucard smiled—

"Do you still have that shell you used to find Cecil?" Zalith asked.

He frowned. "I do."

"I'm thinking that we can break it into pieces and give one each to Danford and Greymore so that they have a little evidence to back up their story."

Alucard nodded. "It's in my office—I can get it when we get home."

"Okay. Thank you."

They continued through the forest in silence, eventually finding their way to the path that led back to Eimwood's gates.

Zalith smiled at Alucard. "You were very brave back there with the big bug man," he teased him.

Alucard pouted, glaring at him. "Are you making fun of me?" he grumbled.

Zalith frowned. "No, baby—I'm not making fun of you," he said with a quiet laugh.

"You probably think it's stupid how someone as old and strong as me is scared of something like an insect," he mumbled. "You laughed at me when I told you I'm afraid of moths."

"I don't think it's stupid," he assured him. "Which is why I said you were brave because I thought you did good. But if you can't accept the compliment then never mind," he said, still teasing him.

Alucard sighed quietly. "I feel embarrassed about being so afraid of bugs. But thank you."

"To be fair, bugs are disgusting—especially ones that are six feet tall and do unsavoury things with trolls."

The vampire grimaced. "I don't... I want to erase all of that from my memory. Why did I have to see that?" he complained.

"You won't have to see them again—don't worry," Zalith said. "At least not together... hopefully."

As they made their way towards the city gates, Alucard sighed and looked at Zalith. "I guess so." He paused before asking, "Do you want to get lunch?"

Zalith smiled and laughed quietly. "Can you stomach lunch after seeing that?"

The vampire pouted. "Maybe. I know I want something sweet, though."

With another quiet laugh, Zalith pulled out his pocket watch—the same pocket watch that Alucard had given him. He took it everywhere, always. He opened it to check the time, and then he smiled at Alucard again, putting it away. "Yeah, we can get lunch."

Smiling, Alucard squeezed Zalith's hand and started leading the way towards the city. "I saw a good place when I was in the city yesterday."

"Where is it?" Zalith asked.

"It's in Bauwell, next to the river."

"That sounds nice," the demon said contently.

With a nod, Alucard began leading the way, and Zalith did his best to put any and all memory of Cecil and that troll out of his mind.

Chapter Twenty-Seven

The Strawberry Saloon and Restaurant

| **Alucard**—*Uzlia Isles, Yrudberg, Eimwood City* |

Alucard and Zalith made their way back into the city, weaving through the familiar streets as the people of Eimwood greeted them with the usual warmth. Some offered smiles from a distance, while others went out of their way to approach, eager to exchange pleasantries. The vampire and demon returned their greetings, maintaining the charm and presence that had already won them the city's admiration. The trust they had cultivated reassured Alucard—when the time came for Cecil's removal, their takeover would be seamless. That knowledge was a relief.

Still holding Zalith's hand, Alucard led them through the winding streets of Oklens, across the bridge, and into the Bauwell Residential District. Once they reached the main street, they turned right, heading towards their destination.

The Strawberry Saloon and Restaurant stood out even among the elegant buildings lining the district. Its rich mahogany exterior was adorned with carefully tended rose bushes and climbing strawberry plants, giving the air around it a faint, sweet fragrance. The ground-floor windows were set with intricate stained glass, their vibrant designs depicting horses, strawberries, and delicate flowers. Outside, a few small round tables were arranged along the walkway, occupied by couples enjoying tea and cakes, and above on the balcony, more patrons dined in the afternoon light, laughter and conversation drifting down to the street.

It was crowded—busier than usual—but as they approached, Alucard's gaze caught on one of the barmaids inside. The moment she spotted them, her eyes widened in excitement. Without hesitation, she darted behind the bar and disappeared through a door at the back.

Moments later, the owner emerged from the back room in a hurried rush, smoothing down his hair and adjusting his suit. A wide grin spread across his face as he strode towards them, his arms outstretched in an exuberant greeting. "Silas! Ezra!" he called warmly, laughter threading through his voice. "How wonderful to see you both." Stopping in front of them, he beamed up at them, barely reaching five-foot-seven—a noticeable contrast to their towering figures. As he spoke, his fingers absently toyed with his paper-thin moustache, a habit that only added to his usual animated charm.

"We'd like a table, please," Alucard said.

"Ah, of course, of course," the owner replied, holding out his arm towards the stairs that led to the upper floor. "I have the back balcony already prepared for you—such a beautiful view of the river," he said with a smile, starting to lead the way over to the stairs.

Alucard glanced at Zalith, amusement flickering in his eyes. He was almost certain that the owner had just ordered his staff to clear the entire back balcony—either that or it had yet to open for the day, and the man had decided to make a special exception just for them. "Thank you," he said smoothly, still holding Zalith's hand as they followed the owner up the stairs.

"This way, this way!" the owner said excitedly as they reached the top of the stairs, his enthusiasm practically infectious. He hurried ahead, leading them to a set of double doors that opened onto the balcony. "Right here, yes," he continued, pushing the doors open with a flourish before stepping aside to reveal the setup beyond.

The balcony was empty, save for a single elegantly arranged table. A private setting—just for them.

"Just for you," the man beamed, gesturing grandly towards the table. A strawberry-patterned tablecloth draped over it, the design charming yet tasteful, and at its centre sat a beautifully arranged bouquet of fresh flowers, their vibrant petals adding a final, thoughtful touch.

Once they reached the table, the owner immediately pulled out Alucard's chair for him. As the vampire sat down, he caught Zalith's irritated glare, which was fixed on the man, even when he pulled out the other seat for him.

The owner clapped his hands together and smiled down at them both. "Can I get you anything?" he asked. "Drinks? Water? Perhaps something sweet?"

"Can I have one of those chocolate milkshake things, please?" the vampire requested.

"Of course, of course," the owner said with a wide smile, nodding. "And for you?" he asked, looking at Zalith.

"Your best white wine, but nothing too dry."

The owner nodded again and then hastily rushed off, leaving them alone—at last.

Zalith smiled across the table at Alucard.

Alucard returned his smile, slipping off his sunglasses and setting them beside him. "Why are you mad at the owner?" he asked.

The demon grunted. "*I* wanted to pull your chair out for you."

He laughed a little and smiled. "I love when you're possessive like this."

Zalith smiled, too. "I just like people to know that you're mine."

Alucard flashed his engagement ring as he shrugged his cape off. "Well, I think this is proof enough of that." He draped his cape over the back of his chair.

"I suppose it is," his mate said flirtatiously.

A little flustered, Alucard's gaze drifted down to the river below. Despite knowing that the water was polluted—and understanding all too well the reason behind it—the view remained undeniably beautiful. Rose bushes clung to the stone walls of the riverbed, their vibrant blossoms cascading over the edges. A few ducks floated serenely on the surface, and a lone man in a small kayak paddled downstream, his quiet huffs of effort barely audible over the gentle rush of the current.

"It's a beautiful view," Zalith said.

Resting his arms on the table, Alucard nodded. "It's been a while since we came out, so I thought it would be nice to come somewhere pretty."

"That's very cute," the demon said, leaning forward a little. He reached out his left hand and placed it on the side of Alucard's face.

Alucard's flustered smile made Zalith smirk, and in an attempt to distract himself, the vampire said, "I hope the food is good."

"Me too," his mate said, picking up two of the four menus that were sitting at the end of their table. "It would be nice to have a place to visit regularly," he added, handing Alucard one of the menus.

"Thank you," he said, taking it from him. "And it would," he agreed. "It'll make a change from having lunch at home all the time."

Zalith smirked. "I suppose you can drink my blood just about anywhere, though," he said, glancing up from his menu as he opened it.

"That's true," Alucard agreed, opening his own menu, smirking slightly. "And it's my favourite thing—I think I like it more than chocolate…and cake."

"Thank you. I'm glad you like it. I make it just for you."

The vampire smiled, looking down at his menu. "I don't know where I'd be without you."

"And I, you," Zalith replied, and then he asked, "So, what do you want other than my blood?"

Alucard couldn't help but blush. "What?" he mumbled.

"From your menu, vampire," he laughed.

Embarrassment smothered Alucard's face as he looked down at his menu. "Oh…well…I like…the sound of this salmon," he said. "What about you?" he asked, looking at Zalith. "Do you know what you want?"

Zalith skimmed his menu. "Hmm…I think I'm going to have the club sandwich," he said, placing it down.

"Your drinks," the owner then called, making his way back out onto the balcony.

They both glanced at him as he made his way over with a tray; on it sat Alucard's chocolate milkshake, a bottle of white wine in an ice bucket, and two glasses.

"Thank you," Zalith said as the man placed their drinks and the glasses down on the table.

"Have you decided what you'd like?" he then asked, holding the tray behind his back. "Or would you like more time? No pressure," he laughed.

"We've decided," Zalith said. "The Salmon for Ezra, please, and I'll have the club sandwich."

"Perfect—great choices," the man said with a smile and a nod. "I'll bring it to you as soon as possible."

"Thank you," Alucard murmured, offering a polite nod as the owner bustled away. His gaze then drifted down to the chocolate milkshake in front of him, a small smile curling at his lips as he plucked the ripe strawberry from atop the whipped cream.

He felt eyes on him.

Glancing up, he caught Zalith watching him, something playful—something *hungry*—lingering in his expression. Smirking slightly, Alucard held out the strawberry in offering.

Zalith leaned in, resting an elbow against the table as he closed the distance between them. His smirk deepened before he bit down on the fruit, his dark eyes locked onto Alucard's the entire time. The slowness of it sent a shiver through the vampire, heat creeping up his spine.

"Thank you," the demon said, his voice low, smooth. He chewed leisurely before swallowing, his smirk never faltering.

Alucard exhaled softly, placing the strawberry's leafy stem on the table. He twirled his straw through the milkshake, taking a sip as he watched Zalith.

"Do you like it?" his mate asked, taking the bottle of wine out of the ice bucket.

The vampire nodded contently. "It's really sweet."

"Good," the demon said, pulling the cork from the wine bottle. "Do you want to try some?" he asked, pouring himself a glass.

He was curious to try it. "Yes, please."

With a smile on his face, Zalith handed his glass to Alucard.

"Thank you," he said, and then, he took a sip. He didn't enjoy white wine as much as he enjoyed red, but admittedly, it was actually rather tasty. "It's good," he said, handing the glass back to Zalith.

"If you want some, let me know and I'll pour you a glass."

"Okay," Alucard replied. "Do you want to try some of this?" he asked, glancing down at his milkshake.

"Sure."

Alucard handed him his milkshake, and as Zalith took a sip through the straw, he smiled

The demon then handed it back to him. "It's good."

"It's probably not a good combination with the food I ordered," he admitted. "Maybe I will have a glass of wine when that gets here."

"All right," Zalith said, smiling warmly at him.

As they waited for their food, they sipped their drinks, enjoying the quiet comfort of each other's company. The world beyond their table barely existed—save for the occasional amused glance at the gawking patrons inside the restaurant.

Let them stare.

Alucard smirked, swirling his straw through his milkshake before taking another slow sip, his gaze flicking back to Zalith's with a knowing look. Whatever came next, whatever chaos awaited them beyond this moment—it could wait.

For now, this was *theirs*.

Chapter Twenty-Eight

— ≺ ✝ ≻ —

Dream-Eaters and Favours

| Alucard—*Uzlia Isles, Usrul, Castle Reiner* |

Alucard was determined to finish Zalith's dream-eater. While Zalith worked away in his office, the vampire remained in his own, fastening the last of the crystals to the delicate, tree-like structure. The thought of his mate finally getting a proper night's rest pushed him forward, sharpening his focus. As he carefully pinned another gemstone into place, Peaches watched from the window, her large eyes tracking his every movement with quiet curiosity.

Only two more pieces of fire agate remained, and then it would be finished—just in time, too. A quick glance at the clock confirmed what he suspected: it was nearing nine. By now, Zalith had likely turned down dinner at least once, maybe twice, too absorbed in his work to eat. Alucard would bring him his meal—he *knew* his mate wouldn't stop long enough to do it otherwise.

Carefully, he caged the second-to-last crystal and secured it to one of the branches. As he did, Peaches leapt down from the windowsill, padding across the floor before hopping up onto the desk beside him. The vampire worked steadily, fastening the final gemstone into place before leaning back in his chair, exhaling deeply. His eyes swept over the dream-eater one last time, ensuring that every crystal was perfectly set.

It was *finished.*

Just then, a knock came at his door. He hoped that it might be Zalith, but he could sense the demon's aura, and he was still in his office. "What?" he called, half-pouting.

Edwin stepped in. "Sir, an urgent letter came for you by owl—the bird couldn't find your window; it landed in the kitchen and scared the staff," he said, his face as vacant as ever.

Slightly amused, Alucard smiled. "Thank you," he said, taking the letter from Edwin once he made his way over and handed it to him. "Could you get Zalith's dinner ready please?" he then asked. "I'll come and get it for him in about ten minutes."

"Of course, sir," the butler said, and with a humble bow, he turned around and left.

Alucard used his claw to open the white envelope and stared at the paper. The writing was Dor-Sanguian, and Soren's signature sat at the bottom.

A,

I've received your letter regarding your request to have me look for a wedding planner. I believe I already have some answers for you. At your earliest convenience, please come and see me so that we can talk. I hope that you and Zalith are well, and I thank you for this opportunity to prove my resourcefulness.

S.B

Placing the letter down, Alucard sighed again and leaned back in his seat. He was surprised to hear that Soren already had answers—he really was eager to prove himself, wasn't he?—and he was excited to start planning the wedding with Zalith. He took out a piece of parchment and wrote his reply, telling Soren that he and Zalith would probably stop by tomorrow. After all, Zalith had to head back to the city to meet with the council to discuss supplies and the water.

Alucard finished writing his letter, sealed it neatly in an envelope, and let out a quiet whistle as he held it up. Within moments, a barn owl swooped in through the open window, snatched the letter from his hand, and disappeared just as swiftly as it had arrived.

With that taken care of, he turned his attention to the delicate dream-eater. Carefully lifting it, he rose from his chair, Peaches trailing at his heels as he crossed the office. He made his way down to his workshop and through the hallways, where Sabazios came bounding towards him, barking happily. Alucard reached down, patting the hound's massive head before watching him trot off into the sunroom, his tail wagging.

Still cradling the tree-shaped dream-eater, the vampire traversed the quiet castle; he ascended the spiral stairs leading to the tower where their bedroom was—Peaches, ever his shadow, followed diligently.

Once inside, he moved to Zalith's side of the bed and carefully placed the dream-eater on the nightstand. Stepping back, he assessed its placement, ensuring it didn't clash with the surrounding furniture. Satisfied, he allowed himself a small smile before scooping Peaches up into his arms and slipping back out of the room.

Descending the stairs once more, Alucard made his way to the kitchen, where he gathered Zalith's dinner, along with a bottle of red wine and a single glass. Balancing everything, he headed towards the tower where Zalith's office was. Knowing his mate was likely buried in his work, he took care not to startle him.

Pausing at the door, he tucked the wine bottle under his arm and knocked lightly. From within, Zalith's voice sounded in acknowledgement. Taking that as his cue, Alucard nudged the door open with his arm and stepped inside.

"I brought you your dinner," he said, a knowing smile curving his lips as he shut the door behind him.

Zalith set his pen down and looked up, a warm smile spreading across his face. "Aw, thank you, baby," he said contently, his voice carrying a quiet fondness. As Alucard approached, the demon shifted his papers aside, clearing space on his desk. The vampire placed the plate down in front of him, and Zalith glanced up at him again. "Are you having anything?" he asked, tilting his head slightly, his tone both curious and inviting.

Alucard poured his mate a glass of wine. "No," he answered, shaking his head. "I'm not really hungry—thank you, though. I just wanted to make sure you ate something."

"Thank you," the demon said, reaching up to caress the side of his face with the back of his hand.

"You're welcome, my love," he murmured, still a little shy about saying it, but he liked calling Zalith something so endearing—he liked the way it felt, the way it belonged to *them*. Once he finished pouring Zalith's drink, he set the bottle down and took the seat across from him, his gaze lingering on the demon.

"Do you want some of mine?" Zalith offered, making himself comfortable in his seat.

The vampire smiled. "Okay," he agreed softly.

As Zalith sliced off a small piece of his steak, Alucard leaned forward across the table. The demon met him halfway, offering the bite with an amused smirk. Alucard accepted it, his lips brushing briefly against the fork before he sat back, chewing thoughtfully.

"It's good," he murmured with a satisfied smile, settling comfortably into his seat.

"Good because I'm not in the mood to fire anyone right now," his mate said with a quiet laugh.

Alucard smiled amusedly. He considered telling Zalith about the dream-eater he'd made for him, but he also wanted it to be a surprise. "What time do we have to leave tomorrow morning? To see the council."

"Around eight," Zalith said, starting to eat his food. "I'm meeting them at half-past eight, but some of them get there early, and they love to see me—it'll give them more time to ask about the water. I sent a message to Greymore and Danford earlier telling them to spread the rumours about Cecil and the cave." He paused and smirked. "After we're done with the council, we'll probably take a walk around the city and wait for people to start asking us about the rumours."

Alucard nodded. "It's a good plan. If we're lucky, maybe Cecil will be out of Eimwood before next weekend."

"That would be delightful," the demon said and sipped from his wine. "Then we can figure out what to do with his estate. I was thinking that it could be a much larger, more comfortable space for Idina to work out of—we'll soon be sending more demons her way, and I know she isn't exactly content in that little townhouse."

"What do we do about the...troll? She and Cecil...they're obviously close. If we cast him out of the city, who is to say that she won't enact revenge or something?"

"We'll have to find a way to relocate her maybe."

"What if she doesn't want to leave?" the vampire asked.

"Then she will learn that unfortunately, as creatures of this world, we don't always get what we want."

"And what if she becomes hostile?"

"We'll deal with it," Zalith said and continued eating.

Alucard nodded in agreement.

They sat in comfortable silence for a while as Zalith ate, the quiet only broken by the occasional clink of silverware against his plate.

Alucard, however, found his thoughts drifting elsewhere—back to his people, his vampires. Guilt crept in as he realized how long he'd left them to fend for themselves. With everything happening in the world, he should have *expected* them to struggle. Why hadn't he? He only hoped that once he met with the Coven Masters, he could start making things right.

Pushing the thoughts aside, he turned his attention back to Zalith, watching as he finished his food and pushed the plate away. Alucard smiled, anticipation flickering in his chest—he was eager to show Zalith what he'd made for him, and he admitted to himself that he was also starting to feel tired.

"Are you ready to go upstairs?" he asked, meeting Zalith's gaze.

Zalith glanced at the time, and then at the papers on his desk, which looked like work he had yet to complete. With a sigh and a nod, he said "Yeah."

Alucard lost his smile and looked down at his lap. "We don't have to," he said with a slight shrug. "It's okay if you still need to work."

"It's okay," the demon said, tidying up his desk. "It's getting late."

"Are you sure?"

"Yeah. I have to get up for my meeting anyway."

"Okay," Alucard said and stood up.

Once Zalith got up, the vampire took hold of his hand and led the way out of his office.

"The meeting is in the townhouse tomorrow if you'd like to come with me, but you don't have to if you'd rather sleep in," Zalith said, following at Alucard's side as they headed downstairs.

Alucard glanced at him. "I'll come," he said, smiling. "The people will be happier to see us both, no?"

The demon smiled contently in response and nodded. "They will."

Also smiling, Alucard then continued to lead the way towards their bedroom.

Once they got upstairs, Alucard started getting undressed; he could feel Zalith's eyes on him, and when he looked over his shoulder, the demon smirked at him before taking his shirt off. Alucard took all but his trousers off and sat down for a moment.

That was when Zalith noticed the dream-eater. As he threw his shirt into the laundry basket, he gazed at the tree-shaped contraption for a moment. "What's this?" he asked curiously, smiling at him.

Alucard nodded shyly. "It's uh…a dream-eater—like mine. It'll help you with your nightmares."

Zalith sat on the edge of the bed next to his nightstand and leaned closer to the tree. "You made this all by yourself?" he asked, looking at Alucard appreciatively.

The vampire shuffled closer to him and rested his chin on the demon's shoulder. "I wanted to help you with your dreams—I know they've been awful, so…I made you something that will stop you from having them."

"Thank you, baby," the demon said, caressing Alucard's cheek. "It's beautiful—I love it." He turned slightly and kissed his lips.

Alucard smiled. "You'll have to let me know if it works," he said with a quiet laugh. "It's been a while since I made anything."

"I'm sure it'll work just fine," he said and kissed him again. For a moment, Zalith then stared at Alucard. He rested his forehead against his, guiding his hand up to his head to start caressing his hair. "I love you so much," he murmured. "And I love all the things you do for me."

Alucard's smile deepened, warmth curling through him at Zalith's words. But before he could reply, the demon's lips were on his again—soft, teasing, insistent. He kissed him once, then again, and again, each press of his mouth sending sparks through Alucard's skin. Then Zalith trailed lower, his lips ghosting over the vampire's jaw, down his neck, and across his chest. He barely had a chance to exhale before the demon was guiding him onto his back, his body yielding willingly beneath him. A quiet, breathy sigh escaped Alucard as he relaxed into the pillows, his fingers weaving into Zalith's hair, *urging* him on as his mate's lips continued their descent.

The warmth of Zalith's mouth traced lower, over his sternum, skimming down towards his waist. Anticipation coiled in Alucard's stomach as the demon's fingers found the buttons of his trousers. But just as quickly, a flicker of hesitation pulled at the vampire. His hand tensed against Zalith's scalp, fingers lingering. He *loved* Zalith's touch, the way his mate worshipped him without hesitation. But tonight... *he* wanted to return the favour.

He lightly gripped the demon's hair. "Wait," he said, looking down at him.

Zalith stopped, frowning in concern as he looked up at him. "What?" he asked quietly.

With a shy but eager smile, Alucard grasped Zalith's wrist, gently pulling him back up until their faces hovered just inches apart. He held his gaze for a moment, and then he reversed their positions, pressing Zalith onto his back and straddling his lap. A slow, playful smirk curved the vampire's lips as he leaned over him. "I want to do it for you first," he murmured.

Zalith's eyes darkened with excitement, his own smirk mirroring Alucard's. "Okay," he replied, the word slipping past his lips like an invitation. His hand drifted upward, fingers gliding over Alucard's chest before settling on his shoulder. With a firm yet lazy pull, he drew him closer, their breaths mingling in the space between them. But instead of rushing, Zalith simply held him there, staring fondly at him.

Alucard let himself get lost in the deep, smouldering gaze beneath him. He traced Zalith's jaw with the barest touch of his fingers, and then he tilted his head with a teasing smirk. "You're so handsome," he whispered, his accent thickening slightly with warmth.

Zalith's smirk deepened. "Thank you," he purred. "So are you."

Smiling, Alucard leaned in, capturing Zalith's lips in a slow kiss.

As their mouths moved together, the vampire let his hand drift down his mate's body, slipping into his trousers. His fingers wrapped around the demon's growing arousal, his touch firm yet teasing as he began to stroke him. The quiet groan in Zalith's breath sent a thrill through Alucard, and when the demon's fingers tangled into his hair, toying with the strands, it only confirmed what he already knew—Zalith's anticipation mirrored his own.

Breaking the kiss, Alucard trailed his lips down Zalith's neck, lingering there. The urge to bite, to sink his fangs into that warm, intoxicating pulse burned through him— but he resisted. He'd already taken Zalith's blood this morning, and as much as he *wanted* to taste him again, he wouldn't.

Instead, he pressed a few more kisses against his throat before shifting lower, slipping his hand free just long enough to unbutton Zalith's trousers. As the demon exhaled a quiet, eager sigh, Alucard continued his descent, his lips brushing over his waist as he passed it; he pulled the demon's trousers down, and when he slowly pressed his lips against the tip of Zalith's dick, he felt his mate tense up ever so slightly beneath him.

Alucard gradually dragged his tongue up the demon's length; Zalith gently gripped a fistful of his hair, relaxing, and a quiet, "Fuck," escaped his hushed moan when Alucard took the demon's shaft into his mouth.

The moment the vampire began sucking—slow at first—Zalith's grip on his hair tightened, and he fidgeted lightly. Alucard loved pleasing him; the demon's pleasured moans delighted him. He gripped either side of Zalith's waist, humming contently as he sucked a little faster. There was something he relished about the feeling of the demon's hard inches in his mouth; the taste, the moans, the subtle flinches. He couldn't get enough. And what he loved most was when he felt Zalith approaching his peak.

Growing desperate to push Zalith closer to the edge, Alucard quickened his pace. The demon moaned loudly, his body tensing, fidgeting more than usual as pleasure overtook him. Alucard could *feel* it—knew without a doubt that Zalith was enjoying every second of it. And knowing that he was doing better than last time, that he was *truly* satisfying his mate only fuelled his determination.

The vampire continued, his mouth working over Zalith's shaft, drinking in every shudder, every breathless sound of delight. And then, with one final, euphoric moan, Zalith climaxed, his fingers tightening in Alucard's hair as his release spilled onto his tongue, his dick throbbing eagerly.

Alucard barely suppressed a quiet groan at the taste—*sweet*, almost intoxicatingly so, like the richest of honey laced with something deeper, something that sent a warm, heady rush through his body. It was euphoric, like liquid desire itself, leaving a lingering heat curling through his veins. He swallowed, savouring it before finally pulling back, licking his lips as he looked up at Zalith with a satisfied smirk.

He slowly made his way back up Zalith's body, his gaze locking onto the demon's as he hovered over him. Zalith met him with a pleased smile, his right hand sliding to the side of the vampire's face. He pulled Alucard in, their lips meeting in a deep, lingering kiss as his fingers trailed lower, gliding over the vampire's skin with a teasing touch.

Zalith wasted no time, his hand wrapping firmly around Alucard's hardening arousal. The vampire let out a quiet breath, his body responding instantly to his mate's touch. Zalith's eagerness to return the favour sent a thrill through him, and Alucard had no objections—*he craved this*, he craved Zalith's attention unlike anything else. And after another slow, heated kiss, he tangled his fingers into the demon's hair and guided him downward, wordlessly urging him lower.

The demon laughed softly, amusement lacing his expression as he let his fingers ghost over Alucard's body, tracing the dips and curves of his form. He kissed a slow path down his neck and over his chest, lingering just enough to tease before reaching his waist. Alucard exhaled, anticipation tightening in his stomach, and when Zalith's tongue traced over his shaft, the vampire inhaled sharply, a quiet moan spilling from his lips. He closed his eyes, letting himself sink into the pleasure—the wet heat of Zalith's mouth, the perfect pressure as he took him in. A satisfied sigh broke through his deep, uneven breaths, his heart quickening as Zalith moved deeper, taking him into his throat.

Alucard's fingers tightened in his hair, his body tensing with pleasure. A quiet, desperate sound escaped him, and as Zalith worked him with slow strokes, he scowled in struggle, a fevered moan tearing free from his lips. "Zalith…" he breathed, his voice unsteady, his body trembling beneath the relentless pleasure. He always unravelled so quickly in his mate's hands, in his mouth, and now was no exception. The wet heat around his dick consumed him, pulling him under, and the deeper he surrendered to it, the more intoxicating his euphoria became.

His muscles tensed, his body writhing as Zalith's grip on his waist held him steady. He moaned, his face twisting in both bliss and struggle, his breaths coming faster, more ragged. And then—he broke. A loud, pleasured moan tore from his throat as his climax crashed through him, his fingers tugging hard at Zalith's hair.

The demon took his time, gradually pulling away before pressing warm, lingering kisses up Alucard's trembling body. As he reached his neck, he nibbled at his skin, teasing just enough to make the vampire laugh softly between his still-shaky breaths.

Smirking, Zalith rested his forehead against Alucard's, his fingers stroking tenderly along his cheek. "How do you feel?" he asked.

Alucard smiled, placing his hand on the side of Zalith's face. "Really good," he breathed. "How do *you* feel?"

"I feel good," he said contently.

The vampire pouted. "You don't feel *really* good?" he asked playfully.

Zalith's smirk grew. "I *always* feel really good when I'm with you."

"Me too," Alucard concurred, fiddling with Zalith's loose, tousled fringe.

Zalith kissed Alucard's lips before they both got into bed, pulling their blankets over each other as Alucard made himself comfortable beside Zalith, resting his head on his chest. Then, as the demon used his ethos to switch off the lights, Alucard sighed a deep, long sigh. Today had been just as eventful as most of their days, and tomorrow was going to be just as so. He didn't exactly want to see that troll or Cecil *ever* again, but he would most likely have to—only once more, though.

Alucard closed his eyes as Zalith moved his arm around him, holding him tightly. Today felt so much different than most others; he hadn't felt a moment of angst or sadness, he'd been able to enjoy his time with Zalith without worrying, and he felt like his excitement for their wedding played a part in his newfound calm. He also loved spending time with Zalith outside of their home when it wasn't work-related. He wanted to do it more—to go on little dates with him. Maybe he'd suggest it more in the future.

But he then remembered that tomorrow, they had more to do than get rid of Cecil. "Oh, we have to go and see Soren tomorrow," he mumbled. "He said he already has news for us about a wedding planner."

"That was fast," Zalith said. "Hopefully it's good news."

"Well, he's always been very good and very fast at finding things and people for me."

The demon sighed. "I suppose that does leave more time in the day for complaining."

Alucard laughed quietly. "Should we talk to him after the meeting? He's in the same house, after all."

"Might as well," Zalith said, turning onto his side so that he could rest his forehead against Alucard's.

Smiling, Alucard moved closer and placed his left hand on the side of Zalith's neck. "I hope you sleep better tonight," he said quietly. "I love you."

"I love you too, baby," the demon said happily. "Thank you for my dream-eater."

"You're welcome," he said, stroking Zalith's cheek. "I'm glad you like it. I didn't really know what shape to go with, but... a tree just seemed right."

"You made the right choice," Zalith said, fiddling with Alucard's hair. "It looks great."

"Let me know if it works," he mumbled sleepily, the weight of the day and the comfort of being in Zalith's arms urging him to give in to the fatigue.

"I will," he replied, caressing the side of his face.

"Goodnight, my love," Alucard murmured.

"Goodnight baby," Zalith said, and then he placed a final kiss on the vampire's lips.

Chapter Twenty-Nine

— ≺ ✝ ≻ —

The Prelude to Cecil's Downfall

| **Alucard,** *Tuesday, Tertium 14th, 960(TG)—Uzlia Isles, Usrul, Castle Reiner* |

Alucard jolted awake at the sharp, echoing knock on the bedroom door. His eyes fluttered open, his mind still clouded with sleep as he lifted his head, instinctively glancing towards the source of the disturbance. The door stood ajar, and in the dim morning light, Edwin's familiar figure came into view. The butler stood in the doorway, watching him with his usual composed expression, though his presence alone suggested something required Alucard's attention.

"Sirs, your meeting is in an hour," Edwin said.

The vampire groaned lazily and rested his head back against his pillow. "Fine. Thank you," he muttered.

"Would you like me to open the curtains for you?" the butler asked.

"No," Alucard mumbled, holding his hand over his face—the sunlight creeping in through the cracks in the curtains scraped at his eyes.

Edwin nodded, bowed humbly, and left the room in silence, pulling the door shut behind him.

Sighing tiredly, Alucard dragged his hand away from his eyes, resting it against the bed beside him. A faint frown tugged at his face—Zalith hadn't said a word. Was he even awake?

Turning his head, Alucard's gaze settled on the demon beside him. Zalith lay sprawled on his back, an open book draped over his face, pages gently rising and falling with each breath. Surrounding them, scattered across the bed, were countless sheets of paper—far too many for someone who was supposed to have been sleeping.

Alucard's frown deepened. He'd stayed up working, hadn't he? The realization sent a pang of disappointment through him. Did the dream-eater not work?

His pout was involuntary, a subtle flicker of frustration curling in his chest. He had *wanted* this to help Zalith; he'd worked carefully...and he wondered whether he'd done something wrong. Too many crystals? Too few? He'd figure it out. He'd fix it.

But right now, he had something more pressing to deal with—if he didn't wake Zalith up soon, they were going to be late for the meeting that Zalith had insisted on arriving early for.

"Zalith?" he asked quietly, placing his hand on the demon's left arm as he took the book off his face. As much as he wanted to let Zalith rest, they had things to do today—important things. "We have to get up."

The demon stirred, uttering a confused sound.

"It's eight," Alucard said, picking up the papers that were spread over the bed. "We only have an hour until the meeting."

Zalith frowned, keeping his eyes closed. "Oh," he muttered sleepily. But as Alucard started moving more of the papers, the demon opened his eyes, slowly sat up, and started trying to move the papers himself. "Sorry," he said.

Alucard shook his head, helping him tidy up his work. "It's fine."

"I couldn't sleep," the demon said sadly as they rounded up the last few pieces of paper.

With a sorrowful frown, Alucard looked at him. "Did the dream-eater not work?"

"No, it worked. I didn't have a single dream. I just had a hard time falling asleep," he said, taking his papers from Alucard and placing them on his nightstand.

"I can...help with that too...if you wanted," he offered. He was sure that Zalith knew he could induce sleep, but what if he didn't and connected the dots? What if he worked out Alucard had put him to sleep several times before?

"How?" Zalith asked.

He shrugged. "I can do this...thing," he mumbled, staring at Zalith's tired face. "I can make people sleep, and make them wake up when I want," he said, angst building in his stomach.

"Oh," Zalith said...and he paused for a moment. "Maybe."

"It's just an idea. We could try other things—I don't know what, but...I want to try and help."

Zalith shrugged. "I don't know. Maybe I should start drinking tea," he said with a roll of his eyes.

"Maybe.... Do you still want to go? If you want to sleep some more, I can go for us," he offered. "Or stay here with you," he added—he knew Zalith didn't want him to go anywhere alone.

The demon shook his head. "No, I should go. Thank you, though," he said with a smile, moving his hand to the side of Alucard's face. But then he sighed deeply and glanced over at the bathroom door. "I should have a shower."

Alucard nodded. "Okay. I'll join you... if that's okay?"

"Of course that's okay," Zalith said softly and took hold of Alucard's hand. He climbed out of bed, pulling the vampire with him. "How's your back today?" he asked, leading the way towards the bathroom.

"It doesn't hurt anymore," he said—and he was glad that the pain was gone. "I don't know if the scars are gone, though."

Zalith stopped walking and guided his hand over Alucard's shoulder. He turned him around, slowly dragging his fingers down his back. "They're gone," he said.

Alucard smiled, but it faded into an almost vacant frown as Zalith turned him back to face him. "With the state my back is already in, I'm sure three more scars wouldn't matter," he mumbled, laughing a little. At first, he thought he was making a joke that might be funny, but he only ended up upsetting himself. "Let's go," he said, pulling Zalith into the bathroom.

"You know that I love you regardless, right?" the demon said, walking at his side.

The vampire nodded. "I know," he said, smiling through the sorrow. "I love you, too."

They showered for the next while, but not for *too* long. They didn't have much time to spare. Once they got out, dried themselves and got dressed—Zalith pulled on one of his best grey suits, and Alucard, as he did most of the time, pulled on a black suit—the pair tidied themselves up and headed downstairs.

"Will we have to see Cecil again?" Alucard mumbled.

"Probably," the demon answered, buttoning his shirt's cuffs as they reached the bottom of the stairs. "But hopefully not as a bug," he said with a smirk, glancing at Alucard, who was still fiddling with his crimson hair. "I was thinking about putting Idina in charge of the troll situation," he said as they approached the cloakroom. "If it ends up becoming an issue, she'll know how to handle her."

"Hopefully the troll will just leave when we tell her," Alucard muttered.

"I don't want to see her again," the demon replied, opening the cloakroom door and taking out Alucard's cape and one of his own black redingotes. "Maybe we should just send Idina from the get-go."

Alucard nodded as he pulled his cape on over his shoulders. "It's probably a good idea. I don't want to go back into that cave *ever* again."

"Are you scarred for life?" the demon asked with a smirk, following Alucard out into the courtyard.

He shrugged. "It's going to take me a while to forget what we saw down there."

Zalith nodded. "Me too."

The vampire came to a halt once they reached the archway leading to the winding path down the hill. His gaze flicked towards the nearby stables before turning to Zalith. "Should we take the horses?" he asked, tilting his head slightly in consideration.

"Yeah," Zalith said, smiling at him. "We'll take them."

They entered the stables, the scent of hay and polished leather mingling in the cool morning air. Zalith swung himself onto Dimitri, while Alucard mounted Noir, settling into the familiar rhythm of the saddle. Zalith took the lead, guiding them out of the courtyard and onto the winding path.

Alucard slipped on his sunglasses, his gaze fixed ahead as they descended the hillside. The sluggish weight of exhaustion still clung to him—he needed more sleep. Yesterday had drained him, especially after giving Zalith so much of his energy. But regret? No, he had none. He loved every moment of Zalith's attention, his touch, his affection. The lingering fatigue was a small price to pay for something he craved so deeply.

His concerns, however, lay elsewhere—with *Zalith*. They had woken late, which was rare for his mate. The demon had barely slept; he'd spent most of the night buried in his work. Now, with no time for breakfast and an entire day ahead of them, Alucard worried that he wouldn't stop to take care of himself.

Glancing over at him, Alucard spoke, his voice light but laced with quiet concern, "Do you want to get breakfast when we're done with the meeting?"

"That sounds nice," Zalith said, smiling at him. "They can make something for us at the house, too—but if you want to go out, we can. It doesn't matter to me."

Alucard nodded, his thoughts drifting as they continued down the path. There weren't many options in the city. Even now, Eimwood was still recovering from the neglect and exploitation it had suffered before he and Zalith arrived. The elves had pillaged it for years, taking whatever they pleased and leaving the people with nothing— not even the bare minimum to survive.

Restaurants like the Strawberry Saloon were a rare luxury, one that most still couldn't afford, especially now. But he and Zalith had done everything in their power to keep the city afloat. They'd poured their wealth into rebuilding, funding renovations for homes and businesses alike. They had created jobs, hiring Eimwood's own people to restore their city brick by brick.

But it had only been a month. No matter how much they accomplished each day, there was still so much more to do. Smaller bakeries and cafés had likely begun reopening, but the city's larger establishments were still far from reclaiming their former prosperity.

"Well...since that Strawberry place is the only big restaurant open right now...I guess if you don't want to go back there, I don't mind waiting until we get home."

"I don't mind going back," Zalith said. "Especially since it's putting money into the pockets of a local business."

Alucard smiled and nodded. "Okay."

They rode down to the meadow, crossing the bridge from Usrul into Yrudberg, the steady rhythm of their horses' hooves echoing softly against the worn path. As they entered Eimwood and made their way along the road, Alucard's gaze flickered over the passing crowd—only to catch sight of something unexpected. At least ten people were wearing makeshift versions of his sunglasses. It was clear that they'd taken ordinary glasses and either painted or stained the lenses black, mimicking the look he often adorned in the city.

His brows lifted slightly, but as they continued up the road towards Bauwell, the numbers only increased. More and more people sported the imitation shades, some subtle, others blatantly obvious. By the time they reached the heart of the district, Alucard wasn't sure whether to be amused or mortified. Was this a trend now? His lips parted slightly in surprise before he pressed them together, glancing away as a flicker of embarrassment settled in his chest.

"Aww," Zalith laughed, looking at Alucard. "That's cute."

Alucard pouted.

Zalith leaned over a little so that he was closer to him as they made their way up the street. "They love you, vampire," he said, smirking.

Alucard frowned unsurely, looked around at all the waving, sunglasses-wearing people, and then looked back at Zalith. "People are going to have accidents," he muttered. "They've just...coloured ordinary lenses with ink," he said, concerned—and as two people wearing the glasses crashed into one another and started apologizing, Alucard looked back over at Zalith.

The demon laughed again. "Cute," he repeated.

Sighing, Alucard stared ahead—

"Ezra!" came a familiar, excited voice. "Silas!"

Both Alucard and Zalith turned their heads, their eyes landing on none other than Mary-Beth, who hurried out of the bakery across the street—wearing, to Alucard's dismay, a pair of sunglasses. Not far behind her, Selena and Cadence followed, their excitement written all over their heavily painted faces. As always, the two women trailed in Mary-Beth's wake, their eager smiles wide as they rushed over.

Alucard offered a polite smile, though there was an undeniable distance to it. Once upon a time, Mary-Beth had been what he might have considered a friend, but things had changed. Since the women's rescue from Nefastus and their settlement in Eimwood, nothing had quite been the same. Their memories had been altered; they couldn't be allowed to remember who Alucard and Zalith truly were, nor the reality of why they had been saved. Zalith had wiped away everything: their knowledge of his and Alucard's real names, their true lives, and everything they had witnessed in Nefastus. Now, they believed what they had been allowed to remember—that they had been rescued from a plague-ridden disaster by Alucard's people, meeting him for the first time on the night they arrived in Eimwood. In this fabricated history, their now-dead husbands had been overseas business associates of Zalith, explaining why they had been given priority in their escape. It was a lie—a necessary one. And though Alucard still regarded them with a certain level of fondness, their friendship was nothing more than a shadow of what it once was.

"I was hoping I'd catch you both down here someday soon!" Mary-Beth called, crossing the road to where Alucard and Zalith dismounted their horses. "It feels like it's been forever," she added with a smile, stopping in front of them as Selena and Cadence stood on either side of her.

"We've been busy," Alucard said, smiling. "How have you all been?"

"Oh," Mary-Beth laughed, waving her hand, fiddling with the makeshift sunglasses on her face. "We've been busy, too—settling in."

Zalith then smiled. "I'm sorry to interrupt, but my husband and I have somewhere we need to be. But perhaps you should all have lunch later and catch up," he suggested, looking over at Alucard as he took hold of and squeezed his hand.

Alucard immediately sensed what Zalith must be thinking. Mary-Beth and her friends were relentless gossipers. If he told them about Cecil, the cave, and the troll, the story would spread through Eimwood like wildfire. But still…a part of him wanted to spend some time with them. Even if their friendship wasn't what it used to be, there was something oddly comforting about their familiar energy. It wasn't the same, but it wasn't entirely lost, either.

Besides, there was an upside to it all. Thanks to Zalith's alterations, Selena and Cadence had been stripped of their more unpleasant traits—their rudeness, their sharp-tongued judgments, and their homophobic remarks. Back in Nefastus, they had been insufferable at times, their attitudes making Alucard feel awkward and hesitant, never quite at ease around them. But now That discomfort was gone. And that, at least, made things easier.

So he smiled and set his eyes back on Mary-Beth and her friends. "We can do that—maybe around…one?"

Selena and Cadence clapped their hands and squealed quietly in excitement to one another as Mary-Beth smiled contently and said, "Oh, we'd love that."

"We'll have tea and cake at my house," Selena said. "It was nice seeing you both," she then called, waving her hand as Zalith and Alucard mounted their horses again.

"Bye!" they all called simultaneously, waving.

Both Alucard and Zalith waved their farewells and then continued up the road.

As they approached the bridge to Bauwell Residential District, Zalith glanced at Alucard and smiled. "When you're at lunch, make sure you spread rumours about Cecil. About him being a bug, the cave, and the troll maybe, too. It'll be helpful since Mary-Beth and her friends are known gossips."

Alucard nodded. "Don't worry," he said. "I know what to tell them."

"Try to get them really worked up about it," the demon said.

"I will. I want Cecil out of here just as much as you do—the sooner, the better."

Zalith nodded in agreement.

With that, they crossed the bridge, their pace steady as they made their way towards their townhouse. Zalith's meeting would begin soon—and with it, the first steps towards Cecil's downfall.

Or so they both hoped.

Chapter Thirty

— ⸰ ✝ ⸰ —

The Townhouse Meeting

| **Alucard**—*Uzlia Isles, Yrudberg, Eimwood City* |

Alucard sat at the head of the table beside Zalith in the townhouse conference room. The space, located at the back of the ground floor, was closed off from the rest of the house—its glass doors shut tightly, with heavy black curtains patterned in gold drawn to ensure privacy; the walls, painted a muted grey, were lined with towering bookshelves, though they were far from neatly arranged. Stacks of books, scattered papers, and disorganized documents cluttered nearly every available surface, and a dark brown carpet stretched beneath their feet, contrasting with the off-white ceiling above. If he and Zalith actually *lived* here, they would have ensured the space reflected their own tastes—something *comfortable*, something *theirs*. But they *didn't* live here, and they had no intention of ever calling this place home.

Around the polished mahogany table sat Zalith's miniature council—a small but carefully chosen group consisting of Bertram, a representative from the larger city council, Mark, the city's sheriff, and Christian, the chief physician. Each man was dressed in a crisp black suit, their expressions serious, reflecting the weight of the discussion at hand.

Sunlight streamed in through the patio doors, casting long streaks of gold across the room. Beyond the thick curtains, the distant hum of the city filtered in through the breeze, a faint reminder of the world bustling just outside.

For the past forty-five minutes, Zalith had been discussing the latest shipments—medicine, building materials, and most critically, water from the lake to the east of the island. Unlike the city's main water source, this lake remained untouched—unpolluted by a grotesque troll and her giant cockroach companion.

The next matter of business was, in fact, the water that ran through the city. Christian, the chief physician, shuffled forward in his seat, resting his arms on the table as he looked at Zalith and Alucard. "What's the situation with the Eimwood River?" he asked as the others nodded in agreement.

"I've recently sent a scientist to test the water and the results have come back inconclusive," Zalith said, looking around at them all. "However, we and the scientist believe that it may have something to do with the rocks upstream. Either that or it's possible that there is something contaminating the water near or in the cave it runs through. We have been looking into sending somebody out there to take a look inside the cave. My concerns about it are growing every day, though. I'll be sure to send someone out there as soon as I can."

Sheriff Mark nodded. "Has there been any news on the Yrudyen Elves?" he asked.

"Nothing," Alucard answered. "My guards haven't reported any sightings."

"Good," Councilman Bertram called. "Now that the city's finally getting back on its feet, the last thing we need is for those thieves to return. But those vampires have been doing a good job keeping them at bay."

"If the Yrudyen return, we'll be ready for them," Zalith said sincerely. "That's if they get past the demons we have patrolling Eimwood's outer borders."

Alucard nodded, his thoughts briefly drifting back to the early days of their arrival in the Uzlia Isles. When he and Zalith had driven out the elves who had been bleeding Eimwood dry, securing the city had been his first priority. He'd stationed his pack of demons throughout Yrudberg, ensuring constant vigilance in case the Yrudyen attempted to reclaim what they had lost. Beyond that, a handful of his vampires patrolled the outer walls, their sharp senses complemented by Greymore's wolves, who prowled the perimeter, ever watchful. The Yrudyen weren't setting foot in this city again—not while he and Zalith ruled here.

Well...almost ruled. There were still loose ends to tie up—Cecil, for one. And, of course, the matter of the city's polluted water. But once those problems were dealt with, Eimwood would truly belong to them.

"When will you be sending people to investigate the cave?" Christian asked.

"As soon as I can," Zalith repeated.

"Would you like to take some of my men?" Sheriff Mark offered. "In case the Yrudyen turn up—it wouldn't be the first time people have been ambushed by them."

The demon sighed quietly. "My main concern is that I don't know who is and who isn't resistant to the toxins, especially when they reach peak potency. Because demons, vampires, and werewolves are naturally resistant to such things, it's better if we send in our people," he said, glancing at Alucard.

"And if they can't find anything?" Bertram questioned.

"Then we'll keep looking for the problem."

They all nodded.

"What about the new homes?" Bertram then asked.

"My contractors said the first phase of new homes will be ready at or before the end of this month," Zalith answered.

Councilman Bertram nodded, his expression carefully measured. "I've noticed that the area you've designated for the next phase of construction is nearly cleared. Will work begin on the next set of homes as soon as the current ones are completed?" he asked, his tone carrying a trace of impatience.

Zalith set his eyes on him. "Obviously," he said. "Unless you and your employer have something to say against it."

He shook his head. "No."

"Then I think that just about wraps everything up," Zalith said.

"There is...*one* more thing," Bertram called just as everyone was about to start getting ready to leave. "There are still some people here that aren't so comfortable with you and your... friends moving into their city."

Zalith scoffed very quietly. "They don't feel safe, yet they're more than happy to take our money."

Alucard frowned. "From what we have seen, everyone here welcomes us and all the things we are doing. It's understandable if some people are still wary, but we have made sure that everyone knows we are only here to help. We have heard no such rumour from anyone."

"A lot of complaints come through me," Sheriff Mark said, looking over at the councilman. "And no such complaints regarding Silas or Ezra have come my way. They have both been nothing but helpful since they arrived—and their people, too."

"That's not the way we see it," Bertram said, leaning back in his seat as he crossed his arms and shook his head.

Zalith smiled. "Then how do you see it? Do enlighten us."

Bertram scowled and said, "You came to our city and started buying everyone's trust with your seemingly infinite source of money; we know you want Lord Cecil's job—you're not going to get it, no matter how many things you fix here. How long is it going to be until there's not enough room here for all of these new demons you're inviting in? Will you start kicking people out of their homes? These islands hadn't seen a demon, a werewolf *or* a vampire in over a hundred years—we don't want your kind here."

Zalith laughed quietly. "And are these words straight from Cecil's mouth? Because I think saying something as bold as 'we don't want your kind here' is a little funny coming from someone like him."

Alucard glanced at Zalith—he was sure that the demon was referring to the fact that Cecil was a man-sized cockroach.

"What?" Christian uttered unsurely.

"Someone obnoxious and irresponsible," the demon lied.

"Lord Cecil has done *a lot* for this city," Bertram argued with an almost cautious look on his face.

"Congratulations to him," Zalith said. "But the city needs more."

Bertram scoffed again, but he didn't say anything. Clearly, he had nothing left to say. Zalith was right, and everyone sitting around the table had to know that.

"If there's nothing else," Zalith said, "then I think that concludes our meeting today."

Everyone looked around at each other. No one said anything.

Then, as Zalith and Alucard stood up, so did everyone else. They both led the way out of the conference room, through the house, and to the front door, where they saw everyone off. And when it was just Zalith and Alucard, the vampire turned to face the demon.

"Are you ready to go and get breakfast?" Alucard asked.

"I am," Zalith said, smiling at him. "Are you?"

The vampire smiled, too. "Yes."

Zalith then linked arms with him and led the way out of the house and down the street, heading for the Strawberry Saloon.

⟵ ❖ ⟶

A little over an hour later, Alucard and Zalith stepped out of the Strawberry Saloon, the warmth of the midday sun greeting them as they exited. Breakfast had been handled, and soon, it would be time for Alucard to meet with Mary-Beth, Selena, and Cadence.

A part of him looked forward to it—once, he had considered them friends. It might be nice to catch up, even if things weren't quite the same anymore. But beneath that sentiment lingered a more pressing purpose. He needed to *use* them. The three women were the perfect messengers—skilled at weaving gossip into something tantalizing, something irresistible. And today, they'd unknowingly serve his cause, spreading the truth of Cecil's wretched secret through Eimwood.

As they stepped onto the street, Alucard said, "I guess I should head to Selena's house and have that tea and cake with them."

Zalith frowned—both sadness *and* worry lingered on his face. "Okay," he said quietly.

"Are you okay?" the vampire asked, concerned.

"Yeah, I'm okay. I'm just a little bit worried that something might happen to you—I'm always worried about that," he said with a hushed, pained laugh.

Alucard frowned despondently. "You could come too—or...I don't have to go. You're more important than some tea and cake," he said, moving his hand over Zalith's shoulder.

"No, it's okay. I want you to go and spend some time with your friends—I'll be fine. I'll probably still be at the townhouse by the time you're done," he said with an assuring smile.

"Are you sure?"

Zalith nodded. "I'm sure."

With a reluctant sigh, Alucard said, "Okay, well…if you want or need me to come to you at any point, tell me," he said, moving closer to him. "I will be listening—you're the only person I let into my head, after all," he said with a smile, gazing into Zalith's dark, captivating eyes.

The demon smiled. "And you're the only person I let into *my* head," his mate said, smirking. "So I'll be listening, too. I hope you have fun with your friends," he then said, stroking his hand to the side of Alucard's face.

Alucard kissed the demon's lips.

Zalith kissed him back and said, "Okay…I'll see you later."

Alucard nodded. "I'll see *you* later," he said, and then he let his hand slip out of Zalith's and went to turn around—

"Wait," Zalith said sadly.

The vampire waited, turning back to face him.

Moving closer, Zalith kissed his lips once more. "Okay…bye," he said sadly.

Alucard smiled—

"No, wait," he said again, lightly gripping Alucard's hand. He kissed his lips once more, held onto his hand for a few moments…and then let go. "Okay," he sighed. "Bye."

"B—"

"Okay, wait—" Zalith interjected, taking hold of his hand again.

"I can stay with you," Alucard insisted, squeezing his hand. "I don't *have* to go."

"No, it's okay," he said, shaking his head. "I want you to go, just…give me one more kiss," he said, pulling Alucard closer.

Alucard smiled and leaned in, meeting Zalith's lips in a slow, lingering kiss. Once. Twice. A third time—before Zalith pressed forward, gently but insistently backing Alucard against the nearest wall. This time, there were no pauses, no hesitation—just deep, unbroken kisses that stole his breath and made him forget everything else.

He wasn't in any hurry to get to Selena's house—not when Zalith was here, his touch warm, his presence grounding. Whether the demon was worried or upset, Alucard would rather stay with him than rush off to spread rumours about Cecil. So they stayed like that, lips moving in a slow, intoxicating rhythm, ignoring the occasional curious glances from passersby—because in this moment, nothing else mattered.

After a few more moments, Zalith leaned into the vampire's ear. "I want to do things to you," he murmured seductively, and then he pressed his lips against Alucard's once more.

Arousal electrified through Alucard as Zalith mumbled into his ear, and as he kissed his lips, Alucard was sure that a flustered expression had appeared on his face.

"But I won't," the demon said with a smirk. "Have a nice time," he said, letting go of him. "Maybe I'll pick you up later."

But as Zalith went to walk off, Alucard snatched his wrist. For a moment, he stared at him confusedly, but he was sure that Zalith had purposely teased him to enjoy his reaction. Alucard, however, was no longer too shy to tell Zalith what he wanted—or at least…to try and let him know what he wanted. "Wait," he said with a pout, glaring at him.

"What?" the demon asked with an innocent smile.

"Do what?" he asked, flustered and almost eager. "What do you want to do?"

The demon's smirk grew. "Things that are too indecent to be said out loud in public," he said quietly as he rested his forehead against Alucard's. "I think you're going to have to use your imagination."

Alucard's pout thickened as he pulled Zalith closer—so close that their bodies pressed together. "Tell me," he demanded.

Zalith's hand drifted slowly down Alucard's body, slipping beneath the fabric of his trousers. Hidden beneath the cloak that draped over him, shielding them from prying eyes, his touch remained unseen—but unmistakably felt. As his fingers wrapped around Alucard's growing arousal, he held his gaze, his smirk laced with amusement and something deeper.

"These kinds of things," the demon murmured, teasing him.

Certain that his face had become bright red, Alucard looked away, trying to hide his embarrassment as the intoxicating excitement shivered through his body.

"But like I said, it's not very appropriate to be doing in the street, vampire," Zalith murmured, still gripping his arousal.

Alucard frowned, trying to ignore his nervousness—that *same* nervousness he felt whenever Zalith acted so confident and seductive. "Then…maybe…we should go somewhere else?" he suggested, slowly turning his head so that he could stare back into Zalith's eyes.

Zalith laughed quietly. "No, baby. You're going to be late."

Pouting again, Alucard frowned and grumbled frustratedly, "They can wait."

The demon shook his head. "Later," he said, taking his hand out of Alucard's trousers.

As his frustrated scowl grew, Alucard sighed. He knew what he wanted right now, and Zalith was probably *loving* his desperation. He craved Zalith's touch—his attention, his affection. He wanted him so badly that he felt as if he might have to *insist*, but he didn't want to pine in front of the people walking by.

Instead, he said, "Fine."

Zalith laughed, kissed Alucard's cheek, and smiled. "I love you," he said.

Sighing, trying to let his aggravated body relax, Alucard rested his head on Zalith's shoulder. "I love you too," he said, moving his arms around him.

"When should I come and get you?" he asked, wrapping his arms around him.

Holding him, Alucard shrugged a little. "Maybe… an hour. They talk a lot, but… it probably won't take me too long to tell them what we need them to know."

"I have to talk to Idina, Danford, and Greymore, so I might be a little late—but I'll aim for then."

Alucard nodded, stepping back as he slowly pulled out of their hug. He then gripped the demon's hand. "So… I will see you then," he said, letting go of Zalith's hand.

"Okay," the demon said, and then he pulled Alucard closer and kissed him.

The vampire returned the kiss before reluctantly pulling away, turning to make his way down the street. As he walked, he cast a glance over his shoulder, watching as Zalith strode off in the opposite direction. A familiar ache settled in his chest; he already missed him. But they both had things to do, and the sooner their work was done, the sooner he'd be back in Zalith's arms.

Chapter Thirty-One

— ⊰ ✝ ⊱ —

Talk of the Town

| **Alucard**—*Uzlia Isles, Yrudberg, Eimwood City* |

Alucard strolled through the Bauwell Residential District. He knew exactly where Selena's house was—just as he knew that she had already remarried, this time to someone of importance within the city. He wasn't sure who, nor did he particularly care—whoever it was, they weren't someone worth his attention.

As he turned onto Donridge Street, the elegant stretch of white-brick road unfolded before him, lined with stately townhouses that bore a striking resemblance to the one that he and Zalith owned. Selena's home stood at the very end, and so he made his way towards it.

Much like everywhere else in Eimwood, the people he passed greeted him warmly, their waves and smiles almost instinctive, and many of them sported their makeshift versions of his sunglasses. The sky had begun to darken, the sun slipping behind a thick veil of clouds; it looked as though it might stay that way for a while, so with a quiet sigh, Alucard slipped off his sunglasses, tucking them neatly into the pocket of his blazer before continuing on his way.

Once he reached Selena's house, he knocked on the door and waited. Not too long after, the door opened, and standing in the doorway was Selena's butler.

"Good afternoon, sir," he greeted, bowing. "Lady Selena is expecting you."

Alucard trailed behind the butler, his sharp eyes sweeping over the house's interior as they moved through it. The space was overwhelmingly floral—too many flowers, too many patterns, even the furniture itself seemed to have been chosen with a relentless theme in mind. It was stifling, suffocating in its extravagance, but he kept his expression neutral.

The butler led him through to the back porch, where Selena, Mary-Beth, and Cadence were—as expected—engaged in lively gossip. Their voices overlapped, laughter spilling into the air as they chattered away, completely absorbed in whatever latest scandal had captured their interest.

Some things never changed, Alucard mused, stepping forward to announce his presence.

"Ezra!" Selena called, standing up. "We were beginning to think you weren't coming," she said, pulling out the seat between her own and Mary-Beth.

"Where's that workaholic husband of yours?" Cadence giggled as Alucard sat down. "Did he not want to join us?"

The vampire shook his head, making himself comfortable as he took off his cape and hung it over his chair. "He has some important things to do for the city."

Mary-Beth laughed quietly as she placed one of the pink, flower-patterned teacups in front of Alucard. "Oh, he's always working on something," she said, pouring him a cup of tea from the flowery teapot. "He probably barely has any time in the day to relax."

"He just...likes to work," he said—and he was certain Zalith *did* like to work, but he knew that his mate's reason for overworking himself lately was because he didn't feel safe; he felt like he had to keep working, to keep getting things done until he felt comfortable.

"Don't *you* work?" Cadence asked. "We've seen your little guards all around Eimwood, but...."

"I have...business overseas," he said with a shrug. "I just help Silas out here."

"What kind of business?" Selena questioned.

He wasn't going to tell them. "Nothing important."

"Oh, you simply *must* tell us about your wedding," Cadence then said as they all stared at Alucard. "I imagine it must have been spectacular."

The vampire didn't really know what to say. He and Zalith weren't married yet; the people of Eimwood had been made to believe that they were to further protect their true identities. But he had to make something up or they might become skeptical. "Well...it was small," he started. "We're not really one for crowds, so we just...eloped in Samjang."

"I've never been to Samjang," Selena said, frowning. "Is it beautiful? Romantic?"

Alucard nodded. He hadn't been to Samjang either, but he'd always wanted to, and it was one of the places where he might want to have the wedding. "There are a lot of pink trees—a lot more fish, too," he said, glancing up at the overcast sky to see if any of the skyfish had come down from the clouds, but there weren't any.

"The fish," Mary-Beth said, smiling. "Once, as a little girl, I was very lucky to have seen one. You don't see them very often these days—it's like the conflict has scared them off."

"I'm just glad we're safe here," Cadence said with a sigh, sipping from her cup. "Did you hear those religious extremists are spreading all around the world?"

"It's crazy—the stuff of novels," Selena agreed.

"Madness," Mary-Beth said.

"What have you heard?" Alucard asked curiously.

They all set their eyes on him.

"Well, I heard that there's a cult," Selena said ominously, nodding.

"Devil worshipers," Cadence added.

"They're looking for someone," Mary-Beth said and sighed. "I'm just glad we got out of Nefastus after everything that happened—thanks to you and Silas."

Selena then sighed as her butler returned and started handing out plates of cake. "What has the world come to?" she mumbled. "I thought the days of religion-focused wars were over—my old husband used to read about them a lot. A long time ago, Lethidism wasn't the *only* real religion," she said matter-of-factly. "There was also Lilidaism, Lucidism, Damodism, and Ephrism."

Alucard felt slightly surprised that this woman actually knew the names of the old religions before they became cults.

"Oh my," Cadence said, frowning. "How did people know what was right and what was wrong?"

"Everything was right back then," Alucard said. "The world was a more peaceful place before the gods got greedy."

Nodding, Selena sipped from her tea. "They fought, and His might Letholdus rose victorious," she said, smiling. "*He* is the true God. And those who won't follow him fell to form these little cults that still believe in these false gods."

Alucard wanted to sigh—Selena was clearly a Lethidian.

"So, are you having kids?" Cadence then asked.

The vampire almost choked on his tea as he sipped from it. "What?" he uttered.

"Kids—children," she giggled. "I mean… you might both be men, but surely you can adopt or… get yourselves a surrogate."

He frowned. "A… what?"

"A surrogate mother. A woman who will have a baby for you," Selena said and took a rather large bite out of her cake. "They just ask for compensation of the shiny kind."

Cadence scoffed. "I'm sure *you* have enough of that right now." She shifted her sights to Alucard. "She married some fancy city council member—he's *loaded*. I might not have loved my ex, but… I sure did love his money."

Mary-Beth lightly slapped her wrist. "Now, now. It's rude to speak ill of the dead. Anyway," she said, smiling at Alucard. "Have either of you thought about it? Children, that is."

Alucard shrugged. "We have talked about it—"

All three women clapped their hands excitedly.

"Are you hoping for a son or a daughter?" Cadence asked.

The vampire shrugged again. "I don't think…it really matters," he admitted. "I would just like to have a family with him."

"That's so cute," Cadence murmured.

"I wanted to have a family," Selena said with a sigh. "Maybe I will…one day."

Alucard then remembered why he'd even come here in the first place. He looked around at them as they sipped from their tea. "Silas and I have been looking into the water situation," he started.

"Oh, that," Cadence replied, waving her hand. "It's been going on for such a long time—my friend Ariel at the little bookstore I visit said that the water here was *always* poison. It used to be a very disgusting colour—green, she said. And it wasn't algae."

"Ew," Selena groaned.

"A lot of people used to think the elves were responsible—take away what the people need, then they'll do whatever they're told to get it," Cadence said.

"Some people don't think it had anything to do with the elves at all," the vampire said and sipped his tea.

"Oh?" Mary-Beth frowned, looking at him as Selena and Cadence did, too.

"I've heard that Cecil has something to do with it. Silas and I were asking around, and a few people have suggested that maybe he's actually a giant bug," he said as the girls gawped at him. "Maybe he's doing something in the cave that the water goes through before it comes through the city," he suggested. "There were some weird noises coming out of there when Silas sent the scientists to investigate the water."

"What?" Cadence asked, dragging out the word. "Are you sure?"

Alucard nodded. "There were also some strange, large pieces of beetle shell near that cave, too. I don't know," he continued and sipped from his tea again. "It's just a rumour."

The women looked around at each other and started mumbling quietly.

"A giant bug?" Mary-Beth asked Alucard. "Like…a pill bug?"

"Maybe," the vampire said with a nod.

"The cave just through the forest?" Selena asked, shocked.

Nodding again, Alucard placed his cup down. "It's just upstream. The scientists did check out the entrance, but it looked like it went on for miles, and it was too dark for them to go very far," he explained. "But they were sure there was something in there."

"Oh, my," Selena uttered.

"Shouldn't we send the sheriff out there?" Cadence asked worriedly. "Some…some hunters? What if he's a giant monster?"

Alucard shook his head. "Silas and I are looking into it. Like I said, though, it's just a rumour."

"What an unsettling thought," Mary-Beth said, holding her hand to her chest. "A man-sized pill bug?"

"A cockroach?" Cadence questioned with a grimace, looking around at her friends.

Sipping from his tea again, Alucard smirked. He was certain that they were going to spread the rumour, and by tonight, half if not the *whole* city would know about Cecil. Everything was falling into place, and all he and Zalith had to do was sit around and wait.

The balcony door then creaked open. "Selena, my dear, have you seen the—"

Alucard set his sights on the man speaking—it was Bertram, the city council representative who had attended his and Zalith's meeting not too long ago.

Bertram glanced at Alucard, a begrudging look appearing on his face.

"Oh, Bertram, my darling," Selena called, jumping out of her seat. She hurried over to him, took his arm, and planted three quick kisses on his face before standing in front of him. "What is it? Did you lose your secret special dishcloth again?" she asked with a sigh.

He took his eyes off Alucard and looked down at his wife. "N-no. What is *he* doing here?" he questioned, looking at Alucard again.

Selena giggled. "Oh. He's here for tea and cake. He's such an interesting man—we love him. But don't go getting jealous now, honey. He's not interested in us females," she said amusedly.

Mary-Beth sighed. "Ezra here is our *friend*," she corrected.

Selena nodded. "Don't you work with him and his husband?" she asked Bertram.

"I do," he grumbled, glaring at Alucard. "And I had thought that our relationship was strictly business. Now we're having tea together?"

"He's having tea with *us*, dear. You're not invited," Selena teased. "Now, what is it that you need?"

Finally, Bertram took his eyes off Alucard and looked at his wife again. "Nothing. I'll talk to you later," he muttered. Then, without another word, he turned around and disappeared back into the house.

"He's a little…strange," Cadence mumbled as Selena sat back down.

Selena exhaled deeply as she made herself comfortable. "*Everyone's* husband is strange in one way or another. *Your* late husband used to insist that he ate with his hands *all* the time."

Cadence laughed and looked at Alucard.

The moment she set her eyes on him, Alucard felt something close to dread grip his heart. He knew what she was going to ask, and he didn't really like talking about his private life with them.

"Surely there's something strange that *Silas* does," she suggested.

"Oh, tell us," Mary-Beth urged him.

Alucard frowned. "Not really," he mumbled.

"Oh, come on," Cadence said with a wave of her hand. "We won't tell anyone."

That was a lie. Alucard was sure that it would be the news of the city if he told any one of them *anything* that Zalith did. "No, he…well…."

"Come on," they all encouraged.

He shrugged. "Well…I don't…think it's strange. He just…he really likes to feed me."

"Feed you?" Selena asked.

Alucard nodded. "And well…I like it, I just…I tried to do it to him, but I didn't understand why he loves doing it."

"Aw," Mary-Beth drawled, smiling. "It's like you're his little baby."

"Aww," Cadence cooed.

As he ate some of his cake, Alucard pouted. "Maybe," he said. "I don't think it's strange, though…I just can't really understand why he loves to do it."

"Everyone has their own little thing they love doing for their significant other. I'm sure there's something *you* do for him that he might not understand," Mary-Beth said, pouring herself another cup of tea.

The vampire thought to himself for a few moments, but there wasn't really anything he could think of that had ever seemed to confuse Zalith. So, he shook his head. "I…don't think so."

"Well, my late husband used to…."

As the women prattled on, their conversation spiralling into another round of mindless chatter, Alucard found himself staring into his drink, barely listening. The mere mention of Zalith had stirred something deep and aching within him—a gnawing sense of longing that refused to be ignored. It hasn't even been thirty minutes, though. And yet, the emptiness felt unbearable. He wanted to leave, to go to wherever Zalith was, to be near him, to feel him.

Focusing his senses, he reached for the demon's presence—still in the townhouse. That was where he wanted to be. He had done what he needed to here; Selena, Cadence, and Mary-Beth had served their purpose. Now, there was only one thing he wanted.

He finished his tea and cake, and then he waited for the women to stop gossiping. Once they had, he leaned his arms onto the table and said, "I think…it's about time I headed out now. I need to meet Silas and talk to the scientists."

Mary-Beth frowned sadly. "Oh, well…it was really nice seeing you again. You need to come spend time with us more—we miss you."

Alucard smiled. "I will try," he said, standing up.

"Tell Silas to come next time!" Cadence insisted.

The vampire nodded as he pulled his cape on. "I'll try to convince him. Thank you for inviting me."

"Oh, it's our pleasure," Selena said. "See you soon—we hope. You two are so busy these days."

Smiling, Alucard nodded. "Until next time."

Alucard stepped off the porch, barely restraining the sigh of relief that threatened to escape him. The butler guided him back through the overly floral house and towards the front door, and the moment he stepped outside, he paused, breathing in the crisp air as if cleansing himself of the conversation he'd just endured. If he'd stayed any longer, they would have drowned him in even more confounding questions.

But at least he'd learned something useful—Bertram was Selena's new husband. And Bertram, like Cecil, seemed to have an unusual fondness for dishcloths.

The vampire frowned, mulling it over. Coincidence? Maybe. But something about it itched at the back of his mind. He'd bring it up to Zalith later—perhaps there was a connection worth considering.

For now, he slipped his hands into his pockets and turned towards the street, his focus set on one thing—returning to Zalith.

Chapter Thirty-Two

— ⟨ ✝ ⟩ —

Plans for the Inevitable Future of Eimwood

| **Zalith**—*Uzlia Isles, Yrudberg, Eimwood City* |

Within the townhouse office, Zalith sat behind his desk, the remnants of his latest discussion still lingering in the air. He'd just finished briefing Danford and Greymore on what needed to be done regarding Cecil—specifically, the unsettling reality of his being a man-sized insect. Idina had been present as well, receiving her own set of instructions. And with everything laid out, there was nothing more to discuss. With a curt nod, he dismissed them, watching as they filed out of his office before he finally allowed himself to exhale.

Leaning back in his chair, Zalith slouched slightly, exhaling a quiet sigh. He missed his vampire. More than that—he worried for him. Absentmindedly, his fingers found the cool steel of the ring on his right index finger—the same one Alucard wore. It was a habit now, a tell he couldn't shake. Every time unease crept into his thoughts, every time the horrible possibility of something happening to Alucard sank its claws into his mind, he found himself fiddling with it.

Where was his fiancé?

He focused, reaching out with his senses—Selena's house. Alucard was still with her and the other two women she always kept around. Relief settled in his chest, but it didn't quite ease the tension beneath his skin. Part of him wanted to leave—to find him and bring him back. But he still had work to do, and more importantly, he didn't want to pull Alucard away from his friends. As much as he loved and missed him, he couldn't be overbearing. So he stayed put, gripping the ring once more before forcing himself to release it.

With another quiet sigh, the demon rested his arms on the desk and began sifting through the stack of papers in front of him. Two hundred and fourteen new demons had arrived the day before yesterday. Idina was handling their housing arrangements, but it still fell to him to determine where each of them would be most useful in furthering his and Alucard's cause.

He scanned the profiles that Idina and Becker had compiled so far, his sharp eyes flicking over names, backgrounds, and skill summaries. Most would fit well within his ever-growing offensive forces, their talents best suited for battle. Others showed promise for defensive roles, their abilities better applied to guarding strongholds, securing key locations, and ensuring the safety of their expanding domain.

It was a slow process—but a necessary one.

A quiet knock came at his door. He looked over there, setting his eyes on Idina, who leaned her head in.

"Sorry, I forgot something," she said.

He frowned, waiting.

"There's a demon among those you sent me the day before yesterday who can't use ethos," she said. "What do you suggest I do with him?"

Zalith exhaled quietly, looking down at his papers for a moment. He didn't exactly have the time or care to work out what to do with an ethosless demon right now. "Just house him like the rest. I'll work out what to do with him later."

Nodding, Idina went to leave the room... but she hesitated and looked back at Zalith. "Are you doing okay?"

The demon frowned harder—*of course* she'd noticed his face. "I'm okay," he said almost vacantly.

"Are you sure?" she asked, leaning on the door. "You don't look okay."

Zalith sighed deeply. He wasn't sure whether he should tell her, but he *was* trying to get over his paranoia. And there was no harm in telling her; she'd already seen that he wasn't feeling his best. So he glanced down at the papers on his desk again, reading through them. "I'm just... worried about Alucard, I suppose," he mumbled.

"Alucard?" Idina asked, making her way over. "Did something happen?" She sat in the seat across the table from him.

He shook his head. "No. Nothing happened. I'm just paranoid."

"About what?"

Sighing again, he sorted through a few pieces of paper. "That he'll get hurt... or killed... or captured," he muttered. "He keeps reassuring me that things are different now, but things don't feel different."

Idina frowned. "It *has* only been a month. You're right to still have your doubts— we all have them. Anything could happen, despite the amount of work everyone's put into making this place safe. You're not wrong to feel like this."

He nodded stiffly. "I hate feeling like this, but you're right," he mumbled. "Lately, I've been concerned that Alucard's going to start resenting me because I always want to be around him, and because I'm always wondering where he is and what he's doing. I'm trying to calm down, though—and I haven't been in the same general area as him for a while now," he said, still sorting through his papers.

She shook her head. "I don't think he would resent you for it. I'm sure he understands. A lot has happened in these past months, and I can't even imagine what you've both been through. And if Alucard really did have a problem with your worry, I'm convinced he would tell you."

The demon shrugged, shaking his head a little as he set his sights on her. "Sometimes I wonder if he just tolerates it because he doesn't want to start an argument," he said—he was pretty sure Alucard tried his best to avoid conflict in their relationship. "I know he cares, but he hasn't really said much about it."

"Well…maybe you should talk to him about it," she suggested.

He shook his head again. "I don't want an argument either. There's a chance that it *won't* turn out that way, but I know what I'm like."

Idina frowned sympathetically. "Every couple has their arguments. It's better to talk about these things rather than leave them unsaid. For all you know, Alucard could be perfectly fine with how you're being right now."

"I suppose," he said with a sigh. But he knew that even if Alucard *was* okay with his behaviour, *he* was not.

Idina smiled. "Just try talking to him."

"We'll see," he said, smiling a little.

The demon then moved his papers aside. "How are things going for you?" he asked, changing the subject.

She smiled. "They're good. Colt's settling in—he's napping upstairs right now. As for myself, I like to keep myself distracted with all the demons you've been sending our way. Soren's a little…odd, but…he gets the job done."

Zalith laughed. "A *little* odd?"

Idina laughed, too. "Well, maybe not just a little, but at least he's not rude."

"Well, he certainly doesn't know when to stop talking. Some might consider that rudeness," he said, smirking—and then he heard the front door open, followed by the alleviating sound of Alucard's voice as the butler greeted him. He felt overwhelmingly relieved—it was a little early, but he was glad that his vampire was back. Maybe now he could let himself relax…even if only for a short while.

| **Alucard**—*Uzlia Isles, Yrudberg, Eimwood City* |

Alucard made his way up the townhouse stairs, sighing away the morning's fatigue, masking his presence so that Soren wouldn't see him from the lounge. All he wanted to do was crawl into bed with Zalith, but he was quite sure that he wouldn't get his wish until much later. Seeing him was enough for now, though. He stepped into Zalith's office, setting his eyes on the demon, who was sitting behind his desk—and Idina was sitting across from him.

"Oh, hello Alucard," Idina said with a smile, looking over her shoulder at him.

The vampire smiled at them both. "Hi," he replied, unbuttoning his blazer.

"Hi," Zalith said contently. "Come sit," he then said, patting the arm of his chair.

"I didn't interrupt, did I?" he asked, making his way over to Zalith.

"No, we're just chatting," the demon said as Alucard sat on the arm of his chair. Then, he set his sights back on Idina as he moved his arm around the vampire's waist. "I was actually going to ask you if you'd like Cecil's manor once we've removed him from the city," he told her.

"O-oh," she said, almost gasping. "Thank you... but that's an awful lot of house for just Colt and me."

"Alucard and I will have to operate out of it here and there to keep up appearances, but I was going to offer the house to Greymore if you didn't want it. So, if you're worried about being lonely, maybe one of us can convince him to move in alongside you," the demon suggested.

Alucard nodded. "Thomas was actually telling me not too long ago how he feels lonely," he said with a shrug. "Maybe it'll be good for the both of you."

Idina smiled and said, "Oh, Colt loves him—that would be great. I'll talk to Greymore." She paused for a moment. "Anyway, I'll let you two catch up—thank you for offering us the house." She smiled, standing up. "I'm sure I'll convince Greymore. Bye," she called, leaving the room.

"Goodbye," Zalith replied.

Once Idina had left, Alucard smiled down at Zalith—the demon instantly pulled him into his lap, which Alucard straddled, moving his arms around his mate's shoulders.

"I missed you," Alucard said shyly, resting his forehead against Zalith's.

"I missed you too," Zalith replied, fiddling with Alucard's hair. "You're here early," he then said with a smirk.

Alucard shrugged. "I don't like to be away from you for too long—I start to feel... empty," he mumbled. "And after I told them what they needed to know, I sort of just lost interest in anything else they had to say," he admitted, pouting.

The demon moved his hand to the side of Alucard's face and frowned slightly. "I'm sorry I made you go. I thought you'd have a nice time."

"I did... especially when I found out that Selena's new husband is Bertram... and that Bertram seems to like dishcloths as much as Cecil."

"Oh?"

"Do you think there's a connection?"

"It's possible," Zalith said. "I wouldn't be surprised."

"Maybe all of Cecil's council are giant bugs," he said, cringing.

The demon looked revolted. "Ugh. I hope they're not planning anything. Although... if they *do* start something, and everyone sees us fighting off giant bugs to save the city, that would make us look really good," he mused.

Alucard smirked. "We already look really good," he said, stroking his hand to the side of Zalith's neck. "The people love us."

"Couldn't hurt to look better."

With a nod, Alucard sighed quietly. "So, what did you do while I was gone?"

"Work," he said as the vampire leaned back and started fiddling with his hair. "I talked to Danford and Greymore about spreading the Cecil rumour."

"I'm sure the whole city will know by tonight."

"I hope so. But I want to let it sit and stew for a couple of days—just to make sure."

Alucard smiled—that meant they'd have a couple of days to themselves. Maybe he could get Zalith to take a break. "Well...maybe we can go somewhere nice for those couple of days."

Zalith exhaled quietly, looking conflicted. "What if something happens while we're gone?"

The vampire shrugged slightly. "I don't think anything will happen. Soren, Thomas, and Idina can keep an eye on things while we're gone."

His mate still looked conflicted, though. There was worry in his eyes.

Alucard was certain that some time away would do them both good, and he wasn't going to give in without at least *trying* to convince him. So he trailed his hand to the side of Zalith's face and quietly said, "We'll only be gone two days. There are already so many demons here; if something were to happen, they would defend everyone. And Soren, Thomas, and Idina will keep everything under control—they are our best people, no? And I've lost count of how many protective barriers and wards we have around these islands—no one will ever find this place. And...maybe we can go somewhere close— somewhere where I can get us back here in no time if something does happen."

Zalith stared at him, a pondering expression on his face.

"Please," the vampire pleaded, pouting.

The demon sighed, clearly trying to hide his smile. "Fine," he agreed.

Alucard smiled contently and kissed the demon's lips. "Thank you."

"Anything for you, baby," Zalith said, tucking a loose strand of his crimson hair behind his right ear. "When do we have to meet Pecker?" he asked with a smirk.

Staring into his dark eyes, Alucard sighed a little. "Well...any time, I guess. He's in the room downstairs."

"Okay," the demon said. "I guess we should go and see him soon, then."

Alucard nodded.

But instead of rising from his seat, Zalith leaned in, his warm breath ghosting over Alucard's lips before capturing them in a slow, lingering kiss. Alucard melted into it, sighing softly against his mouth, savouring the heat of Zalith's touch. And for a while, that was all there was—just the two of them, lips meeting in an unhurried rhythm, the world beyond this moment entirely forgotten.

As Zalith's fingers brushed against his jaw, though, Alucard's mind stirred, a flicker of memory cutting through the haze of pleasure. The desire to remind Zalith of what he'd said earlier quickly ensnared him, and with a smile against his mate's lips, he pulled back slightly and shyly murmured, "So…are you still going to do things to me?"

Zalith smirked. "Well, actually, I was considering bending you over this desk, but all the bug people talk really got to me."

Disappointment consumed Alucard. "Really?" he asked sadly.

The demon laughed and rested his forehead against Alucard's. "No," he said, and then he kissed his lips again.

Amused, Alucard smiled and returned Zalith's kiss, and as they started kissing eagerly, the demon's hand drifted from the vampire's face, fingers deftly working open the buttons of his shirt. A thrill coursed through Alucard as Zalith's palm pressed against his bare chest; their kisses deepened, unhurried but intoxicating, each one drawing him further into the pull of his mate's touch.

With a quiet hum of approval, Alucard tugged at Zalith's shirt, freeing it from his trousers. His hands traced over the demon's torso, his palm carefully stroking his firm muscles, and anticipation coiled in his stomach as Zalith's hand wandered past his waist, teasing him with every slow movement.

"Do you want blood?" Zalith then asked.

Alucard hesitated for only a moment, sinking into the anticipation. He *loved* the taste of Zalith's blood—the rich, intoxicating sweetness of it, the way it sent a rush of euphoria through his veins. His lips curled into a small, eager smile. "Yes, please."

Zalith's own smile deepened, his dark eyes gleaming with amusement as he slid his hand to the back of Alucard's head, fingers threading through his hair. He pulled the vampire closer, tilting his head aside, silently inviting Alucard in—an offering that the vampire had no intention of denying.

Alucard leaned in, trailing his fingers lightly over Zalith's neck, feeling the steady pulse beneath his touch. He already knew exactly where he wanted to bite—where he wanted to taste him. He pressed a lingering kiss to his mate's throat…once, twice, and then, with agonizing slowness, he sank his fangs into the demon's skin. A quiet, pleasured moan escaped Zalith as his grip tightened in Alucard's hair, his body tensing just enough to betray his enjoyment. At the same time, his other hand slid down Alucard's body, slipping into his trousers.

The moment Zalith's blood touched his tongue, bliss rippled through Alucard's body—warm, euphoric, electrifying. And the sensation only heightened as Zalith's fingers wrapped around his arousal, stroking him with the same teasing pace that always drove him mad.

It *always* felt so good. His mate's blood soothed something deep inside him, it made him feel whole, wanted, needed. A soft moan escaped him as he gripped the back of Zalith's head, his fingers tangling in the demon's hair as Zalith let out a low, breathy sound of approval.

But Alucard wouldn't take too much—he never did.

He lingered for only a few moments more, drinking deeply, relishing the pleasure and the intimacy of it. Then, with a final, contented moan, he withdrew his fangs, exhaling against Zalith's skin as he lazily licked the blood from his teeth. "Thank you," he murmured as his hand traced a slow path from Zalith's head and down his shoulder.

"You're welcome, baby," Zalith said with a smirk, still caressing the vampire's arousal.

With a satisfied smile, Alucard tilted his head, wordlessly inviting Zalith closer. The demon didn't hesitate. His lips found the vampire's throat, trailing slow kisses down the column of his neck. A deep, pleased sigh sat upon the vampire's breath as warmth spread through his body, his grip tightening in Zalith's hair.

When Zalith's mouth lingered on a particular spot, sucking gently, a shiver ran through him. Alucard hummed, the sound barely above a whisper, his smile turning languid. He could feel the heat of Zalith's breath against his skin, the teasing graze of fangs that never quite bit down, drawing out the anticipation. He tugged lightly at Zalith's hair, silently urging him to keep going.

As Zalith's touch grew more eager, tension coiled in Alucard's body, the pleasure building with every slow movement. He'd waited too long for this, too long to feel Zalith's devoted attention, to bask in the heat of his hands and the teasing press of his lips. He nuzzled into the demon's neck, his fingers tracing firm, appreciative lines over the taut muscle of Zalith's abdomen. The vampire exhaled deeply against his skin, shivering at the sensation of the demon's mouth still working over his throat, his hand still steadily stroking his dick.

A quiet, breathy sound of pleasure escaped Zalith as Alucard's hand slipped past his waistline, fingers gently grasping his shaft. The demon tensed slightly, exhaling sharply as Alucard pulled off his shirt with his free hand, determined to feel more of him. Zalith responded in kind, abandoning Alucard's neck to recapture his lips, their kiss deepening as he slid the vampire's shirt from his shoulders.

Then, without hesitation, Zalith stood, bringing Alucard with him. He turned the vampire around in his arms, hands roaming possessively over his body. With a slow, teasing drag of his lips up the curve of Alucard's neck, he whispered into his ear, his voice low and enticing, "Bend over," as he stroked his fingers down the vampire's right side and pulled his trousers away.

Alucard obeyed, bracing himself against Zalith's desk as he leaned forward, his anticipation mounting with every passing second. He ever so slightly tensed when he felt Zalith's hands on him, massaging the slick, warm lube into his ass, preparing him with gradual, soft strokes. The sensation sent a shudder through him, and he exhaled deeply, lowering himself onto his forearms, his eagerness growing unbearable.

Then came the first slow push—Zalith eased his dick into him, stretching him with torturous patience. A quiet, breathy moan slipped from Alucard's lips as pleasure rippled through him, heat unfurling in waves. As the demon moved deeper, a shiver ran down his spine, his body instinctively yielding to the intrusion, sinking into the intoxicating sensation of being filled.

But just as Alucard adjusted, his mate grabbed his wrist, pulling it behind his back. Before the vampire could react, Zalith took hold of his other wrist, securing them both, rendering him helpless beneath him. A sharp thrill coursed through Alucard as he let out a soft, surprised grunt, his cheek pressing against the scattered papers on Zalith's desk.

Then Zalith started moving, his thrusts slow but deep, the pressure exquisite. The vampire moaned, his voice muffled against the wood, his body thrumming with pleasure as Zalith took his time, setting a pace that was both maddening and utterly intoxicating.

Zalith's pace quickened, his movements gaining an intensity that sent a fresh wave of delight rippling through Alucard's body. The demon gently tapped his ankle with his foot, urging Alucard to part his legs further, and he obeyed without hesitation, his breath catching as the shift in position made each thrust hit deeper. His heart pounded, anticipation curling tight in his stomach, and when Zalith's grip on his wrists tightened, a quiet, needy whine slipped from his lips.

Alucard *loved* when the demon became rougher, when he took full control, leaving him no choice but to surrender beneath him. The pressure, the weight of it all only made his pleasure more intense. Zalith moaned contently, his own enjoyment evident in the way he held him down, in the way his movements grew more forceful with every passing moment. Alucard responded in kind, a deep, breathless moan escaping him as his body trembled under Zalith's touch.

The demon thrusted faster, still keeping his grip firm, keeping Alucard exactly where he wanted him. The relentless pace sent the vampire hurtling towards his peak, his body strung tight with euphoria, trembling from the sheer intensity. His moans grew needier, a sharp grimace crossing his face as heat coiled at the base of his spine. His legs ached, and the edge of the desk digging into his stomach was a dull, distant discomfort—but it was drowned out by the overwhelming bliss, the consuming pleasure of Zalith's touch and the lingering delight of his blood still thrumming in Alucard's veins.

As always, Alucard couldn't hold back. His body tensed, pleasure surging through him in an intoxicating wave that left him trembling. He moaned deeply, *desperately* as he scowled in struggle, his climax ripping through him with an intensity that stole his breath. His muscles clenched, his grip tightening against the desk as his entire body shuddered beneath the force of his reaching his peak.

Zalith didn't stop. He kept thrusting, his pace unrelenting, drawing out every last pulse of Alucard's pleasure. His grip on the vampire's wrists tightened, his breath turning ragged, and then—he let go. A content, satisfied moan spilled from Zalith's lips as he came, warmth flooding into Alucard, deep and searing, sending another shiver through his already overstimulated body. The sensation—*the fullness of it, the heat*—only prolonged the aftershocks, leaving Alucard breathless, his heart hammering as he sank into the bliss.

The vampire then exhaled deeply, willing his body to relax as Zalith finally released his wrists. His limbs felt weak, his skin still thrumming with the lingering echoes of delight, but before he could fully settle, Zalith helped him to his feet and pulled him back down onto his lap. With a tired sigh, Alucard rested his head against the demon's shoulder, closing his eyes for a moment as he let himself sink into the warmth of his mate's embrace.

All he wanted now was to collapse into bed with Zalith, to lay tangled together and simply *exist* in each other's arms. But their day wasn't over yet. He sighed again, his fingers absentmindedly tracing over Zalith's shoulder. They still had to see Soren, and knowing Zalith, there were plenty more tasks he wanted to get through before they finally took their much-needed vacation.

"You're not allowed to take any work with you when we go away for a few days," he said firmly. "We're just going to enjoy a few days together away from all of this."

"What if my work finds me?" Zalith asked with a quiet laugh.

The vampire shrugged. "I won't let that happen," he said, prodding Zalith's left cheek.

The demon chuckled quietly but shook his head. "Come on. We should go and see Pecker—get it out of the way."

"Okay," Alucard said with a nod of agreement.

He pushed himself up with a quiet sigh, reaching for his trousers and pulling them back on as Zalith cleaned himself up. The demon, ever thoughtful, handed him a few tissues from his desk, and Alucard knelt briefly to wipe away the evidence of their time together, ensuring no trace was left behind.

Once they were both dressed and composed, Alucard cast Zalith a lingering glance, a small, satisfied smirk tugging at his lips. Then, without another word, they stepped out of the office, ready to face whatever the rest of the day had in store.

Chapter Thirty-Three

— ᚴ ✝ ᚵ —

Wedding Planner

| **Alucard**—*Uzlia Isles, Yrudberg, Eimwood City* |

Alucard led the way downstairs, making his way towards the lounge where Soren worked. The moment he stepped inside, the faint scent of ink and parchment filled the air, mingling with the lingering traces of candle smoke. Behind his desk, Soren lifted his head groggily, blinking as if roused from an impromptu nap. His expression shifted the moment he saw Alucard, but the vampire had no interest in hearing whatever excuse he was about to offer. He strode forward, his gaze steady, making it clear that he wasn't in the mood for delays.

"Tell me what you found," he said, standing by the window with Zalith.

"Uh..." Soren drawled, rubbing his forehead with a frown. "I wasn't sleeping—on the job, that is." He straightened up in his chair, quickly reaching beneath his desk as if to prove his point. "I spent all night working on this," he added, standing with a noticeable effort as he lifted a thick, red binder into view. "And just hear me out," he insisted, cutting off whatever sharp remark Alucard had been about to make. He stepped around the desk, positioning himself in front of them with a look of determination, and then he flipped open the cover to reveal the first page. Bold letters stretched across the top, painstakingly neat and dramatically underlined:

Alucard and Zalith's Wedding Planner Pitch

Both Alucard and Zalith rolled their eyes.

"Look!" Soren insisted, holding up a hand as if to silence any objections before they could start. "All I do is sit around in this little house, interview these demons you send my way—not that I hate my job," he added quickly, nodding. "I'm glad you wanna involve me in your grand scheme to kill the Numen." He flipped to the next page in his binder with a flourish. "But I can do more—I *want* to do more. You two are always so busy, so obviously, you want me to find you a wedding planner—*but*—"

With an exaggerated pause, Soren thrust the binder forward, displaying two densely packed pages filled with scribbled notes, floral arrangements, menu ideas, and what could only be described as the frantic energy of a man who had spent *way* too much time on this.

A self-satisfied grin spread across his face. "What if I did it all for you? Skip the finding a wedding planner—*I* can be your wedding planner. You two can sit back, relax, do whatever it is you do, and I'll take care of this whooooole thing for you," he declared, flipping to another set of pages where he had painstakingly glued cut-out images of extravagant wedding outfits. With an eager nod, he gestured to his work. "You like what you see? There's more where this came from."

With a quiet sigh, Alucard rested his chin in his hand, his elbow propped on his crossed arm. "Okay," he mumbled, eyes narrowing slightly. "Like what?"

Soren's grin widened. He eagerly flipped through the pages as he spoke, his energy practically buzzing, "I can sort out everything for you—the guests, the music, the food, the attire, the venue, even—and," he added pointedly, glancing up, "I'm sure you'd feel more comfortable putting this in the hands of someone you know rather than some random wedding planner who's just gonna be more interested in the money than what you two actually want, right?"

"It's their *job* to do what we want," Zalith said.

"Yeah, but," Soren said with a shrug, "I've known Alucard for forever—you won't have to go through the stage of letting your organizer get to know you. *And* I've planned a wedding before, too—this won't be my first time."

Alucard frowned. "You do know, Soren... I'm not the same man I was two hundred years ago."

"Yeah, but... we get along," he said, placing his binder on the desk behind him. "You won't have to deal with no snobby know-it-all."

Sighing, Alucard thought to himself for a few moments. Soren had a point. It would probably be a lot less stressing if they could work with someone they knew—well, someone *he* knew. He knew Soren was good at what he did, and he put his all into everything, too. He wouldn't let them down, that was for sure. But was it what Zalith wanted? He looked at the demon and asked, "What do you think?"

Zalith frowned. "If we're going to rifle through people we know to find someone to do this, what's stopping us from choosing Idina or someone we're closer to?"

Soren shrugged and shook his head. "Has Idina planned a wedding before? Probably not. And she needs to rest, I don't—"

"You were literally just napping over there," Alucard said with a scowl.

"I was brainstorming!" Soren insisted, stepping closer. "Please?" he pleaded. "When have I ever let you down? Now won't be an exception."

Zalith rolled his eyes—his dislike of Soren was clearly growing by the second. "I'll tell you what," he said. "Cecil should be out of power by early next week; I want you to plan a city-wide party celebrating that and the fact that Alucard and I will be taking his position. If you can do that well, then I will consider considering you as our wedding planner."

Soren's face lit up. "Really? Of course—I won't disappoint either of you," he insisted. "I'll organize the best party this city has ever seen!"

The demon sighed again. "Alucard and I are going away for a few days, but depending on the state of the city, we can talk about the budget when we get back."

"No problem," Soren said with a smile, sitting on the edge of his desk. "I'll start thinking of ideas right away—you won't be disappointed."

Zalith rolled his eyes. "You already said that," he mumbled.

Certain that Zalith was tired of Soren already, Alucard said, "Right, well, now you have something to do. Zalith and I have places to be."

Soren nodded. "Oh, yeah. You go do what you need to do—"

"And don't forget," Alucard warned him. "You still have your first job to do, too."

"Don't worry about it. I'll have the rest of these demons figured out before you get back."

"Good… because we will most likely be sending more your way next week."

Nodding, Soren sat back down behind his desk. "I'll keep you updated with everything."

Alucard then glanced at Zalith to see if he had anything further to say, but it didn't look like he did. So, the vampire took hold of his hand and led the way out of the room.

Once they left the house and stepped out onto the street, Alucard sighed and stopped by the horse-hitching post. "I wasn't expecting that," he mumbled.

"Me neither," the demon said.

"Is there anything else you need to do here today?" he then asked.

"No," Zalith said, smiling at him. "I've done all my work here."

"So… should we head home and pack some things for our trip?"

"Oh," the demon replied as his smile became a smirk. "Do you know where we're going?"

Alucard had a few ideas, and he'd decide which one he liked the most when they got home. "I have a few ideas. It's a surprise, though," he said, starting to lead the way down the street.

The demon laughed quietly and kissed Alucard's lips. "I can't wait."

Chapter Thirty-Four

— ≺ ✝ ≻ —

Sleeves

| **Alucard,** *Saturday, Tertium 18th, 960(TG)—Uzlia Isles, Usrul, Castle Reiner* |

The morning was quiet, the air crisp with the lingering chill of dawn. Alucard and Zalith sat outside on their porch, their breakfast table laden with an assortment of eggs, bacon, fresh bread, fruits, and a variety of beverages. Across from him, Zalith ate his fruit and yoghurt parfait, while Alucard idly picked at a plate of strawberries and toast, his mind elsewhere.

He found himself retracing the past week's events, his thoughts circling back to the unsettling reality they had yet to discuss—what if all of Cecil's council were also giant bugs? That question had lingered in his mind since their discovery, yet neither he nor Zalith had discussed it much. And with their trip fast approaching—a vacation where no work would be tolerated, a rule that Alucard had made very clear—this was his last chance to bring it up. It was better to deal with it now than let it fester.

He looked at Zalith and asked, "So, do you think all of Cecil's council are giant bugs, too?"

"I wouldn't be surprised," the demon said. "But how can we prove it?" he asked and took a sip of his coffee.

Alucard frowned, sipping from his orange juice. "I feel like there's a connection with those dishcloths. Maybe we should get someone to investigate the other members."

Zalith nodded. "I'll tell an izuret to send Danford out again," he said, finishing his parfait. "I think we should do a little more research on these Insectumoids, too—Idina can do it, though. This kind of thing is right up her alley."

"What do we do with them if they're all bugs?" Alucard asked, buttering another piece of toast.

"I'm torn between what I want to do and what's moral."

Alucard smiled slightly. "What do *you* want to do?"

The demon laughed. "Call an exterminator."

"What exterminator can get rid of seven giant, ethos-repelling bug men?"

"A smart man with a big can of bug spray," his mate said with a shrug.

Laughing again, Alucard finished his toast. "I guess we should get someone to look around for one such person just in case we end up needing one."

Zalith nodded, sipping from his coffee again. "Or maybe we just need one strong man and a really big fly swatter," he said, smirking. "Either way, I want them gone."

The vampire refilled his orange juice. "Maybe Idina will find out some of their weaknesses during her research."

"I hope so."

Alucard then smiled at Zalith. "Are you excited for today?" he asked, changing the subject.

"I am," the demon said contently. "I can't wait to see where you're taking me."

"I've never been there myself. But I've always wanted to go, and I had no one to go with, but... now I have you," he said, his smile becoming shy.

Zalith's smile grew. "What's so special about it?" he asked curiously.

"It's a surprise," the vampire teased.

"I await with bated breath," the demon said, finishing his coffee.

"We're going to have to take the boat, though."

"How far is it?" Zalith asked, taking a few pieces of bacon and some eggs and adding them to the toast on his plate.

Alucard shrugged, eating his last strawberry. "It's about an hour or so on the steamship."

"Okay," the demon said.

"I heard there's a big festival happening near where we're going, too—do you want to go?"

The demon nodded. "Sounds good."

"Okay," Alucard said, taking one last piece of toast. "Did you pack everything you think you'll need?"

"I think so," Zalith said, finishing his bacon and eggs.

"Good. Well... if you're ready to go, we can probably head to the ship now," he said—there wasn't anything else he could of that they had to do. They'd already sent izurets to inform everyone who needed to know that they were going to be away for a few days. All that was left to do was head to the ship and be on their way.

"I'm ready," the demon said.

Alucard led the way through the castle, Zalith following close behind. They made a final check to ensure Edwin had packed all their belongings onto the ship waiting in the castle's private boatyard. Satisfied, they mounted their horses and rode down the hillside, cutting across the meadow before following the winding path around the hill towards the docks.

The steamboat awaited them, its black-and-gold-painted hull gleaming beneath the sun. Twin smokestacks towered above the deck, a faint wisp of steam curling into the sky as the engine quietly rumbled. Brass fixtures adorned the railings, polished to a shine, and the large paddle wheel at the stern sat idle, awaiting the signal to begin their journey. Crew members bustled about, making final preparations, ensuring their voyage would be smooth and uninterrupted.

Upon arrival, Alucard and Zalith hitched their horses where Edwin would later retrieve them, and then stepped aboard. The steady hum of the engine and the rhythmic creak of the wooden deck beneath their boots signalled the beginning of their much-needed retreat—one where, for once, duty would be left behind.

They headed into the cabin, where Zalith sat on the couch, and Alucard rested beside him. When the vampire glanced at his face, though, he could see that his mate was uncomfortable; he was panicking, wasn't he? Alucard knew that he didn't really want to leave Uzlia, even if it was only for a few days. But Zalith needed a break from everything. Hopefully he'd settle a little once they were away from the islands.

A comfortable silence enveloped them as the ship moved along the sea. Alucard rested in Zalith's embrace, enjoying the warmth of his arms. But the further they sailed, the warmer the temperature grew—it became very humid, and eventually, Zalith took his blazer off and rolled up his shirt sleeves. Alucard also took his blazer off, and then he rested his head on the demon's chest.

"Aren't you hot, baby?" Zalith asked, moving his hand up to the top button of his shirt. "Why don't you roll up your sleeves?" he suggested as he unbuttoned the top two buttons of the vampire's shirt.

Alucard shrugged as he took hold of Zalith's hand. "I'm okay."

"Are you sure? It's pretty hot out."

"I'll be okay," the vampire insisted, making himself comfortable again.

"Are you certain?" he asked again.

The vampire nodded, moving his arm around Zalith.

Zalith frowned despondently, tightening his embrace around him. "Alucard," he said quietly, caressing his hair. "You don't have to hide your scars from me, and you shouldn't feel like you have to hide them from the world, either. I love you just the way you are, and I don't care what other people think. I know how you feel about them, and I'm not going to force you to stop hiding them, but I just want you to know that they're a part of you, and I love *every* part of you."

Alucard held Zalith a little tighter. He knew that his mate was only trying to help, and he knew that he loved him just as he was and didn't care about the scars. And sometimes, Alucard believed it... but only in fleeting moments, mostly when they were tangled up in bed, when Zalith's focus was elsewhere—on pleasure, not on the marred state of his arms or back. But now, in the quiet stillness, with nothing to distract them, the thought gnawed at him. What if Zalith was looking? What if he saw just how ugly they really were?

He didn't want that. He didn't want to be seen, not like this. And worse, he didn't want his own standing—or lack thereof—to tarnish Zalith's. Zalith was rising, becoming something greater, and Alucard feared dragging him down. No wings... it was the greatest disgrace in demon society. If Zalith's growing ranks saw that their leader's mate was something so pitiful, something incomplete... would they still respect him? Would they still follow him so loyally? He felt like a burden, and no amount of reassurance, no matter how often Zalith offered it, would change that.

He frowned sadly and buried his face against Zalith's chest. "I know," he said quietly, his voice muffled against the demon's shirt. "I just... hate them. They make me feel... disgusting," he admitted. "And I know you don't think that, and that means a lot to me, but not everyone will feel that way, and I don't want them to see me with you and think less of you because of it."

"I don't care what anyone thinks of me," the demon said, hugging him tightly.

"I know, but you're trying to build something here, and I don't want to get in the way—because I *will*. The people who have always been with you might not care, but the people you are trying to get to believe in you and what we are doing *will*," he insisted. "They won't respect you for being with someone like me, and therefore won't want to follow you. So I just keep them hidden so no one will see," he said, resting the side of his head on Zalith's chest, staring over at the empty fireplace.

Fiddling with the vampire's hair, Zalith moved his free hand over Alucard's arm and hugged him again. "If they don't respect me *or* you, then I'll kill them," he said simply. "I don't care what anyone else thinks. And right now, it's just us," he said, moving his hand up Alucard's arm again. "Don't feel pressured, but I want you to feel comfortable around me—I love everything about you, Alucard, and your scars are no exception."

The vampire sighed quietly. He felt conflicted. Zalith was right; he didn't need to feel so uncomfortable around him—and he didn't, he just worried that someone might see him and it would get back to Zalith's new followers. But it *was* just them right now, and he was awfully aggravated in the humid heat. "Okay," he said quietly—he felt nervous about it, for he had done his best to shroud his scars all his life, but maybe it was time to stop doing that. He already felt so relaxed around Zalith, and he knew that the demon thought no less of him because of his scars—and he didn't feel pressured, either. "You're right," he mumbled, moving his own hand down to his shirt sleeve.

Zalith helped him unbutton his shirt's right cuff as he said, "Most things that have wings don't have them down here." He guided his hand over the scars on the underneath of Alucard's forearm. "So no one's going to know," he assured him.

That was true, too. Alucard had never seen nor heard of any other demon possessing a second pair of wings—especially not a pair that conjoined with their arms. So maybe nobody would notice—his back, on the other hand...he'd keep that covered no matter what. *Everyone* would notice what had happened there.

"See," Zalith then said with a smile once he finished helping him roll up his sleeves. "You look so handsome."

Alucard smiled, laying back down. He rested his head on Zalith's shoulder, moved his left arm around him, and exhaled quietly. He wanted to change the subject. The increasingly humid heat made it clear that they were close to arriving, and soon, they'd have to prepare to disembark. "I think you're really going to like this place."

"What is it?" the demon asked curiously.

"A secret," Alucard said, smirking.

"Can I have a hint?"

Alucard thought to himself for a moment. He couldn't really think of a hint that wouldn't give away where they were heading, but he also liked watching Zalith try to guess what he was hiding. "Well...it was really expensive," he said with a quiet laugh.

"How expensive?"

The vampire shrugged. "A few hundred."

"A few hundred what?"

"Gold," Alucard mumbled.

Zalith laughed quietly. "That *is* expensive. Do you think we'll be able to afford it?" he said with a smirk.

Alucard laughed, too. "I don't know...we might have to take out a loan."

"I hope we have enough for the wedding," Zalith then said.

"You're not so happy about Soren's offer, hmm?"

"No," his mate answered. "Do you think he'll do a good job?"

"Well..." Alucard paused and sighed. "Yes," he answered honestly. "When he sets his mind to something, he does a really good job. He seems really invested in this, so...I trust him," he said confidently. "He won't let us down—I wouldn't have agreed if I thought he would."

"I think I need some more convincing," the demon said.

Alucard frowned. "Well, I guess we'll see how he does with the Eimwood celebration."

"I suppose we will," Zalith said.

Alucard turned his gaze to the window, watching as vibrantly coloured birds flitted past, their feathers catching the sunlight like scattered jewels. Beyond them, skyfish drifted lazily through the open air, their translucent fins shimmering despite the absence of clouds or rain. The scent of saltwater mingled with the sweetness of ripe fruit and the delicate fragrance of tropical flowers, a blend both foreign and intoxicating.

The heat, however, was beginning to weigh on him. He knew it wouldn't bother Zalith—not when his body burned with a natural warmth unaffected by climate. For a fleeting moment, Alucard envied him. But his body, accustomed to much harsher extremes, was already beginning to adjust. He was born to survive Hell, after all—his small non-demon lineage only made the process take a little longer.

Once he'd adapted, he said, "I think we're almost there."

The demon smirked. "I can't wait to see where you've taken me."

Alucard didn't move as the ship began to slow, the gentle shift of the vessel barely registering against the steady warmth of Zalith's embrace. He wasn't ready to leave this moment behind—not yet. For just a little longer, he wanted to stay right here, wrapped in his mate's arms, where the world and all its worries felt so far away.

ASCENDANT
Numen Chronicles | Volume Five

Arc Three — † — Time Away

ASCENDANT
Numen Chronicles | Volume Five

Chapter Thirty-Five

— ᛉ ✝ ᛊ —

A Short, Tropical Escape

| **Zalith**—*Maluhia, Lunakai, A'okalani Cove Resort* |

As Zalith followed Alucard onto the deck, the view struck him at once—towering mountains rising like sentinels in the distance, emerald forests spilling down their slopes, and a stretch of white sand curving along the shore on either side of the dock ahead. The water below had turned crystal clear, revealing strange and mesmerizing creatures gliding through the depths, their scales catching the humid sunlight in iridescent flashes. The scent of salt and ripe fruit clung to the air, carried by a warm, lazy breeze, while the only sounds were the distant trill of birds and the rhythmic hush of waves. No bustling crowds. No shouting voices. Just stillness.

The quiet settled over him, sinking into his bones like warmth after a long cold spell. It was…peace. True, undisturbed peace. No one clawing for his attention, no demands, no endless calls of his name pulling him in a dozen directions. Just him, Alucard, and the serenity of this place wrapping around him, loosening something deep inside his chest.

"I love it already," Zalith said contently, looking at Alucard as they stopped by the ship's gate.

"Wait until you see where we're staying," the vampire said, smiling.

"Is it on the beach?"

Alucard shook his head. "No. I already told you how much I hate sand," he said with a quiet laugh.

Zalith laughed, too. "I thought you might be trying to change your ways."

The vampire stared out at the dock as the ship stopped, and the crew started to moor it. "I remember what you said about where you wanted to have our wedding—somewhere with water. So, I thought I could take you on a sort of…vacation—somewhere with water," he explained, leading Zalith down onto the bamboo dock once the crew extended the bridge onto it.

"That's very nice—thank you," he said and kissed the vampire's cheek.

Zalith followed his fiancé down the dock, expecting him to head for the beach—but instead, Alucard veered left towards a small, hut-like building. Just before stepping inside, he rolled down his sleeves, concealing the scars on his arms. The demon didn't comment, though; he trailed after him as they entered.

Behind the thatch-roofed desk, a woman looked up, her expression brightening as she stood to greet them. "Can I help you?" she asked.

"I had someone book for Ezra and Silas Wright," he said, stopping in front of the counter.

The woman opened a small notebook and started looking over what must be a list of names. "Sorry, what was that, love?"

Alucard frowned. "Ezra and Silas Wright," he repeated. "Someone booked for us."

"Uh... Vight? I don't see a—"

"Wright," Zalith said irritably. It really wasn't that hard to understand.

"Oh, sorry," she laughed. "Yep, right here," she said, placing the book down. "Two nights?"

"Yes," Alucard mumbled.

Nodding, she reached behind into a small wooden box, shuffled through it for a moment, and then pulled out a set of keys, which she placed on the desk. She also grabbed a small leaflet and what looked like a business card. "So, here are your keys, and this will tell you everything you need to know about the resort," she said, pointing to the leaflet. "And this is your pass to get into the private bars for V.I.P guests," she added, pushing it all towards Alucard.

"Thank you," the vampire said and sighed, stuffing everything into his trouser pocket—he looked embarrassed, and he seemed eager to get going.

"V.I.P guests, huh?" Zalith asked with a smirk, squeezing the vampire's ass as they left the building.

Alucard smiled as he playfully shoved him away. "Well, we're rich, no?" he replied as Zalith took hold of his arm, smiling at him. "We might as well enjoy that."

"Yeah," the demon agreed, following him down onto the white sand beach. "Don't let them hear you, though. They might try to upsell us."

The vampire shrugged, leading him along the beach. "Is that a bad thing? They might have something you really like."

Zalith tilted his head a little and said, "Maybe. But I find people at places like these love to take advantage."

"Well, we won't let them."

The demon smiled and asked, "So, where are we staying?"

"This way," Alucard said.

Zalith walked beside Alucard along the shore, their steps sinking into the soft, white sand. The path curved around a towering chalk cliff, and as they emerged on the other side, a stretch of pristine beach opened before them. Several hut-like structures sat over the water, connected by a long pier; each hut was spaced apart by nearly a mile of crystal-clear sea, with the one they were clearly heading to positioned closest to the island on the left.

Alucard kept leading the way, slipping his hand into Zalith's as they neared the steps to the pier. Zalith felt the subtle hum of anticipation in the vampire's touch—Alucard was eager to see the inside. He likely assumed Zalith was, too. And perhaps he was, in his own quiet way. They reached the thatch-roofed hut, and Alucard unlocked the door with the key the woman at the desk had given him.

Stepping inside, Zalith took in the space as they followed a short hallway into a spacious lounge area. Sliding glass doors led out to a small terrace, where a private pool shimmered in the sunlight, separated from the crystal-clear sea by sleek glass walls. To the left, a compact kitchen and dining area fit for two; to the right, a bathroom and a walk-in wardrobe. It was a comfortable setup—but Alucard seemed far more interested in what waited downstairs.

Zalith followed as the vampire led the way down into the submerged bedroom. The walls were made entirely of glass, revealing the water beyond, where fish glided past in slow, mesmerizing motions. At the centre of the room sat a double bed, draped in crisp white covers with grey pillows, a nightstand on either side, and a single wardrobe in each back corner. Unlike the rest of the space, the wall behind the bed wasn't glass—an intentional design, no doubt. Zalith glanced at Alucard, recognizing the subtle ease in his posture. He loved the view, but a solid wall at his back? That would make him feel more at home.

"What do you think?" Alucard asked as Zalith took a few steps forward, looking around.

"It's very impressive," he said with a smile. "You did a good job."

The vampire smiled as Zalith made his way back over to him.

"How does it feel knowing that at some point, you're going to get fucked in front of all the fish in the sea?" he asked, an unseemly tone in his voice and a smirk on his face.

Alucard's face turned red as he looked away.

The demon laughed as he slowly moved his hand over Alucard's chest and to his shoulder. "I guess we'll just have to find out one of these days," he said, and then he kissed the vampire's cheek. "So, what do you want to do now that we're here?"

His fiancé shrugged. "Well…maybe we can walk around the island and see what's here while we wait for them to bring our things?" he suggested.

"Okay," Zalith agreed, and then he took hold of Alucard's hand. He was excited to see more of the island, and he was eager to enjoy the time away from the chaos of Uzlia.

ASCENDANT
Numen Chronicles | Volume Five

| Alucard—*Maluhia, Lunakai, A'okalani Cove Resort* |

As they made their way along the beach, Alucard pulled his sunglasses out of his trouser pocket and put them on—and as he did, he remembered what sat in his *other* pocket. He looked at Zalith and said, "I made something for you."

"What is it?" Zalith asked curiously.

The vampire stopped walking, and as Zalith did, he smiled at him. "Close your eyes," he said.

"Are you going to do anything to me?" the demon asked with a small smirk.

"No," Alucard said, pouting.

"Okay," the demon said, dragging out the word. Then, he closed his eyes.

Once Zalith had closed his eyes, Alucard reached into his other trouser pocket and pulled out another pair of sunglasses—a pair that he'd made especially for Zalith. Carefully, he placed them on Zalith's face, and once he'd taken a moment to stare at the demon, he smiled again and lowered his hands. "There," he said.

As he opened his eyes, Zalith smiled and dragged his thumb around the rim of his new sunglasses. "Oh, thank you," he said contently. "When did you make these?"

"You're welcome," the vampire murmured. "I made them when we got back home from the city the other day—when you went to work in your office," he said, taking hold of the demon's hand.

"That's very thoughtful—thank you," the demon said and kissed Alucard's lips.

Alucard smiled before continuing along the beach, the warmth of the sand shifting beneath his steps. The steady rhythm of waves and distant birdsong still filled the air, but soon, other sounds crept in—the quiet murmur of conversation, the clink of glassware, and the occasional burst of laughter. As they rounded a sharp corner past the cliff's edge, the landscape shifted. They had stepped into the public part of the resort.

Scattered across the sand, half-dressed tourists strolled with drinks in hand, their cocktails likely from one of the many nearby bar shacks. A volleyball game played out further down the shore, someone walked a dog along the water's edge, and a rather alarming number of people were sprawled across towels, basking in the sun…naked.

Alucard blinked but kept moving, his gaze flicking towards the far end of the beach, where a concrete path led up to a large hotel. Clearly, not everyone here had the luxury of a private hut over the water. He should have found the crowd irritating—too loud, too exposed—but instead, curiosity settled in his chest. He'd never been to a place like this before. From their path, he could see a row of food stalls and open-air restaurants lined up beside the bars. It had been a while since breakfast, and though food did nothing for him nutritionally, he still enjoyed trying new things with Zalith. Maybe they could stop and—

Zalith slowed beside him, his gaze lingering on a small, thatch-roofed restaurant. Alucard followed his line of sight, taking in the place. Wooden tables were scattered beneath the shade, occupied by people chatting over drinks served in coconuts and martini glasses. Platters of steaming rice and what appeared to be…raw fish with tiny sticks sat in front of them.

"Do you want to try something here?" his mate asked.

Alucard took his eyes off the people and looked up at the restaurant sign which read, 'Sappo's Sushi'. Sushi? He looked at Zalith. "What…is sushi?"

"Well," Zalith said. "It's usually raw fish and rice—sometimes, they even put seaweed in it."

It didn't sound very appetizing, but he *was* curious to try it. So, he nodded. "Okay. We can try it," he said. "Have you…had this before?" he asked, following Zalith into the building.

"I have," he said with a nod as one of the waiters escorted them to a window table. "But I didn't have it very often."

"Well…what do you recommend, then? I've never tried it, so…I don't really know what to get," he said, taking off his sunglasses.

Zalith looked up at the waiter. "We'll have today's special," he said. And as the waiter wandered off, he set his sights back on Alucard. "It's been a long time since I've had sushi, so I can't really name anything. We'll try whatever the special is, though," he said, taking off his sunglasses and tucking them into his pocket.

"So…do you like it here so far?" Alucard asked with a curious smile.

The demon smiled and nodded as he rested his arms on the table. "I do. It's beautiful here. How about you?"

"It's a nice change from all the big city and forests. And I can actually enjoy it, too—the sun is no longer my mortal enemy," he said, smirking. "Well…as long as I don't stay out in it too long."

"Good. When I saw we were somewhere tropical, I was a little worried that you might not be comfortable—but you have your cute little glasses," he teased, leaning over the table to tuck a loose strand of Alucard's hair behind his ear.

Alucard smiled again, looking down at his arms as he rested them on the table. "What would you do if I couldn't walk in the sun like most of my vampires?"

"I'd block out all of my windows and only go out at night," he answered.

Still smiling, Alucard gazed at him.

"Why *does* that happen?" Zalith then asked. "Vampires created from your blood can walk in the sunlight, but those created from any other vampire's blood can't."

Alucard shrugged. "Well...I guess it's to do with the...potency of my ethos. The vampires I create are being created with *my* blood, so...my pure ethos, I guess. Then those who are created by other vampires are getting that vampire's blood along with a fraction of mine, so my ethos isn't as potent, therefore these weaker vampires don't gain as many traits as the vampires turned by my blood," he explained.

"That's fair," Zalith said. "Does the blood of the vampires you create turn into your blood?"

He shook his head. "No, they just...get a fraction of my ethos—it's kind of like how I have half of Lucifer's ethos, I guess...well...." He paused. He'd never really thought about it before. A long time ago, Janus had convinced him that *he* had given him the ability to create vampires, but after years of study, Alucard had learned that Aegis couldn't do such a thing—they couldn't give someone the ability to create a species. Only the Numen could do that...and the Numen could do it because they had Lumendatts, ethereal crystalized masses of power that could craft and create life in any way its user wanted. And for a while, Alucard had thought that he could create vampires because he was Lucifer's son, but was that really it? No other blood-born child of the Numen—as far as he was aware—could create life in the way he could. Was he just...special because he was the son of Lucifer, the creator of the most powerful demon races?

"Are you okay?" Zalith laughed.

Snapping out of his thoughts, Alucard frowned and set his eyes back on Zalith. "I'm fine," he answered. "Uh...but no," he said, thinking back to Zalith's original question. "They just get a tiny amount of my ethos—so small that I wouldn't notice even if I made a hundred-thousand vampires."

"Does that bother you?" Zalith asked. "I wouldn't want to share my ethos with anyone like that."

He shrugged. "I don't...think it does," he mumbled. "If I could feel them all...like they were connected to me all the time, then...yes, it would bother me. But I don't feel them unless I want to, so...no," he said, and then he smiled a little. "You wouldn't want to share your ethos like that? You do know, if we have a child together, you would have to share your ethos just like that, Zalith," he told him, smirking. "Demon children always take ethos from their parents."

Zalith chuckled. "I mostly meant with a stranger. I wouldn't mind sharing with our child, of course."

Smiling, Alucard looked down at his arms again. "When do you...want to think about us *actually* having a family?" he asked quietly.

The demon pondered for a moment. "Sometime after we get married. Not *immediately* after, though. I want to enjoy the feeling of being married to you before we have a crying baby to deal with day and night," he said amusedly. "We'll have a nanny, though, of course. But still."

Alucard nodded as he spotted the waiter making his way over. He leaned back, taking his arms off the table as he smiled at Zalith. "Okay," he said contently.

The waiter set a large platter of sushi in the centre of their table, along with two coconut shells filled with what was presumably alcohol. Alucard settled into his seat, glancing over the unfamiliar spread. Zalith did the same, both of them taking a moment to inspect the assortment of neatly arranged fish and rice. As the waiter turned to leave, they murmured their thanks, though Alucard was still more focused on the food.

His gaze flicked to Zalith as the demon picked up a pair of the strange wooden sticks—chopsticks, apparently—and used them to lift a piece of sushi. With a small, amused smile, Zalith held it out to him.

Alucard eyed the morsel warily. Raw salmon-wrapped rice. It wasn't exactly what he would have chosen for himself, but after a beat, he parted his lips and allowed Zalith to feed it to him. The texture was strange—soft yet cool, the rice slightly sticky against his tongue—but the taste was…surprisingly pleasant. Better than he'd expected. He chewed thoughtfully, then glanced at Zalith, arching a brow.

"It's good," the vampire said with a smile.

"Good," the demon smiled. "You can dip them in this, too," he said, pointing to one of the two small saucers, which had brown liquid in it. "It's soy sauce. And this other one is wasabi, but it's a little spicy," he said, pointing to a pot of something green and rather mushy-looking. "This is tempura," he said, pointing to a plate of deep-fried vegetables.

Nodding, Alucard reached over and picked up the second pair of sticks. "And…these?" he asked.

"Chopsticks. You usually eat sushi with them."

Alucard studied the chopsticks in his hand, then glanced at Zalith's, his brow furrowing with concentration. With a curious smile, he attempted to mimic the way Zalith held them—but the moment he tried to grip them properly, they slipped from his fingers and clattered onto the table. He pouted, casting a glance at Zalith, who—of course—handled the utensils effortlessly. The demon picked up a piece of sushi, dipped it into the soy sauce, and placed it into his mouth without issue. Alucard exhaled softly, glancing back down at his own chopsticks. It couldn't be *that* difficult. Carefully, the vampire positioned them in his fingers again, adjusting until they felt…right. They weren't slipping this time. He even felt like he was holding them correctly—just like Zalith. A triumphant little smile tugged at his lips as he reached for a piece of sushi. But just as he went to lift it, the chopsticks twisted awkwardly, the fish slipping free before both sticks tumbled uselessly from his grip.

He scowled angrily at them.

The demon laughed quietly, but not so quietly that Alucard didn't hear. He took his eyes off the chopsticks and glared at Zalith, watching him as he ate another piece of sushi with no struggle at all.

Embarrassed, Alucard dropped the chopsticks and went to take one of the forks—

"Let me help you," Zalith laughed, picking up Alucard's chopsticks. "You hold this one like you would a pen," he said, positioning the first stick in Alucard's hand. "And then this one rests against your middle finger," he said, positioning the other. "Then, you just...pick them up," he said, picking up another piece of the sushi.

Alucard wanted to try. With a determined frown, he very carefully gripped one of the small pieces of sushi with his chopsticks. Sure that he had hold of it, he gently lifted the sushi off the plate...and to his relief, it didn't fall from the chopsticks, and the chopsticks didn't wriggle out of his hand. But he wasn't going to get *too* confident. Slowly, cautiously, he moved the sushi towards his mouth, and once he had raised it close enough, he swiftly ate it before the chopsticks could give way.

"See," Zalith said, smiling at him. "I knew you'd get the hang of it."

Smiling, Alucard carefully picked up another piece of sushi—this time without fumbling. He really was getting the hang of it, and the food was surprisingly good. Better than he'd expected.

Curious, he reached for his drink and took a sip. The taste was sweet and refreshing, like tropical fruit juice with a faint bite of something stronger beneath it. He licked a stray drop from his lip, nodding slightly in approval. That was good, too.

His gaze flicked to Zalith, a quiet sense of satisfaction settling in his chest. He was glad the demon had chosen this place. Maybe once they finished eating, they could wander further up the beach and see what else the resort had to offer.

"Do you want to continue our walk along the beach when we're done here?" he asked, swirling his drink idly before taking another sip.

Zalith met his gaze and smiled. "Yeah."

The gentle lull of waves filled the space between them as they returned to their meal, the hush of the ocean and the warmth of the evening settling around them. For now, there was no rush—just good food, good company, and the promise of more to come.

Chapter Thirty-Six

— ⋜ ✝ ⋝ —

Pina Coladas and Pasta

| **Alucard**—*Maluhia, Lunakai, A'okalani Cove Resort* |

After leaving the restaurant, Alucard and Zalith wandered along the beach, the midday sun casting a golden sheen over the sand. The vampire slipped his hand into Zalith's, and when the demon turned to him with a smile, he returned it, the warmth of the afternoon settling comfortably around them.

The air buzzed with life—distant laughter from sunbathers, the rhythmic beat of drums from a beachside performer, and the chatter of tourists gathered beneath straw umbrellas. Further down the shore, a row of open-air restaurants lined the beachfront, their grills sending up curls of fragrant smoke as chefs prepared fresh seafood over crackling flames; the scent of charred fish and sweet coconut mingled with the salty breeze.

Near a rocky outcrop, a small crowd had formed around a cluster of curious, nimble-fingered creatures—wide-eyed jungle critters darting between legs, eagerly snatching bits of fruit offered by amused visitors. Overhead, bright-feathered birds glided from palm to palm, their sharp calls blending with the crash of waves and the rustling of fronds swaying in the breeze.

Alucard gave Zalith's hand a slight squeeze, his gaze lingering on the scene before shifting back to the horizon. The sun glowed high, painting everything in rich hues, but he found his attention drawn less to the world around them and more to the steady presence at his side.

"Thank you for agreeing to come," he said.

"Of course," Zalith replied contently. "Anything for you, baby. Thank you for suggesting the trip."

Alucard shrugged, a slight smile on his face as he looked at Zalith. "You work so hard; I just wanted to spend a few days with you so we can both relax."

"It was a good idea," his mate said as they continued along the sand. "This island is beautiful."

The vampire nodded in agreement, but before he could say anything more, a sharp bark caught his attention. He turned his head, his gaze landing on a large, light brown bloodhound bounding towards them, its ears flapping wildly with each step. Its tail wagged furiously as it closed the distance, its enthusiasm almost contagious.

Of course, Alucard wasn't about to ignore a dog.

As soon as it reached them and plopped down at their feet, panting happily, Alucard released Zalith's hand and crouched down, scratching behind its floppy ears. The hound leaned into the touch, eyes half-lidded in bliss, its tongue lolling as it basked in the attention.

After a moment, Alucard glanced up at Zalith—only to find him still standing, his expression oddly subdued. There was nothing sharp or obvious about it, but something about the quiet, almost despondent look on his face made Alucard pause. Surely, he wasn't actually upset that he'd let go of his hand to pet a dog?

Before Alucard could say anything—

A voice called out, "Beauty!"

The bloodhound's ears perked up, and with a final, contented huff, it turned and loped back to its owner, leaving them alone once more.

Alucard then stood back up. "What's wrong?" he asked his mate.

"Oh, nothing," the demon said. "I was just worried about you touching that dirty dog."

The vampire pouted and frowned. "She wasn't dirty," he grumbled.

"Let me look at your hands."

"No," Alucard denied, hiding his hands behind his back.

"Just as I suspected," the demon said.

Alucard's pout turned into a smirk—before Zalith could stop him, he pulled his hand from behind his back and started wiping them all over Zalith's shirt.

But Zalith swiftly grabbed hold of his wrists and laughed a little. "That's very rude."

"It's rude to call a dog dirty," he sneered, pulling his hands free.

"Not when it's dirty it isn't," Zalith argued, still smiling.

"She wasn't dirty," Alucard mumbled. "She was just sandy."

"Sandy is *dirty*."

The vampire crossed his arms. "Well, you have sand on you, so I guess *you* are dirty."

"I was clean when I got the sand on me—the dog most likely wasn't," he stated.

Frowning at him, Alucard sighed quietly. "Would you like me to go and wash my hands so that I can hold your hand again?"

"I would," the demon said, smiling.

"Fine," he muttered. "Wait here."

But before he could leave, Zalith frowned in what looked like guilt and lightly grabbed his shoulder. "No, wait," he said.

"What?" he asked with a frown, looking back at him.

"I'll get over it. It's okay," Zalith said.

Alucard shook his head. "No, it's fine. I'll just be a few moments."

Zalith looked reluctant, but he let go of Alucard's shoulder and nodded. "Okay."

The vampire kissed the side of Zalith's face and left, heading towards a small restaurant not too far away. He'd do his best not to take too long; he was eager to resume their exploration of the island.

| Zalith—*Maluhia, Lunakai, A'okalani Cove Resort* |

As Alucard disappeared into the restaurant, Zalith sighed, his gaze lingering on the spot where his fiancé had stood. Something uneasy twisted in his chest. Was it guilt? He didn't want to be fussy—he was starting to sound like his mother. He loved her, of course, but she had always been…particular. Always fussing over the smallest things. He knew what it felt like to be on the receiving end of that, and he didn't want to do the same to Alucard.

With a quiet exhale, he dropped his gaze to the sand, absently shifting it beneath his boot. He wasn't upset. Not really.

Another sharp bark cut through his thoughts.

His head lifted, and his eyes landed on the same bloodhound from before. Of course, it would have to be a bloodhound. His frown deepened slightly. Memories stirred, unbidden. He'd once had a dog just like that when he was a child. He and his brother found the poor thing—a wounded pup, barely old enough to survive on its own—wandering the woods near their home. Zalith had insisted that they keep it; he'd argued with his mother until she relented. He'd nursed it back to health and cared for it, and in return, the dog had become his closest companion.

Until it died.

That was when he had decided—no more pets. No more attachments like that. Losing them wasn't worth it.

But that had been ages ago. *Literally.*

He exhaled through his nose, shaking his head slightly. It was ridiculous to let something so distant weigh on him now.

With a deep sigh, Zalith shifted his gaze to a large group gathered outside the restaurant that Alucard had just entered. They were arguing—voices raised, gestures serrated—but he didn't particularly care about the subject. Still, it was a welcome distraction. Better to focus on them than let old memories creep back in.

At first, he only half-listened, but as their conversation unfolded, something caught his attention. Their frustration wasn't just drunken bickering—it was about the very restaurant they sat at. Apparently, its owner had monopolized every supply line of alcohol and provisions, buying out stock the moment it arrived. Other establishments had been left struggling, unable to source goods because suppliers refused to sell to anyone else.

Zalith frowned. That wasn't a bad idea.

The cults he was currently enemy number one of—if he cut off their supply of poisonous metals and whatever else they were using against his and Alucard's people, taking them down would be a hell of a lot easier. Without their weapons and their tools, what did they have? *Nothing.* They'd be left with nothing but their own flimsy ethos, and Zalith knew that alone wouldn't be enough to stop him, Alucard, or their growing army. Considering that he and Alucard were likely two of the richest people in Aegisguard, buying out the suppliers wouldn't be a problem. And if anyone refused to sell? Well…he had other ways of persuasion.

A smirk tugged at his lips. He'd talk to Alucard about it later.

Speaking of Alucard…

Zalith's gaze shifted, catching sight of his vampire emerging from the restaurant, something held in his hands. When he reached him, Alucard placed a red velvet cupcake into Zalith's palm and smiled.

Of course, Alucard had bought cake. Zalith smiled amusedly. "What's this?" he asked, looking down at the white-icing-topped cupcake and the little strawberry that sat atop it.

"It's uh…red velvet," he told him. "I thought you might like to try one."

"Thank you. I should have known when you went in there that you'd come back with something sweet," he laughed.

Alucard shrugged. "I couldn't just ignore them—they looked so good."

Smiling, Zalith took a bite of his cake and walked at Alucard's side as they walked along the beach again.

"Do you like it?" Alucard asked, glancing at him as he ate his own cake.

"It's a little sweet," he admitted. "But I like it."

Nodding, Alucard looked down at his cake. "It *is* a little sweet," he agreed. "Do you want to head back?" he then asked. "Maybe the crew brought our things to our room."

"Sure," Zalith smiled.

| Alucard—*Maluhia, Lunakai, A'okalani Cove Resort* |

Alucard led the way back to the beach house; their bags had been delivered by the ship crew and left in the lounge. The vampire smiled as he set his eyes on his small suitcase, which was sitting next to Zalith's. "I have something for you," he told him.

The demon smiled curiously. "What?" he asked as Alucard let go of his hand and went over to their bags.

From his bag, Alucard pulled four small crystals. He walked back over to Zalith and held out his hand, showing him the obsidian, fire agate, shungite, and black onyx stones. "They're like the ones from your dream-eater," he said with an assuring smile.

Zalith smiled, too. "Thank you," he said and kissed the vampire's lips.

"You're welcome, my love," Alucard said shyly. "You can just leave them on the nightstand—they will do the same thing as the tree, but they will only last the two nights we'll be here before you would have to cleanse them."

"Okay," his mate replied, taking the crystals from him. "Thank you. I'll go put them there right now."

Alucard nodded and followed Zalith down to their bedroom. As the demon set the crystals on his nightstand, the vampire let his gaze drift to the glass walls, watching the fish glide through the water. Schools of silver-scaled fish flickered like living coins beneath the filtered light, their sleek bodies darting between strands of swaying coral. A lionfish hovered near the glass, its striped spines fanning out like delicate blades, while further in the depths, something far larger—almost serpentine—slithered through the blue. Its elongated body shimmered with iridescent greens and purples, trailing bioluminescent tendrils that pulsed faintly in the dimness. Smaller, stranger creatures flitted past—one with translucent fins that resembled silk ribbons, another with a body like polished obsidian, its luminous red eyes glowing softly in the deep.

By the time Zalith placed the last crystal down, Alucard turned from the mesmerizing scene and sat beside him on the bed, resting his head against his mate's shoulder with a quiet sigh. "I want to just lay here for a bit," he said, still watching the fish.

Zalith smiled. "Okay," he murmured before wrapping his arms around Alucard and pulling him down onto the bed, guiding them both until they were lying side by side.

The warmth of the demon's embrace settled around him, grounding him in a way nothing else ever quite managed. As they lay there, Zalith pressed slow, lingering kisses against Alucard's neck, his jaw, and the crown of his head—each one unhurried, as if savouring the closeness. His grip was firm, holding him as though he had no intention of letting go. Alucard exhaled softly, his own smile growing as he ran his fingers through Zalith's hair, the strands smooth beneath his touch. Another kiss brushed his cheek, then another.

His mate shifted slightly, pressing one last kiss to his forehead before murmuring, "What kind of ocean life do you think we'll see?"

"Well..." Alucard said, glancing at one of the glass walls. "I think we might see some turtles out here—a lot of tropical fish and maybe even some smaller species of sea serpent. They don't usually like to come too close to people, but there are a lot of fish here, and they eat the fish, so...we never know."

"What about sharks?"

Alucard shrugged. "Maybe. Are you scared of them?"

"No," the demon said with a smile. "But I'd like to see one."

"Maybe we will if we sit here for long enough."

Zalith kissed Alucard's neck again. "This is nice," he mumbled. "It's like a magical little painting."

"I would love something like this back home—a room...and all the walls are one big fish tank. The ones I have in my office would probably love the space upgrade," he said with a quiet laugh.

The demon didn't answer right away—maybe he was thinking. He fiddled with Alucard's hair, and eventually said, "We could probably knock down a wall or two in your office and put big tanks up instead. Then there'd be a crawlspace or a closet where there'll be unseen access to the tank for cleaning and feeding."

"Really?" Alucard asked excitedly.

"Of course. But your office might not be so private anymore—unless we do it with a wall that looks outside, but that's not very safe."

"Well...there are so many spare rooms in the castle; maybe we can just turn one of them into a sort of...aquarium."

Zalith frowned confusedly. "I don't know why I pictured a whole room filled with water when you said that," he laughed.

The vampire laughed amusedly. "I mean the walls—they could be tanks."

"Good, because it would take a lot of work to convince me to let you fill a room with water."

"I don't know about that," Alucard murmured, smirking. "I think I could convince you rather easily."

"I don't know," the demon said. "I can be very stubborn."

"And I can be very convincing."

The demon chuckled. "I don't know if I'd be willing to listen when it involves water ruining my floors."

He shrugged again. "We'd take the floors out and put some sort of...waterproof thing in."

"That scares me."

"Why?"

"Because what if it doesn't work, and then I have a pond leaking from the ceiling and into the guest lounge?"

The vampire laughed. "Don't worry, Zalith. I don't want a room full of water. Maybe a few tanks or the wall tanks is enough."

"Good. Thank you," Zalith murmured, pressing a kiss to the side of Alucard's face. He shifted, propping himself up on one arm so he could look down at him, his dark eyes warm with quiet affection. A moment passed, then— "Do you want to go lie on the beach with me?" he asked, his voice soft yet inviting.

Alucard smiled—that sounded relaxing. "We can do that," he agreed. "There's a picnic blanket in one of the bags; we can use that so we don't get covered in sand."

"Sounds good," Zalith said.

They left the bedroom and made their way upstairs. Alucard grabbed a beige picnic blanket from his suitcase before following Zalith out onto the beach, the afternoon sun casting long shadows across the sand.

Once they found a spot, they spread the blanket out and settled onto it, reclining against the soft fabric as they gazed up at the sky. Wisps of clouds drifted lazily overhead, their edges glowing in the golden light; the warmth of the sun soaked into Alucard's skin, though he quickly slid on his sunglasses, Zalith doing the same beside him. And for a while, they simply lay there, the rhythmic crash of waves and the distant laughter of beachgoers filling the silence.

Then came the sound of approaching footsteps, sand crunching underfoot.

"Can I get either of you two any drinks?"

Both of them turned their heads towards the voice. A man stood nearby, dressed in a white, flower-patterned shirt and brown shorts, a string of wooden beads hanging around his neck. A lanyard dangled against his chest, the name 'Dylan' printed across it.

It seemed he worked here.

"Could we get two pina coladas, please?" Zalith asked.

"Of course—anything else?"

"No," the demon said, and as the man left, they both laid back down.

"What is...pina colada?" Alucard asked curiously.

Zalith smiled as he fiddled with Alucard's hair. "It's a rum cocktail with coconut milk and pineapple. But usually, they blend it with ice so it's nice and cold."

"It sounds really good," Alucard said, shuffling closer to Zalith so that he could rest his head on the demon's chest. "I'm excited to try it."

"I think you'll like it."

Nodding, Alucard sighed and closed his eyes, letting himself relax once more.

Once the man returned with their drinks, though, he sat up when Zalith did.

"They look so good," Zalith said as they were handed their drinks.

Alucard nodded—he was eager to try it, so he took a small sip. "It's really tasty," he said with a smile.

"Good. I'm glad." Zalith took a slow sip of his drink before setting it down; he pulled off his shirt and exhaled in quiet contentment. Leaning back on his hands, he tilted his head to the sky, letting the warmth of the sun soak into his skin. After a moment, he turned towards Alucard and started unbuttoning his shirt.

Alucard smiled, setting his own drink aside as he let Zalith work. Once the last button was undone, they eased back onto the blanket together. With a deep sigh, the vampire rested his head against the demon's bare chest, listening to the steady rise and fall of his breathing. His fingers idly traced the gold chain resting against his mate's skin, twisting it between his fingertips as the quiet, lazy atmosphere settled around them.

Then, Zalith's voice broke the silence, "Do you want to see something funny?"

Alucard frowned, shifting slightly. "What?"

Zalith didn't answer right away. Instead, he slowly slid his hand beneath Alucard's shirt, fingers drifting over his waist.

Alucard watched as a smirk crept across Zalith's lips just before his fingers tightened around his waist. The moment he did, a sudden, almost unbearable pleasure jolted through the vampire's body—sharp, electrifying, and utterly consuming. His breath caught, muscles tensing as he fought against the instinct to react. He knew exactly what Zalith was doing; he knew that the demon was waiting for him to break, to gasp, to shudder, to give in. But Alucard clenched his jaw, scowling as he willed himself to stay silent, though the heat coiling in his core made it near impossible.

Zalith wanted him flustered, he wanted him startled, teetering at the very edge. And although he was close, Alucard resisted.

The demon laughed, dragging his hand up the side of Alucard's body. "Sorry," he said, fiddling with his crucifix.

Alucard exhaled sharply before sighing and burying his face against Zalith's chest. Of course the demon's little joke had left him aching, but now he wasn't entirely sure what he wanted to do about it. Initiating something here was out of the question—anyone could walk by, and he had no desire to put on a show. But getting up and heading back to the house? That didn't appeal to him either. More than that, as much as he loved Zalith's attention, he didn't want to be the one receiving it all the time. Not right now. This trip, this fleeting slice of peace—they had come here for Zalith. And if anyone deserved to be spoiled, it was him.

And he had an idea. He sat up and looked down at Zalith. "Roll over," he told him.

"Why?" Zalith asked.

"Because I want to do something for you," he said with a pout.

"Do what?"

A flicker of embarrassment crept in, warmth rising to Alucard's face. He wanted to surprise Zalith—he wanted to do something different, something he hadn't really done for him before. But the demon's questioning was starting to unnerve him, making him second-guess himself.

He shrugged, trying to push down the growing anxiety tightening in his chest. "Something," he mumbled, avoiding Zalith's gaze.

"Are you going to hurt me?" Zalith questioned, smirking.

The vampire frowned. "No," he mumbled.

Still smiling, Zalith rolled onto his stomach, folding his arms beneath his head as he settled in.

Alucard moved over him, straddling his waist and adjusting until he was comfortable. Then, he placed his hands against the demon's back and began to massage him—slow, gentle movements, pressing into the firm muscles beneath his palms.

With a content sigh, Zalith relaxed and smiled. "Thank you."

For a while, Alucard worked in silence, his hands gliding over Zalith's back in slow, measured strokes. But his thoughts drifted back to earlier, to the moment that dog had run up to them. He hadn't missed the fleeting sadness in Zalith's expression, no matter how quickly it had faded. And despite trying to push it aside, the concern lingered. Was Zalith not as happy here as he claimed? Or had the dog stirred something else—something deeper?

Alucard wasn't sure. But he wanted to be. "So... are you going to tell me why you looked so sad when that dog came to us?" he asked quietly.

A frown stole Zalith's relaxed expression as he sighed. "I used to have a dog like that when I was young."

Alucard smiled a little. "I never would have thought *you* had a pet."

"Xurian and I were playing in the woods near our old house with our cousins. But they ran ahead—like usual—and I was just trailing behind. I stumbled upon this little sick-looking bloodhound puppy, and I wasn't going to leave it there. I took it home, and despite my mother's disapproval, I nursed it back to health," he explained.

The vampire smiled. "Did your mother let you keep him?"

"She did, surprisingly. I think it was because I was so attached to him. I had been so determined to save him—I called him Leo. I read so many veterinary books; I had my mother hire the best vet there was around that time, and he made a full recovery," he said with a small smile. "I had him for about a year after that."

Alucard watched the smile run away from Zalith's face. "Did you have to get rid of him?" he asked, still slowly massaging his back.

"No," he said despondently. "But there was an accident...and he ended up passing away."

"I'm sorry," the vampire said sadly.

"It's okay," Zalith mumbled, sighing quietly.

"What happened to him?" he asked, but then he hesitated. "You don't have to tell me. I don't want to upset you more."

His mate sighed again. "We were out playing in the woods—my mother always insisted that we wore bright colours out there because people hunted in those woods. But we didn't put anything on Leo, and a hunter shot him, mistaking him for a deer or something—I don't know. We were just kids, so we didn't know not to take the arrow out...and he died," he muttered sadly, shrugging.

Alucard stopped massaging his back and frowned sorrowfully. He didn't know what to say—he could see the dismay on Zalith's face, and he could hear it in his voice. "I'm sorry," he said again. "No one should ever have to go through that."

"It's okay," Zalith said. "It was a long time ago."

The vampire frowned sympathetically and made Zalith roll onto his back. He straddled his lap, leaned forward, and rested his arms beside his. He stroked the side of the demon's face with the back of his hand, kissed his lips, and then rested his forehead against his, closing his eyes.

Zalith stroked his hand to the side of Alucard's face and kissed his lips.

"I love you," Alucard said, smiling at him.

"I love you too," Zalith replied.

They lingered on the beach for a while, finishing their drinks as the afternoon melted into the evening. The sky deepened into shades of amber and violet, the sun dipping towards the horizon in a golden glow.

As twilight settled in, they made their way back to their beach house. Dinner was brought to them—lemon garlic shrimp pasta, the aroma rich with butter and citrus. They ate on the porch, the ocean stretching endlessly before them, waves rolling in a steady, soothing rhythm. The warm breeze carried the scent of salt and blooming night jasmine, wrapping around them as they dined beneath the painted sky.

"I had a thought earlier," Zalith said, looking at Alucard.

The vampire turned his head, setting his sights on him. "About what?"

"About supply lines. If we were to buy off every single supplier our enemies are getting—"

"No work," Alucard said with a pout, glaring at him.

"But what if it's a really good idea?"

"No work," the vampire repeated. "We're here to relax and think about nothing work-related. You can tell me when we get home."

Zalith laughed quietly. "Fine," he said and continued eating his food.

There wasn't another mention of work. Once they finished dinner, they wordlessly relaxed in their seats.

Zalith broke the silence, saying "The pasta was delicious," as he leaned back a little. "Thank you again for suggesting the trip."

Alucard smiled at him. "We'll have the whole day tomorrow to do things."

"Do you know what you want to do?"

The vampire shrugged as he sipped from his wine. "There's a festival tomorrow. We could go."

"I look forward to it," the demon said contently.

Smiling, Alucard shuffled closer to him and rested his head on his shoulder. "Can we sit out here for a while?"

"Of course we can," Zalith said, moving his arm around him.

For a while, they sat together, watching as the sun dipped lower, its golden light spilling across the waves. Shadows stretched, the sky shifting from fiery orange to deep indigo, stars beginning to flicker to life above the horizon.

The ocean murmured in the distance, the warmth of the evening wrapping around them. And in that quiet, with nothing but the sound of the tide and each other's presence, Alucard felt something rare—something weightless.

Peace.

Chapter Thirty-Seven

— ⟨ ✝ ⟩ —

Tolerable

| **Alucard**, *Sunday, Tertium 19th, 960(TG)—Maluhia, Lunakai, A'okalani Cove Resort* |

The night stretched on, slow and endless.

Alucard lay beside Zalith, listening to the demon's steady, soundless breathing. Sleep should have come easily—there was no reason it shouldn't. His mind was quiet, his body at ease. He wasn't restless, he wasn't hungry, and he wasn't so exhausted that sleep felt impossible.

And yet, it still wouldn't come.

He stared at the ceiling, his thoughts drifting in circles, searching for an answer he couldn't quite grasp. What was the problem?

The vampire exhaled softly, his gaze shifting to the four stones resting on his nightstand—obsidian, fire agate, shungite, black onyx. The same ones he'd given Zalith. He still needed them to ward off his nightmares. And now, so did Zalith.

That unsettled him. Zalith carried so much already—always worrying, always pushing himself beyond his limits. How many times had Alucard found him slumped over his desk, passed out from exhaustion? How often had he drifted into sleep with work still clutched in his hands? Alucard had hoped—*still* hoped—that this trip would be the break that Zalith desperately needed. But the truth was becoming harder to ignore. Zalith didn't want a break. That wouldn't stop Alucard from trying, though. He'd keep pushing, he'd keep making him rest, because whether Zalith wanted it or not… he needed it.

With a quiet sigh, Alucard rolled onto his back, his gaze trailing up to the ceiling, where the dark ocean loomed above. Fish drifted past, their scales catching the faint light of the moons, shimmering like scattered fragments of starlight beneath the water's surface.

And then he heard something.

Not the steady hush of the waves, not the familiar creak of the house shifting with the tide. Scraping. Sharp scraping. Like metal dragging against glass.

Alucard frowned, his body tensing as the sound grew louder. Sitting up, he turned towards the glass walls, his eyes searching the dark waters beyond.

But he saw nothing. Just fish gliding through the water, their movements slow and indifferent. A sea turtle drifted lazily past, undisturbed by anything out of the ordinary. Crabs scuttled along the sandy seabed, their tiny legs kicking up clouds of silt. There was no sea grass close enough to be brushing against the glass, no visible debris caught in the currents. Nothing that could explain the sound.

Alucard's frown lingered. Was he imagining it? Had exhaustion finally started playing tricks on him? It didn't matter. It was late. He was tired. And tomorrow was supposed to be for Zalith. Whatever it was—if it was anything at all—could wait.

Sighing, he lay back down, willing himself to ignore the lingering unease. But as his head met the pillow, the world around him seemed to still. The hush of the waves vanished, the moonlight dimmed, and the shimmering reflections within the bedroom froze in place. Even the slow drift of fish beyond the glass walls ceased, as if time itself had hesitated.

And so did Alucard.

In the water above, something was moving, drifting closer. A face emerged from the darkness, so eerily familiar that, for a fleeting moment, he almost mistook it for his own reflection. But then the truth revealed itself. Eyes began to open—too many, unfurling around the face like blooming petals of a nightmare.

A voice followed, smooth as silk yet dripping with something ancient, something rotten. She hummed his name. *Lilith.*

Alucard hadn't heard her voice since he and Zalith had returned home to their castle. His dream-eater had blocked her out, sealing her away along with his nightmares. And yet, there she was.

Clearly, the crystals beside him weren't enough.

However, what he felt…staring up at Lucifer's face, listening to Lilith's call—it wasn't fear. It was aggravation. Exhaustion. A slow, simmering anger. Knowing that Lilith would soon die by his and Zalith's hand made it easier to feel anything but fear. And Lucifer…Alucard had been seeing glimpses of him ever since that day, since the moment he'd escaped his grip, torn from the chains of that wretched place, only to be dragged down again into Lucifer's prison. But it wasn't really him. It couldn't be him. His father was bound to that hell, trapped for eternity with no way out. This? This was nothing more than his mind trying to process it all, trying to make sense of what happened. Because *so much* had happened that day. He died. He'd lost Zalith in a way far worse than death—Lucifer had stolen his memories of him, stripped Alucard of the man he loved, leaving only an empty space where Zalith should have been. And for a time, he had believed that he would never get those memories back, that he'd never remember the warmth of Zalith's touch, the depth of what they had.

But he had. And now there he was...lying beside Zalith—his fiancé, his mate, his *everything*.

Everything was fine. Everything was supposed to be fine. And yet, he knew—admittedly—that he hadn't given himself the time to truly get over it. He hadn't let himself breathe long enough to heal. And that had to be why he was seeing Lucifer's face now—because the fear, buried as it was, still clung deeply within his heart and mind, a remnant of the terror he had felt the day he almost lost everything.

But he refused to let it take hold of him now.

All he wanted—all he *needed* was Zalith's warmth. His touch, his embrace, the safety it promised. That was always enough to silence Lilith's voice, to push Lucifer's image back into the void where it belonged.

Alucard shifted, reaching out, and placed his hand on Zalith's arm. "Zalith?" he whispered.

The demon murmured quietly in response.

He didn't really know what to tell him—he should just tell him that he wanted a hug, right? "I want...can we cuddle?" he asked quietly.

Zalith murmured again and began to turn over. Alucard smiled softly, shifting closer, settling into the warmth of him. But before he had time to fully comprehend what was happening, Zalith moved—too fast.

In an instant, Alucard found himself pinned, his back pressed into the mattress with a force so sudden and aggressive that a sharp grunt escaped his lips. Pain jolted through him, but it was nothing compared to the ice that flooded his veins the moment his eyes met the face above him.

His breath caught. His body froze.

Because it wasn't Zalith.

It should have been him, it should have been the man that he trusted with his very soul. But the face staring down at him, twisted into a malevolent grin...was his father's, a malevolent grin stretching across it—

Alucard's eyes snapped open as he jolted upright, gasping for air, his fingers digging into the sheets beneath him. His mind reeled, struggling to make sense of his surroundings, of the lingering terror still clawing at his chest. Behind him, Zalith stirred, sitting up as well, his hands moving instinctively to Alucard's shoulders. The sudden touch made the vampire flinch, his body tensing as he sharply turned to look back at him. For a moment, he could only stare, his breath uneven as he took in Zalith's tired, concerned face.

Zalith asked if he was okay, but Alucard couldn't answer. Words felt distant, his voice trapped somewhere between what he'd just seen and waking reality. But then, slowly, the world began to settle around him, the haze lifting just enough for understanding to take hold. It hadn't been real.

It was just another dream.

Exhaling deeply, he let his shoulders sag, his fingers loosening their grip on the sheets as a frown crept onto his face.

"Alucard?" Zalith asked quietly, moving his hand to the side of the vampire's face. "Are you okay?" he repeated.

The vampire nodded, closed his eyes for a moment, and shook his head as he looked down at his lap. "I'm okay—I'm sorry," he said with a sigh. "It was just a bad dream. Did I wake you up?" he asked, looking back at the demon.

Zalith shook his head. "No. I've been in and out of sleep all night."

He exhaled deeply once more, calming down. "Why?"

"No reason," his mate answered, shrugging. "This is just how I sleep now, I guess."

Staring at him, Alucard frowned despondently. He didn't care about his own problems right now; he just wanted to help Zalith—or at least try to. So he laid back down with him and rested his head on Zalith's shoulder. He dragged his fingers over the demon's chest and started fiddling with the gold chain that hung around his neck. "Are you okay? *Really*?"

He nodded. "I'm okay. I'm just worried about everything."

"What are you worried about?"

"You, our people, the city—the list goes on," he mumbled sullenly.

Alucard knew that repeating the same thing over and over wasn't going to help. He could go on and on about how they were safe, how the wards around the city would keep everyone protected. He knew it wasn't going to convince Zalith or help him feel less worried. "I wish I could help you feel better about all of this," he mumbled. "But we *will* be okay, Zalith."

"I know," the demon mumbled.

The vampire moved his arm around him and held him tightly. He'd found a solution for Zalith's nightmares, and now he wanted to try and find a way to help him fall asleep and *stay* asleep. He'd offered before to help…he could put Zalith to sleep any time the demon might want. But Zalith hadn't confirmed whether or not he wanted that. Should he offer again?

Alucard sighed and nuzzled the demon's neck. "I can still help you with sleeping," he said quietly. "If you wanted me to."

"I'll think about it," his mate replied.

He sighed quietly and nodded. "Okay," he mumbled. He wasn't sure if Zalith was actually going to accept his help, but that was okay. It was up to him what he wanted, and whatever the demon chose to do, Alucard would be there for him. "Do you want to try and go back to sleep or do you want to go for a walk?" he asked—maybe a walk would help tire the demon out.

"A walk would be nice. But I don't want to keep you up."

"We can walk," he said, sitting up. He felt like he needed a little distraction before he could try and get some more sleep. "Let's get dressed."

Zalith smiled and said, "Okay."

They climbed out of bed and dressed in silence. It was early—barely three in the morning—and though the air inside was warm, Alucard suspected that it would be cooler outside. He reached for the turtleneck sweater Zalith had given him for Yule, pulling it over his head. The fabric was soft, comforting in a way that made him hesitate for just a moment before smoothing it down. Once they were both ready, they headed upstairs and stepped out onto the pier.

As they walked, Alucard reached for Zalith's hand, threading their fingers together. The demon's palm was warm despite the night air, but when Alucard glanced over, he caught the telltale signs of fatigue lining his mate's face. His thoughts drifted to the plans he'd made for them today—the festival. He wanted them to go; he thought it might be exciting… but now, looking at Zalith, he wasn't so sure.

Would he even want to be around so many people? Was that really what he needed right now?

Alucard had been thinking about what *he* found exciting, but maybe that wasn't what Zalith wanted. Not right now. "We don't have to go to the festival later if you don't want to," he said. "If you'd rather just spend time alone together, we can do that."

Zalith looked at him and said, "Of course, I would love to spend the day alone with you, but I don't mind going if it's something you want to do."

The vampire shrugged. "We can see how we feel later."

"Okay," Zalith said, smiling at him. "So, what happened in your dream?" he then asked.

"Just the usual," he muttered. "Lilith and Lucifer."

The demon nodded. "Did you bring the little crystals for yourself, too?"

"I did. But I guess one of each isn't enough," he mumbled. "I should have brought my whole dream-eater."

"Do you want to use mine as well?"

Alucard frowned. "No. Thank you, but… you need them."

"You need them more," Zalith insisted.

He shook his head. "I'll be fine. The ones I have are enough—they make my dreams tolerable. I'm fine with that knowing that you're not having nightmares."

"But I don't want *you* to have them either."

The vampire stopped walking and turned to face his mate so that he could put his hand on the side of his face. "I'll be fine. It's only for one more night after today. You need the sleep more than I do anyway—you work more."

Zalith frowned and seemed to relent. "Okay."

Alucard didn't really like the sound of his voice—he didn't look or sound content, and he didn't want Zalith to feel annoyed or unsatisfied. "I can send a message and get someone to send an owl with some more for me," he said.

"Okay, good," his mate said, and then he kissed Alucard's cheek.

They continued walking along the beach as Alucard telekinetically sent a message to one of his vampires—an owl should arrive no later than 6 a.m. "Do you feel a bit better now?" he asked Zalith.

"I do," he said with a smile. "Do you?"

Alucard nodded. "I do too," he said. But as he then set his eyes on a few rockpools up ahead, he smiled excitedly. "Can we look in the rockpools?"

Zalith nodded. "Of course."

Eager, Alucard swiftly led the way to the rockpools and curiously crouched down in front of the largest one. Zalith crouched beside him, and they both peered inside. The vampire eyed all of the differently coloured sponges and starfish; hermit crabs scurried along the bottom to hide in the seagrass, and a lone sea urchin clung to the very back wall.

With a smirk on his face, Alucard rolled up his sleeve and reached into the water—

"Be careful," Zalith said.

"I will," he laughed, picking up one of the hermit crabs, which he then held in front of Zalith. "Do you want to hold him?" he asked, moving it closer as a hesitant look appeared on Zalith's face.

"No, thanks," the demon said amusedly, backing off a little.

"Are you sure?" Alucard asked, smirking as he moved it closer to him.

Zalith laughed and gently pushed Alucard's arm away. "I'm sure."

The vampire shrugged and put the hermit crab back into the water. Then, he stood up. "Do you want to head back?"

The demon smiled as Alucard took hold of his hand. "Sure," he said.

"Do you want to try and get some more sleep or do you want to stay up?" the vampire asked as they headed back towards their beach house.

"I'll try and get some sleep," the demon replied.

"Okay," Alucard agreed, giving Zalith's hand a small squeeze before turning back towards their beach house. The sky had begun to shift, the deep indigo of night fading into the first pale hues of dawn. As they walked, the distant hush of waves and the soft creak of the wooden pier filled the quiet between them.

By the time they reached the house, the horizon had begun to glow, the promise of a new day unfolding around them. But before they could start their day, a little more sleep awaited them.

Chapter Thirty-Eight

— ⋖ † ⋗ —

Portrait

| **Alucard**—*Maluhia, Lunakai, A'okalani Cove Resort* |

As morning settled over the island, Alucard and Zalith sat on the porch once more, breakfast laid out before them. The staff had brought sausage and egg over rice, a fresh fruit salad, and a plate of golden malasadas, their sugary coating glistening in the warm light. Zalith had opted for coffee, its rich aroma curling through the air, while Alucard had chosen a chocolate milkshake—cold, creamy, and exactly the indulgence he wanted.

Beside him, Zalith ate in comfortable silence, his gaze drifting towards the horizon, where a small ship moved lazily across the water. The sight seemed to amuse him, but soon, his attention shifted back to Alucard.

The demon watched him with an endearing smile as Alucard took a slow sip of his milkshake, eyes half-lidded with quiet satisfaction. It made Zalith chuckle softly before picking up one of the malasadas and taking a bite. "Are you enjoying your breakfast?" he asked, his voice warm, pulling Alucard's attention away from his drink.

Placing the cake down, Alucard smiled. "I am—thank you. Are you?"

He smiled in return. "I am," he said and sipped from his coffee.

"Do you know if you want to go to the festival today?" Alucard asked.

"We can go if you'd like to go," he said, but he sounded a little reluctant.

Alucard shrugged and laughed a little as he placed his drink down. "It's okay. I know you don't want to go. We can do something more relaxing together."

"Are you sure? I don't want you to miss out on anything."

"I just want you to be happy," he said, picking up another malasada. "It's what makes me happy."

Zalith smiled, leaned over, and kissed the vampire's lips. "*You* make me happy."

"You make me happy, too," he said contently. "Well, I had a few hours booked at this spa for us today—we can head there soon."

The demon looked worried. "Are you going to let the people touch you?"

Alucard frowned. He hadn't really thought about that. Did he really want strangers touching him? *Seeing* him? He shrugged and sipped from his drink, trying to hide the fact that he now felt embarrassed. "Well… it's mostly meant for you."

Zalith laughed. "So, you're just going to sit and watch them do stuff to me?"

The vampire shrugged. "I'll do some things… where they don't have to touch me," he mumbled and sipped from his milkshake.

"They have to touch you for just about everything," the demon said amusedly.

He placed his drink down and sighed. His insecurities were beginning to make him feel a little stupid; he wanted to get over them, but every time he thought about someone other than Zalith touching him, he felt a desperate need to attack, and it made him feel extremely uncomfortable. "Not *everything*," he replied.

"If you say so," Zalith said, smirking at him.

"After that, we can go and get something for lunch. There's this thing I want to do on the beach by that restaurant we went to yesterday," the vampire told him, finishing his breakfast.

"What do you want to do?" Zalith asked curiously.

"It's a surprise. You'll see when we get there."

"Okay," the demon said with a smile.

Once they finished breakfast, they left their beach house and made their way across the sand towards the spa, nestled near the hotel they had seen the day before. The walk was pleasant, the ocean breeze carrying the scent of salt and tropical flowers, the distant sounds of laughter and music drifting from the resort's livelier areas.

Despite his initial hesitation, Alucard let Zalith pull him into the spa for a few hours. He wasn't entirely convinced at first—luxuries like this weren't something he indulged in often—but as the time passed, he found himself enjoying it more than expected. He spent much of it sitting at the edge of the warm pools, letting the mineral-rich water swirl around him while Zalith took full advantage of the experience. Watching the demon relax, his usual tension easing from his shoulders, was enough to make the trip worthwhile.

By the time they emerged, the late morning sun hung high, casting golden light over the shore. They wandered for a while, stopping to watch surfers ride the waves and local artisans set up their stalls along the beach, selling handmade jewellery, woven baskets, and intricately carved wooden figures. It was a slow, easy pace—one Alucard didn't mind.

And as they passed a row of open-air restaurants, the scent of grilled seafood and sizzling spices reminded them both of the time. Lunch was fast approaching.

"Where do you want to go for lunch?" the vampire asked, smiling at Zalith.

"Somewhere nice," he answered. "Or we could eat out on the deck again."

"Do you want to order something?"

"Yeah—unless you want to go somewhere. I don't mind either way."

Alucard shrugged. "Well, if you want to head back, we can, but there's still something I want to do first."

"If we're going to be near that restaurant, we might as well stop by for lunch," Zalith suggested.

"Okay," the vampire said as they stepped down onto the beach and started making their way towards the restaurant they'd eaten in yesterday.

As they walked, Alucard kept an eye out for the small stall he had noticed the day before. When he finally spotted it, a small smile tugged at his lips. The same woman was there, seated behind the display, absentmindedly fiddling with her paintbrushes and pencils. Sunlight filtered through the woven canopy above her, casting dappled patterns over the table, where delicate paintings and intricate sketches were neatly arranged.

"This is where we're going," he said, pulling Zalith towards the stall.

Zalith smiled, eyeing the drawings the woman already had on sale. "Are you going to buy some art?"

"No," Alucard murmured excitedly. "I'm going to get her to draw us together."

The demon smiled. "Aw, okay," he said, following Alucard.

Once they reached the stall, Alucard stopped and looked down at the auburn-haired woman as she smiled up at them.

"Are you interested?" she asked.

Alucard glanced at the sign advertising that she drew couples together. "Would you draw us together?" he asked, looking at Zalith.

She smiled brightly. "Sure, sure," she said with a nod. "Do you want a pencil drawing or a painting? Painting takes longer."

The vampire asked Zalith, "Do you have a preference?"

His mate replied, "A painting would be nicer—do you mind sitting for longer, though?"

He shook his head. "We can do that." Then, he said to the woman, "We'll have the painting, please."

"Of course—it's five gold and two silver," she said pleasantly.

Silver—Alucard couldn't touch it, and he never carried it. "Do you have… change for six gold?"

"I do," she said with a nod, and as Alucard handed her the coins, she started rummaging around in her coin purse. "Thank you," she chuckled, holding out the three silver coins in change, but Zalith took them from her. "Okay, if you both just sit over there on that little bench, I'll set my things up," she instructed, pointing to the dark oak bench placed against the white concrete wall, a potted palm tree on either side of it.

As instructed, Alucard and Zalith moved to the nearby bench and sat down while the woman set up her easel and placed a fresh canvas in front of her. They settled side by side, Zalith to Alucard's right. Without hesitation, the demon slipped an arm around him, his fingers resting lightly against the vampire's waist as he pulled him a little closer. Alucard smiled, his expression softening as he leaned in, resting the side of his head against Zalith's shoulder.

"Are you ready?" she then asked.

"We're ready," Zalith confirmed.

The woman began sketching, her brush gliding across the canvas in smooth, practised strokes.

As she worked, Alucard let his thoughts drift. After lunch, a walk along the beach seemed like the perfect way to spend the afternoon—something slow, something easy. Then, they could head back for a while and simply relax. He wanted Zalith to unwind, to enjoy this trip without worry pressing at his mind. And for dinner…Alucard had something special planned. He was certain that Zalith would love it—that it would make him happy. And right now, that was all Alucard wanted.

He smiled as Zalith squeezed his hand and turned his head so that he could nuzzle the demon's neck. "I love you," he mumbled.

"I love you too," Zalith said and kissed the vampire's head.

The woman smiled at them both. "Aw, you two are so cute together," she giggled.

"Thank you," Zalith replied.

"Have you been together long?" she asked curiously.

"A while," he answered. "We got engaged last month," he said, smiling at Alucard.

The vampire smiled back at him but looked away—he was sure that his face had gone a little red in response to his fluster.

She smiled as she continued painting. "Congratulations," she said. "My cousin's friend is seeing another man—it's not really something you see every day, but I think it's cute; you're not afraid to hide who you are. I've heard that in some places, it's against the law to be with someone of the same sex—I hear people have been hung for it," she continued with a sigh, shaking her head.

"It's true," Zalith said. "Best of luck to your cousin's friend," he added.

She waved her free hand, shaking her head as she worked on her painting. "Oh, well, you don't have to worry about any of that out here," she assured them. "Out here in Maluhia, everything and everyone is welcome. No one cares. It's a place to come and unfold and relax and simply live your life, you know?" she said contently. "Once, we had a Corvian come here—a *Corvian*," she laughed, wiping her brow.

"Corvian?" Zalith asked quietly, glancing at Alucard as the woman kept talking.

"It's uh…a crab…person," the vampire told him.

"Ew," Zalith mumbled.

"…We've had elves, katokirinkata—we even had a djurian prince once."

Zalith glanced over at Alucard again. "Djurian?"

"Uh…animal…shapeshifters."

"I've never heard them be called that before."

"They're…not like other shapeshifters. They can shift into whatever they want until they mature, and when they mature, they can only turn into one animal for the rest of their lives."

"I see," Zalith said, looking back over at the woman.

"…And you—are you…elves?" she asked, pointing to her own ear.

"We are," Zalith lied.

"Oh," she giggled. "What kind? I-if you don't mind me asking. Your ears are a little different," she said, glancing at her painting and then back at them. "I just want to make sure this is perfect."

She wasn't wrong. Alucard's ears were differently shaped than Zalith's—of course they were. They weren't the same species of demon.

"Can't you just draw what you see?" Zalith asked.

"Oh…." She frowned, glancing at them. "Yes, of course. Sorry—I didn't mean to pry," she said, focusing on her painting. "I just like everything to be perfect. Where are you from?" she then asked, looking at Alucard. "You have an interesting accent."

"I thought you didn't want to pry," the demon said.

She laughed and shook her head. "Forgive me, I'm so chatty."

The demon smiled a little.

For a while, silence settled between them. The woman continued painting, her focus unwavering as people strolled past, the distant murmur of the bustling beach fading into the background. Alucard and Zalith waited patiently, their fingers intertwined, warmth lingering between them.

Alucard wasn't sure how much time had passed, but by the time the woman finally set down her brush, a dull numbness had crept into his legs. Taking that as a sign, he shifted and rose from the bench with Zalith beside him. They stepped forward just as the artist turned her easel towards them, revealing the completed painting.

"What do you think?" she asked with a proud smile.

They both stared at the painting—it was beautifully perfect; it looked so realistic.

"It's so detailed," Zalith said.

"It's wonderful," Alucard added, glancing at her.

"Thank you," she beamed. "If you're happy with it, I'll wait for it to dry and gloss over it so it's all nice and shiny."

Alucard nodded. "It's perfect—thank you."

"Thank *you*," she grinned. "Well, it's going to need a little while more to dry. If you need to head anywhere, I can keep it here for you until you come back; it should be dry by then."

Zalith nodded. "We're just going to go for lunch over there," he said, nodding at the restaurant they'd eaten at yesterday.

"Okay. Just head back over here when you're done, and I'll let you know if it's ready."

"Thank you," Alucard said once again, and then he turned around and followed at Zalith's side as the demon made his way towards the restaurant.

Once inside, they settled into their seats and placed their orders—Zalith opted for a chicken salad, while Alucard chose the salmon. Both ordered lemonade, the idea of something cool and refreshing appealing under the midday sun.

As the waiter walked away, they rested their arms on the table, the quiet hum of conversation and the distant sound of waves filling the space between them.

"So, where should we hang our painting?" Zalith asked, smiling.

Alucard thought to himself for a few moments. "What about in one of the lounges?"

"It'll look nice in our personal lounge with the red couch."

The vampire nodded, moving his arms as the waiter returned with their drinks and placed them down on the table. "That woman sure had a lot of questions," he mumbled.

"I didn't like it," Zalith agreed.

"Well, at least it's over—we can just get our painting and go."

"At least she did a good job," he said and sipped from his lemonade. "Sometimes, you never know what you're going to get."

"Maybe we should hire her for the wedding," Alucard suggested with a smirk and tried his lemonade. It wasn't bad; it was just a little sour.

The demon laughed quietly. "Not if she's going to ask questions the whole time."

Alucard shrugged. "We'll find someone eventually—well…Soren will if he manages to pass your little test."

"I hope he doesn't embarrass us."

"I don't think he will. He seemed too happy to be given a chance. Anyway," he then said, resting his arms on the table. "Is there anything you want to do? We only have another twenty-four hours or so before this little break of ours is over."

"I'm content to just lay on the beach with you all day," Zalith said with a warm smile.

"We can do that when we get back."

"We can order drinks again," his mate said, guiding his hand along the table to take hold of Alucard's.

Alucard smiled and nodded. "Okay."

Soon, the waiter returned with their lunch, setting the plates down before them. As they began to eat, Alucard's thoughts drifted back to this morning. He had offered *twice* now to help Zalith sleep. He didn't want to be too insistent, he didn't want to push—but the worry lingered. Zalith carried so much, more than he ever admitted, and Alucard just wanted to help him—whenever and however he could.

"Did you give any thought to what I said this morning about helping you sleep?" he asked, eating some of his salmon.

The demon shrugged. "I still don't know how I feel about it."

"Well…it'll stop you from waking up constantly—and you'll actually get a good night's rest, too," he said, looking across the table at him.

Zalith frowned almost sullenly. "I know," he said sadly.

Alucard didn't really know what more to say. He didn't want to upset him, nor did he want to ruin their vacation. So he ate a little more of his food and asked, "Do you like it?"

"It's good, as far as salads go," he said. "What about you?"

"It's okay," he mumbled. "It's kind of dry."

"They must have overcooked it."

Alucard shrugged. "I'll still eat it."

They ate in comfortable silence, the ocean breeze carrying the faint scent of citrus through the open-air restaurant. Alucard let the moment settle, pushing aside his worries—for now. There would be time to talk later, time to help if Zalith would let him.

For now, they simply enjoyed their meal, the quiet between them needing no words.

Chapter Thirty-Nine

— ⊰ ✝ ⊱ —

The Tortoise

| **Alucard**—*Maluhia, Lunakai, A'okalani Cove Resort* |

Alucard and Zalith lay stretched out on the beach, the late afternoon sun sinking towards the horizon, casting the sky in soft hues of amber and gold. Zalith rested on his back, while Alucard lay beside him, his head comfortably nestled against the demon's chest. The rhythmic rise and fall beneath him was soothing, their quiet shared between the steady crash of waves and the distant murmur of resort life.

Frowning slightly, Alucard shifted, carefully moving aside their sunglasses and the empty coconuts that had once held their drinks. He adjusted his position, finding a spot that felt just right, and as he did, Zalith's fingers drifted into his hair, idly twisting a few strands between them. The gentle touch sent a quiet shiver down Alucard's spine, but he let himself relax, closing his eyes for a moment as he melted into the warmth of Zalith's presence.

"Do you think… the sky here is like… bluer than back home?" he asked, gazing up at it.

The demon looked up, too, and said, "I do. But maybe it just feels that way because the water is reflecting it."

"Perhaps," Alucard mumbled. "The water is nicer too—it's all… oceany back home."

Zalith laughed quietly. "We should just live here."

"Maybe," the vampire said with a small sigh, closing his eyes again as Zalith tightened his embrace around him.

After a stretch of quiet, Zalith sat up before gently guiding Alucard to lie flat on the picnic blanket. The demon leaned over him, resting his arms on either side, his stare lingering as he brushed a few stray strands of hair from the vampire's face. And for a moment, the demon seemed to simply take him in with that quiet intensity that Alucard had grown so familiar with. He met his mate's gaze, his own hand lifting to rest against the side of the demon's face, his thumb tracing lightly over his cheekbone.

Zalith smiled and leaned in, pressing a kiss to Alucard's forehead, another to his cheek, and then the other before finally catching his lips in a soft, unhurried kiss. His touch was warm, lingering, his breath ghosting over Alucard's skin as he pulled back just enough to smirk. His fingers skimmed along the vampire's jaw, his palm cupping the side of his face. Then, with a teasing glint in his dark eyes, he murmured, "Let's take our clothes off."

Alucard frowned unsurely. "What?" he asked, and as Zalith chuckled and fiddled with his hair, the vampire glanced around to see if anyone else was nearby.

"It'll be fun," his mate said, smiling.

"What if someone sees?"

"Who's going to see?"

The vampire shrugged. "I don't know."

"Are you scared?"

He shook his head and pouted. "No. I've just…never been naked outside before."

Zalith laughed as he fiddled with Alucard's hair. "What about that time in the woods?"

"That was different," he grumbled.

The demon laughed again. "Barely. Come on. It's fun—you should try it."

Alucard stared up at him, his fingers curling slightly against the blanket. He hadn't forgotten what Zalith told him on their way to the island, how he wanted him to feel comfortable and secure in his own skin, at least around him. And Alucard *did* feel more at ease with Zalith than he ever had with anyone else.

But that didn't make the hesitation disappear.

The reluctance still lingered, a quiet, familiar nervousness pressing at the edges of his mind. Yet Zalith was right. They were alone here. No one was going to wander onto their section of the private beach, no unwelcome eyes, no interruptions. This trip was meant for them—for enjoyment, for something light-hearted and easy. He didn't want to ruin the moment with his own unease.

Exhaling softly, he nodded. "Okay, but…you go first," he murmured, his lips twitching into a faint smirk despite himself.

The demon's smile deepened, his expression content. "Okay," he agreed before his fingers moved to the buttons of his shirt. He undid them, slipping the fabric from his shoulders before reaching for his belt; he unbuckled it, unfastened his trousers, and slid them off. Now utterly bare beneath the fading afternoon sun, he grinned down at Alucard, his smirk playful yet unmistakably expectant. "Your turn."

A reluctant frown flickered across Alucard's face, but he wasn't about to let his nerves win. Taking a quiet breath, he started unbuttoning his shirt. Before he could remove it fully, Zalith stepped in, helping him, carefully sliding it off his body. Then, the demon's hands moved lower, unfastening Alucard's belt before the vampire unbuttoned his trousers himself. He sat up slightly to pull them off, trying to ignore the tension coiling in his chest.

When Alucard was finally naked, Zalith didn't speak right away. Instead, he stared, his dark gaze trailing over the vampire's body, slow and appreciative. After a moment, he leaned in, bracing his arms on either side of him, his warmth seeping into the space between them as he gazed down at his face.

"Do you hate it?" Zalith laughed.

Alucard pouted. "No."

Smiling, Zalith lightly dragged his fingers over Alucard's arm. "Does the sun feel nice and toasty on your skin?"

He frowned slightly, taking a moment to truly focus on how he felt. Before now, the only parts of his body that had ever truly felt the sun were his face and hands. He'd always done his best to keep every inch of his scarred skin hidden, wrapped in layers of fabric, avoiding exposure. But here, with Zalith—he didn't have to hide. And that realization settled over him like warmth itself. A quiet smile found its way to his face as he reached up, his fingers grazing Zalith's cheek. "It feels...really good," he murmured contently.

Zalith's smile softened, approval flickering in his eyes. "Good."

Shifting onto his side, the demon pulled Alucard closer, their bodies naturally falling into place. Alucard followed the movement, rolling to face him, his hands settling against Zalith's warm skin. The demon positioned himself so that his back was to the ocean—ensuring that if anyone happened to walk by, they wouldn't see. It was a small gesture, but Alucard noticed it, and he appreciated it more than words could express.

His mate then grabbed his trousers and pulled a small bottle of sunscreen from the pocket. "We should put some of this on," he said, unscrewing the lid.

Alucard glanced at it and looked back at Zalith. "Why?"

Zalith smiled, squeezing some of it onto his hand. "It'll stop you from getting sunburn."

"Okay," he agreed.

"Turn around—I'll do your back first," the demon instructed.

Alucard did as he asked and rolled onto his front. Zalith then started gently massaging the sunscreen onto his back. "Elvin got sunburn once," he mumbled, resting his head on his arms.

"He must have looked like a sundried tomato," his mate joked, pouring more sunscreen onto his hand.

The vampire laughed as Zalith made him turn onto his back so that he could put the sunscreen on his front. "Not far off," he said. "Anyway, he thought he was dying. He cried the whole day and night and asked me to take him to a healer."

Zalith rolled his eyes. "Did you take him?"

"I did...and I paid them to keep him there while he healed so I didn't have to listen to his constant crying and complaining. When I went to get him, he insisted they saved his life. He was such an odd little man," he said as Zalith finished massaging the sunscreen into his skin.

The demon laughed as he handed Alucard the sunscreen and laid down on his front. "If he were around, he probably would have begged you to come on our trip," he said as Alucard started massaging the sunscreen into his back.

"If he were around, he would have cried and cried about us getting engaged, and then he would have begged to be my best man or something like that," he said, but sadness was building up behind the amusement; Elvin may have been odd and overbearing, but he *did* miss him, and he still felt guilty about his death. But he wasn't going to let it consume him. "If he was given more time...I think he might have grown to like you."

He laughed again. "But would *I* have grown to like him?" he asked, and as he rolled onto his back to look up at Alucard, who straddled his lap, he smirked. "No, because I don't like to share."

Alucard smiled as he rubbed the sunscreen into the demon's skin. "I don't know.... He probably would have moved on with that Mia girl. Out of everyone from my old life...I think the only one who would still be around is Tobias. He gave me some confidence back then—maybe he even helped me understand how I really felt about you. I never understood all of these feelings back then," he admitted, unable to fight off a sullen stare as he finished putting sunscreen on Zalith.

His mate moved his hand over his shoulder and smiled. "You've come a long way, baby."

"*We've* come a long way," he said with a smile, prodding Zalith's chest with his finger.

"We really have," he agreed, taking hold of Alucard's hand.

"And we'll be married soon."

"We will, and everyone will be so jealous."

Alucard smiled and lay beside Zalith, resting his head on his chest. "Are we going to have a honeymoon? I know some people do that...like a long vacation together after the wedding."

"Of course we are," Zalith said, turning his head to look at him. "Where do you want to go?"

"I don't know yet. But...somewhere nice...and quiet—like this," he said, moving his arm around the demon. "I like being away from the city and all the people."

"That suits me just fine," the demon said.

Alucard then sighed contently as he closed his eyes and relaxed. "Will you tell me a story?" he asked.

"About what?"

He shrugged. "Anything."

Zalith thought to himself for a moment and started fiddling with Alucard's hair. "Xurian and I were heading to a fancy dinner for some important charity that my mother had organized. We arrived, but as my brother got out of the carriage, his leg was asleep, so he fell into the staff carrying these huge silver trays of confectionary, and he got icing and sugar and cake all over himself," he said, laughing. "My mother scolded us both for it."

Alucard laughed. "Why did she scold both of you? You had nothing to do with it."

"That's just how my mother was. If Xurian did something bad, it was my fault, too. If I did something bad, it was also my brother's fault. For example, when he got the girl he was seeing pregnant with his first daughter, our mother was mad at him because the girl was human, but it was also my fault because I didn't talk sense into him and allowed him to keep seeing her—as though Xurian listened to anyone," he muttered.

The vampire laughed again. "Was there ever a time *you* did something bad, or was it always your brother getting you both told off?"

"I did my fair share of bad things, but either way, she was always mad at me for something," he said with an amused chuckle. "She was mad at Xurian more often, though, because he refused to listen to anything she said, and as my mother put it, he brought shame to the family because of his life choices."

"I gather your mother was all about keeping your bloodline pure, huh?" he asked with a frown. "Like most Lilidian demons. A lot of the cultists stopped following Lucifer after he decided to have a witch mother his child—they all thought he'd choose a demon—Lilith or one of her scions. To be honest, I don't even know why he went about it the way he did. It's a good thing, though. If Lilith was my mother, we'd be related," he said with a grimace. "Anyway...I assume it was hard to please your mother?"

Zalith laughed quietly as he fiddled with Alucard's hair. "She had particular tastes and was very hard to please."

Alucard smiled, moving his hand over Zalith's chest. He was sure that talking about his family was making Zalith sad—or soon would. So, he thought he should change the subject. "Do you want to go for a walk?"

"A naked walk?" Zalith asked, smirking.

The vampire pouted. "No. We have to get dressed."

Zalith sighed and smiled. "Fine."

"We can get naked again later," Alucard told him as he sat up and started pulling his trousers on.

"You promise?"

"I promise," he said, handing Zalith his trousers.

Once they were dressed, Alucard took Zalith's hand and led him down the beach. The sand was cool beneath their feet now, the heat of the afternoon fading into the softer warmth of early evening. Zalith, however, had left his shirt behind, choosing to walk with nothing but his trousers; the demon looked completely at ease, the golden light casting a soft glow over his bare skin as the ocean breeze tugged lazily at his hair.

"Do you think the people of Eimwood miss us?" Alucard asked, looking at Zalith.

"Hopefully, everyone's up in arms about the Cecil rumours."

"I wouldn't be surprised if they burned down his home and hanged him in the streets."

"That would be nice. It would really cut our workload down."

"It would. But we haven't heard anything, so, he must still be alive."

"Unfortunately, I think you're right," the demon said, sighing.

Alucard exhaled deeply, his gaze fixed ahead—until a flicker of movement at the edge of his vision caught his attention. Something small scurried into the grass near a cluster of trees, disappearing into the shade. Curiosity sparked in his chest. Aside from the fish in the sky and sea, the dog that had greeted them yesterday, and the tropical birds, he hadn't seen much wildlife since they arrived. He wanted to see what it was.

Without hesitation, he tightened his grip on Zalith's hand and pulled him towards the trees.

"What is it?" Zalith asked as they reached the swaying palms, his tone laced with amusement.

The vampire stopped and leaned forward, searching the small, grassed area for what he'd seen... but there was nothing. "I thought I saw something," he mumbled.

"What kind of something?" the demon asked, sounding a little unsettled.

"I don't know," he replied, but then, as he caught sight of something dark shuffling behind some tall grass, he lost his frown and hurried into the trees as Zalith followed, gripping his hand tightly.

Reaching the grass, Alucard crouched down, releasing Zalith's hand as he carefully parted the blades. Nestled at the base of a tree lay a small tortoise—but not like any he had seen before. Its shell was a pale, off-white hue, its skin a soft, almost ethereal blue, and its eyes—deep red, like fresh-spilled blood—blinked up at him with quiet curiosity. But what stood out most were the small shards of fluorescent crystal sprouting from its shell, clustered like barnacles, catching the fading light with a faint, mesmerizing glow.

Alucard might have stared longer, fascinated by the strange little creature, but his gaze drifted lower; he watched it drag its right hind leg awkwardly through the sand. His frown deepened. Upon closer inspection, he noticed a length of fishing net cutting into its skin, the thin, cruel strands biting deep enough to leave the flesh raw.

Zalith watched as Alucard reached towards the tortoise—only for the little creature to snap at his finger without hesitation. Alucard recoiled, a startled snarl escaping him, and at the same time, Zalith instinctively pulled him back.

"Leave it alone," the demon said, his voice edged with concern. "Let's go."

But Alucard shook his head with a stubborn pout. "No," he muttered. "It's hurt and needs help."

Zalith hesitated before releasing him, exhaling as Alucard crouched again, moving closer to the distressed tortoise.

The vampire's voice softened. "It's okay," he murmured, reaching forward once more.

This time, the tortoise didn't attack, simply blinking up at him as he carefully patted its head with his other hand. Zalith let out a quiet, disgusted sound, clearly unimpressed by the moment of bonding, but he still watched as Alucard shifted focus to its injured leg. The vampire extended one claw, using it like a blade to slice through the tangled netting. Piece by piece, he freed the tortoise's leg, and once the last strand was cut, he smiled, rubbing the creature's head again before tucking the net into his pocket—he wasn't about to leave it lying around for another helpless animal to get caught in.

As Alucard rose to his feet, the tortoise lingered for a moment, its blood-red eyes fixed on him. Then, without ceremony, it turned and disappeared into the grass, leaving them alone.

"Are you okay?" Zalith asked.

Glancing down at his hand, Alucard nodded. "I'm fine. It's already healing."

Zalith sighed in relief—but he made a rather revolted face as he glanced down at where the tortoise had been.

"Let's head back," Alucard said. "It's getting late."

"Okay," the demon said—but as Alucard went to take hold of his hand, he pulled his arm away and frowned. "I can't, baby, I'm sorry. You just touched a turtle and you've got its little turtle germs all over your hands."

Alucard pouted, looked down at his hands, and then back at Zalith. He scowled and sighed, and then he led the way out of the trees. "Fine," he grumbled.

"It was covered in garbage," the demon insisted as he caught up and walked at his side.

"No, it wasn't," Alucard mumbled.

"Yes, it was. And I love that you helped it, that was very kind of you, but who knows where it's been?"

The vampire glanced at him. "Don't get *too* close. I might infect you with my tortoise hands," he sneered, waving his hands in Zalith's face.

Zalith sighed and kept walking at his side, heading back to their beach house.

Once they got back, Alucard led the way in. A white barn owl was waiting in the lounge on the table with a small package at its feet, and as he spotted it, the vampire sighed in relief.

"That must be my crystals—finally," he muttered, making his way over.

"Good," Zalith said.

Alucard picked up and unwrapped the package, taking out the crystals from within. "You can go now," he said, looking down at the owl. Then, he slipped the crystals into his pocket and turned to face Zalith.

"Before you touch anything else, can you please wash your hands?" Zalith requested.

Alucard scowled, huffing irritably as he brushed past Zalith without a word. He made his way into the bathroom and shut the door behind him with a quiet but firm click. From the other side, he heard Zalith sigh, followed by the sound of his footsteps retreating downstairs to their bedroom.

The vampire rolled his eyes, a pout settling on his lips as he leaned against the door. Why was he so easily irritated? The smallest things managed to get under his skin, leaving him aggravated for reasons he could barely explain.

Shaking his head, he pushed away from the door and walked to the sink, turning on the water. As the cool stream ran over his hands, he let his thoughts settle. It was just a tortoise, not some dire situation, not something worth feeling so tense over. And besides, it wasn't as if either of them could actually get sick from any germs the little creature might have carried.

Sighing, he shut off the faucet and reached for a towel, drying his hands before sinking to the floor. His back pressed against the cabinet, legs bent, arms resting over his knees as he glared down at his lap. He needed a moment to cool off. If he went downstairs now, he might let his snark get the best of him, and he didn't want to do that—not tonight. Not when this was their last night here.

Chapter Forty

─ ⟨ † ⟩ ─

Dining Under the Setting Sun

| **Zalith**—*Maluhia, Lunakai, A'okalani Cove Resort* |

Downstairs, Zalith dropped onto the bed with a heavy sigh, rubbing a hand down his face before letting it fall to his chest. He didn't like that Alucard was annoyed with him—that much was obvious. But that tortoise had been filthy, and the last thing he wanted was its germs all over the place where they were staying.

He knew it wasn't a big deal—not really—but he also knew how easily small things could spiral into tension. And the last thing he wanted tonight was an argument. Not when this was their final night here.

Exhaling again, he tried to let the irritation slip from his mind. Alucard would cool off—he always did. So, the demon waited, patient as ever, letting his body sink into the mattress as he forced himself to relax.

He soon heard the bathroom door open—

"I'm going for a walk," Alucard called from upstairs.

Zalith frowned, the weight of the situation settling deeper in his chest. Fine, he wanted to say, but the word came out flat, lacking any real bite. "Fine," he called back, though he wasn't sure if Alucard even lingered long enough to hear it.

A few moments later, he heard the front door shut. The house fell into silence.

With a heavy exhale, he stared up at the ceiling, his jaw tightening. He hated this—he hated that he'd irritated Alucard, maybe even upset him. He didn't want to ruin their trip, he didn't want to be the reason a perfectly good evening soured. Yet, somehow, that's exactly what it felt like. He ruined everything.

But he wasn't going to just lie there and wallow in his frustration.

Pushing himself up, he made his way upstairs, heading straight for the bathroom. A shower. That's what he needed. Something to clear his head, to wash away the weight of his thoughts. And after that…he'd go back downstairs and wait for Alucard to come home.

⊷❖⊶

After his shower, Zalith lay in bed, staring at the ceiling, his damp, tousled hair a mess against the pillow. He wasn't sure how much time had passed—minutes? An hour?—but when he finally heard the sound of the front door opening, relief settled over him. Alucard was back. He was safe.

But the demon didn't move.

The heaviness in his chest remained, pressing down with every passing second. He felt too disheartened, too frustrated with himself to go upstairs and face him. If Alucard was still upset, then forcing a conversation wouldn't help. It was better to wait, better to let his fiancé come to him when he was ready.

So…he waited.

He listened as the vampire moved around upstairs, the quiet sounds of him settling back in filling the silence. Eventually, the soft creak of the stairs signalled his descent, and Zalith turned his head just as Alucard reached the bottom step.

For a moment, neither of them spoke. Zalith wasn't sure what to say; he wasn't even sure if Alucard was still angry. He could only hope that whatever aggravation lingered between them had faded and that they could enjoy the rest of their time here without this hanging over them.

Alucard made his way over without hesitation, climbing into bed and crawling over Zalith until their bodies were close. His fiancé pressed his forehead against his, his eyes flickering between icy blue and hell-fiery red as the water beyond the glass refracted the fading sunlight. The effect was mesmerizing—like molten flame rippling beneath a frozen surface, shifting with every subtle movement of light.

"Are you annoyed at me?" Alucard mumbled, his voice quiet, almost uncertain.

Zalith watched the way the colours of Alucard's gaze danced, otherworldly and striking, before exhaling softly. "No," he murmured, trying to keep his lingering sadness from slipping through. He didn't want Alucard to see it; he didn't want to make him feel guilty over something that didn't matter anymore.

"I have something upstairs for you," the vampire said, smiling softly.

"What is it?" Zalith asked, a hint of curiosity managing to break through his despondency.

Alucard took his hand, his grip firm yet gentle. "Come and see," he said, standing and pulling Zalith with him.

Zalith pulled his clothes on before trailing after his fiancé through the lounge and towards the porch. As they stepped outside, he finally saw what Alucard had been so eager to show him.

The small outdoor table had been carefully set, a white tablecloth draped neatly over it. Candles flickered in the centre, their golden glow casting soft light against the evening air. Their plates were already set, steaming with spaghetti and garlic bread, and beside them sat a bottle of red wine, the deep crimson liquid catching the candlelight.

Zalith's chest tightened, his frown soft, almost sad, as he turned to Alucard. "Is this for me?" he asked, his voice quieter than he intended.

Alucard's smile warmed as he nodded. "Yes."

Zalith's expression brightened, his gaze sweeping over everything Alucard had arranged. It wasn't just the table—candles lined the edge of the porch as well, their soft flames flickering in the gentle evening breeze. When Alucard reached inside and switched off the lounge lights, the entire space was left illuminated only by the candlelight and the rising moons, casting a warm, intimate glow over their dinner.

The demon turned back to him, his dark eyes full of something tender. "Thank you, baby," he murmured, his voice softer now. "I love it." He reached up, cupping the side of Alucard's face, his thumb brushing lightly over his cheek. Then, without hesitation, he leaned in, capturing Alucard's lips in a slow, lingering kiss.

Alucard smiled and fiddled with Zalith's hair. "Good," he said with a small smirk. He made his way over to the table and pulled out Zalith's chair.

"Thank you," he said, smiling as he sat down.

Then, Alucard sat across the table from him.

"This was really nice of you," the demon said, leaning his arms on the table.

The vampire shrugged as he made himself comfortable. "I wanted our last night here to be...well...special, I guess," he mumbled, taking the bottle of wine.

"Well, it's very sweet of you," Zalith said, resting the side of his face in his left hand. "I love you."

Pouring them both a glass of wine, Alucard smiled. "I love you, too," he said and handed Zalith his glass.

"Thank you," he said, taking it.

"I would have cooked it myself, but...I don't know how to cook," he said with a hushed chuckle. "And I didn't want to ruin this with shitty food, so."

"That's okay. I'm sure it's delicious," the demon said contently. He leaned over the table, moved his hand to the side of Alucard's face, and kissed his lips. "I really do love it."

Smiling, Alucard looked down at his food before shyly glancing at Zalith. "It's uh...Lupanese," he said, picking up his knife and fork as Zalith did. "The food. I found a little restaurant on the promenade. Out of all the foods I've tried, I think Lupanese is my favourite. We should go back there one day," he suggested.

"We could go for our next trip," Zalith said and sipped from his wine.

Alucard smiled. "Okay. Maybe we can invite ourselves to another wedding," he laughed.

"It'll be good for inspiration," he said with a smirk before trying his food.

Alucard nodded in agreement. "Do you like it?"

The demon smiled again. "It's delicious," he said, and then he held out a fork of spaghetti, inviting Alucard to eat it.

With a shy, adorable little smile, his fiancé leaned forward and ate it. "It's really good," he agreed, making himself comfortable in his seat again. "I was in Lupa once—a long time ago," he started and took a sip of his wine. "It's where most of my wine businesses are, so I would go there a lot to make sure everyone knew who their boss was. It was a really different place two hundred years ago. It was all…vineyards and fields and scattered villages. It's all glass and cities now. Anyway, I met this really…eccentric man. Antonio—he liked to think of himself as an artist. But nobody bought his work—no one would even look at it, really. The day I met him, he was sitting on a street corner painting the meadow in front of the windmill. And it wasn't actually that bad—not as good as the painting we got today, but it was close. So I was confused as to why no one wanted to buy his work or hire him. I asked around. It turned out that he was a con artist—much like Cecil, actually. He stole the body of the original Antonio and all his skills and knowledge and whatnot. This creature would slink around the town at night and crawl up into whoever he could—he tried over and over again to disguise himself as one of the citizens, and he could never work out why the people always knew it was him. I guess no one was brave enough to tell him his disgusting little tail was always showing."

"Ew," Zalith laughed amusedly. He appreciated the story, but he loved hearing Alucard's voice more.

The vampire shrugged as he ate some more of his food. "Eventually, the people of the town gathered enough money to put a bounty out on this creature. I won't lie…I felt sorry for him. He just wanted to live somewhere. So, I took him away from that little town and had him work for me. I taught him how to hide his tail, and he worked for me for years, infiltrating some very important places. He met his end, however, when he fell in love with a rich girl named Mary. At the time, he was masquerading as a lord, so of course, this girl was all over him—her parents even arranged to have her marry Antonio for his money—well, the money of the man he was wearing the skin of. On their wedding night, he decided to reveal his true self to her—he couldn't keep lying, blah…blah," he mumbled and sipped from his drink. "The moment she saw his weird little spider-like face, she stabbed him in the neck with her hairpin. He bled out, and that was the end of Antonio," he concluded with a shrug.

Zalith laughed as he picked up his glass. "Antonio should have kept his face to himself."

"I guess...love makes you do stupid things," he mumbled.

"Like fighting Gods," he said, smirking.

Alucard smiled but looked down at his food. "Well...at least we know what we're doing."

"Fortunately," the demon agreed, finishing his wine.

The vampire topped up both their glasses and then sighed quietly. "Do you think...Peaches is okay? And Sabazios...and Hanna, Sierra, Molly, and Marcy."

"I hope so. I'm sure Edwin is taking very good care of them. He's good at his job," he said, finishing his dinner.

Alucard nodded, finishing his own food. "I miss Drac."

"We should go and visit him soon. Is he doing okay?"

"They update me weekly," Alucard said, nodding. "He is happy with his girlfriend—they think she might be pregnant, actually. They don't know for sure yet, though."

Zalith smiled. "We'll definitely have to go and see his babies when the time comes—if she *is* pregnant, that is."

Alucard nodded. "They are an endangered species—it would be nice to see more of them."

"I'm sure the fishermen will be thrilled," he joked.

"The people hunted them for their ethos properties," his fiancé grumbled. "Alchemy and medicines that do nothing. The same goes for that tortoise we found earlier."

The demon frowned. "What did people think the tortoise could do?"

"They hunt them for the crystals that grow on their body. They are...ethos crystals—sort of like the ones I make...the ones that explode. People use the crystals for making weapons and whatever else. They can also morph their legs into fins so that they can swim—it's probably why the one we found had fishing net on her leg."

"How do you know it was a she?"

Alucard shrugged. "Only the females grow the crystals."

"Interesting," the demon said before finishing his wine.

They tidied the table a little before refilling their glasses, the warm glow of candlelight flickering around them. For a while, they sat in a comfortable silence, letting the peacefulness of the evening settle over them. It had been a long, eventful day, and Zalith felt a rare sense of ease.

He glanced at Alucard, watching as the vampire shifted slightly, his fingers idly tracing the rim of his glass. When their eyes met, Alucard smiled—small, soft, almost shy. Zalith returned it without thinking, something fond curling in his chest as the vampire looked down at his lap, as if suddenly uncertain under his gaze.

"We have dessert—if you want," Alucard said.

Zalith nodded. "Yeah. We can eat it on the deck and watch the sun set."

"Okay," he said contently. "I can go and get it if you want to go and wait over there.

Zalith nodded and stood up. "Thank you."

Alucard then headed back inside.

With a quiet, relieved exhale, Zalith made his way to the edge of the deck. He rolled up his trouser legs before lowering himself down, letting his feet slip into the cool water below. The gentle current lapped against his skin, the sensation grounding as he sat back, soaking in the stillness of the night.

His fiancé returned soon after, carrying two sundaes. Zalith smiled as he approached, and Alucard returned his smile as he handed his dessert to him.

"Thank you," the demon said.

The vampire sat down beside him cross-legged.

As he ate his ice cream, Zalith smiled at him. "The water's still nice," he said, moving his feet around in it. "You should put your feet in."

Alucard frowned reluctantly but dipped his free hand in to test it. He then put his ice cream down, took off his socks, and rolled up his trouser legs. After shuffling closer to Zalith, he eased his feet into the water until it reached his shins.

The demon smiled and leaned nearer to kiss Alucard's cheek, and then he continued enjoying his ice cream.

"Is it good?" the vampire asked.

"It is," he replied. "Do you like yours?"

Alucard nodded with a content smile. "I had this a few times when I visited Lupa before—it's one of my favourite ice creams."

"Noted," Zalith said with a smirk. "I had some pistachio ice cream a few times back in Eltaria—the one I ordered when we got ice cream in Boszorkány. I think that's *my* favourite."

"I will remember that," Alucard murmured before pressing a soft kiss to Zalith's cheek.

As the last light of day stretched across the horizon, the vampire rested his head against the demon's shoulder, their bodies warm against the evening breeze. Zalith exhaled quietly, feeling a deep sense of relief settle in his chest. The tension from earlier had faded, their disagreement nothing more than a passing shadow now. He hated when things soured between them, even briefly—but they had moved past it, and now they could enjoy the rest of the evening without bad feelings lingering between them.

Chapter Forty-One

— ⊰ ✝ ⊱ —

Their Last Night Away

| Alucard—*Maluhia, Lunakai, A'okalani Cove Resort* |

After a while—and once they had finished their ice cream—Zalith exhaled deeply and straightened his posture. Alucard frowned, watching as the demon suddenly stood and began unbuttoning his shirt; there was a quiet ease to his movements as he shrugged it off and reached for his trousers.

Alucard's frown deepened. "What are you doing?" he asked, curiosity creeping into his voice.

Zalith smirked. "Going for a swim." And with that, he turned and dived into the water.

The vampire blinked, momentarily startled as he peered over the edge, his eyes following the ripple of movement beneath the crystal-clear surface. He watched as Zalith's form cut through the depths, his body moving effortlessly in the water before he finally resurfaced.

As Zalith swam back towards the deck, droplets shimmering against his skin in the moonlight, he tilted his head up at Alucard, smirking in that infuriatingly self-satisfied way. He lightly gripped the vampire's right ankle and tugged on it. "Come swim," he said.

The vampire frowned reluctantly and shook his head. "I'm okay here."

"*Please*," Zalith pleaded, swirling around the thin, crimson hairs on Alucard's leg with his thumb.

He shrugged and mumbled, "I don't know." Despite having been confident enough to take off his clothes and rest on the beach earlier, the same fear of revealing his scars gripped him tight.

Zalith sighed heavily and shrugged. "Okay. I'll just float all on my own in the great blue sea," he droned dramatically.

The vampire pouted. He didn't want him to feel upset, nor did he want to let his insecurities ruin their night. "Okay," he agreed, unbuttoning his shirt.

As Zalith chuckled softly, watching him with amusement, Alucard exhaled and pulled off his clothes. Once undressed, he carefully climbed down from the deck, lowering himself into the surprisingly warm water. The gentle current wrapped around him, and for a brief moment, he let himself adjust to the sensation.

Then, Zalith swam closer. The demon slid his arms around Alucard's waist, pulling him flush against his own; the heat of his body against the water sent a shiver through Alucard, though whether from the contrast in temperature or something else entirely, he wasn't sure. Zalith pressed him back against the dock, his fingers drifting into the vampire's hair, toying with the strands as his dark eyes traced his face with quiet admiration. And without a word, he leaned in, capturing Alucard's lips in a slow, lingering kiss.

"Thank you for dinner," Zalith said with a soft smile, resting his forehead against Alucard's. "And for our beautiful vacation."

"It's okay," Alucard said, gazing into his eyes. "I wanted us to have some time away from everything and everyone—I wanted you to have a nice time."

"I am having a nice time," he assured him. "And now *I* want to do something nice for *you*," he murmured, leaning in until his lips brushed against Alucard's ear, his tone dipping into something seductive.

A shiver of anticipation jolted down Alucard's spine. "What?"

Zalith smirked against his skin. "I think you know."

The demon's hand slid lower, fingers ghosting over Alucard's body, the touch featherlight yet unmistakable. Then, his lips found the vampire's mouth again, claiming it with a slow, deep kiss—one that sent heat pooling low in Alucard's stomach. Anticipation melted into arousal as Zalith's hand finally reached his crotch; the vampire's head tipped back against the dock, a quiet exhale escaping him, his body inviting more. And Zalith accepted, his mouth leaving scattered, lingering kisses along his neck, fingers teasing, barely there, just enough to make Alucard's breath deepen with eagerness.

But Zalith didn't linger there for long. His lips travelled upward, pressing against the curve of Alucard's ear before he bit down—just enough to make the vampire tense—and then exhaled, his breath hot against his skin. "Get inside," he instructed, his voice edged with something dark, commanding.

Alucard wasn't about to question Zalith's demand.

Their eyes met, locked in a silent exchange—Zalith's gaze burned with desire, dark and unyielding, and it only sent another pulse of excitement thrumming through Alucard's veins. His breath quickened, anticipation coiling in his stomach.

He obeyed.

The vampire climbed out of the water, droplets slipping down his skin, but as he reached for his clothes, Zalith caught his wrist. Before he could protest, the demon pulled him forward, his grip firm, insistent. There was no hesitation. Hastily, his mate led him back into the house, down the stairs, and straight into their bedroom.

Zalith spun him around, hands gripping his waist, pulling him in as his lips crashed against Alucard's. The kiss was deep, consuming, filled with undiluted hunger. The demon moved forward, forcing Alucard back step by step until his spine met the wall.

A smirk tugged at Zalith's lips as he pulled back just enough to breathe him in, his eyes drinking in the sight of Alucard's damp, flushed skin. His fingers trailed downward, gradually dragging heat in their wake.

Alucard shuddered, his body tensing with anticipation. Then, Zalith's hand slid lower, wrapping around his arousal, firm and knowing. A sharp, pleasing jolt shot through the vampire, a low exhale slipping from his lips as his head pressed back against the wall.

Zalith's smirk deepened as he pressed a few more heated, lingering kisses against Alucard's lips. The vampire, already lost in the moment, let his hand slide down his mate's body, his fingers curling firmly around his hardening length.

The demon exhaled a low, satisfied breath before leaning in, his lips brushing the curve of Alucard's ear. "I'm going to fuck you so hard," he murmured, his voice thick with adamance. And as if to prove his point, the demon's grip tightened around Alucard's growing arousal, his strokes slow, teasing, measured.

A fresh wave of anticipation surged through Alucard, his body reacting instinctively. Zalith's words sent a sharp thrill racing through his veins, a rush of heat that had him tipping his head back against the wall, his breath coming out in a deep, pleased exhale. "Good," he muttered, matching Zalith's touch as his hand continued to work over him.

But then Zalith moved. In one abrupt motion, he spun Alucard around, pressing him forcefully against the wall. The shift was aggressive, commanding, *intoxicating*. Alucard barely had time to react before his mate's strong hands gripped his waist, pulling him back—forcing him to arch into Zalith's hold.

Bracing his forearms against the wall, Alucard let his head rest against them, his breath catching as Zalith pressed against him from behind, the heat of his body unmistakable. A shuddering exhale slipped from the vampire's lips, his breathing already picking up as Zalith's right hand trailed possessively over his back, his touch promising everything that was about to follow.

"Are you comfy?" the demon whispered, leaning into Alucard's ear.

The vampire nodded, his breath uneven, anticipation curling tight in his stomach.

"Good," Zalith murmured.

And before Alucard could comprehend it, sharp fangs sank into his neck.

A startled sound escaped him, his body tensing instinctively at the sudden bite. Pain flared for only a moment—piercing, fleeting—before it melted into something else entirely. As Zalith's venom seeped into his veins, warmth spread through Alucard's body, slow at first, like a heady, creeping intoxication. His limbs felt lighter, looser, his thoughts shifting into something softer, hazier. The world around him seemed to blur at the edges, his skin hypersensitive to every touch, every breath.

But the feeling didn't stay gentle for long.

The slow haze deepened, it *intensified*, building until it was overwhelming. A rush of pleasure, thick and consuming, spread through his chest, his stomach, curling down into his core. The sensation was all-encompassing, like his mind was being unravelled and rewired at the same time.

Zalith's fingers pressed into his waist, grounding him, but the moment only sent a fresh shock of euphoria through him. Alucard couldn't stop the pleasured moan that slipped past his lips, his body tightening in response to the sensation, his mind succumbing to the sheer, dizzying pleasure that constricted him where he stood.

"Zalith," Alucard whined, his voice breathy and unrestrained as his eyes fluttered shut. His heart pounded against his ribs, his body already trembling beneath the waves of intensifying delight that his mate was pouring into him. Every nerve felt alive, burning, yearning, his mind clouded in pure sensation.

Zalith smirked against his skin, slowly withdrawing his fangs from Alucard's neck. "Yes?" he murmured, his voice dark with amusement as he released Alucard's aching shaft, dragging his hand slowly—*torturously*—up his body.

Alucard barely knew what he wanted to say. The overbearing sensation, the pleasure still coiling through him…it left his thoughts tangled, incoherent. But as the demon's fingers brushed over his throat, gripping lightly, and his tongue dragged over the fresh wounds on his neck, Alucard moaned—soft, helpless, lost in bliss.

Then Zalith's other hand left his waist, and though he was no longer actively feeding his venom into him, the intoxicating pleasure still lingered, pulsing, throbbing deep inside. A moment later, something slick and warm coated his skin as Zalith's fingers worked over him, massaging the viscous lube into his ass with slow, teasing movements.

The vampire shuddered, his forehead pressing harder against his arms, which still braced against the wall. His breath came in quiet, uneven gasps as Zalith pressed kisses along his neck, then up to his jaw, then as much of his flushed face as he could reach.

Alucard let out a breathless, pleased sound, his body tightening around the slow stretch as Zalith eased his thick, hard dick inside him. The first inch burned just enough to make his breath hinder, the ache sharp yet undeniably intoxicating. Another inch followed, pushing deeper, and his muscles clenched involuntarily, his body adjusting to the sheer size of him. No matter how many times they'd had sex, taking Zalith was still sometimes a struggle, always something he had to work himself around. But it was a struggle he welcomed, a struggle he *loved*.

By the time Zalith had worked halfway in, Alucard's mind was already slipping, his breath coming in shaky, uneven gasps as his walls stretched around him. Every inch that followed was exquisite torment, dragging against every sensitive part of him in a slow, torturous descent into pleasure. The pressure was overwhelming, the heat between them unbearable, his nerves burning with each careful movement as Zalith finally bottomed out.

A deep satisfaction devoured the vampire, his body trembling from the sheer fullness, and yet, he hardly resisted. He was already too far gone, too eager—too desperate for Zalith to keep going.

Zalith pressed a few lingering kisses against his neck before he began to move, his rhythm unhurried at first, drawing out the moment. His free arm slid around Alucard's waist, pulling him closer, his grip firm yet possessive, while his other hand remained at his throat, fingers pressing just enough to remind him who was in control.

A soft, shuddering moan escaped Alucard, his trembling legs growing weaker the longer he remained standing. The stretch was deep, unrelenting, a piercing ache spiralling through his muscles, but the pleasure far outweighed the strain. Every inch of Zalith inside him left him gasping, his body forced to adjust, to take him in despite the familiar struggle. The demon's warm, hard frame pressed against his back, his grip firm, *possessive*. And the way he fit—filling him so completely, leaving no space untouched—was almost too much to bear.

Zalith exhaled a low, pleased sound into his ear, his grip tightening around his throat as he buried himself deep with each thrust. Alucard's fingers clenched into fists, his breath ragged, his body aflame with sensation as he moaned loudly. His mind felt like it was slipping, lost in the devouring heat, his heart hammering violently inside his chest.

His mate then abruptly pulled him from the wall, eased his dick from his ass and spun him around, pushing him down onto the bed. Alucard barely had time to react before his back hit the mattress, a surprised laugh spilling from his lips. Above him, Zalith smirked, predatory and clearly pleased with himself; he crawled over him, pressing the vampire further into the sheets, pinning his arms above his head with one hand while the other wrapped once more around his throat.

And then Zalith kissed him. It started slow, teasing, but quickly deepened, consuming. Alucard melted beneath him, surrendering, his body settling, his breath slowing. But even as his heart steadied, his need only grew. How long did Zalith intend to make him wait?

After a while, Zalith pulled back, his lips lingering near Alucard's for a moment before breaking the kiss. His dark eyes roamed over him, heavy-lidded, intense, as if committing every flushed detail to memory. His fingers slipped from Alucard's throat, only to trail slowly along the side of his face, his touch firm yet reverent, like he was savouring the moment.

Alucard's breath was still unsteady, his body thrumming with the effects of Zalith's venom, the high making every sensation sharper, every touch more intoxicating. Even the absence of Zalith's lips left his skin aching for more, craving whatever else the demon would give him.

For a moment, Zalith admired him, his expression unreadable—until Alucard caught the familiar smirk that curled at the demon's lips. Before he could question it, Zalith's hand returned to his throat, fingers curling possessively around it just as his horns and wings emerged, unfurling in full, demonic splendour. His wings stretched wide before folding back neatly, but the display, as always, sent a familiar pulse of exhilaration and submission through Alucard's body.

He stared up at Zalith, utterly entranced. Whenever his mate revealed his whole self, his presence became something more—something greater, overwhelming, dominating. He radiated power, command, and raw desire, and it made Alucard feel so very small beneath him. Meek. Owned. Devoted. To lie there, to serve as something that pleased the demon, was a role he welcomed, one that sent a deep, almost primal satisfaction knotting in his chest.

Knowing that he satisfied Zalith, that he was able to bring him pleasure, that he alone was the recipient of this attention and affection—it left him feeling something he had never known before, a contentedness that settled deep within his very being, warming him from the inside out.

He loved this. He loved Zalith.

And there was nowhere else he would rather be than within the demon's possessive grip.

A deep, breathless moan spilled from Alucard's lips as Zalith eased his dick back inside, stretching him open once more with that slow, unbearable depth. His body clenched around him instinctively, desperate, aching, craving more.

Then, Zalith's hand returned to his throat.

Alucard's breath struggled, his pulse hammering beneath the demon's grip, pleasure curling tighter. A delighted sound escaped him, his body shuddering as exhilaration surged through him, spreading like fire through every trembling limb. His right leg hooked over Zalith's back, pulling him in closer as he drank in the sight of him.

Wherever their skin met, golden, fire-like markings bloomed across Zalith's body, tracing over his skin like embers awakening into flame. The sight alone made Alucard moan again, the sheer intimacy of it intoxicating.

Zalith picked up the pace, his rhythm deepening, faster, harsher, and as the intensity built, Alucard turned his head to the side, eyes fluttering shut, teeth gritting in delicious struggle. He moaned, he writhed, he fidgeted beneath Zalith's weight, his body both resisting and yearning as the demon thrusted aggressively.

Instinctively, the vampire tried to pull one of his hands free, desperate to grip onto something—onto *him*. But before he could, Zalith's hold tightened, a quiet growl rumbling into his ear, a warning.

"Stay exactly where you are," the demon demanded.

The dominance in his touch and his voice sent a jolt of desperation spiralling through Alucard's already overstimulated body; it almost *pleaded* for mercy as he wordlessly obeyed, submitting.

Then Zalith moved faster. Harder. More relentless.

Alucard gasped, his entire form tightening beneath the overwhelming pleasure, his trembling limbs burning with it. He scowled, a quiet whimper escaping his throat before he finally tore his wrist free from Zalith's grip. Without hesitation, his fingers buried into the demon's hair, yanking him down just as Zalith's mouth found his neck, his lips and fangs grazing over sensitive, fevered skin.

But instead of a kiss, Zalith sank his fangs into the other side of Alucard's neck.

A sharp whine tore from the vampire's lips, his body jolting, completely overcome as fresh venom surged through his veins. The high hit him instantly, a dizzying, euphoric flood that left his limbs weak, his breath uneven, his mind blank. His hand shot up instinctively, grasping onto something—

Zalith's right horn. The moment his fingers curled around it, another loud, uncontrollable moan spilled from his throat, louder than he would have liked, but he was too lost, too consumed to care. Zalith, however, grinned against his neck, a quiet, breathless chuckle escaping him through his own erratic breathing.

And then he moved faster.

Alucard didn't want it to end—he *never* wanted it to end—but his body was surrendering, the pleasure becoming impossible to contain. His scowl deepened, his fingers tightening around Zalith's horn, his gasps breaking into staggered moans as his body trembled beneath him. The demon let out a pleased, indulgent hum, nuzzling into the side of his neck as if revelling in every moment.

And with one final, overwhelming wave of pleasure, Alucard reached his peak. A desperate, strained whine escaped him as his body tensed, his climax overtaking him in a shuddering, helpless collapse. Zalith finally stilled, his grip slowly loosening around Alucard's wrist before letting go entirely. His hand trailed down his arm and over his chest, tracing possessively over his trembling form.

Alucard barely had the strength to move, his body still shuddering, his heart racing, his breath uneven as he tried to calm himself. But before he could fully settle, Zalith's fingers gripped his jaw, tilting his head up, forcing him to meet his gaze.

The vampire's eyes flickered open, still heavy, still dazed from the high.

Zalith's lips curled into a slow, unseemly smile. "You're so cute," he murmured, his thumb stroking over Alucard's flushed cheek, delightedly devouring every bit of his wrecked state.

Alucard tried to think of something to say in response, but he felt so completely engulfed that all he could do was exhale deeply and frown.

The demon's smirk only widened, his amusement deepening as he took in the sight of Alucard's thoroughly undone state. Without breaking eye contact, he lowered himself, his lips trailing a slow, teasing path down Alucard's body. Soft kisses, lingering nips, the warmth of his breath ghosting over sensitive skin. Then, his tongue slowly flicked out, dragging over Alucard's cum.

A low, satisfied hum broke Zalith's smirk as he savoured the taste, his voice thick with pleasure. He let his lips linger there a moment longer before making his way back up, his mouth tracing familiar paths—across Alucard's stomach, over his chest, along his throat—before finally settling back at the crook of Alucard's neck.

There, he paused, watching him.

Alucard's breath was still uneven, unsteady, but as the tremors wracking his body finally began to settle, he lifted a hand to the side of Zalith's face, his fingers brushing against his skin. The touch was light, almost absentminded, as if grounding himself after everything that had just unravelled between them.

But then Zalith's gaze darkened. A shift, subtle yet unmistakable. A glint of lingering hunger.

Alucard barely had time to process it before a familiar smirk curved Zalith's lips.

"Roll over," his mate commanded.

The vampire stared at him for a moment, his breath still uneven, his body still buzzing with the lingering aftershocks of pleasure. But he didn't hesitate for long. Slowly, he rolled over, shifting onto his hands and knees. The moment he did, Zalith's hands were on him, gripping his waist firmly, possessively, pulling him closer to the edge of the bed as he stood beside it.

Alucard barely had time to brace himself before Zalith eased his dick back inside.

He moaned sharply, his fingers tightening around the sheets. His earlier climax had left him serene, his body relaxed, pliant, making the stretch so much easier, so much more intoxicating. And yet, as Zalith's thick length sank into him once more, the pleasure rushed back in full force.

Then Zalith began to move.

His thrusts started slow and deep but quickly built in speed and intensity, each motion harder, more demanding. Alucard let out a whimpering, breathless moan, his entire body jolting forward with each forceful snap of Zalith's hips. His mind reeled, his senses flooded, his pleasure mounting too fast, too soon.

Zalith's own moans filled the air—deep, utterly satisfied. The sound only made the coil inside Alucard tighten further, making him crave more, *need* more; his arms trembled beneath him, his body screaming for rest, aching and exhausted— but he didn't care. His body refused to stop responding, it refused to let go of the overwhelming delight overtaking him.

The vampire scowled in strained satisfaction, his heart hammering, his breath short and desperate, his fingers clenching the sheets. Another feverish moan tore from his lips, and he knew that he was close. *Too* close. Despite the fact that he just climaxed, his body was already at its limit, already spiralling towards another peak.

But he held back, biting his lip, his body trembling with the effort.

Zalith, however, had no intention of slowing down.

A pleased growl broke through the demon's hums as he tightened his grip on Alucard's waist, thrusting faster, harder, his movements dripping with possessiveness.

And then Zalith moaned—deep, breathless, laced with both relief and satisfaction.

Alucard whined, his body tensing as he felt it—the sudden, overwhelming warmth spilling inside him, filling him. The sensation sent a fresh wave of pleasure spiralling through him, his walls tightening instinctively around Zalith's throbbing dick, as if his body wasn't ready to let him go.

His breath came ragged, uneven, his entire form trembling. The heat, the fullness, the lingering high of Zalith's venom still thrumming through his veins—it was too much, too intoxicating. He felt weighted, sluggish, trapped somewhere between bliss and desperation.

Zalith pulled him up onto his feet, his grip possessive, as if he needed Alucard as much as Alucard needed him. The vampire exhaled shakily, tilting his head to the side, letting Zalith nuzzle into his neck. His mate's wings moved, curling slightly inward, the edges brushing over Alucard's arms, wrapping around him in something dangerously close to an embrace. Zalith's hands slid slowly, reverently down Alucard's trembling body, tracing over every inch of heated, overstimulated skin.

But Alucard still couldn't calm himself. His pulse pounded in his ears, his body too keyed up, too restless, too desperate.

He needed more.

Without thinking, he turned abruptly, his hands gripping Zalith's shoulders before he pulled him down with him, collapsing back onto the bed.

As he moved, he felt it—the sudden, empty ache left behind as Zalith's thick shaft slipped from his body, leaving him sensitive, overstimulated, craving. A quiet, shuddering groan escaped him as he shifted, the lingering warmth inside him spilling out, trickling slowly down his thigh. The sensation sent pleasure and frustration curling in his gut—he was still too high, still too wired, too desperate for more.

Zalith smirked, clearly amused, leaning in to kiss him.

But Alucard scowled, his fingers threading into Zalith's dark hair, gripping tightly. "I'm not...finished," he breathed, his voice rough, wanting, insatiable. And then he pushed Zalith down.

Zalith's lips curled into a smile—whether it was surprise or excitement, Alucard couldn't tell. But it didn't matter.

His grip on Zalith's hair tightened, a relieved, needy moan escaping him as the demon's mouth enveloped his dick. The warmth, the wet heat, the slow drag of Zalith's tongue over his length made him moan again; his eyes fluttered shut, his chest rising with a deep, shaky inhale as he sank into the sensation, into the sheer bliss. Every careful flick of Zalith's tongue, every shift of his lips only amplified the delight, turning his lingering desperation into pure, unrestrained euphoria.

The demon moved faster, his grip firm around Alucard's waist, holding him in place. Alucard exhaled deeply, whining softly, breath catching as pleasure knotted impossibly tight within him. He wasn't going to last much longer—his body was spent, overstimulated, teetering on the edge of exhaustion.

As much as he craved Zalith's touch, as much as he wanted to bask in every second of it, the pull of sleep was creeping in. He scowled, his muscles trembling as his body fought between pleasure and fatigue. And then—his release crashed over him, his body arching as he reached his peak once more. A shattered, pleasured moan escaped him as satisfaction flooded through his exhausted frame, drowning him in warmth, in delight, in overwhelming, aching tiredness.

He barely registered each soft kiss as the demon made his way back up his body; when Zalith reached his face, he smiled and tucked a few loose strands of Alucard's crimson hair behind his ears. Despite his tiredness, however, the vampire couldn't rest yet. He was almost certain that he knew what Zalith was about to say to him, and he knew his answer. He lazily gripped Zalith's shoulders and swiftly pinned him down on his back—Zalith laughed and smirked up at him, and without a moment's hesitation, Alucard sank his four fangs into the demon's neck.

Zalith moaned in delight, and Alucard in relief, the demon's warm, sweet blood seeping into his mouth. As it poured down his throat, the vampire groaned in satisfaction; the ache in his body waned, and his fatigue lifted. Right now, he felt so...alleviated. Everything felt serene, and all he wanted to do was lie down and rest beside his mate.

So after a few more gulps, he pulled his fangs from Zalith's neck and sighed a deep, relieved sigh. "Thank you" he breathed, nuzzling the demon's neck.

"You're welcome," Zalith murmured, fiddling with Alucard's hair. "Thank *you* for the sex," he laughed.

Alucard exhaled deeply, his body finally relaxing, his limbs heavy with exhaustion. A faint smile tugged at his lips as he shifted closer, resting his head against Zalith's chest, letting the steady rise and fall of the demon's breathing soothe him.

Zalith, of course, knew that he was on the verge of sleep. Without a word, he carefully moved, gathering Alucard in his arms as he eased them both into bed, his wings and horns crumbling away. The warmth of the blankets settled over them as the demon pulled the covers up, wrapping them both in quiet comfort.

Alucard nestled against him once more, his head finding its familiar place over Zalith's heart. He wanted to say something—to keep himself awake just a little longer, to listen to Zalith's voice, to hold onto the moment. But the weight of the day pressed down on him, pulling him further towards sleep with each passing second.

Tomorrow was their last day here, and he wanted to be rested for it. The last thing he wanted was to waste their final moments together in exhaustion. So, with a quiet sigh, he closed his eyes, his arm sliding around Zalith's waist, holding him close as the steady, rhythmic beat of the demon's heart filled his ears.

Zalith's fingers slid through his hair, slow and soothing. "I love you," he whispered, his voice low and tender.

With a tired, content smile, Alucard replied, "I love you too."

And as the warmth of Zalith's presence wrapped around him, the vampire finally let himself drift into sleep.

Chapter Forty-Two

— ⋖ ✝ ⋗ —

Four Hundred and Twenty-Three Years Ago

| Alucard, *Wednesday, Undecim 2nd, 537(TG)—Dor-Sanguis, Diabolus Catacombs* |

Alucard didn't know where he was. Not at first. The world around him was a strange, hazy blur. He blinked sluggishly, his vision sharpening just enough to make out the dull brown brick walls enclosing the candlelit room. He was sitting against one of them, arms wrapped around his knees, the cold seeping through the thin fabric of his clothes. A bitter draft crawled under the door, carrying the scent of damp, blood, and burning ash. Voices echoed beyond the walls—sharp, fleeting murmurs swallowed by the oppressive silence that always followed.

He knew this place. He hated this place.

From where he sat, he listened. The doors opened one by one, each groan of rusted hinges followed by the bellow of Abbess Brânduśa. Such an awful woman—petulant, angry. Her voice was a jagged thing, like the howl of a starved creature, an omen of horror to come. The closer she drew, the louder she became, her fury spilling into the corridor like a slow-building storm. He tensed as her footsteps neared his door.

Five years in this place. Five years of the same thing, day after day.

He waited, eyes fixed on the metal door, watching the shadows of passing priestesses flicker and distort beneath it. Their silent movements came and went like ghosts. Then came the sound of the bolt sliding back, the door creaking open, and he lifted his gaze with quiet, simmering tension.

Abbess Brânduśa stood in the doorway, her wrinkle-lined face pinched with displeasure. Her dull green eyes bored into him, heavy with the same mix of revulsion and wariness she always carried. Alucard knew it wasn't just disgust that made her stare. It was fear. She had been there the night he was born—she had seen what he really was. She'd witnessed the carnage, the bloodstained ruins of those who thought they could control him. Now, she was the last Abbess left. She feared for her life, but she hated that he was still breathing even more.

But what could she do? Her only purpose was to keep him alive until his father came for him.

Would his father ever come for him?

He wanted to leave this place. Desperately. He had been waiting since the day he was born, but he'd been left here—abandoned to these... people. These cruel, irrelevant people. And of them all, Brânduśa was the worst.

She visited him. She visited the others, too—however many of them there were. He never saw them, only heard their cries, thin and miserable as she shrieked at them. She always told them the same thing. They belonged to the Diabolus. Their purpose was singular. Their purpose was to die.

But Alucard was certain that he was different. His mother had told him so.

He wasn't going to die here. His father would come for him. And Abbess Brânduśa would suffer for her cruelty.

But tonight was different.

Abbess Brânduśa and her subordinates were restless, their movements beyond his door more frantic than usual; whispers and hurried footsteps filled the halls. Something was happening. Something important. And then he heard it—a voice he recognized.

Lilith.

The white-haired woman who had killed his birth mother. A Goddess. She had taught him much of what he knew. She taught him to speak, she helped him maintain a human form. She liked to think of herself as his mother, but she never would be. Alucard knew who his mother was, and it wasn't her. Lilith was just someone who loved his father.

Brânduśa lingered in the doorway, but the sharp click of heels echoed down the corridor. Lilith soon appeared at her side, leaned in to murmur something, and sent the Abbess away with a mere whisper.

Alucard never liked being alone with Lilith. He'd have preferred Brânduśa's sharp words, her venomous tone. But Lilith—she made him feel something beyond anger. Beyond hatred.

She glided towards him, every movement as effortless as drifting mist. Lowering herself beside him, she traced a hand over his head and down his back, making him shiver. He didn't want to look at her. He didn't want to meet those crimson eyes. But she grabbed his face, fingers pressing into his cheeks, forcing him to meet her gaze.

And then she smiled. "Caedis, my sweet little boy," she said, letting go of his cheeks to stroke his head as if he were a pet. "Do you know what tonight is?"

He didn't. Alucard never really knew what any day was. He'd been trapped down here in these catacombs all of his life. He never saw the outside, and he knew very little of it. But the first thought that came to his mind— "He... he's here?" he asked excitedly.

Lilith smiled brightly. "He will be," she said. "But he needs your help. Do you remember what I taught you?"

Alucard nodded. She'd spent most of the last year teaching him what he had to do—and what he had to do was help his father into this world. "I'm ready," he said, desperate to finally meet his only remaining family.

"Good," she said, and with a snarl of what might be disgust, she gripped Alucard's wrist and hastily pulled him from his bed.

He followed her through the winding catacomb halls, struggling to keep pace without breaking into a run—if he didn't, she'd end up dragging him across the floor. So he hurried, breath quick and uneven, his small legs aching as they neared the ritual hall.

When they stepped inside, he froze.

Bodies littered the chamber—men and women with their throats torn open, their blood pooled and smeared across the stone in the shape of a massive pentagram. Black candles burned at each point, their wax trickling down in thick rivulets, forming summoning runes along the floor. The scent of copper and hot wax filled the air, heavy and suffocating.

Everything was ready.

Lilith shoved him forward, forcing him into the centre of the pentagram. His heart pounded, and a painful, twisting dread built in his chest, thickening with every frantic beat.

From the darkness, hooded, cloaked people emerged, surrounding the pentagram as Lilith dragged a whimpering woman from the corner and dropped her in front of Alucard.

Lilith smiled down at him. "You know what to do," she said, her voice warm, coaxing—almost motherly. As Alucard stared up at her, she lifted a hand, tracing it over her chest. A crimson rune shimmered into existence, and from within it, she pulled a small, black blade. She pressed it into his hands. "Don't let me down." Her clawed fingers brushed over his cheek before she stepped back, retreating into the circle of cloaked, hooded figures.

Alucard lowered his gaze to the blade, then to the woman at his feet. She lay trembling, her breath uneven, her face streaked with tears and blood. Why was she crying? This was her purpose, wasn't it? Just as this was his. Shouldn't she be happy? Shouldn't he?

He should, but... dread pooled in his chest, tight and suffocating. This was the moment, the one he'd trained for, prepared for. He had spent a whole year practising. Maybe his whole life. And now, finally, he would meet his father.

So why did he hesitate?

The murmurs of the crowd grew restless.

Lilith's voice cut through the low hum, nasty and seething, "What are you waiting for?!"

He frowned, drawing the blade from its sheath and letting the empty scabbard clatter to the floor. Then, without remorse, he knelt and drove the blade into the woman's throat. Blood sprayed across his face—hot, metallic. It splattered onto the stone and soaked into his clothes. The woman choked, gasping for air, but Alucard only scowled. "*Invoco te, Domine tenebrarum, dominum noctis. Haec sacrificia offero, et sanguinem meum offero, quia tuum est. Veni, excipio te in hunc mundum,*" he said, just the way Lilith had taught him. He cut his palm with the same blade, letting his own blood spill onto the ritual markings.

Lilith smiled, pleased, as the pentagram beneath him ignited with an eerie red glow. Around them, the cloaked figures took up the chant, their voices rising in rhythmic unison. At the peak of the crescendo, Lilith called out his father's name.

Alucard stood motionless, watching as his blood dripped onto the stone, the hesitation that had gripped him moments before loosening. A few feet ahead, the air itself tore apart, a rift cleaving open with a deep crack.

This was it.

He was going to meet his father.

His father would take him away from this awful place—from Brânduśa, from Lilith. His father would love him. His father would care for him.

That was all he wanted.

As a shimmer of red flickered within the parting void, excitement stirred in his chest. A slow, eager smile stretched across his blood-smeared face.

A flash of crimson light filled the chamber... and the chanting stopped. The cloaked figures dropped where they stood, collapsing in eerie unison. Only Alucard and Lilith remained upright.

Stunned, Alucard stumbled back, his knees hitting the cold stone. Was that supposed to happen? Did he do something wrong? His gaze darted to Lilith, searching her expression for answers. But she only smiled—until, suddenly, that smile wavered, shifting into something almost... relieved.

Then she moved.

Alucard tracked her with wide eyes as she rushed forward, throwing herself at the figure that had stepped through the rift. And for a moment, everything else—the blood, the chanting, the bodies—ceased to exist.

The rift sealed shut.

And in its place stood a man.

Tall. Crimson-haired. His presence alone cast a statuesque shadow across the floor, his broad stance unmoving, unshaken. Wings stretched behind him, massive and

← 336 →

leathery, shaped like those of a dragon—some smaller ones connected to his arms. And atop his head, ten tall, dark horns jutted skyward, wickedly sharp.

But it was his face that stole Alucard's breath. It wasn't what he had imagined. It wasn't monstrous or unfamiliar. It looked like him. The same hair. The same skin. Even his eyes—well, one of them. The man possessed seven, and the one that sat in the centre of his forehead burned with the same hell-fiery red as Alucard's.

Those crimson eyes locked onto him.

And Alucard exhaled, relief swelling in his chest.

That was his father.

But Lucifer took his eyes off Alucard and set them on Lilith, who wrapped her arms around him and held him tightly.

"My darling," she cried, kissing his face, tears trickling down her cheeks as she pressed as much of her body as she could against his. "I waited so long—I did everything you asked—"

He snarled and shoved her away, setting his eyes back on Alucard. "This is it?" he questioned, his voice deep, unnerving—like an animal's aggressive growl. And it echoed as if the room was empty.

Lilith lost her smile when he pushed her away but flipped her hair back, scoffed, and set her eyes on Alucard. "It is," she confirmed.

Alucard stared at his father, unsure what to feel. This wasn't how it was supposed to be. Lucifer's expression wasn't warm, it wasn't welcoming. He didn't look pleased to see him. No relief, no recognition—nothing Alucard had longed for. Instead, his father's gaze held something cold, something eerily familiar. Disgust. Anger. It was the same look Abbess Brânduśa always gave him.

Had he done something wrong?

"Dispose of it—I don't need it." Lucifer's voice cut through the air like a blade, sharp and absolute. His attention had already shifted elsewhere, as if Alucard was nothing more than an inconvenience. A mistake. "And find me something to eat." He barely spared Lilith a glance as he issued the order.

Lilith didn't question him. She didn't hesitate.

Before Alucard could react, her clawed fingers wrapped around his throat, hoisting him off his feet. The pressure was immediate, crushing; he gasped, clawing at her wrists, his mind reeling. What had he done wrong? His legs kicked uselessly, his vision tilting, darkening. But through the haze, he caught a glimpse of Lilith's face.

She looked... conflicted?

Just as his consciousness began to slip, her grip loosened.

And then she let go.

Alucard hit the stone floor with a sharp, breathless impact.

"Why kill him?" she questioned, looking back at Lucifer. "Why dispose of this...pathetic little creature?" she asked, turning to face Lucifer. "We can use him—craft him into a weapon. That is his purpose, right? To do what we ask. He was born with a Lumendatt—all we have to do is activate it. We could not only use him to kill the others, but we could use him to create an army. Letholdus wouldn't dare test us—this world... it could be ours."

Alucard lay on the cold stone floor, staring in silent devastation. Why? Why was this happening? His father told her to kill him. As if he were nothing. As if he didn't matter. Did he not want him? Did he not love him? A scowl pulled at Alucard's face, but it wasn't anger—not truly. It was something deeper. A hurt that had no wound, no gash, no blood. Just a hollow, crushing ache inside him. And it didn't stop.

Lucifer grinned. "What a marvellous idea," he said, slowly prowling towards Alucard.

That look on his face—Alucard didn't like it. He'd seen it before on the faces of the people who raised him, the ones who had beaten him, used him. He'd always told himself that his father would be different, that Lucifer would save him. But now he understood. His father didn't want him, he didn't need or love him. Lucifer had used him. Lilith had used him. And they would keep using him.

For five years, he was told that he was meant to serve his father, that it was his purpose. That it was an honour. But laying there, staring at the truth in Lucifer's cold, unfeeling gaze, he felt nothing but dread.

This wasn't what he wanted.

He thought that freeing his father would mean escape, that Lucifer would take him away and give him the life he deserved. But now he knew the truth. They would never let him go. They would keep him locked away in the dark. They would hate him and hurt him, just like everyone before them.

So, he ran. He scrambled to his feet and bolted for the door, his heart hammering, his breath sharp and ragged. But he didn't make it.

Everything faded to darkness.

The last things he heard—

Lilith's distraught voice.

Lucifer's devastated yell.

And a blinding explosion of blue light.

Then—

Nothing.

※

ASCENDANT
Numen Chronicles | Volume Five

Alucard wasn't sure how long it had been. He woke in a strange room—the bricks were red, the hue in the air was red, and the sky outside... that was red, too. He lay there, wrapped in sorrow, disappointment, and fear. He had no idea where he was, and however long ago, he had learnt that his father, like everyone before him, didn't want him—he didn't love him.

He felt empty. He felt alone. He felt... worthless.

"You're such... a pathetic little thing," came a cold, heartless voice. "What am I going to do with you?"

Alucard turned his head, setting his eyes on a man he'd never seen before. His face... it was sharp and pale—his eyes... they stared a revolted stare, one blue, one red. And his hair, perfectly split down the middle, one half white, one half black. He stood there by the door, leaning his back against the wall, his feathered wings folded behind him, the tall horns on his head dark and light-devouring. And his aura... it felt like a demon's... but not entirely.

Who was he? What was he?

"It would seem that you belong to me, now," he said with a grin. "I'll find something for you to do. Surely, there's something you're capable of. Well," he paused, looking Alucard up and down. "I don't expect much," he snarled, sitting beside him, glaring down at Alucard as he stared up at him. "You're so... worthless. Not even your father wanted you—who would want you? Such a disappointment. Such a waste. Nobody could ever want you. But I can give you purpose. I'll make good use of you, don't worry," he said, placing his hand on Alucard's chest. "You're mine, now... Aleksei. Don't ever forget that."

Staring at him, Alucard felt a sadness unlike anything he had ever known. It swallowed him whole. He felt... lost. Unmoored. Nothing felt right. Everything he had been told, everything he had been taught—his entire life, since the moment he was born—meant nothing.

It was all a lie.

He had no mother. His father despised and would never love him. And if even his father couldn't love him... then who would?

A scowl twisted his face, hot tears burning at the edges of his vision—

"Don't—" the man snarled, his hand snapping around Alucard's throat. "Don't... do that." The words came quieter, but the grip remained firm.

Alucard choked, eyes wide with horror.

"There's no room for emotional, weak little worms like you here—you'd best understand that." The man's fingers tightened and then released, shoving him back. "I'm a very impatient man."

Alucard gasped for breath.

But the man continued, his voice cold and final, "This is where you'll spend your life now. Forget everything you were told before. I am your master now. And you...you will forever belong to me."

⤝ ❖ ⤞

| Alucard, *Monday, Tertium 20th, 960(TG)*—*Maluhia, Lunakai, A'okalani Cove Resort* |

Alucard's eyes snapped open with a sharp, quiet gasp, his chest rising with the remnants of something cold and suffocating. A faint flinch ran through his body as his gaze darted to the water beyond the glass walls, watching the slow, silent drift of fish weaving through the dark currents. It only took a moment to ground himself, to remember where he was. But the weight in his heart didn't ease. It only settled deeper, pressing against his ribs like an unbearable ache. Tears blurred his vision, pooling at the corners of his eyes before spilling over. The despair clung to him, thick and relentless, a familiar, heart-wrenching sadness, one he had hoped to never feel again.

He frowned, forcing himself to push it down, to ignore it. But it only worsened, tightening its grip on him, refusing to be dismissed. Irritation flared in his chest, burning over the sorrow. With an aggravated scowl, he sat up, quickly wiping at his tears, frustrated with himself for even letting them fall. His gaze flicked to his left, landing on the crystals sitting on the nightstand, the ones meant to keep his nightmares at bay. But there was still only one of each. The extras he had sent for were in his trouser pocket, and his trousers were still upstairs, left out on the deck.

A quiet sigh escaped him, his hands curling into the sheets as he turned his head, looking to his right. Zalith lay beside him, deep in sleep, his breathing slow, steady, and peaceful. Alucard longed to wake him, to curl into his warmth, to feel his arms around him, to let himself be comforted. But he knew how much his mate needed this rest. So he clenched his jaw, looking away. He didn't want to bother him with this nonsense—these *stupid* dreams.

However, he still needed something...something to take his mind off what he'd just seen—what he had just *remembered*. He knew that he should write it down while the memory was still fresh...while the pain was still there. But he didn't have his book, and he didn't want to write about it, to relive it. He just wanted to forget.

He wouldn't wake Zalith, though; he'd let him sleep. He'd find something else to put his mind at rest. So he leaned back and kissed the demon's cheek, and then he carefully and quietly climbed out of bed. He silently made his way over to the wardrobe, took out a pair of trousers and a long-sleeved grey shirt, and got dressed.

The vampire headed upstairs and took out one of his turtleneck sweaters; he pulled it on and walked out onto the deck. First, he picked up their clothes from last night and took them inside. Then, he slumped down onto the couch and stared out at the ocean.

He didn't want to think about his dream...but it was what his mind focussed on the moment he sat down. So, he'd not sit. Instead, he got up and headed outside. As his bare feet touched the warm sand, he sighed and stopped. He looked left, he looked right, but he didn't really know where to go. The day was early, the sun was still rising, and he felt...alone. He didn't want to feel alone.

Alucard turned around and walked down the slope beside the deck. Beneath it was the small, makeshift tent he'd made from some large palm tree leaves and some of the tall grass that grew near them. He crouched in front of it and pulled away the leaf door, and inside, the white tortoise from yesterday greeted him with a quiet chirp.

"Hi there," he said with a smile. "Did you sleep well?"

The tortoise chirped again and started walking towards him.

"Shh," he mumbled, scooping her up in his arms. "I have to find somewhere to put you before Zalith wakes up," he whispered as he backed out from beneath the deck and stood up.

Then, he made his way back into the house and stood in the centre of the lounge. Where to put her? He looked around, and the only way he'd get her home was if he hid her in his suitcase—so that was what he was going to do. He knew he and Zalith were only going to be here for a few more hours, and he had learnt from his research yesterday that this type of tortoise could more or less freeze themselves in crystal, so if she were to do that, she'd not need oxygen or food until they got home.

He held her in front of his face and stared into her red eyes. "I'm going to put you in my suitcase here, okay? So I can take you home. I need you to do the thing you do...freeze yourself," he requested.

The tortoise stared at him for a few moments, but then she pulled her legs and head into her shell and started to crystalize.

Alucard smiled deviously. He was taking her home and no one was going to tell him he couldn't. Once she had completely crystalized, he opened his suitcase and buried her under his cape. Then, he put his old clothes from yesterday inside and zipped it shut. Nobody would know.

Chapter Forty-Three

— ≺ ✝ ≻ —

Souvenirs

| Zalith—*Maluhia, Lunakai, A'okalani Cove Resort* |

Zalith woke abruptly, his mind immediately latching onto a single thought—Alucard. Without hesitation, he reached out, his arm sliding across the bed in search of his vampire, but his fingers met only empty sheets. A flicker of unease tightened in his chest as his searching turned frantic, his eyes scanning the dimly lit room. Panic struck like a spark igniting dry tinder, but before it could consume him, he focused on the bond between them—the connection they shared through their imprints... and he exhaled in quiet relief when he sensed Alucard's presence upstairs.

Sinking back into the mattress, he let out a heavy sigh, yet the tension in his chest didn't fully ease. The familiar weight of disappointment settled over him, sinking into his bones like an old wound that refused to heal. There was still so much to do—so many things he had failed to accomplish. He despised this feeling, the sense of waiting, of struggling to piece everything back together when it had already taken far too long.

But then the rich scent of coffee and warm food drifted down to him, pulling him from his thoughts. Only now did he recognize the gnawing hunger creeping in, and with a slow breath, he pushed himself up. He pulled on a pair of trousers before heading upstairs, following the inviting aroma and the presence of the one person who could make all of this bearable.

As Zalith stepped into the lounge, his gaze immediately found Alucard outside on the deck, carefully setting up their breakfast table. The demon smiled as he moved silently towards the doorway, leaning against the frame while watching his fiancé fuss over every little detail.

Alucard adjusted the placement of a plate, only to shift it again a moment later; he frowned in quiet concentration as he nudged the utensils into what he apparently deemed the *perfect* arrangement, then hesitated, reconsidering. Zalith's smile grew, warmth settling deep in his chest. He was so cute. The demon could never quite get enough of these moments, these little glimpses of Alucard's perfectionism over something as simple as breakfast.

With a quiet sigh, he let himself relax, his arms folding loosely across his chest. His smile didn't fade. He could stand there and watch his vampire forever.

However, Alucard soon caught sight of him, his movements faltering as he frowned in surprise. His gaze flicked towards Zalith, and for a brief moment, an almost *nervous* look crossed his face. "How long have you been there?" he asked, his voice edged with suspicion, as if he'd just been caught doing something he shouldn't.

Zalith laughed a little. "Not long," he said, making his way out onto the deck.

The vampire nodded and looked down at the table he had prepared. "Well... I got us breakfast—are you hungry?"

"Starving," he said, walking over to him.

Alucard pulled out a seat for him, and once Zalith sat down, the vampire sat beside him.

"Did you sleep okay?" his fiancé asked.

"Thank you," the demon said with a smile. "And I slept fine. How about you?"

"It was okay," he mumbled, pouring Zalith some coffee.

He didn't sound so sure, and Zalith was almost positive that something was wrong. It wasn't often—if ever—that Alucard would get out of bed before or without him. "What's wrong?" he asked quietly.

Alucard shrugged as he buttered his toast. "I just... had a bad dream. I forgot the crystals in my pocket last night."

"Well, at least we'll be in our own bed tonight," he said with an assuring smile, taking some toast for himself.

Although he still looked a little unsure, the vampire nodded, eating his toast. "Is there anything specific you want to do today?"

"Not really. I'm content just lounging around with you."

"We can lay on the beach again if you want," he suggested.

Zalith smiled. "Okay," he said, sipping from his coffee. "Oh, should we go souvenir shopping?"

"I saw a place near where I got breakfast from. We could go there?"

Zalith nodded and smirked teasingly as he said, "I'm thinking of getting something for Idina and Edwin—are you going to get something for your *boyfriend* Greymore?"

Alucard pouted. "He's not my boyfriend," he grumbled.

The demon laughed as he took some of the eggs and bacon and put it onto his plate. "He might be when he sees the wonderful gift you bring him."

He rolled his eyes. "I could say the same for your *girlfriend* Idina."

"We can change the wedding to accommodate the four of us—what do you think?"

Alucard sighed and glared at him. "I'm sure you don't like to share as much as I don't."

"You're right," he said, still smirking at him. "And I'm also gay, so that counts Idina out. Unless *you* want to sleep with her."

He pouted. "No, I do not," he muttered and sipped from his hot chocolate.

"Then I suppose it'll just be you and me."

"It's how I like it," Alucard mumbled.

"Good, because that's all you're getting."

Alucard smiled shyly, glancing at him. "Can I have you right now?" he asked.

His words sent a shiver of excitement through Zalith's body. "You can have me whenever you want," he told him.

The vampire stood and took Zalith's hand, leading him back inside. The demon followed without hesitation, letting himself be pulled onto the couch as Alucard fell back into it. The moment they landed, the vampire was already claiming his lips, his kisses eager and demanding, carrying an edge of something unspoken, something desperate.

Zalith could tell what this was—he knew what Alucard needed; he could taste it on his lips, he could feel it in the way he gripped his arm and grasped his hair. It wasn't just desire, it was reassurance, a way to drown out whatever had haunted him in his sleep. And Zalith understood far too well that as much as Alucard knew he was loved, there were moments—especially after his nightmares—where he needed to feel it, to be reminded in ways words couldn't quite satisfy. And Zalith was more than happy to give him what he needed, more than happy to let him take control.

Alucard's fingers curled into his hair as he pulled him closer; their lips parted only for sharp, shallow breaths before meeting again, the hunger between them growing. Zalith's hands moved beneath Alucard's sweater, fingertips tracing over firm muscle, dragging slowly over his abs. But patience was never his strong suit. In one swift motion, he pulled the sweater over Alucard's head and tossed it aside, his hands already moving lower.

It wasn't long before Alucard was bare beneath him.

But then, just as Zalith was about to guide him back down, the vampire moved first. His hands gripped Zalith's waist, shifting him onto his back before straddling his lap.

The demon smirked, watching with amusement as Alucard reached for the buttons of his trousers. With a quiet laugh, he tilted his head back slightly, dark eyes gleaming with admiration. "I like seeing you from this angle," he murmured, his smirk deepening.

Alucard glanced down at him and smiled before swiftly pulling Zalith's trousers off. He straddled the demon's lap once more, leaning forward, lips meeting his in a deep, slow-burning kiss. As their mouths moved together, Alucard's hand slid between them, curling around Zalith's arousal; the demon tensed lightly, excitement spiralling through him, anticipation quickly devouring him. While this was about giving Alucard what he needed, he couldn't help but indulge the pleasure of letting his mate own him every once in a while.

He smirked eagerly, his fingers drifting up to rest against the side of Alucard's neck, his thumb tracing slow, lazy circles against his skin. He let Alucard continue, letting him take control, letting him set the pace, though the vampire's growing impatience didn't go unnoticed. His kisses became more fervent, more insistent, his grip around Zalith's shaft tightening ever so slightly as if silently urging him along.

The demon chuckled against his lips as he reached into his vault and took out a small tincture bottle of lube. "You're going to need this."

Alucard pulled back just enough to see what Zalith was holding, and then he took it without hesitation, sitting up straighter as the demon's hands slid to his waist, his grip firm, steady, waiting. The vampire wasted no time. He uncorked the bottle and poured some of the liquid onto his palm, and then he smoothed it over Zalith's dick with slow strokes. The demon hummed in approval, his hold on Alucard's waist tightening slightly as he watched the vampire work. His heart started beating a little faster, the anticipation growing. But he did his best to wait.

Once Alucard finished smoothing the lube over him, he set the bottle aside. Zalith watched as the vampire lifted himself, shifting forward just enough to align them properly.

The anticipation was unbearable. Zalith's grip on his waist tightened instinctively as Alucard carefully positioned himself, pressing the tip of the demon's dick against his ass. Even that slight contact sent a sharp pulse of anticipation and heat through Zalith, making his muscles tense.

Then, Alucard began to lower himself.

Zalith exhaled slowly, his fingers flexing against the vampire's waist, holding him steady. The initial pressure was tight, hot, *overwhelming*, forcing a quiet groan from deep within his chest. It didn't matter how many times they did this— it always stole his breath, it always made him feel like he was being completely enveloped, completely claimed.

Alucard's body clung to him perfectly, squeezing around his shaft in a way that sent a slow, simmering pleasure spiralling through Zalith, winding tighter with every inch that the vampire took.

The demon hummed contently as Alucard sank lower, stretching around him, his warmth ensnaring every inch. The pace was agonizingly slow, forcing Zalith to feel every pulse, every shiver of tension as Alucard's body adjusted to him. His fingers dug into Alucard's hips, his own restraint hanging by a thread as he let the vampire take him in at his own pace.

When Alucard couldn't take any more, Zalith groaned again, the vampire's weight fully resting in his lap. The heat, the tightness, the undeniable claim of it all sent waves of pleasure through the demon, making his muscles tense and his jaw clench. His head tilted back against the couch for a brief moment, his breathing struggled as he relished the sheer feeling of being buried so deeply inside his fiancé.

And then Alucard began to move. Slow at first—*achingly* slow. His body lifted, just enough for Zalith to feel the delicious drag of every inch leaving him, only to take him back in just as torturously. Zalith let out a low, shuddering groan, his eyes flickering up to watch him, completely entranced by the way Alucard moved.

He *loved* watching him like this. The way his body arched, the way his breath came in quiet, desperate gasps, and the way his thighs trembled faintly as he worked to take Zalith in again and again. The demon tightened his grip on his waist, urging him to move faster; Alucard found a rhythm, a pace that had them both moaning, a perfect push and pull of delight. The sounds Alucard made and the way he rolled his hips just right, dragging every inch of Zalith in and out of that perfect, intoxicating heat—it was too much, too good.

A deep, satisfied growl broke free from Zalith's lips as he watched his vampire completely lost in pleasure. The sight alone sent a needy pulse of desire burning through him, his restraint fraying further by the second.

He needed more.

And the moment the thought took hold, he moved.

His hands tightened on Alucard's waist, his own hips snapping up, thrusting deep inside him, meeting his movements with a new urgency. A shudder of pure satisfaction shot through him as Alucard whined contently; the demon's breath broke into another moan, feeling Alucard's body tensing around his dick. He matched the vampire's pace, thrusting up into him just as Alucard rode him, their bodies moving together in a perfect, intoxicating rhythm. The wet heat, the grip of him, the sounds, the sight, the sheer feeling of it all pushed Zalith further, making him desperate, making him crave nothing but more.

But he could feel it—the way Alucard's body clenched around him, the slight tremor in his thighs, the way his moans grew higher, more desperate. The vampire was close, and the thought only sent a fresh surge of hunger and satisfaction coursing through Zalith. He tightened his grip on Alucard's waist, fingers pressing possessively into his skin, and without hesitation, he thrust harder, faster, *deeper*. The rhythm between them became frantic, relentless, their bodies moving together in perfect, overwhelming synchronicity.

And then Alucard broke.

A sharp, pleasured cry tore from the vampire, his body tensing violently as he came. Zalith felt everything— the way Alucard's walls tightened around his dick, squeezing him impossibly tight, milking every inch of him in a way that made his vision blur with pleasure. Then, warmth splattered onto the demon's stomach, onto his skin, and the sensation sent a deep, primal satisfaction spiralling through him. He had brought Alucard to this—he'd unravelled him, he'd made him tremble, and he'd made him completely his.

The pleasure surged, cresting into something unbearable. Zalith groaned low and deep, his hands gripping Alucard's trembling hips as his own release finally hit. His head tipped back against the couch, his breath stalling, his muscles locking up as pleasure crashed over him. The sheer heat and tightness of Alucard's body gripping him, still pulsing from his own orgasm, only dragged Zalith deeper into his own. A low, pleased moan rumbled from him as he thrust up one last time, burying himself fully inside Alucard as he climaxed, warmth spilling deep inside him, and the sounds that Alucard made forced a delighted cry from Zalith's hurried breaths.

And then the demon let out a sated, breathless growl, his grip finally loosening as his own pleasure slowly, lazily unravelled. Even now, as the aftermath settled over him, the deep satisfaction of filling Alucard completely, of feeling his body still trembling against him left Zalith entirely content.

The vampire groaned quietly, smiling as he leaned forward and rested his body on Zalith's. They both slowly calmed down, their breaths slowing; the demon stroked Alucard's crimson hair, and the vampire slowly moved his hand up Zalith's body and to the side of his neck.

"Sorry I took you away from your breakfast," Alucard mumbled.

"It's okay," he said with a small chuckle. "I wasn't really that hungry anyway."

The vampire rested his arms beside Zalith's and pressed his forehead against his, staring into his eyes. "Do you want to go back out there and finish?"

"Sure," Zalith said, tucking a few loose strands of Alucard's hair behind his head.

Smiling, Alucard reached over to the table, grabbing a few tissues from the box. He slowly cleaned the lingering warmth from Zalith's skin, his touch gentle but thorough, and once satisfied, he pulled his clothes back on, smoothing out the fabric as he adjusted himself. Zalith took a moment longer, his eyes lingering on Alucard as he dressed before finally following suit.

Once they were both ready, they stepped back out onto the deck, the ocean breeze cool, carrying the lingering scent of salt and sun-warmed wood.

As Alucard sat down, he leaned back in his seat and sighed deeply. "We can probably go to that souvenir shop after this if you like. Then we can spend the rest of our time here laying on the beach again."

"That sounds good," the demon said, eating his breakfast.

While they ate, Zalith focused on the lingering satisfaction that Alucard had given him. But when he glanced at his fiancé, he noticed a deep, pondering expression on his face, and it made him feel curious.

"What are you thinking about?" he asked him.

Alucard looked at him, snapping out of his thoughts. He then took a bite of his toast and shrugged. "I was just thinking about how I wish we weren't leaving today."

Zalith smiled as he sipped from his coffee. "We can come back at some point."

"I would like that," Alucard said contently.

| Alucard—*Maluhia, Lunakai, A'okalani Cove Resort* |

After breakfast, Alucard and Zalith strolled along the beach; the warmth of the sun barely touched the vampire's skin beneath the veil of morning mist. Once he spotted the souvenir shop that he'd noticed earlier, he took hold of his mate's hand and led the way towards it.

As they walked, passing the occasional sunbather and a few shirtless strangers, Alucard's thoughts drifted to something Zalith had said—not to taking his own clothes off and embracing his scars but to the night one of their enemies had slashed his back. The agony had been unbearable, but worse than the pain had been the way his body had locked up, how his mind had splintered into disjointed fragments of torment and confusion. He hadn't been able to move, he hadn't been able to think beyond the sheer, suffocating sensation of it. He needed something to keep that from happening again—something that wouldn't tear so easily…something he could wear into battle.

His first thought was his beloved cape—the one he cherished not just for its elegance but for the protection it offered. The dragon fur lining its collar shielded his mind from intrusion, reinforcing his already impenetrable mental defences against those stronger than him—like the Numen. He always kept his thoughts locked away, and that fur made them even harder to breach. The only one he ever let past both barriers was Zalith.

But that wasn't the issue. His back was.

He'd remake the cape. He'd replace the fireproof dragon-fur fabric with something stronger—something that wouldn't tear or break in battle. And he knew exactly where to find it.

He looked at Zalith. "I was…thinking about what you said," he mumbled. "About making something to protect myself—my back, to be more specific. I want to remake my cape with something stronger. And I know what I need, but to get that…we would…have to go Aegis hunting."

"Is the cape the best option?" he asked with a concerned frown. "You're not always wearing it, and someone could get under it if you're moving. Our enemies are also going to be aiming for you and your body, not the fabric."

Alucard nodded. "That's a good point—I can make maybe a whole...outfit. Something I can wear whenever we're heading into battle. I'm in need of a new blazer anyway—or a redingote."

"Is going after an Aegis going to cause problems?"

"No," he said with a shrug. "Letholdus can't find me—he can't find *us*. And he's too busy keeping the other Numen away from his throne to care about his lesser children. It's very unlikely that he'll do much at all—but if you don't want to take any risks, I can look for another source."

"I need to think about it. I want you to be protected, but I don't want things to get worse."

Alucard nodded.

"Do you know how to find the Aegis you're looking for?" he then asked.

"I know where they all are—I have people watching them. I may have stopped killing them, but I never stopped keeping an eye on them."

"Where would we have to go to find the one you need?"

He thought to himself for a moment. There were three Aegis he knew which possessed the strong, armour-like fur that he needed to make his new attire. "Well, there is Erysa—she resides in Avalmoor. Then there is Adenaver—he is in Odessius, as well as Asul. They all possess the things I need."

The demon nodded, a look of pondering on his face.

"Anyway," Alucard then said. "We're not meant to be talking about work things. Do you know what you want from the gift shop?"

"No, but I'll figure it out when we get there. If we can find anything nice for the castle, though, that would be good," he said, smiling.

"Okay," he said contently. Then, they continued towards the gift shop.

Once they got into the shop, Alucard immediately set his eyes on a shelf of animal-shaped crystals. While Zalith looked around the spacious store filled with so many curious and unique things, the vampire made his way over and examined the crystals. There were fish, birds, fruits, and plants carved out of rose quartz, amethyst, aventurine, and clear quartz. What caught his eye in particular was the tortoise carved out of green aventurine. It reminded him of the tortoise he'd hidden in his suitcase—which he missed already. So, he picked up the crystal tortoise, and he then picked up an amethyst wolf; maybe Greymore would like that.

He wanted to get something for Zalith, too. He eyed all of the crystals, and as he set his eyes on a palm tree that had been carved out of green aventurine, he smiled—he knew Zalith's favourite colour was green, and he was sure that his mate would prefer this over a craved animal. So, he picked that up, too, and then he walked over to the counter, where Zalith was already paying the owner for something.

"What did you get?" he asked curiously.

"I got that glass bird for the manor—for when it's ours," the demon said with a smirk, nodding at a large glass bird statue which stood around four feet. "I also got us a nice rug for the castle."

Alucard smiled. "Okay," he said, placing the green aventurine carvings onto the counter. "I'm just going to get these."

"I'll pay for them," Zalith said, taking them from him.

"Thank you."

"Is that everything?" the owner asked.

Zalith looked at Alucard, and as Alucard nodded, the demon said to the owner, "That's everything, thank you. I'll have someone come over and pick up the two larger items shortly."

"Of course," the owner said, handing Zalith his change. "Thank you so much—enjoy the rest of your day!"

"And you," the demon said with a smile. Then, he and Alucard left the store.

Once he put his carvings in his pocket, Alucard took hold of Zalith's hand. "So, should we head back to the beach now?"

The demon gave him a small smile. "Yeah."

Once they returned to the beach house, Alucard led the way inside. Zalith veered left into the bathroom, while he headed into the lounge—only to stop dead. His suitcase was open, its contents strewn haphazardly across the floor. It didn't take him long to piece together what had happened.

The tortoise had woken up.

And she had escaped.

Suppressing a groan, Alucard rushed to gather his scattered clothes, stuffing them back into the suitcase before scanning the room. The kitchen. Under the couch. The deck. No sign of the little menace. Just as frustration set in, a shimmer of white flickered near the bathroom door.

His head snapped towards it. There—his crystal-covered tortoise, making a determined march straight for the bathroom.

That was the last thing he needed. If Zalith spotted her, he was certain that his mate would be furious. Without hesitation, Alucard lunged forward, scooping the tortoise into his arms before hurrying back to his suitcase.

"I told you to stay in here until we get home," he whispered, tucking the tortoise back into his suitcase. Then, he started to zip it up—

"What are you doing?" Zalith asked.

Alucard froze—but he quickly looked over his shoulder. "Nothing," he mumbled, standing up as he turned to face the demon.

Zalith didn't look convinced. "Let me see."

He wasn't going to lie. With a sigh, he dropped his gaze to the floor; he crouched down, unlatched his suitcase, and carefully lifted the tortoise out. Straightening, he turned to face Zalith and held her out, his expression caught somewhere between guilt and reluctant acceptance. He didn't want to see the look on Zalith's face—didn't want to confirm the irritation, the exasperation, the inevitable frustration. He wasn't in the mood to be scolded.

Zalith exhaled sharply, rolling his eyes. "Oh my god. Why?"

Alucard shrugged. "She was hurt and alone, and if I left her there, someone would have found her and killed her and used her for whatever they use them for. I wanted to keep her safe," he mumbled with a sullen pout.

"How long has it been in the house?"

The vampire shrugged again as the tortoise stared at Zalith. "Since this morning."

An uncomfortable expression appeared on Zalith's face. "It's probably got germs everywhere."

Alucard frowned. "She didn't get anywhere or on anything—I put her straight into my suitcase."

"Now all your clothes are filthy. And I touched them—"

The vampire scowled—but he didn't want to get angry or annoyed. "If it makes you feel any better, I put her in there after I got dressed."

"It doesn't," he said. "What are you doing with a turtle—where are you taking it?" he questioned. "What are your plans with it?"

Alucard pouted. "I want to take her home with me and look after her," he said, cradling the tortoise.

"And where are you going to keep it?"

"I'll get a cage for her."

"And put it where?"

"In one of the thirty-plus spare rooms we have."

"Alucard, you're not keeping it in the castle."

Alucard's pout deepened, frustration curling in his chest. He felt irritated and upset. He didn't want to argue—he didn't want to waste what little time they had left here by bickering, nor did he want to push Zalith's patience any further. So he tore his gaze away and stormed past him, heading straight for the door. Zalith didn't try to stop him, and that only made the frustration bite deeper. Without a word, he stepped outside, the tortoise in his arms, and followed the deck towards the beach.

"It's a wild animal—you can't keep it locked away in a room," Zalith called from the house.

He didn't want to respond.

Reaching the sand, he crouched and set the tortoise down. She blinked up at him with sad, glassy eyes, but he forced himself to stand, turn his back, and walk away. He stepped onto the deck, re-entered the house, and passed Zalith without a word. Dropping onto the couch, he slumped back, arms crossed, a deep pout set into his irritated expression.

Zalith sighed. "You went through all that effort to hide it in your suitcase, only to give up the moment I tell you it can't stay inside?"

Alucard stared out at the ocean, his jaw tight. He didn't have an answer. He just wanted to sit there and glare.

Zalith sighed again, but this time, he didn't press further. He simply left the room.

As the demon left, Alucard turned onto his side and yanked a cushion over his head, irritation burning hotter than it should have. Maybe it was the exhaustion of hearing about germs—things that hardly mattered to demons. But they mattered to Zalith. Clearly.

Why couldn't he keep her in the castle? If she was meant to live outside on an island like theirs, she'd die or get sick. It wouldn't be warm enough, especially during the colder seasons. Leaving her here felt just as cruel—poachers could find her, or worse. She wasn't dirty. She wasn't some pest to be thrown outside. But Zalith wouldn't see it that way, and Alucard was too tired to fight a battle he already knew he'd lose.

This trip was supposed to be for Zalith, anyway. He wouldn't make it about the tortoise.

So, he'd wait; he'd let the irritation fade and move on with their day. The tortoise was gone. He'd get over it.

Eventually.

Chapter Forty-Four

— ≺ ✝ ≻ —

Until Late Afternoon

| Alucard—*Maluhia, Lunakai, A'okalani Cove Resort* |

Alucard sighed deeply, letting the last of his frustration slip away. Zalith had been gone for what felt like twenty minutes now, and the initial agitation had finally begun to wane. As much as he wanted to look after that tortoise, he wasn't about to let it overshadow what little remained of their vacation. Exhaling once more, he pushed the matter from his mind, and then he got up and made his way towards the stairs leading down to the bedroom. But he didn't head down.

"Do you still want to go outside onto the beach?" he called.

"I don't know," Zalith retorted. "Are you done with your tantrum?"

The vampire deadpanned—but he wasn't going to get mad. He closed his eyes, exhaled quietly, and scowled. "Yes," he grumbled.

Zalith walked up the stairs, grabbing two towels. "Let's go," he said, but before they could take more than a few steps, he suddenly paused. "Wait."

Alucard stopped, watching as the demon turned back towards the lounge. His mate picked up the small bottle of sunscreen from the table and returned to his side.

"Take your shirt off," Zalith said, his tone leaving no room for argument.

Alucard flicked a glance at Zalith's face, noting the faintly irritated glare lingering in his expression. Not that he was any better—he was sure his own frustration was written just as plainly across his face. But he didn't want to make it worse. He didn't want to argue. So, without a word, he pulled his shirt over his head and tossed it onto his suitcase, and then he turned his head to the side as Zalith carefully applied the sunscreen to his chest.

As the demon turned him around, the irritation in his gaze faded, replaced by something almost sullen. Alucard hated this—the way they barely spoke when they disagreed, the way neither of them wanted to push and risk an argument, leaving only silence to fill the space between them.

But when Zalith finished, he didn't step away. Instead, he wrapped his arms around Alucard from behind, holding him close, and rested his head against the back of his neck with a quiet, weary sigh. The tension in Alucard's shoulders wavered. His frustration still simmered beneath the surface, but the weight of Zalith's despondency pressed against it, softening the edges. He didn't want this distance between them. He just wanted things to be okay again. So he lifted a hand and curled his fingers around Zalith's wrist—the closest he could get to holding his hand.

"I didn't say you can't take the turtle home," Zalith said calmly. "I just don't think it's right to take an animal away from its beautiful home just to stick it in a room."

Alucard sighed quietly. "If I leave her here, someone else is bound to find her before she can heal and go back to the water, and they will most likely take her and kill her and use her for whatever they use these ethos animals for. And if I take her home, the climate won't be warm enough for her to live outside—she will either get sick or just die because it's too cold. You don't want her inside, so I'll just leave her here and hope she heals in time to leave the island."

"We can get a hut of appropriate size built for her that's heated and safe and secure with an attached pen so she can come outside during the warmer months. And we can keep her inside until it's ready."

The vampire shrugged. "It doesn't matter anymore," he mumbled sadly. "She's gone."

"It's a tortoise—she can't have gone very far."

Alucard shrugged again.

Zalith then started to slowly push him towards the door. "Let's go find her," he said.

"We don't have to," he mumbled. "It's fine."

"Yes, we do," the demon insisted.

The vampire frowned hesitantly. They were supposed to be spending the remainder of their time in Maluhia on the beach, not searching for an animal that disgusted Zalith. And this vacation was about Zalith, not about him and some tortoise he'd found. "We're meant to be laying on the beach," he said as the demon led him outside, still holding him from behind.

"We can do that after you find your friend," Zalith said, leading them along the deck.

He didn't want to argue. "Okay."

They walked onto the beach and headed in the direction the tortoise's footprints led. Alucard was sure that she was long gone by now—either that or someone had found her and taken her away. So he wasn't going to get his hopes up—

"Is that her over there?" Zalith asked, stopping.

Alucard followed Zalith's gesture, his eyes landing on the white, crystal-covered tortoise nestled in the sand beside a patch of long grass. Relief enthralled him in a heartbeat. Without hesitation, he hurried over to her, and the moment she spotted him, she abandoned her meal and began dragging herself forward as quickly as she could manage.

As soon as he reached her, Alucard scooped her up, cradling her against his chest. Holding her close, he exhaled deeply, the lingering tension in his body melting away. She was safe. She hadn't wandered somewhere dangerous or fallen into the wrong hands. Overwhelmed with gratitude, he hugged her a little tighter, pressing his cheek lightly against her smooth, crystalline shell.

He turned to face Zalith—he caught the endearing smile on his face before he deadpanned, but he wasn't going to say anything about it. He looked down at the tortoise and then back at Zalith. "I'll clean her... and myself before we lay on the beach," he said, certain that Zalith was worrying about germs and whatever else.

The demon smiled and placed his hand on the side of Alucard's arm. "Thank you, baby," he said, and then he kissed Alucard's cheek.

He smiled and started to lead the way back to their beach house.

"Where are you going to keep her until it's time to go?" the demon asked.

"I don't know," he admitted.

"You could keep her in the bathroom—in the bathtub."

He nodded. "Okay."

Once they got back to the house, he took the tortoise into the bathroom and placed her in the bathtub. He then washed his hands and every part of his body that the tortoise had touched before joining Zalith in the lounge.

"Are you ready to go?" he asked, using one of the towels to dry his hands.

Zalith—who was sitting on the couch—stood up and smiled as he made his way over to him. "I'm ready."

Alucard slipped his sunglasses on, picked up the towels, and without letting go of Zalith's hand, pulled him along as they stepped outside onto the deck. The warmth of the midday sun graced his skin as they descended onto the beach, the soft sand sinking beneath their feet.

Once they reached a good spot, he laid both their towels down, smoothing them over the sun-warmed sand. Zalith wasted no time pulling off his shirt, stretching out on his back with a deep, content sigh. But Alucard had other plans. He straddled the demon's lap, and Zalith, smirking up at him, lazily traced his fingers over his body, drinking him in with appreciative eyes.

Reaching into his pocket, Alucard retrieved the small bottle of sunscreen and squeezed some onto his palm before smoothing it over Zalith's skin. His hands glided over the demon's toned body, his touch lingering just a little longer than necessary.

"Thank you," his mate said as he put his own sunglasses on.

"Thank *you* for letting me keep the tortoise," he said with a small smile.

"If she was here, she'd be thanking you for saving her in the first place," Zalith said as he guided his hand to the side of the vampire's face.

Alucard leaned closer and kissed his lips. Then, he laid down beside him and rested his head on Zalith's shoulder, letting himself relax.

"How long until we have to leave?" Zalith asked, fiddling with Alucard's hair.

"Well... I guess we could leave in the late afternoon if you want to get back and catch up on what's been happening while we were away."

The demon nodded and closed his eyes. "Okay," he murmured.

Alucard was certain that Zalith just wanted to rest for a while, so he closed his eyes and let himself relax, too.

But the longer they lay in silence, the harder it became for Alucard to *not* think about what he had seen this morning. He always tried to make some sort of sense of what he saw when he saw it. After all, the dreams he'd experienced back when he and Zalith were on the run with his people had been of things that were soon to come. He'd known when Lilith's people were catching up, he'd sensed when danger was coming, and the dream that had woken him to tears this morning... it felt like a warning.

He wasn't afraid, though. The warning... it felt more like an answer. He'd always questioned how Janus had apparently given him the ability to create vampires, but... now, if what Lilith had said in his dream was true—or *memory*, in fact, then... Janus never gave him the ability to create vampires, he just... must have somehow activated the Lumendatt that was within his body. Because if he really did have a Lumendatt, there was no way Lilith would have activated it or done whatever Janus had. No, she wanted to own and control him... so she would have made sure that she had control of everything he could do.

He pulled his sunglasses off his face so that he could move closer and nuzzle Zalith's neck. Was *that* why all of the Numen seemed to want him so desperately? Did they just want the Lumendatt? Did any of the other Numen even know he had one—if he did, that was? But... didn't they have their own Lumendatts? Hadn't Lilith stolen Erich's centuries ago? It was, after all, a Lumendatt which gave the Numen the power to create scions, to enter the realms, and to adorn human-like forms.

Wasn't it?

Was it?

He knew that he didn't know everything about the Lumendatts—if he had at one point, though, he needed to remember.

Right now, though, he wanted to know if *he* had a Lumendatt. If he did, then he and Zalith could use it to help them with their cause—with *Zalith's* cause. And that was all he wanted to do. He wanted to be there for Zalith and help him with whatever he could. If he had the Lumendatt, he could learn to control and manipulate it; he could do more than create the standard vampires that he had been all his life. He could literally decide what each and every vampire possessed—he could give them so many new abilities.

There was no point in making plans right now, though. After all, he might not even have a Lumendatt. Damien or Lilith could have taken it from him and hidden the memory. So he tried to think. He tried to remember. Could he recall either of them taking a Lumendatt from him?

No…he couldn't. Did he still have it? There was only one way he could find that out, and he'd need Zalith's help. But he wasn't going to talk about it or ask him for help now. They were still enjoying their time away, and he wasn't going to ruin it.

Alucard frowned and moved his arm around Zalith. The demon was still relaxing, and he didn't want to bother him with conversation. "Do you want me to go and get us something to drink?" he offered—maybe a walk would help settle his thoughts.

"Okay," the demon said with a smile. "Thank you."

"What do you want?"

"Hmm…something with rum."

The vampire nodded—but then he remembered that he'd left his shirt in the house, and he didn't want to walk around without one, especially without Zalith to make him feel comfortable. "Can I…borrow your shirt?" he asked.

"Of course," Zalith said. He reached over, picked up his shirt, and handed it to Alucard.

"Thank you," he said, pulling the demon's shirt on. He tied a few of the buttons, and then he got up, heading for one of the nearby bars. And as he walked, his pondering thoughts faded, letting him focus on what remained of his and Zalith's small vacation.

Chapter Forty-Five

— ⋜ ✝ ⋝ —

One Final Day in the Sun

| **Zalith**—*Maluhia, Lunakai, A'okalani Cove Resort* |

The sun soaked into Zalith's skin, easing the tension he hadn't realized he was holding. Lying there in the quiet, the rhythmic crash of the waves and the distant murmur of voices lulled him into something close to serenity. He didn't get moments like this often—true, undisturbed stillness. He was going to miss it once they returned to reality, but they could always do this again. He *wanted* to do this again.

With a slow exhale, the demon rested one arm above his head, his body pleasantly heavy. Fatigue still clung to him—it always did. Even now, without the nightmares, sleep remained just out of reach. He'd spent so long forcing himself to stay awake and losing himself in work that he hardly knew how to rest properly anymore. There was no excuse for it now, no torment to justify the habit. But he was grateful. He knew how much effort Alucard had put into making sure he could sleep soundly, even if he hadn't quite figured out how to let himself.

Pushing the thought aside, he let the warmth settle into his bones, deciding, just for now, to simply exist.

The familiar sound of footsteps in the sand reached his ears, and he knew without looking that it was his vampire. He always knew. There wasn't a moment he didn't keep track of him, not out of control, but out of instinct—out of love. Worry had settled into him long ago, and it never truly left. He relied on their imprints, not just to reassure himself of Alucard's safety but to keep a quiet pulse on his emotions as well. His fiancé's feelings mattered to him, so he paid attention, though never enough to intrude. If there was something Alucard needed to say, something he wanted Zalith to know, he trusted him to share it in his own time.

But something felt...off. Conflict stirred in Alucard's imprint, a hesitation that made Zalith's brows crease slightly. What was wrong?

Opening his eyes, he turned his head just as Alucard approached. He offered a smile, and when Alucard returned it, some of his concern eased—but not entirely. Sitting up, he reached for one of the coconuts as the vampire handed it to him, brushing his fingers briefly over Alucard's in the process. Whatever was on his mind, Zalith would give him the space to share it when he was ready.

"Thank you," he said with a smile.

"I wasn't really sure what to get," Alucard said, sitting beside him. "But I saw this had black rum, so…I got it."

Zalith felt relieved. It seemed as though Alucard was simply conflicted about the drinks he'd got. "That's perfect—thank you," he said, leaning back on his left arm.

As they made themselves comfortable, Alucard took off Zalith's shirt; Zalith saw him glance at him, and he looked a little hesitant, swirling the ice cubes in his drink around with his straw.

"What's wrong?" the demon asked.

He shrugged and said, "Nothing. I was just wondering if you want to get lunch brought to us here."

Zalith laughed a little and smirked at him. "I don't believe you."

Looking down at him, Alucard sighed and said, "I just…saw that dog again and thought about your dog—it made me sad."

"Did you touch it?" he asked, still smiling.

Alucard pouted. "No."

The demon laughed again and put his drink down. "Come here," he said, holding out his arm.

Putting down his drink, Alucard leaned closer.

Zalith moved his arm around him and kissed his lips. "You don't have to be sad. It was a long time ago."

"Is that…well…is the dog the reason you don't want pets?" he asked, sitting up straight as Zalith leaned back on his arm again, picking up his drink.

He shrugged and thought to himself for a moment. "Probably," he admitted. "That, and the germs."

"Well…animals aren't actually *that* dirty, you know," he mumbled.

"I know, but some are—especially ones covered in garbage."

Alucard frowned. "Why would anyone touch an animal covered in garbage anyway?" he asked, leaning on his arm and resting on his side.

"I don't know—that's something you'll have to ask yourself."

"If you're talking about the tortoise, she wasn't covered in garbage," the vampire said with a pout.

"Then what was she covered in?"

He scowled, still pouting. "Crystals."

"She had garbage tied around her legs."

"That was a fishing net," Alucard argued.

"Fishing net that someone discarded, ultimately making it garbage."

"It wasn't dirty," he insisted. "It came out of the water—the same water we were sitting in last night."

"Yeah, but we weren't swimming in garbage, were we?" he replied amusedly, placing his hand against Alucard's chest.

"No, but the net wasn't dirty and neither was she. If she was, I wouldn't have touched her."

Zalith started slowly stroking his hand down Alucard's body. "Yes, you would have, because you wanted to save the turtle. I'm starting to think you might like garbage," he teased, still smirking.

"I wasn't going to let her suffer," he grumbled. "And no, I don't," he snarled, looking away with a stubborn scowl.

"Of course not, but you seemed a little *too* happy to be taking the garbage off of her—suspiciously happy."

The vampire's scowl thickened as he glared back at Zalith. "I was happy to help her."

Zalith laughed a little. "When I turned my back, you probably slurped up the fishing net line like spaghetti."

Alucard's frown contorted into a revolted glare. "Why would anyone do that? That's disgusting," he grumbled. "*You're* gross," he sneered.

The demon smirked, *still* trailing his hand down Alucard's body, guiding his fingers over his abs. "*You're* the gross one. I wouldn't be surprised if the spaghetti we had last night was fishing line, too."

Pouting, scowling, Alucard snatched Zalith's wrist before he could grip his belt and glared at him. "If I'm so gross, maybe you shouldn't touch me."

"Okay, you're right," the demon said.

Alucard let go of his wrist and slumped down onto his back, crossing his arms as he glared up at the sky.

But Zalith was having far too much fun. He leaned over and smiled down at his fiancé. "What's wrong?"

"I'm not gross," he muttered.

The demon laughed again. "You called *me* gross, but I can't call *you* gross?"

Alucard looked up at him. "You were the one who said we ate fishing net spaghetti."

"Well, I ate every bite, so it couldn't have been that bad," he said, smirking.

The vampire sighed. "And I don't like garbage," he grumbled. "But I would rather touch it to save a tortoise than leave the poor thing."

Smiling, Zalith started stroking his hand down Alucard's body again. Then, he leaned even closer and kissed his lips. "You're very sweet, vampire."

For a few moments, Alucard stared up at him, slowly losing his pout, relaxing beneath the demon.

"What?" Zalith asked, still smiling as he guided his fingers over his fiancé's abs once more.

Alucard shrugged. "I'm sorry I try to help all the animals," he mumbled.

"You don't need to apologize," he said, tracing slow, circular patterns around Alucard's waist. "I love that side of you. It's just the dirt and germs I can't stand." His touch lingered, gentle but firm. "But don't stop helping animals," he added, his voice steady with reassurance. "I'd never want that."

The vampire nodded, but guilt lingered in his eyes.

"What's wrong?" Zalith asked him.

"Nothing. I just…feel bad because we argued about the tortoise."

"I feel bad, too. I'm sorry I'm so fussy," he said, guiding his hand over Alucard's crotch—and then he lightly grabbed his shaft through his trousers.

Clearly flustered, Alucard frowned shyly. "What are you doing?" he asked.

"Nothing," he said with a smirk and started kissing him.

As their lips met, Alucard reached up, slipping off both his own sunglasses and Zalith's before his hand found its way to the side of the demon's neck. Zalith welcomed his touch, but his own hands had a different destination. He unbuckled Alucard's belt, fingers grazing the vampire's waist before slipping into his trousers. A quiet hum of satisfaction left him as he felt Alucard's growing arousal. He didn't need to hear confirmation—he already knew, he already felt the shift in his fiancé's body, the subtle tension, the quiet anticipation. Smirking against Alucard's lips, he wrapped his fingers around his dick and deepened the kiss, teasing him. He relished the way Alucard responded to his touch, the way his breath quickened ever so slightly between kisses. Zalith enjoyed taking his time, drawing out every moment, and he intended to do just that.

"Wait," Alucard murmured against Zalith's lips, pulling back slightly. "What if someone sees?" His voice was hushed, but the nervous edge was unmistakable.

Zalith tilted his head, his smirk unwavering. "Who's going to see?"

Alucard shrugged, glancing around as if expecting someone to emerge from the empty shoreline. "I don't know," he muttered, still hesitant.

Zalith held Alucard's gaze, amusement flickering in his eyes, though there was reassurance there too. He could feel the vampire's hesitation, the push and pull between desire and anxious thoughts. But he also knew him well—well enough to know that if he pulled away now, Alucard would only end up frustrated with himself later, regretting the moment he let slip away.

A breath of quiet surrender left Alucard's lips before he reached for Zalith's face, drawing him back in. The demon smirked against his lips before deepening the kiss, his grip firm as he felt Alucard's lingering tension finally give way.

"I say let them see," Zalith murmured as he pulled back just enough to meet Alucard's eyes. "It'll probably be the highlight of their day."

Alucard exhaled a quiet laugh, his reluctance dissolving. "Okay," he muttered and grabbed Zalith by the face, kissing him again—this time with no trace of hesitation.

After several long, heated moments, Zalith decided that it was time to strip Alucard of his clothes. The vampire smiled excitedly as Zalith unbuckled his belt and slid his trousers down his legs. Pressing a slow kiss to Alucard's waist, the demon dragged his lips upward, following the curve of his body, over his chest, up his throat, until he reclaimed his lips. At the same time, his hand slid between them, fingers wrapping firmly around Alucard's growing arousal, stroking him with a teasing touch.

A quiet moan escaped the vampire as he trailed his hand from the back of Zalith's head, down his spine, then around to his front. He lingered for a moment, palming the demon through his trousers, feeling the heat of his arousal even through the fabric. But patience quickly gave way to eagerness, and Alucard reached for Zalith's belt, undoing the buckle.

With a quiet laugh, Zalith pulled the belt free and rid himself of his trousers, then wasted no time reclaiming Alucard's mouth, kissing him deeply as their bodies pressed against one another.

Zalith exhaled a slow breath, trailing kisses down the curve of Alucard's neck; both of them were breathing unevenly with anticipation. As he dragged his lips over the vampire's throat, he loosened his grip on Alucard's shaft, shifting his hand to his thigh instead. A silent cue. Alucard understood, hooking his leg over Zalith's back in response. The demon felt him relax beneath him, he heard the quiet, pleased sigh that left his lips, and as Alucard's hands wandered up his body, Zalith smirked against his skin.

He reached into his vault and took out a small vial of lube; he poured some into his palm before smoothing it against Alucard's ass. The way the vampire tensed beneath him didn't go unnoticed. Zalith knew that hesitation well. Even now, even after so many times, Alucard's nervous anticipation always returned in these moments. The demon let him adjust, nuzzling against his neck, pressing another lingering kiss to his throat before finally lifting his head to meet Alucard's gaze.

Alucard swallowed, his hesitation flickering for only a moment before he glanced swiftly around them. Zalith could almost hear his thoughts—the fleeting anxiety, the need to make sure they were truly alone. Once satisfied, Alucard's tension melted away, and as he looked back up at Zalith, he offered a small, almost bashful smile. But Zalith could see past it—the way his eyes darkened with need, the way he held onto him. The demon smirked. He knew that look. He knew what Alucard wanted. And he knew exactly how to give it to him.

Zalith met Alucard's lips in another fervent kiss as he slowly guided his dick to the vampire's body. With measured ease, he pushed in, savouring the warmth that embraced him. A quiet, pleased moan left Alucard's lips, his body arching beneath him, and Zalith hummed in satisfaction at the sound. Their kisses deepened, growing needier, and when Alucard hooked his other leg over his back, the demon grinned against his mouth.

He pulled away, trailing hot kisses down Alucard's neck as he rocked his hips, setting a slow, intoxicating rhythm. The quiet gasps and sighs against his ear only spurred him on. As he nuzzled Alucard's neck, inhaling the faint traces of his cologne mixed with salt from the sea breeze, the vampire's fingers wove through his hair. Zalith chuckled—he knew what was coming—but before Alucard could tighten his grip, the demon swiftly caught his wrist and pinned it above his head, pressing his weight into him as he picked up the pace.

Alucard groaned, and Zalith smirked at the breathless sound, moving faster, deeper. The vampire retaliated by gripping his ass, squeezing firmly, and Zalith let out a low, amused laugh against his neck. A sharp nip followed, playful yet possessive, and as Alucard dragged his free hand up Zalith's back, gripping a fistful of his hair, the demon let go of his wrist just long enough to grab both of his hands and pin them above his head, humming contently as he drove into him harder.

Zalith's breath grew heavier, his own pleasure mounting with each movement. He could feel it—Alucard was close. The way his body tensed, the way his quiet moans grew shakier, needier. He knew that feeling intimately, he knew how tight and desperate his fiancé became just before he reached his peak. The thought alone sent a deep, satisfied shiver down Zalith's spine.

Still holding Alucard's wrists above his head, he thrusted harder, faster, watching with pure desire as the vampire's head tipped back, his lips parting in a breathless gasp. "That's it," he murmured against his neck, his voice laced with anticipation. "Let me feel it."

Alucard groaned, his entire body trembling beneath him, and then—he climaxed. His release hit with an almost overwhelming force, his legs tightening around Zalith's waist as a pleasured, unrestrained moan spilt from his lips. Zalith groaned at the sensation, his own excitement tipping dangerously close to the edge as Alucard clenched around him, dragging him into a pleasure that threatened to consume him.

Growling lowly, Zalith gripped his hips, slamming into him with a few final, deep thrusts before pleasure crashed over him in a sharp, intoxicating wave. His head dropped to Alucard's shoulder, his breath coming in uneven gasps as he moaned deeply against the vampire's neck. His entire body tensed, overwhelmed by the sheer bliss of it, and he let himself sink fully into the sensation of Alucard wrapped so perfectly around him. He loved this—the way his fiancé felt, the heat that pulsed through him in the aftermath.

For a few moments, he simply stayed there, catching his breath, still buried deep inside the vampire. Then, smirking against Alucard's skin, he loosened his grip on his wrists and ran his hands slowly down his sides. "You feel so good when you cum," he purred, his voice rough with satisfaction. "It's like every inch of you was made exactly for me."

Alucard smiled up at him. "Every inch of me *was* made for you, and every inch of you was made for me," he said breathlessly.

Zalith's hands slowly traced down the vampire's trembling sides. He loved seeing him like this—breathless, blissed out, completely undone beneath him. And he wasn't quite finished enjoying him just yet. Trailing soft kisses down Alucard's neck, he dragged his lips lower, savouring the heat of his skin. He took his time, moving over his collarbone, down the centre of his chest, pausing briefly to flick his tongue over a sensitive nipple, smirking when Alucard shivered in response. He kissed his way lower, past his ribs, past his navel, before settling between his legs.

The sight of Alucard's cum streaking his stomach sent another wave of satisfaction through the demon. Humming contently, he dragged his tongue up the vampire's abdomen, licking up every drop. He moved with excruciating slowness, his warm tongue sweeping over Alucard's skin, tasting the remnants of his pleasure. The soft, breathy sounds Alucard made above him pleased him further, and he took his time ensuring that not a trace was left behind.

Once he was satisfied, Zalith started his gradual ascent back up Alucard's body, pressing kisses along the way—over his stomach, his chest, the hollow of his throat—before finally reaching his neck once more. He nipped teasingly at his skin, then pressed a deep, lingering kiss there, inhaling the faint scent of his mate's satisfaction mixed with salt and sun.

Smirking, Zalith finally eased down beside him, resting on his side as he traced idle patterns along Alucard's bare hip. He sighed, utterly content. "You're perfect," he murmured, voice thick with contentment, before pressing one final kiss to the vampire's jaw.

"*You're* perfect, my love," the vampire replied, shuffling as close as he could get to Zalith.

They lay there for a while, the warmth of the sun embracing them. But every time Zalith glanced at Alucard, he saw his vampire dozing off—and he knew why. Whenever they had sex more than once or twice in the same day, Alucard started to feel the effect of the energy drain. Guilt enthralled Zalith, but before he could say anything, Alucard switched places with him, making him lay on his back, resting his head on the demon's chest.

ASCENDANT
Numen Chronicles | Volume Five

"Do you have all of your things packed?" Zalith asked.

"Uh...well...most of it," he mumbled tiredly. "I think I have one or two things left in the wardrobe in the bedroom. What about you?"

"I haven't even started," he laughed.

The vampire smiled. "Should we go back soon and make sure we have everything?"

"I'll do it later."

Nodding, Alucard exhaled deeply. "Did you want to go and get lunch? I feel like if I lay here much longer, I'll fall asleep," he said, dragging his hand down Zalith's body.

Zalith nodded as he fiddled with Alucard's hair. "Okay."

Alucard smiled as he sat up and pulled his trousers back on.

Zalith pulled his trousers on, too, and handed Alucard his shirt. He helped the vampire tie the buttons before they both stood up and put their sunglasses on.

"Do you know where you want to go?" the vampire asked.

"No, but I want something light."

"We could check out one of the places down by that sushi place we went to yesterday if you want?"

He nodded and smiled at him. "Okay."

Zalith followed at Alucard's side as they walked along the beach, enjoying the warmth of the sand beneath his feet and the rhythmic crash of the waves beside them. The sun hung lower now, casting a golden shimmer across the water, reflecting in Alucard's hair. Their time here was slipping away, but for now, they were still *here*—not in Eimwood, not buried under strategy and war, but somewhere untouched by the weight of everything waiting for them.

He hadn't realized how much he needed this until recently. The past months had been nothing but battle, sleepless nights, and relentless planning. Here, for the first time in too long, he could simply *exist* without feeling the pressure of expectation, without the constant urgency pulling at his thoughts. And he had Alucard to thank for that.

He took his fiancé's hand as they walked, letting his fingers trail lazily over Alucard's knuckles. There was still a little time left—time to make the most of these last few hours before duty reclaimed them. They'd go back soon enough. But not yet.

Chapter Forty-Six

— ⊰ ✝ ⊱ —

Play Fighting

| **Alucard**—*The Eryndral Ocean, The Steamship* |

Later afternoon came around fast. While the ship crew carried their bags onto the deck, Alucard and Zalith headed towards the cabin. The vampire carried his new tortoise in his arms, smiling contently, and when he glanced at his mate, a small smile lingered on his face, too.

"Thank you again for organizing this whole thing. I had a really good time," Zalith said.

"It's okay. We both needed a break."

"Well, I'm looking forward to the next one," the demon said and kissed Alucard's cheek. He then looked down at the tortoise. "So, have you named her yet?"

He nodded. "She's called Snappy."

Zalith laughed. "A fitting name."

"We'll have to get her some food," he said, laughing a little, too.

"What does she eat?" Zalith asked as they reached the cabin door.

"I think she eats fish… and insects."

"You *think*?" Zalith asked, looking nervous.

Alucard shrugged. "I could only find so much out about her species from the little wildlife board by the reception, but I'm going to do some more research when we get home so I can make sure she gets everything she needs."

"Okay," Zalith said, pushing the door open and inviting Alucard to enter first. "You can do that while I get updates on the Cecil situation."

Alucard frowned as he stepped into the room and looked back at Zalith. "You… don't want me there, too?" he asked, making his way over to the couch in front of the fireplace.

"I do," he assured him, shutting the door behind him before walking to the couch. "But you have to set up things for the turtle, and I want to get to work as soon as we get back."

As Zalith sat beside him, Alucard looked down at Snappy and shrugged. "I can do that later," he mumbled.

The demon shook his head as he slouched back on the couch. "No, it's okay. You can do what you need to do for her, and I can just figure out something else to work on while I wait for you."

Alucard sighed quietly as he patted Snappy's head. He knew Zalith just wanted to get back to work; he'd taken away enough of his time, and he wasn't going to take any more. "It's fine," he said, glancing at him. "You can just tell me about it later."

"I'll wait," he insisted.

"Well..." the vampire drawled. "I could just bring her with me."

"Is that going to stress her out? She's already going to have to endure this boat trip, and then she's going to have to get used to an entirely new home."

Alucard leaned back, making himself comfortable. "I know you just want to get to work—it's honestly okay. You can meet with whoever you need to meet with to get the updates you need, and I will get to work on her temporary home. I also need to do that research, so...you can just find me when you're done."

But Zalith shook his head. "It's okay—I can wait. I'm sure I can find other things to work on."

An idea then made its way into Alucard's head, and he smiled curiously at his mate. "Why don't you help me with her house?" he suggested, but as he watched a reluctant, perturbed look appear on Zalith's face, his idea made him feel a little naïve. He knew Zalith didn't like animals, and he knew he didn't really care about Snappy, so why would he have any interest in helping build her a house? Alucard laughed a little. "It's fine," he said. "I know you don't care—I was just joking. You can go and do your work, and I'll come and find you when I'm done with her."

"I care about *you*," the demon said. "Are you sure?"

He nodded. "I'm sure." But then he smiled deviously and held out Snappy. "But only if you go and put her in the bathtub for me right now," he dared him.

Zalith frowned unsurely as he stared an almost disgusted stare down at the tortoise in Alucard's arms. "I'd rather help you with the house, to be honest," he laughed.

Alucard was sure he'd say something like that. He smiled a little and shrugged. "I'm messing with you," he assured him. Then, he stood up and headed to the bathroom. He carefully lowered Snappy into the bathtub, took a dish from under the sink, and filled it with water. After he placed the dish into the tub and washed his hands, he made his way back towards Zalith. "I put a dish of water in there this time just in case she needs a drink," he said and slumped down onto the couch beside the demon.

"Okay," his mate said, smiling at him.

"And I washed my hands too," he assured him. "Am I allowed to lay on you?"

"Thank you very much—and yes, you are," he confirmed, holding out his arms.

Alucard shuffled closer; he leaned his body against Zalith's, resting his head on his chest as the demon wrapped his arms around him and held him tightly. Instead of resting his hand on Alucard's waist, though, Zalith gripped the vampire's ass and kept hold of it, relaxing.

"I'm going to miss the warm water," the vampire mumbled.

Zalith laughed a little. "I'm going to miss doing stuff on the beach with you."

The vampire smiled and hugged him tightly. "I had a really good time."

"On the beach, or in general?" Zalith asked with a smirk.

"Both."

Zalith kissed his head. "Me too."

They lay there for a while, wrapped in the quiet comfort of each other's presence before the ship finally stirred to life. The deep, steady hum of the steam engine rumbled beneath them, blending with the rhythmic creak of wood and the gentle push of waves against the hull. The ship swayed with the current, rocking in a slow, hypnotic motion, and Alucard caught himself dozing off, his body sinking further into Zalith, limbs weighted with fatigue.

The ocean's lullaby should have been soothing, but he knew better than to surrender to it so easily. Sleep threatened to pull him under, but the thought of a nightmare stealing what remained of this peace kept him clinging to wakefulness. He needed something to occupy his mind, something to keep him from drifting too far into the dark corners of his own thoughts. If he wanted to stay awake, he needed a distraction—something to do or something to talk about.

He frowned, shuffling around a little. Soon, he had a meeting with his subordinates and the leaders of his vampire covens. He wasn't sure how long the meeting would last, and he didn't know how much his people had to say to him, but he was certain that there was going to be a lot to do.

"I have my meeting next week," he mumbled.

"Oh, yeah," Zalith replied tiredly. "I forgot. Will we have to stay overnight?"

The vampire turned a little, laying on his back and resting his head in Zalith's lap. "Probably not," he said, staring up at the ceiling. "If we leave in the morning, the meeting will probably only last a few hours, so we can come home after that and I will plan what I'm going to do. I will have to plan where I'll be going and what I'll be doing there, and once I know what I have to do, we can plan from there. We can plan my visits around your new plans so we're not doing too much in one day," he said, looking up at Zalith as he smiled down at him.

"That sounds good to me," his mate said, starting to fiddle with Alucard's hair. "Are we going to have to kill anyone?" he asked with a quiet laugh.

Alucard shrugged as he moved his right hand up to the side of Zalith's face. "Maybe," he mumbled, slowly stroking his hand down to the demon's neck. "Maybe not. I guess we will find out when we get there."

"I guess so."

The vampire then sighed and rested his hands on his chest. "So, what's next?" he asked, gazing up at Zalith. "Are you still searching for more packs to add to your numbers?"

"I am," the demon confirmed. "I'm actually thinking about confronting Vila, the scion we learned of from Alegan. I had Orin send one of his men to find and keep an eye on her. She has a rather large pack—roughly three hundred members. I'm admittedly nervous, though. Challenging a scion is going to provoke Lilith a whole lot more than killing a few pack leaders. She's bound to react a lot more seriously than sending demons across the country to search for us."

Alucard nodded in agreement. "And then there's also the possibility she will gather her followers like I said the other day—if she isn't already planning to do so. But three hundred would give you over a thousand demons."

"We'll still need more," his mate said with a sigh.

The vampire pondered. He knew they needed more, and he knew of a way for them to get more demons... but he was sure that Zalith wouldn't be comfortable with the idea. Zalith hadn't sounded very confident when he'd mentioned it before. But they didn't exactly have many options. He sighed, staring up at Zalith. "There's always Lucifer's packs. There are so many Diabolus out there, and now that I have a pack following me, it'll be easier for me to add to it."

"I'm not ready to get involved in that."

"Why?"

"Because the wounds are still fresher than I'd like them to be."

Alucard nodded as he turned his head to stare over at the fireplace. "I guess I could always make more vampires."

"We'll need a lot more of everything," the demon said with a half-chuckle.

"We'll work it out," Alucard assured him.

Zalith nodded in response.

They lay in silence once more, letting the time race past them.

Fatigue crept back over Alucard, heavier this time, and he made no real effort to fight it. Instead, he let himself sink into thought—though not the kind he wanted. No matter how much he tried to push it aside, the doubt slithered in, persistent and unwelcome. After centuries of living in Damien's shadow, it was impossible not to wonder... did Zalith not want him to challenge other Lucidian demons because he truly believed that it was the wrong move? Or was there something else beneath it? Did he think he couldn't handle it? He knew that Zalith loved him, that he only wanted to protect him—but to what extent? Did he see him as fragile? As something vulnerable that needed to be shielded rather than something capable of standing beside him? The thought settled uneasily in his chest, nagging at him in a way he wasn't sure how to shake.

No...Zalith knew he was capable. This wasn't about doubt—it was worry, amplified by everything that had happened. Alucard understood that. But they needed more numbers, and he had the ability to help. With a pack behind him, his missing wings wouldn't be the hindrance they usually were when it came to leading. And while he knew Zalith wasn't ready to involve himself in Lucifer's domain, Alucard couldn't shake the feeling that it was one of the few viable options they had left.

Zalith could continue expanding his own forces, but pulling demons from different lineages into a single pack wasn't as simple as it sounded. Different species didn't mix well—there was no telling what kind of tensions might arise if he brought Lucidian, Damodeus, or Lethidian demons into a pack that had been, until now, strictly Lilidian. And while Zalith had the strength to keep them in line, was it worth the potential unrest when Alucard could take a more direct approach? He sighed, running a hand through his hair. Zalith would disagree, of course—but that didn't mean he was wrong.

He looked up at Zalith. "Have you thought about seeking out other demon packs at all? Or are you sticking with Lilidian ones for now?"

"I've thought about it. But I can't decide if it's a good idea or not."

"It could increase your numbers a lot. You don't even have to fight the Alphas yourself; you could send one of the packs you own to deal with them, so it's less work for you. But...the fact that other demon species don't really like each other might cause problems—especially in a time like this when there's talk of the threat of a world war. I'm surprised the Numen aren't fighting each other yet. We've given them all a perfect excuse to start squabbling," he mumbled. Then, he sighed deeply. "But then again, it's possible that Damien is working with Lilith, or that the Diabolus are working with Lilith. We are yet to get any confirmation about that."

"We should get someone to find out what Damien's doing," Zalith said. "We need to find out who is working with who—if anyone even is working together."

"Do you have anyone in mind?"

"The people I'd prefer to do it are busy, but maybe one of Tyrus' guys."

Tyrus...he had tracking ethos on him and had been the reason Lilith's people were able to find them last month. Alucard knew he was one of Zalith's best subordinates, and maybe even his friend. Tyrus would be a good choice, right? "Maybe we can look into removing the tracking ethos off of Tyrus, and then we can send him?" he suggested.

The demon nodded. "Who do we know that can do something like that?"

"Well...if that Opus guy was able to enchant this ring and your chain to keep the Numen from finding us, I'm sure he'll be able to remove a Numen tracking ethos.

Or…maybe we can find someone else directly related to a Numen who can do such things. I don't really want to ever have to see Opus again."

"Agreed. But what's the likelihood of us being able to find someone else within a reasonable timeframe?"

"We could always ask Camael. He seemed very eager to help us when we were leaving Nefastus."

The demon exhaled another deep sigh. "I guess," he grumbled.

With an amused laugh, Alucard pulled himself up and sat in Zalith's lap, moving his arms around his shoulders. "I could get Attila to look for someone else, but I have no idea how long that might take. These people tend to hide themselves well," he said, gazing into Zalith's eyes.

"I'd rather gnaw off my own leg than ever have to even hear that man's name again."

Alucard shrugged again. "I will send a message to one of my vampires in DeiganLupus with him. Should we meet with Tyrus somewhere once Camael has moved the tracking ethos?"

Zalith nodded. "Yeah, we'll meet with him."

"Okay," Alucard said.

He rested his forehead against his mate's and stared fondly into his eyes. He didn't really have anything else to say, he just liked gazing at him, and he loved being so close to him.

Zalith smiled as he stared back. "What?" he asked.

Alucard murmured, "Nothing."

Zalith grinned—but before Alucard could even process it, the demon dragged his tongue across his face, sliding over his lips, his nose, and even his left eye. Alucard barely had time to react before Zalith leaned back, laughing, clearly pleased with himself.

Alucard stared at him, momentarily stunned, caught between confusion and amusement. He didn't know whether to scowl or laugh, but before he could decide, Zalith lunged forward, clamping his teeth over the side of his neck. He didn't bite down, he didn't pierce the skin, but he held firm, a low hum of satisfaction rumbling in his throat. Alucard frowned, gripping the demon's shoulder with a bewildered smile, unsure whether to shove him off or let him carry on with whatever he was doing.

Once the initial confusion faded, Alucard let out a small, breathy laugh. "What are you doing?"

Zalith didn't answer…and he didn't let go.

Frowning, Alucard tilted his head, attempting to pull back, pushing against Zalith's shoulder in protest. But the demon only growled—a low, possessive sound—before seizing Alucard's arms and pinning him down onto the couch with swift, effortless strength. Alucard laughed, excitement sparking through him, though a lingering perplexity remained. He wasn't entirely sure where this was leading yet, but he wasn't about to complain.

Zalith grinned down at him, satisfaction gleaming in his dark eyes as he kept Alucard's wrists pinned above his head. Alucard smiled back, but curiosity furrowed his brow as he fidgeted, testing the demon's hold. When he tried to tug one hand free, Zalith smirked deviously, tightening his grip just enough to make it clear—Alucard wasn't going anywhere. Then, he shifted, resting more of his weight against the vampire's body, the warmth of his skin pressing against him.

Alucard frowned and pouted. "What are you doing?" he repeated. "Do you *want* something?"

"No," Zalith said, still smiling at him.

The vampire pulled on his wrists again. "Then why won't you let me go?"

"Because it's funny," the demon said amusedly.

Alucard's pout deepened into a scowl. Clearly, Zalith was enjoying this far too much. Fine. If the demon wanted to play, he'd put up more of a fight.

He twisted beneath him, yanking at his arms with renewed effort. His left hand slipped free, and he immediately grabbed Zalith's shoulder, using it for leverage as he pushed against him, trying to wriggle out from underneath. But Zalith countered just as quickly, laughing as he overpowered him with ease. In a swift motion, he caught Alucard's wrist, snatching it back under his control before pinning it once more above his head. The vampire stared up at him, flustered and caught between frustration and intrigue, but Zalith only smirked, eyes glinting with satisfaction.

"No." His voice was firm, final.

Alucard narrowed his eyes. He wasn't going to surrender that easily. With a frustrated huff, he squirmed, managing to slip his leg free. He brought his shin up, pushing against Zalith's body in an attempt to force him back, but Zalith only smirked wider. Before Alucard could react, the demon leaned down, his sharp teeth grazing just above his knee before biting—not hard, just enough to startle him, to remind him exactly who had control. His grip on Alucard's wrists never wavered, keeping him effortlessly restrained as he chuckled against his skin.

Alucard flinched, kicking instinctively as Zalith focused on his right leg. Seizing the opportunity, he yanked his left one free and immediately used it to shove against the demon's side. This time, he didn't hold back—he pushed with enough force to finally knock Zalith off balance. The demon barely had time to react before Alucard sent him rolling back, but just as quickly, Zalith's laughter filled the air, his hands latching onto Alucard's waist as he twisted his body.

Before Alucard could scramble away, Zalith yanked him with him, and they tumbled off the couch with a *thump!* The impact startled Alucard, knocking the breath from his lungs, but he had no time to dwell on it. Zalith was already moving, attempting to pin him down again.

Not this time.

Alucard caught his wrist and shoved his knee between them, keeping Zalith from pressing his weight onto him. With his free hand, he reached for Zalith's other wrist, but the demon was quicker—he pulled back, laughing, and instead caught Alucard's hand, swiftly pinning it above his head.

The vampire growled in frustration, squirming beneath him. He wasn't out of the fight yet—he still had Zalith's other wrist in his grasp, and he fought to yank his pinned arm free. His knee remained firmly wedged against Zalith's torso, preventing the demon from fully settling his body over him.

But then Zalith smirked.

Without warning, he released Alucard's trapped wrist. For a fleeting second, the vampire thought he had the upper hand—until Zalith's hand shot down, fingers curling against his waist.

A sharp pinch.

Alucard jolted, his body betraying him as a startled gasp escaped his lips. His momentary lapse was all Zalith needed. In an instant, the demon grinned, snatched both of Alucard's wrists and pinned them effortlessly above his head once more. Then, with a triumphant chuckle, he sprawled over him, pressing their bodies together.

The vampire snarled, thrashing against him, but before he could form a proper protest, his mate blew a raspberry against the side of his face.

Alucard froze.

A beat of silence. Then—utter, bewildered indignation.

He turned his head just enough to glare at Zalith, his expression caught between mortification and fury, but the demon only grinned, clearly pleased with himself.

The vampire pouted and scowled, trying to wriggle free.

"I said no," Zalith said, smirking down at him.

Alucard's scowl deepened. He was certain that this was all so very fun for Zalith, and every time they fought like this, the demon would always overpower him. And he didn't try *too* hard to win. This time, however, he wanted to win. So, he put in a lot more effort. He struggled and tried to pull his hands free—Zalith laughed and tightened his grip, but Alucard was successful. He pulled his right hand free and grabbed Zalith's arm; then, before Zalith could try to stop him, he turned them around and pinned the demon down on the floor, glaring at him.

Zalith laughed as he smiled up at him. "Can I tell you something?" he asked.

"What?" Alucard grumbled.

"Come closer so I can whisper—I'm shy," he teased.

The vampire scowled skeptically. "Are you going to lick me again?"

"No."

Alucard narrowed his eyes, suspicious of the sudden shift in Zalith's demeanour. He hesitated, exhaling slowly before leaning in, half-expecting the demon to kiss him.

Instead—Zalith licked his face again.

The vampire froze. His eyelids fluttered in startled disbelief as the wet sensation dragged over his cheek, and as he jerked back, Zalith burst into laughter.

Scowling, Alucard wiped his cheek with the back of his hand, a deep, embarrassed pout forming on his lips. He should have known.

Zalith only laughed harder, the amusement in his dark eyes making Alucard's scowl deepen. With a quiet, begrudging sigh, the vampire finally released his grip on Zalith's wrists. He pushed himself up, shifting until he was sitting in the demon's lap, but he didn't move away. Instead, he exhaled deeply, slouching slightly as he stared at his mate beneath him.

That was when he felt it.

A slow, creeping warmth settled in his chest, curling low in his stomach as he watched Zalith—his sharp, teasing smirk, his dishevelled hair, the warmth of his hands now resting at Alucard's waist. His body responded before his mind could rationalize it, and desire stirred within him.

He wanted him.

But he knew he shouldn't. His limbs still ached from earlier, from last night. He was already fatigued—if they did this now, he wouldn't have the energy to do anything tomorrow. He needed rest, at least until morning.

With another quiet sigh, he let the tension seep from his body and slowly leaned forward, surrendering to his exhaustion. He rested his chest against Zalith's, pressing his cheek into the crook of his mate's neck.

And that was where he stayed.

The demon wrapped his arms around him and hugged him tightly. "Sorry," he mumbled.

Alucard frowned. "Why are you sorry?"

"For licking."

He shrugged, nuzzling Zalith's neck. "You don't need to be sorry," he murmured with a quiet laugh.

"Are you sure? You seem grumpy."

Alucard lifted his head and looked down at him. "I'm not grumpy. I just… don't like losing," he admitted with a stubborn frown.

"You were play fighting with *me*; many would consider that a win," Zalith assured him.

The vampire flicked the demon's loose, tousled fringe and smiled. "You won't find it so easy next time," he warned him.

Zalith smirked and pulled Alucard closer; he kissed his lips once...twice...and a final time.

Alucard had no intention of moving. He'd let Zalith think he'd won—he'd get the last word in his own way. He exhaled deeply, settling against the demon's chest, his head resting on Zalith's shoulder. The warmth of his mate, the gentle sway of the ship, the rhythmic lull of the waves—all of it conspired against his exhaustion, pulling him deeper into the quiet embrace of sleep.

There was still at least an hour before they reached home, and he was tired. The vacation was over, and while part of him felt a pang of reluctance, he knew they couldn't ignore their work forever. Their responsibilities awaited them, and the sooner they faced them, the sooner they could put it all behind them.

ASCENDANT
Numen Chronicles | Volume Five

Arc Four
✝
Extermination

ASCENDANT
Numen Chronicles | Volume Five

Chapter Forty-Seven

— ≺ ✝ ≻ —

Aniani Tortoise

| **Alucard**—*Uzlia Isles* |

Zalith's soft voice echoed, "Alucard."

The vampire frowned, mumbling in disapproval as Zalith gently shook his arm, waking him up.

"We're home. It's time to get up," the demon said, caressing his hair.

Alucard scowled and nuzzled Zalith's neck. "It's not," he grumbled.

"It is," his mate said.

The vampire pouted and shuffled around. "No."

Zalith chuckled as he stroked his hands down Alucard's back. Then, he prodded his waist—

Alucard flinched and groaned in startle and irritancy.

"Come on," the demon encouraged him.

With a tired sigh and a lazy groan, Alucard opened his eyes and sat up.

The demon stared at him as Alucard sleepily gazed back. "I'll carry you," he offered, sitting up. "On my back."

Alucard stared at him for a few moments. He just wanted to go back to sleep, and Zalith's offer sounded very appealing. "Okay," he mumbled. But as Zalith turned around, the vampire frowned. "What…about Snappy?" he asked, remembering his tortoise.

"I'll get whoever's taking our bags up to the castle to bring her, too," his mate replied.

The vampire nodded and did as Zalith told him, moving his arms around the demon's shoulders. And then he succumbed to his fatigue again.

What felt like mere moments later, Alucard drifted back to awareness, the world around him hazy and slow to take shape. The rhythmic clipping of hooves against gravel filled his ears, mingling with the distant cries of crows and the steady rush of the ocean.

The carriage rocked gently beneath him, lulling him into that strange space between wakefulness and sleep. They were on their way up to the castle. Soon, he'd be able to crawl into bed.

He was *exhausted*. The past few days had been long and demanding, and every ounce of it was catching up to him.

As his senses sharpened just enough, he became aware of Zalith beside him, his warmth familiar and soothing. Alucard exhaled softly and shifted, resting his head in the demon's lap as he stretched out across the seat. He wasn't sure how much longer they had left before they reached home, but he'd take whatever moments of rest he could get. Once they arrived, he'd walk—he didn't want Zalith exhausting himself by carrying him around everywhere. For now, though, he let himself sink into the comfort of his mate's presence, hovering on the edge of sleep once more.

The next thing Alucard knew, he was being tucked into bed. His body felt impossibly heavy, his mind clouded with fatigue and disorientation. The warmth of the sheets should have been comforting, but a faint sense of unease stirred within him as Zalith pressed a kiss to his cheek and murmured a quiet *goodnight*.

Goodnight?

It was too early for that. They still had things to do. He vaguely remembered—Snappy needed a temporary home, he wanted to research Lumendatts, he needed to write down the memories he'd recalled, and there was that meeting about Eimwood. He *wanted* to do those things. He *needed* to. But his exhaustion pressed down on him, trying to pull him under once more.

Before Zalith could step away, Alucard reached out, catching the demon's hand in his own. His grip wasn't particularly strong—he barely had the energy for it—but it was enough. He forced his eyes open, blinking against the weight of sleep as he met Zalith's gaze. "Wait," he mumbled, willing himself to stay awake.

"What is it?" Zalith asked quietly, looking down at him.

Alucard sat up. "It's only like...five—we have things to do."

"But you're tired," the demon said with a concerned frown.

The vampire shrugged. "I'll be fine," he said, pulling the blanket from over himself. "I'll...go and do what I need to do...and then I'll come find you and we can meet everyone to get updates on Cecil."

"Are you sure?"

Nodding, Alucard climbed out of bed. "Where are we going to have the meeting—and...where is Snappy?"

"I had Edwin put her in the bathroom in your office," Zalith said as Alucard took his hand and headed towards the bedroom door. "And the meeting is going to be at the townhouse in the city."

"Do we need to be there at a specific time?"

"I was just about to send an izuret to tell everyone to be ready soon," his mate said as they made their way downstairs.

Once they reached the main hall, they stopped walking and turned to face one another.

"Well...I'll try not to be too long," Alucard said. "I just need to make a comfortable place for Snappy until her house is built, and then I have to do a little research."

"Okay," Zalith said with a smile, placing his hand on the side of Alucard's neck. "I'll be in my office." He kissed Alucard's lips and headed off down the hall.

Alucard exhaled a slow, sleepy breath as he watched Zalith disappear from sight. His body still begged for rest, but his mind had other plans. With a quiet sigh, he pushed himself onwards through the castle. When he reached his workshop, he climbed the stairs up to his office space with sluggish determination.

Upon reaching it, he barely paused before stepping into the adjoining bathroom. The moment he did, his gaze landed on the bathtub—and there, nestled atop a plush cushion, was Snappy. Edwin must have placed it there for her. The crystal-covered tortoise blinked up at him, looking as comfortable as ever in her makeshift resting place.

As he stood there, staring down at Snappy, a frown settled on his face. He didn't have anything suitable to make a proper home for her—not here, at least. His gaze drifted over his shoulder, landing on the large enclosure beneath the window to the right of his desk, where his python, Dante, resided. Something like that could work as a temporary solution, but where would he even find one? He'd have to send Edwin or another staff member into Eimwood to track something down.

With a quiet sigh, he scooped Snappy up and carried her to his desk. As he lowered himself into his seat, he placed the tortoise in his lap, where she nestled comfortably against him. He let her settle as he reached into one of his desk drawers, pulling out a piece of parchment and a pen. He carefully noted down the materials he'd need to construct a proper enclosure. That was one issue taken care of—now he had to figure out what she ate. Surely, somewhere in the vast libraries of the castle, there had to be a bestiary that contained information about her species.

He'd already read through all of the Dor-Sanguian bestiaries in his personal library, and none of them had contained anything that remotely resembled Snappy. If her species had ever been documented, it wasn't in those books. With that in mind, he rose from his seat, carefully cradling the tortoise as he made his way downstairs and through the castle's grand halls.

The main library, situated next to the lounge, was an expansive chamber lined with towering, dark-wood bookshelves that stretched nearly to the vaulted ceiling. Chandeliers of wrought iron hung overhead, their candlelight casting a warm glow over the heavy oak tables arranged for study. The scent of parchment, ink, and aged leather permeated the space, mingling with the faint trace of dust that never quite seemed to settle no matter how often the staff cleaned.

Alucard made his way towards the left side of the room, where the Deiganish books on animals and creatures of this world were stored. There were countless tomes, bound in everything from simple cloth to ornate, gold-embossed leather. Surely, among them, there had to be something about Snappy's species.

He moved along the towering shelves, scanning the rows upon rows of books. The collection covered everything from common pets to dragons, deep-sea fish, and even the elusive skyfish that drifted through the upper atmosphere. His eyes flicked over the spines, searching for anything that might hold an answer.

To his relief, he spotted a tome, 'Tropical Ethos Fauna', its cover adorned with vibrant, iridescent illustrations of exotic creatures. Right beside it sat another book, 'Crystal-Bearing Fauna of the Known World', its binding embellished with delicate silver filigree. Both seemed promising. He pulled them from the shelf, ensuring he didn't touch the silver, and carried them over to one of the heavy wooden desks. Setting the books down, he eased into the chair and let Snappy settle in his lap once more before flipping open the first volume.

He read, flipping through the pages of the first book with growing frustration. There were endless entries on ethos-infused creatures—fish shimmering with elemental energy, crustaceans that manipulated tides, birds that glowed with latent ethos—but nothing resembling Snappy. No mention of a tortoise capable of shifting its form into that of a turtle, nor any species that bore naturally occurring ethos crystals on its body.

Setting the book aside, he reached for the second volume—one dedicated entirely to creatures that grew crystals as part of their biology. He thumbed through the delicate, timeworn pages, scanning each entry until his eyes landed on an illustration that looked familiar.

An Aniani Tortoise, also known as a Crystal-Shell Tortoise. His shoulders loosened in relief as he read. These creatures had the ability to shift between a land-dwelling tortoise and an aquatic turtle at will, perfectly adapting to both environments in the tropical regions they inhabited. Ethos crystals grew naturally from the females' shells, just as the information board in Maluhia said, and sometimes even their skin, each one infused with elemental energy—typically water or sand. They were known to live for centuries if they could evade poachers and the Daimonio Kai, a massive, predatory sea creature often mistaken for a shark.

Alucard exhaled softly, glancing down at Snappy in his lap. "Well, at least now I know what you are," he murmured, gently brushing his fingers over her crystalline shell.

He frowned in curiosity and continued reading, absorbing the details of the Aniani Tortoise's diet. Their primary food sources included sea fish, snails, small crustaceans, and pua berries—a flower-shaped fruit native to tropical islands. They preferred to sleep on land and hunt in the ocean, making it clear that Snappy would need access to water to mimic her natural habitat.

He exhaled, already formulating a plan. He'd have to talk to Zalith about arranging a suitable enclosure—one that included a water source deep enough for her to swim and hunt in. That meant sending Edwin or one of the staff into Eimwood to gather the necessary materials. For now, the bathtub would suffice. She'd be fine there until tomorrow.

With a quiet sigh, Alucard leaned back in his seat. He knew he should also research Lumendatts, but the thought unsettled him. If he truly possessed one, it could change everything. A part of him wanted to delay confirming it for as long as possible. But when the time came, he'd need Zalith's help to figure it out. That was a problem for later. For now, he had more immediate matters to deal with.

He picked up Snappy and left the library, heading for Zalith's office. Slowly, he made his way up the winding stairs, and once he reached the door, he knocked and pushed it open. Zalith—who was sitting behind his desk, writing—took his eyes off whatever he was working on and smiled at the vampire.

"I'm finished with what I needed to do, so... if you're ready, I can meet you in the hall in about five minutes?"

Zalith nodded. "Okay," he said. But then he frowned as his eyes shifted from Alucard's face to the tortoise in his arms. "You aren't taking the turtle... are you?"

Alucard looked down at Snappy, shrugged, and then looked back at Zalith. "No."

"I mean... you can, but it's just a little random."

He shook his head. "I'm not taking her."

"Okay," his mate said, smiling. "I'll be ready in a moment."

"I will just... take her back to my office," the vampire said, looking down at Snappy. "I'll see you down there."

As Zalith smiled and nodded, Alucard turned around and left the demon's office. Once Snappy was back in the tub, it was time to get back to business.

Chapter Forty-Eight

— ⸨ † ⸩ —

Back to Work

| **Zalith**—*Uzlia Isles, Usrul, Castle Reiner* |

With a deep exhale, Zalith leaned back into his seat. He wanted—*needed*—this meeting to bring good news. The last thing he could afford was another obstacle slowing him down, another problem dragging him away from his mission to restore order.

Despite knowing how much work had piled up in his absence, he didn't regret taking time away with Alucard. Those days had been a rare reprieve, a fleeting moment of peace he hadn't realized how badly he needed. But now, the break was over, and it was time to snap back into his work-driven mindset.

Things felt stable—for now. The city was recovering, the people had begun trusting them, and their plans were finally taking shape. But Zalith refused to get comfortable. Stability was fragile, and complacency was a weakness he couldn't afford.

Cecil had to be removed—only then would he and Alucard truly *own* Eimwood and the Uzlia Isles. But even once Cecil was gone, the work wouldn't be over. The Yrudyen Elves had grown far too comfortable under his rule, and if Alucard's vampires were right, they wouldn't take kindly to a change in leadership. Zalith expected resistance, maybe even open conflict, but he was prepared for it.

Once Uzlia was fully under their control, he would ensure that it became the safest place possible—for him, for Alucard, and for their people. No outside force would threaten them again. Not the Yrudyen, not the Diabolus, and certainly not the Numen.

He sent an Izuret not long ago to summon those required for the meeting: Idina, Danford, and Greymore, along with the three demons—Laria, Neville, and Dunstan—who had been stationed around Eimwood to monitor the people's reactions to his work and the ever-growing rumours about Cecil. He had also requested the presence of Castellan, the leader of the small vampire coven Alucard had assigned to keep watch over the Yrudyen Elves. Zalith hadn't met him formally yet—he only knew of him through the reports that he sent to Alucard, which the vampire would share with him. He could only hope that the man wasn't like Pecker or the other associates of Alucard he'd encountered.

So far, nearly every one of them—except for Crowell, perhaps—had been arrogant or insufferable in some way. Whether that was due to the natural rivalry between vampires and demons or simple disapproval of their creator consorting with one, Zalith didn't care. Alucard was *his,* and nothing and no one would change that.

His focus had begun to drift, the weight of his thoughts pressing in as he idly gathered his papers, setting them aside for later. Just as he finished, a faint puff of green smoke curled through the air by his window, heralding the arrival of an izuret. The small creature flitted towards him, landing lightly on his desk; its large, owl-like green eyes blinked up at him before it let out a quiet chirp, delivering its message—everyone was already assembled at the townhouse, waiting for him and Alucard.

Zalith gave a small nod, and then he reached for the second-to-last drawer of his desk. Pulling it open, he retrieved a polished mahogany box, flipping its lid open before holding it out to the little creature. "Pick one," he instructed.

With an excited whistle, the izuret hopped closer to the box and gawped inside. It started to sort through the many trinkets and shiny curiosities inside; it took a few moments, but soon stood there with a gold and silver coin in one hand, and a small ruby in the other. It frowned, muttering to itself as it looked at them both with an indecisive expression on its peach-fuzzy face. But eventually, it placed the coin back down and took the ruby.

Once the izuret left, Zalith put the box away, stood up, and left his office. He headed downstairs, and the moment he set his eyes on Alucard—who was waiting in the hall wearing his fur-collared cape—a smile made its way to his face. Every time he laid eyes on the man he loved, he was always alleviated by a familiar, warming sense of contentedness. He had decided a long time ago that he wanted to see Alucard's face every day—hear his voice, hold him, touch him. And he had exactly that. Alucard was his, and to this day, it still made him feel *so* happy.

"Hey," he purred, stopping in front of his fiancé as he turned to face him.

"Hi," Alucard replied with a smile, guiding his hand to the side of Zalith's neck.

The demon placed his hands on Alucard's waist and pulled him closer. "Are you ready to go?"

He nodded and said, "It's kind of cold, though. I got you one of your coats." He lifted his other hand, holding out Zalith's black velvet redingote.

"Thank you, baby," he said and pulled it on. He linked his arm with Alucard's and opened the front door.

They left the castle and walked across the courtyard, approaching the carriage.

"So... I discovered that Snappy prefers to hunt in water," Alucard said. "She eats sea fish and crustaceans. We'll need to have an enclosure built where she can swim and hunt—is that okay?"

"So, she definitely can't live inside, then," Zalith laughed. "But that's okay."

"We could set something up in one of the gardens?" he suggested. "We have a lot of space out the back of the castle."

He nodded. "Let me know once you've found a place for it."

"Should we...hire someone to build?" the vampire asked as they reached the carriage.

Pulling the door open, inviting Alucard to climb in first, Zalith smiled amusedly and replied, "Probably—unless you want to build it yourself."

Alucard laughed as he stepped up into the carriage. "I would, but I have other things I need to get done before we head to Fort Rudă de Sânge in a few days."

"Very true," the demon agreed, resisting the urge to slap Alucard's ass as he climbed into the carriage. Once they were both sitting down, and after Alucard had shut the door, Zalith relaxed and rested his head on his fiancé's shoulder. "When are we heading there?"

"Saturday," he said, resting his head on Zalith's. "I figured the weekend was best."

"I'll let everybody who needs to know that we'll be gone."

Zalith gazed out of the window, watching the world pass by as the horse pulled the carriage down the hill. When he glanced down at Alucard, he saw him dozing off, but he wouldn't disturb him. He'd let him get his rest.

| **Alucard**—*Uzlia Isles, Yrudberg, Eimwood City* |

Alucard jolted awake as the carriage lurched over a bump in the road. He blinked, momentarily disoriented, before glancing out the window. He wasn't sure how long he had been asleep, but judging by how stiff his limbs felt, it must have been a while—and the familiar sight of houses and restaurants confirmed they had arrived in Eimwood.

With a tired sigh, he adjusted his posture, leaning further into Zalith's warmth. The steady sway of the carriage and the rhythmic clatter of hooves on cobblestone should have been soothing, yet something stirred within him—something restless, insistent. It was the same sensation he'd felt earlier when they were returning from their retreat, an undeniable craving that only intensified in Zalith's presence. His thoughts drifted, lingering on the way the demon made him feel, the pleasure of his touch, the way his body responded so easily to him. It wasn't like his usual longing—it was stronger now, almost urgent, and Alucard didn't understand why. But even through his fatigue, his mind refused to focus on anything else.

"Well, I don't see any smoke or mobs," Zalith said, snapping Alucard out of his thoughts.

The vampire frowned, his gaze settling on the streets of Oklens, noticeably quieter than those of Bauwell. The buildings here bore the weight of neglect—cracked façades, peeling paint, and cobbled streets in need of repair. Many of the houses sagged under years of poor maintenance, their shutters askew, their roofs missing tiles. It was clear that Cecil had little interest in anything outside his own district, leaving Oklens to wither while Bauwell flourished under his favour.

Alucard knew that would change. Once Cecil was gone, he and Zalith would ensure that Oklens was no longer overlooked, restoring it to a standard that rivalled Bauwell itself. No more crumbling homes, no more forgotten streets. It would take time, but Eimwood was theirs now—or it would be soon. And when it was, they would fix everything Cecil had let rot.

"Maybe Cecil has already been hanged," the vampire replied.

Zalith chuckled. "Maybe."

They sat in comfortable silence as the carriage rolled through the city. The bridge to the Bauwell Residential District loomed ahead, its stone arch casting a long shadow over the river below. As they crossed into the wealthier part of the city, the streets grew more polished, the houses grander—evidence of where Cecil had focused his attention.

The carriage slowed as it pulled up to the townhouse that they used as their official residence. As soon as it came to a stop, Alucard pushed the door open, glancing at Zalith before gesturing for him to step out first. Once they were both on solid ground, the vampire instinctively reached for Zalith's hand, lacing their fingers together as they turned towards the townhouse.

With a quiet grunt, the coachman guided their carriage into the small driveway near the horse-hitching posts.

"Is everyone here?" the vampire asked his mate.

Zalith nodded. "They're waiting for us inside."

Instead of letting the demon knock on the door, Alucard pulled him closer and took a moment to gaze into his curious eyes. His mate opened his mouth to say whatever he was going to say to match his smirk, but before he could utter a word, Alucard kissed his lips.

"What was that for?" Zalith asked softly, fiddling with Alucard's hair.

Alucard shrugged, his shyness consuming him as he looked down at the ground. "I just wanted to kiss you."

"It was nice," the demon said, stroking his hand to Alucard's chin; he made him lift his head to look at him. "I could go for another."

He smiled and leaned closer, kissing the demon's lips once more.

His mate laughed quietly and tucked a loose strand of Alucard's hair behind his ear. "Thank you."

Zalith then knocked on the door. Moments later, the butler answered—a middle-aged man with a neatly combed moustache, dressed in an immaculate black coat with silver buttons. He greeted them with a polite bow, stepping aside to allow them entry.

Alucard followed Zalith inside, the cool hush of the house a stark contrast to the bustling streets outside. The polished parquet floors gleamed beneath the warm glow of the gas sconces lining the walls; the grand staircase curved upward to the second floor, its mahogany banister smooth from years of careful upkeep. The scent of beeswax polish and faint traces of expensive tobacco lingered in the air, mingling with the distant clatter of glasses from deeper within the house.

They strode past the drawing room, its high-backed chairs and velvet drapes cast in soft lamplight, and continued down the quiet hallway to the meeting room at the rear of the house. As soon as they stepped inside, the low murmur of conversation stilled. Everyone seated around the long, dark-wood table rose in unison, offering their greetings with a mix of formality and familiarity.

"How did your trip go?" Idina asked as everyone sat down.

"It went good," Zalith said, making himself comfortable in his seat beside Alucard. "The island was beautiful."

"Oh," she replied with a smile. "Where did you go?"

"Maluhia," Alucard answered.

Idina's smile grew with excitement. "I've never heard of it before. What's it like?"

"Peaceful," the vampire replied, resting his arms on the table.

Greymore then laughed. "Maybe next time we'll all go with you."

Alucard smiled a little. "No," he denied.

Everyone laughed amusedly as Greymore guffawed.

Zalith loudly cleared his throat as he rested his arms on the table.

The room fell silent, and everyone set their eyes on their leaders, waiting.

"So," Zalith started. "What's happened in our absence?"

Idina replied, "The rumours about Cecil travelled fast. I sent some of the city volunteers to the cave along with your own men." She glanced at two of the demons Alucard hadn't seen before. "They all saw Cecil *and* the troll together—Cecil was also seen... as his true self. We confirmed that he's a rochkin. The people were outraged, and of course, *that* news travelled, too. Yesterday, people started crowding up outside his house; they demanded he leave and threatened to enter his house and remove him themselves. We relocated the troll to a cave deeper in the forest with no connection to

Eimwood's water source. As for Cecil, he's still hiding in his house along with his entire council."

Zalith smiled. "How pathetic."

"We suspected that Cecil's council were also Insectumoids—bug…people," Alucard said. "I see we were right."

The demon nodded. "We'll let the people of Eimwood decide Cecil's fate. What's next?"

Coven Master Castellan leaned forward and set his eyes on Alucard and Zalith. "We still believe that the Yrudyen Elves aren't going to take kindly to Cecil's removal. He was collaborating with them for years before your arrival, and they've already started making plans to take back this city. We've kept them back, but I fear that soon, we might not be enough. There are a lot more of them than there are us, My Lord," he said, setting his eyes on Alucard. "If we are to keep holding them back, we may need more numbers."

Zalith sighed quietly.

Alucard sighed too and nodded. "That seems to be my main problem these days. I'm working on that. This Saturday, I'm heading to Fort Rudă de Sânge; I will be finding a new brood nurse or two, so we will be able to increase our numbers. I will keep you updated and send more vampires your way when I have them. Is that all?"

Nodding, Castellan leaned back in his seat.

The vampire lord then looked at Freja. "Are you still on good terms with any of the wolves back in Dor-Sanguis?"

She nodded. "I have relatives in a few of them, yes. In my absence, a cousin of mine married into another pack."

"I have heard that things are…bad over there since the attack on my castle. I want you to arrange a meeting—gather as many of the packs as you can. I want to start discussing relations," Alucard instructed.

"Relations?" she questioned.

"We are going to need more than vampires and demons to grow this little empire we're all working on. I think it's time we try to convince some more of the wolves to join us."

Freja bowed her head and said, "I'll contact them as soon as possible—"

"Tomorrow," Alucard ordered. Then, he leaned closer to Zalith. "Should we meet the wolves in Dor-Sanguis or somewhere here?" he asked quietly—so quietly that only Zalith could hear him.

"We'll talk about it later," his mate muttered.

Alucard nodded and set his sights back on Freja. "Contact them and inform them that we will all be meeting at some point. We don't know where yet, but make sure they are ready."

"Okay, she replied. "I'll contact them tomorrow."

Castellan raised his hand slightly. "My Lord. There was one more thing some of my coven members felt it necessary to share with you."

"Go on," Alucard mumbled.

"The Yrudyen have a yearly ceremony approaching. We've asked some of the locals about it, and it would appear that the Yrudyen Elves offer humans as sacrifices. Cecil must have played a part in this practice—people have gone missing around this time every year before, and we believe Cecil must have offered the elves these humans for their practices. There has been talk among the Yrudyen of this year's offerings."

Zalith sighed deeply. "We'll need to increase security."

Alucard hummed in agreement. Then, he said to Castellan, "If any elf passes the border we have set up, kill them. We must protect this city and everyone who lives here. You will have some more vampires sent your way in a few days. Until then…" he paused, shifting his gaze to the Beta of his own small pack of demons, "…send six of my demons to assist them."

The Beta, Quinn, nodded. "Of course, My Lord."

The vampire then looked around the table. "Is there anything else?"

Everyone shook their heads.

"Good. Keep me updated," Zalith instructed, nodding over at the three demons he had watching the streets, and then Danford—and as they all nodded, the demon stood up.

Alucard followed him out of the room; while everyone else filed out and left the house, Alucard and Zalith stayed behind.

"Should we talk here before we head home?" the vampire asked.

"Sure," Zalith replied.

The vampire led the way upstairs, his steps unhurried. Initially, he considered heading for Zalith's office, but the bedroom—the one they'd use if they truly lived here—held a stronger allure. He wasn't sure if it was the lingering fatigue urging him to lie down or the persistent, insatiable need for Zalith's attention that had been gnawing at him all day. Either way, there was no question about where he wanted to go.

Reaching the bedroom door, he pushed it open and stepped inside, the dim lighting casting long shadows across the richly furnished room. Without a second thought, he slumped onto the bed with a deep, weary sigh, sinking into the plush mattress as tension eased from his limbs. The day had been long and demanding—and now, at last, it was winding to its end.

"So, about the werewolf meeting," he said as Zalith sat beside him. "What do we need to talk about?"

"Well, I don't want you going to Dor-Sanguis—it's not safe for you. But I also don't want the wolves to come here and feel like they're trapped and that they *have* to agree to stay. It's bad for morale, and I don't want to deal with the drama."

He was right. Alucard sighed and rested his head on Zalith's shoulder. "Maybe we can all meet somewhere in the middle. I would say Fort Rudă de Sânge, but…I don't think my vampires would take well to that."

"I don't mind meeting them somewhere else; it doesn't matter how far out it is for us, as long as we don't have to go to Dor-Sanguis."

"Okay. What about…DeiganLupus at the end of this month? I feel like it's probably about time I showed you the estate I used to work out of over there. It's safe and secure—hidden the same way as Uzlia."

The demon smiled curiously and said, "Sounds good."

"I'll send a message to Freja later."

Zalith nodded in response. He then looked around the room, and a smirk stretched across his face. "Why are we in here, Alucard?"

Nervous, he shrugged and looked down at his lap. "I don't know," he mumbled. Despite his gradually increasing desire, he felt too shy to tell Zalith what he wanted—what he *needed*.

"Does it have anything to do with the bed?" his mate asked with a quiet laugh.

"Maybe."

"Maybe?"

Alucard sighed, lifting his head just enough to meet Zalith's dark gaze. There was something so effortlessly alluring about those eyes—something that made his stomach tighten, something that made him crave more than just the demon's presence. "I…want you," he murmured.

Zalith smirked, his expression laced with teasing curiosity. "You want me to what?"

The vampire frowned, his pout deepening. He didn't want to say it again—Zalith already knew. Instead, he grabbed a fistful of the demon's shirt and tugged him down with him as he laid back against the bed. His mate followed, crawling over him, his weight pressing just enough to make Alucard's heart race.

Staring up at him, the vampire held onto his pout, though it was losing its stubborn edge. "I want you to fuck me," he mumbled.

Zalith chuckled, resting his forehead against Alucard's, his warm breath fanning over the vampire's lips. "Okay," he said, amused but undeniably pleased. "And how would you like me to fuck you, vampire?"

Alucard barely needed to think—he already knew. "Like this," he whispered, moving his hand to the side of Zalith's neck. Then, without waiting for another word, he pulled the demon's face to his own, claiming his lips in a kiss that left no room for hesitation.

The demon chuckled against Alucard's lips, amusement laced in the first few kisses. But as Alucard pulled him closer, Zalith smirked and responded with a firmer, more demanding kiss—one that left no doubt that he knew exactly what Alucard craved. There was nothing he loved more than when Zalith was commanding, when his touches carried an edge of dominance. He trembled beneath him, fingers twisting into the demon's hair as his body hummed with anticipation. He still didn't understand why he felt so sensitive—why every brush of his mate's hands sent sparks racing through his veins. Was it because the demon had taken so much of his energy these past few days? Or was it something deeper? He didn't know, and right now, he didn't care. All that mattered was quenching the fire that burned inside him.

Zalith made quick work of his shirt, unbuttoning it eagerly. As the fabric slipped from his shoulders, Alucard's hand drifted down the demon's torso, fingers pressing against firm muscle before reaching the outline of his arousal. He gripped Zalith's shaft through his trousers, relishing the way his mate's breath deepened before he exhaled a pleased hum. Smirking, the demon bit the tip of Alucard's ear, his voice a low, teasing growl as he stripped away the last of his clothing.

Alucard wasted no time. He pulled at Zalith's belt, unfastening it swiftly before sliding it from his waist. Zalith mirrored the action, his touch slow, his fingers tracing over Alucard's ribs, down the defined ridges of his abdomen, leaving a lingering heat in their wake. With both of them bare, Zalith shifted lower, pressing open-mouthed kisses down Alucard's body, each touch only heightening the hunger pooling between them.

The vampire's fingers wove through Zalith's hair, his grip tightening as the demon's tongue traced over his arousal. A sigh escaped him, pleasure curling through his limbs as Zalith's tongue trailed up his dick, each slow movement sending waves of heat spiralling through his body. His brow furrowed, his breath shuddering as satisfaction pulsed through him the moment the demon's lips brushed against his tip.

He kept his eyes closed, surrendering to the pleasure—but beneath the satisfaction, there was something else. A dull ache, a strain. It wasn't unexpected; he always felt this after too many rounds in too little time. But the need thrumming inside him was unlike anything he'd felt before—insistent, relentless. It drowned out the discomfort, demanding more.

A quiet moan left his lips as Zalith's tongue languidly traced along his length, teasing him. But it wasn't enough. As if reading his unspoken plea, Zalith kissed his way back up his body, his lips grazing Alucard's throat as his hands wandered lower. A slick touch followed, massaging viscous lube into his ass, and Alucard exhaled sharply. His body responded before his mind could catch up, his right leg moving over the demon's back, pulling him closer. His pulse quickened, anticipation racing through him, consuming every other thought until nothing else remained.

Zalith's fangs grazed his neck, sending a pulse of sensation through him, and Alucard hummed contently as the demon's dick slowly pushed inside him. The pleasure unfurled swiftly, his body arching as a moan escaped him. He dug his claws into Zalith's back, holding him close, but he needed more. His fingers tangled in the demon's hair, pulling roughly as he murmured against his ear, "Harder."

His mate growled his approval, his thrusts becoming aggressive. Alucard exhaled deeply, his body aching under the relentless pace. Each thrust sent pleasure surging through him, drowning out everything else. He tugged at Zalith's hair, lost in the heady satisfaction that burned through his veins, overwhelming in its intensity. His body trembled, his breath unsteady, his mind unable to focus on anything but the fire building within him.

The demon moved faster, pushing him closer to the edge, each motion unravelling him further. Heat constricted inside him, the familiar pull of climax teasing at his restraint. But he held back, dragging the moment out, his legs tightening around Zalith's waist, pulling him deeper. He wasn't ready for it to end. Not yet.

Alucard turned his head aside, his breath coming fast as Zalith's lips left his neck. Their mouths met again, and they kissed through their ragged gasps, the urgency between them reaching its peak. He felt the demon tense against him, his thrusts turning desperate, each movement sending another wave of pleasure rolling through him. He knew Zalith was close—he could feel it in the way his muscles tightened, in the way his breath grew uneven as he nuzzled back into his neck.

The vampire dragged his fingers through Zalith's hair, grasping tightly, and just moments later, a deep, satisfied moan broke free from his lips as his climax crashed over him. His entire body tensed, overwhelmed by the intensity—somehow even more intoxicating than before, leaving him breathless. Zalith groaned at the same time, his own pleasure cresting as he bit down on Alucard's neck, his grip tightening around the vampire's waist. Alucard groaned in delight as he felt the demon's dick throb inside him, as felt the heat of his cum flood his body, drawing out the last waves of his own climax. It sent a final shudder of pleasure through him, leaving him dazed, content, and utterly spent in the arms of the man he loved.

Zalith then exhaled and laughed quietly as he moved from over Alucard and rested beside him. "Whose bed is this?" he breathed amusedly, resting his head on the vampire's shoulder.

Dragging his hand over his face, Alucard laughed and shrugged. "It's supposed to be ours," he said, huffing as he tried to calm down.

The demon smirked and rolled onto his side. "Good," he said, moving his arm around Alucard. "We don't have to explain anything to anyone, then."

Amused, Alucard chuckled but then fell silent as Zalith nuzzled his neck. He waited for his trembling body to settle, his sudden, burning desire having finally been satiated. He felt relieved, pleased, and serene. All he wanted to do now was lay there with Zalith and relax.

"I think we should head home in a moment," his mate suddenly said, dragging his fingers along Alucard's chest. "It's late, and I don't want to be in this house anymore."

Alucard nodded. "Okay," he breathed, exhaling deeply.

As much as he wanted to lay there a little longer, he didn't want Zalith to have to wait. So, he sat up, and once the demon helped him clean up, they both swiftly pulled their clothes on and headed for the door. At least they were heading home now. Once there, Alucard could rest as much as he wanted, and that was exactly what he planned to do.

Chapter Forty-Nine

— ⊰ ✝ ⊱ —

Temptations

| **Zalith,** *Tuesday, Tertium 21st, 960(TG)*—*Uzlia Isles, Usrul, Castle Reiner* |

Zalith woke to an overwhelming sensation—something so intense that it seized his senses before he was even fully conscious. It wasn't a scent in the traditional sense, but a lure, deep and inescapable, like a predator honing in on its prey. His body reacted before his mind could catch up, heat pooling low in his stomach, his pulse quickening. He knew this feeling. He knew it instantly. And there was only one possible source.

He turned onto his side, his gaze locking on Alucard.

That was where it was coming from—the irresistible, intoxicating pull of a demon in heat.

A shudder ran through him, instinct clawing at the edges of his control. His mate was emitting an energy so potent, so utterly alluring that it should have made sense. It should have been familiar. But it wasn't. He understood male heat intimately, and he understood how gay male demons experienced it, too. It was simple. A need to fuck, a need to sate desire, nothing more. There was no expectation of reproducing, no drive beyond temporary relief. And he knew the signs of female heat—the desperate allure, the way it called to a mate, demanding satisfaction and claiming. But it had never interested him. It had never stirred anything in him beyond detached recognition.

But this?

This wasn't the raw, restless desperation of a male, nor was it the receptive pull of a female. It was something else—something that defied both categories. His instincts were being scrambled, thrown into disarray by something they didn't know how to process. His body knew it, though. It reacted with an intensity that made his breath come heavier and his skin hotter, his muscles tensing with restraint that he was struggling to maintain.

Zalith exhaled sharply, dragging his fingers down Alucard's exposed back. His mate's skin was warmer than usual, his body reacting to something that Alucard might not even be aware of yet. The scent—no, t*he presence*—of Alucard's heat wrapped around him, burrowing into his senses and igniting a feeling deeper than lust. He didn't just want to just satisfy Alucard. He wanted to *breed* him.

The realization sent another sharp tremor through him. He'd *never* felt that way when he found himself with a male demon in heat. There was never the desire to reproduce, just the instinct to help his partner cum. But this? This was something else. This was… consuming, an inescapable, primal demand from deep within him, an urge not only to give Alucard what he needed but to create, to ensure that his mate was filled and marked in the way nature had designed.

Except Alucard was male.

Zalith tightened his grip on the blanket between his fingers, forcing himself to remain still when every nerve in his body screamed at him to claim. His rational mind fought against the instincts roaring for control, trying to understand what his body already seemed to know. Was it because Alucard was the son of a Numen? Was that why the aura was different, why the scent was new? That had to be it—that made sense. And as the confusion faded, the desperation flooded back into him.

He wanted him. He wanted to give in, to give Alucard what he needed. But his fiancé was still asleep. He wouldn't wake him up just to satisfy his own need.

With a quiet sigh, he withdrew his hand and settled back, though every inch of him resisted the distance. Instead, he pulled Alucard into his arms, pressing close, his lips hovering near the back of his mate's neck as he nuzzled against him. Maybe this wasn't a good idea. Maybe he was making it worse for himself. But he didn't care—he needed to be near him, needed to feel him. The morning would come soon enough, and then he would explain. But for now, he let himself savour the warmth of Alucard's body against his own, letting his eyes drift shut, even as his mind burned with anticipation.

| **Alucard**—*Uzlia Isles, Usrul, Castle Reiner* |

Birdsong drifted over the distant hush of waves, a gentle reminder of the morning's arrival. Alucard stirred, caught between wakefulness and the lingering heaviness of sleep. Despite having rested through the night, he felt as though he hadn't slept much at all, his body still weighed down with an exhaustion that he couldn't quite place. But the warmth of Zalith's arms around him kept him grounded, a comfort so natural that it lulled away his lingering fatigue.

Exhaling deeply, he shifted onto his back. Zalith's grip loosened, and within moments, the demon propped himself up on one arm, gazing down at him with a familiar, amused smirk. But there was something else beneath it—something more intent, more eager.

"Good morning," the demon murmured.

Gazing up at him, Alucard smiled as Zalith carefully took hold of his hand. "Good morning," he said, moving his free hand to the side of the demon's neck. "Are you...okay?"

Zalith nodded as he glanced down at the vampire's chest and then back to his face. "How are you feeling?"

He frowned. "What do you mean?"

"How does your *body* feel?" the demon questioned curiously.

Alucard's frown thickened, staring up at Zalith as a sense of confusion settled over him. Why was the demon suddenly asking how he felt? Had something happened? But as he searched Zalith's face for answers, the pieces began falling into place. His mate always knew when something was off with him—he always sensed when something was different. And what was happening now...Alucard wasn't entirely sure.

He noticed it yesterday, this strange, restless need that seemed to consume him. He'd been so eager for Zalith's attention, so desperate for his touch, and now that he was awake, the feeling had returned with an intensity that only grew the longer he lay there. It wasn't just desire—it was something deeper, something frustrating and insistent, coiling inside him like a hunger that wouldn't abate. He felt almost feverish, his skin prickling with the need for something that he didn't fully understand.

Zalith knew. Of course he did. And as shy as Alucard felt, he wasn't going to lie, nor would he pretend that this would simply pass on its own. If anyone could help him make sense of this, it was Zalith.

"I feel...I don't know," he muttered, shoulders tensing as he glanced to the side. "Like I really...*need* you." His fingers curled slightly against the sheets, his voice quieter now. "Like...*want* you. It feels like I *really* need to...fuck you," he admitted, uncertainty laced within his words, unsure if that even explained the extent of what he felt.

Zalith's smirk deepened as he slowly ran his fingers through Alucard's hair.

Alucard barely had the words or the patience to process how it felt. The moment Zalith's fingers threaded through his hair, something intense rippled through him, a sensation so overwhelmingly satisfying that it sent a deep, spiralling heat down his spine. It was as if his entire body responded to that simple touch, drawn into a trance of raw desperation. His muscles tensed beneath the weight of it, and no matter how hard he tried, he couldn't stop the pleased, almost dazed expression from crossing his face.

The demon watched him closely as he asked, "How does that feel?"

Alucard exhaled, his fingers instinctively moving to the side of Zalith's face, his voice little more than a breath as he replied, "Really good."

The demon nodded as if confirming something to himself, and he laughed a little. "I think you're in heat, baby."

In what? Alucard frowned in confusion. "I'm... what?"

"Your body wants you to breed and have lots of sex for the next month," he explained, stroking the side of Alucard's face with his fingertips.

Still confused, he kept his frown and stared up at Zalith. "Really?" he asked, unsure whether Zalith was being serious or not.

"Really," the demon assured him, starting to move his hand down Alucard's body. But as the vampire's frown became one of confliction, the demon laughed. "You don't believe me?"

Alucard shrugged.

"I can tell," his mate said with a smirk, guiding his fingers down past Alucard's waist.

"How can you tell?" he asked with a pout.

Zalith shrugged. "My body just knows."

Alucard glanced up at the ceiling, but no matter how much he wanted to dwell on what Zalith had just told him, his body refused to let him focus on anything else. The heat simmering under his skin, the way Zalith's hands moved over him—it all pulled him deeper into this unbearable craving. There was no desire to pause, no patience to slow down. He needed him *now*.

Without hesitation, he slid his hand over Zalith's shoulder, pulling him closer, and as their lips met in a fervent kiss, any lingering doubt vanished. His mate had to be right—this all-consuming need, this inability to think beyond the moment, it was something beyond his usual hunger for the demon's touch. Right now, nothing else mattered.

The vampire dragged his hand down Zalith's body, sighing against his lips as the demon gripped his quickly growing arousal. His mate knew—he *had* to know just how desperate Alucard had become. He wasted no time guiding him onto his side, an arm curling around him to pull him against his body. The cool slick of lube followed, and Alucard barely had a moment to brace himself before Zalith eased his hard dick into him, a deep, content moan slipping from his lips as his fingers clenched into the sheets beneath him.

Alucard's body was engulfed in pure, electrifying delight, every nerve alive with sensation. The heat of Zalith's touch sent tremors through him, each brush of skin against skin intensifying the ache deep within. His breath quickened as he dragged a hand over his own side, then reached for Zalith's arm, tugging insistently. He needed more— faster, *harder*—and Zalith, attuned to his every desire, obliged without hesitation. Their bodies moved in sync, each thrust sharper, deeper, driving them both closer to the edge as their erratic breaths and pleasured moans filled the space around them.

Sinking fully into the euphoria, Alucard felt himself spiralling, caught between tension and release. Every touch, every movement sent another searing wave of sensation through him, his entire body tightening as he teetered on the edge of something far greater than he had ever experienced before. But this time, it was different—more intense, more overwhelming, as though something deep inside him had been building beyond his control. The pleasure coiled so tightly within him that it burned, a white-hot pressure that consumed every thought, every breath.

When it finally snapped, it was nothing like before. His climax surged through him in rolling, near-violent waves, his body trembling against Zalith's as he let out a strangled, gasping moan. The pleasure didn't fade after a moment but instead prolonged itself, drawing out his release until it felt almost unbearable. His entire body tensed and convulsed, wracked with an ecstasy so deep that it left him momentarily breathless, his senses drowning in the sheer intensity of it. He could feel himself pulsing, cum spilling from him again and again, nearly twice as much as usual, and yet the sensation did not cease. His vision blurred, his entire body alight with overwhelming satisfaction, an ache so deep that only Zalith could soothe it.

And then, Zalith followed, his grip tightening as his breath caught against Alucard's ear. The vampire felt it—the deep, rhythmic throbbing of the demon's dick inside him, the way his body tensed in time with his own pleasure. And when he felt Zalith's hot cum spill into him, a new kind of bliss overtook him, something raw and primal. A shuddering exhale left his lips, and his body melted into Zalith's, utterly consumed by the overbearing warmth that spread through him. It was unlike anything he had ever felt before—like completing something vital, something necessary, as though he had just fulfilled an unspoken, instinctual duty. The satisfaction went beyond pleasure; it was relief, like breathing after suffocating, like quenching a thirst that he hadn't known was killing him.

His heart pounded, his limbs weak as he lay there trembling against Zalith. The warmth of his mate's body, the feeling of being filled, of being claimed—it was enough to leave him utterly devoured. As Zalith nuzzled against his neck, holding him close, Alucard exhaled shakily, a lingering tremor running through his body. He felt complete—wholly, utterly complete, as though nothing in the world could compare to this moment.

"How do you feel *now*?" his mate asked, smirking against Alucard's neck as he fiddled with his crimson hair.

After a deep exhale, Alucard turned onto his back. He gazed up at the demon and shrugged lightly. "I feel…really good. This hasn't ever happened to me before," he mumbled.

Tucking Alucard's hair behind his ear, Zalith smiled, his touch warm and soothing. "It only happens when you're sexually active," he explained. "Once every four to six years—it happens to all demons, but it's more intense for men, probably because…." He trailed off for a moment, as if choosing his words carefully, not wanting to say anything that might sound crude or dismissive of what Alucard was experiencing. "Well, because we can keep reproducing, while women only conceive once before their bodies shift to prevent it from happening again."

Alucard nodded slowly, listening carefully.

Zalith traced his fingers down the vampire's jaw, his gaze steady and reassuring. "It's like an instinct embedded into us—to keep spreading our bloodlines, to ensure we pass on our ethos and strength. But it doesn't just make us more…virile, it makes us crave the ones we belong to; it makes us want to be close to them—to bond with them. That's why it feels the way it does. It's not just about sex, it's about a drive to claim and connect…to fulfil a need that, for demons, isn't just physical." He pressed a gentle kiss to Alucard's forehead before leaning back just enough to look at him properly.

"Have…you been through this before?" he asked. "Will it get worse?"

"I have," the demon confirmed, stroking the side of Alucard's face. "And it will. But it'll be manageable—you'll be okay. I'll be here for you when and if you need me."

Alucard gazed up at him, his fingers trailing to the side of the demon's neck as a quiet sigh escaped him. He felt drained, yet at the same time, a restless energy still stirred beneath his skin, refusing to settle. All he wanted now was to be close to Zalith—to bask in his warmth, to let himself rest in the arms of the one who had just unravelled him completely.

He shifted onto his side, guiding Zalith down with him until the demon lay comfortably beneath him. He pressed his forehead briefly against Zalith's collarbone before resting his head on his chest, listening to the steady rhythm of his heartbeat. But even as he exhaled deeply, seeking calm, that lingering need still pulsed within him—a frustrating, insatiable demand that once again needed to be satisfied.

"I still…feel like I need more," he admitted, his voice carrying a tinge of irritation. He had just given his body what it craved mere minutes ago, yet already, the yearning was creeping back, winding around him like a vice, refusing to let go.

Zalith hugged him tightly. "What do you need?"

But Alucard didn't want to move. Despite what he felt right now, all he wanted was to lay there and enjoy Zalith's embrace. "I just…want to lay here," he mumbled.

"Are you sure?"

"I'm sure," he said with a nod. "Do we have to go to the city today?" he asked, changing the subject in an attempt to distract himself.

The demon replied, "We should so that it looks like we live in that house."

"We could always go and have breakfast over there," he suggested.

"That would probably be best. I want to have a shower first, though."

A shower sounded rather inviting. "Okay," he said, sitting up.

"Will you be joining me, vampire?" Zalith asked with a smirk.

He nodded. "If that's okay."

"Of course," the demon said, smiling up at him.

They climbed out of bed and headed into the bathroom. Alucard followed Zalith into the shower; steam curled around them, the warm cascade of water pouring down over their bodies. Alucard leaned back against the wall, his eyes half-lidded as Zalith worked the shampoo through his hair with slow, careful fingers. He sighed quietly, shifting just enough to rest his palm against the side of the demon's neck, his fingers idly tracing over the damp skin as he stared at his face.

His thoughts were beginning to wander again, slipping into the same restless uncertainty that had lingered in his mind since Zalith first told him about this—this *heat*. He still wasn't entirely sure how he felt about it. It was new, unexpected, something he had never even considered before, though his body had already fully embraced it without hesitation. Zalith had explained what would happen—how his urges would intensify, how his instincts would demand more from him—but knowing it and *experiencing* it were two very different things.

A slow frown crept onto his face as he considered the implications. Was this going to cause him problems? Zalith was an incubus, after all, and each time they had sex, his mate took his energy. And now that his body *needed* it more frequently... would that lead to him becoming weaker? Would he start to suffer from the constant demand?

He stared at Zalith, watching the way the water traced over his body, how effortlessly at ease he seemed despite Alucard's silent worries. But... something felt different. He didn't feel drained anymore. Not even the usual, fleeting strain that followed after their time together. If anything, he felt *fine*—more than fine, actually. His body wasn't protesting, and his mind wasn't clouded by exhaustion.

Maybe this wasn't as much of a problem as he thought. Maybe whatever was happening to him, whatever his body was going through, it accounted for the fact that he would need more and gave him the stamina to actually *have* more, instinct ensuring that he could keep up with what it demanded.

The vampire's smile deepened as his fingers slid from Zalith's neck to the back of his head, tangling into his damp hair. Just *thinking* about it—about what was happening to him, about how much he *wanted*—made something molten burn within him, tightening with each passing second. The need was overwhelming, insatiable, and as the heat in his chest grew, he let instinct take over. With a quiet hum, he guided Zalith's head downward, a silent plea for attention that he knew the demon would understand.

And, of course, Zalith did.

An understanding smirk tugged at the corners of Zalith's lips before he complied, kissing his way down Alucard's body with agonizing slowness, leaving trails of warmth in his wake. The vampire shuddered, anticipation curling in his stomach as Zalith reached his waist, a small groan escaping him as the demon's sharp fangs grazed his inner thigh. He didn't have time to react before Zalith's mouth was around his dick, sending a jolt of sheer pleasure through his trembling body.

Alucard moaned, his head tipping back against the tiled wall, fingers tightening in Zalith's hair as euphoria seized him. "This... feels... so good," he uttered breathlessly, his voice thick with need.

Zalith glanced up at him, his dark eyes gleaming with satisfaction. "Good," he murmured with a smirk, and then he returned to his work.

Alucard moaned in delight, his free hand gripping his own thigh as waves of sheer, intoxicating pleasure rippled through him. But the warm water falling over him didn't compare to the warmth *inside* him—the heat racing, tightening, building with every slow motion of Zalith's mouth. The demon worked him over, lips and tongue dragging over his sensitive inches, pulling quiet, breathless gasps from his parted lips.

Zalith's tongue swirled around his tip, flicking over the most sensitive spot with teasing precision before he took him deeper, sucking just the way Alucard loved. The vampire whimpered, thighs tensing as his pleasure intensified, toes curling against the slick tiles below. The deeper Zalith took him, the more overwhelming it became— *too* much, *just* enough. Each bob of the demon's head sent sparks of euphoria through his trembling body, every pull of his lips tightening the knot in Alucard's body until he felt like he might break apart completely.

And then, just like before, he *did.*

His body tensed, a delighted moan breaking from his throat as pleasure crashed over him in a blinding rush. His orgasm hit with an intensity that left him reeling, his body tightening, trembling as he scowled in both struggle and sheer contentment. Again, it didn't stop; the euphoria stretched on, rolling through him in powerful, lingering waves, his release drawn out, leaving him gasping, breathless, utterly lost in the sheer force of it.

His moans turned to desperate, alleviated whines as he came heavily, spurts of hot, thick release spilling into Zalith's eager mouth. The demon swallowed him down without hesitation, his lips sealing around him as his throat worked greedily, not letting a single drop go to waste. The sensation of it, the *way* Zalith took him in so willingly, so possessively, only prolonged the pleasure that wracked Alucard's body. His vision blurred, white-hot bliss coursing through every nerve, leaving him limp, weak, and trembling in the demon's mouth.

And as the last shivers of release ran through him, he exhaled a deep, shuddering sigh, slumping against the wall, satisfied... yet still craving more.

"Zalith…" he groaned, dazed, his voice nothing more than a breath against the humid air. His hand slipped down the demon's back, gripping him weakly as Zalith kissed his way back up his body, slow and indulgent. When their faces were mere inches apart, the demon rested his forehead against his, their breaths mingling in the warm steam.

"I like it when you say my name," Zalith murmured, dragging his thumb over Alucard's bottom lip.

The vampire smiled, taking a quiet moment to admire Zalith's face. He felt good—better than he should have, considering how many times they'd indulged in each other already. Normally, by now, he would have started to feel sluggish, his body drained from giving Zalith so much of his energy. But this time…he didn't. If anything, he felt *more* invigorated than before stepping into the shower, his body thrumming with a strange, lingering vitality.

Whatever this was—this unexpected shift in his body, this *heat*—it was something he could already appreciate. He could enjoy every intimate moment with Zalith without suffering the usual exhaustion, without needing to pace himself or recover. And he had no doubt that Zalith relished the change just as much. It might only last a month, but Alucard was certain he'd make the most of every moment.

"Do you feel tired?" Zalith asked curiously as he guided his hand to the side of Alucard's neck, his thumb lightly tracing his skin.

Alucard shook his head, a small, pleased smirk curving his lips. "No," he murmured. "I feel fine—maybe…*more* awake than when we got up."

Zalith's eyes gleamed with amusement. "Oh, good," he hummed before tilting his head and pressing his lips to Alucard's, sealing his approval with a slow kiss.

"How…bad is this going to get?" he then asked. "We still have things to do; I don't want to be distracted—or *distracting*," he mumbled.

"It's a little different for everyone based on their body chemistry," the demon said, fiddling with Alucard's crucifix chain. "You'll probably feel distracted here and there, but I don't think it'll be *unbearably* distracting. You're not an incubus, so your mind can focus on other things a whole lot easier," he laughed.

The vampire smiled curiously. "How bad is it for *you*?"

"It's pretty bad," he replied. "And it'll drive *you* crazy, too, I'm sure," he said with an amused chuckle. "But we'll cross that bridge when we get to it." He patted the vampire's ass.

With a quiet sigh, Alucard pouted and dragged his hands down Zalith's arms. "I guess we will," he said. "Are you ready to get out?"

"I'm ready," Zalith said with a nod.

They stepped out of the shower, steam curling in the air around them as they reached for their towels. Alucard ran the fabric through his hair, absently noting how much longer it had grown—longer than he usually let it get. His gaze drifted to Zalith as the demon pulled on his white shirt, his damp hair falling in dark, tousled waves. He looked good like this—dishevelled, relaxed—but Alucard knew he'd complain about it eventually. *Maybe they should get our hair cut later.*

Once they were both dressed, Alucard took hold of Zalith's hand and followed him downstairs, the warmth of the morning lingering on his skin. Their brief escape into indulgence was over, but the day had only just begun.

Chapter Fifty

— ⊰ ✝ ⊱ —

Intoxicating, Devouring

| **Zalith**—*Uzlia Isles, Usrul* |

Settling into the carriage, Zalith sighed deeply, allowing himself a moment to relax. He was ready to tackle the day, but the undeniable pull of Alucard's heat lingered in the back of his mind—a constant, intoxicating distraction. Not that he minded. If anything, it only heightened everything about Alucard that already drove him wild. His scent, richer and more potent than usual, stirred something primal deep in Zalith's chest. The way his body responded, the barely restrained eagerness in his touch, the subtle changes in his demeanour—it was all designed to entice, to demand attention, and it worked. Every fibre of Zalith's being urged him to claim, to satisfy, to revel in the instincts that had been set alight by Alucard's heat.

But alongside the overwhelming desire, another instinct surged just as strongly—possessiveness. It wasn't rational, nor was it something that Zalith could simply suppress. His incubus nature made him hyper-aware of the scent that his fiancé was giving off; he had no intention of letting another demon so much as look at Alucard the wrong way. The thought of anyone else sensing even a fraction of what he could made his fangs itch. His jaw tightened slightly as he gazed at the vampire beside him, watching the way he absentmindedly fidgeted with his sleeve, his expression tinged with that restless need he was still getting used to.

Zalith exhaled slowly, forcing himself to shake it off. He knew Alucard belonged to him—he knew that there was no risk of anyone else taking what was his. But his body didn't care about logic. It only cared about ensuring that no one else got the chance.

And yet, he knew he had to focus. There was work to be done, and as much as he wanted to drag Alucard back upstairs and keep him to himself until his heat passed, they couldn't afford to lock themselves away.

Not yet, anyway.

"Should we go and get our hair cut later?" Alucard asked, glancing at him.

Zalith nodded. "Sure—as long as the barber isn't out rioting in the streets."

Alucard laughed quietly as he rested his head on Zalith's shoulder. "Do you think Cecil will be gone by tonight?"

"That would be nice."

The demon exhaled slowly, forcing himself to settle. He needed to focus on the day ahead—on the work that still had to be done, on Cecil, who would hopefully be removed from the equation by nightfall. But Alucard's presence was impossible to ignore. That alluring, demanding scent wrapped around him like an intoxicating spell, clawing at the edges of his control, making it agonizing to think about anything else.

His instincts fought against him, every inch of his being urging him to take, claim, and satisfy. His body knew exactly what Alucard needed from him—what he craved in return—but Zalith had to resist.

He turned his head, nuzzling against Alucard's hair as his fingers absently toyed with the strands. And of course, the worry crept in. He knew how overwhelming his touch could be—how easy it was for him to take too much without even meaning to. Alucard had insisted that he felt fine after this morning, but Zalith still found himself hesitating. He didn't want to hurt him. No matter how much Alucard's body could handle right now, no matter how much his heat suppressed the usual signs of fatigue, Zalith couldn't forget the simple truth: every time they had sex, he drained him. It was in his nature—it couldn't be helped.

And yet…his hands ached to touch him, and his instincts burned to please him.

Zalith shifted, trying to get comfortable, but there was no escaping it. His restraint was wearing thin, stretched taut like a fraying rope. Giving in just a little, he nuzzled Alucard's neck, inhaling a slow breath through his nose.

The effect was instant. His usual scent had always been enough to excite him, but this—this was something else entirely. It wound around him like a vice, squeezing tighter with each second, sinking into his skin, into his bones, into the deepest, most primal part of him. It made him restless. Ravenous. Distressed. His instincts twisted inside him, tangled between frustration and desire. The need to please, to devour—to make sure that no one else got close—it was overwhelming.

It was as if he were some starving beast being lured into a trap by something impossibly sweet, something irresistible. And that was exactly what this was to him—a temptation so intoxicating, so maddening, it bordered on torment. He wanted more. He wanted everything. But all he could allow himself to do right now was sit there, inhale deeply, and drown in the sensation of it.

For a while, as the carriage rolled over the bridge from Usrul to Yrudberg, Zalith remained utterly still. Not a word, not a movement—just the slow, steady rhythm of his breath against Alucard's skin. His lips brushed against the vampire's neck, his arms curled possessively around him as if holding him closer might somehow satisfy the insatiable craving his scent had ignited.

It was all-consuming. Every breath he took dragged him deeper into the intoxicating haze of Alucard's heat, drowning out everything else. He barely registered the distant shouts of protestors gathering in the streets of Oklens. Let them riot. Let the world burn if it wanted to. None of it mattered. The only thing worth his attention—the only thing worth *anything* was right there in his arms. *His.*

And fuck…what he wouldn't give to tear the clothes from his body right now. To lay him out beneath him, to feel every inch of his skin, to drown in the warmth and pleasure and sweetness of him until there was nothing left but this need—this unbearable, maddening need.

"This doesn't look good," Alucard muttered.

Alucard's words registered somewhere in the back of Zalith's mind, but they were distant—background noise to the more primal urges flooding his senses. The pheromones pouring from the vampire's body clouded his thoughts. He could barely think past the overwhelming need—to undress him, to touch him, to feel him trembling beneath his hands. The image flashed in his mind, vivid and torturous—Alucard bent over one of these seats, his flushed skin against the cool leather, his voice breaking in those desperate, breathless moans that drove Zalith to the brink. The way he whimpered, the way he gripped at Zalith's shoulders, the way he gasped his name like a plea—he needed to hear that. It was unbearable. His claws flexed against the seat, restraint fraying. He could take him right here—

"Zalith?"

The vampire's voice pulled him back just enough—just enough to realize that Alucard was touching him, his fingers trailing up his arm. His gaze snapped to the vampire's face, and it didn't help at all. Alucard was staring at him, his expression tinged with confusion, oblivious to just how devastating he was in this moment.

Zalith swallowed hard, fighting the sharp, possessive growl threatening to escape.

"Are you okay?" his fiancé asked.

"Mm-hmm," Zalith hummed, his voice a low murmur of satisfaction as his fingers trailed up Alucard's chest, settling against the side of his neck. His hand flexed slightly, savouring the feel of his vampire's skin beneath his palm. He needed more. Sitting here, inhaling that intoxicating scent—it was torture.

He wanted to taste him.

The urge sank its claws into him, insatiable and relentless. To drag his tongue over Alucard's throat, to feel the warmth of his skin against his lips, to claim him in a way no one else ever could. But no…. No. If he did that, he wouldn't stop. He wouldn't be able to. And they had things to do. He couldn't let himself lose control.

But it was getting *so much fucking harder to resist.*

The demon clenched his jaw, battling himself, the war between want and restraint tightening in his chest.

He was spiralling. Overwhelmed, desperate, frustrated beyond reason. And what made it worse was that he knew Alucard would give him everything he wanted if he asked. That was the problem. One kiss would lead to more, one taste would ruin whatever fragile hold he had left.

His claws twitched against Alucard's skin. He needed it. He wanted it. And he knew he could have it.

"We're almost there," the vampire said, fiddling with the gold chain around Zalith's neck.

"Where?" the demon asked with a quiet laugh, pushing the desire aside as best he could.

"The townhouse."

"Oh." For a moment, he actually forgot where they were headed.

"Were you falling asleep?" Alucard laughed.

"I could never," the demon replied.

Alucard smiled and turned his head to look down at him. "You seem pretty sleepy."

"I'm not sleepy," he said with a smile, resting the back of his head on Alucard's shoulder, gazing up at him. "You just smell really good."

A flustered look appeared on the vampire's face. "Do I?" he asked quietly.

He smirked. "You do."

"What...do I smell like?"

Zalith fiddled with Alucard's hair. "Yourself, but...better—*so* much better."

Alucard smiled and exhaled deeply, relaxing.

The demon spared a small glance to the window, seeing that they were now in the Bauwell Residential District; they were moving along Saint Arkan Street, almost to their townhouse.

"What's the plan after breakfast?" Alucard asked.

Zalith nuzzled the vampire's neck, inhaled quietly, and made himself comfortable again. "We work," he answered, his voice barely above a whisper.

Alucard silently rested his head on the demon's—maybe he was sinking into the bliss, too.

As the carriage eventually slowed to a halt, Zalith barely registered it. His focus remained locked on Alucard. He spared another small glance outside as they arrived at their townhouse; he knew what came next—the moment they stepped out, the real world would demand their attention. Work. Plans. Responsibilities.

But right now, he wasn't ready to let go.

As Alucard shifted to stand, Zalith's grip tightened, his instincts flaring. "Wait." His voice came low and firm, his arms instinctively pulling Alucard closer before he even fully realized what he was doing.

Zalith held Alucard close, nuzzling into his neck as he inhaled deeply, savouring the intoxicating scent that had been driving him mad since the moment he woke. He pressed a slow, lingering kiss to his vampire's skin, and the way Alucard tensed beneath him sent a surge of satisfaction through his body. He could feel the slight way his fiancé's fingers curled against his arm—silent proof that his touch was unravelling him.

A quiet chuckle left him. This—*this* was what he wanted. To feel Alucard's body react so helplessly to him, to know that his vampire craved him just as desperately as he did in return. He dragged his hand along Alucard's neck, revelling in the warmth of his skin beneath his palm.

Then, he rested his forehead against Alucard's, his smirk never fading. He could sense the war happening inside his mate—the struggle to remain focused, to resist the desire clawing at his body. But Zalith knew the truth. He knew how easily Alucard would break if he only pushed a little harder.

He had to wait, though. They both did.

Chapter Fifty-One

— ≺ ✝ ≻ —

Utterly Entranced

| **Alucard**—*Uzlia Isles, Yrudberg, Eimwood City* |

The morning air carried the distant shouts of the protestors as Alucard sat at the small breakfast table on their townhouse's balcony. Across from him, Zalith barely touched his food, his dark eyes fixed intently on him rather than the gathering crowd outside Cecil's manor. The demon's gaze was weighty, unwavering.

Alucard lifted his cup, sipping his hot chocolate as he caught Zalith staring again. He knew exactly what he was thinking about; he'd sensed it since they had woken up, the way Zalith's focus was split between the situation with Cecil and the lingering distraction that had been plaguing them both.

Zalith finally broke the stare, offering a small smile before returning his attention to his plate. At least he was trying to focus on something else. He took another bite of his food, though his occasional glances towards the protesters suggested that his thoughts were elsewhere.

Alucard turned his attention to the streets below. Even from their balcony, he could see the tension rising in the square, the way the crowd thickened outside Cecil's manor, their voices carrying frustration and anger. He narrowed his eyes slightly, scanning the windows of the grand house in the distance. Just as he expected, every window was occupied—Cecil's councilmen stood like statues, watching the protest unfold from behind the safety of glass.

Just then, a quiet knock came at the lounge door.

Alucard and Zalith turned their heads and watched as Idina walked, looking like she had news to share. However, when she came closer, she first looked perplexed, but then she blushed and stopped in her tracks, her eyes focused on Alucard. Evidently, Zalith wasn't the only one who could tell that he was in heat—nor was he the only one who seemed utterly entranced. Idina's stare widened, and she seemed almost stunned.

Zalith growled quietly, *possessively*.

But Idina snapped out of it, shaking her head as she set her eyes on Zalith. "Um... Soren said he has some news for you—he wants to see you both," she said firmly, clearly trying to fight the distraction. "And..." she said, glancing at Alucard, "...Castellan needs to see you, too. He said the elves are planning something."

Alucard sighed and looked down at his plate. "Fine. Tell Soren we'll see him later and tell Castellan I will... see him in about an hour."

Zalith nodded in agreement.

"Soren probably has everything ready," the vampire said, glancing at his mate.

"I hope it's good," he mumbled.

"That's all," Idina said. She then turned around and left the room—but not without one final glance at Alucard.

"I'm sure whatever Soren has planned will be good," Alucard assured Zalith.

The demon nodded. "I hope so. Should we send Pecker away so we can deal with Castellan first?"

He shrugged. "I'm sure he has work to do here, so... he can wait for us."

Zalith nodded and smiled. "Okay."

As they resumed their breakfast, Alucard cast another glance over his shoulder, his gaze settling on the swelling crowd outside Cecil's manor. It wouldn't be long now. The tension in the air was thick and heavy, the people's anger simmering, ready to boil over. He could already see the inevitable unfolding—soon, they would force their way through the gates, storming Cecil's home without hesitation. And the best part? He and Zalith wouldn't even have to lift a finger. The people of Eimwood would remove Cecil themselves, and when the dust settled, they would have no choice but to turn to Zalith. They'd beg him to take control.

A slow smirk tugged at the corner of Alucard's lips. Everything was falling into place. "So, how do you feel knowing you will soon be Lord Silas?"

"Stressed out," he laughed.

"Why stressed out?" he asked, also laughing a little. "Becoming City Lord means you have done everything you wanted to do here."

"Which means it'll be time to do everything I need to do everywhere else," he said with a sigh and sipped from his coffee. "But things are coming along nicely, so I'm not complaining."

"That's true," the vampire agreed, taking another piece of Boszorkian toast. "But you're getting through everything really quickly; you do so much for everyone, Zalith... and I'm proud of you," he said quietly, trying to make sure that Zalith knew just how highly he thought of him, and how much he appreciated the things he was doing. "You've done so much."

"Thank you, baby," Zalith said, smiling at him.

While they continued eating, Alucard started to reflect. It had been a long week, but things were finally starting to conclude. Hopefully by tonight, he and Zalith would be Eimwood's new leaders. Zalith's army was growing, and he was sure that they were soon to convene and discuss their next plans regarding taking out Lilith. First, though, Alucard had to meet with his Coven Masters and sort out whatever was happening in the world of vampires. Then, it would be time to finish growing Zalith's army. They still needed a Pandorican before they set their sights on Lilith herself, but Zalith was the most dangerously dedicated man he knew, and there was no way any of this was going to fail.

He finished his toast and asked the demon, "After we meet my Coven Masters, are we going to organize a meeting with everyone and discuss what's next with the Lilith plan?"

Zalith nodded. "Yeah."

"I sent a message to one of my vampires to tell Camael and Tyrus to meet—he will remove the tracking ethos from Tyrus, and then we will be able to safely meet him," he said, leaning back in his seat. "Maybe we can invite him to the discussion?"

The demon sighed quietly as he rested his arms on the table. "I'm just not sure if I trust that Camael knows what he's doing, or if he even has good intentions."

Alucard understood why Zalith was skeptical—he was, too. He didn't trust any angel, least of all one who seemed so eager to help them for an unknown reason. So, he shrugged but laughed a little. "The only other way I can think of getting rid of the tracking ethos would be to kill him. When someone dies, their ethos withers, along with any other ethos within them," he said, but as a reluctant look appeared on Zalith's face, the vampire frowned. "We'd bring him back to life," he assured him. "Well...not exactly—" he rested his arms on the table. "What I'm saying is...I turned Danford into a vampire—that should be impossible. Maybe I can turn a demon, too."

"I don't know," Zalith said. "I don't want to risk losing him."

He nodded—there would be no risk...if he really did have a Lumendatt inside him. Maybe now was the time to tell Zalith and ask for his help. He exhaled deeply before saying, "Well...I need to...tell you something—this reminds me."

"What?"

Alucard took a moment, trying to work out what to say. But if he gave it too much thought, he might overwhelm himself. So, he took a deep breath and looked down at his arms. "I...the night before last, I had a...it wasn't a nightmare; it was...a memory," he said, looking at him. "I...remember why Lucifer and Lilith didn't just kill me when I freed him when I was younger. Lilith said that...I have a Lumendatt—the thing the Numen use to create and manipulate life—living things. It was...dormant, and when Janus came to me and 'made me a vampire', I think he just...activated the Lumendatt, which meant I could use it to do some of the things the Numen can do; that's how I make vampires, I think—if I *do* have a Lumendatt. It *would* make sense; I mean...none of the other scions or blood-children of the Numen can create a species like I have," he explained slowly. He then sighed, sure that he was dragging on. "What I am saying, is... if I have a Lumendatt, then... I could make Tyrus into a vampire and remove the tracking ethos. As well as that, I could use it to create different, *stronger* vampires for our cause—for *your* army."

"*Our* army," Zalith corrected, smiling a little. "How do we tell if you have one or not?"

The vampire frowned uncomfortably—and he was sure that what he was about to say would make Zalith feel just as so. "Well... I can't do it myself. I would... need *you*... to put your hand into my body and search for it," he said slowly. "From what I've heard over the years... it would be behind or around my heart somewhere."

A conflicted, almost distressed frown appeared on Zalith's face.

Alucard laughed a little. "It's a stupid idea. But there's no other way to be certain."

"It's not a stupid idea," his mate said. "I just don't know if I'm on board with putting a part of my body in that particular part of yours."

The vampire shrugged. "It'll be okay. We're both not going to like it, but... I will heal, and if I do have a Lumendatt, it's going to give us so many more advantages."

Zalith sighed, still looking conflicted. He didn't speak for a few moments, clearly thinking, and then he rested his chin in his hand, sighed again, and leaned back in his seat. "Fine," he agreed.

Alucard could hear the hesitation in Zalith's voice. "We don't have to," he assured him. "I'm not going to make you do something that makes you uncomfortable. We've been managing just fine without a Lumendatt, so we don't really need to know."

"It's worth checking," the demon said with a shake of his head. "Especially if Lilith and Lucifer might know about it—and Damien, too."

That creature's name still sent a shiver down Alucard's spine. He pouted a little, trying to dismiss the flurry of emotions that name struck him with. "We can check later," he said, slouching back in his seat.

"Are you okay?" Zalith asked, obviously noticing his sudden change in mood.

Alucard nodded, glancing inside the lounge. "Can we... go inside?"

The demon nodded. "Of course."

They left the breakfast table and stepped into the lounge. As Alucard made his way towards the couch, Zalith pulled the balcony doors shut, drawing the heavy mahogany curtains to block out the daylight. The vampire sank onto the couch, sighing softly as he settled in. His mate joined him, shifting close until they fit together in a familiar embrace—the vampire resting against the demon's chest, with strong arms wrapped tightly around him.

For a while, he just wanted to stay like that. The steady warmth of Zalith's body soothed him, chasing away the disquiet that Damien's name had stirred. He focused on the comfort of his embrace, the solid reassurance of his presence, and the way Zalith always seemed to anchor him. But even as the lingering ache dulled, something else took its place—something stronger, more insistent. His thoughts drifted, his skin tingling with awareness of the demon's touch, the way his breath warmed his neck. A quiet sigh escaped him as Zalith nuzzled against his throat, his lips barely brushing over sensitive skin.

The melancholy faded. Alucard turned onto his back, pulling Zalith with him. His mate wasted no time in pressing closer, resting his weight atop him, head nestled against his shoulder as his fingers skimmed over his chest before settling at the curve of his neck. Alucard smiled as he felt the demon inhale deeply, clearly entirely captivated by the scent he now carried. He let his own hand drift down Zalith's back, slipping beneath his untucked shirt to glide over his smooth, heated skin.

Zalith exhaled a slow breath, his fingers drifting from Alucard's neck to tangle in his hair. He toyed with the strands for a moment, his touch absentminded yet possessive, before shifting even closer. The warmth of his body pressed in, and then—Alucard shivered as the demon dragged his tongue gradually over his neck.

A quiet hum of satisfaction escaped the vampire, but it wasn't just the teasing stroke of Zalith's tongue that sent a rush of anticipation through his body. He could feel the demon's arousal against his thigh, hardening, pressing insistently against him. His own body responded in kind, his arousal growing. He sighed, tilting his head slightly, offering his neck as his fingers ghosted down Zalith's spine.

And then the demon licked his neck again.

Alucard laughed quietly as he ran his fingers through Zalith's hair. "Why do you keep doing that?" he asked curiously. "Do I taste nice?"

"Yes," Zalith answered seductively as he nuzzled his face against the vampire's neck again.

Smirking, Alucard lifted his right leg, hooking it over Zalith's waist and pulling him in, pressing their arousals together. "What do I taste like?"

"Sex," the demon answered, kissing his neck just below his ear.

He smiled, a little fluster smothering his face; Zalith's answer sent an enticing shudder through his body. His voice, his simple, snappy answers—Alucard knew that his mate was totally mesmerized, and he had no plan to make either of them wait any longer. "Fuck me," he pleaded quietly into Zalith's ear.

Zalith smirked against Alucard's neck. "Okay." Without hesitation, he unfastened the vampire's shirt, peeling it away before tossing it aside.

Alucard wasted no time in returning the favour, yanking the demon's shirt over his head and working at his belt with impatient fingers. As soon as the leather slipped free, his hand found its way into his mate's trousers, gripping his arousal as his own anticipation sharpened into desperation.

The demon caught his lips in another kiss before swiftly unbuckling Alucard's belt and sliding his trousers down his legs. A quiet laugh escaped the vampire, his breath unsteady as excitement coursed through him. Their hands moved in tandem, tearing away the last of their clothing, urgency fuelling every touch. With a low, eager growl, Zalith buried his face against Alucard's neck, sinking his teeth into his skin—not enough to bite down, but enough to claim, to tease. Alucard groaned, pleasure sparking through him as he tangled his fingers into the demon's hair. His other hand continued stroking Zalith's length, his own body trembling with need as the heat between them threatened to consume him entirely.

Alucard hooked his leg over Zalith's back, releasing his grip on the demon's shaft just as Zalith took over, stroking himself and smoothing warm, slick lube over his inches and against Alucard's ass. There was no hesitation, no pause—Zalith guided his dick forward, slowly pressing into Alucard's body. A deep, unrestrained moan slipped from Alucard's lips, his claws digging into Zalith's bicep as the demon nuzzled his neck, releasing a contented groan of his own. He pushed deeper, filling Alucard completely, and the sensation sent a shiver racing through the vampire's already trembling body.

Nothing else compared to this. The bliss, the sheer exhilaration—it was almost unbearable in its intensity. His heart pounded, his breathing ragged as wave after wave of pleasure coursed through him, leaving no room for anything else. Every thrust, every brush of Zalith's body against his own only made it stronger. Alucard whined, moaned, gasped his mate's name, barely able to think beyond the searing pleasure. Zalith murmured his own sounds of delight, his grip tightening, his movements growing faster, deeper, harder. The scrape of claws against skin only heightened the euphoria, sending another shock of pure sensation through Alucard's overwhelmed body. He could feel himself trembling, but there was no exhaustion—only satisfaction, only Zalith.

And then Zalith shifted him, urging him forward onto his hands and knees. Alucard obeyed, bracing himself as the demon grabbed hold of his waist, keeping him steady as he drove forward again. Their erratic breaths filled the space between them, blending with the rhythmic sounds of their bodies moving together. Alucard loved this—he loved the raw pleasure of it, the sounds Zalith made, the way he clutched him with such possession. More than anything, he loved knowing that he was bringing his mate just as much pleasure as he was receiving, and that knowledge only made his own desire burn hotter.

As his arms started to ache, Alucard intended to brace himself on his elbows, but before he could, Zalith pressed a firm hand over his, grounding him in place. The demon tilted forward, his breath warm against the back of Alucard's neck as he continued thrusting deep inside him. A low, satisfied moan left Zalith's lips, and then his tongue traced a slow, tantalizing path along the side of Alucard's throat before his fangs sank deep into his skin.

The moment the venom entered his bloodstream, Alucard whined, his entire body seizing with an almost unbearable pleasure. His legs trembled beneath him, his moans turning desperate, fevered. The sensation was scorching, electrifying—Zalith's venom always heightened his pleasure, but now, in the throes of his heat, it was near maddening. His mate groaned against his throat, licking at the fresh bite as his hands slid down the vampire's back, fingers tracing over his scars before gripping his waist with a possessive, unrelenting hold. He pulled him back into each thrust, deep and insistent, their breaths erratic.

Alucard's body began to unravel, struggling under the weight of the overwhelming pleasure surging through him. Every muscle tensed, a helpless whine slipping from his lips as his climax approached, thick and burning inside him. His arms buckled, and he slumped onto the cushion below, gripping the fabric in a trembling hold. His moans turned breathless, desperate, his entire body tightening—and then the sensation struck him like a tidal wave, drowning him in a release so intense that it stole his breath. He came *hard*, his back arching as his body convulsed with the sheer force of it. It lasted even longer than the last, stretching into what felt like an eternity of pleasure; his own release pooled below him, and even then, the pleasure didn't stop—the residual waves of his climax rippled through him, making him whimper as his body continued to shudder.

Zalith groaned in delight, his hold tightening, and Alucard barely had a moment to recover before he felt the demon's own pleasure reach its peak. A delighted moan sat upon Zalith's deep exhale as his grip on Alucard's waist became bruising, his body tensing before his climax surged deep inside him. Alucard shuddered, his exhausted body overcome with yet another wave of euphoria as he felt the heat of Zalith's cum filling him. Once again, his body was left feeling as if it had just been fulfilled in some life-altering way. His heart pounded in his chest, his limbs weak, his mind hazy with pleasure as Zalith leaned over him, panting against his skin, neither of them moving, both still lost in the aftermath.

Alucard exhaled deeply, his trembling body sinking into Zalith's as he stretched his legs out behind him, the lingering waves of pleasure still pulsing faintly through his limbs. He felt weightless—utterly relieved. Every ounce of tension had melted from his muscles, leaving behind only a blissful haze that wrapped around him like a comforting embrace. As he closed his eyes, another slow, satisfied sigh left his lips.

With a quiet hum, Zalith reached out, grabbing a handful of tissues from the table nearby. He moved carefully, wiping away the evidence of Alucard's release from his stomach and the cushion below before tossing them aside. Only then did he lay onto his side, pulling Alucard against him with an arm around his waist, shifting him until he lay atop his chest.

Alucard melted into the warmth of the demon's body, sighing contently as he rested his head against him. He nuzzled into the crook of Zalith's neck, pressing a slow, lingering kiss to his skin. "Thank you," he murmured, his voice quiet, almost drowsy as he let himself settle into the comfort of his mate's embrace.

"Thank *you*," Zalith said, kissing the side of Alucard's head.

The vampire smiled curiously. "Do I still make you feel distracted? Or now that you've fucked me, has your overwhelming need to do so withered?"

"It'll never wither," the demon said, hugging him tightly. "You're too hot."

Alucard laughed quietly. "You're hotter than me. I find everything about you irresistible. If I were like you, we would be doing this a lot more—every day," he said with a smirk, dragging his fingers over Zalith's left pec.

"*All* day. We'd never get anything done," his mate laughed.

The vampire shrugged. "Maybe it's a good thing, then. We both have a lot of things we have to do."

"Maybe," the demon agreed.

A comfortable silence fell between them. While they rested, Alucard found himself thinking about what Idina had said. Castellan had news about the Yrudyen Elves. They were up to something? Alucard was certain that it could only be bad news. He and Zalith were just hours away from becoming Eimwood's new leaders; the last thing they needed was another problem to deal with once Cecil was gone. What did these elves even do for them here? Nothing. They were just an annoyance. Alucard felt no guilt about considering just killing them or banishing them. The Uzlia Isles belonged to him and Zalith. Anyone who didn't respect that had to go.

"What are we going to do about the Yrudyen?" he asked.

Zalith sighed deeply. "They either accept that we're in charge now or they die."

"From what we've learnt, these elves don't seem like the type to roll over. We can try to reason with them, but…in this case, I feel we would do better to kill them."

"I don't know. I don't want to commit genocide."

"If they don't want to listen, that might be the only option. If we fight and let them go, they could come back with more numbers and cause us problems later down the line."

The demon sighed again. "Is it worth finding a way to resolve things in relative peace?"

Alucard thought to himself for a few moments. "Well…we know that they follow a single queen and that they cherish the natural world. Before this whole queen thing, they worshipped Khila—Khila protected their people from any and all harm. Maybe…we could talk to their queen—become their new protectors. If they had an arrangement with Cecil, maybe they can make one with us."

Zalith nodded. "We'll send someone to see if they're open to negotiating, and we'll go from there."

"Maybe we should go. Elves are...easily offended. If we send a messenger, they might think that we don't respect them enough to ask ourselves. And we will need to take a gift for the queen—something of great value to us. This is the highest form of respect."

The demon sighed *again*. "Fine," he mumbled.

Frowning, Alucard lifted his head and leaned on his arms so that he could look down at Zalith. "You don't sound very happy about that."

"I'm not," he laughed.

"Why? What's wrong?"

"Nothing's wrong. It's just more problems we have to deal with."

Alucard smiled and flicked Zalith's loose fringe. He then relaxed again, resting his head on his mate's shoulder. "Well, why don't you stay here and work on whatever you like, and *I* will go out there with Castellan and deal with the Yrudyen?" he suggested—but he was sure Zalith was going to say no, and he immediately felt stupid for suggesting it, even if he was half-joking. Zalith didn't want to let him out of his sight, and Alucard didn't want to leave him worrying.

"No," the demon said, a possessive, protective tone in his voice as he tightened his embrace around Alucard.

"I was just joking," he assured him. "I won't go anywhere without you."

"Good," the demon mumbled, kissing his head.

The vampire exhaled deeply, shuffling around. "Should we go and try to talk to the Yrudyen soon—get that out of the way?"

"Shouldn't we wait around and make sure the Cecil plan works before we start acting like we own the place?" he questioned amusedly.

Alucard shrugged. "It's going to work," he said confidently. "But we can wait. The question is, though...what do we do while we wait?"

"I suppose we can go and see Pecker," the demon grumbled.

Alucard smirked as sex possessed his mind again. This whole being in heat thing was starting to feel like a problem to him; he wasn't very wilful when it came to ignoring his need for affection, and if it kept happening as often as it had been and didn't stop until he got what he needed, then he was certain that it was going to drive him insane at some point, especially since it felt as though it was getting worse.

He sighed, stroking his fingers over Zalith's chest. "Are you going to fuck me first?"

The demon chuckled. "Can you handle it?"

"Can *you*?" he questioned, his smirk growing.

"I could go for *days*," Zalith said, dragging his fingers down Alucard's back.

Alucard sat up. "We will see about that," he tested.

Zalith slid his hand to the back of Alucard's neck, fingers threading through his hair as he pulled him closer, their lips meeting in a slow, heated kiss. The world outside their embrace faded into irrelevance—there was only the warmth of Zalith's body, the intoxicating scent that clung to Alucard's skin, the unspoken hunger simmering between them.

Alucard melted into it as Zalith deepened the kiss; he settled against him, anticipation thrumming through his veins, his body already alight with the same feverish need that had consumed him all morning. His patience wavered, but he knew it wouldn't be long—not with the way Zalith held him, the way his touch promised to fulfil every desperate craving.

The room around them dimmed into obscurity, lost to the growing heat between them, and as Alucard surrendered to Zalith's embrace, nothing else mattered.

Chapter Fifty-Two

— ⊰ ✝ ⊱ —

The Final Predicament

| **Zalith**—*Uzlia Isles, Yrudberg, Yrudberg Woods* |

Beneath the thick canopy of the Yrudberg Woods' towering trees, Zalith and Alucard rode side by side, their horses moving at a steady pace along the well-worn path. The air carried the fresh scent of damp earth and cedar, the sounds of rustling leaves and distant bird calls filling the otherwise quiet stretch of forest. They were heading towards the Yrudyen village, a place nestled on the far side of the vast mountain range that acted as a natural divide between Eimwood and the elves' secluded land.

Before departing, they'd taken the time to trim their hair back to its usual lengths—something Zalith hadn't given much thought to, though Alucard had been the one to insist. More importantly, they had ensured that they brought a suitable gift for the Yrudyen Queen. A diamond pendant from Alucard's vault now rested securely within Zalith's coat, an offering that, according to the vampire, would be seen as a great sign of respect. Elves placed deep significance on gifts, especially when those gifts came from the personal possessions of the giver. And while Zalith didn't particularly care for such formalities, he knew how important it was to make the right impression—especially given the tensions surrounding their visit.

Zalith was deep in thought, struggling but managing to pull his focus from Alucard's irresistible pheromones just enough for him to be able to think. He felt irritated; he didn't want to have to do this, and he didn't feel like negotiating *at all*. But he'd rather take the time to try and do so rather than kill every single Yrudyen elf. He was hopeful that it would work out—he really didn't want to have to be dealing with any more conflict right now. He and Alucard had enough on their plates.

Perhaps, if negotiations failed, he could just manipulate the elves' minds and get them to do what he wanted. Was that even possible? He didn't know much about elves at all—they didn't exist in Eltaria, and when he moved to Aegisguard, he and Varana had only really learned what they needed to know to blend in and appear as though they were elves. He didn't know about their abilities or resistances, either, but he was sure that Alucard would know—his vampire was very knowledgeable, one of the very many things that he found extremely attractive about the man he loved.

"Are elves resistant to mind manipulation?" he asked Alucard.

Alucard glanced at him as their horses followed the path that led up the side of the mountain. "Some of them are, yes," he answered. "The Yrudyen are vysočina elves, though, and from what I know, most vysočina elves are only resistant to ice-based ethos."

Zalith nodded. "What about fire?"

"Fire is actually one of their biggest weaknesses," Alucard said matter-of-factly.

"Are they made of paper?" he laughed.

"Maybe," he said with a shrug. "But fire is a vampire's biggest weakness—it's similar to that. Vysočina are nocturnal; the sunlight hurts their skin. It's why they are so pale."

The demon smiled at him. "Aw, are you made of paper, too?" he teased.

His fiancé pouted and looked away. "No," he grumbled. "I'm like this because I was meant to live in the Underworld and Hell."

Zalith's smile grew. "My little origami boy," he said with a sigh.

Still pouting, Alucard glared ahead. "I'm not made of paper."

"If you say so," he teased him, smirking.

The vampire glanced at him, and as Zalith smiled at him, he looked down at his lap, pouted, and then set his sights back on the demon. "Do you know what you're going to offer the Yrudyen?" he asked, changing the subject.

"Maybe you can tear off a part of your leg and make them some paper cranes."

Alucard scowled again but scoffed moments later. "So, you would share a piece of me with them, huh? And here I was thinking I was all yours."

Amused, the demon laughed. "It's *your* leg; you get to decide who you give the paper cranes to. Although I *will* be jealous."

"If we did make paper cranes out of my paper leg, I'd give them all to you," he sneered.

"That's very nice of you, thank you."

"Seriously, though," Alucard then insisted. "What do you plan to do?"

Zalith thought to himself for a few moments. "I'll try to convince their leader that we, as Eimwood's new leaders, will agree to take care of their people, too, so long as they abide by a set of rules. If their leader refuses, then…we may have to resort to forcibly removing them. But I'm hoping that their leader will hear us out. After all, we're coming all this way ourselves to talk to them."

Alucard nodded as they rode onto a tree-shrouded plateau, the dense foliage overhead casting dappled shadows across the mossy ground. Ahead lay the designated lookout point where Alucard's vampires and demons kept watch over the Yrudyen, their presence a silent but constant reminder that the elves' movements were being carefully monitored. The air here felt heavier, charged with an unspoken tension, as if the very trees bore witness to the quiet power struggle unfolding beyond the mountain's divide.

"We don't know their queen's name," the vampire said. "We should ask Castellan if he knows—they might find it disrespectful of us to not address her properly—if we are even given an audience."

The demon nodded. "Sounds good."

As they neared the tree line marking the entrance to the elves' land, Zalith's gaze locked onto Castellan, who stood waiting. Though the man was merely one of Alucard's subordinates, a quiet sense of possessiveness stirred within the demon. He knew that there was no real threat, but that didn't quell the instinctual urge to assert himself, to make it clear who Alucard belonged to.

His unease only deepened when two of Alucard's demons emerged from the shadows of the towering trees. Both bore the signature traits of their kind—raven-black, ear-length hair and piercing crimson eyes. As their gazes fixed on them, Zalith immediately noticed the shift in their expressions. Their focus snapped to Alucard, admiration—no, fascination—flashing across their faces. Zalith clenched his jaw. They could sense it. Just as Idina had, these demons had fallen under the intoxicating spell of Alucard's heat, and that realization ignited something fierce and territorial within him. His grip on his horse's reins tightened; if they thought for even a second that they could entertain any ideas, they were sorely mistaken.

He kept a close eye on them, his protective instincts intensifying as his and Alucard's horses stopped a few meters from the tree line. Zalith reached over and took hold of Alucard's hand for a moment, watching as Castellan and the two demons came closer.

"My Lord," Castellan greeted, bowing humbly as he and the demons stopped in front of Alucard and Zalith.

"Idina tells me you have some information," Alucard said.

Castellan nodded. "My coven and I have been watching the Yrudyen, as requested. We know of their tri-quarterly rituals; in just over a week is the end of Tertium—"

"Obviously…" Alucard grumbled impatiently.

"At the beginning of Aprilis, the Yrudyen's month of ritual will begin. They sacrifice things to their deceased God, Khila—humans and creatures seen as a disgrace to the natural order are their usual offerings. Through everyone's joint investigations into Cecil and the Yrudyen, it seems as though Cecil had made a deal with the Yrudyen and let them not only take whatever they wanted from the city but let them take its citizens when this time of year came around. Now that Cecil is no longer in a position to let the Yrudyen take as they please, I believe they may attempt to siege Eimwood."

As Castellan spoke, Zalith rolled his eyes and listened, but he kept a close eye on the two male demons fixated on Alucard, not one of them uttering a word or moving a muscle. He knew what they were thinking, and his protective, possessive instincts became stronger the longer he stood there—as did his grip on Alucard's hand.

Alucard frowned. "Right, well...that won't go well for them. We're heading over there to try and reason with their leader. What is her name?"

"Queen Syllia Caiyarus of Yrudberg, My Lord."

"Thank you. Is there anything else?" he asked, glancing at the demons.

"A morbius was spotted in the west, My Lord," the shorter demon said.

"A small boat of refugees has arrived in the north," the other added.

"Keep them away from the city until we decide what to do with them," Alucard instructed.

The man nodded. "Yes, My Lord."

Alucard then asked, "The morbius—is it feral?"

"It doesn't seem to be, My Lord," the shorter demon answered. "I believe it might be a member of the group of refugees that Alec just mentioned."

Alucard nodded. "Keep it away from the city."

"Of course."

"Keep up the good work," Alucard then said. "I will be sending more vampires sometime next week—if anything happens before then, I will send more of my demons."

Castellan and the two demons nodded. Then, they walked off, heading back to the posts.

Alucard squeezed Zalith's hand, smiled at him, and began leading the way into the forest. "What do we do if this Queen Syllia Caiyarus of Yrudberg doesn't want to see us? Or if she isn't interested in our offer?"

"I don't want to have to kill them," Zalith answered. "But if she leaves us no choice, then we'll do what we have to do."

Alucard nodded in agreement, and they continued their journey in silence, keeping their senses peeled for any sign of danger.

| **Alucard**—*Uzlia Isles, Yrudberg, Yrudberg Woods* |

An hour had passed, and still, the Yrudyen village remained unseen. The forest stretched endlessly around them, its towering trees forming an unbroken canopy that filtered the sunlight into shifting patterns on the forest floor. The winding path led them around the mountain's base, past jagged cliffs where mist clung to the rocks, over windswept plateaus where the scent of damp earth and grass lingered in the air, and across narrow rivers that carved silvery trails through the landscape.

The steady rhythm of their horses' hooves against the uneven ground blended with the natural symphony of the wild—the rustling of leaves, the distant cries of unseen birds, and the occasional snap of twigs beneath their mounts. Alucard adjusted his grip on the reins, his sharp gaze scanning the dense foliage ahead. The Yrudyen village was hidden well, concealed within the heart of the forest. He had no doubt that they were close—he could feel eyes on him, and he felt the increase of ethos auras around him.

"Do you think they'll attack?" Zalith asked quietly, obviously having noticed, too.

"No," he answered. "They have probably been watching us for a while—and just as we have done our research on them, they have probably been trying to find out whatever they can about us, too. They know we are demons, and they can sense how much ethos we have. They won't attack someone they know they cannot overpower. They will just watch us until we get too close."

His mate nodded. "At least they're smart."

"They *will* try to stop us, though; they will protect their queen with their lives."

"Also smart."

Sure that the Yrudyen were listening, Alucard telepathically spoke into Zalith's mind, *"The Yrudyen are listening, so we will talk here. We need to come up with a plan before we get there."*

"We should," Zalith agreed, speaking into Alucard's mind. *"Preferably, I'd like these elves to mind their own business—I don't really want them to become involved in our plans or our lives. But... if we have to come to some sort of agreement, then we will. I suppose that this is their land, after all."*

"Well, there is the option of using their beliefs to manipulate them. They highly respect the gods and their children; if we told them who I am, then it would be easy to have them do anything and everything we ask," Alucard suggested as they continued through the forest.

"I don't want them to know who you are," his mate replied protectively, squeezing Alucard's hand. *"If they figure it out on their own, fine, but I do not condone telling them."*

Alucard thought to himself for a moment. *"The Yrudyen love their land and their privacy. They might not be aware of the war and plague spreading through the world— we should make them aware and offer to protect them and their land from it just like we are protecting the people of Eimwood. We can offer to help them with anything else they need, too—treat them like another Eimwood. Give them food and water and supplies. They need to know that Uzlia belongs to us now, and they can either respect our claim and accept our help or we will make them leave—I'm sure they have seen the amount of demons we currently have in our army, not to mention our other allies."*

"Agreed. Hopefully, this will be quick and painless."

The trees around them started to rustle. Alucard sensed a lot of movement around them, but they didn't stop walking. Up ahead, he felt a mass amount of ethos—so much that it could only be the Yrudyen's settlement. They were close, and he was sure that the elves watching them were soon to reveal themselves and try to stop him and Zalith from going any further.

Alucard rolled his eyes. *"Should we keep walking, or should we stop and tell these Yrudyen that we are here to talk to their queen?"*

Zalith stopped walking and sighed. "Might as well say something," he said aloud. Then, he looked around. "We're not here to start conflict," he announced. "We're here to seek an audience with Queen Syllia Caiyarus of Yrudberg in hopes of discussing an arrangement."

The trees shivered as a cold breeze raced past. They both waited, the sound of hushed voices muttering around them. Alucard could sense the elves' temperament had gone from cautious to almost intrigued. Had they been expecting them to come here intending to start a fight? Probably. But that wasn't their *main* intention; it was simply an option if an arrangement wasn't possible.

After a few moments, one of the Yrudyen emerged from the shadows, stepping cautiously into the sparse light filtering through the canopy. He stood no taller than five feet, his silver-blue hair falling straight to his waist, long pointed ears adorned with gold and silver rings. His pale skin, even lighter than Alucard's, seemed almost translucent beneath the dappled sunlight. Dressed in simple beige robes, he carried a bow on his back, a quiver full of black-feathered arrows, and a curved blade strapped to his leg— which one of his fingers twitched towards with clear unease. His bright silver eyes locked onto them with a skeptical, guarded glare. "Her Majesty will not want to see you," he said, his voice edged with quiet hostility.

Zalith smirked. "Well, surely she must if she's planning to siege Eimwood."

The elf frowned and glanced to his left, obviously looking to his comrades for help, but no one came to him. So, he set his sights back on Alucard and Zalith.

"We don't want to be enemies," Alucard said firmly. "The world is in a very unfavourable state right now, and we plan to protect Uzlia from suffering the same fate. Surely, you have all heard of the wars? The plague?"

Again, the elf frowned and looked into the trees, and as he did, Alucard listened as all the hidden, waiting elves started muttering again.

"War?" the elf in front of them asked.

"The Numen and their followers are sweeping Aegisguard in search of something, racing each other to be the first to find it and destroying whoever and whatever gets in their way," Zalith explained slowly. "Even their own supporters."

"We have heard no such thing—"

"And the plague?" Alucard continued. "People turning into undead, blood-starved creatures. One bite and you are infected."

A look of dread appeared on the elf's face.

"Ezra and I have seen it all, and we are doing our best to keep all of Uzlia safe," Zalith followed.

"That's why you built the wall?" another elf asked, emerging from the trees.

"Yes," Alucard answered, looking over at her. "It's also why we are turning away any ships that try to dock here. We are turning Uzlia into…a paradise. No war, no plague, no conflict. It's also why we're removing Cecil—"

"An awful little man," Zalith said with a sigh. "Poisoning his own people…animals and plant life, too—surely, you've heard about *that*?"

The elf looked to his comrades again, frowned, and set his eyes back on Alucard and Zalith. Clearly, the mention of plague and war had unsettled him. Elves *hated* conflict that would ruin their precious land, and such things as war and plague were two very dangerous threats.

Alucard said, "If Queen Syllia Caiyarus is not aware…then at least let us make sure she knows what to expect—if she does not want to align with us, we will…wall off just *our* parts of Uzlia and let you deal with what is to come however you want."

The elf frowned unsurely—

"If what you speak is true…" another woman called. "Then…Queen Syllia Caiyarus of Yrudberg must know—you are demons; you possess the ability to share your memories—you will show me."

Alucard and Zalith turned their attention to her—a tall, lavender-eyed elf, her silvery hair braided and adored with many white, red, and pink flowers. And just like the man who had first approached them, she possessed a bow and stood dressed in beige robes.

"Show me that what you speak of is true…and I will take you to see Her Majesty," she said.

Zalith and Alucard glanced at one another—neither of them wanted to do it. But when Zalith eventually set his sights back on her, he rolled his eyes, sighed, and climbed down off his horse.

Alucard got off his horse, too, observing as the elf watched Zalith approach and prepare himself. Zalith placed his fingers on the elf's face, and it didn't take very long at all for dread to smother the woman's face as Zalith shared with her what she needed to see. Whatever the demon was showing her was obviously upsetting her, and Alucard was certain that she would take them to her queen.

A few moments later, Zalith stepped back, taking hold of his horse's reins in one hand and gripping the vampire's palm in the other.

"It is true," the woman said, her voice shaky as she stared into the darkness of the trees. "They speak the truth—we must take them to see Queen Syllia Caiyarus," she called. Then, she set her eyes back on Alucard and Zalith. "I am Tianel," she introduced herself. "I will take you to see Her Majesty—you must tell her of these threats. Our land is most sacred."

Zalith nodded. "Thank you."

"This way," Tianel said, hurriedly leading the way forward.

They didn't falter. Pulling their horses with them, they followed the elf into the trees, soon to meet Queen Syllia Caiyarus of Yrudberg—soon to solve Uzlia's final problem.

Chapter Fifty-Three

— ⊰ ✝ ⊱ —

Queen Syllia Caivarus of Yrudberg

| **Alucard**—*Uzlia Isles, Yrudberg, The Yrudyen Village* |

Silently, Alucard and Zalith followed Tianel through the dense woodland, leading their horses by the reins with one hand while holding each other's with the other. Their footsteps were muffled against the soft earth, the rhythmic clink of tack the only sound breaking the quiet. More elves flanked them on either side, watchful and tense, their sharp eyes never straying far from the vampire and demon. Like Zalith, Alucard hoped that this meeting would go smoothly—he had no desire to make an enemy of the Yrudyen. He had dealt with enough hostility back home in Dor-Sanguis—well…was it even home anymore? No. Dor-Sanguis was gone. Whatever scraps remained of it belonged to the past.

He kept his eyes fixed ahead, gripping Zalith's hand a little tighter as they neared the entrance to the Yrudyen settlement. The dense forest gradually gave way to an orderly path, the trees perfectly aligned on either side of a dirt road, their roots cradling patches of wildflowers and moss. At the very end stood an archway woven with twisting vines, delicate blossoms, and hand-crafted charms fashioned from feathers, fur, and string. The distant hum of flute music and rhythmic drumming drifted through the air, blending with the whisper of leaves. Despite the tension that came with knowing they were moments away from negotiating a treaty, Alucard found himself unexpectedly at ease. Even Zalith, whose body had been taut with quiet wariness, seemed to relax.

Zalith glanced at him and smiled, a rare moment of quiet reassurance between them. But the instant his mate stepped through the archway, his horns and wings materialized in a flicker of dark energy. Alucard stiffened. It took him no time at all to understand—the archway was an anti-ethos barrier, stripping away disguises and illusions, leaving only one's true form. Dread twisted in his stomach. He stopped abruptly, pulling back, his fingers slipping from Zalith's grasp. He couldn't go through it.

The air around them tensed. Zalith turned to face him, sorrow and understanding reflecting in his dark eyes. The elves, however, were far less patient—Alucard felt their scornful gazes pressing down on him, their irritation unrestrained. But he barely noticed. His focus was locked on the archway, the invisible force beyond it, and the truth it threatened to reveal.

"Are you okay?" Zalith asked before the elves could say anything.

Alucard shook his head. "I don't...want to go in there," he refused.

"You must!" one of the elves called.

"Her Majesty awaits," Tianel insisted.

Zalith frowned. "It's okay—you wait out here. I'll go by myself," he said and glanced at Tianel. "She only needs to see one of us."

That relieved Alucard. He didn't want to be forced into a form that embarrassed him, a form that made him feel ashamed.

"No! You *must* come," Tianel exclaimed. "Unless there is something you wish to hide from us?"

Alucard sighed—

Zalith went to speak—

But Alucard forced himself to step forward. He had no desire to start a conflict, nor did he want to risk ruining this fragile opportunity for a treaty with the Yrudyen. Swallowing his reluctance, he crossed the threshold, bracing himself for what was to come. The moment he did, a familiar, unwelcome sensation rippled through him—his horns materialized atop his head, undeniable proof of what he was.

Humiliation burned through his veins like acid. His first instinct was to lower his head, to shield himself from the weight of judgment that he imagined pressing down on him. Shame enthralled him, silent and suffocating; without a word, he fell into step behind their escort, his gaze fixed on the ground.

Tianel pressed forward without pause, unconcerned by his discomfort, and Alucard—despite the searing embarrassment—followed in silence.

The demon rubbed Alucard's back and took his hand, smiling an assuring smile at him as Alucard glanced his way. *"These elves probably don't know anything about demon society. They're not going to have worthwhile opinions about what either of us look like, either,"* he spoke into Alucard's mind.

"I know," Alucard replied sullenly, but he still felt ashamed of himself.

The elves led them deeper into the settlement, where the village unfolded like something out of an old fable. The homes were woven seamlessly into the land itself—organic structures of mud, carved wood, and interwoven vines, shaped into ovals and domes that looked almost as if they had grown from the earth rather than been built. The rooftops shimmered with bioluminescent moss, casting a faint silver-green glow in the dim patches of shade beneath the towering canopy.

To the left and right, crystal-clear rivers wound through the place, their surfaces reflecting the soft glow of lanterns strung between the trees. Small, luminescent fish darted beneath the water, leaving behind trails of light like fallen stars. As Alucard and Zalith were escorted, wary gazes followed them. Elven villagers whispered among themselves, some clutching their children's hands and gently pulling them back from the path—not out of overt hostility, but caution, their expressions unreadable beneath their shadowed hoods and bone-carved adornments.

Ahead, a colossal oak tree loomed at the heart of the village, its roots coiling like ancient serpents. Embedded within its gnarled base was a grand arched doorway, framed by curling vines and wildflowers that pulsed faintly with residual ethos. From where he stood, Alucard could already make out the throne nestled within—an intricate seat of wood, interwoven flora, and gemstones that seemed to thrum with life, as if it had been shaped by ethos rather than hands. It was clear that this was where they were being taken.

Silent but watchful, the vampire and demon trailed behind their guide towards the tree. As they neared the entrance, the elves who had led them silently peeled away, taking up guarded positions at the perimeter. Tianel directed them to a fur rug, its surface decorated with elaborate etchings that likely bore some cultural significance; positioned roughly ten feet from the throne, it was obvious that this was where they were meant to stand.

Without a word, Tianel turned and disappeared through a doorway carved into the left side of the throne's base, leaving them alone in the expectant hush of the chamber.

For a few moments, they stood in tense silence, pointedly ignoring the sharp, watchful glares of the guards, whose presence was not simply one of caution—it was a quiet, unspoken warning. Alucard could feel the weight of their suspicion pressing against him like a blade at his back. But neither he nor Zalith reacted, keeping their composure while they waited.

Then, with a sudden shift of movement, every guard in the room lowered themselves into a swift bow.

Tianel emerged from the doorway to the left of the throne and announced proudly, "Presenting Her Radiance, Queen Syllia Caiyarus, Keeper of Khila's Diadem, Sovereign of Yrudberg, and Guardian of the Ancestral Bough. May the roots of her wisdom run deep, and may the stars ever bow to her grace."

A presence moved through the shadowed doorway—a woman, tall and poised, moving with an effortless grace that seemed almost otherworldly. Her long, silken-white hair cascaded behind her, trailing across the polished wooden floor like spun moonlight, pooling at the hem of her flowing gown. Unlike the other elves, her ears extended far beyond the usual length, the very tips beginning to curve downward as though shaped by the weight of centuries. The soft glow of the torchlight caught the delicate shimmer of her skin, as though her very flesh had been kissed with stardust. Upon her brow rested a regal diadem, an intricate masterpiece of woven gold and luminous, iridescent crystals that pulsed faintly with ethereal light. The delicate filigree formed celestial motifs, and in the centre, a larger golden gem gleamed with a soft radiance, casting a faint halo around her, lending her an almost angelic presence.

As she approached, her platinum eyes gleamed with interest, settling upon Alucard and Zalith with an expression that was neither welcoming nor unkind—merely intrigued, as if she were studying something rare and unexpected. And then, the slightest trace of a smile touched her lips.

"*She seems to have taken a liking to me already,*" Zalith suddenly spoke into Alucard's mind. "*This might get done a lot faster and easier if I flirt with her.*"

Alucard fought to keep his expression neutral, though irritation burned beneath the surface. The last thing he wanted was for *his* fiancé to flirt with anyone. But as he observed the Yrudyen Queen, it became painfully clear that Zalith had a point. From the moment she sat down, her gleaming eyes remained fixed on the demon. She leaned forward ever so slightly, the movement ensuring that the low-cut drape of her gown accentuated the fullness of her chest. At the same time, she shifted in her throne, parting her legs just enough for the motion to be unmistakable. Alucard's fingers twitched at his sides. He wanted to roll his eyes, scoff, make it clear just how unimpressed he was—but any visible display of disdain would only cause unnecessary problems. Instead, he kept his face utterly unreadable, suppressing every ounce of his annoyance.

"*Fine,*" he responded.

"*I don't have to. I'm open to other ideas.*"

"*No—it's fine. Whatever works, works—do what you have to,*" he said, his irritancy quickly becoming frustration.

Zalith glanced at him with a small smile. "*I love you.*"

The vampire sighed quietly and glanced down at the ground. "*I love you.*"

"*Don't worry,*" Zalith murmured into Alucard's mind, his voice laced with wicked amusement. "*There's only one person here walking around with an ass full of my baby juice...and their name is Alucard.*" His tone was sinful, shameless, dripping with the kind of devious satisfaction that made it clear that he knew exactly what he was doing to him.

Heat rushed up Alucard's neck, and he was sure that his face had turned as red as his hair. He scowled, a mix of mortification and frustration twisting through him—but beneath the flustered weight of his embarrassment, a traitorous shiver of arousal spiralled down his spine.

"Is something wrong?" Tianel asked with a perplexed frown.

The vampire's eyes shot over to her. "No," he said, trying to adorn a vacant stare.

She then cleared her throat and said to the queen, "Your Majesty, Silas and Ezra of Eimwood."

With a curious smile, Syllia leaned back in her seat and rested her right leg over her left. "You are... brothers?" she asked.

Zalith smiled. "Not brothers, but... really good friends," he lied.

Alucard did his *very* best to keep a pout off his face. If this was going to work, he would have to ignore his possessive instincts despite them clawing at his insides.

She giggled and dragged her finger over her lips. "Why have you come here?"

"To offer an arrangement," Zalith answered pleasantly. "Ezra and I will soon be Eimwood's new leaders, and we'd like to make sure that *everyone* living in Yrudberg is... content."

Syllia's smile grew as she waited.

The demon cast a brief glance at Alucard, and in silent understanding, the vampire reached into his trouser pocket, retrieving the diamond pendant they had earlier taken from his vault. With careful fingers, he passed it to Zalith, who turned back to the queen, holding the gleaming jewel out for her to see.

"We brought you our most exquisite treasure as a gesture of goodwill," Zalith said smoothly—then, with a slow smirk, he added, "though now I see that it pales in comparison to the true jewel before me."

A lilting giggle escaped Syllia, her amusement evident, but there was a flicker of satisfaction, and perhaps intrigue. She waved a delicate hand, beckoning him closer. "Come—let me see it properly."

Alucard clenched his jaw as Zalith stepped forward, every moment stretching the vampire's patience thinner. He knew this woman was devouring Zalith with her gaze, drawn in by the very allure that belonged to him and him alone. He wanted to bare his fangs, to make it clear who Zalith belonged to, but he forced himself to remain still. He had to let this play out.

When Zalith stopped a few feet before Syllia, he extended the pendant towards her, the jewel catching the soft glow of the torchlight as it dangled from his fingers.

Syllia's smile deepened as she traced the pad of her finger over the diamond's smooth surface, her touch featherlight, almost reverent. When she reached the tip, she began to circle it slowly; as if savouring the moment, she lifted her gaze to meet Zalith's, her eyes shimmering with something almost indulgent.

"It is beautiful," she murmured, her voice carrying the silkiness of temptation. "One might even say... delectable."

"May I?" Zalith requested.

She nodded and relaxed her arms.

Alucard watched as Zalith moved closer to Syllia and leaned forward. The demon paused to smile at her, and then he focused on clipping the pendant around her neck. Once he had done so, he stepped back—

"Oh," she giggled, her fingers grazing the unnaturally large swell of her breasts, mere inches from where the diamond now rested. "Would you mind?" she purred, tilting her head, her eyes deep with mischief. "I quite enjoy the sensation of something hard between them." She let her gaze flick down, inviting Zalith to indulge her.

The demon's smile didn't waver. If anything, it sharpened as he obliged, carefully easing the diamond between the breasts that she so proudly presented. The way her chest subtly rose beneath his touch, the almost imperceptible hitch in her breath—it was clear that she was enjoying the attention.

Alucard, on the other hand, was doing everything in his power not to roll his eyes or rip Zalith away from her entirely. He couldn't fight off the anger, the impatience, the *jealousy*, the possessive frustration. He wanted to growl, he wanted to snarl, but he held his breath.

"It suits you well," Zalith said to the queen, stepping back.

Syllia's smile curled into a smirk, her eyes darkening with a sultry gleam as she gazed up at Zalith. Slowly, she traced her fingers over the swell of her chest, brushing against the diamond nestled between her breasts. "Mmm," she hummed, tilting her head just enough to make the movement seem almost indulgent. "Such a thoughtful gift," she murmured, her voice dripping with suggestion.

The demon nodded respectfully and said, "You're most welcome." And then he smiled again. "We would like to discuss the arrangement with you."

She nodded.

"As I mentioned, Ezra and I will soon be the new lords of Eimwood, and—"

"Why does that one not have wings?" she interjected, waving her hand almost dismissively at Alucard.

As Zalith looked back at him, Alucard tried to hide the despondent scowl that struck his face.

"He's a different species," his mate said, setting his eyes back on Syllia.

The queen half-nodded. "Continue," she invited.

"Ezra and I aim to protect *all* citizens of Yrudberg and its sister islands. I have been told that you are unaware of the war and plague that has spread across Aegisguard. Ezra and I have seen it with our own eyes—it has devastated an entire country already."

Through his embarrassed frown, Alucard watched a perplexed expression steal Syllia's smile.

Zalith continued, "I'm sure that you have seen the walls being built around Eimwood—"

"A petty attempt to keep my scouts out?" she questioned.

"Not at all," he said with a smile. "It is being built to keep the city and its people safe in case the plague reaches Uzlia—Ezra and I, however, are doing everything within our power to make sure it does not reach us. We have come here to offer to protect you and your settlement in exchange for peace and an alliance between our people. You are, after all, citizens of Yrudberg, too."

Syllia frowned curiously. "What are the terms of this arrangement? Do *I* get to choose?"

"We can negotiate something that will make the three of us very happy," he answered, smiling at her.

She leaned forward. "I was thinking... more like something that would make *us* very happy," she said quietly, batting her eyelids.

Alucard held back another scowl, but this time, he *felt* Zalith's reaction—maybe through their imprints, or maybe because of his heightened senses. His mate was *revolted* by her offer, and that made the vampire smirk discreetly.

"I'm flattered," Zalith replied. "But I'm a gentleman. I like to take things very slowly because it's so much better in the end."

The vampire couldn't help but sink deeper into Zalith's thoughts—though, this time, it felt as if his mate was welcoming him in. He could feel Zalith thinking of him, reminiscing about the longing that had built before their first kiss, the anticipation, the hunger. And then, the memory shifted—flashes of that night when they first had sex, when they had given in to each other, when desire had unravelled into something intoxicating, something utterly consuming. The relief, the euphoria, the way they had fit together so perfectly. Alucard felt it all through him, a warmth blooming in his chest as he lingered in the intimate pull of Zalith's mind.

But he was snapped out of it when he heard Syllia giggle.

The queen sighed longingly before she deadpanned, leaning back on her throne. "Cecil and I had an arrangement. He'd let me borrow some of his people for my people's rituals, and he'd also let us take what we needed from his city—the city the humans built on *our* island."

"What do you need from the city?" Zalith asked.

"Whatever we want," she said simply. "It varies."

He frowned slightly. "Respectfully, in order for us to honour your previous arrangement, we'll need specifics."

She blinked slowly, obviously growing impatient. "Food. People. Materials."

"How many people do you need for your rituals? And how often do they occur?"

The queen held up three fingers. "Three people every nine months."

"We can provide you with people," the demon said, and at the same time, he spoke into Alucard's mind, *"We could use prisoners the same way you used them for blood back in Dor-Sanguis."*

Alucard replied, *"That works."*

A curious smile appeared on Syllia's face again. *"Will* you?"

"We will," Zalith assured her firmly. "What about everything else that you need? Food and materials—we can supply that, too."

But the queen took her eyes off Zalith and looked at Alucard. "You—come and join us."

Although he still wanted to snarl and hiss, Alucard made his way over, and as he stood beside Zalith, the demon smiled at him. His mate's expression calmed him, but the possessive instincts boiling inside him didn't settle entirely.

"Since your handsome friend turned down my offer, would *you* perhaps like to exchange bodily fluids?" Syllia asked Alucard with a grin.

The vampire deadpanned. "I'm gay."

"Oh," she said with a pout. "What a waste."

"Do you have any other terms?" Zalith asked.

She looked up at him. "We need enough food to feed everyone here—perhaps…materials and resources to build our own farms, better homes. If you can help us with that, and respect our practices, then I believe that we can reach some sort of understanding. We lost a lot when the humans immigrated to our islands, and after so many long years, we still haven't recuperated."

"How many people do you have?"

She dragged her fingers over her chest again. "Currently, there are only fifty-eight of us."

The demon nodded again. "It shall be done—I can set up supply lines and ensure you get everything you need. As for the people for your rituals, I could have somebody bring them here to you."

"That would be wonderful. What are you doing with poor little Cecil?"

"The people of Eimwood have discovered that he's a man-sized cockroach—" he looked to Alucard.

"An Insectumoid," the vampire said. "Rochkin."

"Rochkin?" she echoed, her voice almost mocking.

"Rochkin," Zalith said.

Syllia raised her chin in acknowledgement.

The demon continued, "The city has turned on him for not only that but for poisoning their drinking water."

"Oh," she murmured, frowning.

"I'd be surprised if his home hasn't burned to the ground by the time we get back," Zalith said.

She shook her head. "Well, we knew about the water—*we* were the ones who put that troll in there. She found her way back here, though, after who I assume were your people banished her from that cave. She tells me that she fell in love with Cecil," she revealed, giggling.

Zalith didn't look mad, though. "Good. I'm glad she's safe. Cecil did seem quite fond of her—I've never seen a happier bug in all my life."

Alucard cringed—he felt like he might never forget what they saw in that cave.

Syllia laughed. "We will take care of her."

"Thank you," the demon said.

"Assuming our alliance proceeds," the queen then said, sounding a little more serious, losing her smile. "I must warn you of the Orrivain."

Both Alucard and Zalith frowned.

"They are a clan of elves much like us, though they dwell on the mountain peaks," Syllia explained. "By your expressions, I'm certain that you have not heard of them, and there is a reason for that." She paused, stroking her new diamond pendant. "They are a very secretive clan; they have stolen from and killed in Eimwood under moonlight, and *we* were blamed. We didn't care at the time, but it matters *now*. Once our alliance is announced, the Orrivain are likely to oppose—they may come for us, or they may come for you.

Zalith sighed quietly. "All right. I'll make sure that we're ready in the city, and if you need additional security here, I'll be happy to supply demons—or werewolves if you'd prefer. We also have vampires available."

Alucard sorely hoped that she wouldn't ask for vampires because they *didn't* have the numbers to spare right now.

"Werewolves will do just fine," she said with a nod. "How would you like to keep in contact?"

"I'll have someone draw up a contract," Zalith replied. "I'll send a messenger. But if you need us for anything in the meantime, we're not too hard to find. Any one of the werewolves I send will be able to contact me for you."

She leaned forward and smiled up at him. "Oh, I'm sure I'll be needing you very soon."

As Zalith winked at her, Alucard felt his anger boil—

"You may leave," Syllia then said. "I look forward to seeing you again, though," she added with a smile, slowly taking her eyes off Zalith.

"And I, you," the demon replied. "I can have some supplies sent here by the end of the day," he then offered.

"That would be wonderful."

"Farewell," Zalith hummed.

"*La Revedere*," Alucard mumbled, and as Zalith turned, he followed him out of the tree. The further he got from Syllia, the better—if he lingered even a moment longer, he wasn't sure he'd be able to stop himself from tearing that smug, conniving smile right off her face. The air outside felt lighter, but his frustration still burned beneath his skin,

---

The Orrivain conflict continues in the Numenverse Companion Story, THE SILVER CLAW

and as they strode towards their horses, all he could think about was putting as much distance between them and this place as possible.

Chapter Fifty-Four

—⊰ ✝ ⊱—

The Protestors

| **Alucard**—*Uzlia Isles, Yrudberg, Yrudberg Woods* |

As Alucard and Zalith stepped beyond the settlement's boundaries, their wings and horns fading from sight, the vampire made no attempt to temper his rising anger. Even if he wanted to, he wasn't sure he could. His emotions were tangled in a relentless storm, everything heightened—his irritation, his frustration, his *need*. It was this stupid new phase of his life, twisting everything inside him until it felt impossible to control. He angered faster, his thoughts of Zalith consumed him—the desire for sex even more so—and the longer he went without his mate's touch, the worse it all became. But that insufferable, arrogant elf had only made things worse. Flirting with *his* fiancé—who the hell did she think she was?

His scowl deepened as he swung himself onto his horse, the irritation settling into his bones. It only darkened further as they rode through the forest, the shadows of the trees doing little to cool the heat simmering beneath his skin. If Zalith didn't need this arrangement to work, Alucard wouldn't have just stood there—he would have said something. No, he would have *done* something. Watching that *bitch* try to groom *his* mate, watching her try to lure him in with her pathetic attempts at seduction... it had been almost unbearable. Zalith was *his*, and having to bite his tongue and play along for the sake of diplomacy made his blood boil.

Zalith guided his horse closer, the smirk on his face nothing short of devious. "What's wrong, baby?" he drawled, reaching over to cup Alucard's face with one hand. Instead of something soft or reassuring, he gave Alucard's cheeks an exaggerated squish, his thumb and fingers pressing just enough to make the vampire's lips pout.

Alucard huffed angrily, jerking his face free. "What's wrong? Oh, I don't know—maybe the fact that you had so much *fun* flirting with that whore," he snarled with a mocking tone.

The demon smiled—Alucard could see that he was trying *not* to laugh. "We *did* agree to take this route," his mate said. "It wasn't fun—I'm just a very good actor."

He rolled his eyes. "Mm-hmm."

"You don't have to be jealous," Zalith said, laughing a little.

"You're right. I hope you two have a wonderful time on your date," he growled, and then he stormed ahead.

Zalith chuckled and hurried to catch up to him. "What date?"

Alucard scoffed. "Looking forward to seeing you again," he sneered, mimicking Zalith's silvery voice. And then he mocked Syllia's, "Oh, I'm sure I'll be needing you very soon." He huffed again. "I'm sure *you* know when someone plans to chase you."

His mate smirked. "If you want to have a threesome with us, just say it," he teased him.

The vampire glowered at him. "No, thank you. Maybe Danford would be interested, though."

"I don't want Danford. I want *you*."

"I'm not sharing you with some desperate whore, let alone a woman," he snapped.

Zalith laughed again. "Alucard, I'm joking."

"*She* wasn't," he grumbled. "She will come looking for you now that she thinks you're interested, and I won't be able to tell her to fuck off because we're 'really good friends'."

After another chuckle, the demon said, "I will tell her that even though he's incredibly grouchy sometimes, my good friend and I are in love, and if she can't respect that, that's *her* problem. I'm sure there are thousands of other men out there who she can have her way with."

Alucard rolled his eyes. "If you do that, she'll probably call the arrangement off."

"I doubt it, Alucard. Her people need food and supplies, too."

He exhaled deeply, rolling his eyes as he started to slow down. "Which prison are you going to get the people from that she asked for?" he asked, changing the subject.

"Did you just roll your eyes at me?" Zalith snickered.

"No," Alucard grumbled, pouting. "I'm rolling them at that ugly elf woman."

"You don't have to worry about her. Everything's going to be fine—"

"Fine until she waltzes into the city looking for you—she reminds me of Varana."

Zalith scoffed amusedly. "Does she?"

"Pining after you, throwing her tits around—I'm surprised she didn't ask to suck your dick right there and then," he complained as they approached the tree line.

The demon smiled and halted his horse, reaching over to grasp Alucard's arm. With a firm tug, he pulled the vampire as close as their saddles would allow, pressing their bodies together in a makeshift embrace.

Alucard exhaled deeply. It wasn't as satisfying as he wanted—there was only so much that they could manage while seated on horseback—but they made do. Zalith wrapped an arm around the vampire's waist and buried his face into his neck; he huffed against his skin, his breath warm and soothing, yet the way Alucard clung to his mate betrayed just how much he needed this moment of closeness.

"I'm yours, and you're mine," Zalith assured him quietly. "You don't have to worry about anyone changing that, especially a woman, because I'm gay," he added with a smirk and kissed Alucard's neck.

Alucard kept a stubborn pout, but as Zalith tightened his hug, he managed to let himself calm down a little, sinking into his warm embrace. They remained like that for a few moments, and when he felt the demon inhaling his scent once again, the vampire relaxed and rested the side of his head against Zalith's.

"But," Zalith then said, "if you're still jealous and worried, you can fuck me into submission if you think it'll help," he offered, sounding devious—and then he licked the vampire's neck.

That *did* sound rather inviting, but despite his constant need for affection and attention, he didn't actually feel like acting upon his desires. He felt far too irritated, and all he wanted to do right now was get home and lay down. "Not right now," he mumbled. "I just want to lay down."

Zalith laughed quietly. "Okay."

"Let's go," he grumbled, tapping his horse's side and directing it towards the mountain path.

With a seductive smile, the demon followed beside Alucard as he led the way onwards. They still had quite a way to go.

| **Zalith**—*Uzlia Isles, Yrudberg, Eimwood City* |

As they rode through the city, approaching Saint Arkan Street, Zalith found himself utterly entertained by Alucard's lingering frustration. The vampire had been scowling for the entire ride back, his shoulders tense, his jaw tight, and that little furrow between his brows deepening each time Zalith so much as smirked in his direction. It was adorable how riled up he was over Syllia's flirting. He knew that Alucard didn't actually see her as a threat, but his possessiveness was something that the demon relished. He loved how stubborn his fiancé got, how fiercely he clung to what was his, how unwilling he was to let anyone else so much as look at him the wrong way. It was a side of him that made Zalith want to tease him even more—though now probably wasn't the time.

When they turned onto the road that led to their townhouse, the sight before them made Zalith's amusement quickly sour into irritation. A restless crowd had gathered outside their home, their expressions a mix of anger, desperation, and concern. People took turns knocking on the door, peering through the windows, their voices carrying agitated murmurs. Zalith exhaled sharply, his grip on the reins tightening. He had expected this, of course. He knew exactly why they were here.

"I'm glad we don't actually live here," he mumbled, glancing at Alucard.

"Are we going to see what they want from us *this* time?"

He nodded. "Hopefully no one's too hysterical."

The moment one person noticed Zalith and Alucard approaching, the entire crowd seemed to shift, a wave of frantic movement as people rushed towards them. Within seconds, they were surrounded, a cacophony of voices rising into the evening air—pleading, demanding, desperate.

"Please, you have to do something about Cecil!"

"He won't come out of his house!"

"The city can't take much more of this!"

"There's a giant bug ruling over us, for God's sake!"

"Why haven't you taken over yet? We need you!"

Zalith's gaze swept over the sea of anxious faces, irritation flickering beneath his carefully composed expression. He had known this was coming—the unrest, the fear—but dealing with it after a long ride and an exhausting meeting with that aggravating elf queen was hardly ideal.

Sighing, he dismounted his horse and lifted his hands, signalling for quiet. "I understand your concerns," he said, his voice smooth, calm—though laced with carefully restrained exasperation. "But until Cecil is officially removed, there isn't much I can do. It's not my place to act unless he's kicked out." He exhaled, offering a well-practiced look of regret. "Believe me, I wish I could snap my fingers and fix everything for you, but that's not how this works."

Alucard dismounted his horse, too, and took both horses to the hitching posts, where he tied their reins.

"He's never going to leave!" one woman cried. "He's going to turn us all into flies!"

"The *whole* council are bugs, too!" a man called. "They'll kill us all!"

"You gotta do something! Use ye guards to chase 'em out of our city!" an old man yelled, waving his cane around.

An elderly woman barged through the crowd and snatched Alucard's hand. "Please, do something," she pleaded, looking up at him and then at Zalith as the vampire pulled his hand from hers. "We have no idea what he could be plotting in there!"

"What if he's laying eggs?!" someone exclaimed.

A man followed with, "There could be millions of them by tomorrow!"

"What about our poor children?!" a woman cried, holding her baby in front of Zalith and Alucard, as if offering it up to them. "What are we to do?!"

A flicker of guilt settled in Zalith's chest. As much as he tried to keep himself detached, he couldn't ignore the sheer desperation on these people's faces. They had been deceived, used, and betrayed by the man they had trusted to lead them, left to suffer under his corruption while he cowered behind locked doors.

It was time for Cecil to be removed. Time for him and Alucard to take control. Time to finally see his mission in Uzlia through to the end.

"We'll see if Cecil is willing to talk to us," Zalith said, looking around at them all.

"Talk?" the man with the cane shouted. "We need him gone!" he screeched so loudly that a baby started crying from somewhere in the bellowing crowd—and they were only getting louder.

Alucard dragged his hand over his face and grunted in annoyance. "*Taci!*" he yelled, and instantly, everyone fell quiet.

"Ezra and I will try talking to Cecil and his council; we'll see if we can get any answers for you," Zalith repeated.

"You're not going to go in there, are you?" a very shaken woman called. "What if... what if they eat you?"

"Or turn you into flies!"

"We can't let them take *you*—we'd all be dead if it wasn't for you!" a man wailed.

"We should storm his house!" another man suggested.

"Yeah! Break the doors down!" the woman at his side yelled.

"Burn the house down!" the old man with the cane followed.

As much as Zalith wanted to let the people handle this themselves, he couldn't risk needless casualties—or worse, an all-out riot. And while he wouldn't lose sleep over Cecil's demise, he preferred that the manor remained intact. It would be far more useful in his and Alucard's hands.

"We'll be fine," he assured the crowd, offering them a smooth, confident smile. "We're tougher than we look." He slid an arm around Alucard's shoulders, pulling him in close. Then, he spoke into his fiancé's mind, "*We should get some of our people down here to keep the crowd calm while we deal with Cecil and his little family of bug people.*"

"*I will call some of my demons from Oklens to come up here and keep an eye on them,*" Alucard replied.

Zalith nodded, trusting Alucard to handle it. As the crowd's voices rose again, overlapping in frantic pleas and restless demands, he let their words wash over him, his focus elsewhere. This would all be over soon—one way or another.

Chapter Fifty-Five

— ⟨ ✝ ⟩ —

Silas and Ezra Wright, Lords of Eimwood

| Alucard—*Uzlia Isles, Yrudberg, Eimwood City* |

As they headed towards Cecil's manor, Alucard clung tightly to Zalith's hand, his grip firm, almost desperate. His frustration hadn't waned—not just from that arrogant elf but from the gnawing, insatiable need clawing at him since they had left the forest. It was growing worse with every passing moment, a relentless ache inside him, demanding attention that he couldn't afford to give it right now. There was work to do, and he would have to push through it—no matter how much his instincts rebelled.

Walking in step with Zalith, he turned onto the street leading up to manor, where chaos had already taken root. The crowds up ahead were in a frenzy, voices raised in furious protest, their rage aimed squarely at the estate. But while they could shout and scream all they liked, they wouldn't be breaking in—not with the tall, barred railings cutting off the manor from the city. The black iron gates stood locked tight, thick steel chains wrapped around them as if the added reinforcement would keep the inevitable at bay.

"What's the plan?" the vampire asked as they neared the protesting crowds. "Do we sneak in, or do we try to get Cecil to come out here with an audience behind us?"

"Well, it seems like Cecil is already reluctant to come out, and us being there isn't going to help convince him."

"So, we find a way in and deal with him? We could open those gates and let the people take control of the situation—but like I said, there might be casualties, so... I don't know."

Zalith nodded. "We'll find a way in and have a chat with him."

"Should we tell those people that we're going to confront him?" he asked, gesturing to the crowd as they stopped walking—if they got too close, he was certain that everyone would come running, just like the people waiting outside their townhouse. "Or do we just go and deal with him and then let everyone know the outcome?"

"I don't want to talk to them," the demon mumbled.

"Okay, well, if we take this street, we can get around to the back gate," he said, nodding at a right turning on the road up ahead.

Moving swiftly through the streets of Bauwell, Alucard and Zalith kept to the shadows, avoiding the watchful eyes of the city's restless residents. They already knew what the people wanted—Cecil gone, and today would be the last day he ruled over anything. If he refused to leave willingly, then they would do what had to be done. No hesitation. No remorse.

Their path led them to a vineyard—Cecil's vineyard. Unlike the city streets, which were thick with unrest, the land here was eerily deserted. No workers, no guards patrolling the rows of twisted vines. It was obvious that everyone loyal to Cecil was holed up inside his manor, clinging to whatever misguided hope they had left.

As they moved between the rows, Alucard's mind drifted, briefly comparing this place to his own vineyard back at the castle. Even unfinished, his was far superior. At least his vines would yield something worthwhile, unlike this neglected patch of land.

But that wasn't important right now. As they reached the back gate, both he and Zalith pressed themselves against the pillars framing its entrance, their movements silent, calculated. On the other side, two of Cecil's guards stood watch, rifles in hand, their stances rigid. Clearly, they weren't expecting company—and they certainly weren't in the mood for visitors.

"Let's just sneak past them," Zalith spoke into his mind.

Alucard gave a small nod before taking Zalith's hand. They *could* phase into the space between the Astral Plane and the physical world, but that wouldn't allow them to pass through solid objects like the locked gates—it only granted them the ability to move unseen and unheard. So instead, Alucard dematerialized with the demon, their forms vanishing into vermillion smoke before reappearing behind a gnarled tree roughly forty feet from the guards.

Further from the gates, the grounds were more heavily patrolled than expected, with watchmen moving in staggered rotations, rifles at the ready. But now that they were past the gates, they could use their abilities to remain hidden, slipping through the estate undetected.

The vampire hesitated before moving, though; he was struck by a strange tiredness—fleeting fatigue. It gripped him tight at first, but it eased up after a few seconds. He didn't think much of it. Moving in perfect sync, they manoeuvred through the grounds, keeping to the deep shadows where the sunlight couldn't reach, shrouding their presence. Soon, they arrived at one of the unguarded back doors. Zalith grasped the handle and snapped the lock before pushing the door open.

They stepped inside, emerging into a dimly lit kitchen. The silence was thick and undisturbed, but the air carried a repulsive stench—a cloying mix of stale food and damp. The manor itself appeared well-maintained, but the foul smell was unmistakable. Alucard had no doubt its source was the grotesque creature infesting this house—a giant cockroach masquerading as a man.

"What do we do about his guards?" the vampire asked, speaking into Zalith's mind as they quietly made their way through the kitchen.

"We'll try to be civil and ask to see Cecil. If they attack, we fight back and kill them."

"These kinds of Insectumoids are ethos-proof, so we should use physical weapons against them—I have a few things in my vault. What do you want?" he asked as they silently left the kitchen and crossed a long hallway lined with closed doors, paintings, and a dusty, blue rug.

"A knife will do just fine. Thank you."

Nodding, the vampire reached into his vault and grabbed the only pair of blades he owned that were made with mortem metallum—the same metal that a grim reaper's scythe was made of, capable of cutting close to everything—and handed one to Zalith, who slipped the black blade into his trouser pocket. Alucard eased the other into his own pocket, and then he followed the demon down the hallway.

Moving soundlessly through Cecil's manor, they encountered no guards inside—not yet, at least. Alucard suspected that most were outside, preoccupied with the angry, shouting crowds or patrolling the grounds to prevent exactly what he and Zalith were doing. The house, despite its lavish furnishings, felt eerily empty, the quiet stretching between them like a held breath.

But as they reached a grand ballroom, that stillness broke. Three men stood rigid outside a set of tall black doors, their expressions dark and unreadable. Unlike the guards on the grounds, they weren't armed—not in any obvious way.

Alucard barely needed to exchange a glance with Zalith to confirm what they both already knew. *That* had to be where Cecil was hiding. The stench beyond those doors was unmistakable, the same disturbing reek that Alucard had the revolting displeasure of greeting when he and Zalith found Cecil with that troll.

The guards hadn't yet seen them, and while shrouding themselves, so long as they didn't get too close, it would remain that way.

"If they won't talk to us, you take the one on the left, I will deal with the two on the right," Alucard suggested, speaking into his mate's mind.

Zalith nodded and pulled Alucard out of the hall. *"You stay hidden so that we have the element of surprise on our side,"* he instructed. Then, he unshrouded himself and stepped into the hall.

Alucard watched, ready to jump to the demon's aid if he needed it.

Zalith set his eyes on the three guards, who immediately adorned hostile scowls. "I'd like to talk to Cecil," he said calmly.

"How the hell did you get in here?!" one of them shouted as they all lurched forward, preparing to fight.

"That's the least of your problems," he answered, his hand ever so slightly twitching at his side, as if he was ensuring that he was ready to grab the knife.

"He's here for the boss—get him!" the man yelled, and then the three of them charged.

Alucard barely had a moment to register the sound of scuttling before the three men lunged at Zalith, their bodies twisting and morphing into grotesque, cockroach-like forms—the same kind of monstrous shape that Cecil had taken. Zalith was prepared, grabbing his blade as he moved to intercept the first rochkin. But the vampire spotted the cockroach trying to get behind Zalith, so he vanished into vermillion smoke and reappeared behind the creature. He drove his blade straight through the thick, chitinous armour of its back before it could get any closer to Zalith.

At the same time, Zalith grabbed the leading creature's arm and plunged his blade into its neck. The weapon cut through the shell with ease, but the moment its thick, orange blood splattered across his face, Zalith recoiled with a sharp snarl. The liquid sizzled on contact, burning through his skin. Alucard's stomach lurched at the sight, dread striking him like a blade. He barely heard the dying creature hit the marble floor over the sound of Zalith's agonized grunt as he shoved it away.

And then—horribly—he saw that more of that acidic blood had sprayed across Zalith's arm. The demon faltered, instinctively trying to wipe his face, but the pain was immediate, blinding. He dropped to his knees, clutching his face with one hand, frozen in place. Alucard felt his heart pound furiously against his ribs—his entire body burned with desperation, but there was still one cockroach left.

The final creature turned on him, but Alucard didn't hesitate. With a furious growl, he twisted his blade in his grip and drove it deep into the monster's gut. It crumpled with a shrill, dying hiss, collapsing onto the floor in a writhing heap.

Alucard didn't wait to watch it die. He rushed to Zalith's side. "Zalith?" he insisted, panicking, dropping to his knees in front of him and moving his hand over the demon's shoulder. "Are you okay?" he asked, guiding his other hand to Zalith's chin, trying to make him look at him.

Zalith grunted painfully, shaking his head. "I don't know," he muttered, dread in his voice. He hesitated for a moment, but he let Alucard lift his head.

Alucard stared at Zalith's injuries, his heart racing. The burns on the left side of his face were raw and an angry shade of red, the acid having eaten through the first layers of his skin in jagged, uneven streaks. The demon's expression was twisted in pain, and Alucard felt something desperate and frantic claw at his chest. His gaze dropped lower, catching the damage to Zalith's arm—the acidic blood had burned straight through his coat, blazer, *and* shirt, leaving charred, curling edges of fabric around the ruined skin. The flesh beneath was an inflamed mess of weeping, second-degree burns, mottled red with patches of white where the tissue had been stripped too deep.

Terror surged through him. He had to do something—*anything*—but what? He clenched his fists, trying to think, trying to *fix* this. "We should go back," he pleaded. "Put something on these wounds—"

"No," Zalith refused, shaking his head. "Let's get this over with."

"But you're hurt," he murmured sadly.

"I'll be fine," his mate said, starting to get up.

Alucard frowned reluctantly but helped Zalith to his feet. "Are you sure?"

Zalith nodded. "Let's go," he said, already heading for the doors.

The vampire hesitated for only a moment before forcing himself to move, retrieving Zalith's fallen blade before yanking his own from the lifeless husk of the cockroach's neck. He trailed after his mate, his mind a storm of unease, uncertainty gnawing at him with every step. He wanted to *force* the demon to turn back, to take him home and tend to his wounds before they worsened—but Zalith had made his choice. He was determined to finish this, and Alucard knew better than to argue when he had that look in his eyes.

Still, the sight of those burns made something twist painfully in his chest. They'd heal—of course they would. Zalith's body would mend itself with time, leaving behind no scars, no trace of this moment. But *right now*, he was in pain, and the thought of it made Alucard's fangs clench. He hated it—he hated feeling so powerless to do anything about it. But if Zalith refused to stop, then all he could do was stay close, ready to tear apart anything else that dared to lay a hand on him.

Zalith kicked the doors open, the force of it rattling the walls. Alucard could feel the anger rolling off his mate in waves—*he* was angry, too, but Zalith's fury burned hotter, crackling like a fire ready to consume everything in its path. This was it. Cecil was going to die, and if Zalith didn't do it, *he* would.

But the moment they stormed into the lounge, the air was cut through with a sharp, panicked scream. Cecil's wife shrieked, their children wailing as the man himself clutched his trembling wife and pressed a letter opener to her throat. His grip was unsteady, his expression wild with desperation as he glared at them both.

"Don't come any closer!" Cecil shouted, his voice cracking under the weight of fear. "Or I'll kill her!"

Alucard scowled. What a pathetic man.

Zalith glowered at him. "You need to give up," he said, his tone razor-sharp, cutting through the chaos. "Nobody wants you here anymore. It would be in your best interest to take what little dignity you have left and *leave* the city—in fact, leave Uzlia altogether." He cast a glance at Alucard, his meaning clear: they had been willing to offer him a way out…but not anymore.

Cecil scoffed, his face twisting with fury. "Courtesy? *Courtesy?*" he spat, his voice climbing to a near-hysterical pitch. "You *filthy,* cock-sucking, rat-blooded fucks waltz into *my* city, turn the people against me, slaughter my men like fucking cattle—and now you wanna talk about courtesy?" Spittle flew from his lips as he shrieked, his grip on his wife's throat tightening. "You can take your fucking courtesy and shove it so far up your demon ass you'll be *choking* on it!" He was trembling now, veins bulging against his pasty skin, his beady, bug-like eyes darting between Zalith and Alucard. "*You* will be the ones leaving *my* city, or I'll gut this whiny little cunt right here, and then I'll send my guards out to rip apart every miserable fuck outside piece by fucking piece!" His voice cracked at the end, shrill and high like a panicked, cornered animal.

Alucard snarled. "We should just kill him. We're wasting our time."

Zalith nodded in response.

Before Cecil could spew whatever filth was festering on his tongue, Alucard's blade flew through the air with a sharp whistle—then *crack.* The black blade buried itself deep into the bridge of Cecil's nose, splitting flesh and cartilage with a sickening crunch. His eyes rolled upward, frozen wide in shock, his mouth twitching as if trying to form one last desperate curse. For a brief, grotesque moment, he stood there, orange blood spurting in uneven bursts from the gaping wound, painting the floor in sizzling streaks. Then his legs gave out. He crumpled to the floor like a broken marionette, the impact forcing more blood to splatter across the marble.

His wife shrieked, stumbling back as her hands flew to her face, her body wracked with hysterical sobs. Cecil twitched once, twice—then went still, his face an unrecognizable ruin of shattered bone and pooling blood.

"I suggest you take your children and leave the city," Zalith said, watching her as she hurried over to her crying son and daughter while Alucard pulled his blade from Cecil's head.

She glared back over her shoulder at them as she moved her arms around her terrified children. "Where are we to go?!" she exclaimed. "I've seen those people outside! They think we're…like *him!*" She pointed to Cecil's corpse, and then she wailed.

Zalith sighed. "With us. We'll direct you to someone who can sort things out for you."

For a few moments, she stayed where she was. When she eventually glanced at her dead husband and shifted her sights to Alucard, who cleaned his blades, she sniffled and winced. Then, she looked at Zalith. "We're *not* like him," she insisted. "I…I didn't even know, I…."

"There's a chance that your children are Insectumoids, too, and the people are not going to like that. Even if they're not, it would be best if you left. You can take half of

Cecil's money, but the rest is going towards repairing the damages he made to Eimwood's water supply," he said as Alucard stood at his side again. "We're going to take your dead husband outside now so that the city can see he's been dealt with. *You* are going to go out the back door where one of my people will meet you."

She stared at them, looked down at her whining children, and scowled. "Fine," she huffed. "I'd rather leave than live here with people like you in charge—"

"We just saved your life," Alucard growled.

"And now you're kicking us out!"

"If you stay, the people will never stop trying to kill you. Leave, or we will make you."

Taking her children's hands, she turned her nose up at Alucard and Zalith. "Unbelievable," she uttered, shaking her head as she scurried out of the room with her children.

Zalith sighed. "I just sent one of my demons a message. He'll pick the three of them up in a few seconds."

And with that, it was over—well, nearly.

Alucard turned to his mate, frowning sullenly as he examined the burns on his face. "I'm so sorry, Zalith," he said shamefully. "I didn't know that their blood was acidic."

He shook his head, turning it slightly to hide the wounds. "It's okay, it's not your fault. I just want to go home."

The vampire nodded and glanced at Cecil's corpse; the orange blood was slowly eating away at the marble, which blistered and split. A sharp, chemical-like tang filled the air, accompanied by the stench of burning metal, wet cement, and decaying flesh. He scowled in revolt and asked, "So, who's dragging him outside?"

Zalith exhaled deeply. "We'll leave it here and get someone to take care of it on our way out."

Alucard nodded and took hold of his hand. "I can fly us home from here."

"The people need to know that Cecil is gone."

"But the burns," he said with a sullen frown.

"I'll be fine," he assured him. "Come on—"

"What about Cecil's guards outside?"

"My people are dealing with them."

Alucard nodded and followed as Zalith led the way out of the lounge, moving swiftly through the house.

Conflicted, he couldn't shake the gnawing sense of guilt twisting inside him. Zalith had been hurt—burned—and despite everything, Alucard felt as if he should have done more; he should have been faster, stronger…something. But there was no time to dwell on it. They still had things to do before they could return home, before Zalith could rest and tend to his wounds. And Alucard knew, without a doubt, that his mate was irritated by that fact. Zalith wanted to leave, to heal, to put this whole damn mess behind them—but first, they had to face the crowd waiting outside Cecil's gates.

Stepping out into the cool air, they made their way through the manor grounds, where Zalith's people had subdued the remaining guards—those who hadn't managed to flee. Their bodies lay in defeated heaps, some groaning, others eerily silent. Beyond the gates, the city's people were still shouting, calling for justice, though most were craning their necks, trying to catch a glimpse of what was happening. And when they spotted Zalith and Alucard approaching, their voices surged—cheers, questions, demands for answers all tumbling over one another, hands waving wildly as the crowd pushed forward, hungry for the truth.

The vampire's gaze flicked to Zalith, catching the slight twitch of his jaw as voices in the crowd rose in shock and horror, calling, *"What happened to your face?"*

Zalith sighed, gripping the iron bars of the gate as he pulled them open, stepping forward to face the expectant sea of faces. "We went in to talk," he said, his voice carrying over the restless murmurs. "But Cecil and his men attacked us. We had to fight back, and now—" his gaze swept over the crowd, "—Cecil is dead. The city is free."

For a brief moment, silence clung to the air, as if the people were processing the weight of his words. Then, an eruption of cheers and shouts surged like a tide, relief and celebration taking over. Cries of thanks filled the streets, voices calling Zalith and Alucard's names, but Alucard could already tell—Zalith had no intention of lingering.

Zalith raised a hand, silencing them just enough to speak again. "Ezra and I have more to do today, but enjoy your freedom knowing that Cecil and his band of cockroaches are no longer here."

The crowd hardly needed more encouragement, their cheers growing louder, their attention turning to one another, to their long-awaited victory.

But among the cheers and happiness, there was *anger*.

"Who do you think you are?!" a man yelled.

The crowd gradually fell silent when a middle-aged man shoved through them. His wavy black hair blew around wildly in the breeze as stood before Alucard and Zalith, his sharp features twisted in anger. Deep lines furrowed his forehead, his dark eyes burning with jealousy and rage as they flicked between the demon and vampire. His clenched jaw and tense posture made it clear—he was barely holding himself back.

"Excuse me?" Zalith replied.

"Cecil is our leader!" the man shouted. "Are you all stupid?!" he then exclaimed, spinning around madly, shooting glares into the crowd. "Don't you see what they're doing?! First Cecil, and then it'll be us—they're going to take over this city, they're going to turn it into a demon nest!"

Alucard rolled his eyes.

"Get out of here, Desmond," a man groaned dismissively.

"We can't let this stand!" Desmond cried and set his glower back on Alucard and Zalith. "We don't want you here."

"We don't want *you* here!" a woman snapped at him.

Desmond shoved her away—

"That's enough," Alucard growled, grabbing Desmond's arm—

Desmond ripped away, scowling at Alucard in disgust. "Get your dirty hands off me!"

Zalith snarled and looked sharply to his left, and seconds later, two of his demons moved through the crowd, grabbed Desmond, and escorted him away while he protested and screeched.

"Who was that?" Alucard mumbled to Zalith.

"Desmond Vale," the woman Desmond had shoved told him. "He's a seer—well, barely. He sucks at spells."

"He's threatened," the man beside her added. "He knows that his stupid little shop will go out of business now that people with *real* ethos skills are arriving here."

That made sense. Of course someone like that would feel threatened, and it was likely that Desmond wasn't the only one. "Are there more people like him?"

The crowd murmured.

And the woman replied, "No, sir. The only other ethos-wielder in the city is Willow, and she knows what she's doing—she heals animals."

Alucard nodded appreciatively.

"All right, we need to get going," Zalith announced.

The crowd burst into appreciative commotion again.

Zalith didn't waste another second. He turned down the street, and Alucard was right behind him. "I'll get someone to keep an eye on that guy," he mumbled.

Alucard nodded in agreement. The last thing they needed was Desmond spreading fear and gathering a following.

As soon as they were out of sight, the vampire pulled him close, arms tightening around him as he dematerialized them both. In a flash of vermillion smoke, they shot into the sky, leaving the city and its roaring celebrations behind. It was time to go home.

Chapter Fifty-Six

— ⸲ ✝ ⸱ —

Burns

| **Zalith**—*Uzlia Isles, Usrul, Castle Reiner* |

The moment they landed in the castle courtyard, Zalith let go of Alucard and strode towards the front door, his pace falling somewhere between a hurried walk and restrained urgency. His skin still burned, the lingering sting on his face a constant reminder of what just happened. But more than the pain, it was the thought of how *hideous* he looked that gnawed at him. He needed to see for himself, he needed confirmation of the damage. The wound on his arm was easier to ignore, a dull throb beneath his clothes, but his face—his face was different. If it was as bad as it felt, then he had no desire to let anyone see him like this.

Alucard followed him. "I will go and get something for your wounds," he said as they entered the castle.

Zalith shook his head as he hastily took his coat off, determined to get to their bedroom. "It's okay. I'm just going to go upstairs."

"I'll come with you," he said, still following him. "There's probably something up there anyway."

He wasn't going to say no. The demon hurried up the stairs, pushing into the bedroom before striding straight into the bathroom. The moment he reached the mirror, he froze, taking in his reflection. A flood of anger, grief, and humiliation surged through him, tightening his throat and constricting his chest like a venomous serpent.

He looked *disgusting*.

The right side of his face was marred with deep, raw burns—blackened edges where the acidic blood had seared his flesh, streaks of inflamed red cutting across his cheek. Smaller burns dotted his skin where the splatter had caught him, each a painful reminder of his failure to avoid it. The damage was worse than he had feared, and an awful certainty settled in his gut. He couldn't be seen like this. Not by anyone. Not until it healed.

"Come here," Alucard said, placing his hand over the demon's shoulder, snapping him out of his horrified gaze.

Turning to face him, he frowned sullenly.

"I can't really do much, but I can try to do something," his fiancé murmured, his voice soft as he uncorked a black bottle and grabbed a piece of cotton wool.

Zalith watched in silence, his jaw tight as Alucard soaked the cotton, likely with something meant to ease the pain or speed up the healing. He hated this—he hated standing here, feeling exposed, feeling *repulsive*. The burns throbbed, a dull, relentless ache that only worsened under the weight of his own shame. He didn't know what to say—he didn't even know what he *wanted* to say. So he just stood there, his hands clenched at his sides, waiting for Alucard to tend to his wounds.

He barely resisted as Alucard took his hand, guiding him from the bathroom. As they stepped into the bedroom, Zalith caught a glimpse of the label—Medicus. He knew the name. A healing balm meant to soothe and accelerate recovery. It would help, but it wouldn't fix the way he felt.

Alucard pulled him towards the bed and gave a gentle but firm tug, making him sit at its edge. Without a word, the vampire grabbed a chair and settled in front of him, his pale fingers moving with care as he dampened the cotton wool with the balm. "Tell me if I hurt you," he murmured.

Zalith nodded stiffly. His mind was still caught in the spiralling thoughts of how *wrong* his face felt—how atrocious he must look.

The first touch of the cotton against his burns sent a sharp sting through his nerves, and though he didn't move, his body tensed. He knew Alucard could see it. The vampire frowned, his expression troubled as he worked with the utmost care.

"I'm sorry," his fiancé murmured, his voice guilt-ridden. "I should have spent more time researching Insectumoids."

Zalith exhaled, forcing himself not to snap, not to let the bubbling frustration claw its way out. It wasn't Alucard's fault. It wasn't *anyone's* fault. But that didn't stop the burning resentment curling in his chest—not towards his vampire, but towards himself. "It's okay," he finally said. "It's not your fault."

Shaking his head, Alucard poured more Medicus onto a new piece of cotton wool after placing the first in his lap. "I should have been faster—maybe I could've stopped it from happening."

"Don't blame yourself," he said, guiding his hand over the vampire's arm. "We could have solved things peacefully, but Cecil's men didn't seem interested in doing so."

Alucard nodded, looking down at his lap.

"It's not your fault I'm hideous."

Alucard lifted his head and stared confusedly at Zalith. "You're not hideous," he said sternly. "Wounds or not, you're the most handsome man I know," he said with a smile, coating one of the last wounds on Zalith's face with the balm.

"Thank you," the demon said, but the despair still lingered.

The vampire moved his free hand to the other side of Zalith's face. "You're not hideous, Zalith," he repeated, shuffling closer. "You got hurt and that shouldn't have happened—but we did what we had to do, and…all your work here is basically done. And this," he said, glancing at the burns on the right side of Zalith's face, "this will be gone in maybe…two days—one if we fuck a few times," he added with a shrug and a smirk.

Zalith laughed a little, undeniably turned on by Alucard's suggestion…and by that rare, desire-filled smirk. "Maybe," he said, but as the burns on his face throbbed, the despondency came back.

Smiling, Alucard looked down at the demon's arm. "I have to do your arm."

Zalith held out his arm, and with his right hand, Alucard gently took hold of it and examined his burns. Although he didn't want to see them, Zalith glanced down. The burns looked worse than what he saw on his face; the largest cut very deeply into his arm, and the only reason he wasn't bleeding all over the place was because the acid had actually cauterised the wounds. It hurt, though—it was like someone was digging around in his arm with rhodium-coated claws, slowly peeling away his flesh. And the longer he looked, the worse it felt. So he looked away with a huff.

Alucard carefully covered the wounds with Medicus, and once he was done, his concerned frown returned. "I have to go get something to wrap this up with—I'll be right back, okay?"

He nodded. "Okay."

As Alucard left the room, Zalith let out a heavy sigh and fell back onto the bed, sinking into a pit of frustration and self-loathing. Of all the places to be burned, why did it have to be his face? The thought twisted inside him like a blade. Now, he couldn't leave the castle—not like this. Not while he looked hideous. He hated everything about it: the pain, the way his skin felt tight and raw, the way he had no control over how long it would take to heal. All he could do was lie there, staring at the ceiling, trapped in his own skin as he waited for his body to repair itself.

| **Alucard**—*Uzlia Isles, Usrul, Castle Reiner* |

Alucard stood in the bathroom, staring at the bottle of Medicus in his hand; he felt tired again, just as he had when he'd rematerialized on Cecil's grounds. Why? It *had* been a long day; maybe he just needed to lay down. He exhaled quietly and placed the bottle back in the cabinet. He closed the door with a soft click, but his thoughts remained restless, circling the same concern over and over again—Zalith.

The demon hadn't said much, but Alucard knew him well enough to recognize the storm raging inside him. His mate was in pain, but worse than that, he was uncomfortable—self-conscious in a way that Alucard had rarely seen before... in a way that he understood all too well. And that hurt to see. Zalith, the ever-confident, ever-powerful force in his life, had shut down the moment he saw his reflection.

But this would pass. Alucard knew it would. His wounds would heal, and soon, his face would look just as it always had—striking, beautiful. *Perfect*. Until then, he'd do everything he could to make sure that Zalith knew he wasn't disgusting, that he wasn't ruined, and that Alucard still looked at him the same way he always had—with love, with admiration, with a need that had nothing to do with flawless skin.

He sighed and grabbed some bandages, running a hand through his hair before stepping out of the bathroom. Zalith needed reassurance, and he would make sure he got it.

When he walked over to the bed, Zalith smiled weakly, a flicker of pain moving across his face, the movement clearly aggravating his wounds.

Alucard frowned worriedly as he climbed onto the bed and straddled Zalith's lap; he smiled down at the demon as he gently eased his blazer and shirt off; he took his injured arm and started wrapping it in the bandages. While he worked, his mate moved his other hand to the side of his waist and smiled through the sadness.

Once Alucard was done, he let go and leaned forward, kissing Zalith's lips.

The demon grimaced and laughed a little. "My face hurts," he said sullenly.

Guilt smothered Alucard's face as he sat up straight. "I'm sorry."

"It's okay," he said, moving his hand up to Alucard's shoulder. Then, he pulled him back down and started kissing his lips.

But after a few kisses, the vampire stopped and looked down at him. "But... you said it hurts."

"I don't care," he said, fiddling with Alucard's hair.

"But I *do*. I don't want to make it worse."

Zalith smirked a little. "Touching me will make it feel better," he mumbled, tucking a strand of Alucard's hair behind his ear.

With a smile, Alucard kissed his lips a single time, guiding his hand down to Zalith's chest. "Should I touch you here?" he asked. But then he stroked his hand to the demon's crotch and smirked. "Or here?"

Zalith laughed softly. "The second option," he said, moving his hand over Alucard's shoulder and down to his waist.

The vampire smiled against Zalith's lips, deepening their kiss as his fingers worked open the demon's belt. Slipping his hand into Zalith's trousers, he wrapped his fingers around his arousal, stroking him slowly. The warmth of it and the way Zalith exhaled sharply against his mouth—it sent a pulse of need straight through him. His own arousal surged, his body responding instinctively to the moment.

He already knew what Zalith wanted—he'd told him earlier, and with every second, Alucard felt that same hunger take hold of him. The desire to give, to claim, to lose himself in Zalith completely.

Their kisses turned more fervent, Zalith's hands roaming his body, dragging over his hips before finding their way to Alucard's own growing arousal. A quiet, eager groan escaped the vampire as Zalith gripped him through his trousers, sending a thrilling shiver down his spine. His heartbeat quickened, the anticipation swelling inside him, and soon, he couldn't hold back.

He broke the kiss, staring down at Zalith, his breath uneven. His voice was thick with desire as he murmured, "I want to fuck you."

Zalith's lips curled into a grin, excitement flashing in his dark eyes. "You do?"

He nodded, trying to hide just how eager he was beginning to feel.

The demon's smirk grew. "Okay. But no looking at my face."

Alucard frowned and pouted sadly. "Why?"

"Because I'm ugly right now."

His frown thickened. "No, you're not."

Laughing, Zalith stroked his free hand to the side of Alucard's neck. "Yes, I am," he argued amusedly. "It's okay. I'm just as fuckable from behind."

Alucard kept his pout; although he was eager, he knew that Zalith turning around would be uncomfortable for the demon's arm. So he wasn't going to cave. Instead, he was going to do *exactly* what he knew Zalith wanted. "No," he replied. "I'm going to fuck you like this," he said, taking hold of Zalith's uninjured arm, and as he pinned it above his head, he started to pull the demon's trousers off.

Zalith's expression grew devious. "Okay," he agreed, starting to unbutton Alucard's shirt.

But Alucard's eagerness swiftly spiralled into something more desperate, more consuming. His movements grew impatient as he shoved off his trousers, barely breaking their kiss. Zalith responded in kind, pulling Alucard's shirt over his head and tossing it aside, his excitement evident in the breathy laugh he let out when Alucard reached into the nightstand.

The vampire pulled out a bottle of lube, but before he could open it, Zalith's hands were on him again—gripping his shaft, stroking him with slow, teasing precision. A deep, shuddering breath left Alucard as pleasure curled through him, making his fingers tighten around the bottle. He tilted his head, nuzzling against the demon's neck before dragging his lips back up to his. Their mouths met in a heated kiss, Zalith's lips parting eagerly against his, and as they kissed, Alucard poured some lube onto his fingers and pressed them against Zalith's ass, working the cool liquid into him.

He tried to pace himself, but the more he touched, the more he felt, the more unbearable it became. His pulse hammered in anticipation, the need to be inside him clawing at his every thought.

With one last lingering kiss, Alucard positioned himself and eased forward, moaning quietly as he eased his dick into Zalith's warmth. The demon let out a hushed, pleased hum, his body tensing before relaxing into the sensation. Alucard exhaled against his throat, pinning the demon's wrist above his head as he nipped at his neck.

As his needs consumed him, Alucard thrust with increasing aggression, his movements growing more frenzied as pleasure electrified through his body. Zalith moaned beneath him, wrapping a leg around his back, his own pleasure evident in every sound he made. The heat of their bodies, the friction, the intoxicating way Zalith responded to him—it was overwhelming. Alucard's claws dug into the sheets, his face buried against the demon's neck as he breathed him in, utterly lost in the moment. He moved faster, unable to slow himself, his body driven by something deeper than desire, a primal, instinctual urge.

Zalith pulled his face up into another kiss, their mouths colliding in desperate hunger. They breathed erratically between each fevered meeting of their lips, their trembling bodies pressed so tightly together that Alucard could feel every shift, every shudder of pleasure rippling through Zalith's form. Despite the growing ache in his muscles, the vampire didn't stop—he *couldn't* stop. It felt too good, too necessary, and he feared that if he so much as hesitated, the pleasure might dull, that it might slip away before he could reach the peak his body was so desperately chasing.

And then, it struck—his limbs tensed, the rush of climax *suffocating*. It was relentless. His body clenched, a strangled moan breaking from his throat as he drove his throbbing dick as deep as he could into Zalith's ass, sinking his fangs into his mate's neck in a final act of possession. He came *hard*, waves of ecstasy gripping him, holding him in a state of pure, intoxicating bliss. And with it came an overwhelming certainty—his body wasn't just indulging in pleasure; it was fulfilling its purpose.

A primal satisfaction bloomed within him, instinct whispering that he had *succeeded*, that something vital had just been set into motion. It was as if nature itself was assuring him that he had done what he was *meant* to do, that life had been passed on, that he had *created*. But as his breath slowed, as his mind began to clear from the haze of pleasure, reality struck just as fiercely as his release had. That *wasn't* what had happened. Zalith was a man. There was no child, no future taking root within him, no legacy growing from this union. And for just a fleeting moment, something inside him *ached*.

But the warmth of Zalith's body, the lingering pleasure pulsing through his veins, and the deep satisfaction still humming within him quickly buried that sadness before it could take hold. What they had just shared was still everything. It was still real. His breath slowed as he rode out the last shudders of his release, the sheer volume of it spilling deep inside Zalith sending an extra jolt of satisfaction through him—even more as Zalith whined in delight. The vampire's limbs trembled, his heart pounded wildly, and as he slowly came back down from that blinding high, he remained draped over Zalith, panting heavily, deeply, profoundly sated. His lips brushed over the fresh bite on the demon's neck, and he let the pleasure drown the ache, losing himself in the simple, undeniable rightness of being with the one he loved.

Then, he let himself relax, resting his body against Zalith's and nuzzling into the warmth of his neck. For a fleeting moment, he spiralled into the lingering pleasure, the steady rise and fall of the demon's chest beneath him. But something disheartening crept in, dulling the afterglow. He hadn't made Zalith climax. He never did—not like this. The realization struck him cruelly, disappointment settling like a weight in his chest. No matter how much he tried, no matter how deeply he wanted to bring Zalith the same overwhelming pleasure he was given, it never seemed to happen.

The thought clawed at him, stripping away his satisfaction like the dying embers of a once-roaring fire. His desperate need for affection withered alongside it. Slowly, he rolled onto his back, staring up at the ceiling, sinking into the quiet ache of his own inadequacy.

"What's wrong?" Zalith asked, leaning over to fiddle with his hair.

Alucard shrugged. "Nothing," he lied. "I'm just tired."

The demon frowned guiltily. "I'm sorry."

"It's not your fault," he assured him. "It was just a long day."

Zalith nodded, but he still looked guilty. "It has," he agreed. For a quiet moment, he fiddled with the vampire's hair. "I'm going to go and have a shower—you can join me if you'd like."

He wanted to say no—all he wanted to do was lay there and do nothing for the next short while. But he didn't want Zalith to worry about him. "But I just wrapped your arm up," he said.

"It's okay. I just won't get it wet."

Alucard nodded. "Okay. I'll join you."

They climbed out of bed and headed to the bathroom. Zalith led the way into the shower, and as once stepped inside, he switched on the hot water, and it poured over them.

← 458 →

Alucard leaned his back against the wall as Zalith stood in front of him, moving his hand to his waist. "What do we have left to do for the rest of the week? Before we head out to meet my people."

Zalith shrugged a little. "Nothing big. I'll warn everyone to keep an eye on Desmond, and to keep an eye out for Orrivain Elves."

"Well, we have the city celebration planned for the thirtieth," he mumbled. "And then we all have to convene and discuss our next moves regarding Lilith, no?"

Nodding, Zalith rested his head against Alucard's. "We do."

"Are you ready for that?" he asked worriedly.

Laughing, Zalith stared into his eyes. "No," he answered, a despondent look on his face. "If it were up to me, I'd want us to wait a few hundred years before even addressing that issue."

Frowning, Alucard guided his hand to the side of Zalith's neck. "You've done so much already—I…" he stopped and sighed, starting to fiddle with Zalith's wet hair. "I want to wait too," he admitted. "I want to…enjoy a long, long while with you without having to run or hide or constantly have to work. But…we can't. The longer we wait, the stronger the Numen will become, and the more work we will have to do to be able to kill them. If we wait, we're going to spend the rest of our lives looking over our shoulders—I don't want to live like that anymore, and you don't deserve to live like that either. And—" he snipped before Zalith could say anything, "—out of all the people I have known, *you* are the *only* one who is capable of doing what you want to do."

Zalith smiled a little, stroking the side of his face. "I'd do anything for you."

"For *us*," Alucard said. "This isn't just about me—it's about you, me, and the people we care about. The Numen have plagued this world for a very long time—we can't be the only ones who want to kill them. You were never alone in this, but…there could be other people out there like us. You have me—you will always have me, and we will get through this," he said quietly, staring into Zalith's eyes. "We just…have to hold on—it's a lot of work, so many things to do, but…no matter what happens, I am always here at your side."

The demon's smile warmed with adoration. "I'm always here at your side, too. I love you."

Alucard exhaled and nuzzled the side of Zalith's face, contentment and relief shoving away any other feeling. "I love *you*."

Cecil was gone, the city was theirs, and even if it was only for a short while, he and Zalith could relax. But there would always be more work to do.

Chapter Fifty-Seven

— ⟨ ✝ ⟩ —

To Fort Rudă de Sânge

| **Alucard,** *Monday, Tertium 27th, 960(TG)—The Vorynthian Ocean, The Steamship* |

Alucard and Zalith lay stretched across the couch in the ship's cabin, the gentle sway of the vessel rocking them as they travelled to Fort Rudă de Sânge. Their destination loomed ahead—the stronghold of the vampire Coven Masters. It had been days since their confrontation with Cecil, and in that time, Zalith's wounds had healed, preparations for their rule over Eimwood were well underway, and Snappy's enclosure was nearly complete.

The vampire knew his people would have a lot to report—and even more to ask of him. The disputes and war spreading across Aegisguard had already taken their toll, thinning their numbers and shaking the foundations of their covens. He felt the weight of it pressing against him, but he was ready to listen, lead, and do whatever it took to rebuild what had been lost. His people had suffered enough. It was time to fix what had been broken.

Responsibility pressed against him. He hadn't been as present for his people as he should have been. So much of his time had been consumed by helping Zalith, by simply living alongside the man he loved. Guilt gnawed at him—he should have done more. His people needed him now more than ever. They needed to see him, to know that he still cared, that he hadn't abandoned them to fend for themselves while the world turned against them.

He would make things right. The humans would be reminded of their place, a brood nurse or two would be found, and the vampiric population would grow once more. It would be arduous, but he was committed to ensuring the survival and prosperity of his kind. Their safety, their comfort—perhaps even their happiness—was his burden to bear.

Sighing, he rested his head against Zalith's chest, absently listening to the steady rhythm of his mate's heartbeat as Peaches purred softly from her perch on the arm of the chair. He missed having her around as much as before—she was usually curled up in his office while he worked, but he hadn't spent much time there lately, and Zalith rarely let her into their bed. So this time, he had brought her along.

They weren't far from Fort Rudă de Sânge now. The island of Ascuns was a well-kept secret, a place that existed only to those who knew how to find it. From the outside, it was little more than a towering, uninhabited rock in the middle of the ocean, but within it lay one of the most secure locations in Aegisguard. Aside from his and Zalith's home, there was no place safer.

Zalith shuffled around and lay on Alucard, pressing his body against his. As they made themselves comfortable, he buried his face into the vampire's neck, a content smile stretching across his face as he inhaled quietly.

Alucard smiled amusedly. He knew why Zalith had switched places with him. "Are you okay?" he teased.

"Yeah," he murmured.

Alucard stroked his hand down his mate's back. "Are you sure you're going to be able to sit through this meeting with me?"

"No," the demon laughed. "But I'll try."

He shrugged and suggested, "You could wait here on the boat with Peaches. I won't be too long. I don't want you to have to sit through a meeting if you don't want to."

"It's okay. I want to go—I'm nosey."

Alucard smiled amusedly. "Nosey?" he asked—Zalith had never used that word to describe himself before. "I wouldn't say that...maybe just...curious. And you want to help."

"No, I'm nosey," he laughed.

"Well...I don't think there's going to be much to nose about. Well...it's been a while since I met with them all, so...there could be a lot, I don't know."

"I hope they put on a show."

The vampire frowned. "Show?"

"I want entertainment."

"Well, Eyra—the Coven Master of Atheson—she is rather loud, so maybe she will entertain you."

"What if I want to be entertained by a man?"

Alucard pouted. "What's that supposed to mean?" he grumbled.

Zalith shrugged. "Maybe I want male entertainment. I can see him in my mind right now...he has jaw-length hair—and it's so, *so* red," he hummed, his tone almost flirtatious. "Pointed ears, the most beautiful face, and eyes like hellfire—the most handsome man I know."

Keeping his pout, Alucard fiddled with Zalith's hair and smiled slightly. "He sounds very interesting. It almost sounds as if you're in love with this man."

"It does, doesn't it?" the demon chuckled. "I do really love his body, too."

Alucard's amused smile was turning into a curious one. The longer Zalith nuzzled and breathed against his neck, the worse his instinctual needs became. And he felt no desire to fight them. "What do you love most about?"

"I don't want to say in front of Peaches—she's too young."

"She has seen you doing things to me so many times—she won't care."

Zalith laughed again. "She's probably traumatized."

The vampire glanced at his hairless kitten as she sat on the arm of the couch cleaning her paws. "She looks fine," he said, resting his head back again. "She doesn't really care about anything."

"She's hiding it to be polite."

"How do you know that?"

"She told me."

"No, she didn't."

"She did—we talk all the time."

He frowned doubtfully. "And what do you two talk about?"

"That's between me and Peaches."

His frown thickened. "Then I guess you don't want to know what Peaches and *I* talk about."

"What do you talk about?"

"What do *you* talk about."

"Lots of things, but mostly work. She keeps me company sometimes when I'm up all night."

Alucard smiled. "I never would have thought you'd become friends."

The demon shrugged. "She initiated it, but we enjoy each other's company."

"Good," he said, fiddling with Zalith's hair. "Now all we need is for you and Snappy to be friends, as well as my chickens, and Sabazios too."

"Sabazios and I get along—but I don't think I'll be friends with the chickens or the turtle."

"Why?"

"Germs."

Alucard pouted again. "I keep all my pets clean, Zalith."

"I know, but chickens, for example, walk around in their poop all day."

He wasn't wrong. "You don't have to touch them to be their friend."

"Can I be their friend from a great distance?"

Alucard sighed quietly. "You don't have to like them. I like that you and Peaches are friends, though."

The demon smiled. "Best friends"

"I wouldn't say that. Are you going to sit there and clean her claws for her?"

"No, because that's your job."

"You probably wouldn't do it right anyway," he grumbled.

"Probably," the demon agreed, smirking.

Alucard smiled, but as the ship began to slow, his gaze drifted to the window. The towering, jagged rock of Ascuns loomed on the horizon, its sharp edges cutting into the misty sky like the fangs of an ancient beast. Ominous and unyielding, the island drew closer with each passing moment. Soon, the time would come to disembark.

"We're almost there," he told his mate.

But Zalith didn't respond.

Alucard waited—maybe he was thinking. But after a few moments, he looked down at what he could see of Zalith and frowned. "Zalith?"

"Huh?" the demon replied.

"We're almost there," he repeated.

"Oh...how do you know?"

The vampire raised his arm and pointed at the window. "It's right there," he said as the demon inhaled against his neck once again.

Zalith didn't respond right away, obviously losing himself in Alucard's scent once again. "Oh," he then said. "I see." He stroked his hand up the side of the vampire's neck.

Alucard's felt devious, *eager*. His body needed sex. "We probably have about...fifteen minutes." He paused, guiding his fingers through Zalith's hair. "Would you like to do anything to me before we go?"

He felt the demon smirk against his neck before dragging his tongue over his sensitive skin, leaving a heated, lingering trail in its wake. A shiver of pleasure shivered down the vampire's spine; he closed his eyes, sinking into the indulgent contentment that only his mate could bring him.

The demon's hand trailed down his body, his fingers grazing over every heightened contour as he inhaled his scent deeply. Excitement surged through Alucard as Zalith slipped a hand into his trousers and firmly wrapped his fingers around his stiffening arousal. The vampire tensed, an unbidden sigh of pleasure escaping him as the demon's grip tightened, working him with skilled, teasing strokes. His fingers curled into Zalith's hair, anticipation growing within him as his mate expertly unravelled him.

It didn't take long before Zalith unbuckled his belt and moved lower, his heated breath fanning against Alucard's exposed skin. And then—bliss. The demon's lips wrapped around his dick, warm and wet, engulfing him in a way that sent jolts of ecstasy through every nerve. A deep, alleviating sigh left Alucard as he surrendered to the intoxicating sensation of Zalith's mouth. The demon's tongue moved slowly, tracing over his length, lapping and teasing with maddening precision.

Alucard moaned, gripping the demon's hair tighter, urging him on as the pleasure intensified. Every stroke, every movement of Zalith's mouth, his tongue, his throat—everything sent him racing closer to the edge. The demon hummed around him, the vibrations sending an electrifying shudder through his body, and Alucard's breathing turned erratic. The pleasure built faster than he could control, his body tightening, trembling, completely at Zalith's mercy.

And then it hit like a tsunami—his back arched slightly, his claws dug into Zalith's scalp, and a strangled moan tore from his throat as he climaxed, throbs of intense, almost *unbearable* delight enthralling him. His orgasm came in thick, pulsing waves, his body utterly lost in the overwhelming sensation. He felt the eager, desperate way that Zalith swallowed around him, groaning in sheer delight, drinking down every drop like it was something sacred. The sound alone sent another sharp jolt of pleasure through Alucard, his breath shaky, his body still trembling as the last shudders of pleasure coursed through him.

But he needed *more*. His body—his *instincts* insisted, giving him the stamina to do as he was being commanded.

Alucard didn't give Zalith a chance to move—before the demon could make his way back up to his lips, the vampire gripped his arms and urged him to sit upright. Zalith leaned back against the cushions of the couch, a smirk curling his lips as Alucard swiftly rid himself of his trousers and climbed onto his lap. His eagerness was mirrored in Zalith's eyes, dark with desire as Alucard yanked the demon's belt free, letting it fall to the floor with a quiet clatter.

Sliding his hand to the side of Zalith's neck, he leaned in, capturing his lips in a fervent kiss. The demon kissed back just as hungrily as he reached over to the small nightstand, pulling open the drawer and retrieving a bottle of lube.

Zalith wasted no time, eagerly smothering his shaft with the slick liquid before reaching back to prepare Alucard. The vampire barely had the patience to wait; his body ached for him, *craved* him. With a quiet sigh of relief, he took hold of Zalith's dick, pressing the tip against himself before slowly easing down onto it. He groaned as he felt the thick length stretching him open, inch by inch, every nerve igniting with a heady mix of pleasure and need. His body trembled as he took more of him, a sharp gasp slipping from his lips before melting into a deep, contented moan once he was fully seated in Zalith's lap, filled completely, utterly consumed by him.

For a moment, he simply sat there, savouring the sensation, the perfect pressure, the intoxicating fullness. The demon's hands roamed over his waist, his touch possessive. Their lips found each other again, the kiss slow but heated, as Zalith's fingers pressed into his skin, holding him in place as though he never wanted to let go.

Alucard began to move, lifting himself before sinking back down, each motion sending waves of pleasure rolling through his body. Their moans tangled between breathy kisses, the heat between them building with every movement. His heart pounded, a frenzied rhythm against his ribs, and as his pace quickened, Zalith's grip tightened. The demon's hands guided him, fingers digging into his waist as he pushed and pulled, helping him ride with more intensity, more desperation.

Soon, the kisses became too much—too consuming, too breathless. Alucard turned his head to the side, wordlessly inviting Zalith to his neck, and the demon complied. He latched on, his fangs grazing over sensitive skin before biting down, groaning deeply as he held him close. Alucard shivered, his body trembling, aching in both strain and delight, his moans turning into needy whines as the pleasure wound tighter within him. He clenched around Zalith, every nerve ablaze with sheer euphoria—

And then a knock at the cabin door.

A sharp snarl ripped from Alucard's throat, his head snapping towards the interruption. "*Pleacă!*" he barked in furious Dor-Sanguian.

Zalith choked out a laugh against his throat, utterly entertained even as he continued guiding Alucard's movements, still deep inside him. "You're so fucking hot when you yell at people," he murmured.

Alucard growled, turning back to him with a glare. "Shut up and fuck me," he demanded.

Zalith smirked. "Gladly."

Alucard smiled as Zalith pulled him closer, their lips meeting in a heated kiss. His right hand tangled into the demon's hair, gripping tightly as a delighted moan spilled into Zalith's mouth. His pace quickened, his thrusts desperate, brimming with desire, and he felt Zalith tense beneath him. The demon's claws dug into his waist, a sharp sting mixing with the pleasure that surged through him; his mate moaned, his breaths coming in ragged gasps as he buried his face against Alucard's neck.

And then, with a final, urgent pull on his waist, Zalith groaned a loud, delighted moan, his body trembling beneath the vampire as he reached his peak. A rush of warmth flooded deep inside Alucard, spreading in an intoxicating wave that sent a shiver through every inch of him. The sensation hit him hard, primal, devouring. His instincts roared in satisfaction, once again whispering to him that he had done it, that he had completed his purpose, that something inside him was taking root—

But reality crashed in just as quickly. His body lied to him, deceiving him with its desperate cravings. He couldn't get pregnant—he couldn't create life inside his body like that. He never would. The fleeting ache of realization pressed into his chest like a dull knife, threatening to steal away his contentment.

Zalith exhaled a deep, satisfied sigh, his arms wrapping tightly around Alucard's waist. The lingering pleasure still hummed through the vampire's veins, and as he let himself sink into the demon's warmth, the ache faded, buried beneath the blissful exhaustion, the rightness of simply being here.

With his racing heart slowly beginning to settle, Alucard exhaled and leaned forward, resting his body fully against Zalith's. It was over. For now. He knew this fulfilment wouldn't last long, that the hunger inside him would return all too soon, demanding that he achieve his purpose. But for the moment, he was sated. And that was enough.

"Are you okay?" Zalith breathed, leaning his head back against the cushions.

Alucard nodded, burying his face in Zalith's neck. It was only then that he realized the ship had come to a halt, and through the window, the entrance to the cave where his fort sat was visible. The ship had docked within, and it was time to leave.

He sighed deeply, resting his forehead against Zalith's. "Are *you* okay?"

"Yeah. But I'm not the one who gets his energy drained by an incubus every day," he said with a smirk.

"Well, lucky for us both, I haven't been feeling the effects of that ever since this whole heat thing started," he said, fiddling with Zalith's hair.

"I'm just afraid that a point will come where you'll crash," he said quietly, stroking the side of the vampire's face.

Alucard shrugged and smiled. "I think I'll be okay," he said and flicked his mate's fringe.

"Good."

The vampire then exhaled deeply and started fixing Zalith's hair, using his fingers to comb it back over his head. "We should probably get ready to leave—everyone will be waiting."

"Okay," Zalith said, gazing at him.

Once they were dressed, Alucard fastened his belt, adjusting his coat before reaching for his cape. As he pulled it over his shoulders, he glanced at Zalith, who smirked, clearly amused by the lingering flush on his face. Ignoring it, the vampire exhaled, smoothing his collar before turning towards the door.

With one final glance at Zalith, he pulled the cabin door open and stepped out onto the deck, the salty sea air rushing to meet him, and his gaze locked onto the fort entrance. Their time alone was over—now, it was time to face another conundrum.

Chapter Fifty-Eight

— ⋜ ✝ ⋝ —

The Vampire Conundrum

| Zalith—*Ascuns, Fort Rudă de Sânge* |

Following Alucard across the deck, Zalith's gaze immediately flicked to one of the crewmen, who ran over with a bright smile on his face. The demon frowned irritably at the man, stopping beside his vampire.

"Sir...sir," the crewman breathed, halting in front of them, panting—what an unfit little man.

"What do you want?" Alucard grumbled, taking hold of Zalith's hand.

"We've arrived, Sir."

Alucard rolled his eyes. "Thank you for stating the obvious," he grumbled—and then he dismissed the man with a wave of his hand and continued down onto the stone docks.

As they stepped from the stone docks into a wide corridor, a quiet weight settled over Zalith's chest. This place... it reminded him of home—the home that he and Alucard had been forced to leave. The cold, damp scent of stone, the way the air carried a faint echo of their footsteps—it pulled his thoughts back to his private cavern, the one where he had stored everything that mattered to him. A place of solitude, of security. Now lost to them.

The thought tightened something in his chest, and he frowned, forcing himself to push it aside. Now wasn't the time for nostalgia.

He followed at Alucard's side, their footsteps echoing down the lengthy corridor until they reached a massive black stone door at the very end. As they approached, the door clicked and shifted, its heavy slabs groaning as they slid open to admit them. Beyond was another corridor, but this one was different—polished, inviting. The floor gleamed white marble, streaked with black veins forming intricate, swirling patterns. The walls, smooth black stone, reflected the flickering light of golden chandeliers hanging every thirty feet or so, each cradling black candles whose flames danced eerily against the dark ceiling.

Zalith let out a low, amused hum. "It's pretty. Nicer than the cave I used back at our old house."

Alucard pulled his cape tighter around himself. "It's very cold, though," he muttered.

Zalith couldn't help but smile, his lingering melancholy momentarily overshadowed by affection. He rubbed Alucard's arms, creating friction in an attempt to warm him. The vampire sighed, leaning into his touch, and Zalith smirked before turning his attention to the cavern beyond the windows as they continued down the corridor.

Outside, the jagged walls of the cave stretched endlessly into the distance, their rough, uneven surfaces bathed in the dim glow of braziers hanging from the cliffs. A river snaked its way through the depths far below, its dark surface reflecting the flickering firelight in broken streaks. The entire scene had an eerie beauty—isolated, shadowed, and ancient.

For a moment, Zalith wondered about the purpose of the braziers. Were they simply for aesthetic or did they serve a practical use? Most demons and vampires had no trouble seeing in the dark, so artificial light seemed redundant. But as his gaze wandered further, he spotted movement—a shape clinging to the cliffside, then several others soaring through the air.

Curiosity piqued, Zalith slowed his pace, watching as the creatures dove towards the river, snatching fish from the water. Their dragon-like wings beat the air with powerful strokes, their bodies covered in sleek, overlapping scales. Four glowing eyes gleamed against the darkness, sharp and predatory. Their hind legs were lion-like, built for gripping and tearing, each talon at least a foot long. But what intrigued Zalith most was their tails—long, whip-like, curling around rocky outcrops or suspending them upside-down from the cavern ceiling like enormous, monstrous bats.

He narrowed his eyes, taking in their strange but captivating appearance. "What's flying around out there?" he asked, glancing at Alucard.

Alucard looked at him. "They are...Nox Volant. I use them as sentries here—like how we use the crows back home. They see and hear *everything*. They are also venomous and can paralyze even a demon in less than a minute," he explained as they turned left, emerging into a large hall, the walls lined with doors. "They are a lesser type of demon—there were a lot of them in the Underworld when I lived with Damien," he mumbled.

Zalith laughed quietly. "We need some of those at home."

"Well, we would already have them if they didn't burn into ash in the sunlight," he laughed, leading the way to the door at the very end of the hall.

"Maybe one day. If we ever get our home back, a few of them can guard the cave there."

Alucard nodded. "We will take it back one day," he said, taking Zalith into another corridor.

"One day," he agreed, but he felt doubtful. The Citadel had been pretty much destroyed, and it seemed as though they wouldn't be able to even *think* about heading back over there for a long, long time—and he didn't want to risk returning to their old home until all of their enemies were dead.

As Zalith walked alongside Alucard, his gaze flickered to the cavern beyond the windows, but his thoughts were elsewhere—rooted in the home they'd been forced to leave behind. He missed it. Their old house, their bed, their rooms…even Alucard's study, the office Zalith had spent countless hours in. It wasn't just a place; it was theirs, filled with memories, with moments of peace and passion, and the life they'd built together before it had all been ripped away.

And they hadn't even abandoned it completely. His vault was still there, though he had moved everything of value. Their clothes, their furniture—things they simply hadn't been able to take when Nefastus fell into chaos—it all remained untouched within those walls. Detlaff was still imprisoned there, too. But how long would it be before someone tried to free him? They had talked about it before, the idea of stationing a few people there to keep intruders away, to ensure the house and cave stayed theirs until they could return. Maybe that was something they needed to revisit when the time came to gather and plan their next steps.

Alucard frowned, squeezing the demon's hand. "I miss that house, too."

Zalith smiled sadly and moved his hand around Alucard's waist, hugging him slightly.

When they reached the door at the end of the corridor, Alucard hesitated for just a moment, his fingers resting on the handle as he glanced over, as if expecting Zalith to say something. But words weren't what Zalith had in mind. Smirking, he reached out and gave the vampire's ass a firm squeeze, his amusement growing when Alucard shot him a look—half smirk, half exasperation.

Satisfied, Zalith leaned back slightly, watching as Alucard shook his head with a small smile before twisting the handle and pushing the door open.

As they stepped inside, the room fell stiff and silent. Every pair of eyes turned towards them, their gazes obedient and curious. Sitting at the massive rectangular table were the attendees—clad in sharp suits or elaborate attire reminiscent of Attila's, the kind of extravagant garments upper-class men might wear to a masquerade ball—they all rose to their feet, bowing respectfully. Rich fabrics, intricate embroidery, and dramatic silhouettes filled the space, adding to the air of formality and spectacle. Zalith barely spared them a glance, his focus solely on the path ahead as he and Alucard made their way into the room.

"For those of you who don't know, this is Zalith," Alucard announced, walking to the head of the table. "He is my fiancé."

Everyone called their greetings, and Zalith smiled in response before sitting in the chair to the right of Alucard. And as Alucard sat down, the others returned to their seats.

"This is Rasmus, the leader of my council," Alucard introduced to Zalith, nodding at the crimson-eyed, blonde man sitting beside the demon.

"Nice to meet you," Zalith said, shaking Rasmus' hand.

"And you, sir," Rasmus replied.

"These are my Coven Masters and my council," Alucard added, looking around at everyone else.

Zalith nodded as everyone called more greetings.

Alucard then began, "It has been brought to my attention that you all each have your own problems that need my intervention." He rested his arms on the table as he looked around at everyone's tense faces. "Our numbers are not what they used to be, I want to ensure that every coven has at least a hundred members, and so today I have called here the oldest among our people—I will be assigning one or two new brood nurses so that I can create more vampires. I hope to have a brood nurse for every major coven before the end of the year—once whoever I choose today is ready, they will teach more of the older vampires how to take care of Fledgelings. So, that's that issue covered." He leaned back in his seat. "If anyone has issues regarding numbers, you can tell Rasmus, and I will make note of that when deciding which covens get the first brood nurses."

Everyone nodded.

Alucard glanced at Zalith. "That is Eyra," he told him, nodding at the crimson-eyed, brunette woman sitting in a strapless black gown with red highlights, her skin as white as snow.

Zalith hummed in response.

"Atheson," Alucard said to her.

Eyra's subservient expression intensified, and as she stood up, she stared at him in what looked like dread.

"I hear there have been some problems there—tell me," he invited.

Eyra nodded. "Yes, My Lord. The humans of Atheson—" she started, snarling when she said humans. "They have been causing problems for my coven and for a few months. We have struggled to maintain a position of power—the humans are no longer as afraid as they should be—these demons...they continue to raid the towns, sweep the cities—the humans are too scared of them to even consider us a significant threat anymore. They no longer cower as they should; they hunt us with pitchforks and torches—they have even gone so far as to hire a 'professional' vampire hunter," she explained, revolt in her voice.

Alucard raised an eyebrow. "Professional vampire hunter?"

Zalith was admittedly a little intrigued. A *professional* hunter? This was the first time he had heard of such a person in Aegisguard.

She nodded again. "That's right, My Lord. They call him Silver Claw—the intelligence in my coven has brought it to my attention that he may be a werewolf."

Alucard rolled his eyes. "Has this...Silver Claw arrived in Atheson yet?"

"Not yet, My Lord. But the humans have pooled enough gold together to hire him—he could arrive any day."

He nodded. "I will deal with this Silver Claw, and I will also pay a *personal* visit to Atheson and make sure the humans remember their place—I will come this week."

"Thank you, My Lord," she called. Then, she went to sit down—

"I'm not finished," Alucard snarled.

A look of horror smothered her face as she stood straight, staring wide-eyed at him. Zalith smiled amusedly.

"I have been told that you have plans to go to war with the humans—is that something I need to be concerned about?" he asked skeptically.

Eyra shook her head. "N-no, My Lord. I am certain that won't be necessary."

"Good," Alucard mumbled.

As he waved his hand in dismissal, Eyra sat back down.

Alucard leaned nearer to Zalith. "We can discuss increasing the vampire population later."

Zalith nodded. "Okay."

He then glanced around the table. "I understand that the current activities of the cults across all of Aegisguard are causing problems for all of you. I will not only increase *all* of your numbers so that you can kill these demons but so that you can also live comfortably without having to worry about the humans becoming too confident," he called. Then, he shifted his sights to Rasmus, who was making notes. As the man nodded, Alucard looked out at the Coven Masters again, setting his eyes on the dark-skinned, silver-haired man closest to him. "Garroway, Drydenheim Coven Master," he told Zalith. And then he said, "Tell me how many are left in your coven."

Garroway—a tall, lanky, man—nodded and stood up. "My Lord," he said gracefully. "Tantibus currently has seventy-four members. We lost four—one man decided to leave, and three were killed on separate occasions when the cults swept the land. *We* are not having issues with the resident humans."

Alucard nodded. "The man who left—it's his choice. He does not have to remain in a coven. I will replace your four members and send an additional twenty members once I have assigned brood nurses."

"Thank you, My Lord," Garroway replied, and as Alucard waved his hand in dismissal, the man sat back down.

Alucard piercing gaze settled on the bald man sitting next to Garroway. "Fane, leader of the Boszorkány Coven," he told Zalith.

The Silver Claw's story unfolds in the Numenverse Companion Story, THE SILVER CLAW

Fane stood up. "My Lord," he started. "Bloodworth currently has sixty-three members. We haven't suffered any losses, and the humans are cooperating."

"I will increase your coven to a hundred, too," Alucard said. "The more of you there are, the stronger you will be if you ever do have to fight."

"Thank you, My Lord," Fane said, and as Alucard dismissed him, he sat back down.

As Alucard's subordinates stood one by one, moving in a clockwise order around the table to report their covens' numbers, Zalith listened in silence, his gaze flickering between them. He tried to focus, but his thoughts kept drifting—Alucard's presence was too intoxicating, his scent, his voice, the effortless authority that he carried. Zalith wanted to touch him, to be close, to sink into that consuming need for his mate.

But then the numbers started to add up, and with them, so did his concern. Some covens had fewer than sixty members. That was far below the goal of a hundred per coven—a deficit that meant Alucard would have to create dozens upon dozens of new vampires, a process that Zalith knew would drain him, test his endurance, and demand more of him than the demon wanted him to give. He didn't want Alucard pushing himself too hard, but he knew there was no stopping him. This wasn't just about restoring his kind—it was about reclaiming vampires' place in the world, securing their future. And Zalith wouldn't stand in his way. Instead, he'd do what he did best: support him, protect him, and make sure he didn't burn himself out.

His fingers drummed absently against the arm of his chair as he glanced around the table, watching the last woman beside Eyra stand and give her report. When she sat down, Alucard asked if anyone else had anything to add. To Zalith's relief, no one spoke. The meeting was over, but Alucard's work had only just begun.

Zalith sighed quietly, his concern lingering. He wasn't sure how much he could do to lighten Alucard's burden, but whatever it was, he'd do it.

Alucard sighed deeply and leaned back in his seat. "Remember, if there is anything else, make sure to tell Rasmus, who I will be conferring with soon," he called finally.

All his people nodded in agreement.

"Right," he said, standing up. "I will see you very soon."

Zalith stood up, too.

Once everyone called their thanks, Alucard led Zalith out of the room.

"What next?" the demon asked as they made their way down the corridor.

Alucard looked like he was pondering. "We can... go to my study and work out where we go from here," he suggested.

"Okay," Zalith agreed, and as Alucard led the way, Zalith silently followed, watching the vampire's ass *closely*.

Chapter Fifty-Nine

— ⋜ ✝ ⋝ —

Behind the Heart

| Alucard—*Ascuns, Fort Rudă de Sânge* |

With Zalith following closely behind, Alucard walked back into the vast, door-lined hall; he veered away from the large doors at the far end and instead took a right, heading towards a middle door. He pushed it open, revealing a staircase that spiralled upward and began ascending.

At the top, another long corridor stretched before them, its windows once again overlooking the vast, Nox Volant-filled caves. Alucard glanced out as they walked, his sharp gaze flickering over the winged beasts as they swooped down, talons slicing into the water to snatch fish.

They soon reached the end of the corridor, where Alucard pushed open a heavy wooden door and stepped inside, leading Zalith into his old study. The spacious room was just the way he'd left it, the scent of aged paper and smouldering firewood lingering in the air; the fireplace in the back wall cast eternal flickering shadows over the wide desk—mostly bare, save for a few scattered documents that he'd abandoned some time ago. His work had shifted to his and Zalith's home, and with so much happening, there hadn't been much need for this office at all.

"Once I'm done making vampires for the covens, I can start creating more for us," Alucard said and slumped down onto the black couch. "We still need to see if I have a Lumendatt, though... before I start making vampires," he said as Zalith sat beside him.

"When should we do that?" he asked, sounding reluctant... and looking a little... restless?

"The sooner, the better," he replied, wearily resting his head in his hand; he was starting to feel the weight of the day. "So I can get to work. Maybe... right now... unless you don't want to."

Zalith didn't answer. His conflicted frown thickened, and he looked away, clearly thinking.

Alucard understood why his mate was hesitant. But the fact of the matter was that they needed to know whether or not he really did have a Lumendatt inside him. If he did, it would benefit them both *exponentially* in their effort to grow an army to face the Numen.

"It'll be okay," he assured him, placing his hand over Zalith's. "If it hurts, I'll tell you to stop."

The hesitation remained on Zalith's face. "Are we doing it *right* now?"

"I would...prefer to do it as soon as possible, but if you really don't want to, it's okay—we can wait."

With a heavy sigh, the demon shrugged slightly. "I don't want to," he admitted. "But...I agree that it should happen sooner rather than later. What do I need to do?"

The vampire sat up straight. "I told you where it should be—behind my heart, or around there somewhere. If...it *is* there, then...it will heal the wound you make to get to it—I saw... hat happen a long time ago with one of Damien's associates."

"Okay," Zalith said, but still with a hesitant, almost despondent look on his face.

Alucard moved closer as Zalith did. But as he unclipped and pulled off his cape, something raced to the forefront of his mind—a memory? A warning? "Wait," he mumbled, pausing.

"What?" Zalith asked worriedly.

The memory unfolded...and Alucard remembered. It wasn't an associate that Damien had attempted to take a Lumendatt from...it was one of the children Alucard had been trained alongside. He remembered Damien ripping the crystal from the boy's body, but it crumbled to ash, and the boy died. And so did the next...and the next...and the next. Damien had been so desperate to obtain a Lumendatt, but his attempts to farm them had failed—and *why* was he trying to farm them? He had his own, surely...because he had a humanoid form back then, and a Numen needed a Lumendatt to obtain one. And that had to mean that Damien *still* had one. Did having more than one Lumendatt at a time increase the power? The possibilities?

He was moving away from his worry. Would *his* Lumendatt crumble if Zalith took it from his body?

"Alucard?" Zalith insisted.

The vampire shifted his gaze to him.

"What's wrong?"

He shook his head, the memories still unfolding. No. His Lumendatt wouldn't shatter...because *his* was pure. The children Damien had used weren't like him—they weren't born with the blood of a Numen, they were *made*. Damien grew them using his own DNA; he'd proudly boasted that he'd found a new way to make purer scions, but *all* of those children died—murdered, illness, unstable ethos. *That* was why their Lumendatts crumbled.

"Nothing," he said, putting his cape over the back of the couch.

"Are you sure?"

"Mm-hmm. Just…thinking of Damien—well, you know what that does to me."

Zalith caressed the side of his face. "I'm sorry."

He shook his head. "It's okay."

The demon offered a soft smile before reaching to help Alucard unbutton his blazer. Once it was undone, Alucard shrugged it off and set it neatly atop his cape. Zalith moved next to his shirt, deft fingers working open each button, but Alucard didn't want to remove it entirely. Instead, as Zalith shed his own blazer and rolled up his sleeve, Alucard gently took hold of his wrist and guided his hand to his chest, pressing his mate's palm flat against the steady rhythm of his heartbeat.

But Zalith didn't get right to it. He lightly dragged his fingers around the centre of Alucard's chest, the hesitant frown returning to his face. "I don't want to hurt you," he said sadly, staring into his eyes.

The vampire placed his hand on the side of Zalith's face. "You won't," he assured him. "It'll be okay—we need to do this."

A shadow of sorrow flickered across Zalith's face, his hesitant expression deepening into something almost pained as Alucard gently removed his hand from his cheek. The demon's touch lingered—his fingers continued tracing slow, absent-minded circles over Alucard's chest, just below his pecs. Alucard could tell that he was thinking, weighing something unspoken, lost in silent debate.

But finally, Zalith's gaze lifted, meeting his eyes once more. "Okay," he murmured, his voice quiet, heavy with reluctance. "Are you ready?"

"I'm ready," he said. "If…if it is there, then…you need to take it out and then put it back so it'll heal me," he explained.

Zalith nodded and straightened his fingers, pressing the sharp tips of his claws lightly against Alucard's chest—but he hesitated. "Do you want me to count down?"

Alucard shook his head, trying to relax. "It's okay," he murmured.

The demon didn't look convinced. His brows furrowed, concern deepening the crease between them. But he nodded anyway. "Okay."

Alucard took a deep breath, bracing himself as Zalith's gaze dropped to his chest. And then the demon gently pushed his claws into his skin.

A sharp, biting pain flared in Alucard's chest as his flesh gave way, and a quiet sound of discomfort escaped his lips.

"Sorry," Zalith said quickly, his hesitation growing—but before Alucard could respond, a warmth bloomed from the demon's touch. The pain dulled, softened, replaced by something almost soothing. He knew what Zalith was doing—using his ethos to wash away the worst of the pain, flooding his body with a sense of comfort. It didn't erase the discomfort entirely, but it helped. It made it bearable.

"It's okay," Alucard assured him. "Keep going."

He did his best to mask the pain, but the moment Zalith's claws pierced deeper, a sharp, searing agony surged through his body. His heartbeat stuttered and then pounded faster, a frantic rhythm that made it impossible to ignore the growing ache spreading from his chest. His muscles tensed, his jaw clenched, and a deep frown settled on his face as he fought the overwhelming discomfort.

His body ached—*too much*. Needing something to ground himself, he leaned forward, resting his forehead against Zalith's shoulder, his breath shallow and unsteady.

That made Zalith stop. "Are you okay?" he asked, concern lacing his voice.

Alucard nodded, though the movement was stiff. "I'm fine," he muttered, doing his best to steady himself.

He felt Zalith hesitate, but after a brief pause, the demon continued. His fingers moved carefully inside him, slowly searching for the Lumendatt. The vampire gritted his teeth, every instinct urging him to react—to pull away, to make some noise of protest—but he held himself still. He refused to let the pain win.

After just a few more moments, Zalith's movements stilled. His hand froze deep within Alucard's chest, and as the vampire lifted his head, he met the demon's conflicted gaze. His mate's expression wavered—uncertainty flickered in his dark eyes—but then he began carefully easing his hand back.

The pain was immediate, fierce and overwhelming. Alucard huffed as a strained grunt forced its way through his clenched teeth. His fingers instinctively found Zalith's free hand, gripping it tightly as if that alone would ground him.

Zalith hesitated. He stopped.

"Don't stop," Alucard breathed, his voice barely above a whisper, but firm in its urgency.

The demon's frown deepened, reluctance etched into every careful movement, but he obeyed. He continued, slower than before, his fingers gliding with painstaking precision. And then—Alucard felt it. A faint, reverberating hum emanated from deep within his body, the sensation crawling through him like an awakening force.

His eyes snapped downward. From the wound Zalith's hand had created, a dim orange glow began to pulse, flickering like a dying ember beneath his skin. The moment Zalith's palm left his body entirely, the glow strengthened, illuminating his chest with an ethereal warmth.

And there, held between Zalith's fingers, was the very thing Alucard had suspected all along. Both of them stared, silent, mesmerized by what the demon had pulled from inside him.

A small, diamond-shaped crystal, its surface alive with shifting hues of orange, gold, and crimson. Light refracted off its flawless facets, casting glimmers of molten fire across

Alucard's skin. A quiet, harmonic hum pulsed from within, resonating with an energy so potent that it sent a faint shiver through his body.

A Lumendatt.

It was exactly as he had seen before—yet entirely different. Unlike the fractured remnants Damien had attempted to obtain, this one was whole, unmarred by cracks or decay. The others had been dim, their glow feeble, their essence barely holding on. But this…this was untouched. Brilliant. Thrumming with pure, undisturbed ethos. It was alive. And it had been inside him all this time.

"Is this it?" Zalith asked, taking his eyes off it to look at Alucard.

The vampire nodded, trying his best to cope with the pain surging through his trembling body. "Yes," he answered. Despite seeing it, and despite the memory that reminded him of its existence…he was still in disbelief. *There it was*. The key to creation, the key to winning the fight against the Numen.

"Should I put it back in?" Zalith asked almost desperately.

Alucard nodded again, gritting his teeth, attempting to hide his *agony*.

Zalith didn't delay. He pressed the Lumendatt back into Alucard's chest—but there was no need to push it inside. The moment the crystal touched the open wound, it reacted. A force unseen pulled it free of Zalith's fingers, drawing it back into Alucard's body as if slipping through an invisible threshold. The wound sealed behind it in an instant, smooth and unblemished, as though it had never been there at all.

Not even a scar remained.

The only evidence of what had just transpired was the blood smeared across Alucard's chest—dark, rich, and abundant.

"Are you okay?" Zalith asked as Alucard leaned forward, resting his head on the demon's shoulder.

He nodded.

"Do you need blood?"

Alucard nuzzled the demon's neck, waiting for the lingering ache in his body to calm down. His heart began to slow, and after a deep sigh, he moved his left hand over Zalith's other shoulder. "Yes, please," he murmured.

Zalith guided his hand to the back of Alucard's head, urging him to bite down. The vampire didn't waver. Slowly, he parted his lips and sank his four fangs deep into his mate's neck. As his sweet, intoxicating blood flooded his mouth, a quiet moan of satisfaction escaped him, the rich taste washing away every trace of pain. A light, heady sensation settled over him, warmth blooming in his chest and curling through his limbs. His thoughts felt looser, his body lighter, a pleasant haze dulling the last remnants of discomfort.

He didn't take much—just enough to steady himself. After a few moments, he withdrew his fangs, dragging his tongue over the fresh wound, enjoying the last traces of Zalith's essence as he licked away the lingering blood, the subtle high leaving him feeling soothed, weightless, and just a little more whole.

"I didn't like that," Zalith then said.

"Neither did I," he mumbled.

The demon took off his own bloody shirt and used it to wipe away the blood on Alucard's chest. "I never want to see that much of your blood ever again," he said sullenly, and then he cleaned his hand.

Nodding, Alucard pushed Zalith down onto his back and rested his head on the demon's chest. "You won't have to."

Zalith kissed Alucard's head and held him tightly.

Despite what had just happened, though, Alucard didn't want to postpone the talk they needed to have. "So...now that we know I have the Lumendatt...what's next?" he asked quietly, stroking Zalith's arm. "We have to meet everyone soon and discuss our plans. Do you know what you want to do?"

The demon sighed deeply. "I guess...it's time to figure out what we want to do with Lilith."

"We need a Pandorican. Are we going to ask Detlaff if our people still haven't found one by the time we all convene?"

With a heavy exhale, Zalith said, "I suppose."

"He is...still in Nefastus. Are we going to go there, or will we have him brought here?"

"I *definitely* do not want to go there...but I also don't want to risk him escaping. Do we have anyone who can safely transport him without it becoming an issue?"

Alucard thought to himself for a moment. "Well...what about Tyrus? Camael has taken the tracking ethos off him. I could send Attila, too—I don't know."

"How can we be sure it even worked?"

"We can send some of my vampires to find out where Tyrus' pursuers are and see if they are still able to track him," he suggested.

Zalith nodded. "Okay. We should do that anyway because I want Tyrus back here."

"Rasmus will be coming to me later with a list of everything I need to do. I will tell him to send some people then."

"Okay. Thank you."

Alucard smiled and moved his hand up to the side of Zalith's neck. "Everything will be okay," he said quietly. "You have come so far already—and now that we have a Lumendatt, Lilith will be dead before the year is over."

"I hope so," Zalith said, caressing Alucard's hair. "All I want is for you to be safe."

"That's all I want for you, too."

They lay together in the quiet, the afternoon slipping by unnoticed. Since arriving in Uzlia, the road had been long and unrelenting, every step a battle, every victory hard-won. But now, at last, they stood on solid ground. Lords of Eimwood, rulers of Uzlia—the safest stronghold in all of Aegisguard. For the first time in longer than he could recall, Alucard felt truly settled. Safe. Steady. Unshaken.

But there was still so much left to do. The Lumendatt within him was proof that they were on the right path, but it also marked the beginning of something far greater. Soon, they would gather their allies, set their course, and prepare for the battles to come. Lilith was waiting, and after her...Damien. And whoever else dared to stand between them and the future that they would carve together.

For now, though, he allowed himself this moment. A fleeting peace before the storm.

ASCENDANT
Numen Chronicles | Volume Five

ASCENDANT
Numen Chronicles | Volume Five

THE NUMEN CHRONICLES
SERIES ONE

Nosferatu
The Numen Chronicles | Volume 1

✝

Demon's Fate
The Numen Chronicles | Volume 2

✝

Light
The Numen Chronicles | Volume 3

✝

Demon's Bane
The Numen Chronicles | Volume 4

✝

Forbidden Bond
The Numen Chronicles | Companion Story

✝

Ascendant
The Numen Chronicles | Volume 5

✝

The Silver Claw
The Numen Chronicles | Interlude Story

✝

The Hunt for Niedreid
The Numen Chronicles | Interlude Story

✝

Icarus
The Numen Chronicles | Volume 6

✝

Demon's Curse
The Numen Chronicles | Volume 7

✝

Renascence
The Numen Chronicles | Volume 8

✝

Demon's Reclamation
The Numen Chronicles | Volume 9

✝

[And more...]

ASCENDANT
Numen Chronicles | Volume Five

THE NUMENVERSE
OTHER SERIES/STORIES

Aldergrove Chronicles

Set in the year 1176 after Aegisguard's second world war. After being told he has only six months left to live, Clementine decides to track down his sister's murderers, leading him to Aldergrove Academy, a place where a hundred students must fight to the death to earn their right to travel to the New World. But he soon learns that the students aren't the only ones prowling the corridors at night in search of blood.

✟

Where The Wild Wolves Have Gone

Set in the year 1330. Following Luan, a young transman werewolf who belongs to a pack owned by Lyca Corp., a military-focused organization. The pack have served them for generations, but after a mission goes sideways, Luan begins to learn the horrifying truth about the people they serve.

✟

Greykin Chronicles

Set in the year 1332, following Jackson, a journalist who heads to the snowy mountains of Ascela in search of his missing best friend, Wilson. But he discovers that not only is there a whole different world hidden out there, but death isn't necessarily the end for some creatures.

✟

The Numen Chronicles Series Two

Set in the year 1335. While hunting for his missing friend, Elijah stumbles upon a fiery journalist, who so happens to be looking for the same people as him: the doctors who experimented on him when he was a child. But when the two are forced to go on the run together, Elijah's healing wounds are opened, and he realizes that Lyca Corp. took more than his childhood.

To stay up to date with future releases, follow the author through their website!

www.numenverse.com/

ASCENDANT
Numen Chronicles | Volume Five

ASCENDANT
Numen Chronicles | Volume Five

Discover more at www.numenverse.com

www.ingramcontent.com/pod-product-compliance
Ingram Content Group UK Ltd.
Pitfield, Milton Keynes, MK11 3LW, UK
UKHW041917310325
456929UK00001B/27